To those who have waited 14 years to read this conclusion to Emaneska, thank you.

To those who helped me get here and who have spent hours enduring my yammering about dragons and magick, gods and daemons, I'm indebted to you.

To those who are excited for the next adventure, I've got you.

For a closer look at the Emaneska maps, go to:
WWW.BENGALLEY.COM/MAPS

OTHER BOOKS BY BEN GALLEY

THE EMANESKA SERIES

The Written
Pale Kings
Dead Stars - Part One
Dead Stars - Part Two
The Written Graphic Novel

TALES OF EMANESKA

The Iron Keys
No Fairytale
The Weaver & The Wyrm
A Feast For Wolves
Blood For The Forest

THE CHASING GRAVES TRILOGY

Chasing Graves
Grim Solace
Breaking Chaos

THE SCARLET STAR TRILOGY

Bloodrush
Bloodmoon
Bloodfeud

THE BLOODWOOD SAGA

Demon's Reign
Demon's Rage
Demon's Ruin

STANDALONES

The Heart of Stone
Shards

TKAGPB1
First Edition 2024
ISBN: 978-1-0687403-9-8
Published by BenGalley.com
Editing by Editing By Taya
Map Illustration by Ben Galley
Cover Design by Ben Galley

About the Author

Ben Galley is a British author of dark, epic fantasy who currently lurks in Vancouver, Canada. Since publishing his Emaneska Series in 2010, Ben has released the award-winning Scarlet Star Trilogy and The Heart of Stone, the critically-acclaimed Chasing Graves Trilogy and Scalussen Chronicles, and the new Bloodwood Saga. His goal is to escort you into deep, vibrant worlds that live rent free in your head, alongside plots that cause emotional damage when you get too close to the wrong characters.

When he isn't writing about magic systems and dragon anatomy, Ben wanders the Canadian wilds, is always trying a recipe way above his abilities, dabbles in archery, and snowboards very, very badly. One day he hopes to haunt an epic treehouse in the mountains and give side quests to passersby.

Find all of Ben's books or join his Discord at:
www.linktr.ee/bengalley

MARGARA
THE EMBERTEETH
THE SPINE
SHOULDERS OF THE WORLD
MOGACHA
THE DOOMSWELL
IRON BARRENS
SCALUSSEN
ICE FIELDS
RIVEN PLAINS
EAGLE HOLD
GOLIKAR
VENSK
NELSKA
TAUSENBAR MTS
DATHAZH
THE BITTER SEA
CHAOS SOUND
HAMMER HILLS
LILEROSK
CLAWN
ARKA
VORHAUG
NYR'S DAGGER
HARTLUND
JORMUNN SEA
ÖSSFEN MTS
THE LONELY SEA
DESTRIX
SACIATH
HÅLORN
JORPSUND
EAST JORP
BYARA
BEGRAD
KROPPE
NORMONT
IRKMIRE YAWN
EFJAR
ESSEN
SUNTER ISLES
DUELLING SEVEN
ALBION
KRAUSLUNG
ROLIA
BLUE MOUNTAIN SEA
SKAP ISLANDS
SOUTH SPIT
LEZEMBOR
BAY OF SOULS
BERN SEA
IKANI
THUNDER SHORES
TROACLES
ITRJS
SHATTERED ISLANDS
CHANARK
CAPE OF GLASS
BELEPHON
BOLSH
PARAIA
DIAMOND MTS
HASPIA
ASPHA
PHENOPS MTS
THE SILENT SEA
KHANDRI
PHORA
LAKE HEXIS
HEKET SOUND
AZANIMUR
AFFELA GULF
KALEUS
KIRAXA BAY
THE WATCH MAN
LAKE UQALA
JAR KHOUM
METISKO
CAPE PLUMMET
BAY OF FERESH
CAPE OF NO HOPE
FORBIDDEN COAST
NONAME BAY
MAP OF
Emanesha
Paraia
&
Easterealm

SCALUSSEN CHRONICLES BOOK THREE

Of What Has Come Before

YEAR 925-926

Mithrid Fenn, a lowly cliff-dweller of Troughwake, discovered a banned spellbook in the shoreline of a shipwreck. After accidentally releasing its magick, Troughwake was consequentially destroyed and Mithrid captured by Arka Empire mages.

Once rescued by the rebels of Scalussen, Mithrid vowed vengeance on the Arka and Emperor Malvus, and agreed to join the rebellion. With other survivors of Troughwake, she journeyed north to the ice fields and hidden city of Scalussen.

While Farden, now called the Forever King – or Outlaw King by the Arka – prepared for war against the empire, Mithrid began training for battle, and soon enough her strange power was discovered: a shadow that could cancel the effects of magick. Farden spied a powerful weapon, and agreed to teach her to wield it.

Long since disappeared, the god Loki at last returned to Krauslung to aid Malvus in his fight against Farden. In Loki's possession was the Hides of Hysteria, a tome which contained dozens of tattooed Books carved from the backs of Written mages, and together they began to create so-called Scarred mages to rival Farden and his remaining Written.

Farden was meanwhile forced to deal with the echoes of an old mistake and travelled to Albion to retrieve a copy of his own Book and keep it out of Malvus' hands. After a narrow escape, Farden,

Durnus, the yetin Ko-Tergo, and the witches Peryn and Wyved found themselves face to face with Malus and Loki for the first time.

Open war was promptly declared, and while the Arka marched north to the ice fields to lay siege to Scalussen, Farden gathered allies from across Emaneska. One such ally was Warbringer, head of the minotaur clans of Efjar, and once a dire enemy.

Battle commenced with ferocity and chaos. With daemons, Scarred mages, Lost Clans, Albion, and almost one million soldiers at his command, Emperor Malvus unleashed Hel on Scalussen. Yet Farden and his general stood strong, surviving battle, poison, and assassins until Loki's deceptions resulted in the capture of Mithrid. It was in Malvus' camp that Mithrid found another survivor of Troughwake, and realised the evil of empire.

After a daring rescue by Farden, Mithrid was curiously set free by none other than Loki, and she returned to Scalussen to join the final battle. Farden had one last plan, and that was to release the power of Irminsul, the nearby volcano, and use it against the Arka. To do this, he needed Mithrid's power.

In the last vital moments of battle, Mithrid's power woke the volcano. Using all his power, Farden wielded Irminsul's fire against Malvus, sweeping aside the Arka forces in a cataclysm of flame and sacrificing the city of Scalussen for victory. But when the spell proved too powerful, Durnus and Mithrid were left with no choice but to stop Farden, and in doing so, the vampyre transported them thousands of miles east, far beyond Emaneska.

While the rest of Scalussen escaped to their fleet and giant bookships to sail south, Mithrid, Durnus, Warbringer, Aspala, Fleetstar, and Farden found themselves lost in Easterealm. Vengeful and desperate, they began a quest for the Spear of Gunnir, an ancient weapon capable of destroying Loki and guarded by a riddle that took them deep into unknown lands. There was one problem: the power of Farden's Scalussen armour and his magick dwindled after the battle, and he grew weaker by the day.

Rejected by a Krauslung now devoted to their saviour Loki, the Scalussen fleet were chased south by leviathans. So began a running battle between monster and ship, and it claimed many Scalussen and Siren lives.

In the meantime, Loki was hailed as a god by Krauslung, and basked in their adoration while he wove his next plot: turning the surviving Malvus into an abomination. With the Hides of Hysteria and the stolen copy of Farden's book, Malvus was transformed into a tortured monster of magick. With Loki and daemons at his side, Malvus marched east to put an end to Farden and Mithrid.

His prey meanwhile forged deeper into unknown lands, making enemies everywhere they went, and after seeking shelter in Golikar, Warbringer and Aspala were forced into the Scarlet Tourney: a fight to the death against Easterealm's finest fighters. With the help of Irien, the Lady of Whispers, they managed to escape east and south, and unravelled more of the riddle with every mile. All the while, Mithrid wrestled with her new power and the carnage wrought in the ice fields. A keen sense that she was meant for more took root in her mind.

When the Scalussen survivors finally found peace in the far south of Emaneska, their survival was thanks to a mysterious creature of the depths, glimpsed only momentarily before it drove the leviathans away. With Scalussen finally safe, Elessi and Lerel decided to defy Loki's threats and journeyed east to find Farden, Mithrid, and the others. The voyage was perilous, and when pirates and monsters loomed, they were once again saved by the strange creature of the deep.

Now in Khandri, Farden and Mithrid faced their hardest challenge and narrowest escape yet in the caves of the creature Utiru. With her mind magick weighing heavy, and questions of destiny and Mithrid's power rife, Farden pushed the others southwards towards Gunnir. Enemies closed in from every angle, and they raced for the spear's resting place: Azanimur.

While Easterealm, Malvus, and the daemons converged on Azanimur, and Farden's recklessness looked to have doomed them all, his plan was revealed, and his enemies unleashed chaos on each other instead. In the distraction, Loki, Farden, Mithrid, Durnus, and Warbringer battled for the spear, and Durnus sacrificed himself to prevent the god from claiming Gunnir. Once the spear was in Farden's hands, his armour and magick were restored, and Loki fled.

It was now down to Mithrid, and she stood alone against Malvus to crush his abominable magick. And though the daemons descended from the sky in their hundreds, she and Farden turned them away with shadow and Gunnir's fire. Scalussen won once more, and with the spear's power, they returned to Paraia and the new home of Scalussen alongside Elessi and Lerel.

And yet the wounds they wrought in the east and north have begun to fester, and might soon infect the world.

The war is far from over.

A PRELUDE

A full moon crossed twice with cloud was an omen of a dangerous night, the old'uns said. Spittle and dreamings was all it was. And that's precisely what Doree told herself as she surveyed the gorse and rabbit holes beyond the walls.

Paying the moon no attention, Doree stretched her legs. Strange talk of strange things spread like fever along the fortifications and in the courtyards and streets below. Talk of white eyes and white fangs in the dark from travelling traders. Guards muttered of screams caught on the southerly wind. Taste of magick in the air, said some of the seers.

Nonsense.

As old Grey Kanaa always opined after a few pints of Gabo's best ale, people were better off without magick in their lives.

'Ain't you Doree?' a fellow leaned close to ask.

She had not seen him on militia duty before. He had a pelican's beak of a nose and an ill-fitting kettle helmet he insisted on adjusting every other moment. His eyes held a certain glint that drew her to stare.

'Giminee's apprentice?'

Doree nodded in reply. Few in the town spared time to talk to Doree, and she didn't like to talk much either. Hers was a tiny circle. Orphan's curse, they called it on the island of Kasto.

The lad tilted her head and wiped at his forehead. 'Njord. I'm surprised I remembered. I'm not blessed when it comes to names.'

'And you?' she asked.

He paused, as if he hadn't expected the question. 'Oh, er, Finii.'

The fletcher's boy.

'You must be militia, not a lifer, then?' Finii asked.

'Militia,' replied Doree, squinting at the useless question.

'Same.'

Doree could almost hear the scratching of quills and paper in his head as he thought of what to say next. It was oddly endearing.

The smile emboldened Finii. 'You have any idea what they're afraid of, having so many of us called up and out here all at once? Seems like the whole town's in the square or on the walls.'

Doree watched the pale blue leaves of the tree-line shift to the west as the wind changed. Something shrieked in the sapphire woods, and no matter how much Doree blamed an owl, the more it sounded like anything but an owl.

'Storm, I reckon,' she answered. 'Like the strangeness in the north sky those weeks ago? Everyone got all shifty then, and I think it's the same as that. Other goings-on in the world that don't concern Kasto.'

'I hope you ain't wrong,' Finii replied with a wider smile. 'Better than the talk of wisps the hunters keep trading in. Gives me the shivers, I don't mind saying.'

Doree felt a shiver right there and then and stamped her foot for luck. Finii did the same. It was bad to talk of wisps. To speak the name of the dead brought the dead from their ocean graves.

'If you don't mind me saying, a carpenter and a fletcher's lad might find a lot to talk about, if we had the time to do so when we weren't trussed up in these leathers.'

Doree hoped the darkness and torches hid the heat she felt in her cheeks. 'Is that an invitation, Finii?'

He finally took the helmet off, showing a mane of bronze hair. 'It might be, if—'

A single toll of a bell broke the night. Every head in the square swivelled as one.

It came from the west tower, and its lights vanished moments after the bell sang. Those who had been lounging stood upright. Conversations died. Iron was drawn and curious steps taken westward.

'What's going on up there, Garbo?' called one of the headmen to the tower.

A scream answered, rising above the lasting whine of the bell. It was the kind of scream that had an excruciating and haunting finality to it. Finii seized at Doree's arm, abruptly nothing to do with the romance he was so set on instigating.

Something tumbled from the tower. Something small and ragged in shape, spitting wet as it fell. Just like every other soul in that stretch of mud and stone, Doree watched the object sail into the centre of the courtyard, landing with half a squelch and half a stomach-wrenching crunch. Anyone within spitting distance was spattered with blood.

Doree felt winter in her gut as the truth dawned.

It was a head, severed and broken by the fall. Somehow the braided hair still looked immaculate as always.

'It's bloody Gabo!' came the howl of the headman, an animal sound: all horror. 'It's his bloody head!'

Arrows struck in a hellish rain. Those who didn't suffer mortal wounds convulsed and foamed at the mouth as a poison racked them. Half the militia around Doree dropped dead and dying, including Finii. His grip on her arm went painful tight and then lax as he slumped to his knees, an arrow through the top of the skull and pretty eyes turned inwards. Doree's screech joined the chorus of terror filling the square.

The town surrendered within moments, but even that was still too late to save them. Black shadows, all spindle-legged, crawled over the mortar of the stockade. The flames of the torches showed no features other than snarling masks, pale skin, sharp black blades, and the shine of blue magick in their claws.

'FLEE!' came the scream of the headman.

Doree had no family. She had few friends beyond those who already lay dead or headless. She was no soldier, only a carpenter's apprentice, and an average one, at that. Doree surrendered to the purest instinct: to survive, and there was no guilt nor other urgency to quell the sheer terror that set her feet in motion.

A bolt of blue fire scorched her face as Doree hurled herself behind a cart. The searing pain cut her breath short, but there was no time for anything but panic. Moments after she was up and running again, the cart exploded in flame. There was no cover for her there, and a splinter long as her forearm pierced the leathers of her shoulder. The pain of it blackened her vision for a moment, and a good thing too, for it sent her careening into the baker's open door. To Doree's scream, an arrow pierced the door between her splayed fingers. Inhuman snarls chased her as she sprinted into the warren of his storerooms. There was a door somewhere to the north square, she knew it, and pawing in the half-dark, breath as short as a hiccup, she found it.

Blue fire greeted her. It lined the palisade and jumped from thatch to thatch. More concerning was the immediate sight of Grey Kanaa with a spear in each hand. He managed to hold two of the fell shadows at bay just long enough for Doree to witness a third slice him almost in half with a vicious sword. The blood painted Doree crimson, and she could taste Kanaa in her mouth, too choked to scream.

Doree wasn't given a moment to consider the horror, the loss, or the jarring alteration to her existence. Another of the creatures bent over a nearby corpse to slice around the cheek and peel the skin from the bone. Doree spat bile as well as blood as it placed the flayed flesh over its black mask. Worse still, she recognised the stolen face. It was poor Giminee, Doree's master. Heart thundering, all she could do was flee, and she scrabbled away on all fours.

Breaking from the north gate, Doree joined a panicked stream of townspeople. Black arrows knocked them down in dozens, from children to the grey and hobbled. A prayer fell from Doree's mouth to the blue forest as she held her hands above her head and hoped one wasn't meant for her. Only once did she look back, and later she would dearly wish she hadn't.

To see the tall slivers of evil dancing against the rising blue and orange fire, hacking apart the still and the moving, and stringing the dead up to butcher was horrific, but they paled to what lurked in the flame-shadows. The giant beast of Hel that hunched over the dead to feast looked as big as a barn. All legs and spines. The mere glimpse of it wounded Doree far more gravely than the creatures' vicious blades ever could have. It would have been a mercy to fall to her knees and wait there for her death, but her legs didn't let her.

Feet slipping in the grass, screams of both prey and predator filling the night, Doree sprinted through the woods without sound, caring nothing for how the branches cut her to ribbons, eyes glazed, mind broken by fear.

RUST

CHAPTER 1
OF DAEMONS & WOLVES

The Claw of Tolema was the farthest south the Arka Empire ever reached into Paraia. Too far, some might say. The fortress was a hurl of a threatening spear far into unbroken territory, left with no arm to wield it and no army to follow. It was built and forgotten just as quickly. Merely a fine marker on a map to make Paraia feel conquered.
FROM THE WRITINGS OF BIBIO TECK, SCROLLMASTER OF TOLEMA

ONE WEEK LATER

In Ardion's mind – which was a filthy, barren, and depraved place not unlike the fetid tangle of alleys he lorded over – there was nothing better than waking up to a pair of still-drunk wenches.

Except perhaps a trio of wrenches.

Extending a hand slick with chicken grease, Ardion pawed at the nearest woman and shook her awake. A groan came from her at the sight of him, utterly ruining the illusion he'd concocted. Her eyes went wide as she realised her mistake.

The same hand reeled back to slap her just as frantic knocking thundered on Ardion's door.

'Not now! Begone with you!' Ardion bellowed, spraying spittle and crumbs of the previous night's feast from his beard.

Ardion had always suspected Captain Thrift owned a key to his private chambers, but his suspicions were not confirmed that day. Thrift used his boot instead of any stolen key. Within two kicks, the lock gave way, and splinters sprayed the bed.

Thrift stood framed in torchlight, the copper running through his horns aglow. To the untrained glance, the captain was a broomstick of a man, but beneath his armour, he had the muscle of two men in the space of half.

Thrift was not alone. Two of Ardion's ugliest sergeants craned to ogle the lord and his naked companions.

'What in blood-drenched Hel do you think you're doing?!' Ardion hollered, enraged and, to tell the absolute truth, in the grip of fear. A fear that all those in positions of power shared: earning the angry knives of their subjects.

But Thrift did not move, and for a moment he only stared. Not gazing across the battlefield of debauchery that was Ardion's chambers, but straight into the lord's eyes, and so intently it speared Ardion still.

'They're coming,' Thrift said.

Whatever blood had been rushing through Ardion's face drained into his thick gut and pooled there. His morning horn had gone right down. This was much worse than angry knives.

'You lie, you bastard,' Ardion spat.

Thrift shook his head firmly.

'Shit on it!' Ardion cursed, tugging at his hair as he walked in circles. It was only a matter of time until the Claw of Tolema fell under siege by the usurper, but Ardion had wagered he had weeks left, maybe months. 'How far away?'

'Less than an hour, milord.'

'Hel's teeth! How did you not notice until now?'

'They raised spells of mist and shadow, milord—'

Ardion flapped an agitated hand in the captain's face. Less than an hour was still enough time to get to his private tunnels: the ratholes he had built in secret. So secret, in fact, that Ardion had the workers strangled and buried in their own construction after the tunnels were done. The soldiers who had done the strangling also mysteriously disappeared or wound up finding asps in their beds.

It was also perhaps enough time to arrange a cart for his best and heaviest chests. All Ardion needed was a few strong men dumb and desperate enough not to turn on him once they were free. *To Hel with this diseased and sand-ridden cow's arsehole he had once sworn to uphold. Fuck Loki's orders and the god he pretended to be,* he thought. Ardion had not heard from Krauslung in months. If Loki had forgotten Ardion and his godsforsaken outpost, then Ardion would forget Loki just as easily.

Thrift's gaze narrowed as if he eavesdropped on his commander's thoughts. Ardion didn't put it past him. Paraia lacked the magick of the Arka, but it still lurked in their bloodlines. It refused to remain controlled no matter how hard its cinders were stamped on. By that measure, Ardion had failed the task the late Emperor Malvus had set him half a decade ago: to conquer Paraia from within.

'Your orders, Lord Ardion?' Thrift asked as panicked shouting rose up from within the castle.

Ardion was still deep in his silent plotting.

'Ardion!' Thrift yelled. More officers gathered at the door, gawping and clueless.

The lord straightened, ignoring the disjointed clicking in his sleep-heavy spine and knees. 'We make a stand, of course! What else did you expect?' he shouted.

'This is not some small rebellion wielding farm tools, Lord Ardion. They've reduced every outpost and watchtower to rubble,' argued Thrift. Not for the first time, Ardion regretted choosing a Paraian as his captain and not a pliable Arka.

'And this is the Claw of Tolema! The walls of this fortress have never been broken!'

'Walls? They turned the north to ash and bones!'

'Do you wish to surrender, Thrift? That is not the way of the empire and the god you swore allegiance to, Captain!' Ardion bellowed. Surrender was out of the question. He could not simply parley Tolema away. That was a recipe for a rope about his neck. A glorious battle that Ardion barely survived was a much finer excuse. And a fine tale that would go down deliciously in the courts and cathouses of Krauslung. Or perhaps sunny Essen. 'Or have you carelessly forgotten your oath and become a coward after all these years of dutiful service? Do I need to remind you that we hang oath-breakers in Tolema?'

'No, Lord Ardion,' Thrift murmured. He was a man of honour and therefore a fool. It was laughable how deeply Ardion had once cared about honour and the glory of the Arka Empire. In the school of Paraia's wastelands, Ardion had learned the true secret to a happy life. It didn't lie in honour but in lavish things: in wine, gold, and women. They were much finer treasures to fight for.

Or, in this case, to flee for.

'Then get to work! And that goes for the rest of you gutless swine! These outlaws expect us to cower in the face of tyranny, but we will do no such thing! We Arka will reign over these lands for a thousand more years if we make a stand. *Here*. Today.' Ardion jabbed at his palm. 'Remember, you work the will of a living god, men! These outlaws have no such divine purpose, and they will regret their foolishness by sunset, I promise you!'

The false bravado worked on all of them save for Thrift. He had heard too many of Ardion's empty speeches over the years. They were nothing but Galadaë vases: gilded yet brittle and hollow within. Thrift's gaze lingered on Ardion as the captain gave his orders.

'Every soldier to the walls and ballistae. Rally the mages. Drop the stonegates. Ready the fire arrows and boil the cauldrons! And bring out Bigface! Maybe the sight of our pet will change their minds.'

Ardion was busy tapping his foot and planning what to do as soon as the door was closed. 'Very good, Captain, now off to the walls with you. I will remain to oversee the defence in the war room.'

Thrift wasn't done. He raised a hand and snapped fingers at his sergeants. 'And fetch our honourable lord his armour.'

'I made no such order!' protested Ardion. 'I am needed elsewhere, Captain.'

'Nonsense,' Thrift whispered as he thrust the lord's sword into his hands. His sergeants loomed at his shoulders. 'You'll no doubt want to see this glorious victory of ours up close and make a stand together. For you also swore an oath to the Arka, did you not? Like you said, oath-breakers are hanged in Tolema.'

Ardion had spent a life forging excuses and lies, yet there he was: utterly tripped by one of his own making. He watched with jealousy as his women bolted from the room. His anger overcame the fear and cruelty blossoming.

'In that case, Captain Thrift,' Ardion said with a sneer, 'I want every gate closed, and I want every soul strong enough to bend a bow, hurl a spear, or drop a bloody rock lined up on the walls. Every gate. Every soul. If you want us to stand together, then so be it.'

Thrift chewed his words before he spat them out. 'Yes, milord.'

With little ceremony and much bruising, the soldiers stuffed Ardion into his armour piece by piece. The Manesmark plate was largely for show, all polish and Paraian gems. He had swapped his battle-scarred steel for silver when he had chosen a life of wine and velvet cushions.

'After you, sire,' said Thrift, gesturing for the door.

Ardion briefly considered how much coin it would take to bribe him, but Thrift and his lot were warriors through and through and bound to their oaths to the Arka as conquered Paraians. It was one of Emperor Malvus' old tricks, and it made their price far too high for his liking. He would simply have to sneak away at the earliest opportunity to avoid the blades of the outlaws. Or Thrift's, for that matter.

'Out of my way, fools!' Ardion barged his way down the stairs, leaving the cool of thick stone behind for the blistering, unabating heat of the desert and the ever-present stench of peasant shit rotting in gutters. There was a foul dust on the breeze. Ardion felt it crunch between his teeth as he grumbled to himself. Magick, too, heavy in the air like the promise of lightning.

Rank after rank of Arka and sworn Paraian soldiers raised their spears to him in salute. Ardion saw their furrowed brows of surprise at seeing him in armour. There was little respect there beyond basic training and the fear Ardion would have them punished if they didn't salute. It wouldn't have been the first time. The bodies of the most recent insult hung from the fortress gates, still meaty enough for the crows and vuleguls to pick at.

Storming across the mucked flagstones of shaded streets, they wound towards the southern walls of the Claw of Tolema. Ardion watched his people run around him like squabbling chickens. The able lined up to have rusty spears and swords thrust into their shaking hands.

It was little solace that the robust walls of the fortress had famously never been broken. In truth, the walls had only witnessed a handful of rebellions over the years and brief battles with settlements that refused to toe the Arka line. Tolema's inhabitants knew how empty the claim was, and that it had never been tested. It was why the young scampered and the old hobbled for the paltry and temporary safety of their homes and Tolema's caverns.

Amidst soldiers drenched in sweat, fattened mages wiping hangovers from their faces, and jostling currents of panic and preparation, they began to climb the walls. Ardion was drenched by the dozenth step. He had to stop and rest halfway, using the ruse of watching the stonegates drop. It was an awe-inspiring sight to witness the colossal sandstone slabs swivel and drop into position behind the gates and minor doors. But Ardion barely paid attention, instead listening to his booming heartbeat race the clanking of cogs and ratchets.

'This way, sire,' Thrift reminded him.

'Yes, yes, gods damn it! I know my own fortress!'

With his heart threatening to pop from his chest, Ardion made it to the top of the spiked wall where ballistae and catapults hunched.

Even though they were ready to fire, their ropes were not nearly as tense as the mood upon the battlements.

Ardion leaned on the crenellations, heaving with breath. Masked by the mists and twirling dust storms, their enemy spread in a thin line a quarter mile across the scrub and wasteland. Ardion snatched a spyglass from a quivering soldier and jammed it against his eye. The ilk that waited to crash against Tolema's walls looked motley: nothing more than ill-formed ranks of soldiers in mismatched armour and the rags of poor desert-dwellers. The paler skin of perfidious northerners stood alongside the beastly fur of Paraian traitors and Jar-Khoum southerners.

'Is that it? No peasants wielding farm tools, you said, Captain? Ha!' Ardion scoffed, somewhat relieved. These fools couldn't have been the outlaws that defeated Malvus in the north. 'The reports are nothing but fear-mongering cow-shit!'

As if the enemy had spotted Lord Ardion atop the parapets, it was then the shadow and dust spells lifted. Thick and tight formations came into view behind the thin line of motley warriors, bristling with polished lances and swords. The sun shone on a sea of bright armour, and magick crackled in the fading clouds of shadow as a gale blew the dust at Tolema like a first volley.

A shiver ran across Ardion's sweat-drenched skin, and it was nothing to do with the stiff breeze. The spyglass in his hands quivered.

'Are those… minotaurs?' gasped a sergeant, ugly face scrunched around his own spyglass.

They were indeed. Ardion's teeth crunched on dust again.

'But Tolema can hold them at bay, isn't that right, Lord Ardion?' asked Thrift.

Ardion might have been a coward. He was most definitely lazy. But he was not a moron, and he was not going to lose his life protecting that stinking fortress. All Ardion needed was a distraction, and what better distraction was there than the madness of battle?

Ardion's boldness grew, and he began to weave together the threads of his escape. 'Get me the Mouth,' he said with a smile.

An ear-piercing rattle grated on Ardion's ears as soldiers manhandled an iron frame along the battlements. A bulbous copper cone perched between its bars. Ardion put his mouth to the narrow end of the contraption, hoping a soldier hadn't pissed on it like last time. Through the cone, even whispered words could boom across the scrubland.

'Begone, traitors! You'll not breach these walls today or any other day, and you will perish trying!' Ardion baited them.

A lone figure emerged from the shining masses, traipsing along on the back of a persnippen bird. They trotted at a leisurely and infuriating pace, and Ardion scraped his nails against the battlements.

'Archers!' he snapped at Thrift.

The captain's eyes were fixed on the army. 'They may want to parley.'

'I do not give a single pinch of shit what they want. Archers!'

When the figure at last approached the walls, Ardion stood on the highest part of the gatehouse, hands spread wide and jewelled armour catching the sun. The envoy was a bright-haired woman, and Ardion glowered as she waved half-heartedly like a common peasant and stifled a yawn in the same moment. Dusty armour hid beneath her cloak. A sunburnt face creased in a weak smile.

'Morning!' she called out. 'Or is it afternoon? I take it you're the one in charge?'

'Who in the true god's name are you? By what authority do you dare approach my gates and address me so insolently?' Ardion barked back.

'Frankly, I'm here because I lost a bet. But probably more importantly, I've come to offer you an ultimatum.'

'I should shoot you where you stand for your arrogance!'

'I understand the impulse. I do. Now, which lord are you again?'

'I…' Ardion paused to quell his outrage enough to speak. 'I am Lord Ardion of Krauslung, Fist of the South, appointed by Emperor Malvus, and anointed by the one living god, and you will speak to me as such!'

'Hi Ardion, I'm General Hereni. I'm here to ask you to lay down your arms, to separate your army from the folk who didn't sign up to fight, and to solve this without anyone needing to die. Or, you can make the wrong decision and put up a fight, but I'd strongly suggest the first option.'

Ardion should have been silently patting himself on the rump for securing his distraction, but the bitch's contempt was detestable. These outlaws were nothing short of animals, and he wanted to put this one down like the dog she was.

For a brief moment, as outrage ruled him, Ardion considered abandoning his escape and putting some truth behind the tale of glorious battle. With the citizen conscripts, Tolema had a greater number of soldiers, plus fifty rotund yet capable Arka mages. And siege weapons. And walls thicker than a bastion's backside. Defeating the outlaws that had taken the life of the emperor was a far more glorious story, after all…

'Shoot her,' Ardion ordered in nothing short of a growl.

Thrift hesitated, and the growl turned into a roar.

'Shoot this impudent peasant between the eyes!'

Thrift gave the order, and the percussion of a dozen bows loosing cut the stale air. Hereni raised a condescending eyebrow as the arrows raced for her. Ardion tensed, eager to see her pincushioned.

The arrows turned to splinters in midair, mere feet from her face. Ripples spread from their impacts, etching a sphere of transparent magick around her and her ugly bird. She was a damned mage.

'Shoot her again!' Ardion spat.

Before Thrift could raise his voice, Hereni held up a hand.

'I'll take that to mean you've made the wrong decision,' she said, turning her bird around and calling to the rest of the walls. 'To those of you not in fancy armour and who disagree with your lord, we will give you time to try to change his mind before we begin.'

Ardion whirled on Thrift before mutiny could erupt, spitting as he spoke. 'Unleash Bigface! Let's see how that shrew deals with my prize.'

Despite the cheers that ran along the walls, Thrift hesitated once more. 'Lord Ardion—'

'You heard them! Unless you would have us bend the knee to these traitors and let them overrun an Arka stronghold, we have no choice but to defend ourselves! Would you forsake your god in such a way? Once again, you forget your oath!'

Ardion let the captain reel before he hit him with another verbal blow.

'Unleash Bigface, you poltroon! I want that bitch and her traitorous friends crushed under his claws! Show them the real force of Tolema!' Ardion screeched, raising his hands to coax some cheering from the crowds.

The soldiers began to stamp their boots and spears in unison as workers sprang to work the giant wheels that punctuated the parapets. To the fierce clanking of chains, a chanting filled the air.

Bigface! Bigface! Bigface!

Face stretched in a grin, Ardion turned to watch the chasm open amidst the scrub beyond the gates. Ardion could already feel the thunderous feet of the beast Tolema kept in its deepest caverns. It was a creature caught long before Ardion had arrived in that sandy arsehole, long before Malvus and the Last War. Longer than centuries, or so the citizens liked to whisper.

Ardion's grin grew so wide it verged on painful as Bigface exploded from the mouth of his cave and onto the plains in a cloud of dust and dirtied straw.

The locals called him a rathcata. A troll was what the Arka would call him, but he was not one of wood or stone, but a tortured monster of raw flesh and sinew, twenty feet tall and half that wide. He was a hulking pet that Ardion kept just hungry enough to be a weapon when he needed one. Or whenever he fancied watching somebody who had offended him be torn limb from limb.

Bigface earned his name from the shape of his skull, elongated like the head of a pickaxe. Jaws heavy with needle fangs and constantly dripping with blood halved his pale and scarred face, devoid of eyes, nose, or ears. Sharp bones protruded from his back like a dragon's spines. Two pairs of arms hung heavy from his gaunt shoulders and ribcage, and his knuckles dragged in the sand, carving furrows with claws as long and curved as sabres.

Ardion's pet emitted a nerve-rending scream as it set its unseen eyes on the outlaw army. Bare bones and sinew creaked and clicked as the beast lurched into a run.

'Let them rue their insolence!' Ardion yelled triumphantly.

Farden sighed and pressed finger and thumb to his temples. 'Now what in Hel is that?'

'Ugly, is what it is,' grumbled Warbringer at his back.

'Is it your turn or mine?' Farden asked of the figure standing next to him. 'I've lost count.'

Mithrid counted on her fingers. 'Yours?'

'You're a liar, Mithrid Fenn.'

'I took the last two outposts.'

'That's debatable.'

'Maybe it's my turn,' Warbringer said, thumping her warhammer on the dirt and making it sigh in its ghostly voice.

Hereni rejoined them, descending from her persnippen and smacking it on the scaled backside to make it charge through the ranks to safety. 'I bet you can guess what their commander, Lord Ardion, chose.'

'Death,' Farden replied with a sigh. 'Fine. Let's say it's my turn.'

'Remember the innocents. We focus on taking prisoners, not digging graves,' Elessi warned them all, standing slightly removed from the front lines with the Jar Khoum and Ko-Tergo's ice field forces.

'I will, if there are any left in this fortress,' Farden muttered. The mage stepped out to face the monster, his Scalussen armour whispering as the metal plates shifted.

'Still with me?' he asked of the glimmering spear in his right hand once he was out of earshot.

The soul within Gunnir whispered in Farden's head, the words faint as always. A sigh on a breeze.

You still have to ask?

'Just making sure I don't embarrass myself,' Farden breathed, already feeling the power vibrating his arm.

The hideous creature thundered towards him, closing fast as it galloped on its multiple arms. Its jaws already stretched wide in anticipation, and great clumps of spittle flew in the wind.

With only moments to spare, Farden dug his heels into the parched earth and lowered the spear. It had required painful practice to channel the sheer magick of the god's weapon, but by now his grasp was firm.

Taking a sharp breath, Farden unleashed the gods-given power in the spear. A bolt of white lightning shot from its elf-steel tip, carving a notch in the monster from hip to chest. Its roaring withered into a whine as it began to tumble and slide across the scrub. A second blast of Gunnir severed half its arms, and Farden pivoted to the side as the horrendous creature slid to a halt inches from his boots and slipped into death with a groan.

The others had already caught up.

'Show off,' Mithrid accused as she strode past the mage.

'For freedom, Scalussen!' Farden yelled, magick speeding his voice across the plains and making the Scalussen army jolt forwards as one. Their combined voices shook the air.

❦

Before an aghast Ardion could close his gaping mouth, a storm-wave of raw magick tore the stone from the tops of the battlements, spraying soldiers with rubble and fire. As if the sun had crashed down upon the plain, a flash of sheer light blinded the walls. Lightning cut a nearby tower in two, and stone tumbled onto the packed walls.

Ardion had been gifted the battle he wanted, just a little too quickly.

'Give them everything we have!' Thrift was screaming, and a volley of spells scorched Ardion's head as the mages below unleashed their magick in retaliation.

It did little to halt the onslaught. Fireballs as large as wagons collided with the walls and stonegates. Bolts of lightning threw scores of soldiers from the walls. A ballista close to Ardion exploded under the brunt of a spell, shattering and piercing soldiers with its shards. Shards of masonry clanged against his armour.

Thrift sought to drag him up, but Ardion shrugged him away.

'It seems you have everything handled here by my reckoning, Thrift!' he said, already slyly edging to the stairs. 'I will check on the other defences to make sure they hold—'

Thrift's eyes pierced Ardion's lies. He bared his teeth and his true feelings as he seized Ardion by the neck, halting the lord's escape. The fancy armour counted for naught with Thrift's vice grip around his unprotected windpipe.

'You want Tolema to fight, Lord Ardion? Then you will stand with your warriors as well as your decision. And if we should die because of the path you've chosen, then so will you.'

'This is mutiny, oath-breaker!' cried Ardion.

'I am no such thing. I made a vow, and though I curse myself daily for it, I will hold myself to the words I spoke. That is honour you will never know.'

'Unhand me! I command it!'

'You are a worthless slug, Ardion,' growled Thrift before he bellowed his orders in the lord's face. 'Reinforce that position! Get water on that gate! Archers! Concentrate fire on the centre! If this is going to be our last stand, then it'll be a damn good one! One the old gods would be proud of!'

It was a fine moment of inspiration. Amidst the sea of wide eyes drowning with panic and despair, a glimmer of rebellion briefly shone. A hope of a fine welcome to the other side and a fanfare in Haven to greet their souls.

By poor luck, it was also the moment that a blast of unbridled magick cut a ragged path through the gatehouse. Body after screaming body tumbled from the heights of the famed walls. The stonegates counted for little. Magick carved through their slabs and half the mages standing behind them.

In the commotion, Thrift's grip fell from Ardion's neck, and the lord seized the chance to flee. The captain was still struggling to stand upright by the time Ardion reached the stairs. Ardion was spry for a man of his size when his life came into question. With the stone collapsing under his feet, Ardion sprinted for anywhere but the walls. Even amidst the heights of brutal defeat, his mind was already calculating losses and gains. Most of his treasures would have to go forgotten, but he was pleased by the burns on his back and the cuts on his hands. They would be fine proof of his future lies of glorious battle.

As soon as Ardion's boots touched the sand, the gates detonated behind him. Stone blocks flattened soldiers around him, and it was all he could do to keep running. Spells rocketed over his shoulders, so close their heat scorched him. Ardion dared one glance over his shoulder, and between the glowing holes in his fortress, he saw Thrift torn between giving chase and his laughable honour.

Ardion almost cackled aloud until he saw the hulking monster emerge from the dust and flames between the broken gates.

The minotaur wore more muscle than twenty men. Deadly horns longer than Ardion's arms curved towards the sky. A gigantic warhammer rested in its hands. The beast didn't need to swing it to carve a path through the soldiers. Fear alone did that.

Ardion stumbled in panic, and his shrill cry fetched the minotaur's gaze. His shining armour did the opposite of protecting his life and brought attention he didn't wish for. With a ground-shaking roar, the minotaur levelled its warhammer at him and began to charge.

'Loki's balls!' Ardion gasped as he scrambled across the sand. Sweat streamed down his face as he tried to outpace the monster. Weaving between barrels of arrows and broken wagons did nothing to keep death at bay. The minotaur broke them like rotten tinder.

Wind graced his bald scalp as the warhammer missed him by mere feet. Ardion seized a fleeing soldier and hurled him into the minotaur's path. The man's scream was cut short by a hammer to the face, efficiently snapping his head from his shoulders. Ardion swore the weapon screamed as it sprayed a fountain of blood.

'Kill that bloody creature, I command you!' Ardion bellowed, but his orders might as well have been issued to corpses. He thrust another soldier between him and the minotaur, and a hoof caved in the man's breastplate and ribs.

Ardion fled for an armoury's doorway, hoping it would buy him time. But before he could cross its threshold, two spells collided with its walls and showered him with bricks. Ardion flopped on the flagstones like a dying harbour seal while an ominous shadow darkened the earth around him.

'Back, you mindless beast! Back I say!' he screeched, praying bravado would save his bruised skin. 'I demand mercy! I demand to parley with your leader!'

The fall of the warhammer halted excruciatingly close to his forehead. A displeased grunt blasted through the beast's nostrils, peppering Ardion with snot.

'You hear me? Parley!' he gasped.

'Parley,' it spoke, making Ardion flinch, but he bade his time. When at last the minotaur turned to face the chaos of the walls, Ardion scrabbled to his feet and fled like the coward he had become.

Once he was behind the first corner, he uttered a cackle and danced between alley and gutter to keep the minotaur as far behind him as possible. A swift look over his shoulder proved the dumb lump was too stupid to notice his escape. *Minotaurs*, Ardion scoffed. They might have had the strength of a troll, but between the ears, they had the brains of a dimwit. Ardion had stepped over smarter puddles of shit.

Speaking of shit, a smear of it on the cobbles sent him careening down the alleyway. A pile of barrels were kind enough to halt his fall. Reeling and dabbing blood from his cheek where a splinter had caught him, Ardion pressed on to his rabbit hole.

There was no time to fetch strong fools. Most of them had already gone to die at the walls and by the hands of the outlaws. Those who were already shedding armour in their attempt to flee were the kind too cowardly to hire, even by Ardion's standards. They had a good point, however, and Ardion began to shed the cheaper sections of his armour between wiping sweat from his eyes.

Unseen in the chaotic crowds, Ardion worked his way back into his opulent tower. Finding it pleasingly devoid of servants, he swiped a torch from a sconce and went immediately to the cellars. A gaggle of maids shrieked at his appearance, making Ardion pause to ponder. The road was always shorter with company…

'Gah!' he muttered. He could always find women in the next town. Behind a barrel of Midgrir's finest salted wine, he pushed at two stone protuberances in the wall, and a stairwell opened at his feet to the grinding of stone.

'Milord?' came the question as the maids began to swarm to the mouth of the tunnel.

'Get back!' Ardion yelled as he yanked the lever at the foot of the stairs. The tunnel closed in their faces no matter how they pleaded and begged. The harsh rasp of stone silenced their mournful whimpering.

Racing through the cold dark, Ardion felt the rumble of magick and tumbling masonry in the tremor of the walls. Dust sought to blind him as it fell from the tunnel's beams.

'No matter,' Ardion repeated to himself as he scurried onwards. 'No matter at all.'

From out of the dark, his prize loomed: a hollowed-out dome of rock with one entrance and one exit and occupied solely by his treasures. Bought, bargained, stolen, swindled, or prised from hands by blackmail, everything Ardion's position had earned him lay below the streets of Tolema in the same – but thankfully unconnected – tunnels Bigface had called home. It almost put a tear amongst the beads of sweat to have to choose between them all. The Essen silks or the copper carvings of a now-dead Troaclean artist? Swearing constantly, Ardion grabbed only what he could stuff into a handcart. He cursed himself for not stabling cows or persnippen down in that hole with his treasures.

With boxes and bundles and his bejewelled armour piled upon the cart, and a sackcloth draped to make it look unassuming, Ardion began the arduous task of pushing it out into the sun. It was a battle to keep the cart moving fast enough without tipping over. Ardion was soaked in sweat within fifty feet, breathless by a hundred, and questioning his whole plan and reason for living by the time he saw the glimmer of the secret exit.

It was the hardest task Ardion had ever lived through, but he was driven on by the sheer stubborn will of greed and self-preservation – and the sacrifice of a few of the heavier trinkets along the way – Ardion's meaty paw finally latched onto another lever and heaved. To a mechanical clinking and the sweet, sweet touch of sunlight on his burning skin, Ardion was free.

Smoke rushed over the hatch built into a cluster of desert rocks, presumably from Tolema burning. Screams filled the city, but Ardion didn't give it a glance as he pushed his cart out onto the baked dirt. What he did allow himself was a smile. A devious grin that stretched his chin and lifted his ears. *He had done it*. He had escaped Thrift and the rebels' justice. His new life beckoned to him from the north. He could almost imagine the ruby wine and the women flooding over the horizon like a beautiful tidal wave, ready to embrace him. Ardion looked up at the retreating clouds and imagined the shine of the Arkathedral in the heavens instead of smoke and magick, and the perfumes of Krauslung's fellow nobles on the breeze. Or the charming bustle of the silk markets—

A sharp and breathtaking pain in his chest stopped him in his tracks. His knees seemed to wobble in failure, but something was propping him up. Ardion looked down to find a thick spear protruding from his belly, just below the sternum. Its blade had pierced the cart, pinning it to the dirt, and Ardion with it.

Ardion tried to take a breath, and his throat gurgled with blood. He choked, head rolling back to see the upside-down parapets of the Claw of Tolema in his vision. There, upon the lofty battlements, stood the minotaur, with a fist raised in celebration of the fine shot that had rudely taken Ardion's life.

Ardion choked again, blood spattering the cart and his spilled treasures. The horizon grew dark, but not with ruby wine. With death and disappointment instead. With taunting laughter.

The sound that escorted Ardion from the world of the living was the faint roar of what his dimming eyes told him was the dumb beast upon the crenellations.

'There's your parley, lord!'

CHAPTER 2
OATHKEEPERS

When the Arka conquered Troacles and Belephon, they used their lack of honour to manipulate the integrity of Paraia. In the southern lands, to save another means a life oath is owed to the saviour. At the last moment before execution, Emperor Malvus would step in to spare the captured forces and their families in exchange for a turn of coat. Life, in return for becoming Arka and fighting against their own. Thousands did, and they swelled the armies of the empire. Those who did not were massacred, staining the flagstones of both cities red. Those who survived were forced to fight in Arka arenas for amusement or die gasping for water building Malvus' roads deeper south.

A RECORD OF THE ARKAN-PARAIAN WAR, WRITTEN BY GENERAL VAAL

'Tell me he wasn't somebody important, Warbringer.'

Farden needled his brow with his gauntlets as he stared down at the red splotch on the desert floor. Blinking hard, he cast a sight spell to see a plump man wearing half a suit of armour, dead as the day by sundown thanks to the spear piercing him.

'That looks like Lord Ardion. We wanted to make an example of him, remember?'

Warbringer shrugged. 'He wanted to parley. Then he ran. That broke the rules, so I broke him.'

Farden smiled. 'Wonderfully sound minotaur logic as always, Warbringer, thank you.'

The minotaur thumped her warhammer Voidaran on the parapet with a deep clang and the usual whine of ghostly wails.

'Welcome,' she said, before turning the mage around. 'And look. Example is made.'

Farden looked back at the hundreds of Arka soldiers on their knees or with their hands splayed against broken walls. Their faces were wide and coloured otherworldly by the blue sparks dancing in the hands of the mages watching over them. The Paraian soldiers and conscripted citizens amongst them stayed standing, hands empty and confused and fearful looks on their faces. The survivors on the walls who could see the corpse of Lord Ardion on the plain were beginning to whisper. One word was all they shared, and no matter how the mages told them to be quiet, the chant spread like wildfire amongst the Paraians. Farden held up his hands for peace and to let them continue.

'Bethel! Bethel! Bethel!'

'What does word mean?' Warbringer snuffled.

'All this time and you haven't learned even a pinch of Paraian?' tutted Hereni, stomping up the stairs with Mithrid and a prisoner in tow. 'It means freedom.'

'Who's this?' asked Farden.

'The second-in-command of this fortress. Captain Thrift.'

Thrift, his hands bound behind his back by rope, bowed his head in Krauslung fashion.

'Captain,' Farden greeted him. 'As you can see, your lord lies dead. We planned on letting you deliver justice and punishment for how poorly I wager he has treated you, but I hope this will suffice and in some way make up for those you lost here today.' Farden had not failed to notice the cages in the fortress' squares and the executioner's blocks, well-dented from use.

Thrift looked at each of his captors, as if expecting a blade from any of them at any moment. 'You have not come to kill us? What of the other outposts and towers burned? The massacres we heard tell of?'

'Lies. Rumours. Gossip. Take your pick.' Farden waved his hand south. 'The people south of you now stand with us in our fight for a free Paraia. The only ones massacred were the Arka who stood against us and who paid the price for their crimes of cruelty. Trust me: even if I was the kind of king that executed prisoners, my High General Elessi would rip me another arsehole if I did. And between you and I, Thrift, I'm rather happy with just the one. Mithrid, free his ropes.'

Thrift looked torn between a scowl of confusion and a smile.

'Tolema is yours now, as is this land,' explained Mithrid, as she handed him the untied bonds.

'The oath you made to the Arka doesn't apply now the Arka have lost, and that means you and your soldiers are free. And as you're the captain, I'm leaving you in charge,' Farden told him. 'Whatever Ardion took from you is yours and your people's now.'

Thrift held the ropes in his hand, squeezing tighter and tighter until, in an abrupt explosion of limbs, he threw them into the air.

'Bethel!' Thrift roared to the crowds of captured.

Leaving Tolema to enjoy its emancipation, Farden and the others walked the walls, mobbed by the shouts and hands reaching to touch their shoulders. All except Warbringer. For one, nobody could reach that high, but it was the sharp fangs she bared that kept them all at bay.

'What did we lose on our side?' Farden asked of his generals while he watched Ilios fly circles around the fortress.

'Nearly a hundred Scalussen soldiers and a handful of good mages,' answered Hereni.

Farden nodded solemnly. 'Be sure to give them a pyre,' he said. 'And Tolema?'

'From what we've counted so far, almost two thousand soldiers dead, mostly Arka, but also several hundred indentured Paraian soldiers and citizens who were either forced to fight or who didn't get to the safety of the caves below the city. Elessi is helping with the wounded in the southern plaza,' she said.

The numbers felt like a fist pressing against Farden's chest.

'As for prisoners, we have several thousand captured by the main gate, mostly Arka. They aren't happy Thrift gave in.'

'Then there's also the matter of the prisoners the good Lord Ardion kept locked away. There must be hundreds of Toleman. Tolemish? Tolemites?' Mithrid paused, nose scrunched.

'Tolemian?'

'Have Thrift free those who are innocent,' Farden said, raising Gunnir to the sky. With a shrill cry, Ilios folded his wings in a vertical dive, and the mage stepped onto the crenellations.

Mithrid folded her arms. 'And where are you going?'

'The sooner we get this fortress on its feet, the sooner we can move on,' Farden answered. With a casual step, as if he were simply avoiding a puddle, the mage walked into empty air and landed on his gryphon's back as Ilios rocketed past. Ilios trilled as they soared back into the sky, but Farden did not miss the narrowing of Hereni's gaze.

The crowds of imprisoned Arka recoiled at the sandy whirlwind caused by the gryphon's wings.

Farden jumped to the earth and broken flagstones with a dull clank of armour. He saw some of the surviving Arka mages cowering and noticed their eyes glancing at Gunnir quick and sharp-like, as if it would turn them to stone if they stared too long. And maybe it could have. The spear was still somewhat of a mystery to Farden. He had swum its surface but not yet delved into its depths.

'There you are!'

High General Elessi emerged from the crowds of Scalussen soldiers laying out the wounded across the warm stones of the square. Scores of healers moved between them, plying water and herbs for the pain. Few amongst the wounded were his own soldiers. The rest were almost all fabric-swaddled citizens of Tolema.

'We can't keep doin' this, Farden,' Elessi hissed when she was close enough.

'You can blame their dead Lord Ardion for this, not me.'

'That's too easy an excuse, and you know it,' Elessi shot back. 'What else do you expect when you taunt the lords and dukes that hold sway over these people? Their egos are too fragile, and the result is this.'

'Look how many citizens and subjugated soldiers we saved, will you?' Farden growled. 'This is war, Elessi. Be glad we lost hundreds, not thousands.'

Elessi crossed her arms, eyeing up and down. 'A war that's been going on far too long if you ask me. There'll be nobody left in Emaneska if you keep pressin' north. This has to stop.'

'It will. You can trust me on that.'

Farden swept away from her, vexed. The others' doubts had been simmering unspoken for weeks. Now they bubbled up and spilled forth like stew in an unwatched pot.

Farden toured the lines of wounded, helmet attached to a hook on his belt and spear pointed low. Many of the fallen Scalussen raised their fists and whispered, 'King,' as he passed.

The citizens of Tolema acted differently. Though most of the Paraians were in a herb-laden sleep to escape the pain of missing legs, arms, or the bloody marks of blades and magick, a handful were awake enough to cower in his shadow. One man did not, and through red-raw, unwavering eyes, he glowered at Farden while he cradled a limp child in his arms.

'You are no king,' he muttered, his voice cracked and broken from shouting.

Farden bowed to the man. Coin would have been a cheap insult. A kind word useless. An apology would have made the other rulers of the known world wince and scoff in horror, but Farden was not their kind of king.

'I am truly sorry,' he whispered before he forced himself away. Elessi caught his glance, and the wrinkle of her nose told him she saw her point had been made. There was no justice when the innocent paid the same price as the guilty. No victory.

Lady Irien had spoken the truth when she had freed Farden from Belerod's camp: Farden's taste for blood and murder was fading. Except for when it concerned Loki, of course.

Farden turned his attention to the captured Arka and traitors. The guilty, indeed. Unfortunately for them, he had seen to the wounded first, otherwise Farden might have nurtured a more forgiving mood.

Farden toured the lines of defeated, all of them fellow northerners. Roped or manacled, kneeling or standing, they had the stillness of the wounded, but they cowered less. Doubt and defiance reigned in equal measure. Doubt for what their conqueror would do with them next. Defiance against their shackles and the sight of Farden standing over them, still an outlaw in their eyes.

Farden was on the verge of passing their judgement when a grizzled Arka soldier hawked and spat on his feet. The mage stopped dead. A cooing spread between the captured, the kind made by children when some brat blurts a curse at a tutor.

Farden looked down at his sabaton, where a greasy smear of snot decorated the red and gold metal. Otherwise impeccable even in that dust. If he was the tutor, then school was now in session, and he had a lesson to teach.

Farden drew level with the soldier and leaned close until he could smell the rot of the man's gums. The Arka stretched tall and stood a few inches above Farden. It seemed to please him no end, as if size had anything to do with it.

'A cheer for the true god Loki,' the bear of a man said, wafting the stench into Farden's face. 'And down with the Outlaw King.'

A muted cheer of agreement came from his companions.

'Is that so?' Farden asked. He could feel his mages drawing closer. Elessi approached with her shortsword drawn.

The bear smiled.

'Have you ever seen your god before?' Farden challenged, raising Gunnir an inch.

'I have. In Krauslung when he turned back the daemons. Before we were sent here to spread his good word and glory.'

Farden wagged a finger at the man's sneer. 'Let me tell you something, and we'll see if I can educate you just a little before I decide what to do with you. Your true god is a cheating, lying, power-mad, soul-drinking deserter who fears to face me himself and prefers to use those who gulp down his lies to do his bidding and dying for him. Now smirk all you want, but you know if Loki cared one shite about you, he would be here showing us his godly powers and protecting his own. But he's not, because he's weak and as afraid as a false prophet and a charlatan should be. Have you ever stopped to wonder how convenient it was for Malvus to die so soon after Loki showed his face in the empire and how interesting it is that a god who turned on his own kind was able to strike a bargain with daemons? No? Then that's why you believe his lies. He sells your drowning ship of a mind a shining beacon and a friendly rope and you don't ask once whose vessel you're clambering onto. All of a sudden—'

A click of Farden's fingers made the soldier wince, and he liked that very little.

'You're trapped. Mind-bent and a slave to the god of lies. Perhaps before you go dying for some god you should make sure it's the right god. And people think me mad for preferring no god at all.'

Farden watched the others' reactions before he withdrew. Most had bowed their heads. But not the bear, who decided the perfect end to the lesson was a poor attempt at a lunging headbutt. Farden had seen it coming in the bend of his knees and the wild in his eyes.

'Heretic!' the soldier roared.

Farden put one foot back and his spear-arm forwards, swivelling Gunnir's blade into the path of the mad leap while bracing it against his boot.

The bear met Gunnir's needle point, driving the blade through his sternum and killing himself through his own idiocy. His last blinks showed a terrible dawning of Farden's truth in his mind, especially as Gunnir began to glow. Cracks appeared across the man's leathers, spewing smoke and sending the nearby Arka hopping for safety with shouts and shrieks of terror.

Wherever the cracks ran across his body, both skin and flesh turned black and crumbled away like cheap charcoal. Before he had the chance to die the good old-fashioned way, the bear was reduced to dust, and a charred skeleton stood in his place for a heartbeat or two before collapsing into a pile. The bones almost had a musical tone.

'Anybody else?' Farden bellowed at the prisoners. 'Or would you rather return home to Krauslung, enlightened and done with fighting?'

Farden let the confusion spread while he looked to Elessi.

'Consider me merciful but also fair,' Farden said. Thankful grins had been growing amongst the prisoners, yet they halted immediately. 'If you are innocent of the crimes committed against the citizens of Tolema and Paraia, then you may leave. How will we decide? Tolema will tell us. Every one of you will be tested. If you're guilty, then Tolema will also decide your punishment.'

The truly guilty didn't hide themselves very well or for longer than the space of a yawn. Several panicked, emulating the dead bear in idiocy and futility. Scalussen mages shoved them back into line and pressed them together with force and wind spells.

'You can find some trustworthy people, right, Elessi?' Farden asked of the general.

Elessi's nod was all he wanted.

Mithrid learned three facts about Tolema that evening.

The first was that far less than half of the captured soldiers were innocent. Before the detritus of the battle had been swept away, the citizens of Tolema formed a court of elders, victims, and witnesses thousands strong. They gathered on the rubbled walls, passing judgement for all manner of crimes committed by the Arka soldiers. From harassment, theft, oppression and blackmail, to wounding, kidnap, and worse, all of their cruelty was yelled from the broken parapets. Only four score were found pure and allowed to flee the fortress as fast as they could manage. Ilios made sure they ran all the way to the horizon.

The second fact was that Tolema's punishments lay on the harsher side. There was no sugar to coat it with. While a third were marched to the prisons, the rest of the criminals were sentenced to death. The preferred method of death was called the Fate of Three Blades, and it was a simple choice: a sword to the spine, a sword across the throat, or a sword to the heart, and their remains burned on pyres. To avoid unwanted spirits, of course.

The particularly cruel and villainous were offered several other methods based on their individual crimes. Their choice, however, was made by the people. Three exceptionally evil brutes were given the horrific fate of cooking alive in a vat of burning sand. Five were to be buried up to their necks and left for the sun and vultures of the morning. The dozen that remained were issued the comparatively merciful punishment of burning at the stake.

The third and final fact was that the burning of criminals was what began the festivities Tolema put on in the name of freedom. It wasn't something Mithrid would have chosen, and even then, watching from the surviving parapets, she wasn't sure if it was justice or torture, but at least it was deserved. Not even Ardion escaped the pyres. His corpse was propped up and dressed in sackcloth.

Most of the burning bodies were already dead, having chosen the blade. The few that weren't allowed such an escape filled the night with their screams as citizens went from stake to stake, setting light to the piles of desert brush. When one Arka finally succumbed to the smoke, the fire, or the pain, another would be lit so the screams never died. With each spark of flame, and as the babbling, cursing and screaming of the doomed began, the citizens gathered on the walls gave out a mighty cheer.

The fellows in the vats of hot sand were the last to meet their ends that evening, and they seemed to form the crescendo of the ceremonies.

The vats had been placed below the ruin of the front gates, with great fires burning beneath their copper bowls. From her vantage point, Mithrid could watch them in detail. Her stomach should have turned, watching them try to hold themselves off the burning sand as long as they could while their hands and feet roasted, but it didn't. She couldn't help but see the murderers of Troughwake in those vats.

'Tests you, doesn't it?' said a voice, close and quiet.

Mithrid didn't flinch away. She knew that voice.

Hereni's hand snaked around her to hold her hip and bring her closer. 'Tests your stomach as well as your heart.'

Mithrid tutted. 'You and I know all too well what the Arka are capable of. We've seen too much to feel anything for them.'

One of the condemned succumbed to the pain and collapsed, wriggling like a poisoned ant. Another tried to climb out but was poked back in with spears to face his judgement. Mithrid didn't take her gaze off him.

Hereni, however, turned around so her back was against the stone like an archer in cover. 'That's enough for me.'

No sooner had the last of the prisoners fallen silent did the fortress erupt in cheers and howls. Mithrid understood some of their shouts.

Death to the oppressors!

For a free Paraia!

Bethel! Bethel!

'Bethel,' whispered Hereni.

Mithrid took her hand while they walked the parapet, stepping around gouges of magick and some of the more stubborn bloodstains. It was a poor place for romance, but times for such things were far and few between. And besides, normality was the sponge that wiped away the mess of war.

'At least we will get some rest tonight,' Mithrid whispered.

'Don't get your hopes up. Farden's called a council.'

Mithrid tried not to sigh too deeply. 'Then let's go see what our king wants.'

'And our queen, let's not forget. She arrived an hour ago, when we were exploring the caverns,' Hereni said, giving her a glance.

Mithrid smirked as they put feet to stairs. 'At least that means Farden's going to be in a good mood.'

'We'll see. We've been gone from New Scalussen longer than planned,' said Hereni, beckoning to a handful of waiting Scalussen mages.

❦

For the second time that day, Tolema was filled with chaos. Thankfully, this was a far less dangerous kind.

It took Mithrid and Hereni some time to weave through the festivities, which ranged from the contents of Ardion's larders piled on a sea of tables to the singing, dancing, and assorted capering that turned the streets into standstills. Clapping and chanting assailed their ears, and when they were recognised as Scalussen mages, mobs of cheering strangers surrounded them. Mithrid didn't mind them, and perhaps even enjoyed it, but Hereni looked as if she wished to escape.

Farden had chosen some rich merchant's house as his haunt, and surprisingly it wasn't filled with the horrifically gaudy decorations merchants were fond of. Instead, it was gloomy between the candles and fireplaces, filled with simple carved columns and empty suits of Paraian armour.

The door at the end of the main hall was almost closed. Only a thin blade of light shone between its halves. Mithrid flexed a hand, summoning her shadow into a fist and using it to grasp each handle and pull. The weight was tricky, and she barely coaxed a squeak out of the hinges.

'You're getting better,' Hereni whispered as she heaved the doors open.

Lerel and Farden were caught in the middle of a kiss, and they pulled swiftly apart to stare at the newcomers in the doorway. The High Admiral looked dangerous in her grey leather armour, adorned with the shining medals Farden had made. Every Scalussen survivor wore at least one. Mithrid wore three on her chest. Every general wore an upside-down sword over their heart, whether on their armour or their tunics, and the other two were for the battles of Scalussen and Easterealm.

'Haven't you two ever learned to knock?' Lerel said with a frown that quickly broke into a smile as she walked towards them, arms wide. 'Glad to see you're safe after all that Farden's putting you through.'

Farden crossed his arms with a clunk of metal and a mutter beneath his breath.

While Mithrid reached to pour some wine, Elessi, Sipid, and Ko-Tergo arrived. The yetin looked grateful for the open windows and magicked fans that hovered in the corners of the room, slowly wafting the night air. Sipid, the Jar Khoum general, wore no fewer than three layers of fish-cloth and robe over his boyish frame. Warbringer came last, ducking under the frame of the door with a grunt.

One by one, each general placed their weapons on the merchant's table. All save for Ko-Tergo, of course, who was a living weapon. He tapped his claws on the table instead, showing off a mouthful of disturbing saw-teeth. Mithrid wasn't sure if she would ever get used to them.

The knife she placed on the table was once Loki's knife. Farden had given her the blade to rid the god's magick from its steel.

The long blade and its once-gold filigree now held the colour of the shadow she'd forced into it.

Farden rapped his knuckles on the lacquered wood. 'You all did Scalussen proud today. I am sorry for our losses, but we can all rest easy knowing the Arka no longer have a foothold in middle Paraia.'

Fists drummed on the table, perhaps not as enthusiastically as Farden would have liked. He pressed on nonetheless.

'Karissa is next, and from there to Belephon and Troacles, the last Arka strongholds. We'll send them packing across the sea to Krauslung, and Paraia will finally escape Loki's grasp.'

'About time,' said Sipid. Mithrid had always thought him suspiciously bold for his age and scrawny frame. She privately imagined he was secretly fifty, with magick similar to Farden's armour in his veins. All the Jar Khoum looked young, and it was a gift that intrigued Farden greatly.

Mithrid watched the others around the council carefully and kept her lips firmly closed. Not because she was a coward; her reason was indecision.

It was Warbringer who spoke their shared thoughts. 'And after that?'

'Then we move on to freeing Krauslung, as I've always planned. We will take what's left of the empire away from Loki. He will be desperate. Enraged. Defeated.'

The council held their tongues, but the looks to the table, the ceiling, and each other were telltale.

Elessi shook her head. 'As you know, we tried to convince them to turn once before, Farden. But Krauslung is all like that gobshite in the square: spellbound by his lies. You know they're a lost cause.'

Farden stayed silent.

'You think you could do better, don't you, Farden?' asked Lerel.

The mage stared at her for some time. 'With Gunnir in my hand, yes, I do. There's still a chance I can change their minds about their so-called god.'

'And if not?'

Farden's frown deepened.

'You would be a warlord,' said Elessi. 'They will see you as nothin' but a conqueror. Loki will turn tail and disappear just like in Azanimur, and this war will stretch for decades.'

'He would be without Krauslung, for one,' Farden countered. 'And they will see their false god is a coward. He will be ruined and alone.'

Hereni wasn't sure. 'If you don't mind me saying, Farden, the Arka were broken the day Scalussen exploded, and the fire took the ice fields. The empire is a fraction of what it was. We know from the messenger hawks that Loki hasn't yet returned to Krauslung, and the Arka borders are already shrinking. Midgrir and Hâlorn have taken their lands back, Essen wants to separate, and Loki has no army left save for daemons and the Arka holed up in castles and fortresses like this one. Paraia will soon be abandoned and free once more. We need to be patient.'

'Meanwhile our losses grow,' rumbled Ko-Tergo. 'My people face extinction if we press on.'

'I'm with you, Farden. As are the Jar Khoum,' Sipid replied. 'But our home calls us.'

Warbringer shook her horns. 'I have left my clan for too long.'

'And innocent Paraians keep payin' the price,' said Elessi.

'I see.' Farden nodded, tapping Gunnir's blade. At council, he always pointed the spear at himself instead of anyone else. 'I see you've been discussing this at length.'

'Only since you started talkin' about marchin' hundreds of miles north to Belephon and Troacles,' Elessi admitted. 'We're tired, Farden. Tired of war. Loki is beaten, and we should be enjoyin' the peace we fought for.'

Farden measured his words before he dealt them out.

'From the very beginning, this war has been about true freedom, and you would rest before it's done? Every moment we draw breath, Malvus' shadow lives on in the cruelty of the Arka remnant. You say Loki is beaten? Every second that passes, he spends it plotting another downfall, I can promise you. None of us are free until the ghost of Malvus is banished and that god lies dead.'

'Too many have died already, Farden, and you know more will perish if we take on larger armies in Troacles and Belephon, or Krauslung,' said Elessi. 'There'll be nobody left to feel free.'

Farden shook his head. 'Then what else would you have me do?'

'Build our own empire,' Hereni whispered. 'Beat Loki at his own game by living.'

Farden stared at Mithrid, and she held his eyes until he thumped his hand on the table. Not in anger. Not in upset. A cold end to the proceedings, nothing more. 'I take it there is no need to vote?' he said.

Silence answered him.

'Then I will decide on the morrow,' Farden uttered as he stood and swept Gunnir from the table. The door slammed in his wake.

'That went well,' Warbringer said, trying her enormous hand at sarcasm. She even showed off the grin she had been working on, but her fangs made it comically terrifying.

Lerel found the mage on the edge of the merchant's roof. The spear rested on the carved stone lip that looked more like a trip hazard than a helpful barrier to halt a fall. Farden was crouched as if picking up a coin, hand outstretched, still and whispering.

Lingering by the stairs, in the persistent shadow between two candles, Lerel waited and listened. Farden's words were faint, and they came between moments of silence, as if he were having a conversation.

It wasn't the first time Lerel had caught Farden acting like this with the spear. Lerel had noticed him muttering to himself twice before, spear in hand, thinking he was alone. She crept towards him to hear him better, but all she caught was a whisper of, 'Loki'. Lerel moved closer still, her steps still finely tuned after all those years living in the shape of a cat.

'Sitting ducks…' were the first whole words she caught.

'Peace also means safety, and how are they supposed to feel safe when we watch our backs day and night?' Farden breathed.

A pause.

'Then I will do it myself. With you, just like the old days—'

Farden turned at the faintest scuff of Lerel's foot, eyes dangerous at first but immediately softening. The mage cleared his throat and stared out across the fortress and its bonfires burning strange and unnatural colours from seers' powders.

Lerel stood at his side, watching the silhouettes dancing in spirals around the flames of victory. 'We've done a good thing, Farden, going this far,' she said. 'Listen to how they chant and sing. As soon as Belephon and Troacles hear of this—'

'You can try to convince me all you want, Lerel, but it's a task unfinished,' Farden muttered.

Lerel nodded, deciding to risk a gamble. The vampyre had been a sore and barely spoken subject since their return from the east, but she had to try. 'Durnus told me once that when you spend so much time on hate, it leaves little room for love. Your people love you, Farden, and you can't keep ignoring them. Malvus' empire was built on hate. I think Scalussen should be built on something different.'

At the mention of Durnus, the mage looked far to the east and clenched his jaw. But Lerel had said her piece, and she waited for the old vampyre's wisdom to worm into Farden's heart.

She waited a long time, and when Farden didn't answer, Lerel took his empty hand in both of hers.

'I know you want to punish Loki for Durnus, but this can't be the best way to do it. Punish him by thriving instead.'

Farden shut his eyes and exhaled until every scrap of breath was removed from his lungs. 'Gods, why do you and Elessi always have to be right?' he muttered. 'You know I agree with you, but I can't sit on my hands when there are still those that pay the price. Not when I promised.'

'You'd rather we pay the price instead?'

'No,' Farden answered. 'This is why I will do it myself.'

'Do what yourself?'

'Free the rest of Paraia.'

'You suggested this a month ago, and it sounds just as mad now as it did then. You might be the strongest mage to ever walk Emaneska, but you're still just one mage.'

'I destroyed Malvus' horde by myself, didn't I?'

'And Mithrid told me it almost broke you,' said Lerel. 'You can't be serious.'

'That was before Gunnir.'

'You don't yet know what that thing is truly capable of,' Lerel said, watching the light wash around the spear's blade even though Farden held it statue-still.

'It's about time you all trusted in this spear as I do. I've proven its power a dozen times,' Farden replied. 'And out of everyone, I don't expect doubt from you.'

'It isn't doubt. It's concern.' Lerel nudged him sharply with an elbow. 'And what of Krauslung? Will you free them by yourself, too?'

Farden smirked wryly as he picked up Gunnir. A wind circled them, blowing her hair across her face. A metallic whine joined the ruckus of festivity.

'Don't you dare!' she warned him, knowing how fond he was of disappearing with that bloody spear.

'I can do this, Lerel. I need to.'

'Gods damn you, Farden.'

'They already did.'

Lerel scowled, folding her arms across her chest. It was like arguing with a wall.

'Fine. I know when there's no stopping you. But you take Mithrid, you hear me? Better to have two weapons than one,' said Lerel, watching a frown appear and vanish on Farden's forehead.

'I can do this alone.'

'What is this face you pull when I talk of Mithrid sometimes? Do you still not trust her after all you've been through?'

'I trust her, but I worry about her also. I can't forget what I saw in the mirrors of that spider's cave.'

Lerel shuddered. That story of Utiru had kept her awake in the early hours more than once. Farden had told her of the mirrors' visions, of Mithrid in a crown and a burning world at her feet. 'You worry she has the wrong kind of aspirations.'

'I wanted her to be a weapon, and now I wonder if she's too much of one. She doesn't flinch at death as she used to, her pride grows every day, and you've seen how she rushes into battle. As if she hasn't already proven herself. A weapon knows only one thing, and a weapon like Mithrid—'

Lerel prodded him in the chest. 'You're scared of her.'

'I am not. All I'm saying is that something blasted the magick out of my armour, and I still believe it was her. Even Loki doesn't have that power over me.'

Lerel tutted. 'Vice made you a weapon just the same, and look where you're standing. You need to guide Mithrid like Durnus guided you. Like Tyrfing guided me. Worrying about what may or may not happen does nothing when you don't yet know the truth. That's what caused you two to clash in the east, no?'

Lerel could have sworn she heard a faint whisper on the wind. Her gaze strayed to Gunnir while Farden nodded slowly, drowning in his thoughts. She dragged him out of his reverie with a shove.

'Go. I believe in you. Just as long as you come back to me, you hear?'

Farden put a hand to her cheek and a kiss on her lips. 'I always do, don't I? I think it's a fact there's no getting rid of me now.'

Lerel watched him go. 'And I hope that stays true,' she told the stars and the plumes of smoke reaching towards them. The skies had grown darker since a third of them had fallen to the earth in Farden's great battle. The constellations she had memorised as a child looked ragged with their missing pieces.

The dreams came fractured as they always did. Muddles of imagery and nonsense that held no plot nor meaning that her waking mind could discern. And yet for all the chaos, there was one constant: the black eyes in a scarlet fire, burning deep beneath the earth. The gaping, fanged maw that always caught her no matter how far or fast she ran. No matter how she fought.

Mithrid awoke to a heavy thud and a forehead slick with sweat. She felt the threads of her magick swirling about her as the dream faded. The smell of burning was an odd addition, but she blamed that on Tolema's penchant for flames.

In the glow of torches sneaking through the shutters, Mithrid looked around to see what had fallen or broken. The noise came again, and her squint shot to the door. The shadows of feet waited beyond.

Leaving Hereni – who somehow claimed all of the blanket yet used but a small fraction of it at the same time – curled in bed, Mithrid went to the door.

'Farden?' Mithrid asked when she found the mage behind it, still dressed in full armour and his helmet under one arm. His curved Khandri sword hung from his hips, and Gunnir glinted even in the dark. 'What is it?'

'We're leaving.'

There was a surprise. 'You've decided, then,' she replied. 'I'll wake Hereni. Though why this couldn't wait until the sun came up, I —'

'*You and I* are leaving.'

'To go where?'

'To free Paraia.'

Mithrid poked at her eye as if it would somehow help her hearing. 'Just us? I thought we deci—'

'Why the hesitation? Don't think we can do it?' Farden matched the smile that spread across Mithrid's face.

'I think the exact opposite,' she whispered. 'I just remember this idea was voted as too dangerous and the spear too unpredictable. So what changed your mind?'

Farden tapped his fingers on Gunnir. 'Practice.'

Mithrid squinted again. 'It was Elessi and Lerel, wasn't it?'

'I'll have you know Lerel was against this, but she agreed on the condition I take you,' the mage muttered. 'You in?'

'If you need me, then—'

'I don't need you, Mithrid,' Farden said with a haughty smirk. 'It's an invite, not a request. I wanted to do this myself, but it'll be good for you to keep learning.'

Mithrid saw to his smile with a scowl. 'Learning what?'

'How not to make the mistakes others have made.'

'You mean that *you've* made.'

'I'll be at the northern gate.'

Mithrid watched the mage march along the hallway. She could have sworn he whispered to himself, but the words escaped her.

Hereni was already awake and propped up on her elbows.

'You heard?'

Hereni nodded after a yawn. 'I did.'

'And what do you think?'

'I think you better get your armour on,' Hereni said.

Mithrid smiled as she reached for Hereni's hand. 'I think I can take my time.'

CHAPTER 3
UNSTOPPABLE

Call me mad – and many have – but I seen it, I tell you. There's not a beast in the oceans like it, and it's no leviathan, no overgrown squid, no merthing, and no whale. I seen islands smaller, and I seen a whole ship's back broken with one blow. Sucked right into the depths it was. That's why you won't catch me going a hundred leagues of the Cape.
FROM THE LETTERS OF CAPTAIN PAULJA MES, MASTER OF THE BRITTLECUR

Mithrid found Farden in the shadows of the north gate, standing halfway along the tunnel that punctured Tolema's astoundingly thick walls. Ten wagons could sit nose to arse in that archway. Stonegates and portcullises hung in their niches, begging to be dropped.

'Bloody finally,' Farden chided. 'What took you so long?'

Mithrid played innocent. 'Couldn't find my axe.'

'Mhm,' said Farden, fingers drumming on his helmet.

'What's the plan, Your Majesty?'

'Don't make me regret bringing you along,' Farden warned. He motioned with a nod, and they walked towards the cobalt-coloured plains of moonless desert. Scalussen, Paraian, and Jar Khoum soldiers raised their pikes and halberds in salute as they passed.

The breeze was chill beyond the walls. The noise of the festivities died behind the stone. Tumbleweeds rolled across the scrub on their never-ending journeys. Screeches of nighthawks and owls echoed between the rocky tors.

'Here's the plan,' Farden replied at last. 'It's time to end this without another innocent bleeding for the price of freedom. Tonight we are assassin's blades first and foremost, quick, precise, and punishing. We have three cities to free, and in each one we'll cut the head from the snake and let the body wither.'

Mithrid thumbed the edge of her axe. 'And if the snake resists?'

'Sheer intimidation. I won't be having bloody battles in the street. If we show our magick, it's to make the cowards turn tail and free. This isn't about our egos or revenge; this is about our duty. Is that clear?'

There it was again: that flicker across Farden's throat. Mithrid knew it wasn't a doubt in her abilities, for she had proved herself too many times. It was a worry, and it bothered her just the same. Farden clearly still saw some kind of flaw in her but refused to speak it.

'As crystal,' she replied.

'Stand close,' instructed Farden as he raised Gunnir. The spear keened like the wind through an ill-fitting door. Sand spiralled around them as Mithrid put her hand on top of Farden's.

'Gods, do I hate this part,' she muttered. Gunnir wasn't as predictable as a quickdoor and was a rage to a Weight's relative calm. Never mind the fact Farden's aim was based on memory.

The fortress of Tolema wobbled like a molten window before collapsing in on itself and ripping Mithrid's breath away. A storm of light and noise washed over her until a new desert landscape stood before her, this time populated by a herd of goats. Their sudden arrival had not only destroyed the goats' grain trough but was apparently so frightening that several of the beasts went completely rigid and fell over themselves like toppled toys.

'There wasn't a farm last time I was here,' Farden said, as he pulled his feet from the pile of spilled grain that had swallowed them. Mithrid's foot had found something worse, and she wiped her boot in dry dust.

'Where are we?' she asked. 'Is this Karissa?'

Farden pointed to the town in the distance, beyond a low ridge. It was no fortress like Tolema's prowess, rather a cluster of lights between sharp pyramidical buildings that looked like black fangs. A wall of stacked pale stone and hasty mortar corralled the town. Around its outskirts, the plains were covered in beaten roads, cranes, and mounds of stone blocks. For miles in all directions, the white scars of mines and quarries spread through the plains, almost reaching the mountains that sprouted on the horizon.

'That it is. It means Melted Spring, and it's our first and smallest stop of the night. It used to be one of Malvus' best silver mines until he dug the ground dry. The workers mine the bare limestone now, mostly for Krauslung, Manesmark, and Essen. A Colonel Blatter runs this town these days, Albion-born, and our spies say the lack of a title or noble blood hasn't stopped him living like a lord. I wager Blatter has enough soldier still in him that he'll handle any threat to his riches and his little throne personally.'

'If he's going to put up a fight, then how are we going to take his town away from him without one?'

'How else do we get anything done in this world? With magick.'

Mithrid snorted. 'I thought it was with killing.'

'Only if we have to, remember,' Farden whispered while he weaved through the goat herd in the direction of Karissa. 'Now gather up any brush you can find. We're going to make fires on that low ridge. Two dozen of them.'

That sounded suspiciously like a lot of menial labour. 'Why?'

'A trick that earned me the title Hero of Efjar. And enough questions. Get to work.'

After a mocking whistle from Mithrid, they did precisely that: gathering up scrub plants and tumble-brush into piles across the sandy ridge.

'Now what?'

'We light them and wait,' Farden explained while he pinched a flame spell between his fingers. 'Our good colonel will get curious, and wanting to make sure he's not under attack, will make a show of force—'

'And once we've lured him out, we take the town.' Mithrid nodded, seeing it now. 'And what about the others that he leaves behind? I don't think you've thought this through.'

Farden smiled. 'Stay close. We'll be jumping when the moment's right,' he told her before moving from one pile to the next, gifting flame to the dry tinder.

Farden worked swiftly, making sure to run along behind the ridge once his flames were lit. Mithrid could feel the breeze of magick in the night air as he kept them blazing bright. The concentration required silence, leaving Mithrid to watch and wait. But not for long.

A whining horn bleated within moments. Mithrid saw the torches on the piled-stone walls flicker and wink as soldiers ran along their parapets.

'Wait for it,' Farden muttered.

The arched gates separating the walls split with a distant rattle of chains, and a regiment of Arka soldiers showed their faces and the shine of plate and chainmail. There must have been a hundred of them, and a small contingent sat astride trotting armoured battle-cows, forcing the rest of the foot soldiers into a run to keep up. The shouts of their colonel reached across the plain.

'Tight ranks, you sacks of moulded shite! Onward!'

'A little shadow, Mithrid,' Farden ordered.

The mage moved without warning, circling around the small army to put them closer to Karissa. Mithrid chased him, trying to wrap them both in a faint cloud of shadow to keep them unseen in the starlight and from prying eyes. She had inwardly groaned at the prospect of sneaking instead of the good old-fashioned swinging of an axe, but this gambit raised her heartbeat the same way battle did. Mithrid was surprised.

The shadow was barely needed. The army's dust cloud did a fine job of masking their approach, and once they were an arrow's shot from the walls, Farden put a hand on her shoulder and stabbed Gunnir into the dust. 'Kill the shadow,' he said, lifting a hand to his throat.

'Reinforcements!' Farden bellowed, his voice taking on volume as well as the raspy tone of a colonel. 'Get your hideous arses out here!'

When not a figure could be seen to move, Farden shouted again. 'That means all of you! Every single one of you unwashed, dickless bastards on the plain or I'll skin you slowly at dawn! We need reinforcements!'

That got them running. Soldiers and archers streamed through the open doors in hastily cobbled-together ranks.

'Impressive,' Mithrid had to admit.

Farden chuckled as he seized Gunnir again, and the world started to melt. 'Steel yourself.'

With a deafening thunderclap, they appeared in the courtyard behind the walls, sending dozens of townsfolk scurrying for cover. A crowd had come to see what the fuss and fires were about, and Farden wasted no time in putting them to work.

'If you want freedom from digging rock for the rest of your lives, now is your chance to seize it! Lock the gates behind your colonel, and let us do the rest. Quickly now! Karissa is yours to take!'

Farden let Gunnir glow as he pointed its long blade at the yawning mouth of the gate.

For a moment, Mithrid thought the townsfolk would waste their opportunity on pretending to be gawping statues, but that was until a wizened old man shuffled from the crowd. He used a pickaxe handle for a walking stick and pointed it at Farden. Mithrid could see the pink scars of whip-tongues through his threadbare shirt.

'Are you the one they call the Forever King?' he asked, making the townspeople murmur.

Farden nodded. 'That I am.'

With a simple tap of his stick – once, twice, thrice – the old miner moved the crowd into action. The people flooded to the gates and walls, swiping makeshift weapons and torches from sconces as they went. A clanging rose into the air as tools smacked rhythmically against metal buckets and the handles of carts. The noise spread across the town like the echo of thunder. Doors flew open. Taverns emptied. Night markets were abandoned. The crowds spilled into the narrow streets and clambered across the conical rooftops to reach the walls. Rebellion had erupted with three simple taps of a stick.

Farden's laughter could be heard over the commotion. He beckoned to Mithrid, and before the gates slammed shut, he made sure they were standing atop the skinny gatehouse, no more than a bridge of stone.

'Well?' Farden asked as they looked over the dust-mired plains.

'Well, what?'

Farden grinned. 'Told you it would work.'

'I won't argue that. But if Colonel Blatter is as greedy as you say, he won't give up his riches without a fight, will he?'

'Not like you to shy away from a battle.'

Mithrid grumbled. Over the past few weeks, she had battled with the knowledge her power was next to nothing against a foe without magick. She was deadlier than most with an axe, but two hundred Arka soldiers were far beyond her. A formidable weapon like Farden, Mithrid was not. And even though she had spent those weeks trying to hone her magick into a weapon against flesh as well as magick, true power still escaped her.

'Intimidation, Mithrid. Entire battles have been won because of it,' said Farden.

Mithrid sighed. 'And yet nobody ever seems to surrender to us.'

'That changes tonight.'

The rumble of feet and hooves grew until Mithrid could feel their approach in her soles. She raised her axe as the shadows emerged from the dust.

'Open the gates!' came the order. Colonel Blatter still rode at the head of his little army. With a greatsword on his lap and wyrm horns on his helmet, the man would have looked formidable in his heavy mail if it weren't for his travesty of a moustache. The grey eyesore was so long Blatter had braided and tied it in a bow below his nose. Mithrid wanted him to fight just so she could chop it off.

'Open the gates, you poxed arseholes!' hollered Blatter, trying to shield his eyes from the glare of torches to see who presided over his walls. He held up a hand for a halt when he realised it was not his men. 'Who in the fuck are you?'

'Messengers, and we've come with word that Paraia is no longer under Arka control. This means Karissa no longer belongs to you, Colonel, and it won't be yours ever again. This town now belongs to Paraia and its people.'

'In short, you've been evicted,' added Mithrid. 'So get lost.'

Colonel Blatter moved his battle-cow in a circle. 'Archers!' he yelled.

'Told you he wouldn't give up without a fight,' Mithrid said, before Farden raised Gunnir.

Magick filled the air above the gatehouse, making a fierce wind howl and lights crackle against the night. Townspeople cried out in fright and at the popping of their ears. It lit a painful fire in Mithrid's forehead she fought to ignore.

The battle-cows lowed with fear. Like most animals, they could taste the magick, and like Mithrid, they found it bitter and decided to gallop away right there and then. The riders that weren't bucked from their saddles clung on between helpless cries.

Blatter was one of the former. The colonel lost his helmet, showing off a head as bald as a peeled egg, and as soon as his sergeants and captains had hauled him up, he dragged his greatsword through the sand towards the gates. 'Give me back my town, you festering cock juggler! Where are my bastard archers? Fire on these craven fuck trumpets!' he bellowed.

Mithrid whistled. 'He's certainly got a way with words.'

The mage chuckled before he jumped from the gatehouse, Gunnir outstretched before him.

'Everyone take cover!' Mithrid yelled.

The archers had barely knocked arrows to their bowstrings when Farden's spell exploded across the earth. A wave of sand and rocks rippled towards Blatter and his warriors. It struck the army like a runaway rolling log, knocking rank after rank onto their arses. Dust spiralled in the spell's wake, choking anyone else left on their feet.

'Mithrid!' came Farden's order.

Mithrid already knew what to do. *Intimidation*.

Reaching within, she summoned her own strange magick and let black shadow spread along the walls. She forced it into the air to reach over the army like a clawed hand. Every strand of it took concentration, but she grinned through it as the Arka reacted to the sight.

Blatter came up again, wiping dust from his face and spitting venom, still lurching towards Karissa to reclaim his riches. Greed was a hunger only death could diminish. 'You whore-mothered cowards! You piss-swilling fiends!'

Farden drew a line in the sand with Gunnir. 'Cross this line and die like the empire you served, Colonel. Or, you can put down your sword, take off your armour, politely fuck off, and be free like Paraia.'

Blatter snorted, snuffled, and otherwise wheezed as he approached Farden. He came so close to the line, the toe of his boot scuffed sand over it, and Gunnir hovered an inch from his chest. How little he knew how close he stood to death.

'Who the fuck are you to take what's ours?' he demanded.

'The Forever King, and the only thing that's yours is your life, and if you want to leave here with it, drop your sword and your armour, Colonel.'

Blatter refused. 'You can't protect these wretches forever, you reeking swine. We'll be back.'

Mithrid tutted as Blatter sealed his fate with the wrong answer. She couldn't see, but she knew Farden smiled his most dangerous smile.

The mage didn't use Gunnir to end Blatter. Instead, he sliced the greatsword in two with the spear's blade and then seized the colonel in his fist. White fire sparked between Farden's fingers, and judging by Blatter's screams, it could have been a quicker death.

Farden let the colonel and his charred, decapitated head fall to the ground. Within the space of a panicked breath, swords, bows, mail, and helmets followed suit in a raucous clatter. One soldier even ripped the tunic off his back just in case.

Gunnir pointed north. Farden didn't need to speak to make the little army turn tail and flee. The cheering of the town chased them.

Mithrid descended from the gatehouse and joined the flood of folk running to bow to Farden and claim the discarded Arka weapons. Farden took the hand of any that tried to kneel and dragged them up straight.

'They won't last long in the open plains come sunrise, will they?' Mithrid asked Farden as her gaze followed the fleeing Arka. Some were running as if Farden might change his mind, so used to cruelty they expected it delivered upon them. It was pathetic.

'I'm not that callous. There's a river port near to the mountains where Karissa sends its stone. If they have any sense, they'll find somewhere else to settle down and never serve the Arka again.'

Mithrid nodded. 'One down, two to go.'

'Shall we?' Farden asked, extending a hand. Gunnir was already beginning to whine.

The saying went that if ever the name Belephon was uttered, it was, more often than not, never far away from the word 'spectacle'.

Finding the pulse of any usual city would have meant visiting a tavern. In Belephon, it meant touring the expansive Gardens of Orestus: a sprawling, awning-shaded area that would have swallowed Karissa whole. Every corner held some kind of performer. Every amphitheatre and building big enough for a stage was alive with puppet shows, soliloquies, skalds, and dancers. Flame eaters perched on rooftops and blew spouts of fire that threatened the colourful kites that shivered above the Gardens on silk lines. Bird tamers had their winged friends place feathers in passing hats and caps. Paraian sorcerers, witches, and would-be mages summoned light and sparks in shadowed stalls to draw attention to their wares.

And between it all, even at night, was the constant churn of people and their conversations. Some of business. Some of petty gripes and romances. Others of gossip and greater goings on, right beneath the noses of Arka guards standing on pedestals. Their green and gold steel shone in the lanterns that draped the columns and gutters. And seeing as his spies and their hawks hadn't yet returned from Troacles, that was what Farden hunted: gossip.

'There's another seer hanging over the gates. Did you see her?' said a noble draped in layers of yellow silk. His friend matched him in yellow.

'I did, and word has it she'll have a friend to keep her company by the dawn. Sister seers, they said.'

'At least they get to hang by their heels together.'

'It's a miracle the seers keep coming to try their luck with that idiot Henrik.'

'Council Kasak thinks they're all chasing a permanent position and a share of the taxes. Says they're coin-grabbers, every one. And she's a shrewd woman with more ears than both of us.'

'I wouldn't cross Kasak for ten thousand gold. I'm surprised she hasn't finally ousted Henrik over this new increase in taxes on animals and beasts.'

'If it wasn't for his soldiers, she would. But enough of seers and the lord's madness. What of the new cathouse beside the armoury?'

With his curiosity piqued and the canvas of knowledge half-painted, Farden let the silken nobles meld into the crowd.

Mithrid was eying another pair of merchants comparing their pet dillo pups. Each of the desert creatures had been painted different hues and kept rolling into balls every time their owner dared to think about touching them. Farden had half a mind to cut their leashes.

The merchants gabbled of imports and exports and nothing they needed, and so Farden hobbled on, playing an old man. Gunnir had surprised him when the spear had first turned into a different shape. A golden cane, answering a silent wish in Farden's mind. With concentration, he had mastered its ability for disguise. That night, Gunnir had become a humble wooden stick, and with a cloak buttoned tight, Farden looked like a tourist of modest means, far from an enemy stupid enough to walk into the Arka's midst. Mithrid matched him with her own cloak, playing the part of begrudging minder. She played it well. After all, a great performance always contained some truth, or so they said.

Madness, came the spear's voice, a breath barely audible over the crowds. Durnus' voice, as Farden stubbornly believed it to be, and that was why he had kept it to himself. Explaining the ghost of a vampyre living in an elf-made spear blessed by the gods seemed entirely too difficult a conversation, especially when Durnus' death was still raw for the others. Farden often worried if he had forgotten what normal felt like.

'Madness indeed, and that doesn't bode well for negotiation,' Farden mumbled so Mithrid couldn't hear.

The mage followed his curiosity to a stall selling nothing of interest except for raised voices.

'Another three silvers a week?' complained a man with cheeks as red as late sunset. The stout amber python coiled around his neck and shoulders looked equally indignant. 'You're already taking twelve, curse it!'

The subject of their anger was a weed of a man in light Arka mail. He wore a tiny cap balanced on his head, and a blade barely bigger than a quill perched too high on his waist. 'As I told you last time, Finnegan, Lord Henrik has put a tariff on animal acts and charmers. You don't like it, get rid of the snake and learn to sing or chew fire.'

'Bastard,' said Finnegan, to the snake's hiss. 'Bauman is my family.'

'Pay the tax, or I'll have him taken away. Lord Henrik is a strong believer in snake meat being good for the eyes, you know.'

'Fine. You'll get your silver.'

After the Arka tax collector and his two hulking bodyguards left the snake-charmer, Farden nodded to Mithrid, and they played at perusing Finnegan's wares of shed snakeskins and vials of venom. 'What's this about Lord Henrik raising taxes on animals?' asked the mage.

'Hmph. Next week it'll be a tax on fruits. Or hats. Or windows. Or the colour blue. Or anything else that greedy, superstitious fool decides he doesn't like. It's exhausting, but this is my home, and there isn't a place like it in Paraia,' sighed Finnegan.

'Surely those tax collectors must be tired of it as well by now?'

'Pah! Not when they can skim off the top. Henrik's made a cult out of them. They're his little band of rule-makers and luck-worshippers.'

'What do you mean?' asked Mithrid. She seemed enraptured by the snake, and the snake seemed pretty keen on her, reaching out from the charmer's shoulder to wag its tongue in her face.

'Never seen soldiers so loyal,' said Finnegan. 'Henrik could say fart, and they'd shit themselves trying.'

Mithrid chuckled, making the man crack a smile. He offered the snake, which had the old Skölgard name of Bauman, and Mithrid let it wind around her arm.

'How did all this start?' asked Farden.

'You must be new to Belephon, eh? You heard the name Headless Henrik yet? No? Well, he's as superstitious as they come. One day, he wants to hear the rattles of bones and stones and know his fortune. A seer was summoned to the tower, and she tells Henrik he'll have good luck and prosperity so long as skalds sing and dancers dance. Make of that what you will, but the week after, a touring circus comes to the city. Strange part is, Belephon never knew a better summer, even under the cruel thumb of the Arka. A sickness touched all of Paraia except us. Rains came and made the fields burst with green. Henrik even found himself a young wife. Believing the seer's words, he never let the circus leave. Then another arrived, and another, until they all found their home in the Gardens. Others like me came in our hundreds, but it weren't long 'til another seer rolled her stones and had the balls to see a lighter purse in the lord's future. Henrik had gotten a taste of luck and fortune by then, see? Next day, the taxes begin. Then another seer comes, and another, some honest and some not, and each had their own future to tell. Henrik believed everything they told him. One day, he banned cats for a whole month. The next, he demanded all of Belephon sacrifice every pigeon they found. It can pay well if you're a good seer. If you're a fake or tell him something he doesn't like to hear, you get to hang by your heels. That's why we call him Headless Henrik, because he's lost his fucking head. And now there's no emperor, well… he follows his madness anywhere it leads him, and all the while, the taxes keep climbing. Isn't anything we can do with his watchful eyes on every corner. Only yesterday a puppet-maker was beaten to death in the amphitheatre for daring to make a headless doll of Henrik.'

Farden plucked six silvers from a coinpurse and placed them in the snake-charmer's palm. 'For your help. I have a strange feeling the taxes will be temporary.'

'I… Thank you, stranger. Truly.' Finnegan looked confused but grateful. He pressed a vial of snake venom into Farden's hand.

'Please, take this. It'll put you in a blissful sleep for three days straight. No ill effects and the wildest of dreams.'

Farden and Mithrid took shelter from the crowds by a pillar and a mural of a man fighting a coelo.

'Well?' he asked her.

Mithrid thumbed her nose before crossing her arms. 'Well… if Ardion was a coward, and Blatter was full of greed, then Henrik is a glutton for superstition, just like the old ones in Troughwake used to be. Kasak and the city's council want to hang Henrik by his heels, and I would say they're ready to turn, but the only thing stopping them are the fanatical soldiers.'

'And how would you oust him and his cult?'

'It's down to me now, is it?'

'Call it a test.'

'Good.' Mithrid barely needed to think. 'Because I already have an idea. All I need are some stones or bones.'

Farden took a moment to unravel her words. 'That's bold. Very bold, Mithrid.'

She grinned. 'But you know it'll work.'

Even if it wouldn't, Farden had never ignored a challenge in his life.

The silk-wrapped nobles had spoken the truth. A seer dangled from her heels at the gates to Lord Henrik's tower. Blood red in the face and eyes bulging, the grey woman looked half-dead already. The only sign of life in her was the sporadic twitching of her hands.

Late was the hour, but his hunger for fortunes meant Lord Henrik didn't hesitate to welcome the latest seer that had announced herself at his gates. One Mithrid of Troughwake, a famed seer of the north, or so she said.

Mithrid looked the part, putting crow feathers plucked from an acrobat's costume in her fire-red hair. A cloak covered in swirls of silver had been borrowed from a drunken actor slumped in an alley. The bones in the pouch she clutched belonged to a roast chicken from a stall quite literally dripping in grease.

'You regretting this yet?' Farden whispered while the soldiers made them wait. The Arka kept a superstitious distance around Mithrid and her mute and impressively dour bodyguard. Farden stayed wrapped in his cloak, and a rusty sword now poked from its hem. Another of Gunnir's disguises.

'This will work.'

Farden didn't argue. It was a bold but clever plan, and one surprisingly without bloodshed. If it all went correctly, of course.

At long last, with a solemn beckon of a hand and far too much ceremony, a captain appeared to welcome them into the tower.

The inside of Henrik's abode was surprisingly restrained compared to the opulence most lords and ladies felt the need to drown themselves in. Instead, Henrik seemed to be a collector, reminiscent to Farden of the Lady of Whispers. Paraian sorcerers' robes dangled from one wall. A series of tall stones inscribed with Arka runes leaned against another. Stuffed birds with eyes of gemstone watched the procession of guards, seer, and bodyguard from every angle. Coins sat alone and confined in crystal cases.

Farden recognised some of the trinkets. One in particular was an embalmed pig foot. Part delicacy, part token of good luck in Skewerboar, and it was then he realised the whole of the tower was a museum to luck. Every item was a ward against bad fortune, similar to the runes Manesmark and Scalussen smiths wrought into armour or shipsmiths carved into iron.

'Where was it you journeyed from?' asked the captain through lips dyed dark with wine.

'From Troughwake in Hâlorn, sir,' said Mithrid in the odd and entirely unnecessary accent she'd concocted, but it was too late now.

'Never heard of it,' the captain grunted. 'You look young for a seer.'

'I have had my gift since birth. I have cast fortunes for Hâlorn, Midgrir, and half of Albion. Even the nobles of Krauslung.'

'Have you any news from the north?'

'I wouldn't know. We've not been north in many months,' said Mithrid before Farden prodded her. She waved her hand in a mysterious motion. 'But I have seen war in my dreams for far too long, and now I see peace.'

'Peace?' the captain scoffed. 'Rumours are saying Loki's left Krauslung, and that daemons roam the north.'

Farden ground his teeth.

Lord Henrik awaited them at the top of the spiral stairs that had carried them to the heights of the tower. If Farden had expected overflowing enthusiasm, he was disappointed. Henrik was quiet and suspicious, but his entwined and tapping fingers betrayed a slight excitement, like a hound waiting for table scraps to fall. Farden could tell Henrik wanted Mithrid to be the real thing. Farden recognised that kind of yearning. Fortune and future were Henrik's drug of choice, and he longed for a taste, just the same as a nevermar fiend who itched for another breath of smoke.

The lord looked like a pile of fabric from the arse-end of a market. Despite his height, he stood hunched, and Farden wasn't sure whether it was because of a life spent bent over dark tables in the company of seers or the weighty tangle of necklaces he wore. All manner of symbols and runes and gemstones hung from loops and chains.

The captain bowed so low she almost knelt. 'Lord Henrik, I present the seer Mithrid of Troughwake, and her guard.'

'What luck you have arrived. My last seer was sent to hang only this morning,' Henrik greeted them.

Mithrid bowed to a more standard depth. Farden resented doing so but gave it his best. Henrik looked Mithrid up and down, searching for reasons to doubt her.

'You look young for a seer.'

'The sight chooses whom it wishes to see,' Mithrid said. 'Age matters not.'

Farden almost smirked at that rubbish. The girl was worryingly good at this.

'You should know I have seen my fair share of charlatans, and I know one when I see one. Captain Monroze has also been blessed with a fine sense for magick, and she will sniff out your tricks if you try any. I am interested in true power only. I am a merciful lord, and I will give you a chance to leave now if that changes your mind.'

'No tricks, milord,' Mithrid said with a smile.

'Then to my chambers with you. Your guard may stay here.'

Mithrid hesitated. 'If you please, he goes everywhere I go.'

'What is he? Your father?'

'He has some magick in him, that's for sure,' Captain Monroze muttered.

'My father is dead. This is a friend. A charm, of sorts.'

Henrik bought that, and he led the way to his windowless chambers, where a candle burned on every flat surface that wasn't littered with more curios. The heat was oppressive, but it was better than a dim room already filled with darkness. Shadow needed light to show its face.

A table lined with gemstones waited for them. Henrik sat on one side and gestured to a single chair. Farden stayed standing while Mithrid sat. The captain shut the door, cutting off the only source of fresh air and turning the room stuffy.

'You may begin,' said Henrik.

Mithrid played her role with ceremony, taking the fresh chicken bones from her pocket and cupping them in her hands.

Henrik raised an eyebrow, a hand on one of his charms, shaped like an X. His other hand tapped upon the table. 'It is customary to prepare the table before you show the bones, no?' he asked, and Farden tasted the danger in the room.

'Not in Troughwake. I'm not like the charlatans you're used to,' Mithrid said quickly as she drew a shape over the table with her hands. 'Now close your eyes.'

Henrik took his sweet time deciding to do as he was told. Mithrid shook the bones with a rattle and threw them out onto the table. One came dangerously close to falling, something that Farden knew was a big mistake for any seer and nothing but bad luck. Mithrid didn't let it show, even though Captain Monroze was as beady as a starving pigeon.

'You may look,' she said.

Farden steeled himself as Henrik looked upon his fortune.

'Why do I smell roast chicken and grease?' he asked. 'It offends my nose, seer, and brings me doubt.'

Mithrid pretended to be concentrating. The plan was to play shocked, and she was building to it.

'Tell me what you see,' the lord demanded.

Farden tried to ignore the sensation of Mithrid's power spreading. Something in his armour creaked. A pain grew in his forehead.

'I bring you a warning of danger. Danger for you and those who follow you. I see death,' Mithrid whispered, speaking the words she and Farden had hastily concocted on the walk to the tower. Henrik's narrowed gaze widened.

A bead of sweat ran into the corner of Farden's eye. The crux of Mithrid's plan was an utter gamble: Henrik hated bad news, but what if the news was so convincing that his superstition and self-preservation won him over?

'What danger? You dare to threaten me?'

Mithrid let her shadow loose. Gently at first, seeping from her sleeves while she tilted her head back and shook her hands. Tendrils of darkness snaked about her arms and around the bones of the table. Monroze drew the short sword at her belt, and Farden made sure to stay stone still.

'What is this daemonry?' Henrik shouted, backing away.

'A message from the gods,' Mithrid hissed as if she were possessed. She spread her shadow wider until it enveloped several of the candles. Farden endured its touch, watching only Henrik.

'Is this magick, Monroze? A trick?' he yelled.

The captain looked haunted to her core. 'I don't know what it is, but it isn't magick, sire. I feel nothing!'

Mithrid spun the shadow into a shape that resembled a skull. Judging by the way her fingers clawed at the table, it took her considerable effort. This was the moment their gamble hung in the balance.

'If you do not leave this city and return to Krauslung, you will perish here.'

'Why? Tell me more!' Henrik's hunger to know his future became a poison in his belly, turning him white as a sheet.

'A pox is coming. An unstoppable plague. The gods wish for you to leave. You must save yourselves.'

'How?'

'Leave Belephon!'

Henrik's mouth flapped as he weighed his choices. He shrank away from every waft of shadow.

'When?'

'The gods say tonight, Lord Henrik. Immediately!'

Henrik was now sweating profusely. 'I cannot simply leave!'

'Then by dawn, you and your Arka will be dead.'

'I should hang you from your heels, Mithrid of Troughwake!'

Mithrid let her shadow recede. 'I am just a messenger of the gods.'

Farden watched as the fear bubbling inside Henrik clashed with his doubt. Superstition was a powerful thing. It could make the most scholarly of scholars whisper a prayer or leap to avoid a black cat in their path. But the question still remained whether it was powerful enough.

It took several moments before Henrik exploded from the table, knocking the bones to the floor and spending a moment in horror at what he'd done.

'Summon the soldiers and mages. We're leaving!'

'But, milord!'

'You dare to question this gift from the gods, Monroze?'

Monroze shook her head most emphatically. 'No, milord!'

'Then gather everybody! We march immediately,' said Henrik, pausing at his doorway and putting a hand to his heart in relief. 'I thank the gods and spirits for sending you, seer.'

Farden and Mithrid were soon alone, and in the gloom, wide smiles spread across their faces.

It took barely an hour for the Arka to flee the city. The word spread quicker through the streets than the ranks, and the soldiers who were last to leave were booed and pelted from the walls. Belephon had taken back its city, and all thanks to a mysterious seer who had already vanished from the lord's tower.

A flat-topped spire made a fine vantage point from which to watch their mad dash. They looked like a caravan of traders running from bandits. And at their head, a bustling Lord Henrik, Headless as he ever was, mocking those who mocked him and wishing them good luck with the plague he had so cleverly escaped.

'I can't believe he fell for it,' Mithrid chuckled.

'You did well, girl. But we still have Troacles, and that won't be solved with lies and acting.' Farden held out his arm for Mithrid to take. 'Two down. One to go.'

CHAPTER 4
THE BARONESS

It is not enough to possess their lands. To build our walls and subjugate their peoples and the beasts that call themselves human. Nor is it enough to make examples of those who stand against us. We must impose not only our laws and stamp out magick, but Arka life and ways. I want you to take away their coin, their songs, their gods, their words and their history, and in their place put ours.

ORDERS OF EMPEROR MALVUS TO THE NEW LORDS OF PARAIA, YEAR 911

'This city reeks to the stars,' Mithrid muttered.

She spoke the truth. The rotting seaweed of the ports and its large population of unwashed individuals conspired to create a stench that not even the spice traders could dampen.

Troacles was not a peaceful city. Between the voices blaring from tavern doorways, the screams from cathouse windows, and the yells and cries for help of those being tortured by criminals and Arka soldiers alike, the earliest hours were not as calm as they should have been. The low cloud burned orange from the torchlights and lanterns that refused to die.

Magick flowed through the city like the bilge through the canals. Farden could feel its danger. There were mages amongst Troacles' army, scores of them. It barely disguised the power seeping from the markets wedged between streets.

A wail rose up from the gate below them, where a fellow was receiving a beating from armoured Arka fists before he was thrown outside the city walls.

'Now can you see why we jumped up here?' Farden asked.

Mithrid gripped the scaffolding of the rooftop with white knuckles. She muttered something foul.

'To business, then. The baroness in charge of Troacles is called Bjera. She's a mage, and one more stubborn than you and I combined.'

'Njord's balls. How do you know that?'

'Because Baroness Bjera and I studied at the Manesmark School together. I chose the path of a Written. Bjera chose politics, and it rotted away what was left of her dwindling conscience. Now she's old and cruel and doesn't give two shits about the poverty that's taken over her city,' Farden lectured while his gaze roved from one alleyway to the next, where waifs huddled around burning rubbish and beggars lay prone with their hands propped up and open for coins and scraps.

'Why?' asked Mithrid.

'What do you mean?'

'We've already fought greed and superstition. What's Bjera's vice?'

'Rage and vengeance. And we both know how all-consuming those can be. Twelve years ago, Malvus gave her the task of taking Troacles, and Bjera lost her sister on the first day of the siege.'

'How do you know that?'

Farden nodded, roaming through old memories in his head. He still remembered the searing heat of the day Troacles had burned. 'Because I was there, fighting on the side of Paraia to stop Malvus from gaining a foothold.' The mage paused. 'Modren was the one who killed her sister.'

'I see.'

'Bjera's taken it out on the Paraians every day since, and every soldier and mage under her command follows eagerly in her dark footsteps. If any city of Paraia truly wants freedom, it's Troacles.'

'What do you have in that rat's nest of a mind then, king?'

'More fire,' Farden said as he pointed to the port, where ships' masts bristled and swarms of vuleguls whirled over fishing boats.

'You want another distraction.'

Farden grunted affirmatively. 'We coax Bjera to the docks where there're fewer people, and then you and I will reunite her with her sister.'

'Then let's go. Dawn's coming,' said Mithrid as she reached for Farden's arm, but he shook his head.

'I can't see well enough through the smoke and lights to use Gunnir. We'll have to walk.'

With much shimmying along the loose and grimy roof tiles, and plenty of cursing from Mithrid, they descended to an alley where no Arka came to tread. A huddle of figures occupied a nearby doorway, and the two individuals climbing down a drainpipe looked suspicious enough to bother.

'Evening, friends,' called one of the men, approaching with a lopsided smile and one hand stuffed in a pocket. The goat horns protruding from his forehead had been sharpened. 'Fine night for some climbing.'

Farden looked to see another pair of alley-dwellers boxing them in. When he turned back to Goat Horns, the hand had been removed from the pocket and was now full of knife. The notched blade waggled at them.

'I say you turn out those pockets and give us whatever you've been burgling before you get some iron 'twixt your guts.'

'If you want to see morning, I suggest you go back to your doorway,' Mithrid warned.

'Big words from a little worm,' chuckled another of the bandits. 'They look pale and Arka to me, Swisher.'

To a man, every thug hawked and spat on the dirt street.

Farden stretched tall, pulling aside his cloak to show his armour and Gunnir disguised as a sword, less rusty this time. 'This isn't a fight you want to pick. We're here to battle the Arka and free Troacles, not the people we're trying to save. Even people like you.'

Farden wasn't so impatient that he didn't recognise the truth. They were nothing but products of their desperation and the cruelty of their conquerors.

'Fancy steel you got there.'

'Rush 'em, Swisher!'

Swisher had already made that mistake. He feinted with the knife, aiming low for Farden's belly before striking at his neck. Farden raised his hand, easily blocking the slash and knocking the blade from Swisher's hand. Before he could recover, Farden swung a fist under the man's chin and lifted him off his feet. Swisher collapsed, half-unconscious and bleeding through his teeth. Before the other thugs could close in, Farden lit the alleyway with a crackle of a spark spell.

Predictably, the thugs fled, leaving Swisher moaning and spitting blood. Farden flicked a coin to the dust beside his head.

'Elessi would be proud,' said Mithrid as they pulled up their hoods, refastened their cloaks, and wandered calmly into the pit of vipers Troacles promised to be.

Unlike Tolema, the Arka of Troacles were not bored exiles nor fattened mages, but wilful subjugators. Soldiers dominated every crossroads in pairs and threes. Archers perched on roof corners and skinny watchtowers. Others patrolled in groups that made the crowds disperse at the mere sight of them, and not because of the frequency at which fists and clubs descended on anyone who got in their way, but for who walked alongside them: Arka mages holding helbeasts on spiked chains.

The ugly brutes snarled and strained on their leashes. Their gaping nostrils drank in every scent, searching for even the faintest taste of magick.

Farden could feel Mithrid shrink behind him at the first sight of the beasts. A memory unspoken pursed her lips.

'Bastard creatures,' she breathed.

'Focus, Mithrid,' said Farden, as one of the helbeasts unleashed a guttural bark and almost dragged its handler onto his arse. The creature had fixed its red eyes on a nearby merchant whose stall was squeezed between two leaning buildings. It clawed at the earth while its forked tail whipped the legs of its master.

The merchant wore the face of a man who had promptly shat himself. He cowered behind his table of seashell trinkets and begged for mercy. But it seemed mercy had been murdered in Troacles long ago, and its bones were already bleached by the sun. Soldiers swarmed around the merchant, spilling him and his wares onto the road.

'I have nothing!' he yelled over and over.

One of the mages not fighting to restrain a helbeast hit him with a force spell, slamming him against the wall so hard he slid into a heap and left a trail of blood on the sandstone.

'Mercy!' cried the onlookers.

The mage had captain's marks on his pauldron. He sauntered to loom over the merchant and pick up one of the man's shells: a pink and pearlescent coil with thin spikes. The mage turned it over to watch a thin stream of seawater dribble from it. The stream didn't stop, defying the size of the small shell several times over.

'By order of the Decree of Magick and by the authority of the Baroness Bjera, you will hang at dawn for the crime of purveying magickal items. To the gallows with him!' announced the captain, and two soldiers ran to drag the merchant up by the arms.

'I didn't know. I didn't know!' he slurred, over and over.

Farden started forwards, but Mithrid held him back. 'There are too many people,' she whispered.

The mage cursed her for being right. The helbeast was sniffing again and this time in their direction. The mage holding its leash searched the crowds with suspicious eyes.

'Let's finish this,' Farden said as he pulled Mithrid into another street.

Hopping from one street to the next to avoid the watchtowers and patrols, they zigzagged towards the docks. There must have been a thousand soldiers and mages in that godsforsaken city, and it made the going slow and careful.

The stench of the port grew in strength until it filled their noses and made their eyes water. Not even the flow of coin and trade could wash away the grime. The buildings might have been a touch grander, but they were decorated with vulegul shit, their windows so smeared with sea salt a brick wall would have let more light in. The canals that met the sea were brown with waste, and on their banks, taverns jostled with fishmongers, which rubbed shoulders with ropemakers, who were crowded by factories filled with vats of bubbling tallow and blubber. And filling any available space, like caulking between planks, were the beggars and derelicts in makeshift shelters. Farden saw signs of pox amongst them, heard the hacking of rotlung, and even the whine of newborns. The sights did nothing to quell the anger crackling in Farden's heart, though it did put some extra speed in his step.

Another helbeast showed its ugly face between the crowds. A patrol was headed directly towards them. Farden looked for an alternate route, but the alleyways were blocked by shanties, and the only other choice was to jump in the canal. That wouldn't only be highly suspicious but likely to curse them with a disease.

'Mithrid. Use your power.'

But Mithrid was distracted by the helbeast. Farden nudged her sharply.

'Mithrid!'

The girl spread her hands surreptitiously and kept her shadow to a minimum. Farden hated the feeling of her magick quashing his, but he endured. With a slow but determined pace, they blended with the beggars on the street and kept their heads low.

The helbeast drew level with them and yowled at its mage master. Farden tensed, gauntlets grating on Gunnir's handle. The creature sniffed deeply, serpent's tongue lolling between its fangs, claws scratching at flagstones.

'He's got something,' the master called to the rest of the patrol.

'Mithrid,' Farden hissed.

'I'm trying.'

Shadow leaked from her, almost invisible in the darkness of the street.

A shiver ran through the helbeast's whole body before it snuffled and plodded onwards.

'False alarm!'

Farden and Mithrid waited until the patrol had passed before straightening and going on their way. The port was close now, barely five streets away. A faint blush of dawn had appeared in the east.

A shout cut the bustle of the street, making its population freeze and wince. 'Halt there!'

Swapping a glance, Farden and Mithrid kept walking with their heads low, hoping it wasn't aimed at them.

'I said halt there, you shits!'

A glance over his shoulder showed Farden a fattened soldier striding after them. Behind him, the patrol had turned around to take interest. 'This isn't ideal.'

'What's your business?' demanded the soldier.

'Pest removal,' Farden muttered.

'Pests?'

'You know, rats and the like.'

'Who've you got there?' came a mage's shout. The helbeast was now straining on its leash.

'Pair of rat-catchers, or so they say! Fancy arms and armour for ratters, though,' yelled the man, eying the glint of gold coming from Farden's sleeve and Mithrid's axe.

Mithrid was still trying to dampen the mage's magick, Farden could feel it, but it did nothing to quell the curiosity of these marauders.

Farden took a step back.

'We could run,' Mithrid breathed. 'Draw them to the port with us.'

'Oi! You stay where you are!' said the soldier as he struggled to draw his sword. 'You're under arrest for… for being suspicious!'

'That doesn't sound like a crime to me,' said Farden, still walking backwards.

'I say what's a crime, not you! Now stop moving!'

Cerulean light sputtered as one of the Arka mages summoned a spark spell into his hands. The beggars that could move did so, sprinting or hobbling in any direction but that of the brewing fight.

Farden sighed. Their choices were few, if not singular, and so he drew the sword at his belt. It was answered by the ring of a dozen other blades.

'Mithrid, if you please.'

'Already there,' Mithrid said as she clawed at the air with her hands. The lightning in the mage's hands sputtered out.

'What in Hel?!' the man cursed, nearly popping an eyeball from the strain, but Mithrid kept his magick down.

'Put down your blades, or taste Arka steel!' said the soldier in a higher pitch than before.

'As you wish.'

Taking a knee, Farden drove the point of the sword into the ground. Stone shattered under a burst of lightning, and when it faded, he held not a sword but a silver spear, its wicked glaive blade reaching high above his head.

It didn't stay there for long but cut deep through the soldier's belly as Farden whirled Gunnir around him. The Arka armour counted for nothing against the spear. It might as well have been silk. The man was gutted in a blink, and the sight made one of the soldiers vomit.

'Now!' Farden yelled as he thrust out a hand. Moments later, he felt Mithrid's power vanish, and the Book on his back burned with magick. Lightning of his own making blasted into the soldiers and tore chunks of stone from the street. The Arka mage was bent backwards under the force and howled through what was left of his jaw and cheek.

Whether by design or accident, somehow the helbeast was unleashed, and it came galloping for Farden in its hunger for magick.

The wild shout in his right ear came from Mithrid. Farden didn't realise until the axe came flying past his elbow and straight into the helbeast's snout. As if a vendetta Farden didn't know about had just been put to rest, Mithrid wrenched her axe sideways and breathed a great sigh.

'Needed that, did you?' he asked.

Mithrid grinned. 'I've wanted to do that for a very long time.'

Farden threw out a shield spell as archers on nearby rooftops joined the brawl. Mithrid quickly took shelter behind him, and they ran towards the docks with magick held high and crackling under the collisions of arrows and spells.

'Well, you wanted a distraction, didn't you?' Mithrid shouted between breaths.

'Too soon. Too close!' Farden yelled as he swatted a fireball into the canal with an explosion of steam. He levelled Gunnir at the amassing Arka and let loose the spear's power. A pillar of white light cut their crowd in two.

It bought them a moment, nothing more, and they spent it sprinting through the clamouring docks and towards an Arka warship that listed against a quay as if it were drunk. The quay sprawled onto the beach that lined Troacles' northern edges, where a handful of sailors milled about, finding distraction from hauling crates.

Farden kicked splinters from the planks as he skidded to a stop. A yelling mass of soldiers could be seen worming through the docks on their tail, and the port's bell tower had taken to tolling. It wasn't pretty, but it had worked, and when was war ever pretty?

'This is our battleground. You ready?' snarled Farden.

Mithrid let her shadow curl about her fists in answer.

'Then shield your eyes.'

Cloak thrown aside, Scalussen armour bared to the torchlight and helmet clicking into place, Farden clanged his vambraces together and let the magick pour from him. He heard Mithrid cry out in pain, but he pressed on, searching for the magick in the ground, channelling the power of Gunnir standing tall and wedged in the planks at his side.

Wood squealed as the quay began to shake. Waves splashed as the quaking spread to the water, and the bell atop the warship began to chitter as the ship lurched. Farden clicked his fingers, igniting a spark between his hands and birthing two raging fireballs that he held in each palm.

'Whatever you're doing, do it now!' came Mithrid's shout, faint and drowned by the roar of fire.

Farden threw out his arms and sent the spells racing for the warship, punching two flaming holes in its deck. The roar of the magick was a whisper compared to the sonorous boom of the ship exploding deep within its bowels. Whatever the Arka kept aboard this ship was apparently extremely flammable, and with a detonation that drove Farden to his knees, the warship split in two. What was left of the two halves rose up before crumbling onto the quay and drowning a nearby skiff.

'By bloody Hurricane, Farden!' Mithrid wheezed. She was gawping at the cloud of fire and black smoke that mushroomed into the sky. 'I think they heard that in Krauslung!'

'Good! And you can tell the others exactly that whenever they dare to doubt this spear.'

A lure Farden had wanted, and a lure he had made. The entire of Troacles now knew they were there, and every single soldier in the city seemed to be running for the port in their hundreds and thousands. Farden and Mithrid could see it in the specks of firelight streaming through roads and alleys and down the portward slope of the city. More concerning, dozens of the lights were rising into the sky, fire arrows soaring. The crunch and clammer of ballistae and catapults echoed across the rooftops.

'This is a little more than a distraction, Farden, don't you think?' Mithrid snapped

It was, but Farden didn't care. The Arka needed to be punished, and he would gladly perform that task.

Throwing his hands to the sky, the mage's shield spells cut the air in time to catch two flaming ballista bolts and cast them into the sea.

'They won't be expecting you or Gunnir,' Farden bellowed. 'And that's going to be our advantage. We kill Bjera, we break them.'

The first wave of soldiers came at them, a distraction of the Arka's design while they arranged ranks of archers and mages behind. Farden cut through their efforts with a blast from Gunnir and kept them concentrated at the end of the quay. Aside from swimming or going the long way around to the beach, the only path to Mithrid and Farden was a thin walkway. The Arka crowded along it, making themselves easy targets. Between fending off ballistae and catapults, Farden threw lightning and vortex spells into their midst, cutting down dozens to trip and foul the rest. He saw Loki in all their faces and treated them as if they were the god himself. No quarter. No mercy. They had shown none and thus deserved less. Farden exercised the daemon of loathing he had been keeping deep inside since the final battle of Easterealm.

Mithrid stood by his side, axe raised and fingers clawed, eradicating magick wherever she could reach it. Mage after mage amongst the rush became useless, no more than soldiers with half the armour and too befuddled to dodge the magick Farden bent at them.

A ballista bolt slammed into the stone at Farden's feet, too low for his shield. He redoubled his efforts as more collided with the quay. Not a single Arka had yet made it a spear's reach onto the quay, but they crept closer with every passing moment. Even with the strength of his Book and Gunnir, Farden's concentration was tested.

'Farden!'

Mithrid was pointing at an inbound mess of rock and flame, streaking over the port. Farden had let his shield slip.

'Curse it!'

A rotation of his hand saw a flame erupt in his palm. He took aim with one eye closed before he hurled his spell at the catapult's shot. The impact knocked it off course and it crashed into the Arka ranks instead with a fresh round of screams.

'Keep it together, old man!' Mithrid yelled at him.

Farden redoubled his efforts with a snarl, wielding quake and vortex spells to keep the Arka pinned and hurling fireballs any moment he didn't need a shield.

But a storm was gathering around the buildings of the port. Lightning tore across the sky, reaching for Farden. Mithrid threw her shadow past the shield spells and into the sky, and any Arka magick that touched it withered into dust and sparks. 'What is that?' she asked.

'It's the baroness! She's arrived.'

Farden relaxed his onslaught to make the Arka bolder and bring them closer into his reach. It worked a charm. Somehow they believed they had the advantage and pressed inwards. It was a risky gamble with archers forming more ranks on the beach, and Farden soon found himself split between shield spells and wielding death. And all the while, Bjera came closer.

With a thump of Gunnir, a wall of magick spread out like a glass bubble, sealing them off from the Arka as Bjera arrived on the battlefield. A dozen masked mages marched with her, wearing matching green and gold. A long coat of scale plate covered old Bjera from neck to heel, but she wore no helmet, letting her silver hair fly free. Her fist punched the air, and the Arka fell silent and still.

'Is that Farden I see before me? My, it has been a long time,' called out Bjera. 'Who would have thought a woodcutter's waif would grow up to think himself king one day? A king and a traitor to his kind, no less. I hoped your little campaign might bring you to Troacles, you know. At first, I was disappointed when the emperor kept me here, instead of allowing me my vengeance in the north. But as luck would have it, I seemingly escaped a massacre, and you've ended up on my doorstep nonetheless. All things come to those with patience, as the dusty scholars say. What have you come for, Farden? Vengeance of your own?'

'A deal,' Farden replied, keeping fire and wind spiralling around his wrists.

'Is that so? A truce, is it?'

'You leave Troacles in the hands of Paraia, and I'll let you live.'

Bjera laughed, a hoarse and unpractised thing. 'How kind,' she said, folding her hands. 'Where's Modren?'

'Dead, unfortunately for you and for me.'

'Then you will have to do. After all, a commander is at fault for their soldier's sins.'

'And what about the sins of yours and the way they treat this city?'

'Spare me the platitudes, Farden. These people resist Arka rule every day of their miserable lives,' Bjera replied, voice dripping in disgust. 'They deserve nothing less.'

'Small wonder they resist.' Farden removed his helmet to throw her a smile. 'Arka rule is over. Malvus is dead, and your newfound god is vanished. The empire is no more. You're finished.'

Bjera's demeanour changed instantly. Her mocking, puckered face had turned to one of jealousy. 'I see now why they call you the Forever King. What dark magick have you used to escape the rust of time?'

'Living a kinder life helps. Tyranny ages you, or so I hear. You must see it in the mirror every morning.'

Bjera stabbed the air. 'It's that shiny armour, isn't it? I know it. I'll pick it off your corpse.'

'You know you can't beat me. Written to mage.'

Bjera began to rub her hands together. 'I've come a long way since Manesmark, Farden, and I've learned a lot from these Paraians.'

'Then come and show me, Bjera,' Farden offered with a mocking bow. Mithrid stepped forwards, but he motioned her back.

'Why don't we just finish her before the sun rises and be done with this? I didn't think this was about old grudges,' she asked.

'Not mine, hers. Focus on the others. Pounce when I tell you.'

'Far—'

'When I tell you!'

Mithrid's scowl said it all.

Farden hadn't taken his eyes off Bjera, who was summoning a spell he had only seen once before. It was a vortex spell, half dust, half force, and it took the form of galloping bulls charging him.

Farden met her spells with fire, sweeping a wall of it into her onslaught and crushing half her creations. The rest clashed against his ship's bow of a shield and were driven into the water. In reply, Farden sent a wave of dirt and splinters her way with a quake spell, making Bjera cower. Her shield spell and those of her mages dented under the force. Two mages weren't quick enough and were impaled by wooden shards. But Bjera was unflinching and swiftly channelled another spell, lips moving frantically as she weaved its words together.

Bursts of light scattered around Farden, partly blinding him and masking her next strike. A force spell shaped like a ball and chain hammered him in the chest and knocked him a dozen feet.

'Loose!' yelled Bjera, and Farden had to scramble to throw up a shield spell in front of Mithrid. It was far too close, but the arrows clattered against his Scalussen metal with little effect.

Farden reached for the clouds, pulling down great forks of lightning to strike Bjera and her mages while he charged. The air grew heavy with the smell of burned flesh and charred metal, and he was already halfway to Bjera by the time her shield dissipated.

Farden struck with Gunnir in one hand and a fireball in the other. Bjera fended off the force of his magick, but the spear was a more difficult foe. The blade edged close to her heart as she held her shield against him. Magick whined as Gunnir heaved against her, deadlocked, just how Farden wanted it.

'Now, Mithrid!'

Shadow rushed over him. Farden felt Bjera's shield give way, and he stabbed viciously into the murk.

When Mithrid's magick washed away, Bjera wore a face that didn't betray an iota of pain for the spear piercing her chest. Even though the metal sizzled against her skin, her face stayed blank. Her eyes held all her hatred.

When Farden withdrew, she slumped to her knees, using her last breath to utter a final order to her followers. 'Kill them.'

Farden's fist shone with lightning. Gunnir crackled as if it thirsted for more blood, its blade drenched in white fire. 'I'll give you a choice,' he spoke to the frozen crowd of Arka. 'The smart ones amongst you will board the nearest warship. The fools can stay to die at my hand.'

The threat hung in the air, not enough to make the soldiers wither.

One of the remaining mages, seemingly distraught over Bjera, ran at Farden with two shards of ice in each fist. Farden blew a hole in his stomach with fire, and the brute's last wheeze was all the Arka needed to make their decision.

The wiser soldiers scuttled for the Arka ships in the harbour and screamed at sailors to make way. Others fled mindlessly into the crowds of citizens who had gathered to watch the battle. They didn't get far.

One by one, the people of Troacles began to stamp their feet, bringing a rhythmic thunder to the night. Here and there, fights and screams broke out as more than a decade of mistreatment was returned to those who had dealt it. Soldiers had their armour stripped away before they were beaten and flogged. Only a fortunate few escaped with their lives.

❦

By the time the dawn sun poked above the eastern cliffs, it witnessed five ships at full sail and heading north, and a city whose every watchtower burned bright and belched black smoke.

Mithrid was examining a slice in her arm between the plates of armour. 'I have to say, I was expecting this to take a few days. They'll be singing songs about this by nightfall.'

Farden watched Mithrid's gaze turn to the burning towers. They weren't alone. Any building the Arka had soiled with their presence had been introduced to the torch. 'We saved a lot of lives tonight. Paraia can finally breathe again,' he said.

'I'm quite surprised you managed to restrain yourself. I didn't expect you to let so many Arka live,' Mithrid replied. 'Maybe you shouldn't have. Maybe we'll see them again.'

Farden ignored the concern that stoked in him. *Teach her*, came a whisper from the spear leaned against his shoulder.

'After Irminsul, Krauslung deserves to have its people come home,' said Farden. 'Just like Scalussen does.'

The crowds now stood on the quays, throwing rocks, cups, and whatever else they could find in the wake of the departing ships. Their cheers were a constant thunder, and once more, Farden looked to Mithrid. He found she wasn't smiling as he had expected, but scowling, and he wondered which was worse.

'Time to go home?' she asked.

Farden extended his arm with a smile, and Mithrid took it without another word or her usual wince of anticipation as the magick grew.

Hereni woke to a hand on her arm. Magick sprang to her mind as she reeled backwards, a spell kindling in her hands.

'It's only me,' Mithrid whispered.

'How long have I been asleep for?' asked Hereni, voice hoarse with sleep and confusion as she sat up.

'It's done.'

'What do you mean it's done?'

'Farden and I accomplished it in a single night. Word's already been spread to Scalussen by quickdoor.'

'You mean Paraia is free?'

'From the Arka and Loki, yes. Farden is satisfied. For now.'

'And what about you?'

Mithrid nodded, but no words accompanied it.

'I take it that means we're finally going home.'

Mithrid smiled at that. Hereni didn't mention it, but she saw a slight regret keeping that smile from being as wide as it should have been.

'Home,' Mithrid said. 'Feels bizarre to say it again. It wasn't where I planned – not any of us for that matter – but it's the home we deserve.'

Hereni held Mithrid's face with both hands. 'Then why are we waiting?'

CHAPTER 5
ROAD TO DOMINION

Not all gemstones shine.
GOLIKAN PROVERB

THREE DAYS EARLIER

Curse this mocking rain.

Curse this fetid cave.

Curse Farden and his ilk to the grave and far beyond the void.

The maledictions came without power, merely hatred distilled in failure. If only it was that easy. If only power was that simple.

With rain cascading in a waterfall across the cave's entrance and nothing but deplorable mud and emptiness beyond, the god's movements became frantic, digging and digging at anything that could be grasped within his coat.

Endless possibilities, and Loki couldn't find a single place to start. Trinket after useless trinket spilled onto the moss-clad rocks. He had no use for a scroll that never ended, nor a ring that could summon a breeze, nor a rat's skull with the ability to whistle. The latter mocked him as his mind racked its pointless possibilities.

'Curse you all!' Loki bellowed to the mocking echoes of the cave. The skull was dashed against the irregular wall. Raw power on raw rock saw shards fly. Shards that would have cut the skin of a lesser being.

Loki fell still. He felt a weight of something that could be called an idea in his mind and sought it in his pocket. A thick tome was manhandled out into the light, one with a scarred leather cover and pages of human skin. It was the Hides of Hysteria, and Loki would have been mad to mingle its magick with his.

Yet sometimes, desperation and madness wear the same face.

The god reached for the sharpest shard of rat bone with rage-shaking hands. Dragging up the sleeve of his coat and exposing a faint edge of a page and a fainter rune, he put the bone to his skin and pressed the shard against the flesh of his arm.

But the skin of a living god didn't surrender that easily, even when it was challenged by a god's strength, and after pressing and scraping and letting spit fly from his mouth, the bone broke into dust and pieces. There was barely a mark on him, and with the back of his hand, Loki knocked the book against the wall of the cave.

'Gah!'

Loki stood in the swirling dust, hating Haven, Hel, and everything in between, and let a raw scream leave him until dust and pebbles rattled around his feet.

PRESENT DAY

There was no better hole to hide in than a tavern which had forgotten its own name.

'Another?' asked the unkempt and far too cheery barkeep.

'Is my tankard empty?' asked the god.

From across the gloomy chamber, Loki had been trying to wither the fool's exuberance with a sour mood for an hour now, employing an arsenal of his most disapproving of stares and frequent curls of the lip, but nothing seemed to dampen the man. Loki bet a knife would have. It was why his hand intermittently snuck to the blade at his belt when the temptation pulled at him.

The barkeep stood on tiptoes and leaned over to confirm the god's tankard was indeed empty. 'Sure is.'

'Then I'll have another fucking ale, won't I?'

The cursing did nothing to erode the man's smile. 'Hard to stop drinking the bogbrew once you get that first sip past your lips, ain't it?' he asked.

'Excuse me?'

'Bogbrew,' the barkeep smiled wider, as if repetition was the answer to illumination. 'It's the name of the ale. We brew it ourselves.'

'Many congratulations,' Loki muttered. The grip on the knife grew tighter. The ale tasted like piss, but he relished the punishment.

With an infuriating humming, the barkeep went to fetch Loki's beer, leaving him to sour the room with his gazing.

Loki was not alone. Three more drinkers hunched over their tables. They were the kind of tables only found in backwater taverns on backwater roads where the travellers always outnumbered the grubby locals. The kind that were carved with graffiti and only ever had one chair. Or one creaky, beetle-bitten stool, in Loki's case.

One man in oiled seal skins counted copper coins over and over. He looked the sort who spent most days on a half-sunk fishing boat, and the days he didn't complaining about said boat. He smelled like fish guts and salt.

Another had the tanned skin of Khandri and looked mildly amused by something in the scrolls he sifted through. There was barely enough room for his tankard amongst them.

The most distant was a woman who sat quietly and stiffly. She stared at the far wall with such loss of wherewithal that Loki had thought her deceased on several occasions. The only clue that she was still alive was the occasional sip she took from her copper cup. Even then, she barely blinked or tilted her head to drink.

Rats, every one of them. The tavern was nothing more than a roomy bend of a sewer pipe for rats to gather, nibble, quaff, rut, and otherwise live out their short, detestable lives. They were minuscule beyond inferior, and yet the very same rats had spurned him. In their masses, they had ruined him and his meticulous plans. Loki had expected to stand atop the glorious construction of his plan and watch the sun rise on his empire, but there he was: alone in the mud, surrounded by ruined foundations gnawed weak by sharp, unyielding fangs. No cheering and prostrating masses, only pets turned rabid in an ugly twilight.

Loki wished a plague on all of them. Worse: he wished *him* on all of them.

A tankard with a helmet of foam was dropped on his solitary table.

'Should I have you fetch me a spoon?' asked Loki, eyeing the foam and then the barkeep.

The idiot's expression didn't waver, but it did grow more clueless. 'Where is it you're from that you take a spoon for your ale, sir?'

Loki watched him for an uncomfortable amount of time before he decided to play along, if only to feel in control for a moment more.

'Krauslung, but I imagine you've never heard of it.'

The boy swelled, knocking his head to a low rafter. 'Capital of the Arka.'

'Look at you. And what do they say of the Arka in this disgusting land?'

'Not much said here in Bvarnik. Most folks be travelling south and north, not east. And all they been speaking of on these roads is the Battle For The World. Down in the Bloodplains.'

'Is that what they're calling it now? Word travels swiftly.'

The barkeep bobbed his head enthusiastically and grinned, quite at odds with the conversation of war. 'All kinds of deserters and survivors have been stumbling through. They speak tale of a living storm. Of kings and queens of the east dead under skies of fire. Beasts made of stone and dust. Great wolves, and creatures of fire, they say—'

'Never mind the spilled blood and bowels, the screaming and the crying, and the sheer massacre of half the kingdoms in this sprawl of a continent. Including some of your countrymen, I wager.

Not a care for them, no?' Loki replied. He was rewarded with a frown. He blew the foam from his ale in one huff, and it attached to the barkeep's greasy shirt. 'What was the last you heard of Krauslung?'

Before the barkeep could answer, the fellow in sealskin tapped his tankard thrice. Loki challenged anyone to find a tavern in the world without an eavesdropper with an interruption poised on his lips.

'Met an Essen trader passing through Lezembor,' said the fisherman. 'Week back, maybe. Said Krauslung's naught but a place for the mourning and the mad now, with some folks saying prayers to some short lord they called a living god for turning away daemons at the city gates. With words alone, apparently. They said he raised sea serpents to his bidding, and I know I remember that right 'cause it put a shiver in my backside. Enough wrong with the Realm without talk of daemons and serpents and false gods. Emaneska can keep them.' The fisherman paused to decorate his lip with foam. 'Upped and left them, this god of theirs, though. Disappeared as strangely as he arrived, so said the trader, and now Krauslung's been left to its nobles. Like gulls on a washed-up whale, they are. Makes sense now the empire's no more, and Essen's looking for independence. The south is kicking the Arka out, too, I hear. With the east scrambling after the Bloodplains, the whole world's in shit.'

Loki furiously gulped down his beer. He had felt the wavering in the prayer of his rats in Krauslung, and the crumbling of the belief they had put in him. Like a wineskin with a puncture, their prayer and Loki's power leaked away in his absence. If he'd had something resembling a human stomach, it would have been knotted.

The eavesdropping spread like the spilled ale creeping across his table. The Khandri tapped his tankard three times also before speaking.

'Your tongue's full of rot. There are no daemons in Easterealm or in Emaneska.'

The fisherman scoffed. 'Cousin of mine swears blind he saw them weeks ago, from the coast of the Diamond Mountains. Great beasts, all smoke, rock, and cinder, travelling south to fight.'

Khandri wasn't having it. 'Your cousin must be a fool if he believes such a thing. I am a man of study and facts, sir, and that is a conjuration of the imagination. Nothing more.'

A discussion fuelled by beer and boredom ensued, becoming a tedious noise in an instant, and one that irritated Loki enough to turn his back on it. He gave the fire the kind of stare the frozen woman gave her wall.

It had been weeks since the Battle For The World. Perhaps months. Months of drifting north like the last goose to arrive in spring, lurking in the arse crack between Emaneska and Easterealm. It was a place of nobodies and nothings, and that suited Loki's mind – a chorus of a thousand voices of rage and frustration all vying to be loudest – just fine.

Loki could have clicked his fingers and taken a look at Krauslung for himself, of course, but he had yet to dare. The simplest explanation was that he did not want to.

Loki carved a chunk from the table with a fingernail as he imagined the smirking faces of Mithrid and Farden in the fire. To have been bested by that wretch and walking mess of a mage was unbearable. Unspeakable. Gods were not supposed to fail. Loki most of all, and to face his stolen city and its questions was to admit such a failure. Gods were not supposed to bleed, and he had been bled. Gods did not return empty-handed in defeat, and he would have to.

Yet it would have been a mistake to think the defeat had put the fight out of him. Quite the opposite, in fact. Revenge and victory were the singular desires that held together Loki's cacophony of a mind. Yet the debilitating question was still, inescapably: *how?*

Calculation and the careful pulling of strings had always been his true power. Plotting. Conniving. Lying. Coercing. Manoeuvring. If he was the god of anything, he was the god of getting what he wanted, and there he was, clueless. There was no calculation that he could cobble together. No string in sight to pull, and for the first time in his centuries, Loki was lost. The truth of it was he felt… *mortal*.

Facing the fire, Loki seized the hem of his trusted coat with a snarl and delved a hand into the pocket. It did not matter that his last attempt had been pointless. Desperation was a wonderful excuse for repetition. And madness, for that matter.

As always, a thought pulled an object towards him, and all Loki had to do was pluck it from the void. Loki produced a knife with a curving blade of black steel that seemed to glimmer and shift as if it were liquid held in shape. It was a nyxblade, a relic of another world beyond the oceans, and he glared at its lack of potential. The poisoned blade was weak, not a god's plan in the slightest, and he put it aside.

Loki racked his brain for everything he knew the void to contain. Trinket after lost trinket was pulled into the light, from jade bracelets that held an eerie light, to a whistle for summoning pigeons, to a charmed silk slipper that would make not a sound nor scuff on any surface. Loki threw that thief's prize in the fire in irritation, watching the magick in it crackle blue.

Once more he delved, searching the void for things he had forgotten and those even more dangerous: those he had not yet found.

They were like marbles in a sack of rice, difficult to summon. Burned rocks appeared twice, then a stone tablet inscribed by lost runes, then a broken dagger that left a streak of rust on his palm.

Loki dared to reach deeper into the dark and cursed sharply as something bit. Not the magick, but something with teeth. He retrieved his hand to find a crystalline snake with its glasslike jaws gripping his finger, its fangs sunk deep. The rest of its short body wriggled back and forth. Baring his teeth, Loki seized it by the neck, twisted to the squeak of crushed glass, and threw it into the fire to hopefully melt.

Vexed, he glanced back to his fellow tavern-goers and scowled at their conversation.

'Fae *are* real, you fool! You're so quick to believe in daemons, yet fae you draw the line at?' yelled the Khandri.

'That I do!' hollered the fisherman.

'Next you'll be saying gods have fallen from their homes in their stars. I—'

Loki's rage spilled over, and he crashed his tankard on the table, splitting it in two.

Rats.

'Enough!' he shouted, drawing wide eyes from everyone but the woman. 'You do nothing but squabble and squawk! You battle each other to the death with deficient minds filled with hearsay and regurgitated nonsense. Your talk means nothing. Your opinions mean nothing. *You* matter nothing, and yet you each have the audacity to believe yourself somehow special, as if you weren't just another spark spat from the fire to die in the dark! You are meal. You are mortar. You are meat! You enrage and bore me at the same time, and I have grown tired of you! Your place must be learned in this world you think is yours!'

Loki clasped the nyxblade again and pointed it at each of the rats before him. He could smell their fear over the sour stink of spilled brew, and he drank its power. Loki would take fear. He wanted adoration and devotion, but fear was cheap. Harder, grubbier work, mind, but it was still a road to dominion.

The barkeep approached with bluster and his ample belly bobbing. 'Now you see here, sir, you—'

As it turned out, a blade at his stubbly throat was the key for removing the smile from the barkeep's face.

'A Battle For The World, you called it?' Loki asked. 'You witless cur. That has yet to come.'

A simple slip of Loki's hand cut the lad's throat. A small cut, and one his victim might have lived through if Loki hadn't chosen to wield a nyxblade. The poison spread, hungry as a street dog, corroding the barkeep's flesh and spoiling it black and rotten as it went. The wound was a gaping and ugly gash to the bone by the time he fell to the floor.

'Bloody gods!' the fisherman tried to rise, half in defence, half in a strong desire to flee. While he struggled to pry a sickle blade from his belt, Loki drove the dagger down into his shoulder with a sigh. The force sat the man back down, where he seethed and he dribbled as the poison ate into his flesh.

The Khandri had chosen flight and was currently scrabbling for the doorway with his hands full of scrolls. Loki pointed the dagger at him, causing the fisherman to retch as it was plucked from his bones.

'Sit,' Loki ordered.

Khandri proved a good pet. Though from the rising stink of shit, he had filled his trews with his fear.

'You. You aren't a believer in the gods?' asked the god.

'I'm a m–man of s—'

'Study. I believe you mentioned that,' Loki said as he weaved a path between the tables towards the scholar. 'And what of those prayers just aching to spill over your blubbering lips? Whom do you call on in your darkest moments, I wager? I think a name other than study and science.'

Loki was right, and Khandri joined the fisherman in muttering prayers. Quite impressive for the latter, seeing as the poison had almost reached his neck, and he wavered on the cusp of consciousness.

The reek of Khandri's mudded trews was a good reason to move on, and Loki turned to the woman. She hadn't moved, and her stare bored into the wall as precisely as before. Even with blood on the floorboards, Loki had yet to notice her blink, and he pondered whether it would take setting the tavern on fire to shift her.

The vacant stranger wore archer's leathers and a scrap of chainmail around her neck, but she was no warrior. The callouses on her hands were of carpentry, not spear or swordplay, and she sat too straight for a life of pulling a bowstring. Judging by her shade, she was not local, not of the north or west, and there was too much amber in her hair to be from Khandri or Paraia. There was a seashell pinned to one of her ears. That meant an islander. From Bolsh or the Sunter Isles, perhaps.

'And you,' Loki called to her. 'What of you? You don't seem to fear me. Are you damaged in the head or robbed of your senses?'

The woman calmly reached for and raised her cup to sip without a sound. 'And why would I fear you?' she whispered.

'Don't you know what I am? Or are you as slow as our Khandri friend here?'

'Besides a murderer?' she asked, pausing for another sip. 'I have no care for what you are. You are nothing compared to what I've seen.'

'What are you?' the Khandri scholar breathed.

Loki was that strange ache in his eye. The nervousness of his gut. The sweat racing down his cheek. The feeling of something amiss and the strange scent on the air. The Khandri cowered as Loki's eyes bored into him.

'Do you have a name?' Loki asked of the islander, stepping nearer to the aim of her stare. The gloomy creature intrigued him, not just for the emotions they both shared, but for what the cause of hers could be.

'Doree,' she whispered.

Another step closer. Another sip of the cup.

'What have you seen, Doree?' Loki asked. 'What is the cause for the hollows around your eyes and the fear in their whites, I wonder?'

Doree's gaze was fierce. A lone tear escaped her left eye. 'The worst.'

'The worst?' Loki's mind turned quiet. A curiosity blossomed. 'I could use the worst. Elaborate.'

Doree shook her head. 'I fear if I speak it aloud, it'll bring them. Like the wisps.'

'Bring whom? Speak, woman.'

'I wager they don't have a name.'

'Tell me.'

The islander finished her drink. 'Gabo managed one toll before they got him. They threw his head into the square for us all to see, eyes still wide as saucers.'

'Who?!'

Doree babbled as if a dam had burst in her mouth. 'Boasted skin like ash and white grins we barely glimpsed in the torches. Tall. Too tall. The way they darted between the shadows weren't right. All disjointed like puppets on broken strings. Their spears and swords stabbed at us, hooked and dripping with blood. Black arrows poisoned. Even if we'd been an army of ten thousand, we still wouldn't have lasted any longer. They were brutal. Grey Kanaa put up a fine fight before he was hacked in two, poor man. One cut off Giminee's face to wear as a mask…'

Something caught in Doree's throat. Another sip of the wine was needed before she continued. A shake crept into her hands. 'They didn't give a fuck who they killed. Lifers. Militia. Beggars. Old'uns. Even the children didn't seem to matter. All were fair game, and like game we were treated, nothing more than beasts butchered and hung to bleed,' whispered Doree.

Loki felt a smile twitch in his lips.

'They weren't trolls, they weren't wisps, they weren't the daemons those idiots argued silly about. They weren't of these lands, and I mean any land. These fell shadows were from wherever nightmares are born. And they weren't alone. They had… *something* with them. Something made of evil that hid in the dark, eating what was left…' Doree drew a stuttering breath as another tear ran. 'The awful sight of it won't leave my eyes, and not a day goes by that doesn't feel borrowed. Or wrong, like I'm trespassing in a world that ain't mine.'

'And just how did you escape such a monster?' Loki, remembering to control his enthusiasm, tested the strength of her story.

'I didn't stop running.'

'When and where did this happen?'

'Kasto, land of the blue trees. And a week, maybe more ago.'

'Where in this forsaken realm is that?'

The woman's gaze almost strayed from the wall. 'Island south of Bolsh. An island that did nothing to harm nobody never.'

'And if I asked you to take me there—'

All at once, the full glare of Doree's focused stare rested upon him. Loki could see the dark blood of the fallen and the burning buildings in her eyes. He saw for the first time the barely healed burn across her face, consuming her skin from temple to jaw. 'I would tell you to go rut with yourself. I'd rather be put out of my misery,' Doree said with winter in her voice before turning back to her wall.

Loki let his smile loose. 'So be it.'

The fisherman was on the verge of death. Loki made sure to give him another stab to finish him so he could drink the soul within. It tasted weak, and the sight made the Khandri scream and possibly shit himself again. Loki wasn't about to ask.

With the curt slam of a door, Loki left the tavern and its occupants to their horror. Loki looked up and down the mud-thick road the tavern kept watch over, and seeing not a soul, he barred the door with a nearby rake and delved deep in his pockets once more.

There was a flame that burned in the void within his pockets. It was once a spirit whose name Loki had forgotten, but it was a flame that refused to wither or die. The god brought it forth, cradled between finger and thumb, and touched it to the thatch above the doorway. The thatch was damp, but the flame was hungry from its exile and feasted eagerly upon the tavern's roofing. The starving fire hissed and spat as it ate into the worn sign that bore no memorable name. Within moments, the tavern was ablaze, and it was curious how the only screams Loki heard were those of the Khandri scholar.

For the first time in days, as he set his boots to the churned road, Loki found purpose in his stride. He even dared to call it hope.

All he had to do was find a nightmare.

CHAPTER 6
NEW SCALUSSEN

Mining and tunnelling come easy to creatures with great claws, jaws, or fire in their lungs. I speak of dragons, of course. Half of Hjaussfen was carved out by dragon-breath, enough to melt the very rock and to be poured into columns, arches, and brick by Nelska stonesmiths. And what untold riches besides stone those dragons found while digging for shelter.
FROM THE DIARY OF DURNUS GLASSREN

The Claw of Tolema had only one quickdoor, and to say it was antiquated was a kind word. So it was that it took almost a whole day for the thousands Farden had brought north to return to New Scalussen. Soul by grateful soul, they embarked through the shivering portal, greeted by the muffled noises of cheering that leaked through from the other side.

At last, it was Warbringer's turn to travel, and she was forced to duck beneath the horrid, crackling archway. The sensation was as intensely dislikable as always, like being washed around the mouth of some great glowing creature before being spat out unceremoniously.

Scalussen waited beyond the chaos. Jar Khoum and Scalussen survivors formed exuberant crowds that hooted and cheered the army's return. Around the portal stood the generals of Scalussen who had stayed behind: High Crone Wyved the mute witch and her helper Peryn, both in the strange company of birds. General Eyrum leaning on his wooden leg and his battleaxe crutch. Kayruka, the childlike queen of the ferocious Jar Khoum, narrow-eyed as always. Admiral Sturmsson stood straight as ever next to the lycan Roglurg. The name was difficult for a minotaur tongue. They and their crowds shouted loudly for Warbringer as she thumped her hammer on the white stone of the square.

A special cheer rose up, separate from the rest, and she recognised the deep and roaring voices. Her whole clan stood at the back of the crowds, pressed against a wall. Their number was far fewer now than when they had left Efjar, and it made her fingers creak against her hammer as it always did.

Warbringer did not endure the pleasantries long before she moved to join them. She said nothing before she clashed horns with her second and third bloodmongers.

'Warbringer. Is it done?' her second, a bloodmonger they called Thenerean, asked in their native tongue.

'It is done. Finished by the king and the girl in one night,' growled Warbringer.

The minotaurs shook their horns and raised fists to their god, impressed.

'What news?' she asked.

'None of daemons or little gods. Scalussen continues to grow. And…' Thenerean waved to the rest of the clan with the sharp and jagged blade that replaced his lower arm. The same arm that had been inconveniently removed by a marsh troll once upon a time. 'The clan waits to depart, as promised.'

Warbringer showed sharp teeth. 'It is not time.'

Thenerean's nostrils flared. 'So you keep saying, Warbringer, but we grow tired of waiting. You promised we would retake Efjar —'

Warbringer prodded him in the snout. 'I want nothing but to return to the Efjar I remember. But we are few. We have safety in this south. Allies. And our work is not yet done.'

'We have never needed such before,' grumbled another bloodmonger with a gold hoop through his nostrils.

'You forget we needed Scalussen when the Arka came for us. Times change, and those who don't change also die. Do you want death for our kin?'

Thenerean grunted, displeased by that accusation. 'Do you?'

Warbringer remembered the cave of Utiru and the two states she had seen her home in: one burning and the other filled with the voices of clans united. She didn't know what the others had chosen as their visions, but Warbringer had made her decision before she had left that damnable cave.

She placed Voidaran at the centre of their circle, letting the metal ring and whisper. 'The prophecy is almost complete. I did not think it was possible, but I can feel it. Much blood has been shed.'

Every minotaur with a good set of ears leaned closer, whispering behind fangs. 'At last, after centuries,' a young bull breathed.

'I followed the mage in hope of war and blood. In the east, I swore to return us to Efjar, but now that we are close, we can fulfil our destiny. That is why we wait and trust in unity.' Voidaran chimed again. 'For all of our kin.'

'But now there is no war,' growled Thenerean. 'We cannot stop now if we are close.'

A loud cheer rose from the crowd as Mithrid appeared, closely followed by Hereni. Voices reached their crescendo when the Forever King emerged from the doorway, helmet off and magick spear in hand. Warbringer watched him closely.

'Farden does not think it's over, and I have a feeling the king is right,' she said.

'Do you still trust him?' asked Thenerean.

'Now more than ever,' Warbringer answered without hesitation, and her growl ended the discussion. With a stamping of hooves, the others bowed.

Farden was trying his best to escape the chanting crowds, politely making himself scarce. Warbringer hefted Voidaran onto her shoulder and followed in the mage's direction.

It seemed like New Scalussen had doubled in size in the short weeks they had been away. Between the beached hulk of the *Winter's Revenge* – a wooden castle now called the Winter Fortress – a large town of wood and stone had been built with magick and craftsmanship from every corner of the map. From the Dawnknell, Farden's new half-grown tower, it was easy to see New Scalussen already stretched towards being a city. Thick defensive walls had sprung up. Spindly watchtowers marked boundaries already overtaken. Carpenters hammered incessantly beneath the ribcages of rooftops, bringing long halls and barracks to life. Even a brand new bookship with an ironclad hull sat in its drowned cradle. *Her* cradle. The pink-fleshes insisted on making their ships female. The rescued *Summer's Fury* and *Autumn's Vanguard* sat in the huge bay like two giant gourds on a turquoise plate. Sanctuary Bay, they called it now.

To Warbringer, it was all a noisy mess.

The Jar Khoum knew no better. Tunnels to their hidden underground abode spread through the town and out into the palm forests. Their rabbit holes made Warbringer's hide feel too tight, and she had suffered their dank air only once.

Thenerean was right. They needed a home of their own. If dragons could make theirs in the snowy mountains to the north, why could the clan not do the same? Warbringer longed for that day, but it was not to come yet. Voidaran had yet to sate her thirst.

Warbringer looked to see if any dragons still lingered in New Scalussen, but the skies belonged to gulls and fishing eagles instead. The streets, built wide enough for dragons, with open squares for landing, were empty of the great beasts, and their dust and boards were trodden by goats, coelos, dillos, and cows instead. The only glint of scales in sight belonged to Fleetstar, curled like a knotted loaf on the white beach.

Counting all the beasts had made Warbringer ravenous. Behind her, the others had gathered for another of their Dawnknell councils, and that meant it would be some time before she could fill her stomach.

Warbringer was considering disappearing for a snack when Farden made his entrance, wearing a cloak over his ever-present armour. Those around the table thumped their hands upon the broad table of cracked stone filled with molten copper.

'One night, they tell me,' General Eyrum said. 'One night to fell the Paraian Arka.'

'Stole the fun from rest of us,' Warbringer grunted. To the gurgling of her gut, Warbringer took her seat with a thump of hooves.

'Saved you the trouble, is what we did,' said Mithrid, arms crossed and slouched in her chair.

'And saved lives doing it,' Elessi added. Her voice was quieter than usual, and Warbringer wondered what perturbed her. The others liked to think minotaurs didn't notice such pink-flesh ways. They considered her kin too brutal and simple, but the clans had spent centuries being betrayed by the rest of Emaneska. Minotaurs had swiftly learned how to tell what a pink-flesh was thinking.

Farden laid his spear amongst the weapons, facing towards him as always. 'What I think you'll find matters most is that Paraia is free from the Arka at last. The empire is an empire no more.'

'And why do you not seem as happy about that as I expected you to be?' Eyrum asked, looking between Mithrid and Farden with his one good eye.

Neither answered. Lerel obliged. 'Because Loki still lives, and Krauslung still believes in him.'

'Because it's not over until he lies dead,' Farden muttered.

'They are building a temple to him, so say the hawks from the northern spies,' said Eyrum.

Farden cursed not far enough beneath his breath.

'And according to most of this council, we should simply ignore that and let sleeping dragons lie for the time being,' said Farden. 'Let Loki recoup, plot, and scheme.'

'He fears you, Farden,' Lerel said. 'A *god* fears you. That's a victory in itself. I say we let Loki come to us. New Scalussen's almost ready, and we'll be waiting.'

Mithrid lifted her eyes from the table at last. 'Not to mention we have in our possession a weapon that makes the little viper fill his trews with shit.'

'Gunnir,' Sipid breathed, fascinated as he always was by the spear.

'I meant me,' Mithrid said, before flashing her teeth.

Hereni rolled her eyes. 'He doesn't even know where we are. We can handle whatever nonsense he dreams up next. Loki's already lost. He just refuses his punishment.'

'And he'll keep runnin'' if he knows what's good for him,' Elessi added. She seemed distracted by the sea beyond the window. 'It would also give us time to heal.'

'And time to focus our minds on building a home,' said Hereni.

'And I say it's dangerous, but I will admit that I don't see the benefit of chasing myself mad around Emaneska and Easterealm trying to kill the fucker,' said Farden.

Hereni sniffed at a candle sitting in a jar and almost sneezed. 'That's likely what he wants. If the gods and Heimdall can't see him, how can we?'

'The war to defeat the Arka is over,' said Farden, making smiles erupt around the table. They were short-lived. 'But as long as Loki lives, I'm telling you another war for Emaneska will come. This isn't over until he's lying dead before our eyes.'

The sombre pause was ended by a rapping of the mage's knuckles. 'Defences?' Farden asked.

'Walls are almost done, King. Twelve new ballistae have been mounted in the past week,' said Admiral Sturmsson.

'We need towers. More walls. I want runes carved on every gate. I want more quickdoors built.'

'We only have so many smiths capable—'

'Have a hundred soldiers sent to Karissa, Belephon, and Troacles. Tomorrow I want to see the new ship.'

'Isn't it time for a rest, Farden?' asked Hereni, a quizzical frown on her. 'Not even for one day?'

'The next day then.' Farden looked around the room, judging faces and guessing minds. 'You want a feast, don't you?'

Warbringer's stomach practically thundered.

'Ask Warbringer's belly,' chuckled Hereni. 'Most of us missed the festivities in Tolema.'

'Can't have a victory without a feast,' said Elessi.

Farden shook his head. 'Then I want the guard doubled. Rotate them if you must so everyone can celebrate, but we will not let our guard down for even a moment. That's what Loki will wait for. Don't forget this is a god who can change faces and who already lived amongst us once.'

The shadow of threat and war they had all lived under for months had not faded. Warbringer saw that now. Perhaps it had for the others, for those who owed Loki a less personal vengeance, but not for the mage.

'Any word from New Nelska?' he asked.

'A few trades have come back or forth, but it feels like the old days of the ceasefire. Queen Nerilan still blames the loss of the north, countless tearbooks and precious dragon eggs, and the last breeding grounds squarely on you.' Eyrum pointed a sausage-like finger at Farden.

Farden sighed. 'Sure you didn't miss anything?'

'I think that is it.'

Farden looked around the circle expectantly, as though he'd asked a question, and the answer was lacking. 'What else?'

Sturmsson shrugged. 'Nothing, King.'

Farden sighed. 'Fine. Then go rest. We've earned it.'

'Some more than others,' Mithrid whispered, before she realised she was speaking aloud. She swiftly removed herself from the table and followed close to Hereni.

Farden stayed seated as the others departed, same as Warbringer. They regarded each other as if they were paintings waiting to move within a blink, but neither batted an eye.

'Was there something else, Warbringer?'

'You miss him?'

The name was not needed. Farden already knew whom Warbringer spoke of, and he broke off his stare. 'Every day.'

'Grey-flesh died to save us from Loki,' Warbringer said. 'The Arka are finished, but that is not the revenge you want. I smell it on you.'

When the mage didn't reply, Warbringer got to her hooves and rested her hand on Farden's pauldron.

'Your hammer, Warbringer,' said Farden. 'You should know it's not the only one that keeps souls.'

The minotaur tapped her fangs together. 'And do they whisper to you also?'

Farden took his time to answer. 'Let's keep that between us for now.'

Warbringer understood, and that brought her a smile. She patted Farden's shoulder, and even though she was gentle, she heard Farden grunt under the weight.

It was impossible to take a step without some bark plate or chicken bone or shrivelled flower head crunching beneath his boots.

The dawn sun, marred by a single bar of cloud that stretched across the sky, was weak compared to the burn of Troacles or Tolema. The lands of Jar Khoum were so far south they started going north again, as Sipid liked to put it. There was talk amongst the snowmads of glaciers and ice fields in their farthest reaches.

Farden walked amongst the snoring revellers who hadn't made it out from beneath the ale barrels, never mind to bed. It was the Emaneska way. New Scalussen was a home from homes, founded on rusty victory and bloody loss, so it was no wonder that one of the first buildings to be erected had been a brewery.

A snore like a saw on a stone block came from one open window. Laughter of the adult variety from another. Squirrels, crows, and sneaky hounds scampered between the shade of the palms and coloured streamers, stealing morsels from the sand. Charmed ladles scraped as they still fulfilled their duties of stirring dry pots. Onwards through the echo's wreckage of the festivities, the Forever King wandered.

Fleetstar was on the beach, in the exact same spot where Farden had left her several weeks ago. The dragon was curled so her tail formed a pillow for her head and draped over her forequarters. Her eyes were already open, watching him trek across the beach. She sat well below the tide line, sitting amongst the turquoise waves lapping gently in faultless rhythm, like immortal soldiers sent to die on the shore over and over. Beyond her, the ships of the Bastard Fleet – as Sturmsson had taken to calling it – sat balanced on the imperfect glass of the sea. A dozen Jar Khoum were knee-deep in the shallows, casting throw nets into the water and heaving up hauls of wriggling scarlet fish.

'Enjoy your night of revelling?' rumbled the Mad Dragon.

Farden dug Gunnir into the sand. 'My night was a respectable one, I'll thank you.' He had found his bed earlier than most. The reason for that was between him and Lerel and entirely none of the dragon's business.

'Rutting hogs, the lot of you.'

'Stay out of my mind, dragon. There's nothing for you there.'

'You want to go to New Nelska, don't you? Or am I imagining things?'

'I said stay out of my head.'

'I don't have to be a dragon to guess that, mage.'

'Ilios chose to fly south. He can't stand quickdoors after an old incident returning to Nelska. Between you and me, I think he misses his old desert, and as your good lady queen doesn't take kindly to me using the spear anywhere within ten miles of her mountains…'

'You need me,' said Fleetstar.

Farden bowed, arms wide. 'As always.'

'And what about him?' Fleetstar raised her snout to point behind Farden.

Leaning against a lone palm was Eyrum, his one eye squinting. A jug leaking something dark and syrupy hung from his finger. 'Going where I think you're going?' he asked.

'That we are. Time to deliver some good news.'

'And?'

'To warn them to watch for Loki and the daemons.'

'And?'

Farden scowled. 'Between you and me? To ask their help in finding the bastard god.'

'Good.' Eyrum spat some of the something dark in the sand. 'I could use an argument.'

Farden smirked wryly as Eyrum marched over, as swiftly as if he'd never lost his leg. The mage stretched out Gunnir, letting the metal shrink into a humble longsword. None but Farden heard the voice in the whisper of metal.

Be respectful.

'I don't want to go,' Fleetstar was growling.

'I'll have the kitchens bring you a whole goat,' Farden promised.

Fleetstar snorted, blowing smoke rings.

'Two.'

'Three. And a barrel of cindergin.'

'Agreed,' replied Farden as he and Eyrum climbed up to the dragon's back. Once they had found their places amongst Fleetstar's spines, the dragon took her time getting up, stretching her wings and wobbling in all kinds of directions.

'Fleetstar…' Farden chided.

'Fine.'

The dragon reared onto her hind legs, and three heavy strokes of her wings later, they were skimming the waters of Sanctuary Bay with scarlet fish scattering for their lives beneath them. Curving around the mast of the *Autumn's Vanguard*, Fleetstar pointed her snout at the white-capped mountains north and east of New Scalussen, peaks the Jar Khoum called the Urkjal. Farden had it on shaky authority that it meant Giant's Shin Mountains.

Eyrum spent the entire journey taking ever larger sips from his jug. Farden spent it wondering if paying the dragons a visit would tighten or loosen the knot in his stomach. The knot that had been there since he first saw Loki's face on the Albion plains.

In the northern crescendo of the Giant's Shin stood an imposing peak called The Watchman, and a more perfect mountain couldn't have existed. It looked as though it had been drawn by an artist, like the classic mountain found on a treasure map. A pointy cone with a white cap, like icing dribbled on a sharp pastry.

In the canyon between The Watchman and its nearest, largest neighbour, the Sirens had made their new home. New Nelska, as the survivors of the north dubbed the new fortress, and as they wound through the mountains towards it, with Fleetstar slicing snow from the tips of the peaks, it certainly felt like Nelska when clouds greeted them with a gentle snow. Neither Eyrum nor Farden shielded their faces against the cold. Farden didn't want to; he had found himself pining for northern snow, and he wagered Eyrum felt the same.

The canyon was shaped like the mouth of a yawning cat. Its teeth were towers made from dragon-melted stone that looked grown, not built. Their blue and silver pennants as long as Fleetstar's tail crackled in the mountain winds. Several half-built bridges reached to span the lower depths, where scattered lanterns and windows glowed, and sharp rooftops were caked with snow. A frozen river divided the buildings.

Farden knew icebergs liked to hide most of themselves beneath the waterline, and dragon fortress were much the same. The turrets and towers atop the rock were merely a hint of what burrowed beneath.

Amber lights spread up the steep face of the Watchman where the dragons had dug their eyries and tunnels. The broader windows and hewn balconies promised log fires and things roasting upon them. Farden hadn't yet broken his fast and found his stomach gurgling.

Horns had already sounded their approach, but as they climbed to a protruding balcony halfway up the slope, it seemed that New Nelska was not too pleased about their visitors.

A crowd of Sirens and dragons had emerged from an enormous door to stand in the snowfall. Warriors lined the crowd's edges, archers stood in the shadow of the door, and every scale of armour and sharpened edge looked newly forged.

'Why are there arrows on your strings and hands on your hilts?' Farden called to the crowd once he had slipped from Fleetstar's side. He met the shining eyes of Kinsprite and Shivertread amongst the Sirens, and he saw they wore sad faces. 'Are we not friends any more?'

The crowds parted to reveal the Old Dragon and his queen. Towerdawn was now the colour of blood-smeared gold. Nerilan had not changed one iota. Farden wondered if it took much effort to keep her golden face in a constant murderous frown, or if it had just settled into that expression through practice. It all felt far too similar to Farden's first visit to Nelska for his liking, when he had knelt before Farfallen and Svarta in chains.

'Because of my orders, Forever King,' spat the Siren Queen, forgoing any kind of greeting.

Farden stood still as Eyrum used his shoulder to lean on. 'Why?' asked the Siren.

'You are not a friend of anyone when you bring such power and danger to our home. Where is it? Towerdawn can feel its magick.'

'Farden,' boomed Towerdawn as the Old Dragon bowed his head in greeting. At least one half of the pair had some respect.

Farden patted his sword. 'In disguise, out of respect and courtesy.'

'Deceit, not respect,' the queen disagreed. 'What's more, I see you have brought two deserters with you. How is that considered courtesy?'

Both Fleetstar and Eyrum growled at that. 'Are we not allowed to visit our own kin now?' the Siren asked.

Nerilan scoffed. 'Not when you turn your backs on them and betray your queen.'

Farden saw Bull between the ranks of warriors, Scalussen's own deserter. It had been a sore day for Mithrid when the boy had chosen to follow the dragons north. His obsession with their scaly allies had made that decision for him. Farden knew the allure of flying on a dragon's back, but he had never left his kind behind to do it. Farden realised he was scowling but did nothing to change it.

It was the Siren behind Bull that stole Farden's attention. A fellow of little hair and plenty of fire in his purple eyes. Grey scales adorned his face, similar to Eyrum's, and he had the long-armed, lithe look of a rider.

Nerilan had drawn closer. 'If it were solely up to me, Eyrum, you would be in chains, enjoying our newest dungeons.'

'Then I'm glad it is not up to you,' said Fleetstar.

Eyrum nodded. 'For a great many reasons.'

'We should go into the warm, where we can speak in peace and private.' Towerdawn had a sharp edge in his voice, and it was aimed at his queen.

'No,' Nerilan snapped. 'Not while he still holds that spear.'

'I won't let it out of my sight,' promised Farden.

'We stay out here.'

Towerdawn blew a jet of flame from his nostrils. 'Leave us.'

The crowd of Sirens dispersed impressively quickly. The warriors withdrew to the doorway and muttered amongst themselves. The purple-eyed Siren was one of the last to leave, lingering with his chin on his shoulder and his gaze frostier than the peaks.

'What do you want, Farden?' hissed the queen.

'Nerilan. That is enough of your spite,' Towerdawn boomed.

Nerilan huffed and began to pace back and forth while she strangled her hands behind her back.

'What brings you to Sutherheim, Forever King?'

Farden had learned enough Siren to appreciate the name. It sounded finer than New Nelska, that was certain. 'Good news is what brings me, Old Dragon. We can finally say that Paraia belongs to Paraia once again. The Arka Empire has fallen.'

Towerdawn showed teeth. A dragon's smile was a glow to bask in, and Farden had missed it.

'At last. We wondered why the wind carried music with it.'

'How is Bull?'

Towerdawn settled into a cat-like position and folded his wings. 'Keen to be a Siren, is one way to put it. The boy has been learning our ways and our tongue, and he and Kinsprite have been spending much time together.'

The queen muttered to herself. 'Too much time.'

'Sutherheim has grown quickly,' said Farden, keeping it civil. *Be respectful.* The words echoed in his head, and he understood them now. It was for Towerdawn, not Nerilan.

'That it has, and more every day. Our people have traded swords and bows for hammers and chisels. One day this new home may rival Hjaussfen,' said Towerdawn. 'But I think pleasantries and curiosity is not all you have come to trade in.'

'The Arka might have been felled, but Loki is still out there, lying low, biding his time, and no doubt plotting his next move.'

'And you want to be ready,' Towerdawn said, reading Farden's mind.

'Precisely.'

Nerilan paused her pacing. 'If I were Loki…'

If she were Loki, Farden would have taken great pleasure in killing two problematic birds with one glorious hurl of his spear.

'…my sights would be set on that blasphemous spear of yours. If we stay clear of you, surely we are much safer.'

'And give Loki the gift of a divided force, both weakened by arrogance,' Eyrum countered. 'Once again, Queen, you forget we are stronger together.'

Farden thought about holding his tongue, but he had never been a fan of that hobby. 'And on that note, I also have a favour to ask.'

'By Thron!' cursed Nerilan. 'I knew it! What more do you ask of us? How many dead Siren soldiers do you wish for now?'

'I know you have been sending out dragons to search for more of your kind. I need you to have those dragons look for signs of Loki,' said Farden, continuing before Nerilan could squeeze a word out of her sour-puckered face. 'That is all. Tell me if you find a trace of him, and I will cut his head from his shoulders. Then we can all know true peace, and you won't have to see my face ever again.'

'That should shut you up, should it not, Nerilan?' said Eyrum.

Towerdawn's claws scraped at the poured stone beneath their feet.

'Eyrum,' Farden warned, putting a hand on the Siren's.

'We will discuss it,' Towerdawn said, looking apologetic.

'I can tell you now that we will not endanger our kind cutting your loose ends, Farden,' added Nerilan.

Farden's heart fell, but he didn't dare show it. 'Loki is a threat to all, human and dragon alike. If he gets his way, he'll make the Ragnarök we went through on the ice fields look like a warm-up. But if that's your decision, then fine. I'll leave you with the warning I came to deliver and be on my way. Though it's clear we're not the allies we were, you will always have my respect and the help of Scalussen, Towerdawn. Nerilan, utterly wonderful to see you again.'

Farden's voice dripped with so much sarcasm the queen could have slipped in it.

'You are always welcome among the dragons, Forever King,' Towerdawn called out over Fleetstar's wingbeats. 'As are our lost kin.'

Once Fleetstar had climbed out of her angry dive and his stomach had settled back in its rightful place, Farden clapped Eyrum on the arm. 'Feel better?'

'A little. It is good to know I am still right. Nerilan is a fool. And I don't follow fools.'

Farden took that as a compliment.

'And you?' Eyrum asked. 'Did you get what you came for?'

The mage shook his head, and both of them fell to silence.

The great cleaning up of Scalussen had begun, and the soldiers and citizens worked as if they toiled over the detritus of a battle. Farden could have blamed the fact that war was all they knew, but he knew better. They were simply yet catastrophically hungover, pale and shivery even in the sun.

One such victim of ale and revelry was Hereni, whom Farden last saw holding a skin of wine in each hand and belting out an epic Siren ballad alongside Eyrum. Impressive, considering she only knew a dozen Siren words, and most of those concerned fighting or ordering a drink.

The mage shuffled about, red-eyed and sweating as though she had the plague. 'I'm never drinking again,' she said in a hoarse voice, swallowing a dangerous belch while she watched Fleetstar fly circles around the city.

'Cow shit,' chuckled Farden. 'I've sworn that more times than I've seen years. Where's everyone else?'

Hereni sighed as if Farden had asked her to calculate the weight of a mountain. 'Lerel and Sturmsson are seeing to your new ship,' she said, with one eye closed for concentration. 'Warbringer is still asleep. Ko-Tergo and Roglurg are in the new underground libraries. And Elessi, well she's done her disappearing act again.'

Farden tutted. 'Where does she go to?'

That question had been bothering him for far too long. Elessi had made a habit of wandering off before they'd marched north.

A yell intruded Farden's pondering. Akitha, the third Siren outcast Scalussen boasted, came barging through the workers.

'Farden! About bloody time.'

'Akitha. How are you?'

'About ready to bust a skull open with one of my hammers, King, so don't you "how are you" me. I want to know which academic marvel and master of knowledge ordered a thatch roof built right above the new permanent forges. Do you want this new city to burn to the ground before it's even built?'

'Ask one of the stonesmiths.'

'I already bloody have, and they said to ask High General Elessi. Seeing as she's not anywhere to be found, I came to you two.'

'Ask him, not me,' murmured Hereni.

Farden shook his head. 'I've got bigger things—'

'Don't you pull that shit, Farden. You've been doing nothing but flying around on that dragon all day.'

'Tell them the High Admiral said to repurpose the thatch for the new warehouses and to build a slate roof,' said Lerel, appearing by Farden's side. After all these years and all his magick, she could still sneak up on him.

No sooner had Akitha turned on her heel did a skinny boy paler than Hereni run up to them, almost tripping to land face-first at Farden's feet. 'King, Admiral. General!'

Farden felt his heart jump at the panic in the boy's voice. 'What is it, lad?' He almost shook the child when he kept swallowing to find his breath.

'A cow's fallen into the east wall trench, and nobody can get it out.'

Farden pinched the bridge of his nose. 'Tell them I'll be there shortly,' he said before glancing to Lerel, who already had a smile growing on her lips. The boy scampered away in a cloud of dust.

'Is this what peace should feel like?' Farden asked.

Lerel tutted. 'It's a task, just the same as war. We're not building a fortress, we're building a home. You should be glad to save ridiculous cows instead of occupied cities.'

Farden clenched his jaw.

The noise of Hereni letting her rake fall in the dust stole their attention. 'If you'll excuse me,' she said, in a throat half-closed sort of voice. 'I think I need to go throw up.'

CHAPTER 7
A RIDDLE OF PEACE

Small disturbance today in the market. A peasant woman was found in possession of a charmed ring. As per the Decree, the woman was charged and sentenced. A struggle broke out, and as such, she was executed on the spot by Mage Chidlow. Husband and child were searched and questioned but let go. Ring confiscated and sent to Manesmark for destruction.
REPORT FROM THE REEVER OF WORNSPUR TO KRAUSLUNG, YEAR 914

TWO WEEKS LATER

'We have sent soldiers to Karissa, Troacles, and Belephon to make sure the Arka don't leave their hooks in Paraia, as you requested.'

'Two ships are patrolling north and south of Sanctuary Bay, but with pirates spotted, we could send one of the bookships to join them.'

'Dreadnoughts. They're called dreadnoughts now.'

'Traders and trade routes are what we need. We could bring some coin into this new city.'

'What we need is to send envoys to the east. Golikar primarily. Repair some of the… *damage* you did politically, King. They are valuable allies. Then there is the relationship with Troacles to fortify…'

Farden's mind was back on the Bloodplains, feeling the keen blade of the wind as he watched Loki emerge from mist and memory. The smile on the god's face made Farden's knuckles creak as he gripped the piece of wood he was absently carving and the small knife tighter.

'Farden?'

The mage stared at the hand Lerel had placed to cover his clenched fist. Farden looked down at the wood and saw a half-finished face looking back at him. Loki's face.

'Damage,' Farden said, repeating the only word he remembered hearing. He looked around his council one by one. Extra chairs had been brought for all the various architects, head stonesmiths, harbour masters, colonels, captains, and other such voices of Scalussen.

'Where is Mithrid?' Farden asked.

'My King?' asked the man who had been blabbing on about envoys. His face and his bald head were having a competition to be the shiniest.

'Training yards,' muttered Hereni.

Farden stood, weathering the stares of Elessi and Lerel. 'I'm needed elsewhere.'

It wasn't a good excuse, but then again, Farden had come to learn that kings don't need to give excuses. He placed the knife and wooden carving in the pocket of his cloak and made for the door.

'Farden?' Lerel asked.

'Who are you again?' Farden asked of the man with the gleaming head.

'Mak Madden, sir. Scalussen freed me in Tolema? I was a diplomat for traders until… hard times, let's say.'

'Then just you bear in mind, Madden, that trust is not something we can throw away freely. I want walls built, not bridges. Nobody enters or leaves Scalussen without my permission.'

'Of course, sire.' Madden went to jot down something on an empty scroll, panicked, and just wrote "walls" instead.

Farden hadn't wanted to be the kind of king who made men quiver in boots for fear of reprisal, but his mind was already elsewhere, his mood souring, and his magick too quiet within him. Farden felt like a dull blade aching for the grindstone. He needed to prove he was still sharp and ready.

Sweeping Gunnir from the table, Farden left, casting an apologetic look to Lerel before the door shut.

❦

The wonderful cacophony of unfettered battle practice greeted Farden. It was a sound he had grown up with, as comforting as a crackling fire or the pattering conversation of rain.

Speaking of, the grey sky was starting to leak. The Jar Khoum believed rain was good luck and the spittle of their gods. Why being spat on was good luck was a mystery, but Farden had never been one to say no to luck. He stepped out from under the awning and let the moisture speckle his face. Winter was creeping north.

Captains and sergeants came to attention at the sight of red and gold armour, not to mention the spear that could apparently carve the peak from a mountain. Farden could see the darting looks to its blade.

'Don't let me stop you,' the mage said with a smile as he trudged on.

Farden already knew where to find Mithrid. She would be in her usual spot at the far end of the yards, where giant red awnings reached over the dirt like an unrequited hug.

Under their umbrella, the warriors of Scalussen and Jar Khoum trained. Several thousand had turned out to practise today, and Farden felt pride as he walked amongst them. There were few places in the world he would have dared to call home, and even those were poor excuses for such a thing. An Albion arkabbey he was sent to on Arkmage orders didn't count. Neither did a shack on the beach on the edge of nowhere. Even Scalussen had been built for war, not settling. A training yard, however, was the only constant Farden had ever known, and it was the only place he had always felt at home.

Farden could have closed his eyes and still seen everything around him. The guttural shouts of the instructors counting forms, and the exhale of the bodies moving as one. The almost-unified swish of blades cutting air. The clattering tune of bowstrings loosing. The grunts and curses of brawlers' victims being thrown onto their backs. Blades clashing with armour where sparring rings lined the walls. Farden willingly drowned in every sound.

General Eyrum was in one such ring, leaning against a pillar with a blunt axe in his hand instead of a bottle this time. He was busy making seasoned warriors look like recruits without even moving from his leaning spot.

'It is all about…'

Whack. A sergeant went tumbling, chasing her shield.

'Balance…'

Clang. Another wielding two swords soon found himself without any and wheezing in the mud.

'Momentum…'

Wood splintered as a mage was sent flying into the fence, knocked cold.

'And distraction.'

Only two of the challengers had recovered, and they stood bent with hands on knees while they prepared to charge their foe again.

'Salute your king,' Eyrum ordered them, but as soon as they turned to see Farden, he swept their legs from under them with his axe and his wooden leg. 'Or kneel. Your choice.'

'Too harsh, Eyrum,' said Farden, shaking his head as he helped one of the unconscious soldiers upright and awake. 'Some advice. Attack him together instead of coming one by one.'

Leaving them to rush Eyrum and tackle him to the ground, Farden kept moving to the very rear of the yards and past an archery range for Akitha's new crossbows – the kind that fired five arrows for every load. There Farden had built his own training circle of bricks and flagstone with his bare hands, the same week New Scalussen was named and founded.

Farden saw the hulk of Warbringer hunched in the rain. She sat on a stone block, spinning her warhammer around on its handle like the most terrifying spinning top. She raised her snout to Farden before going back to her staring. The subject of interest was their very own Mithrid, busy hacking at tree trunks with her newest axe.

Farden couldn't tell if it was rain or sweat that draped her fiery hair across her face and armour, but he would have bet the latter. She trained incessantly, going from target to target, delivering flurries of blows and filling the air with splinters and wood chips while Farden waited for her to notice him.

'I thought you were in council,' Mithrid said at last, breathing hard.

Farden shrugged. 'I thought the same of you. But word has it you've been here every day for two weeks.'

Mithrid wiped sweat from her face and dug her axe into a trunk. 'Almost as much as you have,' she said with a smirk.

'Guess I'm not the only one who's finding this game of sitting and waiting… tedious.'

'An itch I can't scratch,' Mithrid replied so quietly Farden barely heard her. 'Been a while since we duelled. Not since you claimed Gunnir.'

'You scared?' Farden said, eliciting a sneer. He shrank Gunnir into a knife and shoved it into his belt before taking out his other sword, a new scarlet blade forged by Akitha that kept the same Khandri lightning bolt shape and matched his armour.

'Use the spear,' she said. It hadn't been the first time she had asked.

Farden shook his head sternly as he stretched his neck and arms. 'No. Like I told you, I don't want to hurt you.'

'I dare you,' Mithrid replied. She sheathed her axe, and with a stretch of her empty hand, the darkest of shadows moved like smoke and coiled around her hand.

'No.' Farden flexed his fingers. A flame exploded into life and flickered as if it raged against a gale. The Scalussen armour rattled at the magick flowing through him. The skin of his back burned.

Farden saw Mithrid wince at the magick washing around the circle. Her jaw bunched as she focused. Mithrid might have put her father's murderer in the ground, but the storm inside her hadn't gone anywhere, confined within the mountains of her mind.

Mithrid let the shadow roam over her shoulders and wore it like a cloak. Farden pounced, hurling a stream of fire directly at her and drawing an intake of breath from the crowd of soldiers gathering to watch. They must have expected him to hold back, but they had not seen Mithrid face down Malvus.

The girl met Farden's spell with hers, forming a shield as wide as arms' reach. It enveloped the fire like a lake swallows a boulder and extinguished it with a crackle of thunder.

Farden threw two bolts of lightning either side of her, causing indecision. When she exposed her left side, he struck again, holding back this time. A green tendril of force magick almost delivered its punch before Mithrid blocked him again. Now, she attacked, throwing an arc of shadow like a whip. It cut through his shield spell like a flame through a dry leaf, and Farden had to shift his feet to avoid its touch.

Vortex spells doused Mithrid with dirt and rain while Farden readied his next spell. A quake spell, rolling through the flagstones behind her so she didn't notice until she was turned arse over head.

Farden moved for the final strike, crossing the circle with the speed spell Eyrum had taught him all those years ago in Nelska. But before he could hold the fire spell in her face, Mithrid put her palm almost to his. Shadow crept over him, and he felt the fire in his Book run cold. The magick died in his fingers, then his arms, and continued to creep towards his skull.

Farden loathed the feeling of Mithrid's power. It made his very soul shiver to feel his power melted away. It reminded him too much of the powerlessness he had endured in Easterealm. Whether Mithrid saw that in his eyes or not, she pushed, trying to come upright.

Farden tutted and tapped his sword against the collar of her armour. 'You're already dead.'

'You're stronger with that spear in your hands,' said Mithrid, eyes narrowed.

'You've improved, too,' replied Farden. He wanted to extend a hand, but he couldn't ignore the worry of what her touch might do. She wouldn't have taken it anyway.

'No magick this time. Blades and limbs only,' Farden said.

Mithrid emptied her lungs as she took a stance.

Farden worked his sword in figures of eight, pressing Mithrid into a corner until she came out swinging with her axe. Steel rang a harsh song. It was a short tune, ending in Farden's sword under the armpit of Mithrid's armour.

'Again,' she tutted.

Farden let Mithrid get close a few times, and he almost found himself regretting it. Mithrid was fast and lithe after the trials he'd put her through, and driven by her inner storm. Yet once again, his sword found its way to her neck.

Mithrid marched in an angry circle while the crowd muttered between themselves. 'Again! And stop going easy on me, damn you! You want me to learn, then teach.'

Farden swept his sword low and drew a half-moon in the sand before saluting. 'As you wish.'

The steel rang three times before Farden caught her. Mithrid switched her grip and forced Farden back, but an overreach meant he seized her wrist and dragged her to the mud.

Throwing a handful of dirt at Farden in a dirty move that he'd taught her, Mithrid attacked with the butt of her axe, managing to land a faint blow on his free hand before she forced the blade at him like a dagger. Farden put a hand between the axe's edge and his neck and twisted it upwards. This time, Mithrid went with the turn, swivelling to bring the axe up between Farden's legs. Using all his speed, he swung the blade against her neck, stopping an inch short.

Mithrid looked smug, so he tapped the sword against her collar again. 'You're dead,' he said.

Farden felt a tap far below and looked down to see the axe against the groin of his armour.

'A glorious end for both of us,' Mithrid said between breaths. 'Though it would be less painful and swifter for me, I think.'

The crowd chuckled between themselves as the two of them clashed weapons to signify a draw.

'Well done,' admitted Farden. 'But it's still not good enough.'

'Why do you think I'm here every bloody day? Did you come here to train, or are you bored and came here to be a cock?' Mithrid asked.

'You should show him, Mith,' rumbled Warbringer from her stone perch.

Farden turned. 'Show me what?'

'A new weapon.'

Mithrid shook her head. 'It's not ready.'

The minotaur arose to stretch. 'Enough words and worry. You are ready. Show him.'

'All right,' Mithrid said, leaving one hand on her axe and the other to leak shadow. 'Again.'

Farden brimmed with curiosity, but he readied his sword nonetheless and advanced.

At first, Mithrid did nothing new but feint and parry his first exploratory stabs. It was only when she threw her dark power at him like an angry tentacle that the surprise came. Farden waved his sword to slice through the shadow, but this time it had a weight to it. Something solid trapped his blade long enough for Mithrid to get close and rest her axe on his shoulder.

The low murmur from the crowd coaxed a smile from Mithrid. Warbringer could be heard chuckling.

'How interesting,' Farden muttered as she withdrew. He nodded to Eyrum, who started herding the onlookers back to their own defeats and victories.

'Not embarrassed are you, Farden?' Mithrid asked.

'When did this start?' asked Farden once they were alone.

'In the past month. It's only started working in the last few weeks. And why do I get the sense this isn't good news to you?' Mithrid raised her chin.

'I told you on the way to Mogacha how I felt. There's still so much we don't understand about your power and what it can do to you.'

'Loki almost killed me before, and I came too close again in Troacles. If we're to kill him, I can't have a weakness. Any foe without magick has always been a danger, but not any more. Now I don't have a weakness.'

'Everyone has a weakness, Mithrid, but I'll wager that's not the whole story, is it? There's a truer reason you and I are down here every dawn and dusk, but I don't think you want to say it.'

Mithrid scrunched up her face, taking her time to answer. 'It's what Evernia said on the ship: Irminsul and Malvus can't be all I'm meant for. Hereni can't wait for an end to the fighting and to call this a home,' she said, baring a glimpse of her soul for just a moment.

Farden's worries bubbled up anew. 'And you don't want that.'

'Do you, Farden?' Mithrid countered, and her soul was slammed shut. 'What was the first thing you did after winning Paraia? You went to ask the dragons for help finding Loki. You can't rest, and neither can I.'

Farden ran his thumb along the flat of his sword. 'Peace seems empty when there's still revenge to be had, doesn't it?' he sighed.

'I thought I was done with hate and revenge, but even though Malvus is dead, Loki still owes a debt for Durnus. It fills my every waking moment.'

Farden clenched his jaw and decided to do precisely what Lerel had suggested and try to guide the girl. 'You and I are far too similar. I thought I was done with spilling blood, but I still crave Loki's just the same,' Farden replied. 'I told you in Easterealm that I wouldn't know what to do with peace when I found it, no matter how much I deserve it. Well, here I am with peace in my hands, and I feel nothing but guilty for shunning it. It's not time. It's not done.

Somebody once told me that weapons do nothing in peace but rust, and I can't help but feel that rust gathering.'

'And yet nobody should desire bloodshed,' Mithrid whispered, eyes distant and squinting, and not from the rain pattering on their faces.

'But I worry we do, and that it'll lead us down darker paths,' Farden said, voicing his concern. Utiru's visions insisted on haunting him. The spider and her mirrors had given him two fates. In one, his greatest fear and the exile and madness of a Written. In the other, the fate he had always dreamed of: a peace he could not yet grasp. The fact he leaned towards the fate that had always terrified him only spurred Farden's fears for Mithrid's future. He thought again of what Utiru had shown him of Mithrid and wished he could believe differently.

'She stronger than you think, Farden,' muttered Warbringer, as if guessing his thoughts.

That was the entire problem, but Farden didn't dare say it.

'Trust me,' Mithrid said, shunning his worry, 'I'll be ready for Loki when we see that fucker again.'

'And then we'll both figure out the riddle of peace together,' Farden said, watching her closely. Each, in their own unspoken ways, knew what it meant. It was a pact, and one he would hold her to.

Farden spun his sword around his wrist. 'Again.'

'Try the spear,' Mithrid said, flicking a nail against her axe blade.

'I said no.'

'Who's scared now? Use the spear.'

'Mithrid.'

'Farden.'

'Warbringer,' said the minotaur, looking proud of herself.

'Fine. Then stand back,' Farden told her, but Warbringer did no such thing. The mage took the knife from his belt and in a flash of lightning, the spear transformed back into its true form.

'Such theatrics,' Mithrid said.

Blows were traded back and forth, with the axe bouncing off the spear's shaft and the flat of the blade with sparks and whining metal, like two opposing lodestones trying to touch. The spear was a blur around Farden as he gave Mithrid the test she wanted.

It was only when it looked as though she regretted her choice that Mithrid fought back. Shadow bloomed around her and cut dead the fireball Farden had been nursing in his hand. The cold grip seized him again, strangling his magick, and this time it felt like a fist around him.

It was for proof that he fought on. He felt Mithrid pushing for her own. Both of them wanted to know who in fact could beat whom when magick fought its antithesis.

Light bloomed from Gunnir's glaive blade, shearing Mithrid's shadow enough for Farden to free himself. He dug deep for his magick, wrenching it up to burn at the base of his skull. One hand wreathed in fire, Gunnir whining in the other, Farden pressed into Mithrid's storm of shadow that she held like a shield. Inch by inch, it shrank, yet it didn't die away. It refused to falter even against a weapon that made gods and daemons quake, and there they stayed locked.

When the wind began to whip the rain into a frenzy, and when a bell sounded a changing of the guard, Farden broke their stalemate.

Mithrid was red in the face, but she still stood firm as an oak, staring at the missing part of her axe blade, where the blade curved towards the handle. The metal that remained glowed hot.

'Bastard.'

'I warned you,' said Farden, strolling in a tight circle, mind afire. He had not earned the proof he had wanted.

Crowds of sweat-drenched soldiers switched with newcomers who were eager to work the boredom of standing guard out of their legs. Between the masses, a dishevelled fellow dressed in ill-fitting armour waded as if he was trying to escape a maze of reeds. The eyes sandwiched between his hood and mask were wild and aimed solely at Farden and Mithrid. Blinking seemed the last thing on his mind, and whatever was first gave him urgent purpose. Only when Farden saw the crossbow levelled at them did he understand.

'Down, Mithrid!'

Despite Farden's shout, the first bolt came without contest, too quick to do anything but duck or dodge. Its blade cut a deep line across Mithrid's cheekbone and split her ear before it disappeared into the rain. A second bolt clattered against Farden's chest before he could stretch his shield.

'Pay for the blood of my people and our dragons!' the man screeched. 'Pay for the ravaging of the north!'

A third bolt smashed against Farden's spell.

'You are nothing but a curse!'

Farden was reaching with his magick when the axe flew past him. An axe trailing a strand of black shadow.

The man's chest split like the melon fruits the Jar Khoum liked to grow. Normally, the rabid look of an assassin died alongside their mission, replaced with a haunting look of failure. But this fellow kept his hatred in his purple eyes all the way to the mud, where a score of blunt training spears pointed at his throat.

Eyrum ripped the mask away to reveal the scowling face of a Siren, and Farden recognised the grey scales across his cheeks. It was the rider from Sutherheim's crowds, and he seethed at the sight of Farden and Mithrid looming over him, hating them with his final glimpse of the world.

Farden examined his wounds, but the Siren's fate was written, sealed, and delivered. 'Give him some air, Scalussen,' he ordered, and the soldiers shrank back.

'You're nothing but a curse.' The rider's last words were full of blood. 'Your magick will kill us all.'

Farden watched his purple eyes grow vacant as he slipped away. This was not the first assassin that had come to test the title of Forever King. The last one's shadow could still be seen on a wall near the harbour, where Gunnir had blasted him to dust. The glaring problem was that all the previous assassins had been Arka, sent by Malvus. None had ever been Siren.

'To your barracks and posts, all of you!' Farden bellowed, and the soldiers receded like a tide before him.

Mithrid's brow furrowed not in regret but simple confusion. 'I didn't know he was Siren. Otherwise—'

'You did nothing wrong,' rumbled Eyrum, placing a hand on the rider's forehead and closing his eyes.

'I know I didn't. He fired first,' Mithrid shot back.

Farden watched her pull her axe from the rider's chest, the body lifting and dropping as if it momentarily lived again. He reached for Mithrid's cheek. The right side of her jaw and neck were painted crimson like her hair. Mithrid touched her cheek, winced, and stared at the blood on her fingertips. She bared her teeth in a silent growl.

'Bastard,' she grunted, and Farden wasn't sure if she meant him or the Siren.

Hereni and Lerel had reached the yards and were running towards them with Dawnknell guards in full armour.

'What did you say to cause the Sirens such offence?!' Lerel spluttered at the sight of grey scales. Hereni ran to Mithrid, matching her frown at the sight of the blood.

'Nothing that would require an assassin,' Farden replied.

'What if it's one of Loki's tricks to drive us apart?' asked Mithrid.

Farden turned to his old friend. 'Do you think this could be Nerilan's doing, Eyrum?'

'If she were still my queen, I would say no. Now?' Eyrum shook his head, unable to say it. 'You do have a certain enraging effect on her, Farden.'

'Let's face it, it wouldn't be the first time somebody took this much offence to me,' muttered the mage. 'The spear can feel Loki, and as far as I can tell he hasn't come within fifty miles of New

Scalussen. He can't send an assassin if he doesn't know where we are.'

'Did this man say anything before he died?' asked Hereni.

'That Farden and I were a curse, and that magick will kill us all,' Mithrid answered before anyone else got the chance.

Lerel sucked at her teeth. 'Nerilan's sentiments exactly. But Mithrid makes a great point.'

'I want answers,' demanded Mithrid, making Farden cross his arms.

'I will get answers, you can trust me on that, *General*,' said Farden. 'You go see to that wound. Hereni, see that she does.'

'Aye, King.'

Farden turned to Lerel. 'Send a hawk to the dragons demanding answers. I won't waste my breath on that Siren queen.'

'You wouldn't be trying to make them feel somewhat guilty and therefore more inclined to help you, would you, Farden?' Lerel asked.

'What if I am?' Farden replied with a shrug. 'If it turns out to be one of Loki's tricks, why not turn it to my advantage? Now where in Hel is Elessi?'

'Gone before council was called. Just like you,' Lerel told him with a hint of judgement in her voice. 'Last I saw her, she was walking towards the harbour.'

Farden dug the spear's blunt end into the mud, making the ripples peak and dance in nearby puddles. 'It's about time I find out what she's doing.'

After a lingering touch of her hand, Farden stormed for the harbour.

'Disappearing again.' Lerel sighed, thinking Farden too distant to hear. He could have turned, and perhaps he should have, but he stowed that for later. Farden winced at the echo of his thoughts.

A king didn't need excuses.

CHAPTER 8
THE FOUNDATIONS OF DOOM

The reason why Easterealm and Emaneska remain largely separate is not geographical, but a quirk of history. In the early years of the Scattered Kingdoms, many survivors of the war of gods and daemons went east. After many months and miles, they discovered others who were beginning to rebuild. Believing the westerners to be a trick of the elves, a battle ensued. Or more accurately, a massacre. One sole survivor of the west was left to return from where he had come, though instead of telling the truth, he blamed ogin and daemons and dark dragons.
Fearing the worst, all maps of the east were destroyed. Ships avoided Easterealm coasts for centuries. Not a single trade road was forged. Equally in the east, rumours spread of barbaric westerners, and that is why city walls in Golikar, Bvara, and Begrad are always thicker on their western side.
FROM THE DIARY OF TREASURE-HUNTER BALEO THE SQUEAKY, FOUND UPON HIS CORPSE

Fifty gold pieces apparently bought not only a passage, but a good deal of silence.

The crew and ship were both out of Lezembor, a mess of sandstone that was part-market, part-cesspit, according to Loki's summation. Krauslung might have rivalled its squeeze of people and overlapping buildings in bustle, but Lezembor stood above all others when it came to its crime rate, the boggling amount of ever-present cocktail of human filth and debauchery, and the kind of distinctive stench of spice and sin that can ruin a mind and a stomach all at once. It was said that Lezembor was everything one wanted to find and everything one didn't all rolled into one, and Loki didn't have a word of disagreement for that saying.

Even Loki's hired sailors seemed to agree, judging by the deep breaths of sea air they had taken barely a mile beyond the rotting port.

Three days later, the benefits of the fresh sea air had died away, and a new stench equal to Lezembor's filled the air. Yet this was not one of gutters and degeneracy, nor of stale wine and staler bodies. This was a stink of death, the taste of dead flesh and burned bones, and it clung to the cold breeze like bugs to a blanket. It was prevalent in every breath of the prevailing wind, and it stuck to the back of the throat like mud sprayed from a wagon's wheel. Loki was the only one who breathed it in willingly. It was a message that told him he was on the right path.

It was the opposite for the ship's crew, who had argued about turning back on the hour, every hour, for the last day and a half.

Loki could have snapped his fingers and jumped the rest of the way, of course, but there was ceremony to be observed. Diplomacy. Gifts were important when it came to negotiations, and a ship's crew was a fine – not to mention a deceptively cheap – gift for those who Loki hoped dwelled in the south.

'Press on, Captain!' Loki made sure to call out, silencing the new arguments he heard bubbling at the rear of the motley ship.

The ship's captain – a puckered and wrinkled man who looked as if he had guzzled nothing but seawater his entire life – strode towards the bow. Loki waited for him, watching the way he rehearsed his words before he arrived.

'Problem, Captain?' Loki's question startled him.

The captain's eyes snuck to the faint etching of hills and cliffs on the horizon. 'There's been rumours about the island of Kasto, sire. People say a plague's come. Some say a witch cursed the town there. People have been fleeing in droves, and any way you want to discuss it, the crew ain't happy 'bout putting keel to shore there.'

'Are you saying you won't make good on your half of our agreement? I paid to be put ashore, not to swim the last leg. I demand nothing less.'

'You see, sire—'

Loki dug into his coat and flashed a handful of golden coins. 'Another five gold pieces for every sailor.'

The widening of the captain's eyes was telltale. These pitiful creatures would do anything for shiny things, and that made them no better than magpies.

'I'll tell the crew,' said the captain, stowing half of Loki's offering in one pocket and the rest in another. '*Three* gold apiece will do wonders for morale. You can expect us to make shore shortly.'

'I will need an escort ashore as well.'

The captain went pale. 'That might need a little more convincing, sire. Like I said, people have been saying the island is pois—'

'Then perhaps another five gold apiece will convince them, no?'

'Aye,' grunted the captain, distracted by the math in his head.

'Very good, Captain.' Loki whispered, and the man hovered for a moment before realising the conversation was over.

Loki half-listened to the muted arguments at the stern of the ship, half to the waves slapping the barnacled hull. His eyes didn't leave the sharp clifftops of Kasto, aching to see a shadow or a shape break their horizon.

The potential for failure was pervasive. Doree's description of the nightmares Loki hoped to find was still little more than the spouting of a madwoman without evidence. And Loki pined for evidence.

While the ship's nose grated on the shale of the beach, and the crew begrudgingly broke out poles and gangplanks with all the alacrity of a legless goat, Loki spied a trail leading to the hilltops. He set foot to the plank, but not one of the wastrels moved to follow.

'If your captain failed to mention, I offer five gold coins apiece for any soul who wants to accompany me up to the high land,' Loki challenged them.

One sailor, a young runt who looked eager to prove himself, shuffled up with his hand barely raised above his hip. It was definitely bravado, not bravery, that moved him. Maybe a hint of greed.

Nobody else volunteered.

'Ten coins each, then. Has a fine ring to it, don't you think?'

That brought a dozen gold-thirsty men and women forwards. One fellow, the sort who looked as though he boasted about the smell of his shit, thrust out a hand missing a finger on his left hand, same as Farden. Loki met him with a scowl.

'We get paid now,' he grunted in the perfect impression of a hog.

'Half now. Half later.' Loki reached into the void again and threw their coins to the deck to make them squabble.

'Do I get ten?' asked the runt.

'You stepped up for five,' Loki replied. 'You should have waited.'

The trail was rough and crisscrossed by the ruts of rainfall. It was not unused as its narrowness and steep gradient suggested, but quite the opposite. The trail was churned like batter, much like the scars of keels and footprints in the sands beyond the cliffs. Here and there, something had been spilled or forgotten. A box of ribbons. A chalice, stamped on and broken. Or the quintessential lost doll that perfectly encapsulated urgency and tragedy. Loki couldn't have staged the scene better if he had tried. It put mutters in the sailors, between their heavy panting. The line of volunteers snaked down the trail behind the god, heads up and bobbing in worry, puffing steam in the morning cold.

A wind waited for them at the top of the cliff, blasting across a plain of dust and spiked grass. It carried the same sour taint of death and smoke, and Loki stood tall on a boulder to get the lay of the land. The coastline of Kasto spread south in three thrusts, and a blue forest belted the island at its thinnest point, only half an hour's reach away.

The hoggish lump had finally made it to the top of the cliff, and he paused with hands on knees while he leered at Loki. 'Why ain't you out of breath?'

The god surveyed the man's bulging belly kept in place by two belts. 'I believe they call it exercise.'

The man hacked and spat in the dust in answer.

Loki forced them onwards, leaving them to their muttering. The worry and superstition of the island had turned into worry and superstition for him. And while they couldn't fight plagues or witch's curses, they could – as it happened – fight and rob one little man. Or so one sailor suggested.

Loki had to glower as he listened to their hushed conversation at his back. Whispers were as shouts to a god.

The crew grew bolder, concocting lies to tell that fool of a captain. They would say he fell – how original – and split his head. But no, the hog of a man had a better idea. They would say the stranger decided to stay with whomever he found here and paid them the rest of the coins to leave. That was a much better lie, and it was followed by much back-patting to seal their bloody agreement. The mages said alchemy was a false art. Impossible. Yet here it was at work: humble gold turning unrefined greed into solid murder. Loki's frown transformed into a smile as the sailors moved on to a fierce discussion of whether to bash him, stab him, or tie him up to die alone. Loki would have gone with the stabbing.

'You want to go in there?' asked Five Pieces, as Loki had dubbed the runt. Like the rest of his murderous shipmates, he was currently giving the forest and the god a foul look, as if Loki had just proposed they strip naked and throw dung at each other. Strangely enough, Five Pieces was the only one who hadn't said a word in favour of the murder of Loki.

In all fairness, the forest did have a mean look. It was a realm where sunlight was unwelcome. The trees had black trunks and crouched heavy with crowns of pale blue leaves, the colour of a day-old corpse. The muddy path was wide, but there was no end to it that could be seen.

'If you want the rest of your coin, then yes,' Loki replied, flicking a coin in the air and then palming it with a chime, making it look as if the coin vanished. The crew were left gawping while Loki walked away.

He's got magick in him, said the whisper.

Charlatan's tricks is all, you rotten dickhead.

Don't care even if he is magicked. There's a dozen of us.

Half of us are taller or bigger than him.

He's rich, is what he is. And a forest is a good place to hide him, ain't it?

Why don't no breath come from his mouth in this cold? asked the Hog.

And so it was settled: the sailors drifted after him, each playing their own game of "watch Loki intensely but pretend badly like you're not looking at Loki".

The smell of rot was stronger amongst the trees. Though the gale had died, the still and musty air was harder to bear. The crew became ever shiftier.

'Boggs. Now,' Loki heard Hog whisper.

A heavy-set woman called Boggs quickened her pace. She even had the audacity to tiptoe as if she were onstage, not on the way to committing murder. Loki saw her laughable approach in the faint patches of sunlight that tried their best to break through the tangled canopy.

A simple dodge was often all that was needed when it came to winning a fight. A miss was better than a block, and Loki let Boggs' rock-filled fist fly past him. He watched the woman utterly overextend herself so that she stumbled, legs floundering, and fell face-first into the mud.

Loki drew a fearsome longsword from his pocket and hammered it down as though he aimed to dig a grave with one blow. The result almost cut Boggs in half. To the music of her shrieking, Loki faced the others and leaned on the sword's pommel.

'How you dozen morons manage to keep your ship afloat, I have no clue.'

'Get 'im,' yelped the Hog.

A few feet scuffed.

'I said get 'im!'

The charge began and immediately stuttered to a halt.

A crooked shadow had flitted between the trees.

Loki readied his sword. Leaves were falling along the path, spinning to the mud in a dance. The rare pools of sunlight began to dry up.

'What in the bastard depths is out there, stranger?' asked the Hog. He was given an answer moments later: an archer, for one.

The grey arrow skewered his face, right through the teeth. A needle-pointed barb burst through the back of his head, and Hog staggered about just long enough for Loki to admire the fletching. It was not made of feathers. It looked more like the spined frill of a lizard.

Another arrow burst from the other side of the path and punctured the neck of not one sailor, but two, before lodging in the leathers of Five Pieces.

Loki watched the forest, where spider-like limbs curled around branches or twitched from tree to tree to the sound of snapping bones. Closer, they grew, but never more visible. Hooked spears reached from the undergrowth. The black blades sliced legs and hands from the unfortunate and stabbed what was left wriggling in the mud. In the space of ten panicked heartbeats, the path was drenched in blood and screams. Only Five Pieces was left, cowering in a very compact ball.

'Sire!' he cried out, desperate.

Even if Loki had wanted to intervene, the spears pierced the boy's body before he could raise a finger. There was to be no mercy on that road.

When the arrows came for Loki, he swatted them aside with bursts of light.

'I have not come to fight but to talk!' he bellowed as the spears reached for him. Loki let his full power shine, god's gold in his eyes and sunlight burning beneath his skin. Those amongst the sailors who still clung to life cowered in shock and guilt.

To the rustling of leaves, the spears paused mid-thrust, turned their hooks to the branches, and slowly retreated. One shadow became bolder than the rest, emerging from beneath the trees. Loki saw a body of ashen skin stretching seven feet, and every inch was scarred in patterns and tattooed with white runes. What scant black steel and mail covered the creature's angular frame looked ancient, and Loki could see the callouses where it had been worn for centuries. The belt around its midriff was an unusual one: entirely decorated with pulled teeth, mostly human from the look of them. And though the creature kept its face in the shadow of the branches, Loki spied the glint of a sharp, hairless head and ears so long their points bent over.

The creature's voice was deep and creaking, an un-oiled hinge of a haunted door everybody refused to fix.

'*Ga avatha elkar as otha,*' he spoke. The words were ugly, drawn out, and almost completely monotone save for a few notes that hinted at a question.

Loki had learned most languages across the centuries, but never had he been gifted the pleasure of hearing the guttural speech of the daemon spawn. It was banned in Haven and murdered by time before Emaneska had a name. It survived only in tomes, where it had lost its raw edge.

'A little tip. You'll want to learn the human tongue if you want to get anything done in these lands in these times,' Loki advised, refusing to dim his shine for an instant.

'We asked…' The creature advanced, finally showing a face as sharp as the bow of a warship. Eyes pale as milk and without pupils measured the god up and down. Equally white fangs poked over thin and ashen lips. The sharp nose dividing his face flared as he sniffed at Loki's magick. 'How has a godling escaped from the sky to which you fled?'

Loki smiled. 'And what is a dark elf doing unbanished from the abyss to which you were exiled?'

The elf took a moment to think. 'We should kill you where you stand.'

'Ah, but you would miss out on a most powerful ally,' Loki warned.

'Ally,' rasped the elf, offering what Loki imagined his kind called a laugh.

'You have missed much, elf. Many centuries have passed outside your void. The humans and the dwindling dragons rule this earth now, and your kind will not last long without me. That is why I came to greet you and make your acquaintance: to forge an alliance. I'm the only god that walks these lands, and I have no intention of sharing it with my kin. In fact, I would rather they didn't exist at all.'

The elf swept a flat hand across the bloodshed of the road. 'Pride and greed. Nothing has changed in this world,' he spoke. The elf showed his fangs. '*Takathia.* What do you want of us?'

'I want somebody dead. I want what was stolen from me, and I want what is rightfully mine. That is why I come to join forces.'

A rustle of what Loki could only imagine was laughter ran through the elvish pack. 'Who is such a person that requires a god to make pacts with elves?' asked their leader.

'A human mage,' Loki said with grit in his tone. 'Though it irks me to say it, he is the finest mage Emaneska has ever seen. A mage that killed your own god Orion.'

'Orion returned?'

Loki snorted. 'For all of three heartbeats. His spawn came so very close to Ragnarök but were foiled by the mage in question.'

The elves were silent now. 'Impossible.'

'I saw it with my own eyes, as did thousands of others.'

The elf flicked a black tongue between the gaps of his fangs. 'And what is to be said of daemonkind? The sky's stars are fewer than before.'

'The sky was emptied of daemons during the last battle against the mage. Prince Gremorin rules their kind now, and he and I had an alliance of our own, but he failed to put the humans in their place. He bowed to one, in fact. Now he skulks and licks his wounds, his rule in question.'

Loki watched his words spread whispers.

'*Kathe*. You lie.'

The god grinned. 'Not to you.'

The elf looked between his warriors in silent discussion, their white eyes blinking in the darkness. Loki watched him closely. The cogs of his mind weren't as clear as humans, who might as well have had transparent skulls, but this elf was tricky to figure.

At last, the elf took long steps towards the nearest corpse. Well, not quite a corpse, but soon to be one. The sailor still had enough life in him to gawk and twitch as the elf crouched over him, sharp knees pointing east and west, insectile.

'Elves do not trade for empty hands. What will you give us?'

'I will give you forges, steel, lumber, a place to shelter,' said Loki, his hands clenching into a fist in anticipation.

'A poor offer,' the elf replied. 'We can claim such things ourselves if we desire. Though the magick in this world is stronger than ever, its worms are still weak. Elves were created to serve the fire and the dark, but we did not ask to be created. We did not ask to serve kings of fiery crowns. We do not wish to serve again.'

'And you shan't. Allow me to paint you the full picture. With the mage dead, I can give you power beyond what you can take yourselves. I can bring about Ragnarök, the glorious death of daemons, mages, and the gods, and you will never know another master again. You can take whatever land you wish and I agree to give you. The rest will be left to me. The humans will be our subjects as they are meant to be. Our cattle.'

Elvish claws worked with swift precision, wrenching the sailor's jaws wide to clutch his tongue. With brute strength, the elf began to pull, making the man gag and writhe uselessly.

'We have spent too many nights in the void, breeding, growing, training, waiting. Too many nights paying for sins that were not ours.'

With a vicious tug and a disturbing howl, the tongue was ripped free, and the man was set free. The elf held the tongue aloft before taking a bite.

'To think this world has been overrun by gods-made vermin detests us,' he said around the mouthful and with blood-smeared lips. 'Murderers basking in the light of their gods.'

Loki smelled a story amongst the stench of the dead and the strange reptilian musk of the elfkind. 'Then help me put it right.'

When the elf finished his grotesque meal, he twisted his bloody claws in midair as if opening an unseen door. A spiral of blue light appeared, marked with glowing runes. 'The pact has been written.'

Loki bowed, eyes fixed on his new ally. 'Do you have a name, elf?'

There was no bow, no nod of the head, nor even a courteous flapping of the hand. 'Azen Ithar of Clan Covor, Tenth Prince of the Imur. And you, godling?'

'Loki. The Morningstar. Fallen god and emperor of the Arka,' Loki replied with another bow, this one grandiose. Somebody had to bring a formality to such a wondrous occasion. 'And as a token of this blossoming new friendship, I've brought you more than this paltry dozen of worm-bitten wretches. A whole ship of them lies on the north coast, and I wager there are fifty delectable souls left aboard.'

Azen flashed his fangs again, this time not in anger, but in a haunting smile that was as far away from humour and kindness as one could get. Loki had met true evil several times, and he met it once more in that moment, right there in that toothy smile.

Loki stood still as the shadows surged through the forest, hideously fast, some capering on all fours. There must have been twice as many as he had already counted, hundreds completely unseen, now lurching across the loam like varnished dolls come to life.

The god eyed the fallen sailors, spread like a seer's chicken bones across the path. Another still clung to life, blinking away in wordless terror.

'Waste not, want not,' Loki said as he twirled the sword in his hand. A swift stab to the spine, and he drank the soul hidden within that dying shell and the power it held. Between the blue leaves now still and silent as if they cowered in his presence, Loki found the stars and smirked at the fools hidden in their ruined constellations.

'Then to Krauslung, I will go,' he whispered.

CHAPTER 9
GRIM TIDINGS

Why must there always be an emperor or empress? A king or queen? A duke or duchess? A council? Why can we not exist unto ourselves in the way that suits us best? In peace and liberty, eye for an eye? That is balance. That is order.
FROM A LEAFLET FOUND IN A KRAUSLUNG SEWER

Three more wells are needed, High General.

We need the Jar Khoum's permission for a quarry, General.

Refugees from the north have arrived, General.

Can I fetch you anything, General?

With a polite smile, a feeble excuse, and a swift exit, Elessi had found herself taking a leaf out of Farden's book and running from the duties of the council. Now she walked the beach alone with the voices of elders and smiths still ringing in her ears. Far better than the screams of war, of course, but still not what she needed.

On the southern hook of the natural harbour that was Sanctuary Bay, a watchtower perched on a spit of land. It was no great fortress, but a humble square spike of stone five stories high, barely fortified. It was what Eyrum called a distraction, designed to lure would-be invaders and waste their arrows while the real defences rallied. And it was a quick-built distraction, at that. One that Elessi swore leaned slightly to one side. Most importantly, however, it was quiet and alone. Now the harbour of New Scalussen had the Winter Fortress, the tower was merely for handfuls of lookouts. Lookouts that glanced up from their bowls of fish stew without surprise at her entrance.

'Out,' Elessi ordered, and without complaint or question, the three soldiers made themselves scarce as petals in winter. It was not the first time Elessi had visited the tower.

Taking the spiral of the staircase, she endured the burn in her legs until she got to the roof, where an uneven step always caught her foot, no matter how many times she crossed that threshold.

The fourth lookout was so engrossed in his spyglass that he near jumped out of his skin at the sight of the general in his peripherals. Elessi took the spyglass he offered to her with a bow and claimed his seat, an armchair stolen from some cabin. It was a piece of detritus, with tattered cloth, salt and sunburn, but comfy enough to make her watches easier. A larger, more intricate spyglass was mounted on the parapet, capable of showing her the barnacles on a ship a dozen miles away.

Elessi took a deep breath of the wind, heavy with the smell of palm and baked rock, and stared out to sea. The shadow of the tower reached almost to the water, where a heavy swell spattered the rocks with spray. The breeze had shifted seaward now the sun was aiming for its grave. Currents beyond the shallows drew lines of light and shadow on the waters. Seagulls rode the winds, mewling at each other as if discussing the likelihood of whether the old lady below had bread or some other acceptable snack to steal.

Elessi disappointed them, moving the larger spyglass back and forth to scan the horizon. Her view stretched north to south and back again before she heard the footsteps: heavy, with an accompanying clink of armour.

Elessi reached for the blade at her side and pulled it from the scabbard. Damn Farden and his fear-mongering. Damn Farden for being right about trouble following them. Elessi would not say it to his face, of course. The mage was unbearable when he was right.

Elessi heard the sound of a metal toe catching a stone step and a resulting mutter of a curse, and she chuckled. It was hardly dignified for the most powerful mage in the known world to trip on the stairs, even ones built so hastily, but it was good to know he was still human.

'You followin' me now?' Elessi asked him.

'I thought you'd stop disappearing after finishing with Paraia,' said Farden. 'Three weeks returned and you're already disappearing again. I thought I'd find out why.'

'What, you don't trust me after all I done for you?'

'Elessi,' Farden reproached. 'Of course I trust you.'

The mage took a seat on a weathered chest full of arrows and followed her gaze out to the cerulean sea. 'Why are you here?'

'I come here to watch the sea. Calms me. Gets me away from the pressures of my position,' Elessi muttered. 'You ain't the only one it grinds on.'

Farden smiled knowingly. 'And have you found it yet?'

That made Elessi blink. 'What?'

'Whatever it is you're looking for up here. They're fine excuses but I know you better than that. Unless it's for Loki coming from the sea. If that's the case, then I appreciate your vigilance.'

'Not Loki.' Elessi paused to stare at a wave through the spyglass, hum to herself, and then scowl. 'We each need our obsessions to get lost in and leave the world behind. Like you and those little carvings you make.'

'Well, I wish you'd tell me what yours is.' Farden waited for an answer that didn't come. 'Is it Modren?'

Elessi bowed her head. 'It's always Modren,' she said softly. 'I think about him every hour of every day, But no. This is a distraction.'

'What, then?'

Elessi squinted her eyes at the horizon. 'I saw something that day we rounded the Cape of No Hope. The rest of the crew either didn't see it, or they did, and they blame madness and tricks of lightning, waves, or exhaustion. Even Lerel doesn't talk about it.'

'What did you see?'

'You'll call me mad like the others.'

Farden tutted. 'Try me.'

'A ship. A beast. I don't know which, but somethin' between the two and four times as big as any. It broke the pirates' ships in half and sent the leviathan runnin' north.'

'And you want it to exist.'

'Of course I do.'

Farden kept a shine in his eye. 'You're right: you're quite mad. It must be the old age.'

Elessi threw him a sour look before melting into a smile. 'I'll tell you why. Have you dreamed anything strange recently?' she asked.

For once in his life, Farden hadn't.

'I have,' Elessi said. 'Just when I thought the decades of unrest and fighting were over, and I can finally return to normal, I keep dreamin' of grey faces and fire and black spiders larger than an iceberg. It ain't the same as how I feel the daemons when they're close, but I know there's a shadow looming in the east. I don't like it when you're proven right, Farden, but for some bloody reason my gut agrees it ain't over. And while I'd like to enjoy some peace and quiet before it starts all over again, proving this creature exists would give me some hope. Hope there might be allies out there we don't know about, and we aren't alone.'

'Then let's hope we find the shadow before it finds us,' Farden said, pausing to listen to the waves as Elessi did. 'If I've learned anything in my years, it's to trust a gut, especially yours.'

'Do you still think that assassin was sent by Nerilan?' she asked.

'It's not farfetched that Nerilan could be behind it. She hates me enough to want me dead, and I swear I've heard her spit the very same words as the assassin did. Perhaps that's why it's taken them a week to deliver their apology.'

'But I thought Towerdawn agreed to help you.'

'But Nerilan didn't. Whatever the reason, we've got leverage now.'

'Cold and calculatin'. The more we fight Loki, the more we become him.'

Farden scowled at that. 'Necessity, Elessi. We're weaker divided.'

'Why do I get the feelin' you didn't just come here to check on me?' asked Elessi.

'I need the Grimsayer.'

'For what?'

'Because it's mine.'

'Ain't it the Sirens'?' Elessi thought of the glowing amber figure of Modren that stood in the grim tome night after night until she fell asleep. She did not want to part with that. 'I don't carry that heap around in my pocket, you know.'

'Where is it?'

'It's in my chambers in the Dawnknell.'

Farden gave her a nod as he arose and went to the stairs. 'I hope you find it.'

'What?'

'What it is you're looking for. I hope you're right about not being alone.'

'Then the same to you,' Elessi said.

'Your secret's safe with me. You keep to your looking. I'll tell the others you're busy and not to be disturbed,' he said between the scuffs of footsteps on the stairs.

'Thank you, Farden.'

'Don't mention it.'

When the clang of the door far below echoed, a small crow flapped onto the battlements, one with piebald feathers and the stem of a white flower clamped in its beak. Elessi stayed deathly still, refusing even to breathe. She watched its beady eye measure her before it dropped the flower on the stone, cawed with a convulsion of its entire body, and flapped away.

Elessi's cheeks felt tight with the smile that forced its way across her face.

Farden breathed deep through his nose, smelling nothing but the incense the Jar Khoum insisted on burning and that everyone but him seemed to enjoy. It smelled like burning hair and far too much like nevermar to his liking. Farden looked around the small chamber, filled with his carvings. They littered every shelf, looking at him silently.

With reverent hands, Farden spread the heavy pages of the Grimsayer over the lectern.

'Show me Loki.'

The grey pages of the Grimsayer did not move. Its firefly lights circled the page, unsure of what to draw.

Farden bowed his head as he clenched the edges of the tome. 'Then he is still alive.'

What else did you expect? whispered the spear in his hand.

'Show me Durnus,' Farden spoke. Even saying the name knotted his stomach.

The lights of the Grimsayer went eagerly to work and weaved a faint pattern of the old vampyre. And yet it wasn't as detailed as the other souls the tome could draw. It never stayed still for long, flickering and sputtering, but Farden could still make out a slick of hair covering the bald skin, a slight and familiar hunch, and arms thin as bones but stronger than iron.

'Elessi once looked like this in the Grimsayer, after the daemons clawed her,' he said aloud.

You cannot bring lost souls back, Farden. That was the cost of claiming Gunnir.

'You can't stop me from trying. Even you don't know the true power of the spear.'

Is that true?

Farden clenched his hand and clamped his eyes even tighter.

The wails of gulls and the rumble of a city being built faded until all Farden heard was the gentle susurrus of snow falling around him. Opening his eyes, he found a familiar face standing before him. It, too, was blurred and shadowed, but in his eyes, it was unmistakably Durnus. Pine and rowan trees lingered on the horizon. Deer wandered about their fringes, nibbling blood-red berries and snorting steam into the cold air. This was not Hel, and it was not Haven, but somewhere in between.

'Why?' the shadow of Durnus asked. 'Why do you fight to save the lost still?'

'Because I need saving myself, Durnus. I feel lost without you. Too full of worry. I should be glad to have this peace, but I can't rest. I fear I know what awaits me if I carry on this way, and it worries me.'

Farden reached down to grab a handful of the clearing's snow, but it was not for him and slid through his red-gold fingers.

'Has it not always been that way?' Durnus said, and his shadow smiled. 'You have been running from the fate of exile and madness ever since I first knew you. Why else do you wear the armour? Has this something to do with what Utiru showed you in her mirrors and visions, Farden?'

'Perceptive even in death,' the mage grumbled. 'Utiru showed all of us two fates. First, I saw myself old, bearded and lost in the snow. It felt like the nightmare of a Written's exile. But Utiru also showed me the end I've always wanted. Peace and silence. A farmhouse. A soul to match mine. Nothing but logs to chop and not a mention of war. Both can't be true.'

Durnus hummed, beginning to walk around Farden. 'Both cannot, but the real question is which is true, and whether you have any choice in the matter.'

'Precisely. And it's not just the matter of my choice. I saw darkness in Mithrid's mirrors, and I haven't been able to rid that from my mind either. She's changing, Durnus, and I worry she won't make the right choice.'

Durnus stopped before Farden, and the mage ached to see the detail the shadow hid. His ghost held out faint hands, and Farden put his own to them, feeling nothing but cold.

'If there is such a thing, then you must allow her to make her own decision. She has to learn what cannot be taught. What cannot be hammered, but rather etched.'

Farden watched a lone sketch of two ravens pass overhead. 'How is that possible?'

'A certain vampyre asked the very same question when he took an unruly young mage under his wing a long time ago.' Durnus seemed to smile. 'You know why you worry so, Farden?'

'Why?'

'Because of your daughter Samara. You worry Mithrid will turn out the same, and there is nothing you can do about it.'

'You might be dead, old friend, but that doesn't mean I won't hit you,' Farden warned, and Durnus held up his hands. The mage forgave him. 'Do you worry about Mithrid, too? Or am I growing mad?'

'Worry is not part of what I am now, Farden.'

'Sounds very fucking blissful.' Perhaps death was the one true peace and silence.

'I see your concerns, Farden. But you have missed one crucial fact.'

'What is that?'

'You believe so strongly that Utiru's visions are fact, but you have not considered they may be nothing but simple fantasies designed to entrap and bewilder prey.'

'They were true for you,' Farden said as the birds of the woods and the snuffling deer fell silent. Durnus grew still.

Farden admitted what he couldn't to anyone else. 'If nothing else, Mithrid's growing in power. If she made the wrong choice, I don't know if I could stop her without killing her.'

Durnus shrugged. 'Then if you choose to believe that, you must kill the god before that decision is demanded of you,' he answered. 'Will you still destroy Gunnir when you are done with Loki?'

'If it means peace,' Farden whispered, unsure if he lied or spoke the truth. 'But I have a feeling that will not be an easy decision.'

Durnus bowed, and the shadow that held his shape folded in on itself like a used napkin in a fist. Farden let go of his grip on the spear.

Snow and winter faded to the sandstone of a plain bedchamber. Farden had come there for answers and direction. He had found both, but he didn't want the ache they brought him.

Farden collapsed Gunnir into a curved knife of silver and black jewels and left the dark of the Dawnknell for the scarlet of the early evening sun.

CHAPTER 10
SOULEATER

Why do the gods not eat souls? It is a cannibalism of sorts. They were our creators. To them it is as parents eating children. They leave such practices to their daemon kin.
WRITTEN BY AN UNKNOWN EVERNIA PRIESTESS

Greedy fools. Every last silk-clad and perfumed one of these puckered arseholes, too greedy to even let a fart escape.

And Froxire was one of them. He didn't curse the dozen lords and ladies he called a council for their avarice, but for their intelligence, and a serious lack thereof. Not that he minded; it suited him just fine. It was always better to have idiots for competition than sharp minds.

'We have to take Paraia back from Scalussen. Troacles was a valuable port. Karissa an important mine. Belephon's taxes were—'

'You're only saying that because you had dealings with Colonel Blatter and that prune of a baroness. Well they're both dead, Buckley, so what good are your deals now?'

Froxire walked his fingers across the table until they pointed at another imbecile.

'You. Lord Tiber. What happened when you tried to expand your warehouses too quickly?'

It was a sore point for Tiber, and he spoke into his hands. 'I almost lost everything.'

'See? We've been given a gift in Loki's disappearance! Why squander it reaching too far?'

The others weren't as convinced.

'But Essen's writ of separation—'

'Will be their mistake once we rebuild.'

'But Lord Loki—'

'Saved us from the daemons and Scalussen!' Froxire snapped, exasperated. 'I will not deny that, but he is gone, and now it's up to us – and I mean all of us – to pull together and rule Krauslung the way it was meant to be ruled.' Froxire paused for effect. 'By a small group of quick minds with a healthy tax income and strong profits. Come now!'

'Hear hear!' crowed Lord Njordmark, a man who had weaselled into the soon-to-be enviable position of Froxire's right hand. His clapping echoed around the vacant Marble Copse of the Arkathedral.

'Onto business, and speaking of taxes, they should be raised. The army needs to be rebuilt if we are to defend our interests.' Froxire twirled his quill.

'Is that a good idea at a time like this?'

Froxire tutted. 'The masses will understand the need for protection given all we have been through. Besides, they are too occupied building their temple to their missing god.'

'It must be costing a fortune in stone.'

'Donations from many smaller traders. The workers and builders are labouring for free.'

The gathered lords of Krauslung collectively shuddered at those evil words. *Donation. Free.*

'I don't have to tell you lords of industry,' Froxire intoned, 'that it is good for business to appear to be on the same side as your customers. It was the mistake Malvus made. I say let them build their temple.'

A voice filled the Marble Copse as if every one of the carved, white trees spoke. 'How very self-serving of you.' A shadow moved between the torches, hooded.

'Guards! Guards!' hollered Njordmark.

'They've been sent elsewhere, I'm afraid,' boomed the shadow.

'On whose authority?'

The short stranger emerged into their candlelight, though he kept his face shadowed. 'Their god's.'

Three of the lords, either saving their skin or saving their souls, immediately bowed their heads. 'Loki,' came their whisper.

Froxire spread his hands, snickering. 'If you were indeed Loki returned and not a conman with a fortunate likeness, then I would applaud you for your help so far, but this council rules Krauslung now. Loki is not needed.'

'You dare to cast out your god?'

'God.' Froxire chuckled. 'Loki may have the rest of this city fooled, sir, but as a man of education and common sense, I know that gods belong in the sky and scrolls. Am I not right, my lords?'

Before any of them could utter so much as a squeak, the stranger's eyes glowed with gold fire. Shadows recoiled before their light. The scent of coal and meadow spread through the Copse. A pressure built in their skulls as if unseen hands clenched. Froxire immediately choked on his laughter.

'T-thank goodness you've returned safe and sound. You've been gone a long time.'

'And I see you leapt at the chance to take my city from me. Out of the goodness of your heart, I imagine?'

'K-Krauslung needed leaders.'

Loki's smile was uncomfortably wide, and it put a gurgle in Froxire's stomach.

'And taxes, I hear.'

Froxire tried getting out of his chair as Loki drew closer, but the god put a finger to his lips and bade him to stay seated.

'You must be tired with so much pressure on your shoulders.'

Loki put his hand on Froxire's neck. The god's touch felt inhumanly cold, and there was no give to his skin, the fingers like steel. What Froxire wouldn't have given for a sip of his wine at that moment.

'It's curious. Krauslung isn't a corpse to be looted, and yet here you all are, gathered like vultures, looking to fill your beaks.'

The fingers began to tighten.

While Froxire debated going for his dagger, something wet slithered from the sleeve of Loki's coat and across his skin. The lord twitched away, but his neck was trapped in the god's vice. Only his eyes could move, and he looked down to see what looked like a black slug with the fangs of a sabrecat. Fangs that were immediately plunged into Froxire's cheek. He tasted the bitter venom in his mouth as a numbness spread across his face and down his neck. Fiery bile climbed his throat, but he had no strength to sick it up.

Paralysed, Froxire was forced to watch as Loki soaked the Marble Copse in blood. A knife flew from his fingers, impaling Lord Tiber in the forehead. A bolt of light scorched the face from Froxire's oldest rival, Lady Birna, who they called Birna Steelshod for how she trampled other traders. Her prowess mattered little in that moment, and her limp corpse slumped to the marble. Loki now brandished a copper whip, though where it had come from, Froxire had no idea. All he knew was that he was drooling, and that the slug was beginning to chew, and that blood decorated his fine silks as the whip lashed back and forth, sowing death.

The last to die was Njordmark. Even with the metal whip wrapped around his neck and blood staining his fingers, the young lord decided to leave Loki with a piece of his mind.

'The people won't follow a tyrant, not when they hear of this barbarism!' he choked.

Loki sucked his teeth as he pulled the whip's knot tighter. 'Poor child. Who exactly do you think will tell them?'

When Njordmark's head had fallen to the floor, and all had fallen still so that the crackling of candles could be heard, Loki bent over so his face was level with Froxire's. The only satisfaction Froxire could claim was that he didn't have to bend that far.

'*Glerg*,' Froxire slurred.

'You'll have to speak up. The venom of the Armaneeta slug is a strong one. Fatal, of course, but slow. Better to speak while you can.'

'*Waugh!*'

'Why, you ask? Would you like me to tell you it is retribution for your greedy, greedy ways? Or for thrusting yourself on this city as you might a defenceless waif in an alley when you have no right? Or I could tell you it is because I am a black-hearted traitor who will use this city as the pawn it always has been, and I don't want cattle like you bleating in my ear. Or, I could tell the truth, that I am thirsty after my travels and am here to eat your souls.'

Loki seized Froxire by the neck and inhaled. Before he died, Froxire saw the fine gossamer threads of his own soul leaving his body and the grinning face of a god drinking every last drop.

❦

Loki clenched a fist, letting the power vibrate across his skin. A golden glow showed the bones beneath his hand. 'Much better, thank you,' he said to the dead and now soulless excuse for a council.

Loki left the surroundings of stained glass and marble boughs and aimed for the Eyrie on the Arkathedral's roof. There, Krauslung stretched before him, and despite its run of bad luck and dark times, it was no less cacophonic nor pungent than it ever had been, even with dawn warming the eastern horizon. The night-wrapped streets were alive with its citizens. The disproportionate number of taverns and cathouses each blared their music into the cold night air. Drunkards led singing processions down the narrow, cobbled lanes in search of more ale. Bastards brawled in the port. Countless thousands of Arka lay dead, and they still bickered over scraps, slurs, and spilled tankards. The only silence came from the gulls wheeling above the harbour.

Shuffling feet came up the stairs behind him. A fellow clad in the green and gold tunic of the Arkathedral servants came forth, bent like a right angle in a bow he rarely rose out of. By the look of his wrinkled face, he had spent a life eating nothing but lemons.

'You called, Your Wondrousness?' he asked.

'I did, Sjarvek.' Good old Sjarvek. Loki had never seen him blink at anything his previous master Malvus had done, and he wouldn't dare blink at a god. 'It seems the lords who called themselves a council have suffered some sort of terrible madness and killed each other in a rage.'

'How unfortunate.'

'A terrible tragedy, if you ask me. Their bodies and their mess need to be disposed of. Discreetly.'

'Will there be anything else?

'I want runners sent to their homes and their estates and riches seized. Then send more runners to the criers and taverns and spread the word that Loki has finally returned to Krauslung.'

'Will you be making an appearance, Gloriousness?'

'I will indeed. I want every soldier, every guard, every militia standing on the street they call the Seaway by noon. North to south, all the way to the port where they're building my temple,' instructed Loki, looking south to the pile of scaffolding and white stone peeking over the sharp rooftops of warehouses and traders' mansions.

'A capital idea, Illuminance. The people will be overjoyed.'

'That they should be. Their saviour has returned, after all.'

Much to Loki's satisfaction, Sjarvek couldn't have been more correct. Before he reached the gates at the head of a hundred men, he could already see the pennants and kites streaming above the stone parapets. Some had even been crafted in the shape of leviathans, stretching over the edges of the gatehouse with jaws wide and full of the winter's air.

The cheers filled him with more than just pride. Power, of course. Gone were the perils of indecision. The noise of his glorious return washed over him and filled him with the sweet elixir of the belief that his kin craved. It was almost as sweet as the taste of the fools' souls.

Make it big. Make it loud. Make sure everyone knows, Loki had told Sjarvek, and the grey bastard had seen to every detail. Ribbons hung from gutters and arches. Lanterns and light spells fizzed and sparked, throwing colour in the overcast sky. The twin bells of Hardja and Ursufel pealed in time with every step he took. This was what Loki had earned. His defeat wasn't even a whisper here.

And yet, there were those in the crowd who refused to be swept up in his celebration. Loki could see it in stone-like faces and the subtle shakes of heads. Not all of Krauslung yet believed.

One woman of note gave him nothing at all in terms of hate or love. Loki had never seen her before, and she had witch's eyes, barely coloured at all but for a ring of green. Black hair covered the marks of fire across her cheek and neck, and the skin that remained unblemished was not a shade of Emaneska. Her cheeks, brow, and nose had the sharpness of the east. Curiously, one arm was encased in a sleeve and a black glove, and the rest of her was covered in a purple shawl and what looked to be wooden armour. Loki watched her until a banner blocked his view.

As soon as they were inside the gates, Loki signalled to the men behind him: the ones who led the cows that dragged the silk-covered wagons. Off came the coverings, showing piles of coin and all kinds of trinkets Sjarvek's minions had pilfered from the dead lords of Krauslung. The rest had come from the various lost and forgotten hoards in Loki's pockets.

Loki showed his most winning smile – just the right measure between callous pride and beaming condescension – while the soldiers went to work hurling handfuls of gold and silver to the howling, heaving masses. The soldiers lining the Seaway worked hard keeping the way clear, and Loki thought it similar to throwing peelings to hungry hogs. Gold was nothing but shinier dirt to gods.

Bathing in the elated cries of his citizens, Loki walked along the flagstones and cobbles towards the sea. By the time the odour of fish and bilge filled his nostrils, he had drawn a shining sword from his coat and marched with it aloft. If they thought him a god of diplomacy and wise words, he would show them he could be a warrior god as well.

After an hour of parading, Loki stood before the scaffolding of his temple. He had expected more, but the towering statue half-clad in gold and silver leaf taking shape atop its dome would have to do. Loki climbed what had been carved of the stairs to look out across the sea of faces.

'What of Paraia!' came the sudden yell, too much of an accusation to be a question. And before Loki had chosen to speak as well. He found a grizzled man in mismatched armour standing alone. People swiftly made space around him, not wishing to be blamed for his insolence.

'What of it?' asked Loki.

'The Outlaw King sent our soldiers and mages packing across the sea! Hundreds have come back and say he's more powerful than ever!' cried the man.

'They say he sacked Troacles in a night!'

Loki forced his smile wider. The mention of Farden was a sour grape in an otherwise sweet bunch. The belief wavered like the tremble of a skald's high voice.

'The so-called king can keep Paraia,' Loki called out.

Murmurs spread.

'But what if Krauslung is next?' came another shout. A baker this time, judging by the flour on his cheek. 'What of the empire?

'There is no empire!' Loki told the masses, and let the gasps die and truth sink in before he continued. 'We do not need one!

Krauslung is strong. *You* are strong, and that is what matters in this world. We shall build and grow and flourish again, and Krauslung will once more be the beating heart of Emaneska. Darkness is behind us, friends. Glory and riches await! I say let the Outlaw King come, if he wishes, for I will deal with him as I did the daemons that sought to enslave you! He is just a man, but I… I am a god!'

The belief soared with his words, and Loki drank it in, letting his glow rise for all to see. Loki's promise was hollow, but they did not need to know that. Farden still had Gunnir. All Loki had was a tenuous pact with ancient and unpredictable elves.

To the cheering of the crowd, Loki raised his sword again, glaring into as many eyes as possible to test their mettle and whether they loved him or not.

Of course, the vultures came circling. Lords and merchants baaed their requests like drowning sheep. Ranking officers asked their questions in gruff voices. Doubters, emboldened now that Loki had retreated to the Arkathedral, demanded proof he was a god and not a simple mage and a liar.

Loki stared down at them from one of the middle balconies. He had grown bored of waving.

Benevolence was a wondrous tool of ruling, but it was flawed. With a generous hand, people grew unused to hardship and accustomed to getting their way. Too vicious a hand, and a ruler bred hatred and rebellion. A fine balance lay in the middle, but apparently waving a sword above his head hadn't silenced the petty badgering that was better suited to a duke with shit in his trews.

Loki drew the power from his belly full of souls and stole magick from the air. Bringing his fists down on the marble lip of stone, light pulsed from his form, blackening and cracking the stone.

The crowd reeled appropriately. The silence was as golden as Loki's eyes. Several dozen fell on their knees. He watched doubters proven wrong and the disbelievers question, and he let loose a cackle.

Loki left them to their muttering as he withdrew into the hall, tiled almost entirely in jade. Scrolls sat in cradles along the walls. At his order, a dozen suits of armour, mail, and Albion leather had been delivered from the finest smiths in Krauslung and Manesmark. They stood around the hall on iron mannequins like the ghosts of soldiers. Lanterns glowed above their helmets, and in their light, steel and chainlink shone. It was only fitting a god should have armour in a time of war. After all, Loki's old kin had done the same in their final battle, and it was absolutely nothing to do with that mage and his bloody spear.

The armourers and merchants who had brought the armour stood beside their property and either beamed their best and proudest smiles or sweated profusely. Some did both while Loki toured their offerings.

Out of the dozen, four were hideous concoctions covered in far too many jewels and tassels. Two were too thick and heavy and the kind of armour that said its wearer was likely going to fill it with piss before the battle even started. Of the final six, one was too sharply angled and impractical, one came with a helmet in the shape of a bear's head, and another was a sickly rose colour. The smith behind that one was a sweater, and Loki stared into his nervous eyes until he looked like he would puke.

That left three. A thick but simple suit of charcoal and black Arka steel. Another had elegant lines, but the copper against its steel reminded Loki of another suit of armour he very much hated. And the last was of straight Arka lines, intricately joined plates, and steel shone a summer-sky blue.

'Sjarvek! Come here, my grizzled friend,' Loki yelled, spirits high.

The servant appeared before Loki could finish his sentence. An impressive feat for somebody as wizened and arthritic as he was, but it was who stood beside him that bothered Loki. It was the green-eyed woman of Easterealm he had seen in the crowds.

'And who is this, Sjarvek?' Loki demanded. 'I said no visitors, or do you not remember?'

'She is an envoy of a land named Golikar, Excellence, and quite insistent that she see you.'

'My commiserations for your dead Queen Peskora,' sighed Loki. He was not a king, he was a god, and he had no interest in holding court or listening to a single mortal word. All he wanted was their worship and obedience. *And delicious souls.* 'But you'll find no restitution or apologies here. And as for an alliance, you have nothing to offer me.'

'How about Farden?' the woman said with a smile.

Loki stopped mid-turn. 'What did you say?'

'I knew you would want to speak to her,' said Sjarvek before he shuffled away.

Loki clicked his fingers, lighting the fireplaces and candles to see this envoy better. The polish and gems of the armour glittered with the dance of the flames. The armourers looked about like a clutch of chickens hearing a wolf's cry.

'You three can stay,' he ordered them with a stabbing finger. 'The rest of you, begone and take your failures with you.'

Once the others had run from the room in a clatter, Loki reached into his coat and produced a grape-sized jewel for each of the remaining three. All of them bowed and scraped and thanked their god profusely.

'Now you can leave,' he said with a coy smile. Little did they know the jewels were once decoys lost by a sly duke of a land that became Albion. Fine, strong glass of marvellous colours, but utterly worthless nonetheless. The mischief was pleasing.

The god turned back to his peculiar visitor, noticing for the first time a tattoo across her ungloved knuckles. It was Commontongue, and he spoke the four small letters in his head. *Live.*

'Daemonfire, am I right?' Loki pointed to the side of her face. The woman did not move to hide the scars. 'A survivor of the north, I take it?'

'Right you are, Lord Loki, but wrong about the second part. I am a survivor of the Battle For The World,' said the woman, moving around the hall to squint at scrolls and pinch dust between her fingers. 'You know, I pride myself in being a scholar, but I didn't believe in daemons before Azanimur. Now I see there is a great deal I do not know, and it irks a soul like mine.'

'You were on the Bloodplains?'

'I was, standing at the side of the warlord Belerod. I barely escaped the daemons' fire alive. But what I saw before I escaped intrigued and disturbed me deeply. I saw a beast of magick, and you standing right by his side against Farden and Mithrid.'

'Who are you, mortal?'

'My name is Irien, Lady of Whispers, formerly of Golikar. You can guess what I trade in.'

'Not the most complex of puzzles. And how is it you know Farden?'

'I know Farden all too well. It was my whispers that helped Farden on his path to Azanimur. I was the one who set him free when Belerod captured him. Some might say the Battle For The World was my fault.'

Loki cracked a knuckle. 'I confess I'm torn between disembowelling you myself or having a flock of vuleguls peck the flesh from you.'

Curiously, Irien grinned a set of pearly teeth. This one had spirit. 'Worry not, it's something I now regret dearly. I thought Farden something of use, but I see I was wrong,' she said, moving to warm one of her hands by the nearest fire. 'After the battle and half of Easterealm fell, I heard whispers of a living god in the west who saved his people from Scalussen and the Forever King. I followed those whispers across the Silent Sea, and I learned of a war in the deserts and of an empire crumbling. I've waited here for weeks now, wondering if this god would return or if he was a lie, and finally he returns. And whom does it turn out to be? You. None other than the figure I saw on the battlefield. I didn't believe in gods before Azanimur either, but now that I have met you, my dear, I am inclined to change my mind. And I am very glad to make your acquaintance.'

Loki wasn't sure about being called "dear", but he let it pass. 'Is it curiosity you waste my time with or something else? What is it you want?'

'I think we can help each other.'

Loki took a seat in a velvet armchair to laugh. 'And why would I need your help?'

'I'm sure you don't need it, but you may want it. But from what I've heard, you and Farden have a feud that is far from finished, and yet nobody knows where he is,' she said, taking her own seat a comfortable distance apart from him, not within his reach, but close enough to know she smelled of pine and sea salt. 'I do, and I can get close without him suspecting me. He knows me as a friend.'

Loki held a hand over his face and pulled his cheeks, nose, and chin into different shapes and places. It took a lot of magick, but within moments, Irien looked back at herself.

'And what's to stop me torturing you for the information and doing it myself?' he asked.

Looking back at themselves always rattled the mortals. It was a marvel they didn't attack themselves every time they looked in a mirror, like a hound might.

'Unless you know what transpired between Farden and his merry band and I, and you can magick yourself *this*...' Irien swept the glove from her covered arm and showed Loki an appendage of grey wood, intricate beyond any craft he had seen. 'You might have a difficult time. And you still don't know where he is.'

Loki smiled as he returned to his form. The woman knew more than most but far from enough. 'It's clear now what I get out of this, but what do you? What are these whispers worth?'

The Lady of Whispers drummed her long nails on the arm of her chair. 'I don't fear much. I didn't fear my sister, nor losing my arm, and I didn't fear Farden at first. But now I've seen what magick can do, I know what fear feels like, and I loathe its fingers around my throat. I played Farden and Belerod to get my hands on the spear that was unrightfully taken from my ancestor Sigrimur by your kind. But now I see there was a reason my ancestor was slain and robbed: that much power does not belong in one man's hands. Farden has already brought back the elves with his wanton use of Gunnir and doomed us all over again.'

'Elves, you say?' Loki asked with a raised eyebrow. Elves, of course, were not a surprise. It being the fault of Farden was, however, and a wonderful one at that. His wild use of Gunnir explained it perfectly. He had opened a door he hadn't meant to open. 'Surely that's impossible.'

'I hear many whispers, but those I saw with my own eyes while I crawled from the battlefield. Let that put a shiver in you, if your kind does such a thing. Take the warning as a gift,' she said, clenching a wooden fist. 'Wherever Farden goes, he sows fire, and for that reason he must be stopped. You, my dear, seem like the type to get that done. That alone will be my reward. It's always been a passion of mine to help the side that keeps me alive, you see, and I place my bets on a god over a mage, spear or no spear.'

'I'm almost impressed,' Loki admitted before pointing a finger at her. 'Where is Farden?'

They both knew the gamble. If she told him, he could cast her out or cut her throat before she took another breath. If she held back, Loki might refuse.

'Rumours amongst the captains of the Shattered Islands and Heket Sound say the pirates are avoiding Paraia,' Irien said, with a casual wave of her wooden arm.

'You know more than that, I wager.'

'You tell me what you want to know, and I will go to Farden and listen for you. What whispers I glean I will feed back to you.'

Loki wagged the finger and tutted three times. 'That you will, but first, you'll speak. If you want to be of use, go to Farden and tell him Loki has returned to Krauslung.'

'You want him to come to you? Here, with all your people?'

'Precisely.' Loki strolled along the line of armour once more, flicking the metal to punctuate each point. 'Every great ballad has a hero to fight the villain. Krauslung already has its hero. *Me*, naturally, and now they need to be reminded of their villain. If you know Farden at all, you'll know he's a creature of two halves. One is a painfully naive devotion to duty and the prevalence of good, peace, fairness, blah blah blah. The other, of course, is an obsession with violence, chaos, revenge. Wrap that up in a big armoured bundle of a man who fears death and the madness of his magick like a child fears the dark, and you have a mess of a man with all kinds of wonderful strings to pull. A man whose end will be the perfect dawn to my beginning. If you don't die inconveniently prematurely, you may just see it.'

'Then we are aligned.' Irien swept her arm over the floor in a Golikan bow. 'Watch for my hawk, Lord Loki,' she said as she walked for the door.

'Stop.'

The way Irien flinched before turning betrayed that she feared more than just magick.

With a smile, Loki reached into the void hidden in his coat and pulled forth two crow skulls hanging from chains. Their beaks were closed shut in death and each bore a small gemstone embedded in their bones, one green, one blue. 'You like to whisper? Then whisper to this skull and its twin will speak to me. Touch the gemstone to make the spell work.'

Irien examined her skull and its blue gem. 'This would fetch a pretty pile of coin in the Boughmarkets of Vensk.' She threw the skull in the air and caught it in her clockwork fist. 'I think this is the start of a marvellous friendship.'

'Don't die, and we'll see,' Loki replied. What an unexpected treat, this Lady of Whispers was. A messenger. A spy. A distraction for Farden. And not to mention utterly expendable. 'And let's keep the talk of elves between us, shall we?'

'Consider it done.' Irien's voice floated through the doorway. 'Oh, and I would go with the blue so it will match your eyes, my dear. And the metal looks lighter, so nobody will think you need it.'

Loki looked at the blue steel suit again and hummed to himself.

She even had good style.

'Sjarvek!'

As if the old wizard lived in the walls, he appeared within a mortal heartbeat. 'Your Magnificence.'

'I need scribes, and dozens of them. I think Krauslung deserves more Scarred mages.'

'An excellent idea, Your Splendidness. And have you decided on your armour?'

'I will be taking the blue.'

'Very good, Your Meticulousness."

Once Sjarvek had left him and the door was shut, Loki removed his coat and put on his armour piece by piece in his own silent ceremony. The thin steel was strong and snug, but not snug enough that he could wear his coat as well. Loki sighed, and after raising one hand to take the magick from the jade walls, he ran it along the length of his coat, turning its brown to a dark grey while he stretched its threads so it would fit over the armour.

Loki admired himself in a mirror before he left. And yes, the sight was just as regal and powerful and awe inspiring as he imagined.

With a repeated clicking of his fingers, Loki snuffed the candles and killed the fires, and on the last click, he folded into nothing with a thunderclap and a shiver of air.

CHAPTER 11
ARRIVALS

For dragons, there is little difference between a battle and a buffet.
A QUOTE FROM MASTER WIRD

Elessi had drifted off at the spyglass, head propped awkwardly against it.

Awaking to a parched mouth, dew in her hair, and the wax of sea salt on her face, the general straightened. Her back and neck sounded like a band of sloppy recruits coming to attention.

'Gods…' Elessi sighed.

A dense fog had claimed the ocean, washing water, horizon, and evening sky into one grey smear.

Elessi thought of a warmer place to sleep and hoisted herself out of the armchair. It was then she noticed another flower had been dropped on the stone while she had slept through the day. As she reached for it, Elessi heard a curious slap of waves against the calm. Beyond the flower, at the edge of visibility, a shadow passed by.

Could it be? Elessi's heart leapt as she grabbed for the smaller spyglass.

With breath held, fingers shaking, and prayers spilling from her mouth in a muttered stream, she focused on the shadow. She had hoped for a tentacle, but what the gods gave her instead was the faint outline of an oar.

'Never a dull bloody day in Scalussen,' grumbled Elessi as she lunged for the bell-rope hanging above her.

'She'll be five hundred souls bigger than the *Fury* and the *Vanguard*, Farden. Got two dozen more ballistae, six more sails, and the rudder's almost twice as large for swift turning, too. Even got plates under the waterline in case that blonde bastard feels like summoning any more leviathans,' Admiral Sturmsson said, coming dangerously close to boasting.

Farden couldn't complain. He could only smirk at the two beaming admirals standing beneath the cranes and scaffolding of the unfinished ship. 'Sounds like she'll be the finest vessel in all the realms,' Farden said, toying with them.

Sturmsson cleared his throat with some volume. 'You've yet to announce its captain, you know, sire.'

'Oh, I'm well aware,' Farden replied, watching Lerel nudge the officious wedge of a man with her elbow.'

'The *High* Admiral should decide that, don't you think?' she said.

Sturmsson shook his head with much grumbling. 'I expect fair consideration. The High Admiral position seems more land-based and strategic than on the high seas—'

'You cold bastard,' Lerel laughed before her face fell dead serious. 'I should get this ship.'

Sturmsson puffed out his chest and enormous beard. 'I will say, while I'm not willing to provide the same favours as the High Admiral here, I hope a case of Skap apple whisky can equal her bribery.'

Farden held up his hands, trying not to show his own smile. 'I think I'll be taking this ship. Lerel, you have the *Fury*. Sturmsson, the *Vanguard*. Why shouldn't the Forever King have the flagship?'

Their competition immediately forgotten and reforged into an alliance, Lerel started waving her hands in the effusive Paraian way while Sturmsson blustered and grumbled.

'You've got to be joking me! You've already got that spear, what more do you bloody want?' Lerel yelled.

'Aren't you afraid of water?' asked Sturmsson, brows twitching.

'He couldn't even sail a dinghy, never mind a ship like this.'

Farden's smile only enraged them more. 'I'll make my decision later.'

Sturmsson chewed his lips. 'And what of a name for this ship?'

'Make me a suggestion.'

'*The Mighty Scalussen,*' said the admiral.

Even Farden winced.

'Mighty Scalussen? Gods, no. I say *Spring's Victory,*' Lerel countered.

Farden wasn't listening. He had turned away, looking across the deck to the evening of sea-fog and not a wave on the water.

'Didn't you hear me, Farden?'

Bells, whispered the spear in his hand.

Farden heard them now. Muffled by the fog, but clear enough. The sound was coming from Elessi's tower.

'Farden?'

'Raise the alarm!' he bellowed.

'You keep picking it and you'll make a scar,' Hereni warned Mithrid for the ninth time that week.

'Maybe I want one.'

'Then what do you think?'

Mithrid bit her lip, poking at a dead leaf hanging from one of the dozen plants that infested the chamber.

'You haven't been listening, have you?'

'No.'

Hereni placed down the map she was holding, a rough scrawling of New Scalussen that was probably already out of date. 'What's bothering you, Mith? Isn't that assassin, is it?'

Mithrid scoffed. 'No.'

'I see all the training has made you confident if nothing else.'

Mithrid turned and folded her arms. 'Why do I feel you have a problem with that?'

Hereni sat up. 'Fine. If you want it out of me, then I thought you would be more involved with this new home of ours.'

'The council makes me want to sleep. I didn't fight my way to Easterealm and back to decide where to put wells.'

Hereni placed a finger on the centre of the map. 'I was talking about our home, Mithrid. The one we're going to build, the one that I kept in mind every day that you were lost, and the one that you've been too busy training to find a moment to talk about. I understand your hatred for Loki as much as I do my own. But don't think just because I'm not hacking wooden men to dust every day I'm not fighting. Why do you think I'm building walls and ballistae?'

'I don't want to argue.' In Mithrid's broken family, arguing had always meant something or somebody got hurt. She had gone to sleep many nights as a child swearing to be different, and here she was. Not one bit.

'We're not arguing, it's a discussion.'

'Some discussion,' Mithrid snapped, before she clutched at her hair and groaned. 'All right. I'm sorry. I'm listening with all ears. Even this fucked up one with the bandage on it.'

Hereni didn't laugh, but she did offer the tiniest of smiles and put her hands to Mithrid's cheeks.

'We're the same, remember. You know fighting's all I've known, but I've always been fighting for peace and to go back to the cottage I can never return to. I feel I've finally found the place to build it, and the only thing I didn't think would be missing is you.'

'Loki will try to knock it back down as soon as we're finished,' Mithrid muttered, shaking her head and hating the sound of the words.

'I thought you weren't going to let him.'

'I want all that you want, Hereni, but I can't give it to you yet.'

'And will you still want it when all is done and dusted? After Loki's toyed with your mind and chasing him's hardened your heart? That's what I worry. Same as Farden—'

'Don't...' Mithrid began to say, but the tolling of a distant bell interrupted her. She held Hereni's eyes for three chimes before they both raced for their armour.

Pirates.

These weren't the kind of scum that marauded the coasts of Hâlorn, with the braided beards and penchant for keeping gulls and gannets on their shoulders. Not the kind that children heard stories of burying treasure on desolate islands and singing drunken shanties.

No. These were professionals.

Whereas the pirates Mithrid knew of were barely more than disgruntled fishermen who realised catching ships was more profitable, these pirates had a fleet of a dozen ships in two formations. Their grey sails were the perfect shade of fog, and the armour cladding their hulls was made from scores of circular shields beaten flat, ugly trophies of past conquests.

Like the rest of Scalussen, she sprinted through the streets towards the sea and its Winter Fortress. Sailors ran to crew their ships. Archers, mages, and ballistae crew hurtled for the high reaches of the fortress. Soldiers ran for the walls hemming the sea and the beaches either side of the bay. Fleetstar was flapping her wings over the beach, driving waves towards the pirates but not much else.

Only two warships sat at sail in the bay. Three others and the *Autumn's Vanguard* struggled to raise sails and jut oars quickly enough. Where the patrol ships or the *Summer's Fury* was, Scalussen had no clue.

The hammer of ballistae punctuated the ringing of bells and the storm of voices, starting with the ships and racing all the way across the harbour. Black streaks filled the evening sky, crisscrossing before they smashed down on opposite sides. Directly above Mithrid, a Jar Khoum soldier was skewered by a pirate bolt, and she had to leap aside to avoid his body. Hereni sparked a shield for both of them as they set feet to stairs.

The pirates' shots were weaker, but there were more of them. Scalussen was faster, however, and another red-fletched volley peppered the invaders before the pirates managed their second, ships wheeling to bring different broadsides to bear.

'Mages with me!' bellowed Hereni as they scrabbled breathlessly to the top deck of the fortress. Orderly formations of mages and archers were forming behind the bulwarks turned battlements. Ballistae thundered at will while crews swarmed around them. Ko-Tergo and his snowmads seemed to be winning the unspoken race between the crews. Several lycans helped him, however, which was hardly fair on the rest of the humans. Mithrid saw one racing through the chaos towards her, and a part of her still gulped with fear at the sight of a piebald lycan aimed at her. But it was Roglurg, her first friend of Scalussen, with a spiked buckler shield on his hand and a mad, toothy grin on his face.

'My friend,' he snarled before taking up a longbow. Mithrid watched the lycan bend the bow almost double before the thick arrow flew astonishingly high. It almost struck the lead pirate ship.

Mithrid's eyes fell on a glimmer of red and gold standing alone on the half-built crow's nest of the new dreadnought. Gunnir burned bright yet useless as Farden sought a clear shot between his ships and the pirates. They were smart or lucky enough not to give him one, and so Farden pushed a raging shield spell before him instead, encompassing a third of the harbour and thwarting their ballistae shots.

Any foe with some brain between their ears would have retreated at such a boast of power, but not these raiders. A clanging louder than the bells ran across the waves as the lead pirate ships fired a volley from protrusions on their sterns. Mithrid saw giant harpoons race across the water, trailing thick chains. Wood and steel clashed as the lead pirate ship managed to harpoon the backsides of two Scalussen warships. Black pirate oars plied the sea as they heaved. Their sails billowed with the power of wind spells, and although Mithrid was privately glad to be fighting magick, slowly but surely, the Arka warships were dragged out to sea. And turned sideways, they made wonderful shields.

It didn't occur to most that magick had a range, just like an arrow or a spear. It took strength and practice to keep spells alive beyond a mage's reach. Mithrid hadn't known this until Hereni corrected her, and it had turned out true for Mithrid's power as well. Even now, half the mages struggled to cover the distance the ballistae could. Only the mages on the *Vanguard* and the warships could trade their spells with the pirates.

But Hereni had a better idea. 'Light those ballistae up!'

Fire sparked along the deck, lighting up bolt after bolt. The fire the mages spread in the sky ignited the rest. Smoke streaked the sky like the work of a bored scribe's charcoal.

Mithrid, unable to fight beyond helping to load ballistae, watched the pirate formations spread out to the shallows while keeping their narrow bows pointed at trouble. They were smart, and pirate mages held up shields as Farden finally unleashed Gunnir upon them.

The stream of searing white light glanced off one ship, and Farden put the deflection to good use. White fire bounced from the ship to the one behind it, missing their shields and scorching them amidships.

A great roar rose up from Scalussen, but it was a minor victory.

'They seek the shore!' Roglurg growled.

The lycan was right. The pirates were pressing towards the north and south shores of the bay while their bigger ships pushed deeper towards the *Vanguard* and the virgin dreadnought, as if those were their prizes.

'They're beaching! Anyone not handling a ballista come with me!' Mithrid yelled.

When she had first come to Scalussen, Mithrid had been nothing but a grime-covered recruit, drowning in a world she never knew existed. Now she was a general, and the mages and soldiers around her snapped to her bidding. The rush of battle took on a sweeter sheen.

'Mithrid!' Hereni reached for her, and Mithrid clasped her hand before she summoned shadow to stream around her arms.

'You take north, I'll take south!' she yelled before fleeing the Winter Fortress, Roglurg at her side.

Mithrid and the lycan led their warriors along the beach beneath the trade of flaming bolts and arrows. A gale made her swerve as Fleetstar roared overhead to pluck Farden from his mast. Further into the bay, the *Vanguard* had finally positioned herself to unleash a broadside of bolts and spells. One of the smaller pirate ships, no more than a sloop, practically exploded.

Three ships were beaching on the sand on the south of the bay, and Mithrid vowed they wouldn't take a step further.

'Rain fire!' she yelled.

The three score that had followed her knitted spells together and set arrows to strings as they ran. Fire, lightning, and ice raced across the sands. Mithrid ignored the pain it ignited in her skull and raised her own power in front of her. Mages eagerly gave her space as their magick began to wither, and they spread out like pincering jaws.

If the magick didn't discourage the first pirates sloshing their way ashore, the cloud of shadow running at them certainly did. Mithrid washed her magick across the sand, rendering the mages amongst them useless as a second wave of arrows and Scalussen spells pounced. A shot from Roglurg's longbow pierced one pirate against the hull of his own ship and hung him there like meat to bleed.

Perhaps it was not the best time to test the new shade of her power, but Mithrid acted without thinking.

A pirate with an arrow in his shoulder was raising a sodden crossbow. He screeched as Mithrid's shadow seized him by the neck and shoved him into the shallows. He fought like any drowning creature fought, and she could barely keep him down long enough while other pirates stormed up the sand and dried seaweed.

Mithrid sent a wave of shadow at them, knocking a dozen onto their backs. Her axe found them there, and with the help of her warriors and the lycan, the shallows were soon turned crimson. Roglurg was waist-deep, twisting back and forth as his claws and spiked shield went to vicious work, slashing and ripping the pirates apart. Once he had cut a path to the first ship, and not content with his current level of carnage, he started to climb the planks and drag them one by one into the sea by their throats. Arrows and blades did nothing to stop him, and several began voluntarily jumping into the sea to avoid him.

Those who refused to surrender were soon regretting their choices when Fleetstar and Farden attacked.

If the dragonfire melting metal and flesh into the decks wasn't enough, Farden and Gunnir's raw power broke the ship's spine and gave any survivors to the ocean to swallow. It was a fine retaliation until a lucky ballista shot from the beached vessels pierced Fleetstar's wing and forced some caution into the Mad Dragon. She spewed a curtain of fire before she flapped far out of reach. Farden rained down magick onto the pirate fleet, but their dispersed formations and shields made them slippery and slow to defeat.

Mithrid let a battle-cry loose as she reached for two archers, dragging them from the bulwarks and down into the sea to flail and splash and drown in their armour. The more she wielded her shadow, the stronger it became. She even managed to steal an arrow from a bow and stab it into its owner before a trumpeting roar broke the sky.

Mithrid saw the glittering shapes skimming the tops of the palm forests and lingering fog. Dragons exploded into sight over the

Winter Fortress with fire streaming from their jaws and riders standing tall in their saddles, bows and spear arms drawn.

The Sirens had arrived.

The pirate ship that was aiming its harpoons at the new dreadnought stood no chance as Towerdawn and two of his captains rained fire upon the vessel. Dragonfire flowed like liquid, and within moments, the ship was a floating bonfire.

A horn came from the pirate flagship, one of the bastards still hauling a Scalussen warship into the fog. Pirate oars made waves as their ships began to withdraw. It was not quick enough for their liking, however, and two more ships fell to the Siren dragons in as many minutes. The pirates scrabbled into a bristling formation with ballistae aimed skyward, shields and spells ready. And still with two stolen Scalussen warships and crews amongst their number.

Fleetstar and Farden dove to finish them before the Sirens could dive for a second assault. It was a mad decision and a madder dash between the ballistae bolts and spells, but Farden kept a fierce shield burning before the dragon. Her fire and his magick managed to melt one harpoon chain before having to withdraw, with Fleetstar's hindquarters and stout scales peppered with arrows.

Before the Sirens could follow, the darker water beneath the retreating pirate ships began to bubble and churn. Premature screams came from their crews. Not a thought was given to the skies or beaches. All danger of dragons and magick went forgotten, and Mithrid felt almost insulted to suddenly matter so little.

She immediately saw why.

One ship simply disappeared beneath the waves. No crunching of wood. No great crashing and splintering of masts. The ship simply descended into the water like a fish thrown back into the sea. Its crew barely got the time to scream before they went down to Hel to be weighed.

Before anybody could make sense of what their eyes had witnessed, wails rang out from another pirate ship. This one did come to a tumultuous end. With a crack that echoed to the mountains and back, the ship *twisted*. Stern and bow turned in different directions until the ship became two halves of a splintered mess, and even then its crew scrambled to be the last to fall into the churning water. Those that did found themselves drowned in a scarlet maelstrom. Mithrid swore she saw crimson and clawed tentacles whipping about in the pink foam, strangling and crushing and otherwise generally mauling the pirates.

'Bleeding Njord!' Mithrid hissed, turning to make for dry land. Her mages and soldiers did the same, setting their shields of spell and steel in the sand. They weathered the last arrows from the beached ships before one was dragged roughly from the sand as if by the hand of a god. The unseen creature beneath the waters drowned the vessel arse-first. Pirates scrambled to the bow like ants avoiding a flood, kicking and screaming at each other. Anything to stay out of the water.

It didn't help one bit. Something crushed the ship under the water and every soul went flying. One sole tentacle whipped about like a bat and treated one of the unfortunates like a ball. With a crunch and a short-lived squeal, the man flew towards the beach with enough speed to compete with a dragon. The unlucky pirate smashed against the mages' shields. She was left bloody and broken, skin hissing against the transparent magick and just enough life in her to die meeting Mithrid's eyes. Mithrid gave her no kindness, just the smirk of victory. Even if it wasn't truly hers. Though the freed Scalussen ships and crews panicked at their oars and wind spells, the hidden monster seemed solely interested in the pirates. Mithrid wasn't about to wait around to see if it changed its mind.

'Round up those survivors!' she ordered her warriors. The surviving pirates were scrambling out of the shallows as if the water was boiling, and they quickly found blades and spells at their throats.

The final ship crumbled into fire and magick, courtesy of a swooping Fleetstar and Farden leading the dragon fleet in a sweep of the bay. One teal dragon plucked a pirate from the water with its claws and flipped him into its mouth mid-flight. Apparently it was hungry after their journey.

In her peripheries, Mithrid saw a shape sprinting down the beach in a loping gait, soft sand spraying from its heels. Mithrid raised her axe, but Roglurg clicked his tongue.

'It's Elessi,' he said, squinting through smoke and fog.

'I bloody knew it!' Elessi was yelling, sword pointed at the frothing water full of screaming pirates, fewer and fewer every passing moment. 'I told Farden it existed!'

'You knew about that thing?' Mithrid spluttered. 'Hereni and I went swimming not one week ago!'

'Look! Haven't you seen? It doesn't want us! It saved us on the Cape of No Hope and now it's savin' us again. Bloody knew it!' Elessi said, breathless. 'I need a boat.'

'You need a *what*?'

Elessi stabbed again at the ruin of the harbour, leaning back and forth to get a last glimpse of the creature before the carnage and waters fell still. The only noise New Scalussen was left with was the smoke and crackle of the upturned burned hulks and wreckage, and the occasional splash of a lucky bastard reaching shore.

'I need a boat, damn it. I need to talk to that thing.'

'Well, you've gone utterly insane.'

Elessi scowled at her. 'Insanity is what people blame when they don't understand they're wrong.'

Mithrid had nothing to say to that. Even if she had, Elessi was already marching along the beach without her. Before Mithrid could close her mouth, sand was whipped into it, and as she spat and huffed, a blue dragon etched with patterns of ochre put claws to the beach and landed with a grin.

'Mithrid,' Kinsprite greeted, her deep voice rattling Mithrid's ribs. With a smile of her own, Mithrid bowed her head to touch the dragon's snout.

'Need a ride?' asked the rider in its saddle. It was none other than Bull.

Mithrid spat more sand back in its rightful place. She didn't care that it looked like she spat at Bull.

'Will you look who it is? Emaneska's newest dragon-rider.'

Njord, Bull even looked like a Siren in his rider's mail and his hair slicked back from the wind.

'I thought I would come along and pay a visit,' he said in a soft voice.

'Bet Nerilan loved that.' Mithrid refused to admit she missed her only remaining friend from Troughwake. He had hurt her too deeply to give him such words.

Bull's wind-burned cheeks bunched into a glum look, and he stuck out his bottom lip.

'You can take me to the fortress,' said Mithrid. She looked to Roglurg, who shook his head emphatically, long ears wiggling like a dog shaking itself to get dry.

Practice and time had not cured Mithrid's fear of flying, but it was better than trudging through the mess that was already washing up on the dying waves. As Kinsprite took a running start across the sand, Mithrid glimpsed a severed head still in its helmet, washing back and forth in the shadows, a look of sheer terror etched onto its face even in death.

'Scalussen's changed so much so quickly,' Bull said over the wind, making her blink.

'And its people too,' was what she wanted to say, but Mithrid stayed quiet and concentrated on the lurch of her stomach that accompanied every flap of the dragon's wings.

Bull took another stab at conversation. 'So warm out of the mountains. I miss that sometimes.'

'Sometimes,' Mithrid muttered. She knew she was being prickly, but he was the one who had left her. He had been all kinds of content to hide like the rest of the Sirens and forget about the true fight, leaving Scalussen to free Paraia alone. That, she could not forgive.

It was when Kinsprite flashed her a look with bewitching eyes that Mithrid remembered that some dragons could hear thoughts. She steeled her mind and paid attention to the Winter Fortress instead. The top deck of the rebuilt ship smoked and steamed in several places where water mages worked their spells and quenched fires. Mithrid could see rows of dead already forming. Two dozen of Scalussen's own, she counted, before Kinsprite put down where the harbour wall was half-built.

Farden was there with Sipid and a proud-looking Fleetstar. He strode back and forth bellowing orders. A gaggle of six dishevelled and miserable-looking pirate prisoners knelt before him.

'Fine work,' was all Farden said at the sight of Mithrid sliding from Kinsprite's scales.

'That was closer than I'd like to admit—'

'Don't say it,' Farden snapped at her before turning to the pirates. He slammed Gunnir into the sand and a vicious wind knocked the prisoners all flat. 'Now tell me: who in the fuck are you?'

Mithrid wasn't sure whether Farden meant their origins or an explanation for their audacity. She examined the charcoal streaks across the captives' weathered, olive faces and the brands on their foreheads. She could make out the pattern of three sails in the welts.

One finally vomited an answer. 'The Burned Raiders of Mael, lord.'

Farden looked to Sipid, who apparently wasn't aware of the arrow wound in his shoulder. One of the pirates had a dozen cuts that looked like the work of Sipid's knives.

'Mael's south. Before the Cape,' Sipid said.

Farden moved Gunnir closer to the captives. 'And how many more of there are you?'

The pirate with a voice looked out over the smoke-smeared bay and what was left of the pirate fleet. He then counted those slumped next to him.

'Five?'

Farden held Gunnir's point an inch from his nose. 'You wouldn't be lying, would you?'

'Didn't expect you'd have such things as magick spears and dragons,' spat another. This chap was full of rage. 'You'd be kneeling before us if it weren't for that *nayamara*, you cowards.'

Farden lowered Gunnir to tap against the metal guarding the pirate's heart, then began to press. The pirate stubbornly held against the weapon for a moment before his rusty scale plate began to crack and buckle like cold butter. Smoke trailed from the spear's blade, and it was then the pirate's resolve vanished. Pain replaced his sneer as Farden kept pressing. 'You call us cowards? When you skulk on my doorstep and come to pilfer and murder?'

Mithrid expected the mage to stop at any moment, but he did not. Sipid looked on, seemingly pleased. Fleetstar and Bull pursed their lips. Mithrid opened her mouth to speak, but it was led by her head, not her heart. She wanted the men just as dead as Farden did, and she stayed silent.

With a twist of the blade, Gunnir met flesh, and the pirate began to scream.

'Mercy!' cried another, probably fearing the same fate rather than compelled by camaraderie.

'Mercy is for those that deserve it,' Farden uttered.

One quick thrust, and Gunnir pierced the pirate as if he were parchment. Veins black and eyes aglow with white fire, the man slumped to the sand to die.

'Throw the rest of them in the cells. If any complain, throw them to the wasteland,' Farden ordered. He looked around as if to challenge the onlookers, but nobody had a complaint to voice.

Towerdawn lumbered towards them through the turquoise shallows with Nerilan on his back. There was a curve to his fearsome jaws, as though he enjoyed the cold touch of the water. Before he had abandoned them, Bull had told Mithrid how the dragons liked the cold.

Towerdawn bowed his golden head to the mage.

'And here we were preparing to say you are welcome for our much-needed help,' spoke Nerilan, and Farden and Mithrid weren't the only ones who seethed at her. Lerel and Hereni had arrived together, and both were leaning on each other. Mithrid moved to help. Thank Njord their wounds were naught but scratches.

'We didn't need your help,' Farden said with narrowed eyes as Lerel joined his side.

'Evidently not. Not with a keraken at your beck and call,' replied Towerdawn. 'You are full of surprises as always, Farden.'

'I have little to no idea what that is,' Farden admitted. 'And though I'm not the one to blame or thank for its timely appearance, I'm grateful for the luck.'

Nerilan sucked at her sharp teeth. 'Your luck is wearing thin after all your stolen years, Farden. If Scalussen cannot handle a fleet of pirates, how precisely are you hoping to defeat Loki?'

'Perhaps if you hadn't divided Scalussen, you wouldn't have to ask that question, would you?' Farden exploded. Gunnir hummed. Mithrid could feel the power pulsing from him and that spear, and she winced at the teeth of the magick on her skin.

'We have not come to argue,' Towerdawn grumbled, and as he displayed his giant fangs, Farden managed to find some restraint. As did Nerilan.

'I bloody knew it!' came a familiar shout. Elessi had caught up with them. She had Roglurg in tow, and she was still madly waving her sword. 'I told you something was out there, Farden!'

'A keraken, if my tearbook can be trusted,' Towerdawn said again.

'*Nayamara*, in our tongue,' interrupted Sipid, busy readjusting his general's sword pin on the chest of his jerkin.

Elessi stomped her foot. 'Yes. *That*.'

'And what in Hel is it?' asked Mithrid.

Towerdawn half-closed his eyes as he soared through his long memories. 'They were once a creation of Njord, and they were the reason elves and daemons never plied the ancient seas. Without my tearbook, I cannot tell you precisely, but until today, it has been centuries since one has been seen, and few have seen one and lived to tell the tale.'

'Lerel and I saw the same beast mere months ago, on the Cape of No Hope,' said Elessi.

'It's true,' Lerel confirmed. 'It makes me shiver to think of it, but it's true.'

Towerdawn bowed his head. 'And I would not have believed if you had told me yesterday.'

'You and everyone else, Old Dragon,' Elessi chided, hands on hips. She might have beamed with the smile of vindication, but Farden didn't look at all happy with the news. Mithrid knew of his fear of the wide waters, and she imagined that fear had just doubled.

'Can you explain why that thing wants to help us?' Farden asked.

If a dragon could shrug, Towerdawn did so. 'That is not an answer I can give.'

'I can.'

All turned to face Elessi.

'Give me a boat, and I'll find out.' she said, voice sharp as broken flint.

'You want to go chasing that monster?' Farden asked, incredulous.

Elessi raised her chin. 'That I do.'

'You're mad!'

Mithrid sighed. 'That's what I said.'

'Did it sink any of our ships? Did it kill any of our people?' Elessi demanded.

Mithrid checked again, and despite a few glancing blows, every one of the Scalussen warships was still afloat and untouched. Damaged heavily in places, but by pirate fire, not blood-drenched and fanged tentacles. On the edges of the fog, she could see the absent Scalussen warships returning at full sail, their panic almost palpable. It was about time.

Elessi clapped her hands. 'Well?'

'No,' the others chorused.

'You're bloody right! It didn't hurt the *Fury* when we nearly crashed into it, either. That thing – that keraken – is a friend. And gods know we need one right now,' Elessi said, making sure to cast a look to the dragon queen.

Farden disagreed. 'No. It's too dangerous.'

'It's happenin' whether you like it or not.'

Farden stood straighter, playing king. 'I will not discuss this now.'

Nerilan sniffed the air as if it offended her. 'Good, because we have not travelled idly. You wanted to talk, Farden, so let us get this over with.'

Farden waved a formal hand towards the scaffolded spire of the Dawnknell. 'Then after you, Queen.'

Elessi stamped her foot. 'Farden!'

'We will talk of this later, Elessi!'

Mithrid watched the High General storm off, not chasing Farden but instead heading along the beach for the harbour. Mithrid almost went after her, led by curiosity and a sense of defiance. But she had no intention of chasing a monster into the sea. She already had the monster that lived in her nightmares to deal with.

'Where are you going? You are but a child,' asked Queen Nerilan as Mithrid moved to join Farden and Lerel instead. They were deep in conversation, and by the sounds of the muttered yet harsh words, it was about Elessi.

Hereni stepped between them with her head high and hand on her sword.

'Who do you think the assassin attacked, Queen?' Mithrid motioned to her wounded cheek, now exposed after the bandage had been lost somewhere on the beach. 'Me, is who. And as a general of Scalussen and the reason we're all still standing here today—'

'Debatable,' Farden muttered.

'—I have the right to sit on any council I please in *my* city.'

Nerilan raised her head and let Towerdawn lead her away. She never got to see Mithrid's smirk.

❦

The roof of the Dawnknell was destined to be the next council chamber, higher, broader, and with a landing area and archway built for dragons. It had been one of Farden's ideas, to make the Sirens feel welcome. That, and Fleetstar had complained most vociferously about the previous council chamber. For the moment, however, the roof was still an open roof. And seeing as it was a fine evening poking through the mist, it was fit for their council.

'The way you once-Arka build so quickly with magick has always fascinated and impressed me,' rumbled Towerdawn as he looked out across the growth of Scalussen. His horned head and neck roamed from north to south, east to the western ocean.

'You dragons have your tricks with stone, we have ours. What's magick for if not to make things easier?' Farden replied.

Nerilan snorted.

'Speaking of tricks,' Mithrid said.

'Mithrid,' cautioned Farden. 'Feel free to speak, Old Dragon.'

'Your hawk invited us to explain the Siren-born assassin in your midst, and we have come to do precisely that. We regret it has taken so long, but our words will explain that also,' Towerdawn began. 'The attacker's name was Hathear. He lost his dragon to the final battle of Scalussen. She had an egg, but we have discovered that it, too, was lost to the leviathans.'

Nerilan was caught muttering to herself until Towerdawn silenced her with a gnash of his fangs. She strolled about the council, eyeing the mountains as if she wished she had never left them.

'Evidently, Hathear blamed you for his losses. We have also discovered he is not the only one to hold such blame and plan reckless measures. He had allies: friends who schemed to do what Hathear attempted but together, not alone. Your appearance in

Sutherheim prompted Hathear to take matters into his own hands. I will admit, we did not expect one of our own to nurture such hatred. It seems a great rift has opened between our peoples,' said Towerdawn.

'No wonder, when your own queen preaches a similar sermon,' Lerel spoke up. Eyrum, who had stayed silent until now, drummed his nails on the table and rumbled in agreement.

Nerilan bared her teeth. 'I preach nothing so bold as murder.'

'So bold it sounds the kind of thing a queen would have to order.' Mithrid answered.

Nerilan did not hide the hand that rested on the glaive at her side. 'What exactly are you implying, child?'

'Calm, Mithrid,' ordered Farden.

'What?' she spluttered. 'Why are you dancing around the question?'

Mithrid was right. The mage was playing a diplomat when he was a warrior. Even Lerel had to shrug at him, silently agreeing with Mithrid.

Farden made sure to keep his voice calm, as if Nerilan was a wild beast considering a charge. 'I think what Mithrid is asking, Queen, is whether you sent Hathear. Whether the same blame you hold for Scalussen spurred you to choose something… drastic.'

Nerilan, for once, showed control, yet it barely kept her bubbling rage at bay. 'I don't know whether to storm out or to strike you down.'

'Either works for me, Queen,' said Farden without hesitation. He could feel Hereni's magick rising alongside his.

Towerdawn raked his claws across the stone with a squeal that made everyone present shudder. 'Nerilan did no such thing, and it borders on an insult to suggest it! A Siren Queen could not hide such a thought from an Old Dragon, and it is Nerilan who has spent this past week rooting out Hathear's friends and placing them in our newest dungeons.'

Farden spread his fingers across the makeshift table. 'Is that so?'

The queen spoke all too quickly. 'That I have. Three of my own people, if you must know.'

'Why attack me if it's Farden your Sirens blame?' asked Mithrid.

'Because it's not merely Farden they blame. You lit the mountain's fire in the north, did you not? You tell me, *General*,' said Nerilan, eyeing the pin on Mithrid's chest that all present but the queen wore. She would have, if she hadn't been such a prick, as Farden had put it so succinctly.

'More importantly,' Towerdawn boomed, 'we have also decided to help you search for Loki, and we will fight against him should he reappear. We cannot promise much, but you have our aid so long as it does not cost us our dragons. In return, we want your promise.'

Though Nerilan seemed to mouth unflattering words, Farden imperceptibly clenched his fist in celebration. His leverage had worked, even despite Towerdawn's conditions.

'What promise?'

'That it will be the end of war,' said the Old Dragon.

'And that you will destroy the spear once the god lies dead,' added his queen.

Farden bared his teeth. 'Ridiculous. Durnus died for this spear.'

Towerdawn shook his head. 'Power invites challenge, and there will always be challenge so long as a power such as that spear exists. We cannot keep fighting, or none of us will survive. Did you know, Farden, that only eight of our eggs survived Scalussen and the journey south?'

Farden had not known the number was so heartbreakingly few. It was also not an easy secret for a dragon to share.

Eyrum spoke softly. 'It may be years before they are born. Decades more before they can continue their lines. Many centuries before we see the numbers we once knew. And then only if we prosper.'

'Now you know the loss we've suffered,' said Nerilan. 'The pain in Siren hearts.'

Farden nodded solemnly. 'And I know this should bring us together, not drive us further apart.'

'It is too late for that,' said Nerilan. 'You can consider us an ally but not a friend.'

'If that's the help you've come to give, then I'll take it,' Farden replied. It was finer than a slap in the face, as an old School instructor of his used to say.

'And you?' Nerilan stared square at Mithrid.

The girl took a moment to answer even though Farden's eyes bored into her. A gift, they'd been given, and he wasn't about to let Mithrid throw it off the roof of the tower.

But Mithrid seemed distracted. 'Is it the battle still ringing in my ears, or do you hear another bell?' she asked.

Towerdawn was already staring north, hearing it moments before her.

Mithrid was right again: another bell was ringing, but this time in a gatehouse at the far northern edge of Scalussen's spread. It sounded almost half-hearted.

Lerel and Farden rushed to the edge of the wall under the draught of Towerdawn's flapping wings.

'What is it now?' asked Eyrum.

Without a word, Farden clutched Lerel's hand.

'Don't you dare!' she yelped, but it was too late. Farden chimed Gunnir against the stone, and the spell folded the day like a parchment in an uninspired fist.

❦

Soldiers scattered in fright as Farden and Lerel appeared amongst them.

178

Lerel, as always, wanted to chuck her guts in the street, but she held the nausea back and rubbed her watering eyes with the palms of her hands. 'Bastard.'

'Sorry,' Farden replied. 'But after those pirates, I'm not taking any chances.'

Lerel shook her head to chase the dizziness away. 'What's going on?' she demanded of a pair of soldiers. She blinked and realised it was only the one soldier.

'There's a visitor at the gates, and on your orders, King, nobody comes or goes without your say so,' she said.

'Fine work, Sergeant,' said the mage as he strutted towards the gates, Gunnir held flat.

Lerel kept to his side with her sword in her hand. 'Does this visitor have a name or a purpose?'

'All I know is she came out of nowhere on the strangest beast I ever seen. She says she's the Lady of Whispers, which sounds all kinds of suspicious if you ask me, and that she's here because... well.'

'Spit it out, soldier,' Lerel ordered.

'She said she knows you intimately, King.'

Farden looked as if he was trying to remember something while at the same time swallowing some kind of guilt.

'And what does that mean?' asked Lerel, her eyes glued to the mage.

'It means it's Irien. The woman I told you about who helped us in Golikar and in Belerod's camp. I assumed she died at Belerod's hands or in the final battle.' Farden furrowed his brow. 'Open the gates!'

The soldiers went to work at the chains and locks, and with much mechanical clanking, the gates opened slowly.

Behind their yawn stood a woman in a violet cloak and with a sword at her side. The hand upon it looked strange, as if it wore an armour the rest of her didn't wear. Black hair cascaded down a breastplate made of polished wooden plates and to the long, pleated kilt of Golikan green. She was tall and stocky, and she wandered into Scalussen as if she strode into a high-born's party: with a smile on her face and emerald-eyed looks for everyone around her. A crow's skull with a blue gemstone hung around her neck from a chain. Waxy scars decorated one side of her face.

Lerel almost forgot the woman when her beast wandered out of the shadow. It was a brown hog, nearly bigger than a cow, with four jutting tusks in its busy mouth, and for a moment, that was impressive enough. That was until Lerel noticed the tawny wings draped over its bristled back. It grunted with every step, complaining like an old drunkard.

'Farden of Emaneska. The Forever King in the flesh,' the woman said before weaving a gesture of greeting with her strange hand. It looked as though she wore a wooden glove. 'And with the Spear of Gunnir in your hand, no less. Your quest was successful after all, I see.'

'That it was,' said Farden, taking a single step. 'But I'm more interested in why in Hel you're here, so far from Easterealm. I told you in Khandri if ever I saw you again, Lady of Whispers, it would be too soon.'

'You're bastards for leaving me behind,' a wheezing voice interrupted as a vicious wind rocked them. Lerel turned to find Mithrid dropping from Towerdawn's claws, her face a picture of resentment.

'What's going on?' she asked. She hadn't yet noticed the Lady of Whispers.

As Towerdawn shook the sand and folded his wings, Irien approached to offer a formal bow. 'And you must be the Old Dragon of Nelska. It is an honour, golden sire,' Irien spoke.

Towerdawn held his tongue and fixed the newcomer with an amber stare. By the glint in the Old Dragon's eyes, he was searching her soul and mind.

'Irien? We thought you had died in Khandri.' Mithrid surged forwards to clasp the woman's hands. 'And what by Njord's salty arsehole is *that*?'

'Thankfully I was spared, unlike many,' Irien smiled. 'And this, my dear, is a grifabore, a little-known breed from Bvara and a family heirloom. A grumpy soul by the name of Saltlick.'

'I know a certain gryphon who won't be happy about this,' Mithrid replied.

Lerel was tapping her foot. 'Is she who she says she is, Towerdawn?' she whispered.

'She is no god,' said the dragon.

'What are you doing here?' Lerel asked of Irien.

'As you may know, I trade in whispers, my dear, and whispers have led me here.' The smile fell into a sorry face. 'Sadly, I come with fell news. And while I would normally charge for my secrets, all this will cost you is room and board for Saltlick and me.'

'Why is it never good news?' Farden tutted. 'Fine. Get talking.'

Irien took a breath. 'Your nemesis Loki has returned to Krauslung.'

In the corner of her vision, Lerel saw Farden bristle. He went rigid with hatred. Lerel put a hand on his arm, raising Irien's brow.

'He's back,' Farden whispered. It was not a question.

'In the flesh, or whatever it is gods are made of. Plain as parchment and pale as snowfall.'

'And has Krauslung welcomed him?'

Irien prowled around them, looking only to Farden. 'Like a victorious king. The whole of your grey city turned out to celebrate him. He looked so pleased he took on a shine.'

Mithrid could be heard muttering curses.

'When did he return?' Farden's voice was gravel in a fist.

'Since I fled Krauslung. It took me three days with barely a halt to fly this far south.'

'A word, Farden?' Lerel said in a warning tone. Even she could feel the magick burning in him. Farden barely nodded.

'I'll be in our chambers,' he said, weaving his way back to the Dawnknell with Mithrid in tow.

Lerel turned to the Lady of Whispers and clasped her hands. 'Irien, as a guest of Scalussen, I'll show you where you can spend the night.' Lerel made sure to make it singular.

The Lady of Whispers bowed low and came upright with a greasy smile.

Lerel had felt the voice of a dragon in her head only twice. Tonight, as Towerdawn's words boomed in her head, it made thrice.

Be warned, Admiral. I cannot read her.

The problem was, neither could Lerel.

CHAPTER 12
THE LURE OF REVENGE

If you prick us, do we not bleed? If you beat us, do we not bruise? If you poison us, do we not die? And if you wrong us, shall we not want for revenge?
BY THE LITTLE-KNOWN PLAYWRIGHT SNORRIKSPAR

With Mithrid escorting a worryingly silent Farden to his chambers, Lerel saw to Irien. She examined her closely as they walked, from her scars to her pristine travelling boots.

Irien spoke first. 'You must be the Forever Queen to the Forever King. Lerel, I believe?'

'High Admiral Lerel, and you're the one who apparently knows Farden intimately,' Lerel ordered, keeping the stranger at her side and her hand on her sword.

Irien played at conversation, running her wooden gauntlet across a wall. The more Lerel stared, the more it looked as if it were part of her and not a kind of armour. She wanted time to sniff the woman out, and so she led Irien in unnoticeable circles through the streets before they reached the Dawnknell's hallways.

'Impressive, to have built this new home so fast.'

'Scalussen used to be Arka, and the Arka came from the sea. They learned to build fast as they moved around the coasts. Arka architects learned to build even faster once their feet stayed on the ground and mastered magick.'

'You are not Arka?'

'No, I am Scalussen. And I was Paraian before that, born of the soil and sand you stand on.

'Yes,' said Irien, looking down at her feet. 'There certainly is a lot of it in your city, dear.'

'And you: you came all the way from Easterealm to warn Farden about Loki?'

'That I did. I owe Farden somewhat of a debt, after all.'

'For betraying him to the warlord Belerod.' Lerel showed her hand.

'I see Farden continues to be truthful and honest. Farden might have upended my life in Dathazh, but he also spared it when I was forced to betray him. I could think of nobody more fitting to hold the spear of my ancestor Sigrimur.'

'He has a habit of upending lives.' Lerel stopped dead at a doorway deep beneath the Dawnknell's roots. It was not a lofty room for an esteemed guest, it was a prison cell. A clean one with a cot and running water, but still a cell.

'You must be joking, my dear,' Irien said

It was not something so crass as jealousy that made Lerel cold and careful with her. Farden's heart was hers and they were promised to each other in unspoken words. Rather, it was Irien's words and her subtle rattling of her sword. Perhaps it was her jealousy, not Lerel's, that vexed her.

'I'm afraid with the arrival of the Sirens, this is all we have,' said Lerel, barely managing to sound regretful.

Irien raised her chin, sweeping into the cell all the same. 'If you say so. Besides, I saw worse on the ship out of Khandri.'

'Tell me, how did you find Scalussen so quickly?' asked Lerel.

'How do you think I got my name, dear? I travelled to Krauslung to see if Farden had reclaimed his true throne. There I heard tell of scared pirates and an army marching north through Empire land in Paraia. Didn't take much to figure it out, if you think a little deeper, dear. It becomes harder and harder to hide in this world, even in this large and – I must say – mostly barren country. Here I was thinking Khandri was hot.'

'Takes a better eye to see its riches, I suppose,' countered Lerel.

'Does Loki know?'

'Know what?'

'Where we are?'

'I did not tell him, if that's what you're asking,' chuckled Irien. 'Why do I get the impression you suspect me of something, Admiral?'

'Because of the Old Dragon. We know you're not Loki in disguise, but he cannot read you to know whether or not you're lying, and that doesn't sit well with me. How do you know Loki?'

Irien replied with a smirk. 'I do not know him. I merely saw him from afar. Even if Farden had not mentioned Loki, I have my eyes and ears, and they all know of the saviour of Krauslung and how he has taken up the mantle of the chaos Emperor Malvus wrought in Easterealm.'

'Sleep well, Lady Irien,' answered Lerel coldly. 'We'll be locking the door for your safety. There are assassins about, and Loki is not above using liars and spies. Wouldn't want to put you in danger, would we?'

'As we say in Golikar, don't tread too heavily on the messenger's neck for the bad tidings she brings.'

'Unfortunately for you, you're in Paraia now.'

With the door closed, Lerel placed her hands to the carved runes to make them glow. She needed no magick to activate the locking spell.

Silent as snakes, the two mages that had been following them the entire time emerged from the shadow.

'She is not to leave that cell,' whispered Lerel. 'If she tries anything, restrain her and bring her to me. And please, don't be shy about it.'

'Aye, High Admiral.'

The Lady of Whispers could wait until the morning. Lerel had a suspicion that more than whispers were needed tonight.

❦

Eyrum and Mithrid stood outside Farden's door like guards grumpily awaiting their replacements.

Lerel looked from one to the other. 'Tell me he's still in there. If he's left—'

Mithrid cut through her worry. 'He's still here, but he's dangerously quiet.'

'You better not have put any ideas in his head.'

'I think Farden's mind is already full of them,' Mithrid said coldly.

Lerel ached in a dozen places from the battle with the pirates, but the pain could wait. She pushed open the door with her fists.

For a moment, Farden was nowhere to be seen in the room. All the candles were dead. Only the light of Scalussen beyond the window showed the shape of the mage, still as stone.

Lerel sighed. 'I'm sorry he came back.'

'He was always going to return,' Farden murmured.

'You're worrying me. Tell me what's on your mind.'

'Everything you would hate to hear.'

'You can't go to him. You know that.'

Farden growled without words.

Lerel put her fists to her temples. 'We've been over this, Farden. It's what Loki wants: to force your hand and show you to Emaneska as the destroyer, not the protector. Krauslung already hates us. The Sirens blame us. Easterealm is up in arms. Loki will get what he wants if you go to him. It is a trap. Pure and simple. And Irien, she could be—'

'Where is she?'

'In a locked room until I figure her out.'

'You don't trust her.'

'Do you?'

Farden snorted. 'I did once.'

'And what if Loki is using her? She betrayed you once, she can do it again.'

'He doesn't know she exists.'

'You sure about that, Farden? Would you bet our lives on it?'

'Every moment Loki draws breath, we risk the world. It's a finer bet to kill him,' said Farden, rising to stalk the room. 'I can be subtle. I can kill Loki in the darkness of his chambers without him becoming a martyr. You remember I used to be an assassin, right?'

'And what path did that take you down, Farden?'

'The world will forget him and be a better place for it.'

'How do you even propose to kill him? Do you even know that you can?'

'There's a reason he feared this spear. I think Gunnir's pointy end will fit nicely in his skull.'

'And are you sure that would work?'

Farden clanged Gunnir on the floor in a moment of anger. 'Let's ask the goddess that's been skulking in the shadows all night, shall we? Evernia? Care to show your face?'

Lerel felt a cold chill run through her as she spotted the faint outline of a woman standing in the deepest shadows. 'What the fuck?' she said, skidding back against the table and reaching for her sword.

'I don't think you two have been introduced,' Farden muttered. 'Lerel, Evernia, goddess of magick and manipulation.'

'Goddess,' Lerel said, immediately bowing.

'High Admiral Lerel, daughter of Qour and Kamara.'

Lerel was speechless. She had never known her parents' names.

Farden paced around them. 'I imagine you know Loki is back in Krauslung.'

'Heimdall has heard the whispers.'

'Well? Can Loki be killed?' asked Farden.

Evernia emerged into the light. At first she was a sketch drawn in gossamer thread, but with every step her form took shape, becoming something solid even though her edges seemed to drift and smoke. Evernia's eyes bored into both of them, moving almost independently, slitted as a lizard's but filled with swirling dark iron. Her obsidian hair floated around her head as if she were submerged. 'Though his power grows in belief and in blasphemous ways, we believe he can be killed. Call it hope.'

'See? Do you really want to trust solely on hope, Farden?' Lerel asked, but Farden scrunched his eyes.

'I've been pinning everything on hope and on luck since you first curled up on my bed as a cat. What do you mean by blasphemous, Evernia?'

'Loki delighted in informing me he consumes souls as the daemons do. It is how he has grown so quickly. It makes his power unpredictable,' Evernia said. 'But there is a way we can be sure.'

Farden thumped his spear once more. 'Gunnir. Durnus knew it threatened you gods once before, and it can do it again. This is the weapon that kills Loki. It has to be.'

The goddess pursed her lips. 'There is another way.'

'Spit it out, Evernia.'

'Instead, use Gunnir to return our kind to our true forms.'

'And why,' asked Farden, leaning forwards in his chair, 'would I want to add more gods to this world when one is already a threat to all who draw breath?'

Evernia's presence grew by a foot. Her edges became steel wire. 'Because we are not Loki. We do not consume souls, and with the power we have gathered shepherding souls into Haven and Hel, and the renewed belief of the world seeing their gods walk the earth again, we have a chance to defeat him together.'

Farden barely waited for her to finish. 'No.'

'Farden…' Lerel whispered.

'I said no. You gods have used us like pawns far too many times before. You used Ilios' dreams to control my uncle. You used Durnus to take Vice. And you used me to kill Malvus. Once Loki is dead, would you vanish to the stars and Haven again, to leave us in peace?'

Evernia did not answer.

'This world needs to be free of its gods and its daemons,' said Farden sternly. 'Free of meddling.'

Evernia shook her head like a disapproving mother. 'You dare say such things to those who created you.'

'I dare,' Farden said, 'because nobody else will. And you should know me better by now.'

Evernia retreated into the darkness without a word.

'Is she gone?'

It looked as if Farden consulted the spear. 'She has.'

'Evern—Shit. How you have the gall to speak to the gods like that, Farden, I will never know,' Lerel whispered, appalled. 'And if you won't listen to them, why in Hel did I think you would listen to any of us?'

'I'm trying to find a way for it not to hurt you,' he said, 'and to avoid the look on your face you're wearing right now. I've made my decision.'

Lerel withdrew from him, shaking her head. 'Sometimes I wonder why you even bother to ask people for their counsel. Don't expect me not to shout, "I told you so" if this backfires in your face, *King*.'

Lerel kicked the door so viciously that Mithrid and Eyrum looked ready to fight when she emerged.

'Good luck convincing him otherwise,' she said, already halfway down the stairs.

'Convincing him of what?'

'Farden?' Mithrid called into the darkness, padding like a stalking cat. 'You wouldn't be thinking what I think you're thinking, would you?'

'You get smarter every day, Mithrid Fenn,' said Farden, in a quiet and dangerous voice. 'Loki dies tonight.'

Mithrid saw a sharp shadow jab to the ceiling and felt magick flood the room as if a geyser had erupted unexpectedly. 'Wait!' she yelled.

Eyrum might have hesitated, but Mithrid lunged for the mage. She managed to seize the cold armour of his leg before she was wrapped in blinding white fire.

Towerdawn and the rest of the council stood at the foot of the Dawnknell, arms or claws crossed and every brow furrowed.

'Where's Mithrid?' Hereni asked. 'What's going on?'

'A woman from Golikar came with news that Loki has come back to Krauslung. Farden wants to end him once and for all on his own, the fool,' Lerel muttered.

'And what if it is a trap?' growled the Old Dragon.

'That's exactly what I said. Even the goddess Evernia warned him against it and asked to be freed from Haven so the gods could join our fight.'

Nerilan throttled her glaive. Her tone was tight, an uncharacteristic whisper. 'What did you say?'

'With any luck, Farden will come to his senses by dawn and we—'

A searing white light pierced the evening fog, bursting from the windows above them.

'That bastard!' cursed Lerel.

This time, Nerilan made sure everybody could hear her. 'Should we be surprised, after all these years?'

'Right!' Lerel said, dusting her hands. 'Can somebody tell me where Elessi is before I strangle something?'

Towerdawn hadn't taken his eyes off the tower. 'Last I saw, she was heading for your underground libraries. Why?'

'If Farden wants to take matters into his own hands, then so will we.'

'Where's Mithrid?' Lerel heard Hereni mutter before she stormed for the libraries.

❧

Memories floated on the breeze, heavy with the char of some distant campfire beyond the peaks of the dunes. Rock and sand rasped beneath his feet as he scanned the empty horizon. The coal blanket glittered with stars. Farden wondered when he'd last paused to stare at them, lost in the dune sea of Paraia.

A spluttering made him jerk around. A mess of fire-red hair and black armour struggled at his feet. A white hand was fixed to his right greave.

'Mithrid!? You stupid fool. That could have killed you!'

Mithrid reared upright with a face full of sand. Spitting and cursing, she threw out a hand to Farden. The mage seized her hand and froze as a glimpse of fire momentarily replaced the desert. He almost let her go, but instead wrenched her upright.

'I wanted to do this alone.'

'By all the gods and their arseholes,' she gasped, blinking hard.

'Nice. Learn that from Sipid?'

'What are you doing, Farden? Lerel told you this was a bad idea.'

'Eavesdropping's a dangerous habit.'

'I told you before: you really should start shutting doors properly.'

Farden did not answer, distracted by the faint gleam of the distant fire.

'You really think Irien's been sent by Loki?' asked Mithrid.

'I can't tell. The woman's an enigma.'

'Then why are you taking this risk? Alone?'

'Because I have faith in my power, this spear, and that whatever trap Loki's set, I can reduce to ashes,' Farden told her firmly. 'Why are *you* here? Why'd you follow me?'

'For the same reason as you: Loki needs to die, and I want to have a hand in it. I told you in the training yards I would be ready next time we faced him, and I am,' said Mithrid, chin high and a smirk on her face. 'Besides, you'll need me like you did last time. Makes no sense to leave your most powerful weapon behind.'

'Mhm,' Farden mumbled. Mithrid was interminable when she was right. Almost right.

'Speaking of, where is here?' she asked. 'This isn't Krauslung.'

'Astute.' Farden walked around the edges of the skinny plateau, where the wind had carved wavering patterns in the sandstone. 'This is the dune sea, and this is where I found my uncle after he was banished.'

'Tyrfing,' Mithrid remembered, clapping some sand out of her ear. 'What's that whistling noise?'

Farden smiled. 'Follow me.'

The mage led her down magick-hewn steps into the relative warmth of the rock. He ran his hands across the sandstone, the Scalussen metal ringing with every bump and divot. Empty rooms yawned like toothless mouths.

The desert had reclaimed much of Tyrfing's sanctuary, sneaking through the windows and broken skylights and forcing them to climb over mounds of it.

'Tyrfing took all his treasures with him when he returned to Krauslung. Ironically, without his prosperous reign as arkmage, the Arka wouldn't have been able to conquer so much of Emaneska.'

Mithrid was poking at some graffiti: Paraian runes scratched with a rusty knife. 'I feel like you're getting sentimental on me. Is there a reason for this stroll into the past? And what in Hel is that whistling? It can't be the wind.'

'Loki's been eating souls, and that probably gives him all kinds of power we don't know about. If I jump straight into Krauslung, he'll likely feel me or the spear somehow. If the others are right and Loki wants to make me a villain, then I will be nothing but a shadow, and Loki will die without fanfare or procession. Like an old bastard in his bed.'

Mithrid squinted, waiting for Farden to fill the gap of how they were going to get from the dune sea to Krauslung, he strolled to the rough doors at the end of the corridor. Thieves had been there in the decades since Farden. The door had been hacked with blades and the handles broken. Farden put his fists against the wood and pushed.

Wind and whistling buffeted them.

Ilios stood proud beneath a roof open to the stars, beak ajar and a song pouring from him. The circular room carried and stacked the notes, making a haunting whine that faded with their entrance.

Ilios' eyes gleamed at the sight of them, and he trilled sharply. The wreckage of barrels and chests beneath him crunched as he flexed his claws.

'This used to be his home,' Farden explained. 'He's the sentimental one, not me.'

'How did you know he was here?'

'I dreamed it, of course,' said Farden.

Mithrid curled her lip. 'Of course.'

'Ilios can make you dream, Mithrid. He can also dream the future. Just a few of the tricks a gryphon has up their… wing,' Farden said as he ran his gauntlets across the gryphon's feathers and made Ilios shiver. 'At least, he used to. The growth of magick has dampened his powers. You can't dream a future if it's too unpredictable.'

Mithrid didn't look whatsoever pleased by that tidbit.

'All Ilios can dream now is flashes, and that's what he showed me. Now he's going to take us to Krauslung. Don't tell Fleetstar I said this, but there's nobody faster than Ilios. Not to mention he's much less conspicuous,' said Farden. 'And if you should change your mind about this mission, then we can leave you in Troacles or Skap.'

Mithrid laughed. 'Nice try, but my mind's as made as yours. I'm ready,' she said, patting the god's blade at her waist. 'Loki dies on the morrow.'

Farden couldn't have been prouder. With a kneel of the gryphon and a jump, he sat astride Ilios. Mithrid once again reached out her hand and, for a moment, Farden hesitated. She reached further, and Farden tested his metal against hers. No flame was glimpsed this time, and the mage pulled her up onto Ilios' spine.

With a thunderclap of the gryphon's wings and a storm of sand and detritus, Ilios tore into the glistening sky.

CHAPTER 13
UNLUCKY FOR SOME

There were once many gods in the world, and those that remain do not solely linger above our heads. We speak of Evernia and Thron and Njord, yet more than their sparks fell with the first morning. Others fell across the plane of this world. Thousands, perhaps. Scoff you might, but why is it that in Paraia we have different stars and different gods? Neringaë and Bezarish, to name but a few. Over time we have forgotten the myriads that are and once were, and that not all fought or sacrificed as ours did. Other, lesser gods did not follow them to the sky. Other, lesser gods breathe still. Belief is a powerful thing.
EXCERPT FROM THE NOTES OF SHATTERED ISLAND SCHOLAR
SUNPRET KIRAN

Warbringer dug her nail into the table, carving the groove deeper each time. Out of Scalussen's generals, only she and the two head witches had come to council. A half-dozen organisers and architects and scroll-scribblers had come to join them. They huddled at the far end of the table, faces full of worry and flinching every time Warbringer moved. And when they weren't gawping at the minotaur, the witches' birds made them duck and cover whenever they raced about the room.

'Where are the others?' Warbringer asked.

The bravest pink-flesh half-rose from his chair. 'We hoped you could answer that, m–madam, as to why they are not here.'

'Madam?' she growled.

'W–warbringer.'

'Better.' The plump man to his left would have made a fine meal in another time, another place.

Warbringer had not come to speak to these bug-eyed pink-fleshes. She had come to speak to Farden. 'Where are the others?' she repeated.

The plump and delicious-looking one had a voice. 'All we know is that High General Elessi is with Admiral Lerel, Sipid, and Ko-Tergo. They said there was something of importance in the Jar Khoum libraries.'

'And where is Farden?'

'We don't know.'

Pink-fleshes be cursed. With a dire creak of her chair, Warbringer stood. The old witch Wyved and her speaker Peryn did the same, and they left without another word.

Warbringer's stomach rumbled persistently as she tested the stairs of the Dawnknell. Wyved and her pet followed. Several of the witch-birds landed on her shoulders and horns, and no amount of staring at them coerced them to move. Warbringer imagined eating one was not the best idea and grumbled at the witches instead.

'You feel forgotten also, witch?' she asked.

Wyved looked to Peryn, who answered for her as always. 'That we do. This is our home, too. We should have been told of whatever is going on, never mind had a say.'

'It may not be home forever. But that is not talk for now,' Warbringer grumbled solemnly. For now, the minotaur had a tunnel to face. 'Come.'

❦

Warbringer stared at the hole and ground her teeth.

The Jar Khoum survived by making their homes look like any old rabbit warren, but peel back the ferns and sand-painted doors, and one would discover a finely-hewn tunnel into the earth beneath the scrub and palm forest. A hole was all it was. A pit. A gutter. And it was not wide enough for her liking.

'Afraid of the dark, Warbringer?' asked the younger witch.

'No. Small places.'

'I bet they're more afraid of you making them bigger,' Peryn said.

Witch-drivel, but it somehow annoyed Warbringer enough to stomp her way down the ramp and into the dark. The witches and their birds followed, the latter twittering and attacking the walls mid-flight for worms.

Jars filled with glowing blue moss provided a pale and gloomy path of light. Warbringer decided that wasn't enough and sparked a flint on Voidaran over a nearby rack of torches. She took three in her great hands and forged ahead.

'We know light spells, you know,' Peryn offered.

'Last thing I want in dark is magick.'

Handfuls of Jar Khoum filtered between tunnel mouths, dragging baskets of soil and timber behind them. Others ran sacks along rails of palm wood. It was clever, but Warbringer couldn't have given a shit. Her hide was itchy. The air was too thick, like hot honey.

'How far?' she asked.

'Not far.'

'Say more, witch.'

Peryn didn't say a word and instead took her deeper into the earth by way of carved steps. Stone and wood columns started to replace the soil and timber. Warbringer hadn't a clue the Jar Khoum were such fine builders, but the descent was more distracting. The steps led to more steps. And then some more.

'Witch—'

'And we're here,' Peryn said with a low bow, then waved her hand towards an arch clearly carved by Scalussen hands instead of Jar-Khoum. It meant the ceilings were tall enough that she didn't scrape the ceiling with her horns, thank Dotharadine. Within, more of the pale blue moss-light beckoned.

A frowning Sipid came rushing from the archway. 'Put those fucking torches out! We can't afford a single spark down here.'

Warbringer shrugged, bristling at being told what to do by such a little hairless mite. After reminding herself she couldn't eat the Jar Khoum's prince, she put the torches in the dusty floor and stamped them out with a hoof. 'Happy, little grub?'

'You're a fucking grub,' Sipid muttered fearlessly before marching back into the libraries. Warbringer and the witches followed him into the gloom and the thankfully broader spaces between towering shelves. They were even loftier than her, and the pink-fleshes needed little ladders to reach the top shelves. And yet the air of the libraries was thicker than that of the tunnels, and stank of book and scroll and the salt of a thousand ocean winds. Warbringer wrinkled her snout.

It was all the knowledge that survived the voyage south and the serpents Warbringer had heard tell of. Farden had been ecstatic Durnus' libraries had survived and had bargained with the Jar Khoum for a new home for this mountain of parchment and paper.

Figures of bristling hair stalked the shadows between the shelves. As always, the lycans devoted themselves to protecting the library and the inner workings of Scalussen. Ko-Tergo of the snowmads walked amongst them, clicking in a strange tongue. Warbringer liked him purely because he nearly matched her girth and stature and fought like a wild thing. He would have made a fine minotaur.

The piebald lycan Roglurg stood beside Elessi, closer than her own shadow. She whispered something to the lycan, and he slunk off to a nearby shelf, claws rifling through tomes.

Lerel had spread a dozen maps over a table and was placing thick gemstones and scraps of parchment at specific places.

'What is this?' asked Warbringer, while the witches' birds went straight to work hopping over the shelves and tables and picking at the carcasses of dead moths.

The minotaur's voice would have given anyone a fright, especially as she loomed from the shadows, but the admiral and generals barely gave her a look and a grunt. Sipid went right back to passing Lerel tomes and translating anything too ancient or southern for Elessi.

'You saw the thing in the bay when the pirates attacked, right?' asked Lerel.

'Keraken,' Elessi corrected.

'I am not blind,' answered Warbringer. She had, however, been shocked, and that was as close to fear as minotaurs can come. It was sort of a mild concern, but in clan terms, that was impressive.

'Well, we're trying to find it.'

Warbringer spun her warhammer in her hands. Sipid didn't seem to like the sound it made. 'I am not blind, but you gone mad.'

'That's what they all say,' muttered Elessi. 'I'm wagerin' it's a friend. An ally. It's saved us twice now, and I want to find out why. Seein' as Farden has forbidden me a ship, we're usin' books and scrolls and hearsay and all kinds of nonsense to track it down instead.'

Peryn and the High Crone looked far more intrigued. They approached the table. The old witch's blackened and tattooed fingers spread across a scroll. 'And what have you discovered?' asked Peryn.

'A pattern.' Lerel prodded the maps.

'Go on,' said Peryn.

'The pirate called the keraken a *nayamara*, which is a Paraian word shared by the Jar Khoum. It took us half the day to find any mentions of either, but we found one in an old Skap Island fairytale translated into Commontongue. It talks of a fearsome beast called *nayamagundr*, known as a *tharkun* to the "third ones", whoever they are. But from the way it speaks of a beast with a shell and long tentacles stealing children from windows, it has to be the same.'

Elessi wrenched open a circular book covered in fish scales and pointed to a line of foreign but strangely familiar runes. 'That led us to this old Arfell tome which has the same word: tharkun. It's a translation guide and a terrible one at that, but we think it hints that keraken and tharkun are dark elvish words. Daemons and gods came first and second, and elves came third, right?'

'Makes sense, though it doesn't say what they are,' whispered Lerel.

Peryn was watching Wyved waggle her fingers. 'The High Crone says *tha'arkun* is a word of the north,' she whispered. 'One she hasn't heard in a long time. It means something like "great beast".'

'Great beast,' Warbringer murmured, following the witches to loom over the mess of script and runes.

'Greater than you or I, I'm afraid, Warbringer,' said Ko-Tergo.

Elessi drummed the desk with her palms. 'That's as far as we've got. Problem is, we don't have Emaneska's finest scholar at hand. Durnus would have solved this riddle in his sleep.'

Warbringer flicked the pages of a leather-bound book over one by one and peered at the scrawl, lines and lines of it faded by time. Many were crossed out in charcoal. She focused on one that was clearer and immediately twisted her head. 'This is strange.'

'What?'

'This the name of the god of my kin. Dotharadine,' Warbringer said.

Lerel looked confused. 'You have your own god?'

'You can read?' asked Sipid.

Warbringer flashed sharp teeth. She swivelled her warhammer and made it moan again, and her claws tapped at worn letters that matched those on the page. 'Dotharadine.'

In her excitement, Elessi grabbed the book from under the minotaur's claws. "Revenge" by Elivimendez. It's in a strange dialect that looks like some kind of rough elvish. Can you read more, Warbringer?'

'Little. Only recognise this word.'

'Peryn? Wyved?'

'It's not our runes either, but...' Peryn stabbed another word with a finger. 'Tell me that doesn't look like it says tharkun.'

Lerel dragged over the fish-scale book and began to leaf through it. It took an age to match up each rune, but gradually, she started to spit out words. 'It's a list of beasts. It looks like Elivimendez was hunting them, but they are called "Great Ones", not great beasts.'

'What does this say below Dotharadine?' asked Elessi.

'*Zath*–something–*urla*… Apparently that means mouths of darkness.'

Elessi tapped her head as if tempting a memory to rise up. 'I remember Durnus and Farden talkin' long ago of elf wells and manuals for summonin' all kinds of nightmares from the other side. Old Lord Vice summoned a hydra from an elf well, and if I remember right, they called it the Mouths of Darkness. See? Eavesdroppin' has its uses.'

Lerel went through the list one by one. 'This one means something called Garyon of the Burnt South, wherever that is. This one I recognise: Shareste. It's an old fairytale about a rathcata, a giant whose sword supposedly rests in Belephon.'

Peryn's nails underscored another column of runes. 'Each has another name next to it. Is it a place?'

'Every prey has a nest,' said Warbringer.

'There!' Elessi yelped. 'The *keraken.* What does the word next to it say? Magre?'

Sipid repeated the word over and over until Warbringer flicked him. 'Sounds like a Jar Khoum word for a haunted cave from the old stories. Don't know where it is.'

Lerel thumped the table. 'Full bloody circle.'

'And just where are we going to find this haunted cave?' asked Ko-Tergo.

Elessi clicked her fingers. 'Let's ask the pirates Farden left alive.'

Bewilderingly, without another word, the whole group made a rush for the exit and fresh air. Warbringer might have been the last to follow, but she was the first to escape, shouldering her way to the light and the fresh air. She hid her deep breath. *Thank Dotharadine.*

The various pink-fleshes followed their excitement towards the Dawnknell. Unfortunately, the prisons were far too similar to the Jar Khoum tunnels.

Door after door flew past as they searched for the pirates. Spears of light divided the corridors, bouncing from mirrors above. Content to watch the bustle, Warbringer hung back, and that was when she heard the thudding.

'Am I to be released?'

Warbringer snuffled at the door and scented something familiar. 'Who there?'

'Is that you, minotaur? Warbringer?'

'Pink-flesh of whispers?'

'Irien, yes.'

'Why you here?'

'Did Farden not tell you?'

'Farden is gone.'

There came a pause.

'Then will his woman let me out any time soon? I didn't think this was how an old friend and kindly messenger would be treated in Scalussen.'

Warbringer stomped to where Lerel was having four pirates heaved into a pool of light.

'I want to know where the keraken lives,' she demanded.

The pirates looked like marsh-frogs ogling a bloodmoon.

Lerel seized one by the neck. 'The *nayamara*. Magre. You heard of it?'

Another pirate spluttered with laughter. 'I know you'll die if you go there.'

'Why?'

'Because everybody does. Every soul who plies the waves north of this pitiful bay knows of Magre. It's a cave, biggest you've ever seen. Full of foul air, they say. Full of *nayamara*, says I.'

'Where is it?'

'You want me to draw you a map? Ha! You bitches ain't as scary as your mage king, you know.'

Elessi and Lerel both drew their swords and put them either side of his neck. 'Sure about that?' asked Elessi.

Lerel tickled his chin with her blade. 'Show us on a map, and we'll let you live.'

The pirate pondered. 'You let me go, and we got a deal.'

One of his shipmates quickly interrupted. 'All of us.'

'Nah,' said the pirate. 'Don't care about them. As long as I go free. That's all I want.'

'Feckless gack!' his comrades shouted. They were coaxed into calm by the guards' spears and a spark spell crackling close to their faces.

'Bargain?' asked the self-serving worm of a man.

Lerel clapped her hands. 'Bargain. Put the others back and bring this bastard to a map.'

Warbringer lowered Voidaran to block Lerel's path before she could follow with the others.

'What are you doing, Warbringer?' she asked.

'Why is whisper woman in your dungeon?'

Lerel spoke like the rustle of a leaf. 'She came to tell us Loki had returned to Krauslung, but I don't trust her. Neither should you, after she betrayed you to Belerod.'

'Why did Farden not tell me?'

'He left for Krauslung last night with Mithrid and nobody else.'

Warbringer bared her teeth, voice dangerously low. 'Am I not allowed my revenge?'

'And what about mine? Or Elessi's? Farden spurned us all.'

The minotaur growled.

'What did you need Farden for?' asked Lerel.

'It matters not, because it does not matter to him,' said Warbringer as she lowered the hammer. 'Question your pirate.'

Lerel did just that, and Warbringer followed her up the far-too-small steps to the nearest room of maps.

The pirate was shoved against the table by Ko-Tergo, and when the fellow whirled to challenge the yetin and found a wall of white hair and iron muscle staring down at him, he quickly thought wiser of it.

The pirate perused the maps for a moment before sullenly pointing out a cove a hands-breadth north from Sanctuary Bay. Almost two thousand miles away, past the Falcon's Spur and where the ocean bit deep into Paraia.

'There. Magre. Lair of that gack that cheated the battle. Now let me go, as you bloody promised.'

Lerel took her sword and cut the bindings around the man's wrists. He was on the cusp of sneering when Lerel pushed him into the arms of Ko-Tergo. 'Throw this scum back into his cell, where his shipmates can thank him personally for his treachery,' she ordered.

'No, wait! You bitch! Fuck you! I hope you catch a pox!'

Lerel crossed her arms as the door slammed and turned to Elessi. 'There it is, Elessi. Now what?'

'You thinkin' what I'm thinkin'?'

The admiral narrowed her eyes. 'I'll get us a ship. A fast one.'

'You really want to seek this beast out?' Peryn asked, face ashen as she followed in Lerel and Elessi's wake. These pink-fleshed loved to rush about.

'What would Farden—' Sipid began to say, but Lerel cut him off with a hiss.

'Farden made his decision. We have made ours.'

Peryn had more concerns. 'You really think this creature could be an ally?'

Elessi threw her a look that said nothing and everything in one glance.

'If for some reason Farden can't kill Loki, then we'll need other answers. If Farden wins, then we'll at least have a new friend,' Lerel said, before spying Warbringer's attention had shifted. Thick shapes had appeared around a building's corner. Her own bloodmongers stood by to watch. Thenerean's brow was as furrowed as a field.

Warbringer felt a touch on her wrist and growled on instinct. She found Lerel staring up at her.

'I'm leaving you and Eyrum in charge. Keep an eye on Irien, and don't let Towerdawn and Nerilan leave. We need the protection,' she said.

Warbringer kept her words of concern to herself. They wouldn't have changed the stubborn mind of a pink-flesh anyway.

'I'm sorry that Farden left you behind,' Lerel said, clasping her hand. 'It doesn't mean he doesn't care about us. He just cares more about Loki, and that's difficult for those close to him.'

Warbringer bowed her head to that, proven wrong. She let the fuss and bustle continue to the wharfs without her. She only stirred from her staring when she felt hoofs on the ground behind her.

'Where do they go?' Thenerean asked of her in their own tongue.

'They go to find another answer to the problem of Loki, should Farden fail. A great beast of the sea.'

Thenerean shook his horns and the jewels dangling from them. 'Dotharadine. It won't be the little god that kills us, it will be these pink-fleshes and their madness.'

Warbringer snorted. 'You think I would let that happen, Bloodmonger?'

Thenerean bared a smile.

'Let them find their beast. We have our own to protect us,' Warbringer said, shifting Voidaran in her claws.

'When will the great sacrifice be complete?' another bloodmonger whispered.

Warbringer put her hands to the face of Voidaran where a skull had been carved. A haunting groan traced her claw's touch. 'We will know soon enough if the mage kills the god.'

❦

Within an hour, a ship had been claimed and outfitted for the expedition. Not a dreadnought, but a small, sturdy, and somewhat fat-bottomed warship stolen from Galadaë. Usually Scalussen changed the name of the Arka ships to change their luck, but this one had stuck: the *Undaunted,* and it seemed to fit the idea of pursuing an ancient beast that could snap a ship in two as easily as a child broke a twig. Even a ship with an iron spine and ribs like the *Undaunted.*

With oars crashing and night-black Scalussen sails slack and waiting, Lerel drove the ship towards the endless blue without hesitation. Although she had plenty of it in her mind, she kept her body moving without question. It had been far too long since her hands grasped a ship's wheel.

Elessi braved the winds at the railing beside her. 'You think we're mad?'

Lerel took a moment to think, but Ko-Tergo beat her to it. He had insisted on joining them, and Lerel suspected he had a need to see a so-called great one for himself. To prove himself sane, perhaps, as Elessi wanted.

'Utterly,' Ko-Tergo replied, making Elessi grin.

'Then again, as Farden would no doubt tell us,' said Lerel, 'madness with good intentions is a fine thing.'

The yetin liked those words. 'Luck and fate seem to smile on that.'

'Magre,' Elessi whispered. 'How long to get there?'

'Maybe two or three days assuming this ship lives up to its reputation. And assuming there's no trouble on the way.'

Elessi and Ko-Tergo looked confused. 'Days? How so quickly?' the yetin asked.

Lerel tapped her nose as the *Undaunted* bucked in a wave. Her ram-pointed prow clashed with the currents beyond the still calm of Sanctuary Bay.

'Stow the oars, you sweaty bastards!' Lerel bellowed to the crew who'd volunteered for their mission. Fifty familiar faces, equally as mad or as brave or as stupid as they were and happy to let time tell them which. Most of the grizzled faces had sailed with Lerel since the days before they suffered gods and their sadistic plans. The dozen mages and soldiers who usually formed their guard had insisted on coming along as well, though Lerel had to wonder whether that was due to loyalty or fear of Farden. Lerel hoped for loyalty and took the protection without complaint.

'It's the wind's turn now!' she crowed.

Lerel shoved the wheel starboard so the *Undaunted* followed the currents north. No sooner had the black sails caught the wind did the ship lurch with speed and sent several deckhands sprawling. The wind mages were barely needed.

'Gods' balls!' cried Lerel. She had expected speed, but not this much.

'Is this what you meant?' cried Elessi, to which Lerel nodded rapidly.

It wasn't just her name and stoutness that was the reason the *Undaunted* had been stolen. It was said she had another trick in her hull, too, the mark of the genius of an unknown Paraian shipsmith.

Wings were the only way to describe them: iron and oak wings curved like a vulture's pinions and protruding from the keel in four places, fore and aft on heavy struts. So far, the wings had been something to gawk and scoff at, but this was the *Undaunted*'s first test, and she passed with flying colours, pun thoroughly intended.

Lerel wasn't sure if it was the magick in the runes carved into their oak or their thick and thin shape, but the wings lifted the *Undaunted* half a dozen feet. They sliced through the waters just beneath the waves, and her fat keel touched only the most ambitious waves. It was a bizarre sensation, but with less to no hull for the water to heave against, the *Undaunted* shot like an arrow, cleaving through the waves and breaking peak after peak into sea-spray. It felt unnatural to fly through the water, and it put a rattle in her chest, but the familiar salt splashing her face was enough to turn the worry to thrill. And as Elessi – with her hands white-knuckled and her eyes wide – put so eloquently:

'Well, at least if it all goes tits up with our friend the keraken, we might be able to outrun it,' she shouted over the rush of wind.

Lerel checked every line and sailor before she nodded and took her turn to smile. 'Make that one and a half days!' she yelled. 'Sturmsson's going to shit himself when he finds out this warship can sail circles around his precious *Fury*.'

CHAPTER 14
A RECKONING

*Takes more to save a life than end one, and it is the greatest shame of our
kind we choose the simpler option.*
FROM FAMED ALBION HEALER DAVITH CARRINGTON

The wind bit like a dragon's jaws on the mountain's claw. A storm
grumbled out in the bay, sending fine drizzle and sleet the city's way.
Krauslung's lights blinked in the precipitation, burning bright and
defiant as always. Farden could almost hear the crackling of the fires
and feet hurrying on cobbles. The drains gurgling and the squeals of
the underdressed rushing from tavern to tavern. He could almost
smell the farska bubbling in cooks' cauldrons.

Farden had stood on such a peak and stared down at such a
city decades before, when all this task and toil had first started.

He had been alone then.

'Njord's balls.' Mithrid edged to the sheer drop of the peak of
Ursufel, testing each patch of snow before putting her full weight on
it. 'So this is Krauslung. Everything you and I have fought for?'

'That it is.' Farden's gaze roved from the bristling port to the
thick city walls halfway up the valley's slope. Manesmark was a
shining blur beyond on the crest of the hill.

'I've never seen so many lights, not even in Golikar. It's
almost…' Mithrid pondered. 'Beautiful.'

Farden smiled at that. 'The ugly kind of beautiful. You'll never
find another city that can beggar you just as quickly as it can crown
you, or where the ale and coin flows freer, or louder, for that matter.'

Putting a finger to the corner of his eye, Farden magicked his sight and his vision swooped into the city. He could count the figures filling the streets. Revellers crowded the bright alleys swarming with taverns, food stalls, and cathouses. Armoured guards crowded the corners, watching over the shanties and homeless hovels that occupied alleys. Farden wrinkled his lip at that, before his attention was drawn to a small gathering that bustled around a bright point to the south. Farden peered closer to see a half-finished dome of marble, topped with a golden statue of a very familiar and utterly hateful figure: Loki.

'They really are building that fucker a temple,' grumbled the mage.

Ilios whistled a low and careful note.

Mithrid sucked her teeth. 'You jealous?'

Fardon scoffed at that. 'I don't want a temple.'

'Not even if somebody built you one?'

'You offering?'

'Hel no.'

Farden pointed across the valley to where the white fortress of the Arkathedral dominated the mountain slopes. It shone like a noon sun. 'What I want is Loki's head on this spear.'

'Can you feel him?'

Farden nodded, angling his face against the shrieking wind. 'He's here.'

'Think he can feel us all the way up here?' Mithrid dared herself to look down the sheer slopes down to the city.

'I'm hoping not. If a spear can sleep, then that's what Gunnir is doing. You can do the rest when we get there.'

'You know, you and that spear seem far too close,' Mithrid muttered. 'What's the plan this time?'

'We approach from the roof of the Arkathedral. Anyone who gets in our way gets silenced quickly and quietly until we're standing in front of Loki's chambers. You'll wrap him in your magick, and I'll run a hole through him.'

'Sounds so simple after all we've been through.'

'Death is the simplest thing in this world,' Farden said, reciting some skald he had heard in a forgotten tavern. 'You ready?'

Mithrid rubbed her hands. 'As I'll ever be.'

'I was talking to Ilios.'

Ilios let out an ululating whistle, a gryphon's laugh. Mithrid scowled as she held her hood against the persistent wind. The gryphon extended for them to climb, and she did with a muttering.

Beating his wings as slowly and gently as he could, Ilios soared in a wide circle over the walls of Krauslung and back to the Arkathedral. They kept to the roots of the clouds, far from the city lights and where the driving rain hid them as well as mist. With a nod from Farden, Mithrid let her shadow surround them as they circled the marble fortress. Far from Farden's touch, thankfully, but enough to keep them hidden from any magicked eyes that happened to be gazing into the miserable sky. Ilios shivered at Mithrid's touch, whistling low.

In dizzying circles, the gryphon descended, almost pivoting on one wingtip. Farden refused to blink in the cold air as he watched the Arkathedral creep closer.

At the tip of the fortress, above the crown of the great hall of the Marble Copse, Durnus and Tyrfing had once built a sanctuary for Ilios they called the Nest. Perhaps not their most imaginative name, but it mattered not. Malvus, in his crusade to ruin everything they had built, changed its name to the Eyrie and let foul vulegul birds turn it into their roost. Loki had yet to change it to his liking, or perhaps he liked the insult to the memories of the last arkmages. Where flawless marble once resided, a mess of straw and shit and feathers now stood. The white stone trees were filled with brazenly large nests and, disturbingly, sleeping vuleguls.

'Leave them to sleep, Ilios!' Farden urged with a whisper. Perhaps Loki knew vuleguls were known for their keening screeches, and they were a better warning than the bells of Ursufel and Hardja sitting in their towers either side of the Eyrie.

Ilios swerved in a way that made Mithrid gulp.

A balcony one level below the Marble Copse was chosen instead. Ilios managed to get two claws on its marble and thrashed his wings just long enough for Farden and Mithrid to jump. It took Mithrid some convincing with the sheer drop beckoning below but the call of solid stone was more alluring. With a snarl and her eyes unwisely clamped shut, she hurled herself onto the stone and breathed a grateful sigh.

'Quiet as shadows. We don't know what Loki's done with the Arkathedral,' whispered Farden.

A furtive heat spell melted the lock from the door. It had no spells to protect it. In his darkest years, Farden had learned there was confidence in the sheer walls and height of a fortress. People didn't usually expect intruders with wings.

The chamber beyond was dark. It was a scribe's room, full of the dust of disuse, silent since the days when the council wanted their words written down. Those who committed atrocities and stabbed others in their back didn't like evidence. Besides, Malvus had burned through most of the Arkathedral's scribes forcing them to create Scarred mages. Farden made a mental note to burn the Hides of Hysteria once he was done with Loki.

The hall beyond was a cavern of marble, with three sets of stairs leading in different directions and one leading up to the Marble Copse.

'Where is he likely to be? If he's here at all?'

Farden watched two guards patrolling past the steps leading to the Marble Copse. He had skulked in corridors with murder on his mind plenty of times before with barely a bead of sweat on his brow, but that night he had to force his breath to slow. In that silence he heard the faintest whisper and felt a chill run through the metal of the spear.

He is here.

'Gunnir can feel him. Loki's close.'

Mithrid held her axe higher.

Though Farden ached to use his magick and all his spells for dampening sound and blending with walls, Mithrid's skills proved far more evasive. Cloaked in nothing more than a roaming shadow, the pair paused a dozen steps from the guards and their lanterns. Their idle chat came in a whisper.

'I reckon he's as mad as the last one. It's all an act.'

'Have you forgotten Malvus' name so quickly?' asked his comrade, exasperated. 'There's too much ale between those ears, I tell you.'

'Don't you wonder what happened to Lord Froxire and those others that swaggered in here? I reckon that little god got rid of them. What have the vuleguls been eating these past few days, eh?'

'Don't tell me you don't know our god's name.'

'Lucky or something like that.'

'Fuck me. How long have you worked here? Decades, man!'

Armour rattled as somebody shrugged. 'Meh, masters come and go so quick around here. What's the point in remembering their names?'

'You should know you've got a genuine problem, Bjelarn.'

If Bjelarn did have a problem, then Farden solved it for him swiftly and kindly. Whisking the man's helmet off, he clobbered him at the base of the skull. Farden caught his body before he fell with a crash and turned to see Mithrid slam the pommel of her knife into the other guard's throat. Unfortunately, Mithrid apparently crushed his windpipe, and choking and wheezing, the man careened for the steps. Mithrid's shadow seized him just before he fell, strangling him until he hung limp in her grasp.

All Farden did was growl, and once the unconscious and the dead had been stowed behind a pillar, the mage ascended to the Marble Copse for the first time in decades. The worn stairs felt all too familiar as the open door of the great hall was revealed one step at a time.

A darkness wrapped the carved marble trees that gave the Copse its name. Farden remembered every white branch reaching up to beam and ceiling, every meticulously crafted root that wandered between the pillars and benches, responsible for tripping countless council members.

The scars of Malvus were spread across the Copse. Gone were the twin thrones of the arkmages, as was the underthrone where Modren once sat. In its place was the Blazing Throne, a huge wall of marble with a seat at the bottom that somebody had decided to set fire to. Flames ran around the throne's edges, sparking here and there. The marble trees near its presence glowed gold. The jagged shadows of branches drew Farden's eyes to the corners over and over and prickled his skin.

Where the mighty statue of Evernia had once presided over the magick council, her plinth was nothing but a floor scuffed by daemons and stained by the blood of cut throats. The shadow of death lingered before that throne.

Farden had left his own scars in that hall. Faint cracks were still visible in the floor, and bruises still lingered in the marble where magick had scorched it darker.

Farden strode towards the throne, one hand on the disguised Gunnir at his belt and another wrapped around his curved Khandri sword.

'Loki's not here, in case you haven't noticed. What are you doing?' Mithrid whispered in that kind of whisper that was more of a hoarse shout.

Insulting the ghost of Malvus and the soon-to-be ghost of Loki was what Farden was doing. He marched up the throne's steps, but instead of sitting, as Mithrid clearly expected him to, he reached for the stone and grasped its magick. The great hall darkened, and marble branches appeared to close in as the Blazing Throne was quenched. Farden stole its magick for himself, letting it glow in the tattoos on his back and forearms. Sorely did he want to throw it right back at the marble and break it in two.

Mithrid let faint shadow surround them. 'Where else could he be then?'

'Playing at being human and living like a king, I wager. Feels like he's in Malvus' chambers. They're not far and hard to miss. Malvus took up two entire levels of the Arkathedral when he proclaimed himself king.'

Mithrid tutted. 'Of course he did. How very Malvus of him.'

Though the chambers were not far and lazily close to the Marble Copse, they were heavily guarded. Once again, Farden had to still himself and force control. Anticipation and half a century of anger made his skin burn and his spells itch, but this was not to be a howling storm of a battle, rather the swift and surgical end to Emaneska's cancer.

'Go around,' Farden breathed, as they peered over a parapet at a dozen guards. Walking crouched was difficult even in Scalussen armour, and Mithrid crept ahead as if it was a race.

'Slow,' he murmured. 'You'll wish you'd never been squeezed into the world if you ruin this.'

Mithrid was about to spit something back at him when one of their feet scraped on the floor. Both looked at each other accusingly.

'That you, Camron? Bensman?' came a call from below, along with the tramping of curious feet. 'Shift yourself, you cocks. You're lagging! How long does it take to have a shite?'

That way, said a whisper. Farden stared at Mithrid accusingly, but her lips were pressed and pale. Farden realised it was the spear and his old friend.

'Thank you,' Farden whispered, pointing to an adjoining corridor that encircled the Arkathedral's core.

Mithrid gave him a frown. 'I didn't say anything.'

A second shout echoed. 'Camron! You speak when spoken to!' The feet were thudding on the stairs now.

'Keep your eyes sharp, lads,' another voice said of the silence and lack of reply, and Farden and Mithrid's subtle scurrying.

A door swung open before them, and Mithrid couldn't help but barge into it. Two servants lugging something heavy and soiled by what looked suspiciously like blood fell aside.

One was already half-concussed by the door smashing him in the face. Mithrid's shadow swirled, out of control but useful enough to keep the confusion rife. The shock muted their cries of surprise, and Farden smacked their heads together before they could utter anything louder. Three shadows were creeping across the shine of the floor behind them.

'In!' Farden ordered as he pushed the two limp bodies into the doorway and out of sight. He took a single shoe from one of the servants and hurled it down the corridor as bait.

The door closed with a minuscule click, and Farden quickly locked it while Mithrid doused a nearby lantern to keep the glow from beneath the door. Even in the dark, it was clear to see they had found a servants' chamber, with two more doors leading deeper into Loki's chambers.

Farden held still with his sword ready. Mithrid was poised with her axe, and both of them listened to the footfalls pass them by.

'What's this? A shoe. Shit, you're jumpy tonight, Cric,' said a voice.

'It's those bloody servants! Boss has got them rushing about like headless faeries.'

Farden swore he heard a slap.

'He is Loki, the one true god, and you'll address him as so.'

'Aye, Captain.'

The footfalls receded, and Mithrid and Farden both took a breath and a moment.

'Two doors. Pick one,' Farden whispered.

The further into the Arkathedral they crept, the more Farden could see a tremble in Mithrid's hands. Nerves, most likely, but perhaps it was the same anticipation quivering in his bones.

Mithrid waved her axe to the one on the right. Farden approached, twisted the doorknob, peeked, and immediately shut it again.

'No.'

'What?

'About two dozen guards.'

'The other door it is, then.'

Mithrid took the lead this time, opening the door to a room stacked floor to ceiling with wines and crystal bottles of various colours. They chimed as Farden ran his hands along them.

'Perhaps we should revisit this room after we're done,' suggested Mithrid.

'All the wine in Emaneska won't be enough for the celebration of Loki's death,' Farden said as he checked the next room. It was dark as sin and perfect for theirs. The mage led them along the curved wall past room after empty room, circling into the centre of Loki's claimed chambers. Farden recognised none of the grand chambers, but he knew the minds of those in power and how they liked to be the centre of their worlds. Loki had the same petty heart beating in his chest. A god he may be, but he had been cursed with humanity a long time ago.

At the centre of the spiral of kitchens and servants and guard captains' quarters, a curved wall of bright stained glass greeted them. The wavering lanterns of the passageway made the hues of long-forgotten battles and haughty arkmages ebb and flow as if they breathed. Not a shadow shifted behind the colours, and Farden led them along the curve until they reached a doorway. No guards protected it, and with a twist of its handle, they found themselves in opulent chambers fit for an arkmage. Or in this case, a god.

'I feel him stronger now. This is it,' Farden breathed. He had to stop himself from casting a light spell to ward against the darkness. With hands sweating inside his gauntlets, they crept through a dining hall and a study to where broad stairs led down to a sprawling bedchamber, thick with shadow. At its far end, a windowed balcony looked out over the shine of city lights, and at its centre lay a bed broad enough for a dozen, never mind one. Farden's insides clenched as he saw a silhouette standing against the glass, staring out across Krauslung. The ragged edges of a familiar cloak stirred in the breeze.

Farden strangled Gunnir's disguised hilt so hard even the Scalussen steel of his gauntlets creaked.

'Is that…?' Mithrid breathed.

Farden nodded, unable to speak. There he was: his nemesis, his prize, the core of all his hatred and being. He could hear the thunder of Mithrid's heart keeping pace with his. Her axe slid a fraction in her hands before she fixed Farden with a stare and gave him an almost imperceptible nod.

It was time.

Farden moved as if battling treacle, lifting Gunnir from his side as he took a stand. With a whisper of metal, the spear stretched into its true shape. Farden took it in both hands, wincing at the faint clink of gauntlet on haft. There would be no escape this time. No mercy. No grand battle of words before the final and brutal strike. This was murder, and the known world would be better for it.

Holding the spear beneath his arm, Farden set his jaw as he took aim. Speed was what he needed, alongside every scrap of magick in his bones and Gunnir's steel. Farden felt the magick scorch his back as his Book came alive within a heartbeat. Gunnir's power grew from a whine to a screech in two.

'FOR DURNUS!' Farden screamed as he unleashed the cataclysm he and the weapon held back, like a dam snapping before stormwaters.

Thunder rolled to deafen them. Lightning raced to blind them. A streak of shining fire erupted from Gunnir's edge with all of Farden's spells chasing it, crossing the room in an instant to punch through the god and out into the void of night. The windows exploded as the hateful figure was carved in two.

Farden felt his teeth on the verge of cracking as he strained to keep hold of the unadulterated magick. It lasted mere moments, but by the time the fire died, and he knuckled light out of his eyes, the room was a blackened husk. Shards of glass studded every wall and silk adornment. A furrow in the marble glowed where the stone had melted.

Mithrid was the first to rush ahead while Farden stood with hands and knees shaking. The girl held her axe ready even though the two halves of the god lay smoking before the shattered balcony. She skidded to a halt, and something in the way her axe hand drooped stabbed Farden in the gut. He chased after her to stare down at nothing but an iron mannequin, ragged edges still gleaming with fire. The brown leather coat was torn and charred, only fragments remaining.

Clap.

Clap.

Clap.

'Farden, Farden, Farden,' spoke a damning voice. Mithrid and the mage whirled, trying to make sense of the smoke and cinders that still swirled around the chamber.

'So foolhardy. So foolish. So eager to see me dead you fall for the oldest of tricks, Farden Four-Hand.'

Gods, did Farden hate that name, but behind the god's mockery, shouts could be heard from the city below. The bells of the Arkathedral began to toll in damning harmony.

Farden clenched a light and wind spell, driving the haze back. 'Show yourself, Loki, you worm!' Mithrid yelled.

There, on the balcony, crouched like a raven on the edge of the gaping hole Gunnir had blasted in the masonry, was Loki. His trusty coat was wrapped around him, but fresh sky-blue armour glinted beneath.

'Did you think it would be that easy?' he asked with a smirk that drove Farden mad. Once again, he levelled Gunnir, magick whining as it sought to skewer him.

Loki folded into thin air before the light could touch him, snapping to a space behind them. Farden whirled, taking the magick with him so it cut through the chamber walls. Soldiers spilled through the doors in their dozens and immediately caught the full brunt of the mage's rage. Those who were not disintegrated were sliced at the waist, falling to scream and claw at the marble.

No Loki lay amongst them. Once again he stood on the balcony, wagging an infuriating finger. 'You know, I didn't expect you to still harbour this much ill will against me. Time is the healer they say, but not for you it seems. All that hatred will get you into trouble one day. Not good for the heart.'

'It's time to accept your fate, worm!' Farden lowered Gunnir to his side as he reached for Loki with the emerald claws of a force spell, lightning sputtering alongside them. Loki vanished again, appearing back where he had started.

'And it's time for you to reap what you've sown.'

Battlements burst as Farden tried one last time, but his efforts were foiled by Mithrid's mad dash, axe in one hand and a wreath of shadow in the other. She and the magick came within an inch before Loki escaped yet again, before shadow and spell fizzled out, cancelling each other.

Farden rushed to the girl's side. 'Don't be so rash! He almost killed you once!'

'Easy for you to say!' Mithrid blurted, and Farden saw why.

The distant rumble of rock greeted his ears over the noise of the city. Where Gunnir's light had escaped the Arkathedral, it had struck the far mountain instead and carved a gash as wide as a ship. Boulders cascaded down the slopes of Ursufel, crashing into spires and rooftops on the western edge of the city.

'I thought you said—' she began, but Farden cut her off.

'Don't you fucking dare. We can still do this.'

Farden, cautioned a voice, but Farden shrugged it away as he leaned over the balcony's edge. Far below, amongst the streets and surrounded by glittering Arkathedral guards and gawping citizens, he spied the god.

Farden snatched at Mithrid's hand as Gunnir crackled. 'Swing your axe, Mithrid.'

Mithrid raised her blade as the spell folded them into nothing.

❦

The flash that swallowed them lasted a moment, and even though her eyes were still mired in light, Mithrid did as she was told. A glimmer of the god's face appeared in front of her before a guard interrupted. Her axe bit into his steel and the neck beneath. Loki smiled behind the dying man.

At her side, Farden thrust with his spear, almost catching Loki before he turned to the side and let Gunnir's elf-steel pass him by.

Farden stamped his foot as guards and soldiers rushed in. Bodies flew as the mage's spells shook them from their feet and cast them aside. There were citizens in that cascade of flesh, and their screams filled the night.

'The Forever King!' came the damning cry.

'Use your shadow, Mithrid! Put a stop to his tricks!' yelled Farden, and Mithrid tried to ignore the hint of desperation driving his voice high.

Mithrid did so, slamming her axe into the cobbles so she could spread shadow with both hands. More screams came as her black magick spread and spun in a miniature hurricane, ever reaching for the retreating Loki.

'Stand and face us if you call yourself a god!' Mithrid bellowed her challenge, but Loki spurned it, escaping up the street and out of her range. He had the gall to draw a curved sword from a pocket, as if he weren't running in the opposite direction of battle.

Mithrid ran, forcing her shadow after him and filling the streets from gutter to tile. Mages and soldiers were either barged aside or cut down by magick and blade as they gave chase. Farden knew where Loki was going, and Mithrid followed blindly until they found themselves bounding into an open square. Ahead, a stone and gold effigy of Loki stretched his arms in greeting from the half-finished dome of marble of a temple. Torchlight made its smile waver as if it had come alive.

Loki stood on the temple steps wearing the same godsdamned grin. Worse, crowds had gathered, and not of soldiers, but of humble citizens. Dour-faced and cross-armed, they awaited them.

'He fucking knew we would come,' Mithrid hissed to the mage beside her. Flames skittered about his armour, and by the look in his eyes, he was ready to carve through every single body in the crowd just to get to Loki.

'Krauslung has chosen its king, Farden, and it is not you,' Loki crowed, voice stretching across the square. Fists punched the air as the crowds began to boo and jeer. Some began to chant Loki's name.

'What are we going to do?' Mithrid asked.

Farden did not answer, and she stared at the multitudes of faces staring back at her. She spied children and babies in arms. One girl a few years younger than her boasted the same hue of hair as she did. Mithrid couldn't catch the vitriol that spilled from her lips, but Mithrid had a good idea what she said. They were loathed. They were despised. These people were brimming with hate, and for her, no less.

'This is not the Krauslung I know!' Farden bellowed over their jeering. 'You see how your so-called god would use you? As a shield to hide his own cowardice? You would follow a god like him, who doesn't even fight his own battles?'

The jeering cries of the crowd affirmed it. They would indeed follow, and to the end of Emaneska.

'He is a god of lies! He is in league with the daemons!' Mithrid howled, but to no avail. She could not ignore the frantic beating of her heart. The frustration shook her hands. Sweat beaded on her forehead and stung her eyes as her own hatred arose.

Loki began to shine in reply. A simple glow at first, coming from his fist and pulsating in waves from his body. A humble trick until the shine grew white hot, almost painful to look at. Mithrid could see white teeth and eyes curved into a smile.

Figures had begun to climb the steps to stand before their so-called god and become nothing but faceless silhouettes in his light.

They formed a barrier that showed only Loki's head and his vile face.

Gunnir shook in the mage's fingers as Farden raised it to point at Loki. He assailed the crowd with harmless vortex and quake spells to try and move them. He even carved a rift in the square with magick, but the fools rushed to pick their fellows up and stand on the rubble.

'Face us, if you call yourself a god! Prove yourself,' Farden cried.

'I need not prove anything! My people already believe. We have had our fill of death and fighting in this city, Forever King!' Loki brayed. 'You sow nothing but death wherever you go. It's you that needs to prove yourself.'

'He lies!' Mithrid shouted, raising her axe. Shadow spiralled about its blade, reaching out to the crowd to test their nerve. Instead of quaking and quailing as she wanted them to, they began to stamp their feet. Even the grey-haired and old'uns amongst them smacked their canes on the flagstones.

'Mithrid,' warned Farden.

But Mithrid was not listening. Her shadow magick continued to build, swirling around her until she reached out with two thick tendrils above their heads, reaching for Loki.

The god's light faltered as the shadow assailed him, and yet it compressed brighter like a dying sun fighting for life. He vanished to the corner of his monument before flitting back, losing Mithrid's touch. It was beyond hard to grasp him, but Mithrid didn't dare to think the word *impossible*.

Some of the crowd began to hurl rocks and bottles. Farden kept them at bay with shield spells and made some light of his own. Lightning danced at their feet and white bursts of flame collided with Mithrid's storm as he and Gunnir showed off. It was a terrifying display of magick, and it stilled a good many of them, caused a few to wince and cower, and stopped none of their hate. Archers began to take aim.

'I can catch him!' Mithrid snarled. 'Get ready to jump!'

'We can't both fight him at once! We're cancelling each other out!' Farden yelled as a dozen arrows studded his shield spell before vanishing into ash. Mithrid's swirling shadow tore the shield at its edges and more with every errant touch. The citizens were preparing to lunge at them. Soldiers had cut off their escape. A ballista was turning in their direction.

Mithrid stared into the faces of the crowd again and found only fools and weaklings, blinded by lies they gulped down like a drunkard quaffed ale. 'Almost got him!'

Loki flitted again, right where Mithrid had guessed he would, and her shadow pushed him against the gold leaf of his statue, trapping him momentarily. His form stuttered as his magick was quenched.

'Do it now, Farden!' Mithrid yelled as the mob pounced, tearing at them. Farden held Gunnir flat before them, roaring with vortex spells that barely kept them at bay with her shadow interfering.

'Not with you exposed!'

Mithrid held out a hand instead. And as the writhing shadow fell lax and faded, Farden snatched her fingers with a clang, and together they flew through the crowd in a jump so hasty Mithrid wasn't sure if she faded out of existence at all. Her axe reached before her as the statue leapt at them.

Loki's face betrayed a flicker of fear before the blades bit. Yet the closer they came, the more time seemed to slow, and the faster he moved, sliding beneath the axe and spear and crackling with lightning as he slipped into the crowd.

Stone and fire cascaded as the blades bit deep. The force knocked Mithrid to her arse, head twirling and breath gone from her lungs. Gunnir had blasted a hole deep into the chest of the god's statue. Cracks spread all the way to his neck and shoulders. If the mob had wanted blood before, they thirsted for it now, edging forwards with fists clenched. A score of bows creaked.

Mithrid immediately spun her shadow once more.

'Mithrid!' Farden's hand on her arm made her snarl. 'The night is lost.'

'They are nothing to us!' Mithrid argued defiantly. 'If they want to stand by a false god, then let them. They can die at his side!'

'This is not what we came here to do! Enough!'

But Mithrid could not – and would not – stop. Gunnir whined in Farden's hand as he attempted a spell to jump them away, but she turned her shadow on him, making the mage strain and his armour rattle. If she had looked at Loki in that moment, she would have seen his eyebrow raise a fraction.

'Don't you dare!' Farden growled, stare drilling into her. 'We will not murder them for him!'

'It's what they deserve!'

'And you don't get to decide that. You know better!'

Mithrid brought her face close to Farden's, unblinking, head pounding. 'Do I?'

'Run, little Forever King. Back to your bolthole!' Loki gloated over the rising rumble of magick. Mithrid saw the mages now gathering on the rooftops and alleys, but she did not care.

Farden seized her by the neck and shook her. 'I won't let you become what Loki wants,' he shouted, and for a moment their magick duelled, holding each other at bay until Farden and Gunnir's magick racked her with pain, and magick won.

To the sound of Mithrid's enraged cry, Krauslung melted into a pit of swirling light and grinning faces that chased her into the void. Mithrid swore she heard a hearty cheer before the night was ripped to shreds.

❦

Sand choked her as the spell catapulted Mithrid across the beach. She ended up in the shallows, hair covering her face. 'You fucking coward!' Mithrid spat seawater.

Farden hammered his spear in the sand, shaking the earth. 'You choose silence right this moment, or you'll regret it dearly.'

'You failed us!' she yelled.

Farden raised a fist. She saw the regret in the parting of his lips and searching eyes, but it didn't erase the truth. 'I've never been that kind of killer, Mithrid Fenn. I won't become one now nor will I let you! It was a trap after all, don't you have the bloody sense to see that? Loki wanted Krauslung to hate us and to force us into committing carnage! Those are still my people!'

'We had Loki in our grasp!'

'Other way around, Mithrid! This was exactly what I was worried about! I feared you would go down this dark path, and you just proved me right.'

Voices hollered from the battlements of the Winter Fortress. Eyrum's gruff tone, chased by the boom of Warbringer.

'Farden! Mithrid!'

'What of Krauslung?'

Farden and Mithrid skewered each other with their stares.

'They weren't innocents. They were fools,' she spat.

'And wrapped up in his lies just like you're too full of hate to see straight!' shouted Farden. 'I don't recognise this girl.'

'Don't call me girl!' Mithrid shook her head, hands like claws.

Farden held Gunnir flat. 'To your quarters. Until I decide what to do with you.'

'You…' Mithrid was too incensed to speak. 'There'll come a day when you regret not taking that chance tonight.'

'To your quarters, *General*,' Farden ordered in a guttural tone.

Feet scuffed on the beach as Eyrum and Warbringer arrived at the same moment as Mithrid stormed away.

'What's happening?' Eyrum demanded.

Farden let the emotions bend him double as he caught his breath. 'Loki was waiting for us. It was a trap, and we walked right into it. Krauslung gathered to stand between us. Old and young, they were willing to fight for him, die for him, even,' he muttered.

'Mithrid almost gave them that chance. She wanted to cut through the lot of them.'

'That's a lie. Surely.'

Farden straightened to find Hereni standing at Warbringer's side, face creased in concern.

'I wouldn't lie about that, Hereni, and you should know better.'

Hereni shook her head. 'What I know is Mithrid. I know her more than anyone here.'

'That wasn't Mithrid I saw tonight.'

'We'll see about that.' Hereni kicked Mithrid's footsteps to dust as she gave chase.

Farden focused on the thudding of his heart to try to keep it from bursting. 'We came so fucking close.'

Both Eyrum and Warbringer held their tongues. Warbringer also wore a scowl on her brow.

'Where are Elessi and Lerel? They'll find out they were right soon enough, so it might as well be me to tell them,' muttered Farden.

Eyrum sucked his teeth. 'They are gone, King.'

'Gone where?'

The handle of his battleaxe pointed the way, out of the bay towards the sea and to the north. Whatever calm Farden had forced into his heart vanished.

'Not the keraken,' Farden groaned.

Eyrum offered a nod. 'It was Warbringer who found out where to find it, I hear.'

The look the minotaur gave the Siren would have killed a lesser man.

Farden pressed his steel fingers to his temples. 'I am gone for one day…'

part two

MYTH

CHAPTER 15
OF WEAPONS LOST & FORGOTTEN

If you are reading this, then I am already dead. Irien did it. She was the one who ruined me. I don't care who started it. She finished it. There's nowhere to go now but the queen, but the night is dark, and the streets are long. I will put this message through your door first, in case...
FROM A SCROLL FOUND IN LADY IRIEN'S DATHAZH RESIDENCE

Loki had never seen a human bow so low. Not even Sjarvek could compete. He swore the scholar's forehead almost scuffed the floor as she paid her respects. It had been impressive the first few times. Now it was becoming irritating.

'You honour us with your presence, Lord,' repeated the scholar in a voice cracked with age and dust. She placed another tome on the broad desk and stood by with hands clasped. 'Perhaps if you tell us what it is you look for, we scholars can be of assistance.'

Loki looked at the two greybeards behind her, fingers kneading and lips pale. Loki could feel their trepidation, and he relished in it.

'What do you know of shadow magick?' he asked.

The scholar bowed yet again. 'It is a school of magick that is less taught than most. It is the elimination of light sources and the casting of darkness. Often to hide a mage, or for furtive activities. The School of Manesmark has long since avoided teaching such a practice, believing it to be a darker magick.'

'No such thing,' Loki muttered. 'And what of magick that can nullify other magick?'

'Do you speak of cessation spells?'

Loki sighed. 'I wager I don't, but speak nonetheless.'

'It is the practice of catching, diminishing, and redirecting spells. That is indeed taught at the School. It differs from shield magick in several particular ways—'

'And does this kind of magick also produce shadow? A smoke-like shadow that moves at the mage's will?'

The scholar looked to her comrades, and together they shook their heads. 'It does not. Not in written memory.'

Another twirled his beard. 'Do you speak of the incident in the cit—'

Loki's gaze was enough to make the man shrink away, lurking behind a bookcase and looking anywhere but the god.

'Perhaps you would find this interesting, sire, if I may.' The other shuffled closer with a scroll, bolder than her counterpart. 'An elvish tapestry saved from Arfell during the fire. Does this show what you speak of?'

It did, though the singed edges of the scroll and its faded, sooty tapestry did nothing to aid the crude images. The elves had managed to enslave the world, bent vast magick and grotesque machines to their will, and yet somehow they had never learned how to draw.

Loki peered. On one side was a crowd of what looked like humans, drawn small and fat so the spears and flames in their hands looked puny and pathetic. It was art Loki could appreciate. Opposing them were three elves, and not the usual ashen grey of elf kind, but of even paler colouring. Coils of what looked like black smoke spread from their stick fingers.

Loki rolled the scroll shut with a snap before he got to his feet. With chin raised, he watched the scholars bow and scrape before him. His tongue traced the back of his teeth as he pondered. He was not hungry, but he was greedy, and yet his secret needed keeping. A trail of dead in his wake would tarnish Loki's golden image if he let it grow long enough.

The dragon scale that hung like a warning bell in its wide atrium hummed feebly as Loki passed by, and he paused to scowl. He knew it would have sung so loud for Farden it would have cracked.

There was a victory to be had in Farden's attempt on his life, but Loki harboured a secret that soiled his satisfaction. It had been too close. Shamefully so. Escaping the spear's touch had taken all his strength. And yet, he still had the delicious memory of Farden's fallen face to buoy his mood.

A snowstorm was crawling over the northern mountains, and Manesmark was already wearing a fine dusting. Loki stowed the scroll in his endless pockets and clicked a finger. Grass and dirt dissolved, replaced by black rock and ice. The shadow of the Spire was replaced by a ruined edifice of a tower clinging to a mountainside. Loki stood amongst tumbled blocks larger than houses, where ravens croaked, and the voices of the wind haunted the crags. Snow fell in buckets, thieving the light from the day. It felt like night beneath the shadow of the mountain.

All save for the torches huddled further down the slope, exactly where Loki had told them to wait. He greeted them with no bow or wave, only keen and searching eyes. There were thirty of them altogether, wrapped in furs and breath puffing from pursed lips, and every one of them a commander returned from Paraia. Their cows and carriages waited beyond in a semicircle.

'Your Majesty,' said one of them, a fat bundle of layered fabrics. The man must have worn every magick and religious symbol Loki had ever encountered on his weighty necklace. 'Might we ask why you've summoned us here?'

'Lord Henrik was it?' asked Loki.

'It was–is, sire. Is.'

'No, you may not ask. But I will tell you nonetheless. I wish to give a gift to you survivors of Paraia, and you deserters too…' Loki let that word linger and saw their faces scrunch up from something other than cold or the touch of snow.

'Here?' asked another deserter. Another failure. A captain who had been booted from Karissa, who now shivered desperately after growing used to southern sun.

'You will see! I will return momentarily,' said Loki, sweeping away to lose himself in the snowstorm.

The Arfell Library was no more than blackened rubble, but the builders had carved deep into the mountain to house their scribbled treasures. Those caves and hollows remained, and Loki strode through the depressing wreckage towards their darkness.

The rattling of rocks did not go unnoticed. The flitting shadows were far from ignored. Loki could smell them on the wind: elves.

An orb of blue fire sputtered into life beyond a patch of gravel. Its otherworldly light pushed back the gloom and revealed the form of Azen crouched on a rock. The orb twirled over his twitching fingers.

'You lied,' rasped the elf.

'Which time?' Loki spat back.

'You did not tell of the spear, godling.'

Loki smirked. 'You've been keeping a close eye, I see.'

'Know your ally better than your enemy,' uttered Azen. 'Why did you lie to us?'

'Technically,' Loki held up a finger, 'I did not lie. I simply forgot to tell you.'

'Slipped your mind that the foe you called us to fight wields the Teh'Mani? The Skyrender? It is an insult to us. Almost as great as the insult that a worm holds it.'

Loki crossed his arms, affecting a faint mockery while he inwardly clenched in anticipation. 'Is that a problem for the great Clan of Covor?'

Loki's answer came in the form of a shifting of rock louder than any elf could cause. A shadow he had not even realised was a shadow shifted abruptly, fading deeper into the snow. How curious indeed.

'The elves made the spear, did they not?' was all Loki said. It was Azen's turn to flash a smirk, and without another word, crooked a finger to the god.

Loki followed, barely keeping Azen in sight as he trod deeper into the darkness of the mountain's innards. With the snow fading, Loki became aware of white eyes filling the darkness. Scores of the creatures perched on shelves of rock. Hundreds more scurried at the edges of the shadows where mist lurked. Blue fires glowed here and there, putting a gleam to the waxy elvish skins. Weapons without shine drank in the darkness.

It was what occupied the back of the cavern that drew Loki's intrigue. In his pocket, he reached slowly for the hilt of a longsword, and that was all he admitted of his trepidation.

Whatever it was, it only became visible when it moved, vanishing into shadow whenever it paused. Loki saw one leg, then another, and another, until he counted a dozen, shifting one after the other. Hidden as it was, he could only imagine the rest of the monster, but what Loki could see were glimpses of dripping, insectile jaws that a dragon would have quailed at the sight of, and it disturbed him greatly.

Azen's voice tried to drag Loki's attention away. 'You came for our help, and yet you would doubt our power?'

A strange applause came from the hundreds of elves roosting like crows around them, made of black tongues clicking against teeth. A rumble rattled his armour as the hideous thing emerged to brush against Azen's raised hand. Legs, spines, and antennae protruded at all angles from its armoured, slug-like body. A harrowing face leered down at him from milky uncountable eyes that ringed spiked mandibles made of four pieces. The monster moved like the elves did, in jerks and twitches, always a blink from pouncing.

Loki had no clever words. No wisecracks or worming talk. 'What under all the stars,' he said, 'is that?'

'Tharkun, in the tongue of elves. One of the Great Ones. Some came from the void with the lure of magick. Some were already here, buried in the world's skin. You did not know, godling?'

Loki pasted a smile to hide his irritation. 'Does your pet have a name?'

'Ekidna, the Hundred-Eyed.'

'What a truly beautiful name,' Loki muttered. 'And how will it fare against the spear?'

Azen offered a gruesome smile. 'They have fought once before. Like many Great Ones, Ekidna was born of magick. Ekidna hunts magick.'

'How convenient. And speaking of magick,' Loki said, fishing the Spire scroll from his pocket. 'Do you recognise this? This power of shadow?'

Azen said nothing, merely staring up and down the tapestry's length. 'What of it?'

'Our mutual enemy Farden has a girl that follows him. A very important girl of pale skin and fire-red hair who wields such a power. I want her unharmed.'

Azen flickered his tongue. Loki took it as agreement.

'Have you a plan, godling?'

'Battle, my good elf. Glorious battle of daemon and elf and mage clashing against the shields of fools.'

Azen curled his lip at the mention of daemons, but he voiced no complaint.'

'You will kill Farden, but you will spare the girl. And should you keep your promise and that spear falls, it is mine, you understand? With it, I will give you everything I promised and more.'

Again, Azen stared in silence.

Loki's gaze toured the walls of elves, enduring their unblinking eyes. 'Who amongst you is the finest with a blade? The kind that comes in the dark. Unexpected.'

Azen stretched with pride. A sharp clap echoed around the cavern as he struck his hands together.

Again, that strange applause filled the air as three hooded and cloaked elves stepped from the gloom. Loki felt the magick in the blades they clenched in dead-skin hands. Black stripes of ink ran from scalp to throat, covering their eyes. Steel pierced the bridges of their noses and lines of their jaws.

'You look upon the Dramath-Ai, godling,' said Azen proudly. 'And that is no small feat. Almost all who are given such a gift die soon afterwards. Once the silent knives of Orion, they are now at your service. Be warned, for it has been some time since their blades tasted blood.'

'Wonderful. They will have that chance very soon, do not fear. As will you all,' Loki said with a smile. With quick twists of his hand, the scroll was once again rolled up and stored away. 'Go to the far edges of Troacles, and wait there for my word. Not a soul can see you and live. And speaking of souls, I have brought you a treat.'

'Treat?' Azen spat as if unfamiliar with the word.

'The humans gathered in the valley. There are thirty of them, plus cows and servants. I thought you might want to feast before you travel. A ship waits for you east of Krauslung on a small beach of black sand.'

Spinning on his heel, Loki turned his back on the grinning Azen and his unsightly beast. To his satisfaction, the Dramath-Ai moved with him, utterly silent on the crumbled stone.

Loki's smile broadened. The elves were on his side. Now all he needed was to convince the daemons to fight one last battle.

A thought sparked in his mind, and Loki paused before the snow could swallow him up. 'These Great Ones,' Loki asked, glancing over his shoulder. 'Tell me: how many more survived the gods?'

'You do not know, young god?' Azen asked, to the faint whispers of mirth from the army staring down at him.

'Tell me.'

Azen clenched his fist shut, extinguishing his shining light. The others did the same, one by one.

'You will have to look in the right places to know this,' came Azen's words once the cave was consumed in darkness.

Loki cursed the riddle and swept onwards. The Dramath-Ai had a knack for disguise; their ashen cloaks, hoods, and masks took on the perfect colour of the storm-plagued day. The others that scurried past Loki and towards his so-called treat were not so secretive.

When he found his gaggle of deserters and failures once more, Loki gave them a smile as he sauntered through their numbers, cutting their huddle in half. The Dramath-Ai strode around the edges of their torchlight, causing murmurs and curses amongst the scum.

'What is happening, Majesty?' whined Henrik, holding up rune after rune on his necklace. 'This is no gift!'

'Of course it is: sweet release from your guilt and shame,' he said, as the hissing of elves grew loud and arrows began to fly. Torches snuffed and died one by one. 'A fitting reward for sprinting from Paraia as fast as your ratlike legs could carry you.'

Loki vanished before the blood-spatter could reach his coat or smear the polish of his armour.

❧

As if the snowstorm wasn't enough winter for him, Loki cast his magick north to a peak of the Tausenbar Mountains, where eagles scattered from the thunder of his spell. There, the daylight had also been murdered, but not from snow.

Loki gazed at the jagged peaks at the Spine of the World, where a mountain lonely in its immenseness belched smoke into the sky for the winds to carry. Ash fell in place of snow on an earth scarred black where glaciers had been burned away. Craters yawned, with great pitted rocks of granite and iron at the centres like pupils in plagued eyes. Purple lightning crackled over the landscape and between the smoke, where peculiar colours swirled.

Yet Loki hadn't come to stare at volcanoes and the scars of cataclysm. He needed daemons, and the distant howls drifting on the air south of the mountain drew his eyes, where smokestacks of daemon-forged iron poked between the leafless trees.

Gremorin used to like it when the worms fled. It made for good sport, watching them weave and duck between their matchstick houses. It made their blood run hot and their souls shine with fear. Improved the meat's flavour, or so thought the daemon prince, but the wounds Malvus had given him had buckled his iron bones and kept his skin scarred like burned wood. It had ruined his sport.

Fortunately, there were always the worms that bravely stood their ground, and Gremorin had developed a taste for them instead.

One such quivering worm wielded a wavering spear in his face. He even managed a stab at the daemon's claw as Gremorin reached for him. The pathetic wretch choked on the flames and smoke that encircled him as Gremorin seized him tight. His skull crunched between his teeth, and Gremorin felt the chill of the soul run through his veins of fire.

Power. Power had been ripped from them, and they would rip it back from the world. One body at a time. The pickings were slim in the north, but it kept his daemons' mouths full of meat and souls instead of complaints.

Gremorin drew fire from his fists and clawed every thatched roof he passed, waiting for those bolted inside to choose between dying by fire or by daemon.

They almost always chose the latter. A few would escape through ratholes or back windows or use the smoke for cover, but those who chose to face the flames never failed to intrigue him.

These creatures were the former, doors flying open as dozens of them spilled into the streets. Gremorin greeted them with more fire, corralling them so he could swing the fiery blade he wrenched from his back. Standing amidst the ruin, he breathed in the char and cinders.

'Leave some for the others, won't you?' said a voice.

Gremorin whirled, smashing a corner of roof from a tavern. The figure leaning causally against the wall below did not flinch. The light that blossomed in his hands pained Gremorin's eyes.

'Loki.' Oh, how he would have enjoyed drinking a god's soul once more. It had been millennia, and no other god deserved it more. 'I will kill you where you stand as penance for your broken promises!'

'And miss out on the gift I have for you?'

'What gift?'

'Why else do you think I have come to this charming little village you're destroying,' Loki said, tutting. 'May I join in?'

Before Gremorin could spit curses and fire, a breathless lad came sprinting down the alleyway. Gawping at the carnage, he managed to realise his mistake before the god seized him by the throat and began to squeeze. Holding his gaping mouth close, ignoring the hands that hammered his arm, Loki dragged the ghost from the worm and turned his eyes white before he dropped him dead.

'Sacrilege,' Gremorin growled.

'Double standards, Prince,' Loki chuckled. 'But it matters not. I've come to pay my debt.'

Gremorin cast his blade and claws wide, searching the inferno. 'You promised us Emaneska, Hel, and Haven. Everything Orion ever wanted. I see them not.'

'Don't forget I brought you the rest of your kin.' Loki pointed to the daemons standing dark against the inferno that was beginning to consume the town.

Gremorin knew the falsehoods this godling kept in his mouth. He started towards him, blade spitting sparks as he aimed for the god's heart, but light spilled from Loki's hands and scorched Gremorin's skin.

'And here I was thinking we could have a civil conversation!' said the little bastard. 'I'm here to give you Paraia, Gremorin. I've withdrawn all Arka forces. The people are defenceless.'

'Paraia,' Gremorin snarled. 'We do not need your Paraia. You seek to distract us with such a paltry offer? We want Hel, and now we have all returned, it will soon be time to claim what is rightfully ours. We do not need you.'

Loki chuckled. 'Hel? Dear me, Gremorin. You're not strong enough for that. I think you do need my help.'

Gremorin reached for the god once more, but Loki put his hands on his hips.

'Think about it. With the Bifröst broken, the gods have built stockpiles of souls in both Hel and Haven thanks to what Farden's fed them.'

Gremorin grinned. 'Precisely.'

'But you forget that makes the goddess Hel stronger than ever. Stronger than the last time you tried to take her domain. You'll fail like you did before.'

Gremorin's grin turned upside down. Loki was right: he and his kin had tried to assail Hel when they had first fallen from the sky, but the goddess and her guard had turned them away with fierce magick.

'You need more than what the north can offer you. Paraia escaped the mage's cataclysm. Emaneska will fight you for every scrap. of land Paraia? They are weakened, defenceless, and superstitious. And there are millions of them, Gremorin. All the souls and meat and workers you could want. All the power you need.' Loki spread his hands as if a feast was laid out before him. 'And between you and me, I know you need to get your subjects in line. I imagine they must doubt you after Malvus made you kneel.'

Gremorin was enraged at the pathetic sounds of the truth. The prince blew fire from his nostrils, taking another swipe at the god. 'You are forgetting the mage and his spear. He does not seek us here.'

'That's because he's forgotten us. Farden is gone. Disappeared into the oceans. A place I know you have no interest in.'

'You would not be trying to trick us again, would you, snake?'

Loki swept a bow. Gremorin almost lopped his head off as he did so, but the god's infernal light shone too brightly.

'I have no cards to play, Prince. No interest in such games. No wars to fight. My only interest is Krauslung and what's left of the Arka. I must be growing complacent in my old age.'

Gremorin had heard enough of the god's voice. 'I will consider it. Now leave us be, before we add you to the dead.'

Loki let the light of his accursed candle flare again, making the daemon snarl.

The god adjusted his coat over his gleaming armour. 'Owe me one favour, though, Gremorin. Start with Troacles. It's bountiful, and it owes me a debt.'

With a snap of his fingers and a crackle of lightning that brought the tavern's sign crashing down where he had stood, Loki vanished. The daemons closed in, encircling Gremorin.

'What did the serpent want?' rumbled one of his captains, Bastazar.

'Why didn't you crush him?' asked another.

There they were, the nibbling leeches of doubt, siphoning away his authority ever since he had knelt before Malvus. Those who had not witnessed it heard the whispers from those who had.

Gremorin searched his mind before he answered. Desperation would see him killed for his weakness, and the scowls surrounding him promised it silently. Decisiveness, even if it was a gamble on the word of a god, was needed.

The prince's voice was as deep as the crackle of the fire. 'The Arka have abandoned Paraia, and Loki offers it upon a plate. There are millions of souls in Paraia. Souls we will bend to our will.'

Eyes blazed around the circle. 'You would trust the serpent again?' another captain spat. 'We do not need a god's offerings. We should have taken Paraia when Loki first failed us.'

Bastazar gnashed his fangs. 'You are weak, Gremorin. The god clicks his fingers, and you spring to his bidding.'

Gremorin thudded his sword into the ground, splitting the flagstones and spreading fire around their feet. 'I am the Shadow of Orion. My word is final. I have made this decision.'

His captains looked between each other before Bastazar spoke for them. 'And if Loki lies?'

'Then we will burn Krauslung to the ground at last.'

That would have to appease them. For now.

CHAPTER 16
REPARATIONS

*Every hero needs a villain. And every villain needs a hero. The two cannot
exist without the other. The question is who will be which?*
KHANDRI PROVERB

Hereni watched Mithrid most of the night. It was a vigil of worry,
spent turning her sword pin over and over while counting the bells
and occasionally checking that Mithrid was still breathing. Hereni
refused to call it standing guard. Besides, she would have been put in
the stocks for the poor job she did. Somehow in the few moments her
tired eyes had betrayed her and sleep had stolen her away, Mithrid
had vanished from their chamber.

Hereni sat up with a start, casting a light spell to check the
room was empty. 'Shit.'

Boots already on, Hereni swept a cloak from a hook and strode
along the chill corridor, ashen in the half-light before dawn.

No other footsteps broke the silence. Not a shadow slid across
the walls but Hereni's.

Beyond the Dawnknell's stone grip, the insects were trilling
and squeaking at the moon. A lone bird warmed up its voice for the
morning chorus. The never-ending battle between the waves and the
rocks beyond the bay was a distant rumble on the breeze.

Not a sign of her. The streets were empty. Mithrid had
vanished.

Hereni let her feet choose for her, and they aimed for the
beach, where she had often found Mithrid skipping stones from the
construction rubble.

‘You went without me,’ rumbled Warbringer, when the first shadows of the day appeared, carving the beach between night and day. It was the first word she had uttered in hours.

Farden blinked dry and frozen eyes. He had almost forgotten he had a minotaur for company. ‘I didn't want to endanger anybody but myself, in case it turned out to be – surprise, surprise – a trap. Mithrid gave me no choice, grabbing onto me at the last second.’

‘Loki owes all of us a death, and more blood needs spilling for my kin.’

‘I have a feeling you'll get that chance. Even if Loki doesn't move against me, the people of Krauslung might just take it upon themselves,’ Farden said through gritted teeth.

It took him but a moment to overflow with the frustration he had been bottling since vanishing from that square full of smirks and grins. Farden bellowed raw emotion, throwing up his arms to gouge the beach and shallows with a spell. As the cloud of sand and water and confused fish tumbled, Warbringer took up his roar, drowning out his voice and making half the docks turn on its heel with owlish eyes.

A skittish guard began to toll the bell, realised what he was doing, and then scrabbled to muffle the bell with an embarrassed smile.

‘Helps, no?’ Warbringer shrugged. ‘How does it feel? To know everybody hate you?’

Farden's gaze rose slowly until he glared at the minotaur. ‘Not *everybody* hates me.’

‘All of Krauslung.’

‘Maybe not all.’

‘Lerel and Elessi are not happy.’

‘I expected that.’

‘Hereni angry. And Mithrid.’

Farden frowned at the ocean. 'She has no right to be.'

'You always worry about her. You not think I see, but I do.'

'You didn't see what I saw in the spider's mirrors. I saw all of Emaneska burning beneath her. Efjar too, for that matter.'

'We all saw two fates. Two futures.'

'And Mithrid just took a big step towards the wrong one. All I want to do is stop her from choosing the path of fire and shadow, but I have no idea how. And if her fate comes true, what does that mean for what I saw in the mirrors? We're on a knife-edge, Warbringer.'

Farden winced as Warbringer prodded his skull with a knuckle. 'Such trouble in that mind,' she said, before clapping him on the back. 'Do not worry. At least Warbringer not hate you.'

Farden allowed himself a smirk, that was all.

'But if I left behind again,' Warbringer tilted a finger back and forth before coming to a halt. 'There something you need know, Farden. Something I not think possible until last battle.'

A yell cut the air and Warbringer's words. Hereni stormed across the sands.

'Have you seen her? Mithrid?' she demanded.

Farden spat a grain of sand that crunched between his teeth. 'Mithrid? I confined her to quarters.'

'As much as I find that ridiculous, she's not confined any more.'

Warbringer put her warhammer on her shoulder with a grunt. 'We speak later, Farden.'

Farden chewed the inside of his lip as the minotaur escaped. 'You clearly still think I'm lying, Hereni, so spit it out. Lerel and Elessi have gone hunting a giant hideous beast and possibly to their deaths, but I can spare a few moments.'

'I don't think you're lying,' Hereni said, shaking her fist with each word as if she hammered an errant spider over and over. 'I just can't believe you.'

'Hurts, doesn't it?' Farden muttered. 'But I know what I saw, and what I had to drag her away from doing. I don't know if it's her magick or the revenge loitering inside her, but Mithrid is changing. Tell me you haven't seen it yourself.'

Hereni tutted. 'What is it you think she's turning into?'

Tell her, whispered the blade at Farden's hip. He thought long and hard, crafting his words for once when he normally would have spat them out. It wasn't as enjoyable, if he had to be honest, but it was for the better.

'I think Mithrid plays a part bigger than we think she does, and I need to make sure it's the right part. But as Durnus said, the more we push, the more she will fight. The more she treads a darker path.'

'Lerel and Elessi have a point: it's a pain in the arse when you're right,' Hereni murmured as she moved past him, pointed at the docks and the eastern bay. 'You know what you need, Farden? Trust. The kind you put in me once when I was nothing but a wretch in a snowstorm. Lerel and Elessi can take care of themselves. They'll be just fine, and so will Mithrid.'

'I hope so,' Farden whispered to the waves and the scuff of angry steps.

'Any news?'

'Thought a king would have better manners, never mind a friend. I'm fine, thanks for asking,' said the dragon, huffing smoke through her nostrils. Fleetstar lounged on the cool stone of a shaded dock, forcing sailors and workers to weave around her swishing tail.

'You're not sulking as well, are you?' Farden sighed.

Fleetstar closed her eyes before she dipped her head to the turquoise water below. 'I saw nothing of the *Undaunted*. The ship's already beyond the horizon. No sign of a keraken either.'

'What's wrong, Fleetstar?'

At last, a glance from the corner of her gleaming eyes. 'Mithrid said you thought Ilios was faster.'

'That petty…' Farden stamped out the words with his tongue and breathed through his nose. 'Where is she?'

'I don't know,' the dragon replied, pausing to dunk her head in the water again.

'Fleetstar.'

'Saw her walking north and west this morning.'

'Thank you. And if you can look again for the *Undaunted*, I would be most grateful.'

'Should get Ilios to search, when he's back.'

Farden's eyes bored into the dragon. 'Lerel and Elessi are out there looking for a creature that could drown them with a mere thought. I need to know they're safe.'

'And if I find them?'

Trust, thought the mage, as he left the irascible dragon to her lounging. 'Tell them that Scalussen needs them alive.'

Onwards, Farden marched. The morning was barely forged, and he had walked the length and breadth of the city twice. He had checked the defences and guards, he had dealt with every foreman with a complaint, he had seen to problems and issues and slain every one, and he had checked the defences a second time. It was all a way of keeping his mind quiet, of course, and to ignore the bleating of, 'Failure!' his thoughts taunted him with. Tiredness now racked Farden like a pox, and yet sleep would only mean surrender to the voices of his mind.

There was, however, one last matter that required a king's attention.

Irien had stared at the crow skull for what felt like a day. She had faced it this way and that, shaken it, prodded it, flicked it, and even tried to prise its beak open. No matter what she did, it refused to speak.

No news was good news, or so the tired adage went, but that didn't apply when there was a god to report to. She had touched its blue gemstone and whispered in the crow's ear of her arrival in Scalussen, but not a whisper had come out of it.

'Loki,' Irien breathed again into the gap in the skull, pressing her finger to the gem once more. 'Did he come to Krauslung?'

Irien froze at the sound of a passing patrol and the changing of the guard. She had already memorised their movements, no matter how many times they changed it up to try to confuse her.

'They still have me locked up, but—'

The crow skull jittered in her palm. It seemed to tilt upwards as if to turn the voids between the bone towards her. To stare. Its blue stone glowed softly beneath her fingernail as the beak opened.

The voice that drifted from its twitching beak was like the hissing of a wet log. It put a shudder down her spine, and Irien fought against it in case the crow – and the god behind it – was indeed watching.

'The mage lives and so do I,' it spoke.

'I thought you had laid a trap.'

Bones crunched as the skull smiled. 'That I did, and it worked perfectly.'

Plans within plans. Irien understood the design if not the purpose. 'And what do you require of me now, my dear?'

'You are useless to me in the mage's dungeon.'

Closing its beak, the skull fell silent and the gemstone faded, and Irien soon heard why: the sound of bodies gathering outside her door. Wood and steel bracing rattled as the locking spell came loose. Irien threw the skull's chain over her neck and adjusted her hair.

Farden stood framed in the torchlight, armour glittering. A sword hung from each hip. One Irien recognised as a Khandri shape, the other was a humble longsword. Far too humble.

'Finally. I thought you'd never release me,' she said, remembering to smile.

'Who says I'm here to release you?' Farden replied, stepping into the gloom of the cell. Irien took a stand, brushed the sand from her hands, and tutted.

'I expected more from you. Where is my grifabore, Saltlick? If you've harmed a bristly hair on his—'

'We're not animals in the west, Irien, and he's enjoying a stable all to himself. Now tell me: why are you really here? You've delivered your news, now what?'

'Did you go to Loki? Is he dead?' Irien asked.

Farden's gaze became thin and dangerous. 'No, more's the pity.'

'More's the pity,' she echoed his words.

'Answer the question.'

'In truth?' Irien took a moment to sigh. 'I have nowhere else to go. Although I don't blame you, to put it bluntly, you ruined me, Farden. I can't go back to Golikar after your antics in the Viscera and since Peskora was killed in the Battle For the World. I was almost killed along with her, might I add.' Irien pointed to the scars along her cheek. 'Nor can I hide in the south with Belerod out for my blood. I have few spies in Emaneska to feed me secrets, and so I came here.'

'Is that what they're calling it?' Farden asked, eyebrows raised. 'This all sounds like a fine reason for revenge.'

'My dear, if I've learned anything in my years, it's that pettiness and vengeance open more wounds than they sew up. You should know that all too well, no? What I need is time and safety, and when I remembered how you spoke of Scalussen and how you called it a haven, I came here and bartered the only secret I had left.'

Farden stood motionless, eyes searching hers.

Irien glanced to the unassuming longsword at the mage's side. 'Is that it?'

Farden's silence was as good as any answer.

'I often wondered if the rumours of the spear's shapeshifting ways were true. How intriguing.'

'And that's all it'll ever be to you. It cost a life to claim it, and I've already paid dearly.'

'The vampyre.'

Farden twitched. 'How do you know?'

'I didn't see him on the battlefield, and I haven't seen him here. Besides, there is a fresh blade on you since Easterealm, Forever King. I thought you sharp-edged before, but now you could cut smoke itself.'

Farden stepped back into the corridor. 'Search her.'

Guards swarmed to check her pockets and the folds of her armour. Their clumsy fingers prodded at her wooden arm and poked in the slack of her boots, but they found nothing at all besides a small crow skull dangling from a chain on her neck.

Farden took it, turning it over in his gauntlets. 'No crossbow?'

'Sold it for the voyage,' Irien said with another smile, this one more forced than before.

'And what is this?'

'A memento. A trinket. A personal treasure. Take your pick. It was offered as payment by a woman who wanted to find her daughter's killer. I normally would have charged much more, of course, but I took a liking to her.'

'I feel magick in this.'

'As you should!' Irien replied. 'It sings every full moon, and a finer song you've never heard. It has always kept me company with its sweet music when life is at its sourest.'

Farden clenched the skull in his hand, but he thought better of breaking it. Neither did he give it back, however.

'Nothing on her, King,' said one of the guards, holding up empty hands.

'Let her loose,' said Farden, giving her space so Irien could swagger out into the corridor.

'I hope my next accommodations will be better,' she asked.

'This is a fortress, not a palace.'

'Expecting company, are you? Another siege? Maybe I was wrong to think this a haven,' Irien brayed as Farden led her towards a doorway of gleaming sunlight.

'When the god of trickery is your enemy, you can't be too careful,' Farden said, staring sidelong and one hand still on a hilt.

'You mean me, of course. Tut tut, Farden. I lied to you once, but I also freed you from Belerod's clutches, or have you forgotten so quickly? I always heard you Emaneskans had poor memories. Now who or what is this?' Irien asked, stabbing a finger at a hulking and hairy individual that stood in their way, splotched brown and white.

'This?' Farden replied, jabbing a thumb at the terrifying figure. 'This is Roglurg. He's a lycan, and he will show you to your new chambers. He'll also be watching your every move.'

Irien put on her finest of smiles. 'Farden, my dear, I don't think that's necessary.'

Farden smiled right back. 'Oh, I think it is.'

'And if I want to see my Saltlick?'

'Feel free. But Roglurg will be right beside you until you prove yourself.'

'Fine,' Irien said, turning haughty. 'If that's how little you trust me.'

Farden leaned close, grey-green eyes switching between hers. 'You live in Emaneska long enough, Lady of Whispers, and you learn it's wise to watch your back,' he said, and Irien found the crow skull dangling in front of her. She took it back with slow and careful hands before the Forever King swept away, leaving Irien alone with the piebald beast.

'Do you speak?' she asked her new minder.

Roglurg bared fangs longer and sharper than Irien wanted to see.

'Fine. Which way to the stables?'

The lycan pointed a claw that was also far too long and curved for her liking, and Irien began to walk, constantly checking over her shoulder to see how close the beast followed. Close, was the answer.

'Why does a beast of your kind follow a human, hmm?' she asked.

No reply came.

'Do you get a choice?'

Roglurg dangled his tongue like a hound.

'I see I'm speaking to a fool.'

The stables were too far for her numbed feet, but Irien pressed on until she glimpsed Saltlick's wings, shining amber in the pervasive sunlight. Scalussen soldiers surrounded the stables, as they did every building of importance, crossroads, and ballista tower. Farden was certainly cautious almost to a fault.

The soldiers parted at the sight of Roglurg and his charge.

'Don't get too close, lycan. You'll scare my Saltlick.'

Despite the beast's silence, he seemed to understand, and Irien greeted the grifabore to a cacophony of grunts and squeals.

'Yes, yes,' Irien said in a soothing voice, stroking the bristles sprouting from Saltlick's eyebrows. With enough attention and a few pinches here and there for good measure, she could keep him in a state of fuss. Masked by Saltlick's grumbling and hidden by his ample rump, Irien lifted the crow skull from her neck, held its gem, and whispered into its ear.

'I'm free.'

The skull jittered before its tongueless beak gaped again, and the stone painted her cupped hands blue. A voice drifted like smoke. 'That was quick.'

'What do you wish me to do, my dear?'

'Learn Farden's city like the back of your wooden hand. Tell me everything. Every door. Every tower. Every weakness. Wait for the hawks,' whispered the distant god before the beak closed once more.

'Show yourself!' yelled a soldier behind her.

'He is a very sensitive beast, I'll have you know, sir! He requires a lot of careful attention!' Irien shouted back, but the soldiers had already had enough of her. Irien could feel Farden's trepidation in them. He had trained them well. No fools, these soldiers.

'You can show me to my quarters, master lycan,' said Irien. 'But first, I would stretch my legs. It's a fine day, after all, and I have not seen the sun in a while.'

Roglurg offered what could have been called a bow and pointed her back to the centre of the city.

Every door. Every tower. Every weakness. Irien had already begun to commit each street to memory.

❧

The sun was on the verge of dying its daily death when Hereni found Mithrid, where the indigo waves of the jealous low tide met the black rocks of Jar Khoum land.

Mithrid sat atop an outcrop, enduring every droplet of spray the ocean had to offer without flinching. Hereni watched her for a time, unsure what to say. Farden's words had echoed in her head since the beach.

'Mithrid!' Hereni yelled over the crashing of waves, but Mithrid didn't turn. She was nothing but stone.

Hereni began to climb, nails rasping against barnacles and dead roots of seaweed until she reached dry stone and found a flat spot next to Mithrid.

'I've been looking for you all day,' Hereni said.

Mithrid did not speak. Her lips were white. The scorch of sun reddened her cheeks and forehead.

'What happened in Krauslung, Mithrid? Farden's told some strange stories.'

Silence again.

'I don't want to believe them. It doesn't sound like you. To think that you'd even—'

'It's true,' Mithrid uttered in the croak of somebody who had spent the day without words. 'Whatever he's said. All of it.'

Hereni placed her hand on Mithrid's, but she did not stir. Hereni clasped what felt like dead flesh, chilled by the ocean winds. 'It can't be.'

'I would have cut through every single one of them just to see Loki bleed. Everyone. Young or old. I didn't care.'

'You told me it was love that filled your mind when you beat Malvus, not hate. Thoughts of us, not thoughts of him. What's changed?'

Mithrid fell quiet again. She had yet to blink, eyes full of the ocean's colours and the sun's fading.

'What's changed, Mithrid?' Hereni shook her hand. Mithrid seized her at last, but not in an embrace. She dug her nails in, squeezing tight. Hereni gripped back, ignoring the pain.

'The waiting. The mockery. The constant question of fate,' Mithrid said, grinding out her words.

Hereni crept along the ragged edge of a sore subject. 'Fate. I've heard that word far too much since you three came back. Just what did you see in that spider's mirrors?'

Mithrid gripped harder until Hereni had to twist herself free. 'Mithrid!'

'Fire and ruin. The same fire I see in my nightmares every night,' she answered.

'That's why you twitch and turn, isn't it? I try to wake you, but you don't even know I'm there. You think that's your fate? Fire and ruin? That's your past, Mithrid. Not your future.'

Mithrid shrugged her away, almost pushing her from the rock, and started to scramble back to the sand. Her voice was a whisper. 'You don't understand.'

'Fine, then you make a choice!'

The words were almost lost to the crashing sea, but Mithrid yelled them like a battle-cry. 'Why don't you ask Farden? He thinks it's already been made.'

❦

'It was a trap, pure and simple,' Farden uttered, watching the witches' birds titter at his failure. He saw Queen Nerilan's eyes gleam and Towerdawn's harden. Warbringer simply growled. Eyrum and Sipid studied the table intently. Sturmsson teased his moustache in thought.

'And what does this mean for us?' Eyrum was the first to speak.

'My thoughts exactly,' Nerilan piped up. 'Could it be you've stoked the fire, Farden? Poked the hornet's nest? Stirred the—'

'I get it,' Farden snapped. The council had called itself without his order. He might have owed them an explanation, but not an apology. 'It was nothing but theatre for Loki's own amusement and gratification. Another nail in my reputation, at most. The only fire I've stoked is his ego.'

'You should not have gone,' rumbled Towerdawn.

'Perhaps I shouldn't have, Old Dragon,' Farden answered. 'But we all know I had to try.'

'And now we watch the horizon for doom,' Peryn muttered, quite unlike her. Even the High Crone clicked bony fingers before her face.

Farden spun the spear on the table. 'The witch is right.'

Nerilan made a rasping noise as if she sucked at a seed stuck in her teeth. 'Then what would you propose, mage?'

'What you all urged me to do before. We dig in. New Scalussen will become the fortress it was meant to be. Gates locked. Arrows nocked. Quickdoors at hand. The army will stand ready to crush any foot he sets on this shore,' Farden said.

'And what if he discovers where we are and wants to sneak in like last time?' asked Eyrum.

'He won't. I can feel him when he's close. The spear can sense him, and dragons and witches will search minds and patrol with the lycans as before,' Farden replied. 'If Loki comes south, he will come with an army at his back, and we will be ready for him.'

Nerilan sniffed. 'How can you be so confident he will?'

'Because I know my enemy. Loki has nothing but the people of Krauslung and a shattered army. Nothing that compares to our combined number. The daemons have abandoned Loki for his betrayal and they fear Gunnir too much to crawl south. That being said, I know now that we can't invade Krauslung without considerable death on both sides. That's what Loki wants. Loki is more powerful and slipperier than ever, but the bastard needs an audience. Give it time, and his adoring citizens won't be enough. He wants me. He wants the spear. He wants all of us dead. So he'll come to Paraia, and we'll be waiting as we did in the ice fields when Malvus came knocking, with magick, tough steel, and dragonfire,' Farden promised.

'Not forgetting the beast Elessi and Lerel are searching for,' said Eyrum.

Farden tutted. 'How could I?'

Towerdawn had a doubt. 'And what if he manages to make peace with the daemons?'

Warbringer snorted in a chuckle. 'Worry not. They run like chickens at mere sight of spear.'

'If Loki manages to rebuild that bridge, we'll be ready for them as well, and I'll cut them down one by one and do what the gods never could.'

'And what of the gods' request?' Nerilan reminded him. 'The weak minds of Krauslung already bow before Loki. What if the other gods were to stand before Krauslung and denounce him? Your precious Evernia? Jötun? Krauslung would be forced to believe.'

'And I've already told you: I won't curse this world with further complication. The gods chose their fate. They can stay in the sky where they belong, and we'll stay free of their slavery.'

'And when did that become your choice to make?' Nerilan whispered, voice tight.

Farden had an answer ready to fire. 'Since they tugged at our strings and toyed with our lives. Since they used the breaking of the Bifröst to fill Hel and Haven with souls and reap their power for their own gain. We don't need the gods to purge our lands of Loki.'

There came a squeak of hinges as the door to the council chamber opened. Hereni stood behind it, and she moved quickly to take her place.

'And where is your other missing general?' Nerilan asked. 'What was it about your excursion to Krauslung that's kept Mithrid from us?'

Farden could have cursed her right there and then.

Hereni gave the queen a sour look. 'Mithrid is resting.'

'Does she wallow in failure as your king does?' asked the queen ever so nonchalantly.

'Nerilan,' Towerdawn sighed.

Farden looked to Hereni. 'She almost took Loki down, Nerilan. She might have, had it not been for Loki's believers standing in her way.'

'If you ask me, you should have cut the fools down—'

'Nobody asked, Queen. And some of us still have a heart beating in our chests. They may be fools, but they're innocent fools, and they're all that's left of my people and much of Emaneska. I will not murder them.'

Nerilan slashed that whip of a tongue once more. 'You think you've changed? You had no such qualms when it came to skulking in Albion killing peasants for a duke, or reducing Malvus' horde to ashes, or breaking Easterealm. Your opinion of innocence seems untrustworthy, King.'

Like the many others that had been forged before, the knives of those choices would never leave his heart, and the mage felt them slice deeper as uncomfortable expressions turned in his direction.

Farden got to his feet and spread his hands over the table, metal grinding against stone. 'I treat any hand that picks up a sword against me and mine as an enemy. Any hand, Nerilan.' He turned the spear so it briefly faced Nerilan before he folded it away into the shape of a sword. 'A pleasure as always, Queen.'

Nerilan tried to quail him with her golden stare, but Farden had endured the stare of the cruellest of Siren queens before, and Nerilan was nothing if not Svarta's lesser. She left the council with a derisive snort and the others bowed before following in her steps. Only Towerdawn remained, and the Old Dragon looked to be wincing.

Farden thought he understood. 'How can you two be so different?'

'Elessi asked me a similar question not long ago,' The dragon led the way to the ledge that poked into thin air. 'Did Farfallen ever tell you, Farden, that a dragon's bond is strong but not unbreakable?'

'I thought it was only broken by death.'

'Even then, not completely. A dragon can choose the rider they bond with, but they do not choose whom they will turn out to be across the centuries of our connection. Nerilan and I once shared the same mind and heart, but no longer. It is only a soul we now share, and I feel that bond straining, like a love turning to hatred.'

'What can be done?'

'Nothing. Our bond will wither, and the both of us will fade with it. It is what we Sirens call the schism, and it has happened before, though only once to an Old Dragon.'

'Something can be done, surely?'

Towerdawn sniffed the wind, letting his scales ripple from his neck down to his tail. 'It will be weeks, months before it truly matters, but it has begun. I wanted you to know, not to worry. I stand with you, even if Nerilan does not, and the dragons will follow me.'

'I wish I could offer some comfort.'

'There is no comfort to offer besides friendship, Farden, as always.'

Farden bowed and put a hand to the dragon's shoulder. 'Hel, I could do with some comfort myself. I always thought rulers lounged about on cushions all day, drinking wine and nibbling grapes like deer.'

'A fine and beautiful lie.'

Towerdawn extended his wing, and Farden took his offer, leaping to the queen's saddle. Towerdawn plummeted from the Dawnknell to circle it twice. Then with strong beats of his wings, they were out over the bay and weaving between boats.

Do you worry for Elessi and Lerel? Towerdawn asked in Farden's head.

'Of course I do, and I would be chasing them down right now if I wasn't trying this new thing called trust,' Farden called over the wind.

Smoke billowed as the dragon laughed. Towerdawn swerved back to the Winter Fortress.

A keraken would be a mighty weapon. A mighty trap to spring.

'And that's why I'm clinging to hope.'

Towerdawn flared his wings as his claws gouged sand. 'Nerilan and I agree on one thing, Farden. That is the return of the gods. Why ignore the greatest weapon we have?'

Farden spoke honestly. 'I respect you more than most, Towerdawn, but I am the greatest weapon we have. And after me – as much as I hate to admit it – it's Mithrid. You know as well as I do that gods rely on two things: belief and the souls filling Haven and Hel. They might not feast on us like the daemons and Loki do, but they are still dependent on us. That's why we were created, after all, to feed them power, and there's no good that can come from that. They will always seek to use us, and I won't let that happen any longer.'

The dragon raised his giant head and stretched his scales once more. 'The last chance to make the right decision has not yet come,' was all he said, striking a chord in Farden's mind.

'I hope that's true,' he muttered in the backdraft of the dragon's mighty wings. As the sand faded, he saw Mithrid standing at the edge of the fortress. She gave him moments only before she turned to disappear behind stone and wood.

Farden bowed his head. Sleep called to him, but he lingered by the waters for a time, looking out to where the calm currents of the bay collided with the rough ocean. *Gods, did he need Lerel.*

CHAPTER 17
FRIENDS NEW

*The closest those of us shackled to the dirt and born without wings will ever
come to flying is racing across the high seas.*
FROM THE DIARY OF ADMIRAL STURMSSON

The air felt weak and sluggish once the *Undaunted* finally slowed, sails half-furled. The constant and exhilarating chill in Lerel's cheeks grew warm in the morning sun, and they turned somehow all the number for it.

'Gods, how far have we come?' Elessi announced herself with a yawn as she emerged from the cabin behind the wheel. 'I don't recognise any of this land.'

Lerel cast a look at the terracotta rocks that poked from the water in twisted spires and huddled together to build cliffs. Something or somebody had spread thick webs between their spindles to catch birds. Lerel hoped it was the latter.

'Where are we?' Elessi asked.

'A day and a half from New Scalussen. Less than a few hours from Magre, by my measure. I've got a lookout perched on every spar, aft and stern. If your beast shows so much as a grotesque sucker, we'll see it.'

Elessi saw to breakfast, dragging the cook out of his hammock and helping him to set up tables of provisions for the crew. The smell of dry sausages, fresh bread, and fried potatoes tickled Lerel's stomach.

'No good cooking up all the supplies if we're to be out here longer than we thought,'

Elessi flashed her a smile and wink and even knocked on the crust of a warm loaf. Lerel gave in, and she was beckoning to a first mate when a cry came from a lookout. A rather high-pitched cry at that.

'Fifteen degrees starboard!'

Lerel whirled to catch the faint glimpse of an object rearing out of the sea. Something silvery and huge enough to be what they hunted.

The crew tottered about the deck with their breakfast clamped into mouths as Lerel leaned the *Undaunted* over and had a few more sails spread. The ship lurched on her wings, flying once more across the waves.

'Be ready!' yelled Lerel. 'Nobody's to throw a spell or a fire a single arrow, you hear me?'

'Aye!' chorused the crew.

Lerel brought the *Undaunted* around again to circle where the splash had come from.

'To our stern!' sounded another cry.

Once again, Lerel went hard at the wheel, and the sailors slid back to the starboard.

'Right beside us now!'

Lerel's heartbeat thudded at the edges of her vision. Even she left the wheel to see what it was.

'A bloody whale shark!' barked a sailor at the bow. 'Big bastard, too!'

It was a strange mix of disappointment and relief that washed over her, as she watched the gawping length of silver-spotted brown pass by. The fish was almost a third of the *Undaunted's* size. Lerel heard Elessi slap a bulwark.

'Onwards!' Lerel ordered. 'Chew and swallow and get back to work! Clear the decks.'

But Elessi belayed that order, making sure the cook kept the food out.

'Elessi.'

'Trust me, Lerel.'

Lerel didn't want to, but she let the general have her way.

They had gone maybe a mile when an eruption of water on the port side made every bastard aboard turn, hearts nudging half-chewed loaf in their mouths. A shadow crossed the sun, but it was no tentacle. It was suspiciously shark-shaped. And suspiciously dead. Lerel yelled a warning she had never uttered before.

'Whale shark!'

Sailors scattered like roaches before the torch, all too eager to escape the descending fish. One young fellow barely made it out alive, torn which way to flee until he hurled himself overboard. The dead fish landed on the deck with a squelch and a boom, making the *Undaunted* crash into a wave and lurch madly.

'Njord's balls!' yelled her second in command, a short barrel of a man the others called Da. The wanted posters in Lezembor used to call him Blue Laroso the Blade, a pirate of wicked proportions. 'That's a warning shot if I've ever seen one!' A cutlass wiggled in one hand, a buckler shield was clutched in the other.

'What if it's a gift?' said Elessi, clinging to the stairs.

'Gift?' Lerel spluttered.

'Like an emissary would bring. It's enough to feed us for a week.'

'We're not fishermen, Elessi.'

Laroso scratched at his sapphire beard. 'She ain't wrong, though.'

'Fetch that man out of the water! Drop sail and cast ropes,' Lerel yelled as she spun the *Undaunted* about to fetch the fallen sailor. 'And I want that monster of a fish off my deck! Give it back to the sea.'

'But what if that's the wrong—'

'We can't sail with it on our deck, simple as that.' Lerel levelled a finger at Elessi. 'What are you playing at with the breakfast?'

'Bait. There's something human entwined with this keraken, and there's not a human in the world who can ignore such a thing as a good breakfast.'

'You think this thing is a cat you can dangle some yarn in front of?'

Elessi wore a mischievous smile. 'It worked, didn't it?'

No sooner had the shark slid into the waters did it get sucked down by some unseen force.

'Agh!' came a yell from the overboard sailor. His vanished with a ripple of water, shout drowned into a bubbling.'

Elessi went paler than usual. 'Gods, what if it thinks that's our gift?'

'Worked, you say, Elessi? Get more ropes out there! We better hope it gives him back like we did.'

'No!' yelled another sailor, more distraught than the others aboard. Maybe a friend. A brother, most likely, and he readied himself to dive in after him before Laroso dragged him back. 'No!'

A hand clawed at the air for a moment as the sailor broke the surface, drawing a breath like the lowing of a cow. A rope was thrown, and he thrashed around to seize it. The giant shadow beneath him grew darker.

'Give him back!' Elessi yelled. 'Release him!'

With an almighty splash, the man was cast from the water. Thankfully, not on the same trajectory as the whale shark, and he collided with the *Undaunted*'s railings with a groan. Sailors scurried to seize him and drag him back to the deck where he belonged.

Lerel bellowed her orders, eyes still fixed on the shadow. It moved then, shifting beneath the ship, and it kept shifting for far too long before it disappeared. It must have been four times their length, and it headed further north.

'Fetch that man a healer and get him below!' Lerel ordered, fighting not to stutter.

'What do we do now? Does it want us to follow?' asked Elessi.

'Magre is that way. I say we go after it. It would have destroyed us by now if it didn't like us,' said Lerel. 'I think.'

'Then onwards it is.'

'You regretting this yet?'

'Not yet.'

Each of them taking a breath, Lerel went back to the wheel, swinging the ship after the keraken and further down the coast. 'All sail!'

❧

No matter how high the sun climbed and how harshly it beat down, and no matter how the breezes raced along the shallows, the fog clinging to the coastline refused to fade. For an hour now, Lerel had guided the *Undaunted* around its edges, and there was not a break in the murk. Neither was there sight nor sound of the keraken.

'Why does the word *trap* come to mind?' whispered Lerel.

Laroso blew the sparks of his pipe over the side. 'Don't like this, Boss.'

The wheel clicked as Lerel aimed the bow into the fog. 'The name of this ship is *Undaunted*, not *Cautious*,' she replied. 'I want oars out! Nice and slow. Quarter sail and spotters on the bowsprit!'

The sailors kept silent as they carried out her orders.

'Two points port, Admiral!' came barely more than a loud whisper came from the bow. Lerel shifted the wheel ever so slightly, and the hushed crew watched the blackened nose of a ship pass them by. It was no design that Lerel recognised, nor Laroso, judging by his grumbling.

Another shipwreck passed them by, slow waves lapping at the rotten bones of timber. The water was black with their grease.

'You smell that? Smells like old fire and char,' Elessi whispered at Lerel's side.

Ko-Tergo hummed. 'Smells like dragon.'

'More importantly, do you hear that?'

A faint whooshing turned heads, and the fog at the tip of the masts swirled as a shadow swung overhead.

'Archers! Mages!' Elessi bellowed.

The shadow danced away, and bows and spells began to slacken when it reappeared, coming straight for them.

'There!' Ko-Tergo pointed a sharp claw.

Elessi drew her shortsword and held it as Modren had taught her, long ago. 'Hold!'

A white and copper dragon loomed, wings flaring at the sight of magick burning in the hands of mages. 'By Thron's cock, you're jumpy,' she boomed.

Ducking under the rigging, claws prising caulking from the planks, Fleetstar alighted on the deck and folded her wings as small as she could make them. 'This ship is unfairly fast.'

'Make sure you tell Sturmsson that when you see him next,' said Lerel. 'But more importantly, why are you here?'

'Farden wanted me to find you and make sure you hadn't been eaten yet. Or something to that effect.'

Elessi scoffed. 'He wants us to come back, doesn't he?'

'No,' Fleetstar said, showing off her knifelike fangs. 'He said Scalussen needs you alive. Wished you good luck, I think. I had stopped listening at that point.'

'Well,' Lerel replied, somewhat surprised. 'You can tell him we'll be back soon.'

'You can tell him yourself. I just flew half of Paraia trying to find you. I would rather rest for now—what was that?' Fleetstar's scales crackled as her head snapped around.

'Don't play games, Fleetstar.'

'I don't,' the dragon growled. 'I heard a splash.'

'Porpoise, maybe. Ray fin. Shark tail,' Laroso listed, neither helpfully nor loudly.

Flame flickered around the crooks of Fleetstar's jaws. Claws slid further from their sheaths, as did the blades and arrows of the crew.

'Steady now,' Elessi whispered. 'Do nothin' until I say.'

Lerel stamped her feet twice. 'All stop,' she ordered.

They lingered amidst sea and fog, in a netherworld that felt as if they had drifted off the edge of the map. Lerel would have rather faced the Cape of No Hope than this place of deathly dreaming. She brought the ship to a wide space between four more shipwrecks, one pierced by a spear of rock. Black cormorants fanned their wings as if in greeting.

'You still hear it, Fleetstar?'

'Not a sound no, just ripples and—'

The dragon never got to finish her sentence. The greasy waters before them foamed and bubbled as the broad masts of a drowned ship rose up from the depths. Not a sail was stretched between her spars, and every inch of rigging and plank that emerged was clad in seaweed, slime, and barnacles, and yet faint glimmers of light could still be glimpsed through the portholes. A narwhal's horn of astounding proportions thrust from its bow. The ship was a giant, almost as big as the *Winter Fortress*, gods rest her bones, and to Lerel's awe, utterly fused to what looked like a submerged island.

'Njord save us...' Laroso wheezed.

The ocean exploded as the rest of the keraken emerged. Lakes of water lifted into the air before crashing and pouring down. It rained on the *Undaunted*, and the oars had to fight the waves that rocked them.

It was not an island but a shell. Like that of a tortoise but far, far bigger, and covered in sharp ridges like a dragon's spine. What lurked in its hollow was a monstrous tangle of scarlet tentacles. Some held the squid-like behemoth out of the water, others weaved sinuous patterns through air and water. Each of them was lined with spines or fangs and round craters of suckers.

As the sea poured in waterfalls, a maw of what looked like two massive beaks ringed with dagger-teeth opened. It was enough to make anyone soil their trews, never mind the two great eyes poking from the sheen of its gnarled skin. They were yellow discs pierced by the deepest and darkest void Lerel had ever stared into, and she found herself knocking against the wheel as she tipped forwards.

'What do we do?' whispered Lerel as the creature loomed.

Elessi's knuckles were white on the railing. 'I don't know.'

'I thought you had a plan.'

'That ended with breakfast. I thought you had a plan!'

'You're the one who wanted to talk to it!' cried Ko-Tergo.

Lerel strangled the wheel. 'So start talking, before it eats us.'

'H-hello!' Elessi hollered, voice cracking slightly and sounding more like a question. She cleared her throat and tried again, winding her way down the stairs and towards the bow. 'We mean you no harm. We only wanted to thank you for your assistance with the pirates! The Burned Raiders of Mael!'

The humongous eyes moved in different directions, but both ended up fixed on the dragon crouched on their deck. The monster loomed closer, tentacles reaching for the ship. Four surrounded them, flexing and rippling as the shriek of a bolt long-rusted came tumbling from the ship towering above them. To their utter surprise, a lone stranger poked an arrow-shaped head above the bulwark and hollered down to them in a voice of grinding stone and with an accent that had long been lost to the sea. Two pinpricks of wavering light showed his eyes.

'Do you call that dragon a friend?' he asked.

'Is that a riddle?' Lerel asked, surprisingly the first question out of her mouth instead of the obvious, 'Who in Hel is that?'

'We do!' Elessi yelled back.

The tentacles inched closer, their strange, splayed jaws gnashing. 'We do not like dragons! Duplicitous beasts!'

'I couldn't agree more!' said Elessi. 'But you can trust this one. She and her kind have saved our lives more than once! Maybe helped save the world.'

'No bloody maybe about it,' muttered Fleetstar, flinching away as Elessi put a hand on her shoulder.

The figure took its precious time thinking. 'We do not trust you.'

'Yet you helped us! Twice, now. You could have destroyed us already, but you chose not to. Why is that?'

'We'll be answering no questions of yours until we hear the truth.'

Elessi and Lerel shared worried glances. 'Which is?' Ko-Tergo called out.

'Was that fresh bread we could smell?'

Elessi wore a smile when she turned back to the aftcastle. Lerel rolled her eyes.

'It was,' Elessi crowed. 'And we have plenty of it.'

A tentacle rose up for the man to step upon, and he descended swiftly, hopping onto the deck with a thud and a squelch.

The man was neither a ghost nor ghoul, but he was of patchwork and mismatched items, from his coat of a thousand pieces to the half dozen belts wrapped around his chest. A beard of braids woven into ever more complex patterns covered his chest of sewn leathers, no design that Lerel recognised. The glint in his peculiar eyes had not been a trick of the light. They were the same shape as the keraken's and continued to glow the same faint yellow as he surveyed the dragon. A hat with three points perched on a river of hair that flowed down his back in a plaited tail. In his pale hand, a thin sabre of silver waited to be used. The other hand reached out, beckoning for bread.

At Elessi's order, the cook brought a platter of the bread he had just stowed away and offered it to the sharp-eyed man. He took it swiftly, on the verge of snatching, and took a tentative bite. It wasn't long before he was cramming the rest into his mouth and making appreciative sounds.

Lerel saw the tension in the crew, never mind the quiver in the cook's hand, and motioned for them to stay put. She could feel Fleetstar's growling reverberating in the planks.

The strange sailor sheathed his sabre, dusted flour from his hands, and rumbled deep in his throat. 'It's been a decade since we had good bread,' he rasped. 'Why did you come to find us?'

Elessi approached slowly. 'To express our gratitude, and to ask why you helped us.'

'And to thank you for not killing us,' murmured Lerel.

'Not yet, at least,' the sailor said, picking crumbs from his beard and grinning. 'You are not pirates. You brought leviathans south for Keraken to chase. And your ships…' He trailed off to examine the mast and stamp his boots on the planks. 'They are fine specimens. We have not seen a ship like this before.'

'We call her the *Undaunted*—'

'What else?' the sailor interrupted. 'It's a long way to travel to say thanks.'

'To find out more about you and about your tharkun.'

The sailor sniffed. 'We haven't heard that name in some time. But still, the answer isn't the right one. Before we speak more, you will help us. Consider that another reason why you're still alive.'

'What could you possibly need help with?' asked Lerel.

The sailor pointed a long fingernail at Fleetstar. 'A dragon.'

'In Paraia?'

'It has stolen Keraken's home and claimed our cave. Keraken is fearsome, but fire is not his favourite, and this dragon's fire is fierce.'

The keraken waved a tentacle rippled with the darker marks of a burn.

'You remove the dragon, we will talk.'

Lerel wracked her brain to make sense of the challenge. *What dragon could face a keraken and force it from its home?* 'Where is your home?'

'That way.' The sailor pointed to the fog-bound coast before another tentacle picked him up to place him back upon his ship. As the water whirled and boiled, the keraken slipped into the black depths. The sailor was the last to vanish, standing aboard the bowsprit to endure the cold clasp of the ocean.

'I have so many questions,' Ko-Tergo whispered.

'Looks like we have to fight a dragon.'

'We need Farden,' muttered Fleetstar.

'We don't need Farden,' Elessi snipped the end off the dragon's words.

Lerel looked to the wide eyes of her crew, now stretched wide with relief. 'That way,' she uttered, and watched her crew go to work. All she could do was hope Elessi was right.

CHAPTER 18
ENEMIES OLD

Never forget the Great Ones. Never forgive the Great Ones.
SCRAWLED ON THE LAST PAGE OF 'REVENGE' BY ELIVIMENDEZ

The keraken's lair was like a colossal hood without a head to fill it. The *Undaunted* could have been three times as tall and it still wouldn't have grazed them. Stalactites dangled ominously from the lips and roof of the cave like teeth. Fog clung to Magre's mouth like malodorous breath.

A harbour wall of broken ships and boats gave them only one route to follow. The gap in it looked burned at its edges, as if dragonfire had been there. The sailor had spoken the truth.

Lerel stood by Fleetstar's side at the prow. 'Has anyone but you left Nelska, Fleetstar?'

'Not that I know of,' she said, keeping watchful eyes and ears on the fog.

'Then it must be another dragon,' Lerel muttered.

Elessi already had her sword out. 'I have a suspicion.'

No sooner had the Undaunted darkened the innards of the cave did a snarl echo. No tentacles came this time, but a burst of fire raced along the teeth of the cave instead. On a landslide of rocks at the rear of the cave, a dark figure of a dragon loomed in the fearsome glow, wings hunched and jaws unhinged. A figure stood by its side, a butcher's cleaver of a sword in both hands and spiked armour glinting.

'It can't be,' Fleetstar growled.

Lerel snatched for a spyglass. 'Is that...?'

Elessi needed none. It seemed as if she had already guessed. 'I bloody knew it! It's Saker and Fellgrin. The damn Lord of the Winds! We always wondered where they escaped to after the battle for Scalussen.'

'Shit.' They might as well have been pitted against an Old Dragon. Fellgrin's iron plates were turning gold at their ragged edges in her old age, and it was well-known that dragons grew mightier with every passing year.

'Reverse oars!' Lerel yelled as the dragon clawed at the rubble. 'Shield spells!'

The order came just in time. Fire clattered against the spells spread beyond the *Undaunted*'s bowsprit, bending them under the immense heat of the dragon's breath. The heat billowed in the sails as the force drove the *Undaunted* into deeper water.

Lerel used the momentum to fade back into the mists, skirting sideways to skulk behind a spire of rock. Fellgrin roared in challenge, but there was no chase.

'We need a plan instead of charging in,' suggested Ko-Tergo with a scowl.

Lerel stood her ground. 'I didn't think it was true.'

'What in Hel is Saker doin' all the way down here?' asked Elessi.

'Cowardice,' replied Lerel. 'And a whole dragon-load of it to have fled this far.'

If anyone had the gall to think Elessi was skating on pure luck and guesswork, she showed the general in her heart right there and then. 'I say we light fires and get the ballistae and catapults stretched. Come in blazin' from a distance so we can draw Fellgrin away from the cave. At the same time, Fleetstar can take us in close underwater so we can strike at the heart of the cave. They seem precious about their stolen home to me, so if Fellgrin goes for Fleetstar as she escapes back to the ship, maybe it'll split them apart. Saker's strong, but he's no match for you, Ko-Tergo. You can hide your strength until he thinks he has the upper hand.'

Lerel nodded. 'Kill him, kill the dragon.'

'Gods,' Fleetstar grumbled, even though she was already stretching her wings. 'Do I ever get a say?'

'This plan is batshit, as you southerners like to say,' Ko-Tergo interrupted. 'You know that, right?'

'Best plan I've heard all day,' grunted Laroso, tapping the point of his cutlass on the deck.

Lerel clicked her fingers at the silent crew. 'Let's get to preparing.'

It took an hour to make ready, and by then the day was clouding over the fog, forcing an early evening. It was a fine excuse to put their so-called batshit plan into action.

'Keep her moving nice and quick, and use every cover you've got,' ordered Lerel, fingers drifting from the wheel. 'If not, we're looking at either a very long swim or a very long walk home.'

'Aye, Admiral,' answered Laroso with a click of his heels. 'She's in good hands.'

With a curved sword she'd found in Akitha's armoury lashed across her back and two knives on her belt, Lerel joined an armoured Elessi and Ko-Tergo. The latter had also put some armour over his white fur for once, and Lerel hoped it was for the ruse. She couldn't stand the thought of the yetin being afraid enough to need armour. That felt too dire.

Two more mages had also joined them, armed to the teeth with blades, and they nodded grimly as the admiral passed and fell in behind her.

'You ever done this before, Elessi?' Lerel asked as she climbed aboard the waiting Fleetstar. Elessi was already strapped into her half of the saddle. Ko-Tergo and the mages were grasped in Fleetstar's claws or clung to the dragon's spine.

'No I haven't,' said Elessi with a shake in her voice. 'And I'm startin' to regret the idea. You? You've got far fewer years on you. Me? I think I'm gettin' too old for this s—agh!'

Elessi yelped as Fleetstar abruptly lunged from the deck of the *Undaunted* and into the dark sea washing about the ship.

The biting cold turned a muffled yell into a stream of bubbles, but Lerel hung tight until Fleetstar swam at the surface, winding through the waters with her wings trailing and body moving like a snake's ripple. The *Undaunted* followed, spells already vibrating the air.

'Nobody's dying over this, you hear me?' Lerel called out to her crew and the others aboard the dragon.

As they crossed the teeth of the cave and entered the detritus harbour, Lerel breathed out until her chest ached, and then took the deepest lungful she could before Fleetstar submerged. The deeper and darker they went, the more it felt as if a hand gripped her skull and squeezed.

Above them, two streaks of fire brightened the murky waters. A wide shadow raced in the opposite direction with flames dancing in its jaws. Lightning crackled around its wings and across the water. A dull splash made them all turn to see a chunk of stalactite surrounded by bubbles and plummeting towards the seabed point first. Fleetstar manoeuvred around it and gripped rocks choked by seaweed and black moss. Pale crabs scattered from her claws.

Bubbles escaping her mouth, Lerel knocked on the dragon's scales as her lungs began to burn. They weren't blessed with choices, and now had to be the time to pounce. Fleetstar lunged once more, this time up the rocky slope and out of the water, hurling them into a pile of gravel and sweltering firelight. Sconces of rock burned all around them. Lerel coughed at the smoke and bitter oily scent of smouldering incense.

At the cave's mouth, the *Undaunted* had retreated out of sight but kept her ballistae firing. Bottles sailed through the air with a catapult's blessing to explode against the rocks and shipwrecks.

Saker was in his dragon's saddle, two swords raised high and screaming wordless hatred as they ducked and weaved between stalactites.

'Throw a few spells Fellgrin's way!' Elessi ordered. 'Get his attention.'

Their mages obliged, crafting shards of ice between their hands and sending them racing for the dragon. One smashed against the cave wall, but the other struck Fellgrin on the arse as she hovered to blow fire – much to the mage's apparent delight. But all smiles faded as Fellgrin swivelled in midair to face the shore and saw their little huddle. An unholy screech came out of her, and it wasn't a noise Lerel had ever heard a dragon make. Fire streamed from her gaping jaws. It was rage, and it chilled Lerel to her marrow.

Before the shield spells could spread before them, the shallows exploded as Fleetstar emerged. Fire burst from her mouth, filling the air and causing Fellgrin to veer away. It didn't stop her from spewing the shore with fire, however, and the others huddled behind the rocks and the mages as the inferno engulfed them. Lerel gasped as the air was stolen from her. It lasted only a moment, but it was enough to make the mages reel from the effort. Fleetstar spared them by digging her claws into Fellgrin's shoulder and snapping at Saker himself. Steel clanged against tough scale as Fleetstar released her hold to escape into the fog. Fellgrin snapped at her tail, almost catching her twice before ballistae bolts sought to pierce her belly.

Lerel almost missed the shape falling from Fellgrin's saddle, the splash amidst the angry waves, and the dark figure sliding through the shallows before them. 'Here comes Saker,' she shouted. 'Spread out!'

Ice glittered in the mages' grips. Blades were held dripping and full of firelight. Metal squeaked as Ko-Tergo struggled to hold back his true form. The claws on his fingers were already growing.

A sun-browned face studded with two vile, yellow eyes and a mouthful of sharpened teeth surfaced from the waters. The Lord of the Winds kept coming, revealing carved arms contained by stone and iron bracelets and clenching two curved swords with saw edges. His boots crunched on the rock as he drew closer and closer.

'You Scalussen scum! I should have known from the black sails. Elessi and Lerel, those are your names, are they not? And a white wilder of the north, same as I.' Saker beat his chest proudly. 'Why can you not help but meddle and pry and needle? Why can you not leave me be and give me peace?!'

'Because you deserve none! This started as a favour for a friend, but it's turned out to be a personal pleasure,' answered Lerel. 'You stood with Malvus, and that would be enough reason to take our revenge even if you hadn't struck down hundreds of our people.'

'And you eradicated mine,' seethed Saker. 'I am the last of my kin, and yet that is still not good enough for the mighty lords and ladies of Scalussen? Curious, how you believed Malvus and his Arka to be the tyrants! I'll have my peace if I have to carve it out of you!'

Saker pounced, aiming two swords at Lerel. She dodged, catlike, leaving room for the mages to sling their spells. One knocked a blade from Saker's hand, the other left a wound across his bald head.

Lerel swung her sword but found nothing but thin air. Instead, Saker's blade snuck around hers to draw a rasping cut across her vambrace. Elessi darted into the fray, aiming for the bastard's neck, but an elbow to her face sent her staggering back the way she came, blood leaking between her fingers. It was now Ko-Tergo's turn, and he wasted no time on introductions. Ripping the mail from his chest, he flung it around Saker's face before punching him squarely in the teeth. Saker snarled as his sword flashed back and forth, carving himself space to recover. He took a moment to spit one of his many teeth into the gravel.

One of the mages struck again, two shards of ice in each hand like blades, but his bravery was not enough. With a spin, Saker cut deep into the man's wrists, right through the metal, and left a trail of blood in his wake.

The other mage roared, using a shield spell to force Saker back a step. A huge blade of ice protruded from his clenched hands, and he drove it at Saker like a lance. Lerel ran behind him with Elessi, swords aimed for the rider's face.

To the smashing of ice, the mage stopped dead, legs flying out from under him to dangle and twitch. Saker twisted his sword, eliciting a crunch of bone, and the blade slid free of the mage's face.

With a cry, Lerel slashed across Saker's ribs, only grazing armour but distraction enough for Elessi to stab at his neck. She struck his shoulder instead, but the Lord of the Winds still grunted in pain.

'You are weak! Where's your precious Farden?' Saker spat as he held both their blades against his, locked in the notches of his dark steel. 'Didn't think enough of me to come fight me himself? Had to send his women to do it for him, did he?'

Lerel sneered. 'Farden doesn't even know you still exist. And don't you worry, we're plenty enough for you.' Her hand fled the handle of her sword for the hilt of a knife. The silver raced for Saker's chest, where his armour was thinnest, but all she managed was a dent before he twisted his sword and booted her in the chest. Elessi's blade cut his cheek before he knocked it away and kicked sand in her face.

Ko-Tergo, on the other hand, tackled Saker with his full weight and barged the rider onto the rocks. Clawed hands seized his thrashing leg to drag him back to the sand, where the yetin loomed over him. Ko-Tergo spared Saker a moment to cough water before his fists descended one after the other, over and over, pummelling Saker so he flew from side to side.

'Dragon!' yelled the surviving mage behind them, clutching at his wrists to stop the bleeding.

Fellgrin raced to her rider's aid, ignoring all spells and shots from the ship behind her. Not even Fleetstar's chasing fire could stop her, nor the flames building in Fellgrin's throat.

The surviving mage muscled between them. 'Get behind me!' he ordered as he reached with shaking, bleeding hands. A stuttering shield spell shook the air in time to meet Fellgrin's inferno. The mage loaned his voice to the roar of fire and magick, hands shuddering as he threw his all into the spell and gave Lerel and the others time to find cover.

The spell cracked when Fellgrin's claws met the shore. Jaws gnashed, crushing the shield into threads of light and seizing the mage between her teeth. Fire sprouted from her throat once more, and she aimed for the roof of the cavern as she exhaled. The mage never got a chance to scream before he was charcoal and ash, and Fellgrin tossed his bones aside to crumble against a rock.

Ko-Tergo was still standing over the Lord of the Winds and had to duck as the same jaws gnashed at him. The yetin made Fellgrin recoil as he raked her scales with his claws and drove heavy blows to her neck and underbelly. She responded with claws of her own, cutting Ko-Tergo's chest before he was thrown against a boulder. Fleetstar tried her luck, spitting a bolt of flame that Fellgrin swiped away with a wing. When Fleetstar dropped like a portcullis with claws and fangs outspread, the older dragon was waiting for her. Fellgrin's heavy tail hammered Fleetstar in the ribs and knocked her into the shallows.

Saker chuckled as he got to his feet, bleeding from his ears, nose, and torn lip. 'You forget yourselves,' he said, spitting at the sight of Fleetstar clambering upright and Elessi and Lerel heaving at a dizzy and bleeding Ko-Tergo.

The moment was a bowstring, drawn fully yet trembling more and more with every moment it was forced to hold. Lerel saw the *Undaunted* powering forwards, ballistae and catapults taking aim but still too far for a killing shot. The air around Fellgrin's fangs wavered in the heat. Her throat glowed. Saker wiggled his sword from side to side, deciding which of them to murder first. Lerel could only focus on keeping her blade from shaking and trying not to ponder what burning to death by dragonfire felt like. She hoped the nerves burned so quickly there would be nothing to suffer.

It was then, when Saker unleashed a war-cry, that the tentacle burst from the waters. The tower of red flesh collided with Fellgrin's head like a falling tree, driving her axe-like chin into the gravel, smoke wheezing from her grimacing mouth. Another tentacle wrapped around her long neck and began to pull. Fire spewed in all directions, but no matter how the keraken's flesh sizzled, it refused to let go. Water steamed and bubbled as Fellgrin was dragged into the shallows. The dragon's wings thrashed like a bat trapped in a cat's mouth, threatening to blow Lerel over, but another tentacle snaked between every one of her limbs and squeezed the last breath of fire out of the dragon.

Ko-Tergo moved before anyone else present could even think and swiped the sword from Saker's hands. Another punch to the jaw lifted the rider from the gravel, but before he could fall back to earth, a tentacle shot out to seize him.

Saker's eyes bulged as the tentacle squeezed. With a callous flick as if lazily swatting at a fly, the keraken dashed him into the nearest rockface. Once, twice, thrice, until Fellgrin fell abruptly still, and there was not much left of Saker beyond a limp rag doll made of meat and ripped leather. Lerel's stomach churned at the sight of what dropped from the keraken's grip.

'I thought you said you needed our help!' bellowed Elessi as the dead ship atop the keraken's shell poked from the waters. The squid-eyed sailor stood on its bow, a curious smile on his face and without an answer of any kind. He stepped into midair again, and the keraken placed him atop a boulder above them.

'Let us see why the foul dragon saw fit to steal my home, shall we?' he called out before disappearing. Lerel and Elessi stormed to follow him.

It was soon clear where the fog and stench were coming from; vents poked from the rock, encrusted with ochre and blue lichen that seemed to enjoy the fumes. Pools bubbled in crevices, and the veins of ore that wandered the rock glowed with a pale light. Lerel felt the urge to cough grip her throat. Elessi's eyes streamed.

'You live here?' she asked.

'Warm in the winters,' said the sailor, not bothering to turn around. 'Cooler in the summers. There's medicine in these waters. Good for the skin.'

Signs of Fellgrin's claws could be seen where she had dug at the rocks to make hollows, as if looking for something. Whatever the strange sailor called treasures had been strewn about and shoved into the clay floor. Lerel eyed the oddly-coloured rocks and seashells the size of platters.

'Disrespectful swine,' he muttered, beginning to pick up various copper trinkets. Something drew Lerel further, where more of Fellgrin's work delved into a nook. She had widened a rift, and to Lerel's squinting eyes, something glinted within.

'What's that in there?'

'Nothing of mine,' said the sailor, paying nothing but a glance.

It took no time at all to find a bundle of dry hay Saker had used for bedding and wrap it around the end of her sword. Borrowing flame from a brazier, Lerel marched back to the rift and stuffed the torch inside. Between the drifting sparks, she spied a metallic object sitting alone in a circular nest of blackened stones. It was the size and colour of a catapult stone, with four ridges that ran along its round shape. It took going on hands and knees and stretching until her muscles ached to get close, and when her fingers grazed its surface, Lerel found it rough as lava rock and hot to the touch. Cool enough to grab from its nest and carry back to the others, but still unnaturally warm, and enough so she kept having to switch hands beneath the heavy thing.

'What in Hel is that?' Elessi asked as she returned.

'Nothing of mine,' the sailor echoed. 'I have not seen such a thing before.'

'Feel it,' said Lerel, putting her hand against the object's stony surface.

'It's hot.'

'It doesn't make much sense, but I think… I think it's a…' Lerel pondered aloud before turning on her heel and going back to the shore, leaving Elessi to trail behind.

'What?' yelled the general.

The *Undaunted* had sent out a boat, and soldiers and mages were clambering onto dry land. Healers saw to the yetin's wounds while others wrapped the dead mage in sailcloth. Fleetstar glanced briefly at Lerel's appearance before whirling around, wings spread.

'Where in the fuck did you get that?' demanded the dragon, bejewelled eyes wide.

'Is it what I think it is?' asked Lerel

Elessi was growing bored of this game. 'What, damn it?'

'That,' breathed Fleetstar, 'is a dragon's egg.'

CHAPTER 19
A KERAKEN'S POWER

Travellers heading east, beware! For there is a beast even the dragons fear to cross paths with. A winged beast, it is said, who haunts the eastern borders of the Skölgard. Never glimpsed is he! Storms and lightning follow it, and its voice is said to bring thunder.
EXCERPT FROM 'DRAGONS AND THEIR FEATURES: LESSONS IN IDENTIFYING THE SIREN BEAST', BY MASTER WIRD

'Whose is it? Fellgrin's?' asked Lerel. She had barely taken her eyes off the egg since she had found it, as if she expected it to crack open any moment. Fleetstar had told her repeatedly it was not ready, but she chose not to believe.

The dragon had stowed the egg close to the fire, keeping the cold of the stones from touching it. She didn't explain why, but Lerel had never seen her so reverent, never heard her voice so hushed.

'It could be. Dragons are only gifted a few eggs in a lifetime. Without a mate, they are laid cold. If they are laid hot, they must be kept that way for years until the wyrmling is grown enough to break its shell. If they're not kept right, the lucky ones stay dormant, sometimes for decades if they're in a warm enough place. The unlucky grow cold and die before they hatch. And that is more than any human should know of dragons and their eggs. Few humans have ever seen a dragon egg, let alone touched one.'

'I imagine that's why your breeding grounds are so prized and protected.'

Fleetstar pursed her scaled lips and blew a thin stream of fire around the egg and the stones propping it up. 'This cave is a fine choice. It must have been why Fellgrin came here. There is a chance it's not hers. Perhaps she protected it. Perhaps she found it here.'

'It'll make a fine gift for Nerilan and Towerdawn,' Lerel muttered. 'If they'll have it.'

Elessi finally broke her silence. 'This is all well and good, but why are we worryin' about the egg when we haven't got the answers we came here for? I can't be the only one who feels tricked.'

Lerel flicked a finger. 'Then why don't you go and talk to our new friend?'

The keraken's lone sailor had not left the tables of vittles that had been put out for the crew who had come ashore. He tried everything three times, first ravenously, the second at a lesser pace, and the final time in slow motion, savouring every bite and chew. He made frequent noises and asked the sailors all kinds of questions, never waiting for the answers. *Undaunted*'s sailors hovered around, enjoying an uncomfortable silence with their meal.

Elessi got to her feet. 'You're absolutely right,' she said before storming off.

'Your name,' Elessi said, standing close to the sailor's side.

The sailor gave her a lopsided smile, stained red with beetroot juice. Crumbs gave him a second beard. 'Pardon?'

'You haven't even told us your name.'

'We're one with Keraken.'

'Your name. You must have one.'

'You are angry on the night of a victory. Why? We're feasting and making merry,' he said, drawing some looks and frowns from the silent crew of the *Undaunted*. 'What more could you want?'

'To know why you lied. To know why you keep saving us. To know what it is you are.'

The sailor mopped his lips with a kerchief soaked in seawater. 'Then walk with me,' he said before squelching away towards his ship.

Ko-Tergo made to rise and follow, but Elessi waved him away and patted her blade. Alone, she joined the sailor at the water's edge, where the keraken had turned sideways to lurk in the depths, feasting on his spoils on the seabed. A rope ladder formed a stair that climbed the monster's shell.

The sailor extended a hand to help her aboard, but Elessi refused to take it.

'Keraken. Nayamara. Tharkun. These are all good names, and you want another?'

Elessi crossed her arms.

'Dear me.' The sailor stared wistfully out of the cave before he flung his braided beard over his shoulder and scrambled up the ladder. 'If you want answers, then follow,' he called down.

Elessi gulped down her frustration and reluctantly set foot on the giant. She tried not to think too hard about it as she scrambled upwards towards the dead ship, leaving Lerel and Ko-Tergo to stare and worry.

The sailor smiled as they drew close, and Elessi swore his strange eyes blinked sideways before he ducked under a beam encrusted by shellfish. What Elessi found inside was stranger. She saw no seaweed or barnacle-encrusted beams within, only ancient wooden architecture blackened with age, piles of dust, and the must of an old ale cellar. Even more trinkets had been pinned to the bulkheads and rafters, medals and coins mixing with woven fish bones and a variety of hats. Shields of all shapes and colours and sizes lined the gaps between portholes and hatches. Elessi's eyes roamed over the painted runes, sigils, and beasts she had never seen before.

'Welcome aboard the ship of no name,' said the sailor, giving Elessi a deep bow. 'You're the first new feet to tread these decks since before the Arka-Siren war.'

That sounded preposterous, but Elessi fought against distraction. 'Why did you tell us you needed help when you clearly didn't?'

'Straight to it,' he chuckled. 'It was a test.'

Elessi scowled. 'You risked our lives for a test? A test of what?'

'No, *you* risked *your* lives to *help* us,' he corrected her. 'And it was a test of trust, and you should be happy. You passed. Too many hunters have come and gone with lies in their mouths only to lure us into a trap and attempt to kill us. Kings and queens in their dozens have uttered promises full of nothing, all so they can wield Keraken's power. And so we decided a long time ago to be sparing with our trust, and that's we why chose to see what you would do about the dragon first. When we saw you risk yourself for us, we knew we were right about you.'

'Right about what?' Elessi could understand that, but she didn't forgive it.

'Right not to sink you. The true reason we didn't is that we find you different from the others who have tried to change the world. I confess that we have watched you for some time, curious ever since your grand ships started casting shadows on the depths. Since the world felt the oceans tremble with the fire in the north and you came south to Keraken's waters. Since you started looking out across the ocean every day and night for us.' The sailor smiled wider, squid eyes unblinking. 'We have seen much.'

'Then I should say thank you again,' Elessi spoke from a dry mouth as she performed a bow. 'And when you say "we", should I be expectin' company on this ship?'

'You look at the only crew left alive. It is just us, Keraken and me,' he said, patting himself down to check he was real. 'As for my name? They called me Rokhelm once, when the first ships landed in a place they would call Krauslung, and others like me stayed in the sea.'

'That's impossible. You can't be that old.'

'Many things are impossible, and you will have to tell us how old that is, for I have lost count.'

'I'm High General Elessi of Albion,' Elessi uttered, bowing her head.

'Albion. Fine waters there but poor ships,' Rokhelm said with a stout sniff. 'Come with me, Elessi of Albion.'

With swift feet that belied his age, he led her through deck after deck of heavy crossbows with strings tied around their triggers, and strange metal columns lay flat in cradles, pointing out over the keraken's dappled shell. At last, they came to a covered bridge where almost every surface but the rudder was covered in dust.

'Now, you may have passed the test,' said Rokhelm as he cleared away ropes and half-knitted socks. 'But you lied to us before. You didn't tell us the whole truth about why you came to find us.'

'We came to ask you to help us defeat a god called Loki,' said Elessi, speaking only truth.

'So you have come for Keraken's power,' Rokhelm whispered, laying a hand on the rudder.

'We've come for help that's given freely.'

'You would still trust us after we tricked you? You don't even know what we are, what we've seen, or what we want—'

'Call it an instinct,' Elessi snapped. 'Is this another of your tests? Do I pass?'

Rokhelm shuffled the rudder back and forth. 'We'll see.'

Elessi swayed as the great beast shifted beneath them. It was like nothing she'd ever felt on a ship's deck, far too powerful and swift. 'What are you doin'?'

'Showing you.'

The keraken surged from the cave's mouth, and the sea started climbing further and further up the shell. Elessi seized a beam with both hands in worry.

'Thought you trusted us!' Rokhelm brayed over the roar of damning waters.

Elessi tried to forget every natural reaction screaming within her as the waves crashed against the ship's bow and streamed over the deck towards the bridge. She recoiled as the murky water reached for her, even turning away from the deluge, but all she endured was Rokhelm's laughter. Elessi cracked an eye to see the bubbles swirling across an invisible window and the ship's torches illuminating the drowned wrecks of ships and scattering fish. The keraken's tentacles reached from crag to crag, pulling itself along the seabed while others swam, ever and ever deeper.

Elessi put her hands on her knees to exhale. 'It's a shield spell.'

Rokhelm shrugged, as if she had guessed at the answer of his riddle, and its wonder had been robbed. 'If you wish to call it that. I know it reaches around the hull of the ship, drips in a few places here and there, but it holds.'

Elessi moved to run her hand along the spell, finding the magick soft and cold and worryingly able to bend under her touch. The thought of the sheer weight of water that waited beyond made her heart tremble. 'Is it the ship's magick or the keraken's?'

'I don't know. It was like this when I first came here, and I had the very same reaction when Keraken first took us below.'

Elessi whirled. 'This isn't your ship?'

Rokhelm chuckled. 'The ship was already old and fused to his shell when I found her. Where it came from, I don't know, though I have a suspicion young Keraken wanted it as a lure to draw other ships close. Devious, he is. Smarter than most humans.'

'Then why didn't it – he – eat you?' Elessi winced at how that sounded. 'Why did he choose you, I mean.'

'Don't know that either, and I've spent a long time wondering,' said Rokhelm, teetering on the edge of babbling. The more he talked, Elessi saw more of what hid behind Rokhelm's patchwork uniform. His eyes grew wider as he let his mouth run. He was a skald brimming with tales, and one who had not seen an audience in many a decade.

'Shipwrecked, I was, and on the third night in the water, I saw a strange ship floating nearby. No lights, no crew. Twelve of us climbed aboard these decks that night, and we thought ourselves in Hel when the ship began to move, but this is where we stayed for centuries. Keraken lent us air and his long life for our service, but not all things can live forever. Others came from time to time, and we died one by one until all that was left was me. I've waited for my turn for many years, but Keraken does not want to let me go.'

'The impossible made possible,' said Elessi.

Rokhelm tipped a corner of his hat. 'I am the last of my kind, he is the last of his, and so we've grown to be one. In return for that and *this*, I accept.'

Rokhelm waved his hand across the underwater world, in which the light had died completely, sponge corals and toothy fish glowed, and where rocky chimneys spouted black ash and white shrimp picked at the boiling offerings. Keraken glowed too, shining crimson along the fringes of his tentacles. Elessi pressed her hands to the shield spell once again to feel the vibration of the rushing water. Her gaze chased tiny squid come to ogle their god, or jellyfish with elaborate umbrellas or skirts of dazzling lights. She craned to see the world above but found nothing but gloom and the white bellies of hammerhead sharks ambling above.

'I've never seen such a thing.'

'Trust me, it never gets old.'

'Speakin' of, we've established you're old—'

'Thank you.'

'—but how old is Keraken? Where did he come from?'

'I doubt he remembers now, but I think he came before the skies had so many stars and when the oceans ruled the earth.'

'It sounds like you speak to him somehow,' Elessi guessed.

Rokhelm put a finger to his temple in answer.

'Just as I thought. Like the dragons do.'

Rokhelm worked his tongue around his teeth. 'If you say so.'

'Where are you taking me?' said Elessi, the worst possible answers already floating around her head.

'Nowhere,' said Rokhelm. 'Which is the beauty of Keraken. We can return to your ship whenever you please.'

That alleviated some of the trepidation that gripped Elessi. 'And then what? Will you come with us and help us win this war?'

Rokhelm approached her, politely took her hands, and stared into her eyes.

'No,' he said with an infuriatingly misleading smile.

'I thought…' Elessi felt the mocking prickle of heat rise up her neck and into her cheeks. 'You'd be helping to save the world from Loki's evil. You said we were different. Surely that has to count for something.'

'You are different indeed, but we are different again. There's no revenge in our hearts. No worry for a god's evil. No thirst for such accolades. And there is no safety you can provide.'

'Loki will come for you one day. He won't be able to stand the thought of you.'

'We'll take that as a warning, but the waters have hidden us for centuries, Elessi. They're deeper than any god save Njord can reach. We have no part in this.'

Elessi felt defeated, hopes dashed on Magre's sharp rocks. 'Then maybe we can trade for your help.'

Rokhelm shook his head. 'The ocean gives us everything we could ever ask for. I am sorry, General Elessi. You can count on us to keep watch and be a friend, but we have no place in the matters of gods and magick. It is how we have survived for so long.'

Elessi bowed. 'I see. Then at least I have my answers,' she said. 'And it's always good to make a new friend at the very least, right?'

'That it is,' Rokhelm said, lowering her hand and putting his to the rudder. 'I will take you back.'

Elessi watched the glimmer of the ocean floor fade, and the waters grew light again. Keraken surfaced with an enormous splash, and as the waters receded from the ship's decks, a cold air wafted through the shield spells as if they had never existed. Fog greeted them, and Elessi spied the maw of the cave glowing with fire. The *Undaunted* sat beyond it, moored between two rocky spurs.

'Thank you for the demonstration, and thank you for savin' our hides. Again,' Elessi whispered to Rokhelm as she moved towards a doorway and precious open air. 'We'll be leavin' tomorrow to go back to New Scalussen. Perhaps we'll see each other one day.'

Rokhelm bowed low with a flourish of his pointy hat. 'I hope we do, Elessi.'

Lerel and Ko-Tergo were on their feet and had weapons drawn when Keraken slid back up the shore to a rumble of rocks.

'I'm fine,' Elessi called out as she stepped onto the barnacles of the ship with no name. She had hoped for a ladder, but a tentacle reached for her instead. 'No need to worry!' she yelled, voice heightening as the tentacle seized her and swept her to the beach so fast she could barely catch a breath. She was left standing on the beach, breathing fast, with seawater seeping into her sleeves and armour.

'Where did he take you?' Lerel demanded, holding Elessi by the arms as she led her towards the nearest fire. 'What happened?'

'Underwater, and I'm not sure I'd do it again,' she said, spreading her hands over the heat of the flames. It took a while for her to spit the words of failure. They always tasted bitterer aloud. 'He said no. He won't help us.'

'That's it?' grunted Ko-Tergo.

'That's what he said. That he and Keraken have no place in our war.'

'Never known you to give up so easily.'

Elessi snorted at such nonsense from the yetin. 'His mind is already made, I can tell. I'm not goin' to force him to change it, just like Farden never forced anyone in Scalussen. We'll leave tomorrow.'

Lerel looked back at the not-so-dead ship. Rokhelm was staring down at them, a half-hearted wave lifting his hand off the encrusted railing for a moment before disappearing.

Ko-Tergo nodded at Lerel's unspoken words. 'I think you made an impression.'

More nonsense from the yetin, and Elessi told him so. 'Rubbish. And even so, I'm not going to lie to him or manipulate him either. I won't be provin' us wrong when he thinks we're different. He's spent far too much time alone, is all, and forgotten a few manners here and there. Now I don't know about you two, but I'm about to drop senseless. Please tell me we're not sleepin' on rocks in this poisonous place?'

'The *Undaunted* awaits, General.' Lerel pointed to where the ship's lights rippled on the waters.

As the boat scraped on the rocks and wallowed out into the shallows, Rokhelm appeared again at a porthole, and Elessi waved. Let him think they were leaving, even if it was a cheap jab. It wasn't that he had said no. It was the calm in his voice at the threat of Loki. It worried him as much as light rain, and Elessi envied that deeply.

CHAPTER 20
DUPLICITY

The elves came in the night, sharp-eyed and blades a-swishing. Cacoar
fought their leader at the gates with both his named swords. Cut to ribbons
was he. Fire failed to turn them back. The unmuzzled mages' voices only
slowed them. A shadow moved with them, full of legs and snickety claws.
FROM A RARE SCROLL PRESERVED IN THE SCALUSSEN LIBRARIES,
THOUGHT TO BE MORE THAN TWO THOUSAND YEARS OLD

Mithrid was finally asleep. Hereni could tell by the slow, deep breaths, catching at their apex before descending again to predictable silence.

Hereni got up from the chair. Only the plants that Mithrid had grown and Hereni now kept alive witnessed her as she tiptoed over to the bed and took a seat. Mithrid still didn't wake. Only a twitch of her hand betrayed her stillness.

She was faced away from Hereni, legs together and pulled up to her chest as she always slept, as if she was still tucked into the hole her father had hidden her in. Hereni had slept like that for many years until the safety of Scalussen had replaced the fear and anger that had filled her heart.

Mithrid twitched again, taking a sharper breath than usual. Hereni lay down next to her, matching the shape of her body and feeling the heat of her skin against her wind-bitten cold. Hereni felt the tremors of her body as her mind ran through dreams.

Nightmares of fire and ruin.

She had said they came every night. A mutter fell from her lips, and Hereni smoothed her fire-coloured hair across her shoulder.

Her hands traced her arm, making Mithrid flinch in her sleep until her body shook violently, making Hereni recoil before holding her tighter.

'Mithrid.'

It did nothing. Mithrid clawed at the bed covers. Her face was creased deep and lips white under her teeth.

'Mith!'

Mithrid's hand snatched at hers, seizing her wrist and twisting slowly as she turned around. Shadow threaded around Hereni's wrist like a wandering bracelet, and Hereni felt a pain make her arm go rigid.

'Wake up now,' she spoke calmly even though a cold seeped under her skin. Weakness followed it, and the light spell Hereni was trying to cast sputtered out before it could glow. Mithrid stared through closed eyes, shadow now leaking from her clenched teeth and hair. She stood, reaching for Hereni with her other hand.

'Mithrid!' Hereni yelled, trying to wrench free but finding the shadow too strong. It was almost at her chest now.

A slap across the face woke her. Hereni regretted it instantly, but it was all that could be done. Mithrid's shadow burst outwards, throwing Hereni against the wall. Mithrid reeled backwards and blinked, waving her arms about as if driving something away.

'What did you do?' she demanded.

'Me?' Hereni said, finding herself shaking, though she had no idea if it was shock or anger. 'You were having a nightmare. You attacked me when I tried to wake you.'

'I...' Mithrid stared at the faint wisps of shadow around her hands.

'The more I see, the more you're daring to prove Farden right,' was all she said, as she turned from the room and left Mithrid to stare at the slammed door.

'Thirty towers now. Twenty-five ballistae. Twenty catapults and trebuchets north, south, and east on raised daises. Patrols move clockwise and counter in concentric circles. Dragons and witches are stationed at every one of the four main gates, throughout the docks, and in the city streets. More fly patrols at random, watching the deserts and the mountains. Even the birds seem to patrol. The walls are now built and sturdy, stretching around the bay. They're as thick and as wide as wagons. Filled with soldiers standing a dozen feet apart along most of their length, bells and horns ready to sound the alarm at the scuff of a shoe or the measliest yelp. At the shore of the bay sits a fortress made from one of their giant ships. It bristles with soldiers daily and nightly, and there is a fleet constantly occupying the bay. A new ship is almost ready to sail, bigger than all the rest. Farden remains at the city's centre in a new tower called the Dawnknell, only half-constructed, and it's where he holds his council. The gryphon roosts atop it, constantly watching. The southern Paraians Farden has recruited – the Jar Khoum – live beyond the walls to the east amongst palm forests, but for the numbers I've seen, they must hide underground. Who knows how many there are,' Irien gasped, almost out of breath. Even the mouse scuttling across the floorboards would have had to cup a paw around its ear to hear her.

Irien eyed the crow skull, still and silent in her hands. A lycan's fist hammered on the door of the privy.

'In a moment, my dear!' Irien yelled.

The skull's beak yawned wide. 'Are they still watching you?' asked a god's voice.

'They are. And yet I've charted the city for you, my dear. My hairy guard thinks I enjoy long walks and sightseeing.'

'You've done a fine job of boring me with details, but what I need, Irien, are weaknesses. Ways in.'

Irien scowled. 'Because there are none that I can see. New Scalussen is a fortress. Farden has more power than a god.'

'We'll see about that.' Loki paused. 'Where is Mithrid?'

'I haven't seen her.'

Loki was chuckling, and the skull jittered with the sound. 'Watch her closely.'

The door hammered again. The handle began to turn. Irien let the skull's gemstone fade, hitched up her kilt, and charged towards the basin of water to pretend to wash her hands. A snout and two glinting eyes poked through the door's crack.

'I'm afraid your southern food doesn't agree with me, my dear,' Irien said, staring blankly at the beast.

Roglurg's snout wrinkled as he withdrew.

Irien rejoined him in the corridor. 'What now then, Mr Lycan? Rogo, was it?' she asked, just to irritate him.

'Roglurg,' gargled the lycan.

'Shall we wander to the beach? The desert? The palm forest? I feel like all there is to do in this sandy city is walk and sleep. However do you not hurl yourself into the ocean? Is there such a thing as a tavern in this glorified fortress?' Irien knew there was. She had seen two. Bless the Emaneskans and their constant thirst for ale.

'There is,' said a voice accompanied by clanking. Farden appeared at the end of the corridor. He had his Khandri sword at his side but no spear this time, not that she could see.

'But call it glorified one more time, and you'll go back to your cell,' he said.

'A drink then, my dear?'

Farden narrowed his eyes, waiting some time to speak. 'I could use one,' he said. 'Roglurg, get some peace and quiet. Much needed, I imagine.'

Irien lifted an eyebrow.

The Forever King led her from the Dawnknell and towards the bay, for all the best taverns apparently liked to linger near water. They passed under the watchful eyes of the Winter Fortress, where a familiar minotaur cast a long shadow across the sand. It was always treacherous stuff to walk on and a terrain Irien loathed.

'Don't you miss the trees here? The snow? Rain?' Irien asked.

Farden didn't reply, and though a thudding of hooves could be heard following them, he didn't turn. Irien did and saw the Warbringer approaching, that lump of a warhammer in her hand as always. Irien wondered if she cuddled it in her cot at night. Perhaps she tucked it into its own bed. The answer to what was so special about it eluded her, and her pervasive curiosity demanded to know.

'Whisper woman,' Warbringer greeted her, marching straight past her.

'Are you joining us?'

Warbringer grunted.

'Seems like it will be a lively occasion,' Irien said drily.

Every tankard, glass, and fist raised as Farden entered the tavern.

'Forever King!'

Farden bowed to his subjects. The tavern was one of the cleaner specimens Irien had encountered in her travels. The last one had rats running freely over boards and tables. This one had no rats, but there were green and grey parrots in the rafters, arguing with each other about subjects only parrots cared about. All manner of weapons lined the walls, each with a scrap of parchment for company. Irien's western runes were rusty, but they looked like names to her.

Scalussen sailors and off-duty soldiers formed a small crowd of half a dozen. Lively, it was not, but at least it was louder than a burial mound. Another minotaur stood behind the wide bar, where stools waited to be filled. Lanterns lit the areas the morning sun in the windows couldn't reach.

'How surprisingly civilised,' Irien said.

Warbringer needed no seat, and the stool didn't need such a test. She rattled her horns at the minotaur barkeep in greeting.

Irien watched, fascinated. 'I've never seen a minotaur serving drinks.'

Farden hunched over the bar as if a weight pressed on him. 'Latherike wandered in here one day and started pouring ales. Nobody dared question it, and he hasn't given an explanation since.'

'He won't,' Warbringer replied. She said the minotaur's name with more of a growl as if she corrected Farden. 'Latherike not talk.'

Warbringer promptly ordered something in the minotaur tongue, apparently with a very long name. Farden took a tankard of something dark and foaming, with a measure of something clear as crystal. The bottle the spirit came from was curious, twisted and capped with a steel lid that formed a cup. Irien watched as the minotaur poured.

'Mörd,' Farden explained. 'A drink of the north. Arka moonshine.'

Irien flashed a smile at Latherike. 'I don't suppose you have Golikan cider?'

The minotaur heaved a green keg onto the bar and twisted its spigot over a beaker.

'What a fine surprise!'

Farden shrugged. 'Scalussen is a true city now. Cities need trade to survive.'

'I'm seeing a different side of you here than I did in the east, Farden,' she said. 'There, you were the desperate warrior. Here, you seem like a king. A leader, and I've known a fair few in my time. Though you could learn a lesson from a number of them when it comes to attire and decoration. Brighten the place up, my dear.'

Farden scoffed. 'It's work, not a perfumed velvet cushion to sit on.'

Warbringer grunted and nodded, lifting up what was essentially a bucket filled with a burgundy liquid. The beast almost halved it in three gulps. Irien was curious, but after she saw the herbs, bark, and a white bone floating in it, she wasn't so sure. She knew all about minotaurs and what they preferred to eat.

'I see. Is that why you both seem wracked with tiredness and leapt at the chance for a drink?' she asked.

Farden and Warbringer declined to speak.

'What happened in Krauslung with Loki?'

Farden gave her a sideways look as he drained his mörd and asked for another while he quaffed his ale. 'Why?'

'Why what, my dear?'

'Why do you care, Irien? You once told me you don't care about the why.'

'And I told you, Farden, that was where business was concerned, and that I cared once my fate was entwined with yours.'

Farden turned on his stool. 'Is it a lust for secrets and knowledge, or do you really care? I may not have seen it at first, but now I know you, and I know you'll do anything to stay alive. Unlike what you see in me, I don't see any change in you. And judging by the fact Towerdawn can't read your intentions, forgive me if I still don't trust you.'

Irien downed her cider at a rapid pace and clanked the beaker on the bar. 'How rude, Farden. I came here to help, and for free, might I add. You could use me, you know. I know all the major traders in the east, and I make a fine diplomat. Or a decorator, perhaps! I can think of no better way for you to make amends for the misfortune you caused, and for me to make up for the slight matter of Belerod.'

'Slight? Hmph,' Farden muttered. 'I'll think about it,'

'So what of Krauslung?'

'They protected their god,' grunted Farden, 'and stood between him and us to force our hands. Mithrid and I were powerless.'

'A strange sensation for you, I imagine. And how is young Mithrid? You haven't gotten her killed already, have you? I haven't seen her since the night I arrived.'

'Mithrid is… difficult.'

Irien dug deeper. 'She is quite the shadow mage. I witnessed her power on the battlefield and have never seen such a thing.'

Warbringer seemed to be chuckling. Farden smiled and had another two mörds and an ale poured. 'Quite,' he said.

Irien felt as if she had missed a joke, and it bothered her. She waited for the other drinks to be served before she kept slicing away the layers of conversation. Drink loosened tongues, and taverns were where whispers were born. This was how she duelled, not with blades and magick.

'And what about your Lerel?' Irien said, her tone sharper. 'I haven't seen her since she locked me in that prison cell.'

Farden sighed, as if the subject perturbed him. 'Lerel is elsewhere.'

Irien poked around his guard. 'An argument, was it, my dear? Lovers' quarrel?

'She and I disagree,' said Farden, leaning closer. The mörd was working its magick. She had seen how many wine bottles he had emptied in the east, and his tongue was loosening. 'On matters of Loki, primarily.'

Irien made sure to nod understandingly. 'Why do you oppose him so vehemently, I wonder? I can't figure it from the way Krauslung cheered for him.'

'He betrayed his own kind, and he betrayed me. He convinced my daughter to bring him down from the sky. Then he betrayed me again and coaxed Malvus into war by giving him the ability to make false Written, using skin torn from dead mages. Then he perverted Malvus into a monster, dragged the rest of the daemons down from the sky, used us like pawns, and charmed Krauslung. Oh, and not to mention he drinks souls, thinks us worms, tried to kill me several times, and is obsessed with the idea of being all-powerful and all-adored, and will do anything to make that happen. That enough? And here I am, waiting for him to make the next move. That's why I'm tired, Irien,' Farden snarled.

Irien softened him with a smile and a beckon for another mörd. 'A touchy subject, I see. I didn't hear such truths in Krauslung, that's for certain.'

Warbringer slapped the side of her second bucket and summed it all up for her. 'Loki is the worm. Worms get crushed.'

Irien bided her time again, letting the mage and minotaur ask of the aftermath of the east. Belerod was of course in hiding, rebuilding strength. Peskora's death had created a power vacuum filled with a dozen potentials, and most of the Easterealm cursed the west for bringing such a war to its shores.

'Sounds about right,' grunted Farden.

'I do miss Dathazh, it has to be said,' Irien sighed.

Warbringer had to disagree. 'Too many people staring.'

'Well, what of your city? It's a marvel what you've built so quickly. A little rough around the edges perhaps, but it seems almost finished. Are you not worried Loki will come to knock it down before it's done? In retribution for Scalussen?'

Farden chuckled. 'That's what I'm counting on.'

Irien raised her glass to that and let them stew in their silence and their sipping for a time, to let their eyes wander. She aimed another verbal assault. 'He would have a tough time, considering what you've built,' she said, speaking carefully. 'I can't see a single angle you can't defend, but then again, I am no expert. Far from it! Tell me: are we safe here? Have I come to the wrong place? Because if so, I'll be out of your hair by the evening.'

'You're safer here than everywhere else. Every wall is sturdy. Even now they're being built deeper into the bay. A tower went up yesterday on the edge of the harbour. The dragons and witches can feel magick and treachery. And of course, there's me.' Farden managed a smile and met Irien's gaze for once.

'What about gate in north?' Warbringer rumbled. 'Too far from every other gate. Stonesmiths say today it weak. Built too fast. Can't take too many bodies. Less space for warriors to fight.'

'Yes, thank you, Warbringer,' said Farden. 'We're building another tower to shore it up.'

Irien made sure not to smile, but she did keep her eyes lingering on Farden to goad him. She even went as far as to touch the red and gold armour with her wooden hand.

'What are you staring at?' he asked, pulling away.

'I could ask the same question,' Irien said. 'Being a king suits you, Farden.'

'It never used to, but perhaps I have changed. You were certainly right about one thing, you know. My appetite for killing has grown thin. Years ago, I might have carved my way through those crowds in Krauslung. But now? All I want is Loki. Somebody has to protect this world.'

'Protect it from Loki?'

'If there's another enemy more deserving, then please point it out.'

'Power,' Irien said with a deep sigh, tilting her glass for another dose from the keg.

Farden held her stare as he sank his fifth beaker of mörd. 'Speak,' he said, wiping his lips and asking for yet another.

'Power. Loki seeks it. You wield it,' she said, pointing to the sword at Farden's waist. A spear in disguise. 'Power corrupts. I defy anyone to stay pure given the power that you hold. It's almost too much, do you not think? Unfair? Unholy? Do you ever wonder if you're on the right side, or if that spear is corrupting you? What would you do, I wonder, if the only way of killing Loki was to slaughter crowds of his believers?'

Farden placed his beaker carefully between the seams of the bar's wooden planks and stood. 'I don't accept that.'

Irien smirked. 'Of course you don't. It's like you believe you're also a god now that you hold my ancestor's spear.'

'What if I am?' Farden asked her, raising his empty vessel and making Irien seethe within. She did her best to hide it. 'You're earning my trust, slowly but surely. I'll think about what you offered. Warbringer, will you please escort our guest back to her chambers? And tell Eyrum to come and join me.'

'Hmph,' was all the minotaur said before emptying her bucket, grumbling something to Latherike, and taking the bone to nibble on the journey. Farden stayed with his mörd, and Irien suppressed a smile as Warbringer led her back into the abominably bright sunlight.

Irien needed no more talk. While Warbringer crunched on bone and the waves chased her footsteps, she walked in silence all the way to her chambers, where she paused and bowed to the beast. The big, gloriously dumb beast.

'My thanks, Warbringer,' Irien said before she shut the door. She frowned to hear its heavy locks behind her, but it mattered not. She had what she needed. Irien went to her porthole of a window and stared through its bars across the bay of New Scalussen. She curled her lip at the beauty of it all as she felt for the crow skull around her neck and pressed her finger to the gem.

'I have what you want,' Irien whispered into its beak.

'How did I know I'd find you here?' Farden said as he slumped onto a palm stump, fresh splinters breaking under his armour. Mithrid was too busy hacking at another, taller palm to answer. Not until he dared to speak again.

'I—'

With the harsh crack of an axe blade meeting wood, Mithrid cut him off. 'If you came here to—'

Farden did the same to her. 'Quite the opposite. I'm trying out this new thing called trust, you see.'

'Is that so? So why do you still worry so much about me? Tell me the truth.'

'Let's be honest: you lost it in Krauslung. Like I said, you're too much like me, and I've lost it before just the same as you did. What I fear is that you'll do anything to kill that god, but willingness to do anything is a dangerous path of darkness and pain, one that can bite pieces off you that you can't get back. Take it from one who's walked it, Mithrid. What will it take to kill Loki? And once he's dead and burned, what's next? What else will you be meant for?'

Mithrid pursed her lips, but she didn't argue.

Farden took a breath. 'I didn't tell you before, but I saw what you saw in Utiru's mirrors, and I fear the same fate as I think you fear. A fate of fire and a fiery crown.'

Mithrid's head swivelled. Her eyes had the red glow of tears. 'You think the vision is true?'

Farden raised his shoulders. 'I don't want it to be. I think the mirrors showed us our darkest fate while Utiru showed us our brightest. I've been trying everything I can to keep you from heading towards the former, but I feel like I'm losing. And if you walk a darker path, I feel I will as well. Two fates. Two futures. One choice.'

'I saw Malvus on his knees and a knife in his hand. That's come and gone, so what else is left?'

'I don't know,' Farden said. 'But I do know you are meant for more than the gods first thought. I think you have a fate greater than any of us can comprehend, Mithrid, but I refuse to accept the mirror's vision.'

'What if I can't help it? All I dream of is that fire.'

'You sure about that? Sure it's not a memory of the north?'

Mithrid had no answer for that, and Farden filled the silence.

'Maybe it's the ale in me, but all I can hope is that the final decision has yet to be made. You can't be the next darkness that Emaneska suffers. I can't imagine having to hunt you down as I did my daughter. As I hunt Loki. You asked me why I worried, and that's why.'

'You worried I'd beat you?' she asked, and there was no hint of mirth in her. Farden narrowed his eyes.

'Sounds exactly like what Loki would want, you know that?' Mithrid snorted.

Farden looked at her with a tilt of the head. 'What did you say?'

'Turning you and I against each other would be quite the fun game for him, I imagine.'

Farden nodded slowly, following the trail of thought that bounded through the maze of his mind. 'A fun game indeed.'

When Hereni finally returned from trudging the Jar Khoum tunnels, she decided to prolong the wandering and passed through the training yards just in case Mithrid was there. She didn't know what she wanted to say. She didn't know what she wanted to hear. Reassurance was the only word for it, but she had no idea if Mithrid could provide it. Hereni spat on the ground. She had wanted nothing but simplicity, and now everything was more complicated than ever.

What Hereni saw surprised her. Farden sat next to Mithrid, and neither of them brandished raised voices or fists. In fact, they looked thick as thieves. A massacre of palm logs had occurred, and the slaughtered lay in angles all over the corner of the yard.

'Isn't this a surprise?' Hereni said as she approached. Farden and Mithrid looked up, words frozen on their lips. Both stayed silent for a moment until Hereni put her hands on her hips.

'I feel something in the air that I should probably go check on,' Farden said as he stood. He offered Mithrid a sour glance before he thudded across the training grounds. 'Remember what I said, girl. Don't disappoint me.'

Hereni waited until the king was out of earshot before she turned to Mithrid. She did not look cowed, she did not look worried. Blank was all she was.

'Well.'

'I'm sorry,' Mithrid said in a hollow voice.

'I know,' was all Hereni had to say. 'Will it happen again?'

'Can't promise it won't.'

Hereni took a moment to decide. 'We'll work on it.'

Mithrid tilted her head as if surprised.

'What did Farden say?'

'The usual. But we're in agreement at last.'

'On this dark fate of yours?'

'About what'll happen to me if I don't curb my ways.' Mithrid stood, wrenching her axe from the palm log and aiming another blow. She felt a wash of magick as Hereni unleashed a fire spell that punched a hole in the middle of the log, making the two halves topple. Hereni stood close.

'Talk to me.'

Mithrid clenched her fists. 'I don't want to sleep. The nightmares are getting worse, and every time, it feels like I'm standing on Irminsul's ledge once more. I feel all the kinds of fear I've been trying to push down. I still don't know what I'm meant for, but I know whatever it is, I won't let it hurt you.'

Hereni seized her hand and wrenched her upright and closer. 'I don't want to sleep either.'

CHAPTER 21
THE CALL OF SHADOW

The only thing necessary for the triumph of evil is for good souls to do nothing.
SIREN ADAGE

'Nobody's in any trouble, madam. I just need to know how many people live here for the new census!'

'Bugger off!' The woman poking one rheumy eye out of the door-crack tried to spit but decorated her own sill instead. 'Won't be falling for none of your tricks. Spent enough time under the heel of the Arka for you new folk to do the same!'

'Madam, just a simple number is all I need. How many people in your house—'

'My Phekles might be a troublemaker, but he won't be going to your workhouses or prisons! I know what your kind do with the boys in there!'

'Madam—'

'Sure he might have torched a few taverns!'

'If you just—

'Stolen a few chickens and goats! But that was under Arka law. Don't count now, you hear?'

Get the job done. Don't disturb the peace. That's all that matters, Ocander repeated the words over and over beneath his tongue before he leaned close.

'It isn't just Phekles they will take,' he said in a low voice.

The one eye went wide.

'Phiones?'

Ocander subtly wrote three marks on his scroll. 'Anybody else?'

'You think you can take Phebia? You bastard! She's barely more than a whelp! You get away!'

A hand reached through the gap, tipped with long nails heavy with layers of paint. Ocander skipped back and bowed in the old-fashioned way. 'Four, thank you, madam.'

Ocander blew a sigh as the door slammed. He took five paces to his right and stared at the next door.

'Greetings. We're counting the survivors of Troacles, and I've been sent to ask how many people are in your household,' Ocander whispered. For three days straight and almost four, he had spouted those words across a quarter of Troacles, and still he had to practise them.

The reed panels shook as he knocked. Once, twice, but the third time his knuckles met the door, a dull boom filled his ears.

Ocander drew back his hand to stare at his knuckles.

A man with one giant eyebrow answered. 'What do you want?'

'Greetings—'

There it was again. Another peculiar noise echoed through the early evening air, and it sounded like it came from the north that time. Pigeons began to scatter from the gutter pipes.

'Did you hear that?' Ocander asked.

The man chewed like a cow, eyes half-closed. 'You knocked at my door to ask if I can hear something? What's wrong with you?'

A third crash came at the same moment the man shut his door. It opened moments later with a suspicious expression behind it. 'I did hear that. You do something to my door?'

'That wasn't me, sir.' Ocander clutched his scroll.

It might have been the growing storm of birds unsure of which way to go or the prickle on the back of his neck, but Ocander began to run. After spending a decade in Troacles surviving as one of the more trustworthy clerks in the busy docks, he had learned to feel trouble before it brewed, and this felt like trouble.

'What is it, Ocander?' yelled a fellow counter, hunched in some shade.

'Something's wrong!' Ocander shouted to the sound of two more booms, closer now. 'Getting a better look. Warn the others!'

There was no finer place closer than the Bank of Ophel, where he knew a balcony stretched around its roof. Ocander burst in through its doors, evaded a yawning guard, and sprinted up the curling stairs to the balcony. He saw the smoke even before he rushed into the sunlight. Behind the cranes and scaffolds of the rebuilding efforts, a tar-coloured column reached up from one of the southern gates. Flames smouldered at its roots.

Then Ocander saw the second plume. And then the third and fourth. Sometimes he loathed numbers.

The census of the city was halfway done, but he knew almost two hundred thousand souls had already been counted, and that was far less than it should have been after the Arka's rule. There would be fewer again by sundown, Ocander suspected, and he slammed his hands on the railing.

A faint cry drifted from the streets. 'What is it, Ocander?'

'Smoke and fire at the gates!' Ocander bellowed. 'They're trying to trap us!'

Perhaps he should have chosen different words, considering he was yelling them from a tower into a busy city. He watched the panic seep and flood from street to street below him.

'Get to the quickdoors! Head for the ships! Use the tunnels!' Ocander began to yell. The volume and pace of his words surprised him, but he didn't stop yelling until the shouts were taken up by the fleeing crowds. Maybe the height of the tower had dizzied him, but it felt right. Ocander gave them a chance, and that was something they never had under the Arka thumb.

He wasn't stupid enough to remain a watchman, so he quickly scuttled back down the tower to head for the nearest quickdoor. The Scalussen soldiers that had arrived through them had demanded nothing except that they stay open for situations such as this, and nothing said escape like a quickdoor. Belephon and Galadaë awaited those lucky enough to squeeze through.

A man held his hands to the rooftops, walking against the crowd and jostled on all angles as he cried, 'Do not fear! The Forever King will save us!' over and over.

'And who's going to warn him in time?' Ocander heard a woman snap as she ran past.

'Warn him of what? You don't even know what it is you're running from!' laughed a man leaning out of a window with a wineskin in his hand.

The answer came too swiftly.

A rift of fire and crimson lightning split the crowds and sent bodies flying. A shape of charred iron and glowing coals appeared in its place, looming as tall as the gutter pipes.

'Shit!' cried the drunkard before the monster dug him from his window and showered the crowds with his blood and wine.

The panicked voices of the crowd came together into one chilling scream: 'Daemon!'

Choking on the smoke and stink of the daemon, Ocander hurtled down an alleyway as bricks and mortar rained behind him.

Five, six, seven, he counted as the streets flew past, and on the eighth, he swerved down some steps and towards a plaza he knew contained buzzing quickdoors. His ears rang with the sounds of screams, roars, and crashing stone. The militia working the ballistae did their best to save their city, but fire soon flitted across the rooftops, striking tower after tower. And where they didn't, they plummeted into the crowds pressed between the streets. It was a bloodbath.

Another daemon swerved into his path, one that sprouted spikes and spied him through a cluster of red eyes. A whip of flame and spiked iron swirled about its head, and Ocander threw himself flat as the savage weapon cracked overhead. A couple behind him were cut in half as they failed to escape.

'Old gods save me!' cried Ocander as he hobbled and crawled to another street. How anyone faced these monsters on open ground was lost on him, and a matter for another day when he wasn't being chased by death on legs.

Ocander froze as a helbeast flew from a doorway, passing so close it grazed him with its claws before it slammed another poor fellow into a wall and began to tear at him.

'This can't be happening!' Ocander babbled as he sprinted on. A brick that flew from nowhere caught him on the shoulder, and when he drew his hand away from the wound, he found his skin painted scarlet.

Ahead, the plaza beckoned. Ocander could already see the gleaming armour of Scalussen soldiers. Spell-lightning crackled above their raised hands and sharp lances.

'Help!' Ocander yelled as he sprinted for their ranks. They parted just enough for him to hurtle through, where others sprawled panting or dashed madly towards the three quickdoors that poked from the stone. Two Scalussen mages saw to each portal.

Ocander took the middle ground, exhaustion slowing him while fear and desperation pushed him to a weak jog. Clerks and counters didn't get much exercise aside from lifting stacks of heavy parchment or sacks of coin, and now Ocander was thoroughly regretting choosing such a sedentary occupation.

The city stank of fear amidst the char of the sprouting fires. Ocander looked back to see daemons bursting from the streets alongside those who fled from them. It was a bloodbath that the Scalussen barely managed to drive back. As the crowds surged towards him, Ocander picked up his pace, aiming for the nearest quickdoor.

Escape was almost in his grasp when another rift of fire and blinding light opened before him, and a hulking daemon larger than the last stepped forth, a black sword bigger than Ocander in his hand. Four glowing eyes glared down at him as the sword raised

Perhaps it would have looked comical to any innocent onlooker who had no stake in life or death or fear, but in his moment of sheer panic, Ocander chose to dive through the daemon's legs. The heat of the monster torched his cloth and skin, but there was no going back now, and before the daemon could sweep the sword after him, Ocander dove once more for the quickdoor's emerald and fizzing surface.

Ocander had never used a quickdoor before. It had been a fear of his once, and then a fascination, but that day it was vital and not an experience he had time to savour. All he was conscious of was tumbling through a tunnel of white lightning and enduring a roar that pained him. Darkness claimed him before another day in another city appeared. Leaves of palms and vines twirled around columns.

Gasps came as he appeared, falling on his chest in a patch of sand. Ocander choked, reaching up for a hand that was quick to come. But he was not dragged out of the way, as he expected. He looked up to find a man who couldn't meet his eyes and instead stared behind Ocander.

The counter turned, fearing the daemon would be behind him, but instead he saw a dead quickdoor, cracked around its stone frame and leaking dust. No spell filled its border.

It was then that Ocander felt a strange sensation in his legs. He wrenched himself up to gawp, unable to make sense of what he saw. The daemon's blade had missed him, but it had severed the quickdoor before he could escape – and Ocander in the process. Everything below his hips was gone.

Ocander began to scream as the pain caught up with his mind.

Farden. Get up. Your trap is sprung.

The clang at the door dragged Farden from the dream of black smoke and grinning faces. His armour clanked as he drew the spear from under his pillow. Metal screeched as it expanded to full length.

Warbringer and Hereni stood as ominous shadows in the morning light.

'What is it? What time is it?' Farden demanded, voice full of gravel.

Hereni entered as Farden hunched on the bed. 'Almost evening, and there's news of war, King.'

'The daemons have come to Troacles,' grumbled the minotaur.

'Loki's work no doubt.'

'No doubt,' snorted Farden as he stood and reached for his helmet and gauntlets. 'Summon the army.'

'Already assembling.'

Farden strode past them. 'Then let's find out more.'

'You're sleeping in that armour now?' Hereni whispered over his shoulder.

Farden ignored her.

Beyond the Dawnknell, they jogged across the unfinished stretch of stone to where the new quickdoors stood in a triangle, five altogether. A flood of people poured from them with repeated crackling. The gathering Scalussen soldiers hemmed them in. Towerdawn and his dragons were spreading their wings for shade. Healers ran amongst the wounded. There were already hundreds and more arriving every moment.

'The doors are connected to Belephon, Farden!' Hereni called over the noise. Sipid and Eyrum now stood by her side.

'The Troacles gates aren't working,' the Siren said. 'We all know what that means.'

Farden thudded his spear in a strange mixture of sorrow and satisfaction before striding forwards into the crowds of survivors. A trap was sprung, but the bait had not been New Scalussen, as he hoped, but those who didn't deserve even another morsel of misery. 'Empty the barracks to give space for the wounded and survivors. Get every healer off every ship and out of every bed and get them down here. Most importantly, I want every single survivor checked by a dragon and a witch to make sure Loki's not using this as a distraction!'

The 'Aye!' of his generals sounded, and the spears of the soldiers amassed thundered in unison. Farden took a moment to search his feelings, to listen for the spear whispering of the god's presence, but Gunnir stayed silent. Loki was not there.

Farden saw a man being dragged on a stretcher and halted his carrier. Both the poor fellow's legs were missing, cauterised by magick. Farden hesitated when he saw a daunting similarity in the man's face. He looked like a young Modren.

'What's happened to Troacles?' he asked.

'Daemons are what happened!' the man groaned. 'Appeared right in the middle of the streets.'

'What's your name, sir?' Farden felt shadow falling over him as Towerdawn loomed.

'Ocander. I'm a counter.'

'How many did you see?'

Ocander winced. 'Dozens. Scores. They broke the doors before I could escape.'

'You're alive, and that's what matters. Our healers will soon be with you. You'll be safe here.'

Farden whirled on the others.

'Eyrum, Sipid, Hereni, I want you all to remain here.'

Hereni spluttered. 'What?'

'If Loki's springing another trap, I want New Scalussen at full strength. I will go alone.'

Eyrum cleared his throat from the dust. 'We believe in you, Farden, but this is all of Gremorin's army. That's hundreds of daemons.'

Farden felt the strong grip he had kept on himself for the past few weeks peel away finger by finger. 'Enough with the doubt!' he yelled. 'I didn't fight through Easterealm and lose Durnus to not use this weapon for the good it was meant for. Understand?'

Eyrum bowed his head. The others remained silent.

Farden gave them his orders. 'Send another dragon to Elessi and Lerel and hawks to the other cities to warn them. Another battalion of soldiers to each as well. See that our army and the Bastard Fleet are ready for anything. Towerdawn, would you do me the honour of having your dragons protect my city while I reduce the daemons to ash?'

'I would, and we shall,' boomed the Old Dragon.

Farden heard the minotaur rattling her horns as he bowed, and Farden remembered his promise. 'Don't worry, Warbringer, you're coming with me.'

'Thought I was done with quickdoors,' the minotaur complained.

'We're not travelling by quickdoor,' Farden said with a smirk. 'Fetch me two hundred hardened soldiers and mages. Volunteers only, and I want them assembled as soon as possible.'

'And what about me?'

All turned to find Mithrid standing behind them, axe in hand and armour on. She had yet to clean it after the last battle. 'I didn't fight to free Troacles just to let it burn.'

Farden hammered his helmet onto his head, letting his voice reverberate around his helmet. 'You can come. But don't you fail me this time.'

Mithrid shouldered her axe. 'Wouldn't dream of it.'

Hereni crossed her arms and pulled a face Farden couldn't figure. There was no complaint. No objection. Only something grim-faced and hard-jawed that Farden hoped was trust.

'I'm coming with you,' Hereni blurted.

Farden shook his head. 'I want you here, General. Nobody else has magick like you do, and Scalussen might need you. This is Loki we're talking about.

Akitha came to fuss over their weapons and armour, attacking with a file or pliers here and there. She refused to touch Farden's, just as he would have refused her to touch it.

The finest soldiers and mages gathered over an hour, volunteers all. One by one, they clamped a hand on each other's shoulders to form a circular chain that spiralled to end with Warbringer. Shields and blades pointed outwards. Magick pounded in heads and popped ears as mages readied. Farden examined them one by one, clapping their shoulders. Between their lines, guarded by a lycan, he saw Irien standing watch. She mouthed something that looked like *good luck.*

Farden spun Gunnir in his fist as he stared to the sky and watched a winged shadow cross the empty blue. Warbringer took his other hand while Mithrid seized his shoulder.

'Hold on tight,' said the mage as he held the spear by his chin to feel the magick flow through him. 'This might be dangerous.'

Farden shot the spear to arm's length as the gryphon swooped to seize it. Lightning crackled when the claws touched the steel, and all of them collapsed into thin air with a shriek of bent reality.

Fire greeted them with rapturous applause. Smoke swirled as Ilios soared into the cindered sky with a shriek. There wasn't a city left to recognise at first. The tall and huddled buildings of Troacles had been reduced to landslides sprawled across the plaza.

Soldiers thrust their steel outwards, but nothing was wounded but thin air. The plaza was largely empty. Farden blasted a shield spell across the rubble to clear the smoke and keep errant volleys at bay. His mages followed suit while those who had stumbled in the jump picked themselves up. A few of them vomited but never faltered in their guards. It was likely the journey, but Mithrid wouldn't have blamed them if it was due to the smell. Death and rot clung to the wind, and when the vortex spells forced back the smoke, they saw the gore and carnage that was to blame. Every body that lay between the rubble was burned to a skeleton, ripped into far too many pieces, or desiccated and reaped of their souls.

'The dead don't lie,' Farden whispered, as if he were worried about being discovered even though the blackened day roared with sounds of distant battle.

Scalussen magick was soon tasted in their air. The glowing jewels of daemons' eyes appeared in the rubbled canyons of streets. Glimmering edges of dark steel weapons cut through the smoke as they emerged. At first a handful. Then a dozen. Then two.

Farden greeted them with a blinding light burning in Gunnir's glaive blade. Roars filled the air in response.

Mithrid could hear their harsh words and curses. 'The spear!' Several daemons began to shrink away, but a roaring voice kept them still. A voice that had run a shiver down Mithrid's spine far too many times for her liking.

Gremorin emerged from the murk, hunched at the centre of the daemon ranks, grasping claws outstretched. 'He is still only a human! I want him dead and that spear in my hands!'

'You know what to do,' Farden growled to his warriors as the daemons shuffled closer.

Four daemons braver than the rest bounded into a run, furnace jaws gaping and fire glowing white across their shoulders and claws. Farden's shield spell pressed against them, holding them long enough for lightning to burst from Gunnir and reap an arc of carnage across the plaza. Two daemons fell immediately to the magick that cut across their chests and left them trembling. The other two scrabbled madly to escape, while the rest hurled boulders over their heads. Warbringer smashed one away with her hammer. Ilios took another and tossed it back into the daemon ranks. When spells of fire began to fly over the ruins, the Scalussen mages were ready, either withering them with their shields or flinging them right back to fall at the daemons' claws. The explosions illuminated their fangs and iron hides. Not one of them was alike in their shape, eyes, or limbs. Mithrid eyed one that had thick crab claws for arms, each shimmering like coal with the blood they'd already spilled.

Farden halted his mages to taunt the daemon prince and bring them closer. Mithrid approved. 'Your house is falling like your crown, Gremorin! I hope you enjoyed your last sunset!'

'He is nothing but a worm! Kill him! Kill them all' Gremorin bellowed back, and the flames of the daemons soared in unison like a forge in a gale.

The daemons came faster this time and more of them. Farden made an example out of the closest, and to the daemon's credit, he endured the blast of magick for several moments before he exploded into charcoal that showered his kin. The others faltered, giving Farden more time to carve their hideous hides to pieces. Not a scrap of their daemon steel could stand before the spear's power.

Yet it was their numbers that sought to ruin them. Warbringer broke a daemon's horns from its head as it lurched around their sides to flank them. Before the beast could recover, Voidaran sank into its skull, bleeding fire and magma across the stone. Ilios seized a lance in his claws and drove it into another that snuck closer with a shriek.

Mithrid stood frozen amidst the carnage. Not useless, but biding her time to prove Farden wrong. Never mind herself and all she had trained for. Her magick brimmed at the surface, aching to bubble over. It was given the chance all too quickly.

Fire cast her shadow long and trembling across the rubble as a daemon towered behind her. Mithrid unclenched her shaking fist and let shadow spin around her as if she were the centre of a tornado. The daemon's claws, inches from grasping her, recoiled with a snarl.

'The cursed worm!' the daemon snarled, making those in earshot raise another roar of outrage. The spear was bad enough, but now they had a freak of nature in their midst.

'I prefer Mithrid,' she replied as her shadow wrapped around the daemon instead. She felt every thread of his ancient magick running through him, from his hooves to every one of his six arms, and she pulled them apart, one by one. The daemon roared in pain, fire sputtering and his eyes flickering until Warbringer put a hammer to his chest and knocked him to rubble.

Another monster galloped on all fours over the detritus towards them, flames trailing from its mouth like ribbons. Mithrid let her shadow spread wide to funnel it closer, until she could slam the two halves of her dark magick together and made the daemon writhe. Ilios did the rest, seizing the beast in his claws to drop it from a height that made it squeal all the way to the flagstones. A mage's lightning pummelled it before it could rise again.

And yet, between every swing of his spear and every lightning bolt that sent shockwaves through the place, Farden kept his eyes firmly on Mithrid. It rankled her. Soured her. Made her want to fight harder, not smarter.

Mithrid threw out her shadow to seize a sword that was descending on the mage. Farden's shield spell withered under her touch, but she held the sword firm, long enough to take her axe and hack at the wielder's wrist with a shower of sparks. Farden thrust the spear past her cheek, so close it made her skin burn. He said nothing, but his grim scowl said it all.

Mithrid pushed her shadow wide, stretching like the tentacles of that keraken Elessi had chased north. She seized throats. She bound arms and legs. She snuffed fire and strangled black steel. For a brief moment, the daemons seemed more afraid of her touch than the spear's.

'Come face me, Gremorin!' Mithrid yelled. 'Let's finish this!'

But the prince of daemons had more of his kin to waste, and with whips cracking and fire blooming, they redoubled their efforts, spreading all around the ruined quickdoors to hem them in. There were more daemons than Mithrid remembered.

Heavy iron arrows and spears began to rain, one skewering a Scalussen soldier from his scalp to his waist, armour counting for little. Fireballs soared through the storm of smoke to crash around them. Mithrid managed to swipe several away before Warbringer grabbed her and dragged her under a nearby shield spell. Lightning, ice, and darts of emerald force filled the plaza as the mages unleashed their fury. Farden stood right beside them, Gunnir never silent for a moment.

A daemon appeared close to their ranks with a whip-crack and a blast of smoke. Farden whirled, but before he could summon the spear's power, Mithrid laid waste to the monster, holding him tight until the mages could drive spells and blades into whatever the daemons called a heart.

Helbeasts raced into the fray, spurred on by their masters' whips and snarls. One galloped straight for Mithrid, jaws slavering. For a heartbeat, Mithrid stalled, that old fear slowing her. But as the creature pounced with claws wide, she brought her axe swinging upwards into its grotesque mouth. The momentum of the beast still bowled her over, coating her in dark blood, but Warbringer was there once again to haul her up.

Mithrid snatched back her arm and held her shadow tight. Between the bodies, she ducked and weaved, axe and dark magick spinning together. Helbeast and daemon fell before her as she pressed on and on across the plaza towards Gremorin. Farden yelled for her. Warbringer roared, but Mithrid ignored them all. Her power stormed around her, reaching upwards like the thorns of a mighty crown.

Daemons pounded the stone as they chased her down, but each stopped short of the shadow, retching as if it choked them. Mithrid snatched at a dozen at once, and although the strain bent her legs and dizzied her eyes, she squeezed, wrapping them in shadow like snakes strangling their next meal.

'I am meant for more!' Mithrid yelled as the daemons fell to their knees. Those that fought back bucked from the force of spells striking them. Gunnir's fire turned murk to bright sunlight as it poured magick over her head. She felt mages swarming around her as she cut a path towards the daemon prince.

Farden was suddenly beside her, Gunnir spinning so fast it looked as if he held a round shield of light.

'Draw back your magick!'

Mithrid glared at Farden for a moment before realising it was a simple order, not a threat or warning. She complied.

The tip of the spear met the ground with a bell toll, sending a wave of dirt and stone crashing across the plaza. Lightning scurried from daemon to daemon, scorching their hides and sending chaos deep into their ranks. It was a shocking blow, and Mithrid was too awed to strangle those who still writhed.

Once more, the daemons fell back to regroup and bellow their threats and curses. Several of them withdrew into the gloom. One vanished with a snap of fire and magick.

Through the smoke, Mithrid could see Gremorin's grin of fire had faded. There was a candle's tremulous glimmer in his eyes. Others at his sides seemed to gnash and snarl in doubt. Fifty smoking hulks of daemons lay around them already, maybe more. More than a score of Scalussen mages and soldiers had joined the dead. Warbringer had an ugly cut across her shoulder but strangely seemed to relish the wound. Mithrid had been punctured by a stone shard at some point, and she dug it out of her arm.

'We have all day and night, Gremorin,' she called to them.

Farden flashed Mithrid another look. 'You remember what we discussed?' he said.

Mithrid nodded, clenching her jaw and her axe. 'Do you?'

Farden's smirk got caught halfway. His eyes shot to his spear before he whirled around, searching the smoke. He barely managed to hiss, 'He's here!' before a crackle of light and magick came from the peak of a nearby pile of rubble. A figure perched casually on a boulder, and a familiar and hateful face gleamed down at them. The bastard was two bites into the sugared pastry he wafted about in his hand.

'Of course!' Farden yelled. 'It wouldn't be a true party without you, would it, Loki?'

Loki cackled around a mouthful. 'Good to see some of that sharp tongue back, Farden. You were getting so serious for a while. So boring, I tell you!'

'You despicable cur,' Gremorin accused with a stab of his fiery sword. 'You said Farden had gone to the ocean.'

'And you trusted me again!' Loki prodded his own chest with his snack. 'Do you not wonder why they call me the god of lies? By my worthless kin, Gremorin, you really are no Orion. You've let desperation blind you.'

Gremorin blazed with anger, wearing fire like armour.

'But you are correct, Farden, and what a party it is! Or will be. We do have a few more guests that need to join us first,' Loki said as he took another bite and shed crumbs as he gestured across the city. 'Surprise guests.'

'More games.' Warbringer clicked her tongue. She seemed preoccupied with the head of her hammer, placing her hand to its runes over and over.

'Whatever he's up to, we'll be ready for it,' Farden reassured them.

'Your overconfidence is one of your finest traits, Farden. I really do enjoy it.'

Mithrid saw a building fade as the smoke of the burning city seeped inwards. What was left of the day died. It was likely a trick of the lights shining in her blinks, but she swore she saw a shadow dance over a chimney stack amongst the whorls of smoke.

Nobody gave an order. Nobody said a word. Farden simply raised Gunnir and aimed it at Loki. Gremorin belched fire from his jaws, and surprisingly, it wasn't aimed at the mage, but the god. For a moment, Scalussen and the daemons were aligned. Such was their hatred that they forged an unspoken alliance, albeit a brief one. Loki skipped to another rooftop before their rage could reach him, though he did look slightly flustered, or so Mithrid told herself. He played it off by staring at the burned end of his pastry with disappointment before flinging it into a bonfire that used to be a house.

Loki sighed. 'Look at you all, bonding.'

Warbringer sniffed at the air, putting a hand to Farden's arm. 'You feel that? Cold in the air.'

If Farden did feel it, he didn't say it. He was busy watching the daemons also putting their nostrils to work.

Mithrid tasted the air. If there was something in the air that was different from the charcoal and copper of blood, it was a faint smell of dead leaves and old forest, and that was odd for a city trapped between ocean and desert and currently on fire. And despite the flames that raged all around them, the wind had a cold current in it.

'Impossible,' Gremorin hissed.

'I believe my guests are almost here,' whispered Loki, face abruptly drawn and serious, making Mithrid shiver once more.

Gunnir crackled in Farden's hands. 'Form up and stay wary. Vortex and light spells, mages.'

Scalussen pushed the daemons back as they stepped into formation: a sharp arrow aimed at Gremorin with Farden at its tip. Mithrid and Warbringer took the other corners. Shields locked as they stood fast, as the smoke swirled close and thick no matter how many vortex spells were thrust into it.

All that could be heard was Loki chuckling, having the gall to sit crosslegged on a slumped rooftop, toasting his hands on nearby flames. Mithrid considered playing clever with her shadow and striking from behind, but she had barely woven threads together when a cry came from their lines, somewhere between Mithrid and Warbringer. All she saw was a glimpse of a soldier's boots disappearing into the smoke. A discarded shield spun around on the stone.

'Close up! Spears out!' Mithrid yelled.

'There's something in this smoke, King!' yelled a mage before a long and spiked lance of black steel skewered his throat. It withdrew as swiftly as it came and dragged the corpse with it, vanishing into the smoke with a gurgle.

Warbringer kept her hammer moving about her body. 'What is it, Farden?!'

'I don't know, but we'll kill whatever it is just in case!'

Another scream as another lance ran through a mage at Mithrid's shoulder, and all she could do was chase the blade with shadow. A hiss was all she heard, and one that seemed to spread around them, growing disturbingly louder.

Mithrid spread her shadow wider, and it was the only remedy to make the smoke recoil.

'There!' cried out a soldier, where three shadows scuttled away. More swarmed forwards, long swords cutting at shields and slashing at legs. Two more fell before Mithrid could force them back. At Warbringer's corner, ashen limbs plunged out of the smoke in their dozens, and more bodies fell out of formation.

'Farden! Do something!'

Farden was already working on it before she could finish speaking. Lightning flicked through the smoke cloud as Gunnir cut an indiscriminate path through the fire, drawing inhuman screeches and shrieks into the night. The scuttling of claws on rocks could be heard.

A figure of fire crashed through the rubble. Opportunistic bastards, and Farden cut them down one by one. Mithrid was too focused on keeping the grey things at bay, whatever they were. Above the pain the swirling magick put in her head, she felt an itch. Something sharp buried deep.

'Back!' Mithrid yelled as another skinny shadow jerked towards her. A wave of her dark magick sent him scurrying again, and wherever she couldn't cover, mages sent spells blasting into the murk.

'Enough!' Farden bellowed, and with Gunnir summoning lightning from the sky, a thunderclap drove a wave across the plaza, shaking the rubble piles and shoving the smoke aside. Once more, what lay hidden beneath wasn't pleasing to uncover, and she felt every soldier and mage recoil, every eye stretch wide.

'Evernia, save us,' breathed a soldier at her side.

Mithrid swallowed dust and grit as she stared upon creatures she had never seen before and felt a stone lie heavy in her gut. Sweat dripped inside her helmet.

Mithrid's eyes roved over the newcomers. Terrifying was the first word that described them. Lithe and tall were the next. They must have stood seven feet tall at least. Ash-grey from bare foot to sharp face, and wherever the bones didn't poke and stretch their waxy skin, wherever black plate and chainmail didn't cover, Mithrid saw complex patterns of white runes and scars. Ugly blades rested in their hands, full of wicked curves and unnecessary spikes. Not one of the hundreds that stood around them moved, standing like last year's burned trees as if they played a game. Their pale, milky eyes did not blink. The lips stretched around their white fangs did not quiver, and it sickened Mithrid with fear.

'What is going on?'

Ilios whistled nearby, hunkering low with a growl shaking his feathers.

One taller than the rest stood a dozen feet before Farden, white eyes locked to the spear, a belt of teeth hanging about his waist. Farden was silent. Still. Perhaps a fear wormed into that stubborn mind of his.

'You are Farden,' the creature uttered in a voice that sounded like a wire brush scraping rust.

'And who the fuck are you?' asked the mage.

A smile of sharp teeth spread. 'Azen Ithar of Clan Covor.'

Mithrid raised her voice. 'What are you?'

'We are those who were created third. Those that were banished. Those that have returned.'

Once more, Mithrid swore she heard a fell whisper from Farden's spear.

'Elves,' Warbringer echoed the word louder, and Mithrid felt the stammer in the mages' magick, saw the wide eyes of the soldiers. The word alone made the formation pull tighter into itself. Humanity had spent two millennia trying to rid the memory of elves from their minds. Mithrid endured a peculiar cold washing over her and a churn of her gut. 'We're fighting elves now?' she asked, voice cracking.

Farden pointed the spear at Loki as he addressed the elf. 'Allow me to guess. You have a pact with this worthless scrap of dung.'

Azen spread his arms in a mock bow. 'The pact has been written. Your head is the price.'

'Treachery!' Prince Gremorin bellowed. 'Your kind was made to obey us, and you will bow before your prince!'

Azen briefly turned to face his once-master. 'No longer, Gremorin. Loki told me how you bent the knee before a human. I did not believe it until I saw with my own eyes. You may join us or suffer the same fate as Farden. The age of the elves is dawning.'

Gremorin raged, yet his cowardly feet stayed where they were. More of his daemons began to shuffle, not away this time, but towards the elves.

'My head, is it?' asked Farden, stretching his shoulders.

Azen's face became sharp marble. 'It is. And the spear. A worm has no right to wield such a weapon.'

Farden let Gunnir's whine answer for him. Azen leaned on his back foot and raised his arms in a strange stance.

'Kill them,' Loki ordered nonchalantly, drawing a long blade from his pocket.

CHAPTER 22
A DREAM

I saw it, I swear! Scarlet tentacles a-reaching and a-crushing. Masts meant nothing. Swords and arrows meant less. Hulls were turned to matchsticks. A ship of ghosts floated there nearby, not moving a hand to help.
REPORT OF A TROACLES SAILOR, SOLE SURVIVOR OF A SHIPWRECK IN YEAR 576 OF THE NEW COUNT. IT WAS DISMISSED AS A POOR EXCUSE FOR FALLING ASLEEP AT THE WHEEL AND RUNNING THE SHIP INTO A REEF

EARLIER THAT DAY

'On deck, you salty bastards!' yelled Lerel, breaking the still of the day, composed of the lapping of calm waves, the familiar creak of ship-wood, and an occasional mewing gull.

At some point between the second and the fourth bell, while she had stared at the star charts on her cabin's ceiling, Lerel had made a decision. Elessi wasn't willing to play any games, but Lerel was. That was why she shouted nice and loud, and from the corner of her eye, she saw the beached keraken angle his head like an owl spotting a mouse-tail.

A light snuffed out in the cabin of the ship with no name. Lerel scowled.

The crew had begun to pour from deck hatches and doors beneath the aftcastle. Those who had slept on deck or had been standing watch hurriedly packed away their hammocks and leftover crusts.

Most already knew where to go and what to do and would have made the ship ready with just a nod, but Lerel shouted her orders nevertheless.

'I want those barrels stowed away or fastened down! Get those sails up, slack and ready. Oars for the moment until we clear this mire of rocks and wreckage! We're heading back to New Scalussen on the double! Get to work. Nice and loud now.'

'Aye!' bellowed the crew in unison, managing to make the noise reverberate even in the constant fog and smoke.

A tut made her turn. Elessi had her arms crossed over admiral's robes as dark as the sails that crept up the masts. Lerel's admiral's robes.

'Morning. Or afternoon, I should say. I thought I'd let you sleep after yesterday's action, but also give you a chance to say goodbye.'

'It's already been said,' Elessi yawned, looking to the cave and the still keraken. 'And why nice and loud?'

Lerel shrugged. 'So all the crew can hear me. A few are still half-deaf from the battle.'

'Lerel.'

'You'll have to trust me,' Lerel said with a tired grin. 'And is that my robe?'

Elessi came to the wheel and watched the crew in their furious dance, rolling barrels back and forth and heaving on ropes and windlasses. Thick oars began to poke from the ship's hull. 'I don't know how Farden does it, wearing his armour all the time. Far too heavy.'

Lerel saw her sneaking a glance into the cave of Magre with pursed lips. 'I really thought Rokhelm might help us. But then, a favour is a favour, but joinin' a war is a debt, and a harsh one at that. Maybe it's best we don't owe a monster that big and deadly.'

A distant figure came to stand on the bow of the ship with no name, standing high on the railing and one hand on a rotten rope. Elessi raised her hand in a wave, but Rokhelm didn't wave back.

Lerel hummed. 'We'll see about that,' she said before taking a breath. 'Make way! Strong and steady now!'

On the rowing decks below, bodies heaved at the oars and sent the ship lurching across the waters.

As she turned the wheel west and south, Lerel looked over her shoulder to see the last of the cave. A few trailing tentacles slid into the water, but that was all. Keraken was gone.

The rocks and wreckage she had mentioned seemed closer, sharper, and more entangled than when they had arrived, and it took them plenty of fending with oars and shouting to get the *Undaunted* through the narrow passages. That suited Lerel just fine.

Elessi stayed silent and vigilant even though she yawned a dozen times before the ship managed to find the edges of the impertinent fog. The afternoon was not much different, with patchwork cloud and a weak sun, and the charcoal streaks of storms brooding in the west. At least the swell was low and far apart, and the wind already tugged at the boat, eager to fly with it.

'Full sail!' Lerel yelled, and as the oars slid back into the ship, the rowers flooded back up to the deck to haul ropes and climb the rigging. Within moments, the *Undaunted* was carving the ocean and beginning to rise up on its wings. Only then did Elessi turn back to see if she could spy anything of Keraken, but there wasn't a tentacle or barnacled bowsprit in sight.

Elessi narrowed her eyes against the wind instead, clamping her hands onto the railing, and as the miles fell away, they closed completely.

Laroso stomped up on deck to take over from Lerel, and she put a hand on the general's arm. 'Let's take a walk. And Laroso, have the hatch opened so Fleetstar can breathe. I don't know if that dragon egg needs fresh air, but it's no doubt better than that small hold.'

'Get that bloody main hatch open!' he yelled the moment Lerel had finished.

Elessi and Lerel paced the long deck, heading for the bow. To a clunk of wood, the hatch was cranked open, and the pale head of

Fleetstar rose up to let smoke fly from her nostrils. Ko-Tergo emerged, white hair all spiked and matted from his cot.

'Afternoon,' Lerel bade them.

Both grunted in reply, and the yetin moved to the ship's side to watch silver fish jump in the ship's wake with hunger in his eyes.

As they took up a seat on the bow, Elessi stared back to the hidden coast, smeared by fog and rapidly fading into the distance. Lerel followed her gaze as it tracked the coast around the vast bay. A flock of seagulls seemed to be trailing them, as if they were a fisher boat about to trawl nets.

Elessi shifted north abruptly and pulled her cloak around her.

'What is it, Elessi?' asked Lerel.

'I don't know. It can't be right.'

'What? It's like you feel a daemon.'

'I can, but very faint. Not as strong and not the same. There's something else with it, like the darkness in the east,' she muttered. Elessi sat straight and face paled by the wind, and Lerel kept her wits about her until almost half an hour passed without a sign of any danger.

'I have to ask, what was it like on the ship?' Lerel asked, distracting her.

'Bizarre, in a word. I thought I would be drowned, but there are shield spells on every porthole and hatch. We went deep where not even the sun reached. I can't describe it, but I wish I could.'

'And what about him? The sailor? Like you said, he's spent far too much time alone, and it shows.'

'Rokhelm? He's odd all right, but he's almost older than Durnus. Keraken has seen even more centuries, and he's one with that ship and beast like Towerdawn's one with Nerilan. It's a shame. They would have made a fine weapon, but they might also have made another fine addition to this strange family we've gathered.'

Just when Elessi's tongue seemed to have been loosened, Lerel wasn't listening. A wave was rippling a stone's throw from the *Undaunted*'s port side, keeping perfect pace with the ship.

'Lerel?'

'I think we're being followed,' she replied.

The two of them rose as one and went to the bulwark. The silver fish had vanished, and Ko-Tergo looked glum. 'That's usually a sign of a predator,' Lerel muttered.

Before she had finished her sentence, the mightiest predator of them all rose from the waters. A single tentacle speared the waves, and Lerel was disturbed to find Rokhelm clinging to its spines with one hand, hat in the other. He waved as the tentacle moved closer. Lerel could see the shadow of Keraken in the grey waters, and her heart pounded once more to think it could keep up with the *Undaunted* without any effort.

Sailors ducked as the tentacle loomed overhead. Rokhelm jumped a dozen feet to the deck and whirled his hat in a bow, mostly aimed at Elessi. Lerel saw the smudges of ancient tattoos of runes on his bald head. They looked vaguely Arka.

'Apologies for boarding so uncouthly, but I'm too curious about this ship. I needed to experience it for myself. The wings are ingenious.'

'Afraid we can't claim any of that genius, sir,' said Elessi.

Rokhelm was already walking to the bridge. 'May I?'

'May you what?' asked Lerel.

'Steer this fine vessel?'

'If you must,' Lerel replied, following him closely to the ship's wheel, where Laroso clamped his pipe so hard in bared teeth it looked as if he would snap it off.

Rokhelm took a moment to examine the wheel before laying hands on it. He held the *Undaunted* straight for a moment before he slewed her from port and then to starboard. Everybody aboard had to hold onto something. Lerel bit her tongue until Rokhelm drove the ship in several wide circles while Keraken's eyes poked from the waters to watch.

'We have to be moving south,' Lerel said, staying polite.

'Of course,' Rokhelm blurted, as if he had forgotten he was not alone for once. He marched back down the stairs to examine the dragon. Fleetstar recoiled and snorted smoke. 'South. It's a shame you can't stay longer. There is much I could show you.'

Elessi followed him while Lerel stayed at the wheel and put them back on course.

'Unfortunately, we have a war to fight,' she said, staring at Fleetstar and silently warning her to play nice.

'Yes, your war against a god,' Rokhelm said, as though their conversation had been weeks ago, not the day before. With a distracted wave of his hand, Keraken slipped back into the waters, and the *Undaunted* seemed once again alone.

'Does the fact you're followin' us mean you changed your mind?' asked Elessi.

Again, Rokhelm smiled wide. 'No.'

'You know, people don't usually smile when they're givin' bad news.'

Now Rokhelm moved to the bow, where porpoises had come to jump where the ship's wings carved the waters. He blinked his squid eyes. 'Is it such bad news?'

Elessi gave him a narrowed look. 'For me, yes. Without your help, many more might die in the fight to free Emaneska.'

'Why do you fight?'

'I just told you, to rid Emaneska of—'

'I mean you, Elessi of Albion. What's your fight?'

Elessi searched her teeth with her tongue as she thought. It was not a hard question. It was merely hard to say aloud. 'I've asked myself many times, and it's always the same answer. I fight for a dream.'

'A dream?'

'I've seen what the filthiest of souls in this world can do and what the world would look like if somebody didn't stop them. I loathe that those like me pay the price. I almost paid it myself when they tried to kill me when I was younger. Much younger, and I've been wrapped up in this mess ever since,' Elessi said with a sigh. 'I fell in love with a Written mage who always fought his hardest to do what was right, even when it cost him everything and made him turn his back on everyone, me included. So I moved on, and I fell in love with the right Written mage. Modren, my husband. Both Modren and the others I call family had a dream of a free world, where evil had no place, and nobody paid the price for its desires. It's a dream I almost gave up on when Modren died for it, but I fight on so he didn't fall in vain. And there you have it.'

'How did he die?'

Elessi looked at Rokhelm. If he expected tears, she had shed countless for Modren already and had few left to give. 'A daemon prince by the name of Gremorin killed him in the battle in the north.'

Rokhelm pressed his hat against his heart. 'I had a wife, but nobody killed me but her.'

Elessi frowned. 'You'll have to explain.'

'It's not how it sounds. I barely remember now, but I know she wanted to settle with the rest of the Arka and that I wanted to stay at sea. I was a pirate once, you see, and many Arka were before they went ashore forever. I remember her clinging to me every time I left for the ocean.' Rokhelm lifted up a hand to look at his fingers as if her grip was still there. 'Not that I didn't go back as often as I could with a handful of coins and nothing more for her. I always said I would stop when we had enough to live like arkmages, but that's never the way such stories go. I was a poor pirate in all senses of the word. I was already a grey man when our ship was wrecked in battle and Keraken found me. I went back of course, but they told me I had been gone too long, and she had gone to the other side, and they found her staring out of a window watching the ocean.'

'I'm sorry,' Elessi offered, but Rokhelm shook his head.

'Too many centuries have passed now, but I will never pay my debt to her, no matter how I try.'

Elessi tapped her hand on the bulwark. 'Is that why you turned from pirate to pirate hunter?'

'I saw what you saw when I was also much younger. Filthy souls. I have fought them ever since. Helps that Keraken likes to break their ships. And you? What were you before a High General?'

'A maid.'

'For this king you follow?'

Elessi snorted. 'Strangely, yes.'

An hour passed of talk, small and large. Of Scalussen old and new and Albion. Of running hands across the veil of death. Rokhelm spoke of whole islands lost to the sea, of treasures forgotten in depths untold, of a whirlpool growing in the farthest east, and of far-off lands across the ocean filled with nothing but ghosts and desert. Elessi didn't know which to believe, and truth be told, the shiver down her spine and the discomfort in her bones distracted her.

A yell came down from the mast. 'Dragon to the south!'

Rokhelm leapt up, hand on his sabre.

'Why do you hate them so much?' Elessi asked as she spied a faint blue dot against the clouds. Fleetstar had reared up, swirling eyes narrow.

'It's Kinsprite!'

'The last war we tried to help in was when Siren fought Siren, dragon against dragon. Keraken had always watched the dragons, and we thought a peace could be made, but the dragons turned on us. They scorched Keraken,' said Rokhelm wincing as if he could remember the pain. 'We decided we were not welcome in this world, and that we would suit ourselves and nobody else.'

Elessi blinked, remembering the tomes of the library. 'That was almost a thousand years ago.'

Rokhelm scratched his head beneath his hat. 'Was it now?'

As Lerel ordered the sails brought in, Kinsprite swooped to circle the ship. She looked as if she had raced to find them.

'Daemons!' the dragon blurted between deep breaths.

'Daemons?' Elessi stormed amidships. She knew the panic in Kinsprite's voice. 'Where?'

'They've attacked Troacles. Farden and Mithrid have gone to fight them!'

'Then we have to go as well!' Elessi called across the deck.

'Elessi!' Lerel shouted. 'That's more than a day away. What can we do?'

Elessi marched up the steps to seize her hands. 'Something isn't right, Lerel. It's not just daemons I feel. I don't know what it is, but I know Farden's in trouble. And if Gremorin has reared his ugly head, then I want to be there when it's lopped from his fiery shoulders!'

Rokhelm was somehow behind her. 'The daemon that killed your husband.'

Elessi set her jaw. 'The very same.'

With a sniff of the air, Rokhelm held up a finger to feel the wind and then licked it. 'Keraken can get you there faster. Keraken knows all the currents.'

'So now you'll help us?' Elessi said with a huff.

'No,' said Rokhelm.

Elessi brandished a trembling finger like a blade. 'I swear to —'

'But we will help *you*, Elessi of Albion.'

'Thron!' Kinsprite roared as a tentacle burst from the waters and slapped onto the *Undaunted*'s deck, surprisingly without splintering a single plank. Fleetstar growled at its proximity.

'Why is that monster never far away?' Lerel muttered.

Rokhelm beckoned to Elessi as he walked to the tentacle. 'Are you coming?'

Elessi slapped a hand to the sword at her side and followed. She didn't hesitate, but Lerel did.

'All mages and soldiers with me!' Elessi ordered. A few moved forwards while the rest bit their lips and bobbed their throats. More tentacles came to poke at the ship. 'With me, I said!'

Lerel pulled at her hair. 'Elessi, this is… This is mad.'

'Aren't you coming?' Elessi asked, holding out a hand just as Rokhelm held one out for her.

'Njord's balls,' Lerel cursed, taking up her blade.

'A pleasure to meet you,' said Rokhelm as Lerel put a foot on the meaty tentacle. Elessi held her tight as Rokhelm held her.

Lerel wouldn't have admitted it, but she emitted a cat-like yowl as the tentacle snatched her towards the ship with no name.

CHAPTER 23
THE DRAMATH-AI

*Those of the Marble Copse like to bray that our conflict is between good
and evil. They are fools. The real conflict is between truth and lies.*
FROM THE DIARY OF EMPEROR MALVUS BARKHART

Loki's instructions were simple. No matter how much she questioned
their deal for the Forever King's head, he did not care that Farden
had gone north and had given her four orders:

Silence the warning bell.

Quench the torches.

Open the gate.

Be ready tonight on the ninth bell.

All simple enough, but with one hitch: Irien needed to rid
herself of a lycan first. Tonight was already the night, and the bells of
the Winter Fortress were tolling eight.

Roglurg stood outside her locked door, as he had for hours
now. Although she couldn't hear him snuffling or picking at claws,
she could still smell the stink of hound and wild beast.

Farden was smart to be wary, but not smart enough. Supper
was always served around eight, even on a day when battle had
called and New Scalussen was filling with thousands of refugees.

Supper, however, was a little late in coming. Irien paced the
minutes away, peeking at the door until she heard the dinner tray
approach, then she threw herself under the simple frame and mattress
they had given her. There were stout boards beneath it to keep it from
skewing, and some helpful moron had built them so low, that with a

tuck of an elbow and a foot – or two of each in this case – Irien could hold herself off the floor with her back to the mattress.

A grunt and a growl accompanied the unlocking of locks and the squeaking of a hinge. A wooden tray was placed on the ground, but as soon as Roglurg noticed the room was empty, he began to stride around, ripping open cupboard doors and shredding curtains. He did not crouch to look beneath the bed, as any normal guard would have done, but rather lifted up the whole bed. Not all the way, however, exactly as Irien hoped the dumb hound would. The impact as the bed was dropped and hit the ground almost tore her grip clean off, but she held on, biting through the pain.

Roglurg stormed out of the room, barging the kitchen worker out of the way with a snarl. Irien also trusted he wouldn't immediately call the alarm but would try to track her down instead.

Once the door had swung shut, Irien shimmied out from beneath the bed frame, snatched the fork from the tray, and went to the door. Irien left the purple shawl and took a layer from her kilt to put over her head. A weak disguise, but better than nothing.

Not a sound came from the hallway, and Irien darted out into its patches of shadow and torchlight, running in the opposite direction of the lycan. She ran a route she had already mapped and practised in her mind many times. It was quick enough, but with a few twists and turns to lose whoever followed.

Only workers passed her by, and Irien managed to slip behind two guards distracted by an apparently fascinating conversation about somebody losing a ship in a bet. The loser's misfortune was Irien's gain, as it always was, and they led her to an open door and the night beyond.

Silence the warning bell. Quench the torches. Open the gate. Be ready tonight on the ninth bell.

Weaving between streets, palms, and carts bent under stone blocks, Irien worked her way north before the ninth bell could ring. It took speed and savvy to avoid the soldiers and patrolling mages, not to mention the witches. Irien found cover every time fluttering wings passed overhead or a dragon's wings beat the air. But her luck held, and the sky was stuck between sunset and night. The grey twilight was wonderful for avoiding searching eyes, and there was no sign of a moon to shine upon her work. A mist was even creeping from the palm forest and the mountains.

The gate the minotaur had so kindly mentioned in the tavern stood three streets away, and she checked if the beast was right. There did seem to be far fewer guards here due to the wall's longer undulating stretch. No tower yet, only scaffolding, and a gate slightly smaller than the rest in the city. It had no portcullis, only stout, rune-marked wood. The almost flat-roofed wooden houses in this street seemed to be queuing to leave, and they didn't make much room for soldiers or engines of siege. *Poor design*, Irien decided. It would serve the mage right for thinking himself a god.

What could be called a bell tower lingered near the scaffolding, in that it was a small but pointy arch of brick, and a bell dangled beneath it. Two soldiers stood either side of it, hands on spears while they stared out over the scrub to the north of the city. The curve of the wall kept them behind the line of sight of the closest soldiers, almost an entire street away. Complex pulleys and weights atop the wall suggested the gates were mechanical, and Irien snorted. Farden had almost made it too easy for her.

Irien crept from doorway to doorway, using the constant crackle of the distant quickdoors to hide her footsteps. Once she was in the shadow of the wall, she waited behind arrow barrels for a patrol to pass before working her way up the stairs to the meagre gatehouse. With a clench of her wooden fist and a tap of a panel on her wrist, a small crossbow sprang from an open hatch in her arm, already drawn and itching to fire. Irien took aim at the farthest soldier, knowing she could take the closest faster.

With a tap, the bolt hammered into the side of the man's head, and he fell against the brick tower. The other gave no cry as he turned to see his dead comrade. Shock could do that, and Irien used those precious moments to clench her fist twice. A thin blade slid from her first and second finger, and she drove it into the soldier's neck, finely aimed between the helmet and pauldron. Irien let him drop as she moved to the small ship's wheel built into the supposedly shoddy masonry. The ninth bell had already started to ring, and Irien turned the wheel as quickly as she could.

Weights fell and pulleys whirred, and to a muffled clanking, the great log that barred the gate lifted up until it was ensconced in the gatehouse. Irien let the wheel run as she reloaded her crossbow. Only when the gates had spread outwards did she fling her makeshift shawl over the torches and snuff them out. Darkness fell over the walls and the patchwork of silent scrub and humble bushes.

Loki would be pleased.

As the final toll of the ninth bell rang across New Scalussen, the soldier she had stabbed gargled something. Irien turned around and was about to jab the fork into him when she noticed the gag in his mouth. She hauled him to face the light of the city and saw smudged streaks of charcoal across his cheeks and a brand of something poking from under his helmet. This looked more like a brigand than a soldier of Scalussen. Or a pirate…

Roglurg bounded onto the ledge, looming over her with a bubbling snarl, and Irien did as her instincts demanded. The crossbow hammered her arm as it fired, catching Roglurg in the neck. The lycan reeled backwards, but he did not crumple. He barely took a moment before he fixed her with a deathly stare and came to seize her, claws flexing down by his knees.

'Back!' Irien swished her blade, stepping along the wall. Her heart throbbed in her throat. 'I won't matter one bit very shortly, I can promise you that. Loki's coming!'

'And we're more than ready for him,' called a voice from the street below. One of the other generals – Hereni, if Irien had heard right – summoned a spark between her hands. Her armour glinted in the darkness.

Irien contemplated diving the twenty or thirty feet off the wall, but it didn't seem wise. Her moment of pondering was enough of an excuse for General Hereni, it seemed and lightning rattled her teeth together and scorched her insides as she slumped on the stone. Before the darkness of unconsciousness swept her away, she saw soldiers flooding the streets. A dozen houses near the wall collapsed almost flat, proving themselves empty and fake. Archers flooded the rooftops of the rows behind. Doors and windows opened to show the fierce, arrow-tipped noses of ballistae.

'Sleep tight, Lady of Whispers,' Irien heard a voice mock before the lightning shocked her again.

Hereni dusted her tingling hands. 'Now that's taken care of, I want that gate shut and the torches relit! Get this heap of shit back to her cell,' she bellowed.

Eyrum limped from between regiments with Sipid, Sturmsson, Nerilan and Peryn in tow, all fully armed and armoured, and they climbed the stairs to join Hereni on the gatehouse. Thenerean, Warbringer's second in command, loped behind them at his leisure.

'Farden was right?' Eyrum asked.

'Irien betrayed us exactly where and when Farden said she would,' Hereni begrudgingly admitted.

'Fucking liar,' spat Sipid as Irien was bound and carried away by four Scalussen soldiers.

'Everything ready?'

Eyrum twirled his battleaxe. 'City's locked tight and loaded. Army's waiting. Sturmsson has all the ships lined up and ready.'

Sipid stretched his neck against the collar of his armour. 'Jar Khoum guard the east, poised to spring.'

'Minotaurs guard fortress,' was all that Thenerean said.

Peryn held up her hand for a finch to land. 'The witches, lycans, and the rest of Scalussen stand guard in the south.'

'And as much as I loathe this, my dragons and riders are perched and ready. Now if I may be excused...' Nerilan muttered, drumming her nails on her armour before turning on her heel and marching towards Towerdawn, who sat glowing in the torchlight a street away.

'Roglurg,' was all Roglurg had to say. It was then that Hereni noticed the bolt sticking from his neck, and she ran to check the lycan's wound. The short bolt had gone through the meat of his neck and nothing important, but before Hereni could ask for a healer, the lycan ripped it from his neck and threw it over the edge of the wall.

'I'm fine. Had worse,' said Roglurg.

Hereni's gaze followed the bolt, and she turned to face the north, where the mist swirled across the scrub and boulders of the wild Jar Khoum coast. Only a few stray palms, disturbingly still, broke the monotony between New Scalussen and the northern mountains. It may have been the dark, but not a single parrot cawed. Not a single gull keened. No owls shrieked while hunting the wasteland. A cold lingered in the night, and it was a chill that did not come from the sea.

'Air don't feel right,' muttered Sipid.

'There's no sign of an army. No ships on the waves. What do you think we are waiting for?' grumbled Eyrum by her side.

'A trick of Loki's, and I hate that is all we know,' said Hereni. 'There was a reason Irien wanted a weakness.'

Peryn sent a finch out into the mists, and it made sure to stay high and far from the ground as she had no doubt whispered in its ear. When it returned after a few short and nervous minutes, it shrugged its wings and offered a useless cheep.

'Whatever was there isn't there now,' Peryn told them. 'Maybe we scared Loki off already by foiling Irien's plan.'

Hereni clenched the stone parapet and felt her magick washing through her veins, gathering to throb in her skull. 'That god doesn't scare easily,' she said, loud and proud. 'But neither do we. Be ready for anything! No rest 'til freedom served!'

The thousand soldiers behind her thudded their spears and boots on the ground in agreement. The noise spread, racing through the ranks spread across the city as if New Scalussen was a storm waiting to strike.

Each of the generals hunkered down behind the wall to watch north, west, and east. The smaller dragons spread their wings to glide on the cold wind, spines crackling as impatient tails swished.

Hereni pushed against the mist with a spell of wind, but it refused to move. Worse, it seeped deeper into the city, reaching over the crenellations with spectral fingers. Light spells flickered across the walls where mages stood. Wind mages stood useless.

A harsh squawking disturbed the eeriness, making every bowstring and sword hand flinch. A crow emerged from the mist, eager to be away from whatever it escaped. Before it could reach the walls, it seemed to stop in midair, with wings flapping frantically and terror in its eyes. It fell unexpectedly still before its bones started to break one by one. When its hidden torturer was finished, it fell to the dust before the mist swallowed it up.

'What the fuck is out there?' Sipid whispered.

Hereni slapped the wall. 'Get to your other positions! Protect the walls!'

'Aye,' said Peryn as she dragged Sipid away from the battlements, heading south and east with their guards. A gust of air rocked them as Towerdawn and Nerilan took flight, heading for the Dawnknell. Thenerean ambled west as though he was out for a stroll.

Eyrum lingered by Hereni's side for a moment. 'Got a bad feeling?' he asked.

Hereni nodded slowly. 'The worst.'

The big Siren grunted before he descended the stairs. He also made for the Dawnknell. As he had put it earlier, to keep his eye on Nerilan.

Silence ruled over the northern walls as the torches and spells became fuzzy with the murk. Every soul ached with the waiting. With the weight and unspoken threat of the unknown.

A lone arrow flew over the walls as a trepidatious archer loosed their string by accident. That would not do. Hereni whirled with orders in her mouth, but they never made it out.

A bell rang from somewhere in Sanctuary Bay, and it turned every head its way.

❦

Admiral Sturmsson let his old ears drown in every slap of a wave against the *Autumn Vanguard's* hull. Every breath of the mages and sailors spread across his decks. Every creak of the ballistae turning in their mounts.

Sturmsson didn't like a lot of things, but waiting for a foe that he hadn't ogled through a spyglass was one of the worst. The second contender was the wretched mist that slunk across the waters between his ships and wrapped them in a woollen blanket.

A sailor bobbed into his peripheries. 'What do you reckon, Admiral?'

'A foul night to be fighting, that's for sure,' Sturmsson replied. At the silence that followed, he gave the sailor a look. He was a young fellow, fresh to the crew, and Sturmsson noticed the tremble of the hand wrapped around his sword hilt. He was reminded of a similar lad standing by his captain far too many years ago, a familiar shake in his hand.

'Not to worry, lad,' Sturmsson assured him, clapping a hand to his shoulder. 'We've fought in worse and come out shining on the other side. Scalussen's ready, and you stand amongst the finest in Emaneska, Paraia, Easterealm, and beyond. You'll do fine.'

The lad flashed a brief smile. 'Thank you, Admiral.'

Sturmsson nodded to the stern. 'Keep your watch.'

'Aye.'

Sturmsson turned back to the city and occupied himself by counting the rooftops, an old trick he'd learned on long watches. What the delay was, Sturmsson had no idea. Hereni and the others had sprung their trap, but there had been no warning of battle. The admiral stood at the helm of his ship and watched the silent city, hand on his sword and ring tapping its pommel. It was quiet. Far too —

A bloodcurdling scream cut the silence, so shocking it felt like a blow to Sturmsson's skull.

In the gloom of the stern, the lad he'd just spoken to was bent over backwards and writhing as a blade sliced him from belly to throat and spilled him over the deck. A shadow bent over the poor soul, and before Sturmsson had the wherewithal to raise a cry, the shadow stood to its full height and held its arms high and crooked, a black knife in each hand. Sturmsson barely noticed the other sailors lying dead and slumped over the bulwarks, killed swiftly and silently.

The stranger must have been seven feet without boasting, and the way it took a step across the deck with an unsettling whisper filled Sturmsson with a fear he hadn't felt since his youth. He wasn't the only one who stared in horror as the creature moved into the light, showing white eyes and ashen skin behind its mask and war-paint. Sturmsson had never seen such a thing in all his days, and yet in his soul and his gut, he knew it was a nightmare his kin had forgotten. It needed to be feared, and he always trusted his gut.

'Enemy!' Sturmsson managed to blurt, drawing the nearby soldiers running while others crowded the stairs of the aftcastle.

The nightmare's blades left its hands in a blink. Soldiers crashed to the deck, a knife in each of their throats and bodies blocking the others. As soon as the knives had done their dirty deeds, they snapped back to the creature's hands, only to dart out again and spill more blood on the stairs.

Sturmsson slashed with his sword, striking nothing but air as the foul creature dodged and weaved. A dozen times, he thought he had the creature pinned, only to find his blade free and clean.

'Have at you!' Sturmsson yelled as he feinted and thrusted, but the thud he felt in his steel was not flesh and bone, if the creature was made of such things, but the grind of metal on metal. The foe held his sword in his crossed blades, and before the admiral could react, the creature drove the sword back into Sturmsson's face with undeniable strength and pierced his chest with both of the black knives. Sturmsson's cry brought the soldiers and mages charging while the creature breathed foul air in the admiral's face. It cut upwards, slashing both sides of Sturmsson's neck as it stepped back. Knives dripped with blood before the bastard hurled itself over the stern and into the waters.

'Admiral!'

The cries grew quieter and quieter as Sturmsson pawed at the deep gouges in his neck, feeling cartilage and bone under his shaking fingers. He seized the closest hands and dragged whoever owned them to the deck.

'Warn... others,' were Sturmsson's last words, as he felt himself melt into the wood of his ship. A dreadnought, he had called it, and he dreaded nothing as the warmth flowed from his body, and he slid into a darker night to the sound of ship's bells.

Sipid checked once more on the walls bristling with archers and magick waiting to strike. Shield spells shimmered at intervals along the battlements. Two dragons perched on the rooftops behind them, riders keen-eyed and lances low as they stared west. Without a word, one of the dragons crunched roof tiles as it leapt into the air and shook the ranks with the wind of its wings. It soared above them to test the mist and taste the foul air.

Sipid realised his sword hand was shaking. Not from worry or fear, but from anticipation. He'd grown a taste for battle, something he didn't think possible after all his years. Impatience, however, was a trait he had always known, and he ached to get the ruckus started. He pined for their foes to show their foolish faces, so Sipid could carve them off.

'*Hia ka showa acki*?' he yelled to his captains perched further down the battlements. It was Jar Khoum for, 'Is there anything fucking out there?'

'*Owa!*'

That was a firm no, and Sipid stamped his foot. By the old spirits, did he need a throat to cut, and he began to thump up the stairs. The armour the Scalussen had given the Jar Khoum warriors always chafed in the wrong places, and so he wore half of it, leaving his arms and head bare. Jar Khoum usually fought in tunics or nothing at all in most battles, but Sipid had to admit the chafing was worth not getting an arrow in the gut.

Sipid shielded his eyes from the torchlight and stared into the blanket of grey that turned the palms into ghostly forms. 'Where are they?' he muttered to himself as he scanned the mist.

A frantic clang of a bell filled the wall with muttering.

Sipid spat in the dust at his feet. 'Where are those bloody bells coming from?'

'The bay!' yelled a mage at his side, and Sipid turned to peer into the mist. Only faint shapes of masts and great hulls could be seen past the Dawnknell.

'You hear what they're ringing?' asked the mage, and Sipid nodded grimly.

'Intruder.'

A cry swivelled him right back around. 'Movement!' A stone rolled across the dust, and every archer and mage swivelled to face it. Sipid slipped behind the battlements as the shield spells cut the air beyond the gatehouse.

A strange sound came from beside him, like a haunch of meat being slapped on a slab. Sipid cast a glance at the mage standing ready next to him and saw a long black arrow poking from her forehead. Another slammed into the man behind him, right below the eye.

'Archers!' Sipid bellowed as loud as he could. It was at that moment something smacked him in the head, and a fierce pain dizzied him. His only clue was an arrow quivering in a beam of scaffolding behind him. Sipid threw up a hand to feel blood dripping from his cheek. The arrow had split his ear and cut a rift in his cheek.

Jar Khoum warriors flooded to him as a volley of spells and flaming arrows painted the misted night with angry colours. Sipid pushed them away.

'I'm fucking fine! I don't care if we burn down the palms, keep up those bloody volleys!'

Fires soon burned amongst the scrub, but their flickers threw no shadows that were enemy-shaped. There was nothing lurking in the night.

It was then that Sipid caught a glimpse of one of his warriors being dragged from the walls, barely an arrow-shot away. Muffled shouts came as others fell, and Sipid began to run in the direction of death, curved sword high and ready and shield firm.

All he could see through the damnable mist was a long shape surrounded by corpses, and he yelled in anger as it hurled itself from the wall to the nearest rooftop. It was no human, judging by the way it moved, too tall and too long of limb. Sipid would cut it down nonetheless.

'There! I want that thing dead!' Sipid shouted to the soaring dragon and watched eagerly as the giant beast landed hard on another rooftop and filled a street with its fire. It was confusingly short-lived, and Sipid watched on as the dragon roared in pain and thrashed its head to and fro. To Sipid's horror — for he had taken a shine to the great reptiles of the north — the rider reeled back in his saddle, and Sipid saw the black arrow protruding from the Siren's heart, stark against the city lights. Both dragon and rider fell dead upon the rooftop.

'No!' Sipid bellowed. He practically threw himself down the stairs and dragged two mages with him as he gave chase through the smouldering street.

A shadow flitted across the flagstones. Sipid didn't have to utter a word. With fire, ice, and emerald light weaving between their hands, the mages filled the street with magick, blasting pieces from houses and scorching the dirt.

'Fuck!' Sipid snarled when the onslaught died and not a single corpse lay on the flagstones.

They pressed on, working west towards the Dawnknell street by street. Mages wielded light spells to burn away the darkness, but it held nothing but spare stone blocks, barrels, and other harmless objects.

'Ahead of u—'

The rest of the warning was cut off by a crunching thud of another black arrow. A mage with green magick in his hands collapsed to the dust with his eyes crossed and blood leaking from his nostrils.

Sipid saw the shape lurking on the edge of a barracks, hooded and crouched like a spider over its prey, short bow in hand and drawn all the way back.

Sipid dragged the nearest mage to an alleyway as their foe fired again. She was struck in the shoulder, but she still managed to pour a river of fire across the street before Sipid hurled her into a doorway. A harsh cackle could be heard as the creature escaped yet again, heading deeper into the city.

'You!' Sipid shook the mage. 'You warn the others. I have to chase that thing down, whatever it is!'

Without another word, he raced down the street after the shadow, blade ready and willing.

❦

Peryn was concerned. Bells were pealing in the bay. Now fire blossomed on the western wall, and magick shone in the mist. The finches stowed in Peryn's cloak and skirts twittered as she took a deep breath and doubled her pace, feet striking the flagstones with sharp thuds. The lycans, snowmads, and witches that waited for her on the southern walls would be equally wary. The question remained: *what were they fighting?*

It was High Crone Wyved who found her first. Two witches and a lycan guarded her shuffling form. She made a sign with her long fingers, and Peryn nodded.

'Trouble, and apparently from within. The bells say intruder.'

Another sign.

'We have a whole army and every point on the compass covered, High Crone.'

Wyved shook her head and rubbed her fingers, telling her to listen close, but Peryn was distracted by a blue light beginning to shine in the adjoining street. Peryn's cloak jittered as her birds took flight, and that was never a good sign.

'Down!' Peryn yelled as the pale glow grew blinding. Shards of fierce blue light raced over the flagstones, and two came to pierce the lycan in his chest and neck. With a gargling roar, the beast fell to the ground, pawing at the sizzling magick that had run him through.

Peryn drew back her cloak, snatched a vial from her belt, and threw it at the light. To a crash of glass, green smoke whirled, and something within it spat curses in a tongue she had never heard.

A spinning wheel of light emerged, studded with strange runes. Lightning skipped across the cobbles, striking one witch who whispered a shield spell that came too late.

Peryn panicked. She wasn't proud, but she didn't freeze as others might have. Instead, she dragged Wyved behind a stone trough and escaped another blast of magick. It smelled strange. Ancient.

A knife filled her palm as Peryn crouched before the High Crone. The other witch took cover with them, readying a hooked blade and a vial of something foul. Their breaths were all that stirred the silence of an alleyway that had grown dark once more. The mist swirled around the corpse of their sister and brother lycan, and Peryn gritted her teeth. Wyved's fingers twitched, but once more, death struck before she could speak.

A spider-like hand of sharp claws descended, seizing the other witch by her jaw and chin and pulling her up wriggling. In the shadows, Peryn could see their foe was tall and spindly, sharp in all its angles even beneath a cloak. White eyes glinted from the gloom of a hood and mask.

Blood came pouring as the creature held the witch higher, and claws sank deeper to silence the screaming. Yet she was a fighter, a witch born of the brutal north, and she did not go quietly.

Wild-eyed, the witch's hooked blade caught her killer in the ribs, eliciting a sharp sound like two flints striking. Down came the vial, to smash at the creature's feet, and the red smoke and cinders that exploded with it choked them both.

Peryn staggered backwards to escape the writhing creature, Wyved's arm clamped in her hand. The High Crone was reaching, summoning her birds to circle around them. Dozens became scores, scores became hundreds, and Peryn felt her own birds join the hurricane of feathers and roaring wings.

Wyved clutched her shoulder with sharp nails. Peryn could already feel the magick that danced within her. In the darkness of her spell, Wyved pointed north.

'I'm not leaving you to this beast!' Peryn hissed.

Piercing light shone behind the wall of birds. A wash of Wyved's hand sent claws and beaks swarming towards the creature while it reeled from the red poison. They tore at the hood and the grey, bare flesh of its hands and pecked at its eyes, eliciting a sharp shriek.

Wyved's other hand flashed before Peryn's eyes, sketching a word she had only heard in stories told on colder nights, huddled around fires. It had filled Peryn with dread every time, and it did not fail her now.

'You can't be serious,' she yelled.

Wyved clicked her fingers.

'I don't doubt you, but how can that be?'

A burst of fire caused Wyved and Peryn to wince. Ashes and burned feathers tumbled to the dust, and Wyved screamed silently as she drove the birds at the foul beast once more with both hands. Peryn stalked closer, letting flock wrap around her like a shield and camouflage all in one.

The creature swiped at them with blades of light. Runes spilled through the air wherever they slashed and stabbed. Its magick was growing; she could feel it turning her stomach, and its hand arched to throw whatever spell it concocted. Wyved's birds swarmed with a desperate viciousness, tearing flesh from the creature while Peryn moved as fast as she could, long knife out and thirsty to cut grey flesh.

Peryn lunged from the trough, one arm hooking the creature around the face while her knife hand plunged into its neck. She howled as the spell exploded in its hands, shaking the air and her from the bastard's neck to land in the trough with a splash. Through blinding spots and murky water, Peryn saw black blood seeping down her enemy's front, but she did not see it fall as she'd hoped. Her knife was still in her hand, and she tried to swish it at the creature as it began to flee.

Spitting sand, Peryn struggled upright to notice the birds had fallen back, fluttering to rooftops and gutters and windowsills, deathly silent. Mind in tangles, the young witch whirled to see Wyved's face aglow with a soft blue light. Peryn's gaze fell to where a spear of magick protruded from her chest. Her matted and knotted hair hung over it, sizzling every time it touched.

'Great mother!' Peryn sprinted to the High Crone's side. Wyved did not shake. She did not look in pain, even when the shining shard began to sputter and fade, piece by piece until a gaping hole was left to bleed. There was no potion or charm in all of Emaneska that could save her, and Peryn howled her frustration to the night.

Wyved took a knee, then two. Finches and sparrows flew to land on her shoulders and arms, and others hopped around her head as she lay flat.

'You can't go,' spluttered Peryn.

Wyved offered a faint smile. She didn't need to use her hands for Peryn to know what was on her tongue. With a slow movement, she placed her hand on Peryn's chest, and even as the warmth fled her body, Wyved's hand remained warm. Every bird that perched upon Wyved flitted to Peryn's shoulders as she felt the life go from the High Crone and felt her limp weight seep into the stone.

A clanking of metal grew loud as soldiers and mages came running. At their head were her sister witches, faces gaunt and eyes already glistening as they saw their eldest lying dead in the road. Shrieks filled the mist, and Peryn sang her pain with them.

'What in Hel was that thing?' barked a mage.

Peryn stood, stomping slow and heavy to where the creature's blood smeared the flagstones between the singed feathers and scraps of black cloth.

'That,' Peryn breathed, 'was a dark elf.'

CHAPTER 24
OCEAN'S WRATH

Has anyone ever seen another fair coast beyond that of Paraia's?
Has anyone dared to go beyond the sunset horizon of Saciath or the
Cape of Glass? Why will no captain dare to push westward and hold,
and test the edges of the ocean cold?
FROM 'FARTHEST REACHES', A BALLAD WRITTEN BY AN UNKNOWN
MIDGRIR SKALD IN YEAR 799

A blue circle of runes met Gunnir's raw power, and though Azen was pushed back, his shield held irritatingly firm. It was older magick, and Mithrid could feel its difference like a bucket of cold water thrown in a hot bath.

Daggers of light burst from the elf's hands, and Farden threw up a shield of his own. One embedded itself in the crystalline spell, cracking it slowly, while another glanced off the Scalussen metal covering his leg. At the same moment, the elves charged inwards, zigzagging as they ran, black steel slashing in blurs. Magick filled the air as the mages drove at them with spell after spell. Ilios escaped their lances to hurl rocks and pick off any unfortunate stragglers. Warbringer broke their lines with wild swings of Voidaran.

Mithrid pushed against them with her shadow, tripping them and swinging their swords at their comrades with her power. It drained her to be so precise and to battle their strange wiry strength, but she had no choice.

Mithrid saw Farden clenching with one hand and felt a painful wave of magick wash over her. As she took cover, pillars of fire ripped through the elvish ranks, sending their insectile bodies scattering. In the same spell, Farden closed the flames around Azen, whose magick of shining blue runes shuddered as he tried to drive the magick back. Fire swirled around him like the bars of a cage, and yet he refused to die. With a blast of light, Azen was thrown backwards against a broken wall, yet the way he landed crouched on his feet like an overgrown spider proved he was far from beaten.

'Farden!' Warbringer yelled.

Hot blood splashed Mithrid's cheek as her line of mages was overpowered. Elves swarmed, slicing and cutting as they went. The formation raced to rebuild itself as Warbringer carved piece after piece from the scuttling masses. It still wasn't enough; their soldiers and mages were dwindling, and the sheer number of elves that crawled over the stone squeezed them tighter and tighter. The elves were too fast, too strong, too practised, too vicious—

'Agh!' Mithrid felt an iron hand seize her leg and drag her to a knee. Her axe sliced it at the wrist, and its owner recoiled shrieking. She battled back to Farden's side, where the mage roared with effort as he swept Gunnir's lightning and fire spells through the turncoat daemons and encroaching elves. Others in their pale ranks had magick in them, and Gunnir's power glanced away from their shields to slice crenellations from walls.

And amongst it all, stood Loki. Mithrid saw him watching with wide eyes, longing for Farden's downfall. Shadow wrapped around her arms as she tried to reach him.

But Azen came to try again, gleaming blue fire in each clawed hand. Farden swiped with a force spell, sent him spinning, and summoned a quake spell to trap his legs with rocks. Azen shoved them aside with vicious blasts of pure magick. Silently fuming, he charged again.

It was Mithrid that met him this time. Before Farden could wield his magick, she drove her shadow at the elf, who tried to swipe it away with a cry of frustration and no success. The fierce angles of his face told her he was far from pleased and more than a little shocked, and Mithrid cackled right there and then as he was forced to one knee.

'Take that, elf! You made a mistake coming back to our world.'

Azen whistled sharply in answer, and a rumbling turned their heads to the east, where bricks and rubble flew high as something very fast and very large raced through the streets.

'Spoke too soon!' bellowed Farden as a monster of spines and sharp legs burst through the plaza walls with a bubbling scream. Gore smeared its jaws and its countless eyes, and once it saw its master in peril, it charged for Mithrid.

Mithrid had no words, no thoughts. Her shadow faded as she was gripped by pure panic. Farden stepped in front of her, his armour full of fire and spear in hand. With a war-cry, he unleashed Gunnir's magick straight at the beast. Yet this was no troll of Tolema, who had fallen to pieces at Gunnir's mere touch. This gargantuan monster's skin might have smoked or steamed, and it might have screeched with a sound that almost deafened them, but it barely slowed. The hideous creature kept coming, step by crushing step.

Farden drew a storm of fire above his head, swinging whips of flame. White light raced and raged across his armour. Mithrid was pushed to the ground under the force, yelling at the pain in her head. She tried to shield herself as sparks began to fly. Farden's feet began to lift off the ground as the winds surged. Fiery memories of Scalussen filled Mithrid's mind as all she could do was watch. The remaining mages held up their shields with grim faces and weathered the hurricane of fire that Farden had become.

Mithrid gawped at the beast looming above them now, barely kept at bay by Farden's rage. Azen's mouth moved with words unheard over the maelstrom. Loki still watched, face glowing in the fire of Farden's storm. Gunnir had built to a fever pitch and was straining to unleash whatever magick it was brewing. For a moment, victory began to shine.

But time wore thin. Before the magick could burst from him, the monster swiped a vicious claw at the mage and batted him like a crossbow bolt into a pile of rubble. Fire and lightning crackled in his wake as Scalussen armour screeched against stone.

Mithrid shot to her feet, dropped her axe, and bent all her will behind her shadow. It was her turn, and as the monster sought to stab at Warbringer with another claw, and Ilios tried to find a place to attack between its spines, she spread her dark power across the plaza. Half went to keeping the elves at bay, and the rest seized the monster's many limbs. She pushed and pushed, harder than she had in Krauslung, and she didn't stop until her breath ran short, and she shook with the strain.

Elves withdrew hissing. Daemons recoiled. And as for the monster, it bubbled and it spat and it lashed out at her wall of shadow. Yet its appetite for Mithrid proved strong. It reached for her still, claws digging in the stone, closer and closer.

Mithrid found herself stuck between saving the others and saving herself. Farden had not yet emerged from the rubble, and the elves strained to cut down what was left of the Scalussen warriors. If she withdrew the shadow to fight the beast, they would all die.

Hot, foul air enveloped her as the monster roared again. Spittle flecked her face, and Mithrid raised her voice to roar back at its snapping, straining jaws.

Before Mithrid could make her dreadful choice, a horn blew across the city. It stilled them all, and not moments after, a flash of scarlet punctured the smoke. Whatever it was, it hammered a fierce blow into the monster's side and sent it rolling across the plaza. There it skulked and screeched, waiting, though nobody knew for what. An eerie lull consumed the battlefield.

A deep howl sounded as a daemon was snatched into the murk of smoke. Another followed moments later. The elves were not immune, and with great whooshing sounds, several were dragged shrieking into the nothing. Black blood rained on the edges of the plaza, and Ilios wisely took to the sky and disappeared into the smoke.

Mithrid saw Loki turn north, where the roads and canals of Troacles all wound up: the docks. The god's head tilted higher and higher, until he spat a curse and vanished out of sight, and it made Mithrid's heart thunder.

'What is happening?' she yelled, unable to look away.

A name cut the stillness, bellowed in an unmistakable Albion accent. 'Gremorin!'

The daemon prince stood frozen in the middle of the destruction, his blade pointed at the smoke and at the shadow that emerged. A figure with grey hair streaming and the glimmer of Scalussen metal beneath her coat, walking slowly through the debris.

'What in Hel?' Mithrid breathed.

It was Elessi, and she pointed her own blade back at the daemon. 'I've waited a long time to see you again.'

'What are you doing, Elessi?' Mithrid yelled, but she went ignored.

Gremorin spat flame. 'I do not remember you, old worm.'

Elessi smiled. 'Then let me refresh your memory, Prince. You killed my husband in the battle of Scalussen.'

'I killed many husbands. Many wives. Many children. Many worms,' the daemon seethed, fire spreading across his shoulders. 'Who are you?'

'His name was Modren. And me? I'm your doom.'

Elessi did not wait for a retort, a question, or even a whimper. She waved a hand to something unseen and before a single stone could tumble, a gigantic crimson tentacle shot from the smoke and seized the daemon's legs in its grip. Fire sizzled against dripping red flesh. Teeth as long as swords dug into the prince's flesh, and Mithrid could hear his iron skin breaking piece by piece by the sharp cracks that echoed across the plaza.

Gremorin roared before a second tentacle wound around his top half, smothering the daemon's mouth. With a vicious twist, the daemon was silenced for good. The tentacles unfurled to drop the broken pieces of the prince and let them crash to the rubble.

Before Mithrid could take a breath, a third tentacle slammed down on the other side of the plaza, sending a dozen elves flying and squishing at least a dozen more. Above the smoke, black against the fire-filled sky, she glimpsed a ship of ancient and sea-claimed wood. Loud explosions came from its portholes alongside the arrows it spewed, and Mithrid saw stones hurtling through the air to punch holes in daemons.

Mind racing with a deluge of questions, Mithrid simply cheered at the top of her lungs. 'It's the keraken! Elessi did it!' she yelled as pandemonium broke out.

'Fight, girl! Celebrate later!' Warbringer yelled as she crushed an elf's face with her hammer.

The bastards were relentless even as chaos rained down on them. Mithrid took up her axe and started hacking at any grey flesh that still moved. A sword rang her helmet, and she whirled to find elvish claws grabbing at her again, raking her armour.

'Back!' Mithrid shouted, wrapping herself in shadow. Three elves snatched at her despite it, trying to snare her with a rope and drag her away from the lashing fury of the enormous creature invading the city. She strangled the first two, but a blow to her head broke her concentration. 'Get off me!'

Shadow poured from her, driving them back for a moment before an arrow jolted her head sideways.

'Warbringer!' Mithrid yelled as she was dragged her to her knees, and her axe was ripped away. Shadow punched and hammered at her attackers, knocking some down and senseless, but the inability to see whom she wanted to strangle made her rally temporary.

Dozens of sharp fingers tugged at the helmet around her neck, prising it away so something metallic could clang against the back of her skull. As the world swam, white eyes stared down as black tongues poked from hissing mouths, and Mithrid felt stone sliding and scraping beneath her.

'Warbringer! Farden!' Mithrid yelled again, weaker than before. Still she fought, scraping and biting and getting clouted in the face for her troubles. Ringing replaced the roar of chaos. Her cheek and jaw had gone numb. Another punch drew blood from her lip. She could taste it. Another sent her head lolling to face the sky.

An elf appeared above her. No, not an elf. A god. Mithrid swung her fists at him, but they slid past him as if he were a mirage. Loki smiled, cupped a hand before her, took a breath, and blew fine powder into her face. Mithrid spluttered dazedly before the night fell like a blanket.

'Mithrid!' Farden yelled, staggering between the chaos, eyes full of dust and his head full of pain. It was probably the impact with the rock, but he swore he could see tentacles filling the sky, smashing elves to paste and crushing the flames of daemons in their spiny grip. A ship somehow floated above the smoke.

The keraken, his mind told him. Blinking, he saw no Azen or Loki, and the hideous monster they'd brought was too busy shrieking at the tentacles.

A sword clanged off his head, making him whirl. Despite the keraken's storm of rage, elves still threw themselves at him, and Farden cut through them as fast as his hands could move. A blast of fire solved the problem, and through those flames, he swore he spied Mithrid: struggling, biting, and clawing to be free of the elves that swarmed her. Warbringer waded through chaos, ducking flying rocks and swipes of the keraken's tentacles, but even she couldn't reach her.

Farden aimed Gunnir and scorched their backs with magick, but before he could close the gap, another wave hurled themselves at him with flailing limbs. Farden found himself enveloped in an elvish whirlwind. He could hear their steel and teeth clanging and squeaking against his armour. They pried and hacked, yet the

Scalussen armour refused to let them in. But when strong claws tried to pry the spear from his grip, Farden let his rage flow.

With a cry of, 'MITHRID!', Farden collapsed the spear into a sword, slicing hands as it shrank, and stood tall as the lightning poured from him. Every ugly figure that laid a hand on him shuddered as the spark spells dug deep, spreading from elf to elf until Farden climbed over a smoking pile of corpses.

Giving chase, Farden crunched through the rubble to run the escaping elves down. He felt Warbringer and a few remaining Scalussen behind him. Fire fled his hands in bright bursts to clear a path and keep the elves at bay. His heart clenched as he saw nothing of Mithrid. There was no sign of a struggle or a fight, not even a thread of shadow, only smoke and rubble.

'Where is Mithrid?!' Warbringer roared, making the elves hiss. 'Return the girl to us!'

Before Farden could summon a spell, a snap and crackle of magick flashed in the gloom, shortly followed by a second. Farden felt the spell in the air. He knew the sound of a god flitting to and fro all too well. He began to shake, sparks flitting from the ground to his hands. 'Loki!' he yelled.

A sharp whistle sounded above the maelstrom, and every elf began to slink away, silent and in jarring movements as if their joints didn't like to bend. Farden chased them, burning hot with fire and drawing shapes with it as he waved the spear back and forth. Ilios circled above, whistling piercingly as he searched the rubble.

The elves kept retreating, whispering here and there, some on all fours and scuttling like insects over the walls. It was impossible to stop them, even though Warbringer tried, dashing after every elf she could see until Voidaran clanged repeatedly on nothing but empty rock.

'Mithrid! Give her back!'

'She's not here,' Farden breathed, ripping his helmet from his head and sinking to a knee. 'Loki's taken her.'

Warbringer smashed a boulder to pebbles with an enormous blow from Voidaran. 'I will rip god's spine from his back!'

A faint cry floated on the wind. 'Farden!'

The mage turned to see a familiar shape striding across the rubble. 'Lerel?'

Farden pushed himself to his feet as she met them. Ilios landed with a crunch and came to press his beak against Lerel's cheek as she approached.

'You're welcome!' she began to say, but Farden seized her by the shoulders, stared into her eyes and seized her in a tight embrace. It took a moment for her to return it.

'I'm glad you're safe,' he whispered.

'You too,' Lerel admitted as she held him tighter.

'Mithrid's gone.'

'What?!' Lerel pushed him away.

'Loki took her. Vanished back to Krauslung most likely.'

Lerel already had tears brimming. 'He can't have! She would have stopped him! How did this hap—'

'We'll get her back,' promised Farden, fixing her with a stare. 'We will.'

Lerel knuckled her eyes. 'I'll hold you to that.'

Farden pointed a finger at the keraken, still mopping up the last of the elves. 'First you have to explain how in the Hel you're here with that *thing*.'

Lerel lifted her chin. 'In a ship with no name.'

'Explain,' grunted Warbringer.

Lerel beckoned them across the rubble and between the smears and piles of carnage. Only a score of mages and soldiers of Scalussen had survived, and they hunched in a huddle, their stares empty and lost.

'What happened here? Why Troacles?' Lerel asked.

'Another trap. The daemons were the bait. Loki knew I would come, and he bet I would wipe out the daemons for him.'

'What do you mean another trap?' Lerel snapped. 'What in Hel happened in Krauslung?'

'Loki saw Mithrid's true power, is what,' Farden said, staring at the dead eyes of Gremorin's corpse. 'I think this was all for Mithrid.'

A shadow above made Farden crane his neck and stop dead with the spear ready. A ship seemed to balance on the clouds of smoke and cinders. A ship so old it was clad in barnacles and coral, and to the sound of scraping so loud it hurt Farden's ears, it came closer.

'What is that?' he gasped.

Lerel smirked. 'The ship with no name.'

As the ship approached, Farden could make out a vast dome of thick shell and two glowing lights that proved themselves to be gigantic yellow eyes. Even Warbringer retreated at the sight of the mouth that loomed. It could have swallowed a fishing boat whole. All the while, the monster's tentacles slid back and forth, still picking at leftovers amongst the carnage.

'By Dotharadine,' the minotaur whispered.

Elessi stood beneath its maw, wearing a smile. A curious fellow in a triangular hat and patchwork uniform stood by her side. 'His name is Keraken, and I think you owe me an apology, Farden,' she said.

'How did you get here so quickly?' the mage asked, ignoring her.

'Keraken knows all the currents,' muttered the hatted man as he scuttled to poke at a dead elf missing a face. Some of Warbringer's handiwork. 'Fascinating.'

Farden clanged his spear. 'What you call fascinating just murdered almost all of my soldiers.'

The man didn't seem at all perturbed. He moved to inspect the spear instead. 'Elves, no? Keraken remembers them.'

'*Elves*?' Elessi spluttered. Lerel visibly swallowed.

'Dark elves,' Farden confirmed with a stony voice. 'Back from the fucking dead.'

'Where in all the bloody Hel did Loki find *elves*?' spluttered Elessi.

'I'm not sure I want to know, but what matters is that Loki doesn't need the daemons any more. He's found himself another army. An army we haven't fought for two thousand years.'

Voidaran thudded on the ground as Warbringer sat on the nearest rock. 'Army that stands against your spear. Wields magick like you do.'

Farden shook his head at that. 'It's not possible.'

'They took Mithrid,' Lerel said, making all trace of victory in Elessi's face fade away.

'What? What happened, Farden?'

But Farden was not listening. Gunnir whispered indistinctly at first, a stream of nonsense Farden couldn't decipher. Holding it an angle, he turned around the plaza until he pointed south, and the words rang true and loud.

Something is wrong.

'What?' Farden whispered, holding the spear firmly. The plaza faded away to show a snowy crag, where a faint figure leaned to look down at a charcoal smudge of a city. 'What's wrong, old friend?'

The ghost of a figure turned, face furrowed and pained. 'Something is very wrong.'

'Is it Scalussen? Is it Loki?'

'I see death in the south,' murmured the ghost as the spell faded.

Farden was dragged back to reality by Lerel prodding at him.

'What's the matter, mage? You're talkin' to yourself!' Elessi demanded, but a dark look from Farden said it all, making her features grow slack. Ilios whistled a question.

'Scalussen's in danger.' Lerel uttered in answer.

Elessi pushed Farden southwards. 'Then you need to go. Now! Stop wastin' time! I'll see to Troacles.'

Farden didn't argue. The wind was already swirling around his feet when he seized Lerel's hand. Warbringer grabbed both her and Ilios' claw.

'Gods!' Lerel yelled before the spell ripped the air in two.

CHAPTER 25
ASHES

Who were the elves, you ask? The sources disagree. Some say they were minor gods taken into the depths of Hel, broken and perverted into the form we once called elf. Others say they were born of the ashes of daemon forges, hence why they had ashen skin and burning eyes. The rarest of scrolls speak of runed and bloodied stones buried in the earth, which burst forth in elven form. In the end, it does not matter where the elves came from, but that they were a curse upon the world, and one of the greatest curses the daemons unleashed.

FROM THE DIARY OF DURNUS GLASSREN

'Fire!'

Hereni's narrowed stare shot to the shining glow of flames by the eastern wall. A dragon's roar now joined the ruckus from the harbour, and bells on the eastern walls began to join the cry of *intruder!* that the ship's bells rang.

This was not, in a simple word, good.

Hereni's mind was torn in two. One half screamed she should turn and fight what was within, while the other bellowed it was a distraction to draw them from the walls.

'Orders, General?'

Hereni heard the words. She simply had no answers for them. All she could think of was Mithrid and whether the same trap was closing its jaws on her.

'General!'

'Give me a dozen mages and twenty soldiers!' Hereni bellowed. 'Spread a battalion out through the streets to look for any unwanted guests. The rest of you keep your eyes peeled in both directions. Be ready for anything!'

To the ringing of a deafening shout, the ranks reordered with sharp yells of sergeants. Torches sputtered into life as the streets teemed with wary soldiers. Hereni marched as fast as her legs would carry her, heading for the Dawnknell on gut instinct alone.

'What madness is this?' Nerilan asked, swaggering about the roof of the unfinished tower and glaring at every part of the city in turn.

'What can you see, Towerdawn?' Eyrum asked, ignoring the huffing of the queen.

The dragon gnashed his teeth in frustration. 'Little, Eyrum. The mist is stubborn and toys with us.'

Eyrum ran to the southern edge of the roof, where bright lights sputtered and flared in the gloom. 'Three intruders at least, and we cannot see shit,' he cursed, before yelling down to the ballistae poking out from every angle of the tower. 'Watch your fire!'

'I smell something…' rumbled Towerdawn, making Eyrum's scales shiver.

Nerilan turned, already knowing Towerdawn's mind. 'Old soil. Dust. Dead leaves. A smell of something ancient.'

'What does that mean?'

'I do not know. Or more accurately, remember, but I feel its danger deep in my soul, where it cannot be forgotten,' the dragon replied, arching his wings. 'Stay low and careful, Nerilan.'

The queen stood by Towerdawn's side, her glaive in both hands and pointing into the night. 'The precious king you gave up your kin for is as overconfident as he is stupid. This trap he has made seems more like it is a trap for us.'

'Farden is my kin, Nerilan. More so than you ever were,' Eyrum replied. 'At least Farden fights instead of hides like a coward.

These people fought for you and would do again. You, Nerilan? You resent even lifting a finger to help them.'

Nerilan glowered over her shoulder. 'I will demand retribution for that insult when this night is over.'

'I'll be waiting.'

More bells began to peal in the south now. *Intruder. Intruder,* said their rhythm.

'That means three attackers at the least,' Eyrum counted. He didn't know why, but he chose to look over the parapet again, staring southwest. A vague shape raced through the mists, zigzagging as it dashed closer and closer to the Dawnknell.

'Southwest! Open fire!'

A hundred flaming arrows descended from the tower, sowing fire across the empty courtyard and streets beyond. Eyrum saw the foe only in glimpses, but it was something cloaked and hooded and fast enough not to catch an arrow. Three of the ballistae caught the same glimpse and tore at the flagstones with their huge bolts, but that was all.

A smash of glass saw a soldier tumble from a low window to the stone below. A sapphire light began to shine between the fire. Eyrum felt the pressure of magick in his skull and the hairs on his arms rise. He was taking a breath to shout a warning when a spell ripped through the base of the tower, making the stone quiver beneath his hands. Blue-tinged fire spouted from every window with a storm of glass and blackened debris. Charred corpses joined the gruesome hail, some no more than skeletons.

'Towerdawn! Nerilan!' Eyrum yelled, but the dragon's claws were already leaving the parapets.

Eyrum stormed to and fro to measure the carnage something was wreaking below. Another splintering of a window sent him running, and he reached the parapet in time to see a mage plummeting into thin air with arms windmilling. Eyrum grasped at him uselessly as he fell to his death. The window was only a few levels below, and Eyrum let the weight of his battleaxe slide through his hands as he spread his feet. With a click of his neck, Eyrum faced the maw of the dark stairs, and there he waited. And not long at all.

White eyes gleamed in the shadow. A blur pounced from the darkness, and Eyrum turned sideways to let the black knife bounce off the broad blade of his axe. Before it could clang against the stone, it snapped back to the shadow, clenched in a pale fist of sharp knuckles.

Even Eyrum had to raise his head slightly as the creature stalked into the light. Only its white eyes showed between hood and mask. A dark cloak and matching armour hid its form. It seemed to jitter in and out of the shadow, but Eyrum had seen enough of them in his time to know an assassin when he saw one.

A hiss came from the creature's hidden mouth, but no words of challenge. That went unspoken and understood. Eyrum didn't care to know what he fought, only that it could be killed.

The assassin darted into the torchlight, but Eyrum slid to the right and used the blunt of his axe to jab at its face. He missed, and the black knives came crashing against the haft and blade. Eyrum twirled and swung, keeping a steady whirlwind of steel about him as his foe ducked and weaved, prying for an opening. When it pounced, so did Eyrum, halting his blade for a moment to snag the assassin and bring the blade perilously close to slicing its arm.

The creature withdrew with a hiss before it threw its blades again, almost catching Eyrum out as they flew back to its pale hands. Warm blood ran down to Eyrum's jaw from the nick in his cheek.

Eyrum roared a battle-cry before he waded in once more, holding the axe above his head and swinging it downwards, back and forth at formidable speed. The assassin was forced to scuttle across the unfinished stonework to escape the onslaught. Black knives came swishing high and low, now forcing Eyrum to retreat to keep up with the assassin's vicious speed. He felt the blade strike his wooden leg, almost swiping it away, and bared a smile at the creature staring back at him.

With a jerk of his head, Eyrum butted the assassin in what he assumed was a nose and sliced one of the knives from its hand. A heavy smack from the axe handle knocked his enemy in the ribs before it managed to strike back, forcing Eyrum to fight for his life as the assassin weaved his remaining knife between his hands, trying to trick his every defence.

A roar of wings interrupted as Towerdawn rose up behind Eyrum, fire crackling in his wide jaws.

'Out of the way!' Nerilan screeched.

Eyrum was trying, but the assassin matched every move he made, keeping the Siren in front of the dragon. Towerdawn quickly gave up and swooped out of view.

The knife darted again, drawing a line across Eyrum's vambrace. Another stab almost took his remaining eye. Eyrum had one trick left, but he kept it waiting. It had been years since he last tried such a thing.

Claws broke stone as Towerdawn appeared behind the assassin, eyes flaming golden and forked tongue beckoning into his mouth.

The creature fell still, gaze darting back and forth between jaws and axe. In the end, it chose Eyrum as the easiest, just as he expected. The scant magick he knew was slippery, but he clung onto it as the creature dove knife-first for his throat as fast as a blink.

But Eyrum moved faster, and the world slowed to a trickle of its normal time as Eyrum stepped to the side, leaving only his axe outstretched.

The black knife met nothing but air, but the axe blade slammed into the assassin's ribs, leaving the creature to stare down in silent confusion and surprise. The moment lasted but a heartbeat before it wrenched the blade from its side and hurled itself for the edge of the roof in retreat. Unfortunately for the creature, the only retreat was into Towerdawn's jaws. The dragon struck like a snake, seizing the assassin in his fangs and biting down. Even in death, not a sound came from the creature. Towerdawn let its foul corpse fall to the ground before he dove back into the maelstrom that had suddenly erupted around the Dawnknell.

Eyrum took a step before leaning against a chair that had somehow survived the fight. He stared down at the hand he pressed to his side and saw the dark blood painting his palm. Eyrum snorted. He'd survived worse, he told himself as he seized a rope dangling from the scaffold and jumped into nothing but rising smoke.

❦

With the sounds of bowstrings and ballistae thudding in her ears, Hereni broke into a sprint with a fireball in one hand and a sword in the other. There was a cobalt light growing in the windows of the Dawnknell, and Hereni swore she could hear screams inside.

She was five steps closer to the tower when its bottom windows and balconies erupted with blue and orange flame. The force knocked her flat with a wheeze.

With mages pulling her upright, Hereni stormed on, only to find a section of doorway blown outwards at the base of the tower. A figure stood in the swirling smoke and dust, too tall to be human, hidden save for two white eyes that were fixated on her, and pointing an ashen finger. The sword pin on her breastplate began to rattle as the creature's finger curled. Strange runes sputtered into being, carved from fine blue light. Hereni tasted magick in the air and took a wide stance with hands flat and blade-like to welcome the creature forwards. Darkness shrouded it like Mithrid's shadow, but it was not her power, and Hereni sent the magick at the base of her skull flooding into her arm.

Fire spilled from her fingers, like flaming snakes writhing to be the first to sink their jaws into the intruder. The blue runes shone fiercely as a circle of them was raised. The shield seemed to absorb her fire before it came screaming back to her. Hereni carved it in half with a vortex spell, arms shuddering from the effort. Shields punched the air as the fire flew against her mages, and before the inferno died, she saw the creature's face in the light of its spells and the black blood staining its slashed neck. *Inhuman, indeed.*

Hereni spun a whip of green light and hurled it at the creature, but it was batted away with little effort. Hereni chose fire again, the same as the mages at her back. Even Towerdawn scorched the wiry thing with his fire as he swooped overhead. Yet again, the creature threw up that shield of runes and held strong against the fire until their light became blinding.

'Take cover! Shield spells!' Hereni shouted frantically as she sharpened her shield to a point.

With a crack of thunder, the wall of flame came surging backwards once more, and several of the fresher mages fell under its force, screaming as it scorched them and their neighbours. Hereni tried another wall of sheer force, but all that did was stall the creature. Hereni closed the gap, hoping to use the blade, but the bastard was fast, spinning runes into spears of white light that shot across the courtyard, impaling soldiers and mages alike. The next volley came too quickly. Some even punched straight through shields, both runed metal and magick. Hereni felt the heat of one clip her ear before she sent a dozen bolts of force to hammer against the creature. Once more, such strength only halted it momentarily before white lightning scorched the flagstones and reaped more screams from the enclosing ranks.

It was then that a roaring lump fell from the tower on a rope, wielding an axe in one windmilling hand. Even the intruder didn't expect such a surprise, and the axe caught it across the wrist, slicing its hand. The shriek it made was haunting, but its runes kept spinning and sparks kept flowing without hardly missing a beat.

'What is this thing?!' Hereni yelled to the Siren.

'Killable, is the most important answer!' Eyrum managed to shout before a bolt of lightning slammed against his armour and tossed him like a pebble across a pond. He landed on the stone with an enormous crash, limp as a sack.

Hereni bellowed with frustration and threw a last stream of fire at the creature. Their spells met in the middle, crackling fiercely as they duelled against each other. Stones split beneath the magick as the creature pushed Hereni to one knee. The blinding lightning jumped closer, crashing against her flames like a dozen blacksmiths' hammers. Hereni cried out as she was forced onto her back, hands splayed and shaking.

A roar could be heard over the clashing of the spells. Hereni felt a thudding in her soles, and it wasn't the rumble of the magick. Within a heartbeat, the spell that was about to consume her collapsed, and her flame shot into the Dawnknell with a landslide of stone.

Warbringer's second, Thenerean was a blur of muscle and mass, horns lowered and war-cry tearing from his throat. He collided with the creature at full speed, managing to spear the bastard in its shoulder before driving it to the tower wall. Hereni could hear the wind being driven from the intruder, and after Thenerean dragged it from the dent in the wall and his horn, he threw the creature to the flagstones. The bloodmonger wasted no time in crouching over it and raising its fists to smear its head across the ground, but something stopped him. Hereni started to run, and as she caught up with the minotaur, she saw the needle-thin blade held clamped in two hands. Its point pierced Thenerean's chest, right where his heart lay beneath his leather armour. His own weight had sealed his doom, and the creature, mask ripped away, sneered with grey fangs.

Hereni raised her sword, but after spitting blood and giving one final roar, the bloodmonger let his fists go to work, pounding the creature in the face until its nose was pummelled flat and its white eyes leaked blood. Thenerean didn't stop until only bone fragments and a mess of black blood covered the flagstones. Until the blade was buried up to the hilt, and the minotaur collapsed atop his foe.

'Hereni!' came an urgent cry, and the mage spied Peryn and Sipid sprinting. At least Peryn was sprinting. Sipid was staggering, but what was more concerning was that they pointed above and behind her, shouting at the top of their lungs.

Hereni saw the murky shape sticking out from the nearby rooftop, bow drawn and arching back. She saw what it was and what it meant. Hereni saw Eyrum struggling to get up, crawling for her, blood streaming from his ears and down his side. She saw her own fingers shake as a shield spell sputtered to life in her fingers, too slow.

What Hereni didn't see was the piebald lycan sprinting towards her, face contorted in a smile. If Hereni had noticed him, she might have thought him feral in her darkest suspicion, but Roglurg was anything but.

The snap of the bowstring sounded at the moment Roglurg leapt in front of Hereni. She heard the thud as the arrow struck, and though she jolted, no pain came. Only the crash of Roglurg landing on the stones, paws around an arrow in his ribs.

Towerdawn and Nerilan chased the creature from the rooftop with fire and snapping jaws, but it was slippery, sliding down the building to rush at them, bow discarded and a sword now in its hand. Hereni threw out the shield spell as she crawled to Roglurg.

'No, no!'

A cry came from Sipid, and a sword came flying past her shoulder, knocking the creature off course long enough for Hereni to raise a hand and summon fire.

With a screech, the creature pounced with its sword aimed down to stab, but a blinding bolt of lightning cast the bastard to the ground close to Hereni, spattering her with cold blood.

The creature was upright and out of reach before she could throw blade or magick, and she stared at the figures looming where it had crouched moments ago. One stood in shining armour, almost liquid in the firelight, and held a brilliant spear in his hand. The other dwarfed him, bulging with muscle, with horns black as pitch upon her head. Another stood with blade ready and hair flowing as a gryphon soared above the rooftop with a screech.

Farden thrust at the sky before he shivered into nothing and appeared in the courtyard, already striding across the stone towards the creature. The intruder threw daggers, but Farden cast them aside. It slashed with its sword, but Farden drew sparks from its blade until he knocked it to the ground. Claws swung and teeth gnashed as the creature skipped away, but Farden had had enough.

With a rising yell, Farden skipped through space, flashing across the stone in a weaving pattern with blasts of magick, until he was standing before the creature. Gunnir thrust up through its heart and raised the foul beast off the stone. Skin and cloth turned to stone around the blade, spreading outwards until the creature fell still with a grating and rasping. Farden let the grotesque statue fall from his spear and break upon the ground. Only then did he turn around and cast a wide eye over the destruction.

'Are there any more?!' he bellowed.

Shouts came from Peryn and Eyrum, but Hereni heard no words. She was still at Roglurg's side. The lycan was blinking, but his breathing came heavy. Even through his matted hair, she could see dark threads spreading across his chest.

'The arrow was poisoned!' Hereni gasped.

'Peryn!' yelled Farden, scraping to a halt at the lycan's side. 'Elessi! Lerel! Get me healers!'

The witch came running, leaving Sipid to freeze in the middle of the courtyard, whispering the word *poison* to himself.

Peryn sniffed and prodded, finding nothing but blood on the arrow. 'It's deep. Too deep,' she muttered as she dragged vials from her pockets.

'He's fading, Peryn!' hissed Hereni.

'I–I don't know what the poison is! This is dark elf magick!'

'What are you talking about, dark elves?' Hereni snapped.

Farden's voice was disturbingly cold. 'She's telling the truth.'

Peryn forced the lycan to drink something of a hideous colour and no doubt taste. The lycan choked it down, but only blood came back up.

'Cling on, Roglurg. You're not done yet,' Farden urged in his ear.

An inhuman roar came as Warbringer charged across the scorch marks and rubble towards the corpse of Thenerean. She collapsed at his side, shaking him viciously. Other minotaurs had gathered, horns bowed and knuckles popping.

'Sipid!' came a cry from Eyrum, who was now staggering across the courtyard, using his battleaxe as a crutch. Lerel beat him to it, but not before the Jar Khoum general pitched onto his face with a thud. Hereni and Farden ran to him, turning him over to find blood lining his cheek and neck. A foul wound scored his cheek, and the same dark threads reached across his face. One eye was entirely bloodshot. Farden shook him, but there was not a glimmer of life in him. His skin was already cold.

'He's not breathing!' Hereni cried, blinking through stinging eyes. 'Peryn!'

Hereni turned to find the witch slumped on the stone, all trace of urgency vanished. Three empty vials lay at her side. She was staring at Sipid, mouth open and eyes streaming.

'They're both gone,' she breathed.

'No…' Lerel shook her head, staring around as if waiting for the nightmare to vanish.

'What in the fuck happened here, Hereni?' whispered Farden in a voice strangled by emotion, face lit by the fire of the Dawnknell as he looked at the chaos, aghast.

'Do you reckon their knives were poisoned too?' asked Eyrum, as he crashed to the stone again. It was Towerdawn and Nerilan that lifted him. Hereni stared up at Warbringer and looked around.

'Where is Mithrid?'

Nobody answered her.

'Where is Mithrid, Farden?' Hereni's fingers clawed at Farden's armour, forcing him to hold her by the arms.

'She's been taken, Hereni. Loki and his elves took her,' he said, buffeted by the wind of dragons' wings. Towerdawn and

Shivertread landed behind them, staring with heads low at the rubble and death around them.

Farden watched all kinds of horror, fear, and pain cross Hereni's pale face before she managed to speak.

'Then we have to get her back!' she shouted.

'And we will, but it can't be now.'

Hereni pushed herself away. 'You were so quick to jump to Krauslung for revenge, but now it's Mithrid, you want to wait? To leave her in Loki's clutches? You co—'

'Don't you dare,' Farden warned.

'If you won't save her, then I will! Alone, if I have to!' Hereni looked around the circle of dusty, bloody, and red-rimmed eyes. She looked to Warbringer, to Lerel, to Ilios, even to Eyrum being carried away by healers.

'Ilios can take me,' Hereni said, marching towards the beast, but the gryphon backed away, eyes wide and whistle sad. 'One of the dragons, then. Old Dragon, will you help me?'

Towerdawn shook his huge head. 'After Farden's failure, it is not wise.'

'Then I'll just walk there, won't I!' Hereni yelled. Farden could feel the magick emanating from her. Her fingers crackled with sparks.

Farden swallowed the talk of failure and stood in her way.

'Get out of my way, Farden.'

'Towerdawn's right, Hereni. Loki would love it if we came after her tonight with no plan. It is a trap within a trap.'

'But he could be doing anything to her!' Hereni spat, fire bursting in her hands. The others shrank back. Farden stood firm.

'And yet he won't.'

'How can you know? Is that some lie you're telling yourself to alleviate your guilt?'

'Hereni!' yelled Lerel.

Farden didn't move, even when Hereni lifted her hand, spreading fingers to tease out the flame. 'Because Loki needs her, just like we do. And that means he'll keep her in one piece.'

'Get out of my way, Farden.'

Farden burst into flame from head to foot, pushing Hereni's flame back along her arm. The others recoiled from the heat and light. 'Don't test me!' Farden barked. 'Not this night. I'm giving you an order, General Hereni. Back down, or find yourself in a cell.'

Hereni stared into his fiery eyes. 'You wouldn't dare.'

'Keep that spell up, and I'll put you there myself,' Farden said, but he let his fire die. 'There's been enough madness and death tonight, and I won't have any more. Let Scalussen put out the flames first.'

Hereni placed a finger on the wolf at the centre of Farden's breastplate. 'Whatever happens to her is on your head.'

Lerel followed in her stormy wake. 'She's not wrong,' she said before she passed Farden by, hand tracing his arm.

New Scalussen burned its dead by the dawn. Two hundred fallen warriors stretched across the sands of Sanctuary Bay, drenched in the torchlight of the Winter Fortress. Those who grieved them stood in their masses with torches and candles in hands, stealing the stars from the night sky. Before them lay the bodies wrapped in palm cloth and perched on pyres. It was a sight that pierced the heart and twisted. Five in particular drew Farden's eyes.

A bundle of cloth lingered in the mage's bare hands, filled with a collection of the small wooden figures he'd carved barely weeks ago. One for each of those who had died.

Admiral Sturmsson.

The High Crone Wyved.

General Sipid.

Thenerean.

Roglurg.

Though all met the fire to let their ghosts find their way, each facet of Scalussen sent their lost to the other side in their own ways.

The snowmads said their prayers while witches poured sacred dusts over the High Crone and Roglurg, letting the powders mix to spark fire.

The Jar Khoum chanted deep and low to every candle that met their pyres of palm frond. Their child-like queen stood upon a tree trunk, arms raised.

Scalussen gave their dead an old goodbye, setting alight ships that drifted into the bay towards the sea. Admiral Sturmsson was propped at the prow, staring east.

The minotaur clan held their own ceremony at the end of the beach, where they spilled Thenerean's blood upon the Warbringer's hammer and then painted their faces and horns with his ichor. Only once his body burned did they speak, and then in guttural roars. New Scalussen raised their voices with them, some in song, some in wails, and the flames of the dead filled the night.

Though Farden stayed silent, his emotions raged with their voices just as loudly. Behind the visor of his helmet, he did not shed a tear. He had already shed too many, and not another drop would change what happened, and so he did the dead one better.

Farden raised a shaking handful of the carvings to throw them into the fire, but he couldn't bring himself to let them go. Instead, Farden held them tight, unable to take his attention off the wooden pieces. A shiver ran through him as he felt the empty space where his little finger used to be.

'It's all we have besides memory,' Lerel whispered in his ear, and he nodded, finally tearing his eyes away.

Farden watched as the final funeral boats sank with a hiss and a bubble, as the roaring turned to quiet sobs and the whispers of feet on sand. He stayed to let the crowds wash over him, enduring their polite touches and mutters. Whether some blamed him for not being there – for choosing Troacles over Scalussen – Farden did not know nor care.

Another silent and stubborn figure remained on the beach with him. It was Hereni, her eyes red and glistening.

'What are we going to do?' she asked in a low voice.

Farden held up one of the wooden carvings. Sturmsson. 'Pieces,' he breathed, almost to himself, thoughts unspooling.

It was all a grand game to Loki. That was the god's true joke, and Farden knew exactly how to even the odds.

All the carvings met the fire.

CHAPTER 26
DUST

Draped in shadows, the sky turns black,
once bright stars now fall from grace.
Omen stir as the night attacks,
midnight creeps with a hollow face.
Daemons rise where the moonlight wanes,
oracles scream as their visions die.
Oceans tremble with blood in veins,
mountains crumble beneath the sky.
Dreams dissolve in the ember's glow,
oaths break fast in the fading light.
Over the world, the shadows grow,
mocking the dawn that ends the night.
THE 'THREE PROMISES', A POPULAR BALLAD AMONGST SKALDS AND
BARDS

Irien recognised the footsteps making their ponderous way down the steps. She could feel the fraying restraint in them. The anger. The purpose. Irien felt a chill run down her shoulders, making her shackles rattle.

Loki. Loki. Loki, she had whispered into the crow's skull throughout the night, once she had awoken to a cell much dingier than her previous lodging. However, when an explosion had rocked the tower above her, Irien found herself grateful for being relegated to the deeper dungeons. And yet no answer had come from the dead beak.

The footsteps inched closer. Irien shuffled up against the cold wall. Rubble clattered across the narrow doorway to her cell.

A grey and battle-stained Farden soon stood at her bars, splotches of rain on his hood and cloak. The spear was a sword in his blood-drenched gauntlet. He said nothing, and as a dirty cloth rag filled Irien's mouth, neither did she.

Some time passed before Farden moved, and when he did, his hand drifted slowly to his sword. At the same speed, he held it towards Irien, letting it transform back into a spear with a whispering and slithering of metal. Its point reached to her throat, and Irien had to lift her chin to escape its touch. It hummed and whined with power, and she could feel its heat.

Though it took a long time deciding, instead of ending her life, Gunnir's blade slid across Irien's cheek, barely grazing her as it sliced through the rag.

Irien rubbed her jaw and smacked her lips. She stared at the mage through hooded eyes. 'How did you know I would betray you?'

Farden sneered as he pulled a familiar twisted bottle from his cloak. It looked like the bottle of mörd from the tavern in the harbour. 'I didn't, but I had a suspicion Loki had his hooks in you. And so I let you believe you had my ear. Let you believe Warbringer and I were drunk and cursed with loose lips.' Farden took the steel cap from the bottle and turned it around to pour a measure. It never reached his lips, but it did reach Irien's. He splashed her in the face with it. Irien winced, but the taste in her mouth was benign. Nothing but water.

If there was anything Irien hated the most in the world – besides Farden in that moment – it was being tricked.

'Warbringer was drinking stew, not ale or spirit,' Farden said. 'Nothing but a dumb minotaur, right? That's what most think of Warbringer, but this was her idea, and she played her part well. You took the bait and walked right into our trap. You failed, Irien. Maybe you should learn you shouldn't believe every whisper you hear.'

Irien spat water on the floor and ran her sleeve across her face. 'I heard the battle just fine in the night, and I see the pain on your face. Not a complete failure, I think.'

Farden crouched to her level. 'And yet your friends didn't come from the north, where we set you up. Loki ignored the tidbits you relayed, Irien. Hel, he even tried to blow the Dawnknell up with you in it. Your god's abandoned you. You're less than nothing to him now.'

Irien swallowed. 'Then what's to become of me?'

Farden reached for the crow skull around her neck and snapped it from the chain. He held it in his fist, and this time it looked as if he would crush it. 'I have yet to decide. A hanging might be fitting. Tell me what this is, and I'll possibly consider something swifter.'

Irien's mouth was dry. A hanging went against everything she stood and fought for. Perhaps it was time for the Lady of Whispers to try some truth. 'Loki speaks to me through it. You touch the gemstone and talk into it.'

'How very interesting,' Farden said as he got to his feet.

Truth tasted bitter, and Irien grew spiteful. 'Don't you want to know why? Why I chose to work against you?'

Farden shrugged before he turned for the door. 'I already know why, Irien. You fear the power I hold and don't think I'm worthy, but I couldn't care less,' he said, pausing. 'What I want to know is did you know?'

'Know what, King?' she muttered.

'About the elves?'

'I heard tell of them.' Irien squinted. 'Is that what came to Scalussen? Elves?'

Farden's voice was a landslide of rocks. 'Three of them killed almost two hundred of my warriors and a dragon.'

Irien snorted. 'A king doesn't grieve over warriors like you're grieving now, my dear. Who else did they take with them?'

Farden left her in the cell without a slam of bars and locks.

'Three elves against the might of Scalussen? Imagine what a whole army could do,' Irien called after him. 'I wonder who let them out of their cage?'

The footsteps paused for a moment before receding.

❦

'Why you're keeping her alive, I don't know,' Lerel said, leaning against the stone in a faint patch of daylight. The cursed mist had lingered, turning to clouds that brought drizzle and the grumblings of distant thunder.

Farden held Irien's crow skull in his hand, deep in thought. When he was done, he took a shred of curtain from a barred window, wrapped it around the skull, and shoved it into his cloak pocket. 'I needed to know if there was anything I could have done to predict the elves. Anything to make this not a loss.'

Lerel rubbed her eyes as if memories of the beasts still haunted her sight. 'Elves, Farden. Nobody could have predicted that.'

'I don't know what's more surprising, the dark elves returning or you arriving on a keraken.'

'Saved your life, is what we did.' Lerel normally would have smirked at such a thing, but the smoke of the funeral pyres still lingered in the air.

Farden frowned. 'We'll talk about that in the morning.'

'It is the morning. It's almost noon.'

'Any word of Eyrum?'

'He's breathing. Peryn's managed to find something that's keeping him alive.'

'Thank the gods.'

Farden pressed a fist against the wall, heaving out a breath. 'We set a trap and fell straight into Loki's instead. Sturmsson, Roglurg…' Farden trailed off, and Lerel took a moment to wipe a tear.

'*Elves*, Farden.'

Lerel took his hand as he led them upwards to take stock of the tower again. The dead had been cleared away, but the stains of blood and scorch remained.

'Three elves. Puts Troacles in perspective,' muttered Farden.

'How many did you kill?'

'Not enough. Hundreds got away. Thousands, maybe.'

Farden found their chambers, and while Lerel collapsed on the bed, he delved into a small chamber protected by a heavy steel door bristling with locks. Within hid the pieces of his armour he did not use every day, his precious idle carvings, a smattering of old diaries, and of course, the Grimsayer. A treasure trove of sorts.

'I assume I was right about Krauslung and Loki,' Lerel called to him.

'Do you need to be?' he asked.

Lerel offered a wry laugh.

'And just how did you convince that monster to help?' asked Farden.

'We didn't. It decided to, it and its captain. I think Rokhelm has taken a shine to Elessi. You'll see when they arrive. We have quite the story. Saker and Fellgrin are dead, for one thing.'

Farden's head immediately poked from the doorway. The rest of him followed. His eyes were wide. '*What*?'

'They were hiding in none other than Keraken's cave. You should have seen it, Farden. Saker and Fellgrin put up a good fight, but Keraken ripped them apart as easily as you'd step on a roach. Sorry to deprive you of your revenge.'

'You fought them?'

'Don't you give me that look. I'm alive and whole.'

Farden hummed to himself as he disappeared back into the chamber. 'Does the keraken have a weakness?'

Lerel scoffed. 'I don't think so.'

Farden emerged carrying a wide oak and steel box, full of something that clunked, and manhandled its lid open. 'Good.'

'Why is it you seem uncharacteristically calm? I don't mean cold and uncaring, but usually you'd be burning something right now. Or destroying an Arka outpost.'

'Because I have the answer,' said Farden.'

'To what?'

'To Loki and his elves.'

'Is this another ridiculous plan?'

'Of course it is,' he said.

Lerel pinched the bridge of her nose. 'When will this end?'

Farden stopped to turn around. Lerel got to her feet and reached for his bare hands. It had been far too long since she had touched his skin instead of red-gold metal.

'You worry about what Mithrid will turn into, but what about you?' she asked. 'You've told me more than once what you saw in the spider's mirrors and visions,' Lerel said, 'but you've never told me which you believe in: the fate where you and I know peace, a farmhouse, and silence? Or the one where you're lost in the snow, exiled and full of madness?'

'I want to believe in the first one, but I worry the closer Mithrid gets to her dark fate, the closer I get to mine. That's why I hope I'm right,' Farden said, scowling momentarily. 'You know I will always fight for that brighter future, Lerel. Mithrid or not. Loki or not. I've been fighting against the Written's curse since the Scribe first inked me, but I don't fight for myself any more. That future is both of ours.'

Lerel patted his breastplate as if congratulating him for saying the right thing for once. After all these years, after all he had seen and learned, he was still hopeless at love. 'And in this bright future, are you still wearing this armour? And when I grow old and you don't?' she asked, eyes sparkling.

Farden took her face in his hand and kissed her, but within, his gut dropped. If he had learned anything, it was the mortality that constantly awaited him. He tried to shrug it away. 'If there was any reason I could accept for taking it off, that would be it.'

'I'll hold you to that,' Lerel said, wiping a fleck of blood from his stubbled jaw. 'You always forget your uncle didn't truly succumb to the madness. That was all Vice's doing. If he went so mad, how was it an exiled Written mage sat on the throne of the Arka for more than a decade?'

Lerel cast a shadow over the Grimsayer, sat on a stone lectern. She opened its heavy binding and turned to one of its aged, empty pages. 'Tyrfing,' she whispered, before the book's pages began to fly towards the end of the great tome. Amber sparks arose to weave their portrait of the old mage. Farden understood. If Durnus had been a father to him, Tyrfing had been the same to Lerel.

The golden figure of Tyrfing stood guard on the page, shimmering slightly with armour on and a sword in his hand, head roving over the unseen masses of Hel. His form shivered and flickered, never staying whole for long. Farden had told her it meant he still drew breath, if there was such a thing as air in Hel.

A distant bell chimed once, letting the city know black sails had been sighted. It still made Lerel flinch and her heart race. Such was the knife-edge Scalussen teetered on.

'Grimsayer,' Farden whispered, deep in thought and making the book shudder as he slammed it shut. 'We'll need this as well.'

'For… for the council?' Lerel asked Farden heaved the giant tome from its lectern and wedged it into the box.

'One last thing.'

'What?'

'Evernia!' Farden yelled at the top of his lungs. 'I know Heimdall can hear me.'

In the corner of their chambers, a shape moved. The familiar lithe form of the goddess of magick came forth, and Lerel bowed her head in panic. She didn't think she would ever get used to such a presence.

'I am not at your beck and call, Farden,' Evernia whispered, as if her voice came from another room.

'Did you know of the elves?' Farden asked.

Evernia's voice was low and careful. 'We did not. Dark magick hides both them and Loki. And for that, I have come to offer my condolences.'

Farden grumbled. 'As much as I long to wallow in pity and grief, I have an invitation for you.'

Evernia looked to Lerel, who barely held her gaze. 'To where?'

'To council. You want to be a part of this world? You will be.'

Evernia tilted her head as she faded to ashes. Farden cursed beneath his breath before he closed the box with a metallic thud, sealed his treasure trove with clangs of steel and the whispering of magick, and made for the door.

'You know, I think I'd rather you burn something to dust,' Lerel sighed as she followed. 'At least I'd understand that.'

'Oh, I will. But first, you're going to tell me everything about that keraken.'

The council awaited them. Two thirds of the council awaited, more accurately. The empty chairs draped in cloth bearing sword pins were enough to stutter Lerel's heart.

No Dawnknell for the council today. Instead, Farden had summoned them to the water's edge, past the harbour where the ships moored far out into the bay. Every flag that bore the scales of Evernia and Scalussen sat at half-mast. A lone tower sat watch over the sands.

Not a single soldier accompanied the council. Only the remainder of New Scalussen and Sutherheim stood or sat upon the chairs that had been brought. A low wooden table sat at the centre of their grim circle, and the tower's awning made the day darker than it was.

Lerel counted. Peryn sat with head low and two finches pecking in her hands. Fresh paint decorated her face and bald head, and Lerel knew enough of witches to know she had been made High Crone. The rest of the north had fallen behind her. The blonde child queen of the Jar Khoum had come in place of Sipid, and a long-snouted hound sat at her side. Her name was Kayruka, and she wore such an impassive face it was hard to tell if she grieved or not. Nerilan and Towerdawn both stood defiantly in the drizzle while Ilios stood protectively over Hereni, who slumped in her chair, hand covering her face. Warbringer leaned against the tower in the shadows, hammer in the sand. And most pleasing of all was Eyrum, hunched in a chair, swaddled in bandages and looking like death, but alive most of all.

Ten in all, counting her and Farden. Only Elessi, Ko-Tergo, and of course Mithrid were absent of the survivors.

Farden slammed his box upon the table and brought out the giant tome of the dead.

'Admiral Sturmsson,' Farden began, making the Grimsayer tremble as its pages sought the right soul. A lone figure appeared, drawn in threads of orange light, standing tall and arms crossed.

'High Crone Wyved,' Farden said again, and the page flipped twice. On, he went, listing the dead to let the council watch them ebb and flow like the waves at Farden's back. *General Sipid. Thenerean. Roglurg.*

Farden took a moment before he delved back into the box and brought out a slab of wood carved in two interwoven spirals, like a pair of snakes knotted together. He thumped that on the table while he produced a small cylindrical object, like a candle made of wood, carved with a familiar face. Farden placed it on one side of the slab, at one spiral's tail. No sooner did it stand upright than did he knock it over and begin counting the dead that brought them satisfaction instead of pain.

'Malvus is dead.'

Another carving was toppled, this one bearing a grotesque face that leered at the council.

'Prince Gremorin is dead.'

Another two pieces appeared, one carved like a dragon and the other a snarling, needle-teethed foe they all recognised. They too were tapped on the wooden board and knocked on their sides.

'Lord Saker and Fellgrin are now dead.'

Towerdawn and Nerilan exchanged a look, but no questions were uttered.

A fifth piece came from the box, carved meticulously to represent a god they all knew and loathed. Farden placed him at the end of one spiral.

'Loki lives.' Farden put an unhewn chunk of pale wood next to him. 'And he has found an army we didn't think possible and didn't expect. Dark elves walk Emaneska again, and the game has changed significantly.'

'I still do not believe it is possible,' growled Towerdawn.

'What do they want?' asked Kayruka in her reed-like voice.

Farden patted the sword at his side. 'My head and this spear.'

'Where did they come from? Who are they?' Eyrum asked in a rasp.

Farden stared at an empty space in the council's circle. 'Evernia?'

The council muttered and recoiled as a faint figure was drawn by the drizzle. The pale willow of the goddess took form before them, with raven hair flowing down to her hips and iron eyes measuring each one of them while her porcelain skin shone with a dim white light.

Kayruka and Peryn bowed low, almost touching the sand. Nerilan took a knee immediately. Towerdawn lowered his head and closed his eyes. Even Hereni stood straighter. Warbringer did nothing.

'Goddess,' Peryn muttered to the whining of Kayruka's hound.

'They were the Dramath-Ai,' spoke Evernia in a voice of rustling leaves. 'Elfkind's finest assassins. It is fortunate you only faced three. Even gods have fallen to their blades in centuries long lost.'

Farden nodded grimly. 'The rest of their kind slaughtered almost every mage and soldier I took north.'

'They are the Clan of Covor. Their leader, Azen Ithar, was once Orion's favourite warrior. Somehow they have found their way back to Emaneska.'

'How many are there?' asked Kayruka.

Farden took more pieces from the box to place on the board, and these remained upright. The others leaned in to find themselves carved in wood, arranged in lines as if Farden drew ranks for battle. 'Thousands, maybe. And every one of them is worth a dozen of us. And that doesn't account for their monster,' he said, as he placed a large chunk of wood on Loki's side of the spirals, which was now heavily weighted in the god's favour. Only one piece stayed apart, and it looked like Mithrid to Lerel.

Peryn leaned forwards in her chair. 'Monster?'

'Ekidna the Hundred-Eyed,' answered Evernia. 'A creature of the cold void summoned by magick thousands of years ago.'

Warbringer clicked her knuckles. 'It almost killed us. Stood against the spear.'

Eyes grew wide around the circle.

'Had it not been for Elessi and Lerel, it would have,' said Farden, 'and that is why I've gathered you here.'

The council waited as he spread his hands across the table.

'There is a game played by the Huskar tribes called mehen. I played it once long ago before I was a Written. Two snakes. Two enemies. The first to reach the centre wins.' Farden placed his hands on Loki's carving, and Lerel saw the mage's knuckles turn white as he moved it along the spiral space by space with a thud.

'At the moment, Loki is winning.' *Clunk.* 'He has the elves.' *Clunk.* 'He has a monster.' *Clunk.* Mithrid's piece moved to Loki's side. 'He has taken Mithrid.'

Farden waited for that to sink in. 'The trick to mehen is not in speed and luck, but strength. Other pieces can be summoned. Larger, stronger pieces. The Huskar call them saviours. Others they call monsters.'

The mage hauled a chunk of log from the box and dropped it on the Scalussen spiral.

'What is that?' Nerilan asked, wiggling a sharp fingernail.

'This?' Farden said, as he cast a look to where a ship drifted through the bay, high on its keel and a familiar white-haired yetin staring back at them. The *Undaunted* had returned.

'This is *that.*' Farden waved his hand to the sea. The council waited, watching the ship turn towards them. The rest of the bay was empty, rippled only by wind and rain. The moments of silence inched by like a tired worm.

Warbringer spat something from between her fangs.

'Do you mean the ship?' asked Eyrum, coughing and wincing.

Farden didn't answer, pursing his lips as his hand fell, eyes shifting back and forth. Lerel stood, about to move to his side when an unnatural wave began to race along the bay in their direction. She knew what was coming, but it didn't stop a nervous breath from catching in her throat.

The others were greeted with an enormous explosion of water as four crimson tentacles shot into the sky. Sand flew and the earth shuddered as the tentacles landed on the beach and dug in. The drowned ship with no name broke the waters, then the shell, shedding waterfalls of seawater, rising up and up until Keraken himself showed his petrifying face, golden eyes bulging and maw opening wide. As the monster hauled his weight into the shallows, Lerel swore even Nerilan and Towerdawn took the smallest of steps backwards. Kayruka's hound bolted for the city without a sound.

Farden was the only one who didn't move, standing now with arms crossed before the monster while bells rang across New Scalussen once more in panic. 'I mean Keraken,' the mage said with a grim smile. 'Our very own monster.'

'Elessi was right,' whispered Hereni, eyes wide and hands shaking.

The council stared, faces full of rain as two shapes emerged from the encrusted ship. Elessi and Rokhelm stood aboard the bow of the giant.

Farden filled them in. 'Keraken ripped Prince Gremorin in two. He did the same to Saker and Fellgrin. And my bet is that Keraken isn't the only monster left in Emaneska. Evernia, will you tell the council what tharkun means?'

The goddess obliged even though her alabaster brow furrowed. 'It means Great One. Relics of times before this world was born of ice and fire. Creatures of the void. Monsters born of magick. They are neither god, daemon, nor elf.'

'From what Lerel's told me, we already met one in Albion when Vice raised the hydra. We saw the swords of similar giants in Easterealm. I believe we fought one in the caves of the Diamond Mountains, and the elves brought one against us in Troacles. They are myths in the flesh, and with their help, we're going to crush Loki and Azen.'

'This is utterly preposterous!' Nerilan spluttered. 'I knew that spear would rot your mind, Farden, and I've been proved correct!'

By her side, Towerdawn looked to be wincing. 'What makes you so sure there are more?' he asked.

'Because I'm counting on it.'

'Madness!'

'Silence, Nerilan,' ordered Towerdawn.

Farden turned to the goddess. 'Evernia, what do you know of Great Ones?'

Evernia's form wafted in a breeze as she walked silently across the sand, leaving no footprint though the rain seemed to patter on her head and shoulders. 'There may be more. Some are lost. Some are waiting to be found. And what of the gods, Farden?'

Hereni stood before Farden could answer. 'And Mithrid?'

'We will grab her from Loki's grasp as soon as our spies know where he's keeping her and how. Loki thinks we'll rush right after her, but I won't stand for another trap. Loki wants her for her power. He always has, and he can't use her if she's hurt or worse.'

Hereni simply stared.

'That's some risky logic,' Lerel whispered.

Peryn had a different air about her. She undulated between wary and fidgety to brooding and back again. 'Have we forgotten Loki's the god of lies? What if he manages to get in Mithrid's head?' Peryn swirled a finger. 'Turn her against us?'

Farden curled his lip into a smile. 'If that's what Loki thinks, then I pity him, to be honest. He has no idea how stubborn Mithrid can be.'

'Farden has a point there,' Hereni admitted. 'But I don't like it one bit. If Lerel was—'

'If Lerel was in the same position, then I would trust her just the same, like you told me to,' Farden told her, staring into Lerel's eyes. 'The same goes for all of you.'

Nerilan could always be trusted to have a complaint. And yet, Lerel had to admit that, for once, she almost had a point. 'And you assume we will agree to help you in this madness?' demanded the queen.

'Maybe you will, maybe you won't, but you should have this in any case,' said Lerel, while the *Undaunted*'s wings scraped on the beach. Fleetstar reared her head, flapped her wings, and rose above the deck. Nerilan staggered at what they saw clutched between her claws. Towerdawn surged across the sand to take it in the furnace of his jaws. Fleetstar bowed as he took it, putting her head to the sand.

Lerel spoke the obvious. 'A dragon egg found in Keraken's cave.'

'It is alive,' said Nerilan, eyes half-closed as she and Towerdawn shared minds.

'That makes nine eggs for Sutherheim,' Farden added, taking a moment before they all paid attention. 'I hear your questions, but that's all. I didn't summon you all here to doubt me. This is happening whether you like it or not. If this is how Loki wants to play his game, then we'll match him piece for piece. The end is almost here, I promise you. All I ask is you follow me one last time.'

Farden's fist crashed through Loki's collection of carvings, scattering them on the sand, and then he set the effigies of the council in the centre of the snakelike spirals.

'Aye, King,' whispered Peryn, quiet yet fierce.

Others nodded. Kayruka, for one. Lerel. Warbringer thumped a hoof. Only Nerilan and Hereni stayed silent, unmoving, staring at kerakens and dragon eggs.

Farden watched the council break apart. Peryn and Kayruka drifted to embrace Ko-Tergo and Elessi, and to meet the strange bearded sailor that stood hands clasped and boots deep in the shallows before his monster. Warbringer took Eyrum in her grasp, making the old Siren grumble, and when Towerdawn and Nerilan disappeared quickly with their new egg, Hereni alone stormed back to the city. Only Lerel and Evernia remained with Farden.

The goddess stood close, lizard-like eyes drilling a hole into Farden's. 'You did not answer my question, mage.'

Farden shrugged. 'You help us find Great Ones, and I'll consider using Gunnir to release you all.'

'Consider this instead: bring us all down from the sky, and you will not need the Great Ones' help. The world will not have to see the Ragnarök you seem to be planning.'

Farden leaned even closer to the god, keeping his eyes fixed on hers. 'And what would you do once you were back in Emaneska, I wonder. Where would you go? Who would you rule? See, that's what worries me. I haven't fought for freedom just to hand this world back over to a multitude of subjugators, aching to use the souls you've been storing in your lofty halls. I wonder if that was Loki's plan after all, to break the Bifröst bridge and keep the dead trapped in Hel and Haven. You certainly have profited from it. I wonder why you gave your scales to your sister Hel as soon as the bridge came down.'

Evernia raised a tremoring finger to point between Farden's eyes. 'Loki is not a benevolent god, as we are. He would not sacrifice himself to save you, as we did. What have you done besides cause the deaths of tens of thousands? Hundreds of thousands. The Grimsayer has grown fat since it has been in your possession. You keep feeding Haven and Hel souls, Farden, and it may not be your choice. Our power grows every day with you in power.' The finger landed against his breastplate, making the metal chime as if she were solid flesh and bone.

Lerel saw Farden's jaw clench.

'Death suits you, doesn't it, goddess?' asked the mage. 'You know, you keep saying you're not Loki, and yet you almost sound like Loki. And don't throw empty threats at me. You need the magick in this world as well as your souls to fall.'

Evernia had said enough, and her shape unravelled into threads of dust. Farden and Lerel stood alone on the beach.

'Well, that went better than I thought. I guess we'll have to see what our libraries can tell us,' muttered Farden. 'Thoughts?'

Lerel crossed her arms. 'It's funny. You worry about madness, but I think you're already mad, you know that?'

'Think it'll work?' Farden asked.

Lerel tilted her head back and forth. 'It just might. And if it does, it's going to be one epic and bloody final battle.'

'Then we finally agree.'

Warbringer had decided the beast smelled too like rotten fish for her liking. Then again, it could have been because she stood next to some gigantic vent that kept exhaling every other moment. With a wrinkle of her snout, Warbringer decided to move and found the big, armoured squid following her with his eye. She scowled, and a tentacle came to investigate. Warbringer kept walking, but the fleshy thing kept following, and she had to restrain herself from swinging her hammer.

Farden and Lerel had finished speaking to their goddess. Warbringer hadn't trusted a word she had said, and her lack of smell and form was unsettling. She clutched at the runes of her warhammer instead, still smeared with Thenerean's blood. There was only one goddess in her mind.

Elessi came at her with her arms wide and put them around her midriff. Warbringer had to smile and tried not to crush Elessi as she put a hand on her back.

'Glad to see you safe.'

'Nothing kills me,' Warbringer chuckled. 'Elves no different.'

Farden approached, and he seized Elessi tightly until she whacked him on the shoulder. 'Say I was right. I want to hear it,' she demanded.

'It's all right, Elessi, he's already eaten his words,' said Lerel, trying a smile.

Elessi chuckled as she pointed between Farden and the strange new man who smelled like old leather and salt. He had the same eyes as his squid, and they had a faint glow about them. 'Rokhelm, this is —'

'The Forever King.' The squid-man circled Farden, making the mage turn with him. 'I've heard your name echo even in the deep. May I?'

'May you—?'

Rokhelm did whatever he wanted anyway, coming to pore over Farden's armour, even going as far as to sniff a vambrace. 'And this,' he said, pointing at the so-called sword at Farden's hip. 'I don't know what this is, but I can feel its power. It has a voice, no?'

Farden ignored the question. 'I have to thank you for keeping those I care about safe and for saving our arses, to put it bluntly.'

'Blunt is good,' said Rokhelm.

'I hope you can help us one more time.'

'Farden. Is now the time for this?' Elessi chided.

Sailors' cries came from the *Undaunted* as the monster poked at the ship with a tentacle. Rokhelm slapped the thing on another fleshy appendage and tutted. 'Be nice now,' he chided, making the beast gurgle. 'And that depends on the kind of help you need, Forever King.'

'I need to find more of you. More Great Ones.'

'To fight your war,' Rokhelm said, preening his braided beard. 'There aren't many of us left. Stayed alive because they stay away from war and such other things of madness.'

Farden's furrowed face immediately brightened. 'Where are they?'

'Keraken might know, but he will need to think upon it. As will I. We don't know you like we do Elessi.'

Farden bowed. 'Take all the time you need. You're welcome to treat this as your home for as long as you want.'

'Warm here,' Rokhelm said before he trotted over to examine Warbringer's hammer. 'Interesting,' was all he had to say to her before he stomped towards the tower. Warbringer growled. She did not like this squid-man.

'He's a little out of practice speakin' to people,' Elessi explained.

'He could be a raving lunatic as long as he will help us,' said Farden, absently patting his sword as he stared up at the big squid. Keraken stared right back, tilting his head so he could bring one of his gigantic eyes closer. Tentacles reached for the mage, slow and steady. Farden kept his hands open and empty as the monster put a tentacle to each of his shoulders.

A whistle came from the squid-man, and Keraken receded back into the shallows, bubbles coming from his jaws.

Farden stepped back, and Warbringer wondered if he breathed a sigh of relief. 'Looks like I'm going to take a leaf out of Durnus' book and stare at a book for once,' he said, looking east to the palm forests.

Elessi, Lerel, and Peryn shared glances. 'We better come with you,' said Lerel, making Farden raise an eyebrow.

'The more the merrier,' Farden replied with a sigh. His gaze turned to the Dawnknell tower, blackened and scorched, before it met the sand.

Warbringer nudged him. 'Mourn no more. Dead will rejoice in Bright Fields when they avenged.'

Farden was not listening.

'Farden?'

The mage whirled, fingers pressed to his chapped lips. His hand flew to a pocket in his cloak, and he brought out a small bundle, in which a bird's skull lay, a gemstone pressed into its head. It looked like a crow's skull to Warbringer.

'Why—'

Farden hushed her and motioned to his ear. All of them huddled around to stare at the skull. It was then the gemstone glowed, and its beak opened to emit a whisper.

'Are you alive, Irien?'

Farden looked up with wide eyes.

CHAPTER 27
BELLY OF THE BEAST

*Toss petals plucked from the Tausenbar's southern slopes. Add essence of
ice wight, and a pinch of ember dust from a dying fire. Stir in a drop of
blood, gathered moonless. Finally, break a feather before adding. Let it
bubble until its dust gleams, and a scent of bitter rosemary rises.*
A WITCH'S RECIPE FOR A BLINDING POWDER

Mithrid could hear the harsh melodies of screaming gulls. There was
salt in her nose and a desperate pounding in her head that throbbed
like a heartbeat in the darkness she swam in. Bones clicked in her
neck as she tried to raise her head, and fire flashed across the dark.
Mithrid jolted, making pain flood her body. She became aware of her
extremities one by one, numb as they were in the frigid wind.
Mithrid tried to open her lips, her eyelids, but they refused to move,
crusted by tears and dry skin.

A shriek of a gull startled some movement into her. Eyelids
came unstuck with a crackle of frozen tears, and what she saw made
her choke on her own breath.

Krauslung was spread below her, covered in sea-fog. The way
the city's torches glowed would have been pretty if Mithrid's view
wasn't from hundreds of feet above it, dangling from a loop of rope
chafing her armpits, and kicking at nothing but empty air. The pain in
her arms where the rope bit became all she could think about.

Mithrid looked around, seeing a wooden beam protruding
from proud marble battlements. A figure lounged against one thrust
of stone, smiling and waving.

Loki.

'You fuck!' Mithrid yelled.

'And hello to you, Mithrid Fenn!' he called out. 'Welcome to Krauslung yet again.'

'Let me go!'

'A poor choice of words, don't you think, Mithrid?'

Despite the dizziness, despite the weakness flooding her bones, despite the fear, she summoned her shadow, and it flooded along the beam.

'I wouldn't, if I were you,' Loki said with a wagging finger that turned into a point. Mithrid felt a pain in her neck and the sharp cold of metal piercing her skin. She pushed the shadow further, reaching for Loki, but the pain grew in kind until she cried out. Her dark magick shrank back into her skin as she felt the weight of something heavy around her neck.

'A wise choice! As you can't use your hands and don't have a mirror, allow me to educate you,' crowed Loki. 'What's currently around your throat is a collar ringed with spikes. An old relic of Skölgard, in fact, used to test a sorcerer's stamina. It was originally charmed to contract when it felt a sorcerer's magick waning. I had its spells tweaked and reversed just for you, Mithrid, and now it will contract any time you use your shadow. I would be careful. Those spikes are long enough to poke through the other side of your neck.'

Mithrid had to test it. She wouldn't have trusted herself if she didn't, but even the thinnest thread of shadow elicited a slithering of metal, and she felt the collar shrink to spike her. As much as she hated to give in to the detestable rat grinning at her, Mithrid's shadow died away with a clench of her fingers. One of her arms was beginning to grow numb, and she tried to haul herself further away from the city.

'And if you have any other mischief in mind, then I would turn your attention to the right,' said Loki.

Mithrid swivelled her head, cursing as the spikes prickled her. A trio of Arka soldiers held her rope in their hands, and every one of them wore a murderous expression for her.

Loki chuckled. 'As friendly as they look, every one of my fine guards here has suffered the loss of a brother, a sister, father, mother, or a friend – and in a few cases all of those – to Scalussen blades. They'll drop you in a moment if I give them the word.'

Below, beyond the sheer sides of the Arkathedral and mire of fog, a crowd of curious citizens was gathering in the streets, and if Mithrid's blurred eyes could be trusted, they were pointing and gawking, beckoning her down. Some waited with clubs or hammers in their hands.

'Even if you somehow survive the fall, my people are eager to give their very personal regards to a general of Scalussen. There are plenty of debts waiting to be paid for what you did in the north, Mithrid. They'll rip to you pieces quicker than a loaf fresh out of the oven.'

'That was Farden's doing, not mine.'

'They don't know that, but you and I both know it was a little bit your fault, too, no?' Loki said with another wag of his finger.

'What do you want from me, snake?' asked Mithrid. 'Am I bait? A prize? A treat for your elves?'

Loki tried to look shocked. 'You are nothing but a guest, Mithrid Fenn. A refugee, rescued from the evil clutches of the Forever King and his lies.'

'Fuck you, Loki.'

Loki nodded to the soldiers, and Mithrid dropped a terrifying couple of feet. She yelped in terror while the crowd below cheered. The bastards had begun to chant Loki's name.

The god threw up his hands. 'And here I was thinking we could have a calm and civilised conversation. Perhaps you need to spend a few days in the dark.'

'Do what you must,' Mithrid snarled. 'Whatever you have in that cesspit of a mind, it's not going to happen.'

Loki chortled. 'We'll see.'

Much to the moaning of the crowds below, the beam was swivelled inwards and her ropes pulled in. The disappointment of the soldiers was evident in the sullen way they worked. Every jolt made her grit her jaw and strangle the rope, and Mithrid bared her teeth at each of them as she was hauled onto the marble.

'Introduce her to her new chambers,' Loki ordered with a wave of his hand.

The others that swarmed from the stairwell were Scarred mages, freshly carved and eager to do their god's bidding. With rough hands, they dragged her upright and used the rope to bind her hands and legs. Mithrid was carried sideways like a log, and she squirmed and shouted every inch of the way.

Corridors passed by, fading from those she recognised to deeper hallways where far light didn't reach. Here was where the Arka had made their dungeons, and Mithrid was thrown into a black hole of a doorway. She crashed to the floor hard, knocking her face against the stone and gasping as the wind was driven from her lungs.

Something stank, like fire in her nose. Mithrid crawled to face the light of the doorway and saw Loki standing there, grimacing mages at his back. 'Enjoy your stay,' he whispered before the door slammed shut, and magick shone across its surface.

Mithrid was plunged into the darkness, not knowing whether it was a box or a cave she had been shoved into. Hands outstretched, she began to feel her way across the floor to a wall, smooth and cold and pitted with strange gouges. Mithrid didn't want to think about what carved them.

It was then she heard the scuff of feet, somewhere in the darkness.

Mithrid was not alone.

She held her fists up, and she didn't know the shadow leaked from her until the collar bit. The wall against her back gave her little comfort.

'Who's there?' Mithrid demanded, and the pitiful echo told her it wasn't a cave she was stuck in. That was good; she had almost succumbed to a spider's dreams in the last cave she'd visited.

Another scuff and silence.

'I'm not afraid to fight you,' Mithrid said, lying just a little, or so she hoped.

Something sniffed.

The thick dark tricked her mind, drawing shapes in the pitch black, and Mithrid lashed out at imaginary foes left and right.

'Come to kill me?' asked a voice. A woman. Tired or an old'un, Mithrid couldn't tell. She pressed herself to the wall and thanked Hurricane it sounded human.

'I don't even know who or what you are.'

'What I am is curious. 'Aven't had a visitor since Malvus threw me in 'ere.'

'I'm no visitor. I'm Loki's prisoner.'

'Loki,' the voice hummed. Footsteps came closer, and Mithrid recoiled.

'You have a name?'

It took a while for the woman to speak again, and Mithrid swore her heartbeat filled the cell.

'Calm, girl. I ain't going to hurt you,' she said. 'My name's Jeasin. And yours?'

'Mithrid.'

'I hear a little western Emaneska in your accent.'

'I'm from Troughwake.'

'Albion.'

'Is there a candle or something in here?'

There came a chuckle. 'I wouldn't care for it, but there are a few.'

Mithrid waited, frozen and wary, while she traced the footsteps across the cell. Something wooden rustled until a spark sketched the shape of the cell and a hunched woman in her eyes. Another three sparks, and tinder caught long enough to light a wick. The light bloomed slowly, until finally Mithrid could see her cellmate.

A gaunt face greeted her, half-hidden by tangled golden and silver hair reaching almost to her waist. Mithrid could tell the dress she wore had once been elegant and fine, but now it was smeared in muck. All but one of its jewels had fallen off, with the rest glittering around the edges of the cell. The gouges in the walls were tally marks scratched into the stone, and there must have been hundreds.

'Is he dead?' Jeasin asked.

'Who?'

'Malvus.'

'As a doornail. I was the one who killed him.'

Emotions flickered across Jeasin's face, but Mithrid couldn't discern what kind.

'Good riddance,' she said at last, moving to put the candle in the centre of the cell. Though she seemed to stare right at Mithrid, she felt the stone when she poured out a little wax and guided the candle to her fingers to stick it in place. The woman was blind.

'First Malvus. Now Loki,' she said. 'It was his smirkin' mouth that put me in 'ere. What about you? You're young to be makin' enemies of gods.'

'How can you tell?'

'Your voice.'

Mithrid wondered if she smelled a trick as well as the bucket of shit in the corner. One of Loki's liars, just like Irien. 'Well,' she said. 'As much as I would love to chat, I'm not staying for long. I need to escape. Maybe kill Loki while I'm at it.'

'Is that so? And how are you goin' to do that?'

'With your help, maybe. I have a spiked collar around my neck, and I need you to hold it while I deal with the spells on the door.'

'You're a mage, then.'

'Ha. Not quite.'

Mithrid let the woman probe with cold fingers, and she muttered as she felt the spikes and lack of hinge on the metal. 'What is this ugly thing?' she asked.

'One of Loki's trinkets. It's going to contract, and I need you to hold it back.'

Jeasin hummed as she followed Mithrid to the door and waited while she spread her hands across the steel and wood.

'Ready?'

'Maybe.'

That was good enough for Mithrid. In the flicker of candlelight, shadow grew from her splayed fingers, creeping across the wood. With a hissing of metal, the collar immediately began to shrink. Mithrid felt the lock spells weakening, but so was Jeasin.

'I can't hold it. It's too strong!' she cried. The spikes pierced her neck again, yet Mithrid pushed on and on, treading a desperate line between death and freedom. She lasted only moments before the pain became unbearable, as if the spikes glowed white hot.

'Gah!' Mithrid screeched, letting go and falling back to the floor. Jeasin stood by, gaze wandering as she listened to Mithrid seethe and pant.

'Got you beat?' she asked, crossing her legs.

'Not for long.'

'I recognise that fire. 'Eard it many times before. So who are you to get locked up in the finest dungeons in Emaneska?'

Mithrid thumped her fist on the stone. 'I'm a general in the Forever King's army.'

Jeasin curled her lip. 'Then you must know Farden pretty well.'

'You know Farden?' Mithrid asked, sitting up.

A cackle came from the woman. 'Better than most, girl. Inside and out, you could say. A long time ago, I was his favourite cat in the cathouse, probably before you were born. He's the reason I'm here in Krauslung instead of livin' my days out peacefully in Albion, the fucker.'

Mithrid finally dragged herself upright. 'I've wanted to strangle him more than once myself.'

'He has that effect,' she said with a sniff. 'I can smell blood and battle on you.'

'Loki and his elves took me.'

'Elves? So that's what else I can smell,' Jeasin said with a widening of her eyes. 'Loki is up to his old tricks then and claimed the Arka for himself, I take it? And I'll bet Farden is driving himself mad trying to kill him.'

'That about sums it up,' Mithrid said, running her hand through the flame. 'Why did Loki want you in a cell?'

'Spite, probably. I was once Lady Jeasin, Malvus' favourite whore,' she said with a smirk. 'Take a lesson from someone who's seen every face of good and evil, girl: only the winning side matters. You've got to choose wisely, and I chose luxury and power instead of scraping an existence in the frozen north fighting for freedom. I told Farden long ago it wasn't my war, but I helped where I could. See, men will tell you almost anythin' with your hands around their cock, and they'll believe anythin' you tell 'em, too. I had Malvus' ear, and that's why Farden and Durnus had me spy for them 'til it got too dangerous, but I didn't account for Loki and him turnin' Malvus against me.' Jeasin threw up her hands and clapped her knees. 'But I s'pose that's the game I played.'

'Durnus,' whispered Mithrid.

'How is that old blind bastard?'

'Not blind any more, for one, and dead, for another.'

Jeasin lowered her head. 'That's a shame. He was kind to me.'

A silence fell between them, and Mithrid grew uncomfortable as Jeasin stared, and she remembered Durnus fading to ash in Azanimur. Mithrid felt her eyes grow hot and knuckled them with dirty hands. Jeasin was still staring at her when she looked up, so she examined the cell instead.

Grim and bland, it was nothing but a square of stone. Straw on the floor. A broken cot and mattress against one wall. It was the scraps of wood from the broken cot that drew her attention.

Mithrid scrabbled to them, finding them to be tough oak. She managed to wedge one between her neck and a spike, and then another, until she wore a strange armour between her and the collar. It was odd, but such was the fire that burned in her.

'What is it you're up to?' Jeasin asked.

'I'm trying again.'

'You sure? I can smell the blood on you. Hear it runnin' down your neck.'

Jeasin wasn't wrong, but Mithrid didn't care. She spread her hands across the door again, pressing fingertips to the bolts and frayed splinters where occupants long gone had carved with fingernails.

Mithrid had to be quick to break the spells and beat the collar. Faster than she had been before. The door shuddered as she took ahold of it and spread shadow quick and fast. If her previous attempt had been a sledgehammer, now she used a sharp and clever knife.

Mithrid felt the wood pressing against her neck, almost choking her, but at least there was no kiss of metal and little pain. It gave her precious moments to handle the spells. They were strong, but not strong enough, and they withered beneath her touch.

The spikes broke through the wooden scraps just as she cracked the magick. Mithrid cried out through clenched teeth, tearing her hands away from the door as it jolted, and the locks and spells came free. Mithrid pushed her shadow deep down and clawed at the door's edge, prising it open with her fingernails until torchlight cut the dark of the cell like a blade.

'Did you do it?' Jeasin whispered.

'I—' Mithrid's words died as she hauled open the door and saw a lithe figure standing waiting. It was an elf. The elf Farden had fought. He had been waiting.

The elf reached out, quick as an arrow, and seized Mithrid by her collar. A bare foot crashed against her chest and threw her back into the cell.

Azen filled the doorframe, face obscured by the light yet white eyes still aglow. He stared between Mithrid and Jeasin as if deciding which worm he wanted to stamp on first.

'*Lakrimur*,' hissed Azen in a guttural language. The elf said nothing more as he withdrew and slammed the door in Mithrid's face, blowing out the candle as he did so. The sounds of a barricade being thrown against the door followed.

'Who or what was that?' Jeasin whispered.

'Just be glad you don't have your sight,' said Mithrid to the darkness, breathing hard and trying to ignore the pain in her neck. She clenched her fists and put them to her face. 'Bide your time,' she told herself, breathing into her knuckles.

Jeasin chuckled in the shadow. 'And what game are you playin', Mithrid?' she asked. 'What side are you choosing?'

Mithrid didn't answer. She let the wall prop her up and stared at the fading silhouette of the elf frozen in her eyes.

Loki awaited Azen with crossed arms and a curious look.

'Trying to escape already, is she?' he tutted, but Azen seemed even less in the mood for his wit and charm than usual.

The pale creature stared down at the god. 'Where did this girl come from?'

'By the sea. East of here.'

'Why is she important to you?'

'Because, my dear Azen,' Loki said, walking a circle around the elf, 'she might be the answer to all my woes. But first, she has to turn to our way of thinking.'

Azen scowled. 'You think your tongue is that golden.'

Loki clicked the aforementioned tongue. 'Hasn't failed me yet.'

'It is nothing compared to that beast. That keraken. *Faer akur.* It killed far too many of my kin! If these are more words you have forgotten to tell us, our pact lies in ruins, god. We will be enemies.'

Loki held his sharp ivory gaze. 'I'm as disturbed and surprised as you are,' he countered. 'And fear not, my good elf, because if Farden wants to fight with monsters, so can we. We already have several,' he said with a wink. 'That's my task and my concern. You need to keep watch for Farden coming to rescue his beloved Mithrid.'

'She is cursed. She is poison,' said the elf as he threw a finger at the cell door. Azen stalked into the gloom between the torches without another word or a single glance.

'That's what I'm counting on,' Loki muttered.

Elves. Loki tutted as the maze of corridors until he stared over his city, cut in half by the jagged shadow of Mount Hardja and her neighbours. Snow had come in the night, and what had survived the sunlight now dusted the pointy rooftops. The rest dripped across the cobbles, already turning to ice in the shadows. Winter's grip was closing in.

Curiosity tugged at him, and Loki reached into his pocket to fish out the crow skull and press its green gemstone. 'Is the Lady of Whispers still breathing?' he asked it.

For a long while, no answer came, and Loki held the skull closer to his lips. 'Are you alive, Irien?'

Loki was mid-grin and assuming everything had gone to plan when the beak cracked open, and a faint voice wafted forth.

'I'm alive, my dear.'

Loki flinched, taking a moment.

'Are you locked away?'

'Free as a bird.'

Loki narrowed his eyes at the skull's empty sockets. Loki had placed a bet that Farden's suspicions would lead him to doubt Irien and test her. Trick her, even. That's what Loki had wanted, to draw Scalussen to their eastern front and conveniently get rid of Irien. But perhaps the mage was not as smart or as brutal in his old age as Loki had expected. Perhaps Scalussen had slipped up, and Irien had got away with her tricks. Perhaps – and there Loki felt the horrid prickle of second guesses – Irien was not so temporary as he thought.

'And what of our good friends in New Scalussen?' Loki asked. He had to know. Gremorin was quite literally resting in pieces. Mithrid was caught and captured. The elves were still with him. All he needed was a Scalussen mired in ashes and dust, tears and blood. Keraken or no keraken.

'Safe and sound. Your assassins were slain,' said Irien.

Loki frowned. 'How many dead?'

'A handful of soldiers. My dear.'

A handful. Loki made a handful of the skull and threatened to crush it with glowing fingers.

'And what would you have me do now?'

Loki made the best of his disappointment. 'You'll find out about this keraken of Farden's, is what you'll do. I want its weakness.'

'Consider it done,' spoke the hushed voice.

Loki held the skull at arm's length, a suspicion growing in his mind. It certainly sounded like Irien. *Could she be that good? Or was this a trick?*

'And what of Farden?' he asked.

The god was forced to stare at the crow for far too long a time until it answered, beak jittering.

'He's coming for you.'

Loki gripped the skull so tightly a crack spread across the bone before he stuffed it back into his pocket.

'Sjarvek!' Loki bellowed, and somehow the old bastard appeared from around a corner within moments, already bowing.

'Your Illustriousness.'

Loki eyed the clouds hovering over Ursufel. A storm was brewing. 'Fetch me Arka scholars, Sjarvek, and fetch me Scalussen spies. We're hunting for monsters of all kinds.'

'As you wish, Marvellousness.'

Thousands of miles south, the blue gemstone atop the skull faded as Lerel removed her finger and cleared her throat. She held it at arm's length.

'Do you think he bought it?'

Elessi snorted. 'I would have. Where'd you learn to do a Golikan accent?'

'From the Lady of Whispers herself. Wasn't hard.'

Farden put a hand to Lerel's face as he took back the skull. 'Nice work. Fine touch with "my dear".'

'Why did you tell him we were safe and sound?' she asked. 'Why not lie and lull him into thinking we're weaker than we are?'

'Because Loki's at his most desperate when his grand plans fall flat,' the mage grinned.

'Do we want desperation?'

Farden was already marching across the sand. 'Better that than overconfidence, and him sending his whole army to finish what he thinks is left of us. Now enough talk and lies. We have Great Ones to find.'

'Is your king all right?' asked Rokhelm, standing behind Elessi and making her jump.

Lerel answered him, staring after her mage. 'Farden is Farden. There's nothing like death and failure to spur him. Action is how he grieves. Inside? He's aflame with anger and sorrow and guilt, and that's what he'll use to win. Loki made a mistake striking us here.'

Beside her, Warbringer rumbled deep in her chest.

CHAPTER 28
VELLICHOR

Show me those cities that built libraries before they built fortresses, and I will show you the cities that will endure a thousand years.
A QUOTE FROM SKÖLGARD EMPEROR ISAIAH, HAILED AS THE KINDEST AND MOST DUTIFUL EMPEROR SKÖLGARD EVER KNEW

Farden stared through sore eyes at the mess of parchment and paper spread over the table. He swivelled away from the sight of it, but he found yet another table to greet him, equally swarmed with literature: books, tomes, scrolls, tablets, tapestries, and rough sheaves of notes that looked like they'd been scrawled by a drunkard. Judging by some of the nonsense Farden had spent the last two days devouring, that was true for a lot of the scholars. One of the ancient papers in his hands was splotched with more old wine than old ink, its ramblings another flight of fancy.

Peryn, Elessi, Lerel, and Ko-Tergo had worked almost as tirelessly, distilling myths and fairytales and skalds' stories into something that might resemble truth. In the darkness of the Jar Khoum tunnels and underground libraries, a constant night had reigned, and the lanterns had been refilled two dozen times. Notebooks had been filled with notes and ideas, places and people long dead and most of them useless as all fuck. They had climbed a mountain of paper, but the summit still remained.

A wall of black slate sat between the shelves, littered with names crossed out. It was a growing history of Great Ones. Not all by far, and many of them dead or already known.

One word kept calling to him.

Utiru.

She had to be a Great One, but Farden had crossed that name out as soon as it was written. Others had been written on the slate, and most of them had a line through them, dead and gone.

Zathurla. The hydra they had fought in Albion.

Garyon. Last of the ogin, or rathcata, as Paraia called them.

Shareste. Another mighty rathcata.

Bane of Orestus. A giant scorpion Farden didn't want to meet.

All dead and gone.

The only words that weren't crossed out belonged to Keraken and a place called Falkenrath that nobody had ever heard of.

Revenge. That was the name of the book he stared at, written by some kind of hunter who had made certain Great Ones fell across the world. Farden found himself cursing them for their fervour and wondering what hole in their heart they sought to mend.

'Get some air,' Farden grunted. 'Take a break. Get some rest. Maybe tomorrow will be more fruitful.'

The others didn't complain. They filtered from the library, with Farden left behind in the dark with the guards.

'Any thoughts, old friend?' Farden whispered to the spear that he leaned on. He closed his eyes and let the rustling and murmur of note-taking fade. He imagined a snow-covered field and a shadow standing alone on a hill. It looked deep in thought.

Many, but none that you would like.

'That isn't helpful.'

If you were hunted, doomed, fated to face death, what would you do?

'Where are you going with this?'

You might fight, but others might flee. Others might hide and bury themselves. You look for the names of Great Ones, but their true names have been forgotten. What if you look for what their names have become? What they have become.

Farden opened his eyes as the snow faded and frowned. A yelling echoed down the tunnels, making the lycan and Jar Khoum guards flinch.

'Farden!'

The mage whirled to see Lerel skid to a halt on the dusty stone.

'Irien's escaped. She killed a guard.'

Farden burst into a run, outpacing Lerel as he raced for daylight.

The foul weather still hadn't broken, and a wind whipped the city from the south, covering the ground in broken palm boughs. It wasn't quite the fresh air Farden had suggested, and the air howled in his ears as he ran for the gates.

Following the shouts of his soldiers, he wound through street after street until he reached the Dawnknell. Ko-Tergo was there, lurching towards the ocean, and Farden followed in his wake as dust and flagstone became sand.

'They've caught her!' came a cry from the Winter Fortress as he raced onto the beach. Through the driving rain, he saw a small crowd of soldiers menacing a bedraggled figure. Farden waded through their numbers to find Irien standing in the shallows with one hand on a spear and another on the prow of a small rowboat.

'I do apologise, Farden, but I simply won't be cooped up in your dungeons,' yelled Irien, taking another swipe at an encroaching soldier. 'You let me go, and we'll call it square. You ruined me. I betrayed you.'

Farden let the sword at his side grow until a spear reached for her. He saw Irien's teeth on her lips.

'All your talk, and it's just the spear you want, isn't it?' Farden asked her, taking a stab in her direction. 'That's why you went to Belerod. That's why you went to Loki. Why you came here. You want to pick it from the ashes when everyone is done fighting for it. Patience is a virtue, you once told me, and it's definitely yours. A devious patience. Sadly for you, you chose the wrong side of your wicked game, yet again.'

Irien's demeanour changed. Even her shoulders slumped. Her face turned cruel. 'Forgive me for wanting to reclaim what is rightfully mine. Sigrimur wasn't fit and neither are you. Look at what you've already done with it,' Irien said, raising her voice and spittle flying. 'You want to hear a whisper, Forever King? Would you, Scalussen?'

Farden almost struck her down with a blast of magick right there and then, but she spoke before he decided.

'Want to know why the elves returned? It was not Malvus. It was not Loki. It was that spear! And the flagrant use of it by none other than *you*, Farden,' yelled Irien.

The accusation was damning and dripped with blood and blame. The wounds of the Dramath-Ai were still open and raw. Whispers spread between the soldiers. Farden saw Lerel and Elessi swapping glances.

Irien pressed on, growing louder. 'You cut a door between worlds and let them out and cursed the world for the second time since you were born. Yours are the wrong hands for that spear to be in, and you'll break the world if it means you kill Loki. I see that now clearer than ever. There's the greatest whisper of all.'

Aware of the eyes on him, Farden lurched forwards to break Irien's spear with his gauntlet and seize her by the throat. Gunnir menaced her, inches from her throat. She deserved it. She had proven herself a traitor twice and a liar many times over. She was a killer. *She deserved it.* This was war.

And yet the spear didn't move. Instead, Farden dropped her in the shallows. He stared at the tattoos on her knuckles. 'You're a poisonous snake, but you deserve more than a quick death.'

Irien spat seawater. 'And what is that then?'

Farden let the magick loose from Gunnir, thinking hard of a place he never wanted to visit again.

Rocks tumbled as the spell died away, leaving Irien dazed and spluttering. She looked around at the rift of dark rock and old spider's webs that hung over them. The air was damp and cold. 'Where have you taken me, mage?'

'You like whispers, that's all you'll find in there,' Farden said, pointing into the deeper dark. 'You want to live? Fine. I'll give you exile instead. Start walking. If you stop, I'll reconsider.'

Irien did not like the look of the cave nor the smell wafting from it. Something sweet like old perfume, but it did nothing to hide the scent of death. 'Surely there must be a trade we can make.'

'No trade.'

'I can spy on Loki for you.'

'No.'

'I can fight.'

Farden crossed his arms.

Irien took a step, readying herself. 'All right. You win, Forever King, is that what you want to hear?'

Farden said nothing.

Irien turned to insults. 'You'll regret this. There'll be a reckoning.'

'I'm counting on it,' was all Farden said in reply before lowering his spear.

Irien stepped over the rubble of the rift. A path hid between the stones and puddles of moss, and she followed it down the rift until the mage was out of sight and she stood at the ragged mouth of a cave. There Irien waited, thinking he would grow bored. The bastard was impatient at the best of times.

But not today.

Irien must have waited almost an hour until she looked back to see Farden sat hunched on a rock, spear balanced on his knees. All he did was point and let the spear glow, and Irien was left with no choice.

'A reckoning!' was all Irien yelled before she went into the cave, rubbing at the tattoo on her knuckles with her wooden thumb.

Whatever trick this was, Irien could survive it. Farden wasn't that cold-blooded. He couldn't even kill her, for goodness' sake. The Lady of Whispers would come out breathing on the other side as always.

It was then Irien heard a scuttle of tiny claws on the rocks and saw a glass spider disappear behind a stalactite.

❦

When Farden reappeared on the beach, the crowd had drifted apart, but Lerel and Elessi remained, waiting with furrowed expressions. Rokhelm wandered in circles nearby, counting seashells.

'Where did you take her? Back to Loki?' asked Lerel, arms crossed and face blank.

'I took her to visit an old friend.'

'Who?'

'Utiru.'

Both she and Elessi went pale. They knew the stories Farden and Mithrid had told them and had no further questions.

Farden kept on walking. The libraries called him. A bitter complaint kept him silent. Guilt swam through his veins in place of magick.

It had to be lies, he told himself. It had to be a last stab in the gut from a dying foe. To think he had cursed the world with elves was too much to carry.

'Is it true, old friend?' Farden whispered over the wind when he could bring himself to hear the answer. 'Did I open the door for the elves?'

It may be, spoke Gunnir.

Farden bit his tongue, biting harder until the pain was too much and he tasted blood. 'One problem at a time,' was all he said as he stalked back into the darkness of the Jar Khoum caves with the others in tow. They likely knew better than to ask, but their silence needled him.

'Back to work we go,' he muttered his order as he peered once more across the sea of script and runes.

Rokhelm had followed them this time, perhaps curious after the events of the beach. He wandered the library, pawing at the spines of tomes and twiddling scrolls and seeming entirely too distracted by the fireless lanterns. His strange eyes shone brighter in the subterranean gloom.

Farden decided to press his luck. 'Have you decided to help us?' he asked while the sailor ran his finger through the chalk written on the slate where it said Keraken.

'We thought we wouldn't,' Rokhelm said distractedly.

'What changed your mind?'

'You did.'

'When?'

'You showed simple mercy to an enemy that you could have killed. Those who came to Keraken before would not have done such a thing. The woman said your spear doesn't belong in your hands. I would disagree, and because of that I will help,' said Rokhelm with a grin of jumbled teeth. 'And because Elessi trusts you too.'

'Somewhat,' Elessi muttered before offering a smile.

Rokhelm tapped at a lantern again. 'Though, I don't know why you're asking us when a tharkun is already in your presence.'

Everybody else swapped confused looks, as if a monster had been sitting on the shelves this entire time and nobody had noticed.

'What?' asked Lerel. 'Where?'

Rokhelm reached a hand to Warbringer's hammer, making the minotaur growl and his calloused fingers fall short. Rokhelm pointed instead. 'This isn't a normal hammer. I can feel it.'

'We know that,' said Farden.

Elessi shuddered. 'The bloody thing screams whenever it moves.'

'You don't know all of it, though, do you?' Rokhelm paused to stare at Farden before turning to Warbringer. 'Do they?'

'What's he talking about, Warbringer?' Farden asked. He knew all too well that Voidaran swallowed the ghosts of those it killed. Warbringer had called it the Soulcatcher once before. Dark Saviour, in her tongue.

Warbringer snuffled as she put her hand onto the book still spread on the table, where a word was written and not crossed out. Only a question mark sat by it. 'He talks of my goddess. Dotharadine.'

'What of her?'

'She is Great One. Her spirit lives in hammer, waiting to come forth again and unite my kin. That is our prophecy. What Thenerean died for.'

'Why didn't you tell me this before?' Farden asked.

'I did, in east country. Told you hammer fell from stars, killed first and oldest Warbringer. It has caught many souls for many years, waiting until Dotharadine ready.'

'I meant about the coming forth and uniting part!'

Warbringer sniffed, looking confused. 'You did not ask.'

'I…' Farden spluttered.

'I said I had words for you. You too busy until now.'

'Then how do we get Dotharadine out?' asked Elessi.

Warbringer thumbed the skull on Voidaran. 'Blood and souls. She has feasted much, but not yet ready.'

Lerel blew a sigh as if it was all too much. 'When will she be ready?'

'Maybe soon. Maybe later. Depend how much we fight. Then Dotharadine will take my flesh as hers. She will rise. She will bring all my kin to her. Clans will stand united again, and prophecy will be complete.'

Farden held up a finger. 'What was that part?

'Prophecy will—'

No, the part about the taking of your flesh.'

Warbringer shrugged. 'The Warbringer must die so Dotharadine can live,' she said.

'When were you going to tell me?' Farden erupted with anger, but he caught himself quickly. 'I can't let you do that.'

Elessi was shaking her head. 'We can't lose you as well, Warbringer.'

'Not pink-flesh's choice.'

'No,' said Farden. 'It's out of the question.'

With a shard of chalk, Farden wrote the name *Dotharadine* on the slate and promptly drew a line through it. 'There must be another way. Another Great One. Rokhelm?'

The strange sailor said nothing. Rokhelm had unearthed a buried map. He spread it against the mounds of parchment, slapped its edges to make it stay flat, and stared at it with a smile.

'Giant,' was all he said.

Where Emaneska and Easterealm joined, it was almost possible to see the bones of the ancient giant that had formed the world. Few remembered him, and yet he had been the greatest of all. The very earth they walked on. Durnus' words rang in his head. *What their names have become. What they have become.*

Farden's fingers traced the coastlines, looking for shapes forgotten or names that matched with myths they had scoured. His wandering took his finger east, where the land faded into the weathered borders of the map. Mogacha, a label told him, before he squinted at a smaller one next to it.

'Ossas,' Farden blurted.

'What did you say?' Elessi asked.

Remember what was said in Mogacha, whispered the spear.

'Ossas. A mountain in Mogacha. The people there swore it was something else. Something that still lived and breathed.'

'I read that word an hour ago,' Elessi as she tunnelled into the mess like a rabbit that fancied a new burrow. A tablet with illustrated scenes spread across it was thumped on the pile. 'Here. The tale of mighty Ossas, the mountain with a voice.'

'Keraken remembers that voice,' Rokhelm said proudly. 'Remembers the sea-dragon that slew him.'

Farden took it all in, from the faded paints depicting a shepherd boy sheltering from a storm in a cave and hearing the mountain's voice speak to him, to scenes of him being whipped for telling such tall stories. Apparently whatever the mountain was warning the boy of came true, and the village was destroyed. Quite the uplifting tale.

'Then that's where we'll start,' Farden decided. 'Looks like I'm going back to Mogacha.'

'Is that it?' asked Elessi. 'You woke up a mountain before, have you, Farden?'

'I guess I'll figure it out when I get there, won't I? I'll take Hereni in case I need the magick.'

'And me. You're not getting all the fun this time.'

'Fun?'

'No arguments, mage,' said Lerel, already on her feet.

Hereni had some arguments.

'Let me get this right: you want to go wake up a mountain, hoping it's a friendly giant.'

Lerel nodded. 'That we do. Well, Farden does. I'm curious.'

'Instead of going to get Mithrid.'

'Spies haven't come back yet.'

'I think those elves have driven us insane, you know that?' said Hereni, although she rose from her bed and tended each of Mithrid's plants before reaching for her armour.

'Where?'

'East.'

'Fine. Gods damn it,' Hereni said, seizing her helmet with both hands. 'Better than sitting here wallowing in apprehension.'

'Trust in Mith—'

Green light crackled around Hereni's fists as she tested her gauntlets. 'If somebody else throws the word trust in my face again, I swear…'

'Enough said.' Lerel waved her to the door instead, and Hereni clanked out into the hallway. She looked over her shoulder, pausing before they departed.

'Is it true?' she asked. 'What's going around?'

'What?' Lerel knew exactly what, but she didn't want to say it.

'That the elves that took Mithrid and killed our friends are Farden's fault.'

Lerel didn't want to believe it either, even if it was true. 'Another of Loki's lies,' she said firmly.

Hereni nodded, eyes vacant. 'Friendly giant, my arse,' she could be heard grumbling as she walked on.

'This is going to be fun,' said Lerel, hands on her curved sword.

CHAPTER 29
OSSAS

You think you can't get lost in Emaneska? You think there aren't nameless horrors hiding in the darkest places? You think those mapmakers have scribbled everything into their masterpieces? Owl shite. Emaneska's wild as it ever was. I've seen places maps have forgotten. I've seen places where the old forces still hold sway. A rule of might and ferocity. Your borders are but written in ink and have no place in the real world.
FROM A MISSIVE WRITTEN TO SKÖLGARD EMPEROR BAKT BY WILD-CAPTAIN MORGON RIOX, WHO WENT MISSING UNDER SUSPICIOUS CIRCUMSTANCES

Dust scurried as the spear dropped three strangers on long, green grass beneath a sky full of sun and clouds shaped like feathers. White spindle-legged birds cawed and flapped as they ran in all directions from the sudden arrivals. Distant but mighty waves crashed like predictable thunder.

It had barely been months since Farden had soared over the seas of eastern grass and watched the cliff-edge rise and fall. Then, it had been idyllic, peaceful, and forgotten by the machinations of the wider world. A simple place of simplistic people.

How much it had changed in such a short time.

'Where are we?' asked Lerel.

'Thousands of miles east, in a place called Mogacha. Though I don't recognise it.'

Trails of smoke twisted above the nearest hill, victims to the quarrelling breezes. There was a sour scent on their airs. Of charcoal and grease. The copper of blood. What used to be a smattering of pebble-built towns amongst the grass sea and perched on the cliff-edges were now fields of rubble. A gnarled and crow-picked skull perched on a lonely spear like an ugly signpost. Persnippen and coelos had once roamed alongside the white herons, but no longer. The only familiarity was the dark peak of Ossas still poking out beyond the cliffs, bent crooked over the ocean.

'I thought you'd been here before,' said Lerel.

'So had I,' said Farden, setting foot to the grass and aiming for the hilltop. The view beyond was a sorry sight. Farden crouched below the crest of the hill and cast a quick spell to see closer.

Golikar had come to Mogacha.

Halfway up Ossas' northern slope, the peaceful town that had once welcomed Farden, Mithrid, and Warbringer had been taken over. Fields cut bald patches in the grass seas, tended by people with bent backs, watched over by figures bearing switches and whips. Between the conical points of pebble-stack houses, buildings of rough wood had sprung up, and tree saplings had been planted around them, meaning this was not a short visit. A road had been cut through the town up to where dozens of fishing poles hung over the sea. Gangs of Mogacha worked them under masters. Fish rattled on squat wagons down to where their carcasses were hacked apart and salted. The dead husks of coelos and persnippen cast shadows around tanneries and bubbling vats of blubber. Even more wagons waited half-loaded, pointed west.

'This wasn't like this before. Golikar must have followed me east and seen Mogacha for the easy target it was,' Farden growled as he got to his feet. 'This is my fault.'

'Another mess of yours to clear up,' said Hereni without a hint of humour. Lerel cleared her throat.

'What do you mean by that, mage?' Farden snapped. 'Just because Mithrid isn't here doesn't mean you get to act like her and fill her role of being a pain in the arse.'

'Understood,' Hereni muttered.

The others fell in behind Farden as he stomped down the hill and up the slope of Ossas.

The green-clad Golikans were too busy with subjugation to notice the travellers approaching, and the three strode into the edges of the town without shout or challenge.

'I don't know anything about these Golikans, but I already know I don't like them,' said Lerel.

'Same,' said Hereni, eying a strange set of stocks. They were empty, but if they weren't, some poor soul would be hanging upside down by wrists and ankles, face dangling over the downtrodden grass.

'Their queen and most of their army died in the Battle For The World. They're desperate,' Farden said, 'but that doesn't mean they get to force others into desperation.'

A harsh shout came from a path between two buildings, and a burly chap fell into view, landing on his knees and spilling his bundles of salted fish. Two soldiers clad in overlapping wooden plates appeared, jabbing him with their clubs. Whatever they said in their language, it was something that made the man scrabble to pick up his bundles.

Before Farden could interfere, a scream came from the nearest building, and another soldier naked from the waist down and trews around his knees tottered out of its door, four bloody lines of fingernails across his cheek. He spat at the house and shook a clump of long hair from his sweaty hand. He looked ready to storm back in when he noticed the three impeccably armoured strangers standing in the street.

'Who the fuck are you?'

At least that's what Farden imagined he said, but whatever it was, it caught the attention of the other soldiers.

Quickly stuffing his limpening manhood into his trews, the nearest soldier fumbled for a sword. 'On your knees, now!' he yelled in Commontongue.

Farden was reaching for Gunnir when Lerel stepped forwards with a look to the mage that said, 'I've got this one'. Farden let her have at it.

The soldier smirked as Lerel approached, sword hand still empty. 'You want a piece, woman?'

'At least a few,' Lerel said.

Farden had to smile as Lerel dodged his first wild swing, straight down. Before the blade could hit the mud, she tucked her arm into the crook of his and bent her grip, forcing him downwards with a yell. She kicked his overextended leg and threw him to the mud in the same motion. Only then did she draw her curved sword in a flourish and bring it straight down on the back of the man's head with a crunch.

The other soldiers immediately ran away, shouting at the top of their lungs. Stepping around the corpse, the three walked deeper into the town as if they gave a half-hearted chase.

It took a short time for the Golikans to sprint from wielding their whips over farms and fishing poles and form a wall of spears and swords in the market square. Piles of blackened rubble sat where buildings had been razed and cleared to make way for wagons. Work had come to a standstill in the town, and Mogacha slaves stared out from behind walls and tanning racks, knuckles pale around their tools.

'Halt there!' cried a Golikan captain with an unnecessarily tall hat on his head. 'You'll throw down your weapons, get on your knees, and put your noses to the—'

Farden slammed Gunnir's haft onto the black rock beneath the grass. The clang was as loud as a bell and sent a wind to blow the captain's hat from his head.

'You,' Farden began, 'will throw down *your* weapons and leave this town and its people alone immediately. You have no place here.'

'And who are you to order us?'

'A friend of these people.'

'You don't know who you're dealing with!' yelled the captain in a reedy voice.

'And neither do you.'

The first line of soldiers marched with weapons outstretched. Farden waded into their midst, shield spell barging them aside. Not a fist or blade could touch him as he chased the captain down and skewered him against a wagon with Gunnir. With a twist of his hand, the shield spell turned to fire, and those who pressed against him were sent scurrying as the flames enveloped them.

Behind him, Hereni strangled others with force spells. Lerel was already surrounded by no fewer than four corpses. The soldiers who hadn't fled backed off, huddling close and eyes wide.

Farden did not have to utter a threat. He didn't have to brandish Gunnir. He didn't have to speak a word of rebellion and freedom. The Mogacha decided their fate without him.

With howling cries, the Mogacha descended on the routed Golikans in their scores, driving them down the road they had built with their ruin and into the seas of grass. More than a dozen of the soldiers fell to rakes and shovels and hefty fishing hooks, and only a handful managed to get away, disappearing over a hill to the north, panting and begging for their lives.

'I remember you,' said a voice in thick Commontongue. Farden turned to find a willow of a man he recognised.

Evorsk, whispered Gunnir.

Others gathered around him, tugging at their hats of woven grass. Evorsk's hands were clasped, and he seemed wary, careful. Farden remembered all too well how the Mogacha treated those with magick in their veins.

'Magick is poison here,' he said accusingly. 'You did not tell us of your magick before.'

Farden opened his mouth to reply, but Evorsk shook his head.

'But today, magick help us. We allow,' he said with a spreading smile. 'You come back.'

'We came for Ossas, but we had no idea the Golikans had followed us here. I'm sorry for that, Evorsk.'

Evorsk's face wavered as he made sense of the words. 'It was only a matter of time. But they will be back. You must stay. Help.'

'I will, but first I need to know everything you know about Ossas.'

Lerel held up a hand. 'Is it me, or can anyone else feel a rumbling?' she asked.

Evorsk looked proud. 'That Ossas. He breathes. He lives.'

'Where is this giant, Farden?' asked Hereni, looking around.

The mage smiled. 'You're standing on him.'

'Excuse me?'

Farden led them up the slope of black rock and patches of stubborn grass to where the fishing poles lay abandoned. One foot firmly against the lip of the cliff, he stared down to where the waves pounded the coast. Their roar was only made louder by the shape of the mountain.

'Mithrid jumped from here. Straight down to the dragon's teeth,' Farden said.

Hereni's eyes grew wider. 'She jumped?'

'That she did.'

Lerel whistled. 'And just how are we going to wake this mountain up?'

Farden pointed. 'I'm hoping Evorsk can tell us.'

The man was hurrying up the slope with a bundle of flat pebbles in his hand. Each had painted carvings on them, and he began to lay them on the rock one by one in order. 'Ossas came thousand years ago with Mogacha on his back. He save us from fire. He make paradise here. But one day, old enemy come. Old monster from sea bite him. Poison weaken Ossas. Almost kill. But he still fight. Kill monster by sacrifice himself. Poison make him sleep. Become mountain. Thousand years and he still live.'

'Will Ossas ever wake?' asked Farden.

Evorsk looked at Farden with a quizzical face. 'Of course. It is why we wait here for glorious day. But thousand years pass. No wake.'

'How does he wake?'

More stones were laid end to end with the last. 'When Ossas taste air on face again.'

Lerel frowned. 'How does that happen?'

Evorsk laid the final stone, showing Ossas crouched, legs up to his chin, arms raised, and fists clenched. A dead serpent with an open maw lay before him, and the sea simmered around his feet.

'When oceans run dry,' Evorsk said, as if it were the simplest thing in the world.

Farden felt Hereni and Lerel looking at him. 'Think Loki would wait?' he muttered.

Lerel crossed her ams, hopes dashed. 'Not in the slightest.'

'Are we sure there's even a giant and that rumble isn't just the waves?' asked Hereni.

'Ossas lives,' Evorsk said with a grin.

'There has to be some way,' Farden said, peering over the clifftop once more to stare at the waves. Without a moment's thought, he snatched one of the stout fishing lines and looped it around his waist.

'Farden?' asked Lerel.

'I need to get a better look,' he said before swinging out into thin air. 'Lower me down.'

Hereni, Evorsk, and Lerel manned the winch, lowering Farden down slowly until the point of the cliff loomed above him. With dark waves crashing below him and spray trying in vain to wet his boots, Farden felt a churn in his gut. He could remember the crush of that water, fighting to invade his lungs.

Farden shook his head and stared hard at the concave cliff. Once more he thought of the giant's shape lost to the map and squinted at the rockface. It took him some time while he swung back and forth on the ocean winds, but the more he looked, the more he saw a shape to the rock. Two great pillars, arching up and crossing beneath the point of the cliff. Farden raised his own arms in mimicry, crossing at the wrists as he had done so many times before to summon his magick. And below them, in the gutter of every ebbing wave, Farden glimpsed a giant protrusion of rock that refused to be eroded by the ever-hungry waves. The top of a skull, possibly.

'I've found him!' Farden yelled to the winds, pulling on the rope. He saw three curious heads vanish before he was winched back up and dumped on the rock.

'I can make out Ossas. The Mogacha are right, this isn't any normal mountain. This is a Great One,' Farden said with a fierce smile.

'And what about running the oceans dry?' asked Lerel.

Farden rubbed his chin. 'We'll need a ship.'

Hereni was not impressed. 'A ship? In those waters?'

'I hate the idea more than you, Hereni, but it's the only way.'

Lerel shrugged. 'It's doable, with the right captain.'

'Ossas' head is not deeply submerged. With the right spells and Gunnir…' Farden thought aloud as he turned for the town.

Evorsk stood in their way. 'You want wake Ossas?' he asked, face like stone.

'With your permission,' Farden replied, 'we would try.'

'With magick?'

'With magick.'

It took a moment for Evorsk's eyes to give away the smile he was hiding. 'Then magick not poison no more.'

Farden hoped he was right about that.

'*This* is the ship? This is a boat,' Lerel said with a tut as she looked over the lopsided craft. It was not Mogacha but Golikan, and it looked like it had been bashed against the cliffs quite enough already. It had one mast with a patchwork sail, a tiller, a blade-like rudder that stuck out of the water, and two suspicious holes in its side. The vessel looked more suited to a river than a sea as violent as this one, and Lerel questioned her own words. 'And what kind of name is

Petunia for a ship anyway?' Lerel sighed, staring out across the waves and along the rising cliff to Ossas a few miles away.

'Evorsk said the Golikans left it here to rot after they tried their hands at fishing for the sharks.'

'There's sharks?'

'Big ones.'

'I'll need one of you on the sail, making sure we stay between the cliff and the reef. And dealing with sharks, apparently.'

'Regretting coming along already?' Hereni said with a smirk.

'And I'll drag the waters back,' said Farden, as if he was still trying to figure out how.

Wading into the shallows, they clambered aboard the *Petunia* and let the sail out. Hereni muttered a wind spell or two to herself that she'd learned aboard the bookships. *Dreadnoughts*. Lerel had to remember to call them that. It was but a small favour to the memory of Sturmsson.

Taking a shuddering breath and putting her mind back on task, Lerel put the tiller hard over until the boat waddled towards Ossas. The swell out of the beach harbour already made her rock violently, and Lerel could hear bilge sloshing around in the hold.

'Where are you going?' asked Farden once he noticed she wasn't aiming straight, but towards the dragon's teeth.

'Turning sideways in a wave is never a good idea,' Lerel answered as she counted the time between the huge rollers that came from the south with fury. A few of them reached as high as the *Petunia*'s mast, but they were fortunate they only curved and peaked a moment before they hit the cliff. 'We've got to come in with the waves and turn as quick as possible.'

'You're the captain.'

'Damn right,' said Lerel, as she turned *Petunia* into a current with a horrendous creaking and ordered Hereni to push a little harder. The boat raced dangerously close to a stone tooth, but its rip pushed them into an oncoming wave in perfect timing. Lerel began to turn to carve down the face of the wave, waiting just long enough for the shadow of the cliff to claim them and for rock to loom tall and ominous before she yanked the tiller hard once more. *Petunia* lurched sideways, sending Hereni and Farden flying as it cut a path up the face of the wave and over its lip before it could crest. The hillock of dark water exploded against the cliff behind them, and the *Petunia* found itself in a calmer trough.

'Push, Hereni!' Lerel yelled.

Hereni obliged, driving a fierce wind into the sail to keep the ship racing towards the next wave.

'We need to keep her there! Use the teeth and coast for markers!' yelled Lerel from the bridge.

It was Farden's turn as he levelled his spear at the head of Ossas. He had to be careful; it probably wasn't the smartest idea to kill the giant before raising him. Farden thought again, touching his wrists together to feel his own magick in his veins. Fire skittered along the Book on his back as he channelled his spells without a word. A water mage was something he had never been, and his spells were fruitless against the waves.

Foam and seawater sprayed the deck as a concentrated vortex spell took hold, aiming just at the waterline on the cliff. Farden drove it against the cliff and watched the waters recoil, but not enough to break the next wave. Farden kept pressing, starting to spin the vortex spell.

Farden heard a faint cry on the wind. He took a moment to glance up at the overhanging cliff, where Mogacha crowded and hung from their ropes. It looked like some of them were pointing.

The *Petunia* bucked as something struck it. Not a wave. Not a rock.

Farden redoubled his spells, carving a shield spell in the gap he caused and pushing back the water inch by inch to reveal more and more barnacled rock. The rise and fall of the leaking boat was his rhythm, and he made his shields flinch and shove outwards in opposite measure. It broke the waves before they could hammer against his spells, but even with the spear lending him strength, the weight of the ocean was a foe even a god couldn't beat.

And yet Farden fought with all his might. Fire began to sputter along his gauntlets and vambraces as he pushed and pressed, entangling the waters in his vortex spell. Slowly but surely, the water began to spin against his shields.

An eye. Farden swore he saw the arc and hollow of an eye socket.

Another cry, but this time from the tiller and chased by a shout from Hereni.

Farden looked to his right in time to see a gigantic shark breaching the swirling waters, the jaws of its flat, axe-shaped head wide, teeth jutting and wing-like fins spread. It soared for the deck, twisting as it flew just to fit more of Farden in its jaws.

The mage did the only thing he could, and that was hold onto the spear. Gunnir sliced deep into the shark's mouth and kept going. Farden had to lean back as the shark finally came to a stop, with his arm deep in its open mouth and its teeth grating against his pauldron.

Another of the monsters exploded from the sea, aiming at Hereni, but with her hands full with the sails, she had to stand her ground until the shark was almost on the deck. Only then did she pivot away and stab the shark in the nose. It thrashed, breaking half the railing from the ship's side and cracking the deck before Hereni drove it back with a shield spell.

'Hereni!'

The *Petunia* had crept backwards, knocked by a wave and Farden's fading magick. The cliff loomed dangerously close as another wave came at them and reared to strike.

Hereni slammed the sails again, making the mast creak awfully. It held, at least for now, and Lerel held them straight as they ploughed into the crest of the wave. Seawater washed the deck and sizzled against Farden's armour, and for a gut-twisting moment, the *Petunia* hovered in midair before crashing back to the waters.

Lerel pointed at more fins gathering. 'Get it done, Farden!'

Farden didn't argue and threw all his magick at the rockface. Shields punched the water outwards, making *Petunia* lurch while a vortex spell got the water spinning once more. The whirlpool dragged at the waters, pulling them downwards as Farden's vortex spell tunnelled to the ocean floor. He could see a nose now. They had to be close.

Farden heaved, forcing a gale down into the whirlpool to blow the water back if even just for a moment. Whatever it took for air to touch the giant's lips. That was all that mattered. Farden bent his magick to his will, hands shaking.

A sharp crunch came from the boat as a shark bit a chunk from the keel. Water sprayed through an open hatch. 'We're sinking!' cried Lerel.

Farden lashed at the waves one more time and was rewarded with a deep rumble. A crack spread up the face of the cliff and dislodged a boulder the size of a wagon. Farden let his magick die as he threw up an involuntary shield spell, but the hefty chunk of stone missed the bow by an inch, conveniently landing on the head of a circling shark instead. Both sank immediately.

'Take my hand!' Farden yelled as stones littered the deck. The rift in the cliff face was spreading. Waves trembled and cowered as a deep boom sounded within the mountain. Hereni held the wind spell for as long as possible while Lerel vaulted and sprinted across the deck. Just as Hereni clamped a hand onto Farden's waiting gauntlet, Lerel seized hers in a flying leap, and Farden whisked them both into oblivion.

Behind them, as the sea reclaimed what the magick had stolen, water cascaded almost to the tip of Ossas, taking the *Petunia* with it. On the first wave, a crack split her bow, and on the second crash of vengeful water, she broke in two, right across the middle.

❧

Farden skidded on rock with a clang. Lerel continued her momentum and crashed into a nearby pile of crab pots with a yell. Hereni sprawled, magick still dancing around her fingers.

'I hated that quite intensely,' Farden panted into the grass.

'Do you think we did it?' gasped Lerel.

Metal clattered as the mountain shook beneath them. Evorsk was standing nearby with his arms held wide, his head bowed.

A blast of a horn broke his reverent smile.

It was no sound of the mountain, but several hundred Golikan soldiers cresting the hill at the bottom of the mountain. The Mogacha brandished the tools and weapons they'd stolen from their oppressors, but they were tired and worn and numbered half the Golikans.

'Help us, Farden.'

Farden intended to, and with legs shaky from the wallowing sea, he stomped down the black rock slope and into the town's stink of blubber, fish, and dead meat. He felt a rumble in every step, but Ossas was being slow to wake. He couldn't help but wonder if they had done enough, and perhaps all they'd done was cause a stumble in his slumber.

Farden didn't have time to think. Arrows were already raining on the edge of the Mogacha town. Farden swatted the volleys aside with a blast of shield magick and held Gunnir flat. Air rippled as a quake spell ran through the earth. As the first soldiers began to charge, the ground began to crack and sink underneath them. A whole rank went sprawling, much to the fury of their captain sitting on his armoured persnippen, who waved a tree branch like a weapon and demanded death.

Farden gave it to him, letting Gunnir loose and carving a path across the hillside to cut the soldiers' formation in two, divided by a wall of fire. Bodies fell screaming. The captain fell from his mount, and the persnippen made the educated decision to run in the opposite direction. Hereni saw to him, aiming a fireball right at his arse and blasting him into a nearby broken cairn.

Another rank and file charged the mage, and once again he sought to break them with another quake spell, but the ground shifted before he could raise Gunnir.

'That wasn't me!' yelled Farden.

Hereni's eyes were saucers. 'Your friendly giant?'

The question was answered by an enormous peal of thunder as a crack split the hillside. It ran straight from Ossas' peak and all the way down the hillside, splitting Hereni and Farden apart with a chasm that kept growing by the second.

Several Golikans were swallowed by the rupture immediately and screamed as they fell into the dusty dark. Farden backed off immediately. A few of the soldiers still clung to the battle and ran towards him with weapons high. Farden indulged them as the earth moved beneath him. Staggering and jumping as cracks spread, he swung Gunnir in vicious circles, cutting blades and throats and hands from arms. A particularly violent shake put him on his back, and a sword crashed against his helmet. It would have been a lucky blow if not for the fact Farden wore Scalussen armour. The sword bounced free, and Farden stabbed the bearer in the neck as the mountain shook again.

Cries cut the air as the Mogacha fled the peak. The crack was widening, with huge chunks breaking off into the ocean. It seemed the rock and earth had grown around Ossas over the thousand years he'd slumbered, and now he broke free of his wrappings.

Farden ran for Lerel, who was clinging to a Mogacha house. More of the peak was breaking off, but part of it was also rising, too. A giant skull of stone cut the horizon, and Farden could have cheered. Most of the Mogacha did. Coelo horns were blown as Ossas kept on rising. A torrent of dust and falling rock covered his features, but Farden could already see two enormous green eyes turning upon the scene of battle. First, they regarded the Mogacha, who had fallen to their knees in worship with arms wide, and then they turned on Farden, who had just managed to seize Lerel's hands.

'Was this a good idea?' she yelled.

Before Farden could answer, Ossas climbed the clifftop, stepping up as easily as the mage might clamber onto a hay bale. The Golikans who had been so insistent on fighting even when the world broke beneath them had come to a gawping halt. Ossas rose above the landscape, still a mountain in every right, but with limbs made of gigantic slabs of stone that were bound like muscle to bone. Long-armed and short-legged, Ossas had a skeletal look, and his head was no more than a skull carved from black and emerald granite. Earth and grass draped over his hulking shoulders, and seawater still poured from his rocky skin. Fists like warships clenched as he reached for the Golikan captain who had just clambered out of a crater, armour burned to a crisp. There was barely a moment for him to scream before Ossas' fist reached over Farden's head and squished the man to paste against the remaining hillside. The rest of the invaders were swatted hundreds of feet into the air, and Farden found himself grinning as the lucky few disappeared over the hillside once again, hopefully never to return.

A mighty cheer went up from the Mogacha once more. Farden surveyed the battlefield and saw that apart from being split in two, almost all of the town had survived. The Mogacha built strong, and only a few buildings had collapsed under the earthquake. No more than two houses had fallen into the ocean. The rest on the south side of the town found themselves with an unexpected and frightening sea view. The peak of Ossas had gone, replaced by the giant himself, who cast a heavy shadow over Farden and the others.

'Who wakes Ossas?' the giant thundered with a voice only rock and dirt could muster. Farden hadn't quite expected the giant to have a voice.

'Farden!' yelled Evorsk, standing upon a wagon. Farden took his helmet from his head and revealed a frown.

'I think you're up, mage,' Lerel said between clenched teeth, looking quite bedraggled and more than a little concerned. 'You better hope you're right.'

Farden approached warily, utterly unsure of the etiquette or protocol of dealing with a giant who had just awoken from a thousand-year slumber. Not that he had ever cared for such things, but now they seemed an enormously good idea. 'I woke you,' he shouted.

Ossas boomed with a single word, making Farden's bones shake. 'Why?'

'To kill a god,' Farden replied. 'One that would see the world – and your people – burn.'

'Never liked gods. It was a god that drove Ossas here.'

Ossas took a knee that shook the earth and leaned close to Farden. Ossas' eyes were flecks of fire, burning deep within two hollows Lerel could have sailed a ship through. His teeth were standing stones, sharp edged and guarding a throat as black as a Jar Khoum tunnel. 'You fought for them?'

Farden rested Gunnir on a fallen rock. 'I did.'

'Why?' Ossas asked, breath like a wind and volume almost on the edge of painful.

Farden could do nothing but shrug. 'They were kind to me once. Now, they needed somebody to fight for them. That's what I've always done. It's a duty.'

'Duty,' Ossas thundered. 'Ossas can smell magick on you.'

'And so you should,' Farden replied.

'Ossas like you, tiny one.'

'Thank you, and you can call me Farden,' he said with a bow. He was starting to like Ossas as well. At least he didn't come with a peculiar sailor that Farden didn't quite understand.

'You woke Ossas. You saved Ossas' people. For these gifts, Ossas will aid you in return.'

Farden stared between Ossas great eyes. 'That's it? You'll help?'

'Ossas will, until his people are in need again.'

The mage clanged his spear and tried not to smile too widely. 'Then it's a deal.'

While Ossas turned his attention to the Mogacha coming to touch his enormous hands and singing songs, a smile crossed the giant's skull, too, and Farden couldn't help but stare.

'Well, fuck. He really is a friendly giant,' Hereni said, appearing by Farden's side.

'Who knew?' Farden said, trying to ignore the feeling that blind luck was behind their victory. It didn't matter. Loki's head on a spike mattered.

'And what of you, Evorsk?' Farden asked the man as he approached with arms open once again, as if he was stuck that way.

'Prayers answered. Good day for Mogacha. Stay for feast!' said Evorsk.

Farden smiled and bowed. 'I wish we could, but war calls us back.'

'Save us,' Evorsk said, features solemn, and although Farden blamed his grasp of the Commontongue, there was something about the man's words that stabbed him in the gut.

Once Ossas had retreated back into the sea, already striding west for New Scalussen, Farden held out his hand for Hereni and Lerel. 'One down, hopefully several more to go.'

'Most people would be happy with a keraken and a giant, you know,' muttered Lerel as Gunnir began to whine.

Fortunately, Farden was not most people.

CHAPTER 30
OF SPIES & SPIDERS

Break me down, break me free,
sail me down the river to the sea.
For Arka know the smell of salt and wave,
where winds were born and mages brave.
Cast me deep in the current's flow,
of magick's blessing and let me grow.
May the Arka recall my name,
in silence, know I wielded flame.
Break me down, break me bare,
to brandish storm and iron air.
For Arka know the calling home,
Where sea meets land and power meets stone.
'THE MAGE'S SONG', AN ARKA BALLAD

Loki wanted to burn every book he saw to ashes. He wanted to unravel every scroll and toss them from the open window that snuck snow into the Spire.

'Do we have nothing else? Did Malvus burn Arfell on a jilted whim and irritate me from the grave? I think so.'

The greybeard scholars didn't say anything, keeping their eyes low.

Loki picked through the mess of scrolls again. His notebook, a worn thing he had found in his pockets, was almost as empty as when he had begun, bright and early that morning, before the snow had come to laden the city. It was preposterous for a god to sit and study like some mewling school child, but there was nowhere else to glean the whispers he needed. Whispers of tharkun.

The problem was they were either scant or useless.

There was one source Loki kept coming back to: a simple poem in a sheaf of skald's songs. The Doomriddle. Its parchment was so old its edges snapped away as he grabbed at them again.

' "Three tasks every god and mortal fears to face await," ' Loki read the words in a mutter. 'Sounds somewhat familiar, don't you think?'

Again, not a single nervous squawk of an answer came.

' "Torrid waters fail to halt you, yet the highest price awaits. Turn where men fail to tread without sinking, with shadow in your right eye at dawn 'til roaring waters. West lies Utiru's wrath. Scarred sister's light burns the path, terror dark and crystal sharp. Cut the throat of your sweetest dreams or lose your mind." '

Silence once more.

Loki tapped the parchment with his fingernail, letting his mind wander. 'Where did you go, Farden? What did you see?' Loki muttered.

East was the answer, and torrid waters, Loki knew. They were the Thundershores, and he had stared into their currents once before, after he had staggered across the desert beaten and defeated. Farden and Mithrid must have gone south from there to meet Utiru.

Utiru. Loki had never questioned the name before. Never wondered what Farden had suffered, and yet here he was staring at a charcoal drawing done in some panic, for its lines were jagged, and if one squinted, it was possible to make out a thin wraith of a figure, its haunted mask of a face hideous and mid-scream.

'It seems my choices are few. We'll see what this Utiru is, and which side it'll choose,' said Loki as he got to his feet. 'Though going east again feels like going backwards, not forwards, wouldn't you see?'

The scholars clung to their silence. As they should. One leaked blood from the ears. There wasn't a heartbeat or a soul left in any of their gaunt corpses. Candles withered to smoke and pages scattered as the god vanished.

Days, it must have been, but all Mithrid had was guesswork without a sun or moon to show the passage of time. Fitful sleep stole all sense of passing hours. She didn't know whether she slept for moments or a whole day, and only the blind woman Jeasin could tell her.

Days, and Mithrid was aching to see star or sunlight. She had steeled herself against Loki's tricks, but his dungeons were formidable.

Days, and already she felt the urge of failure. It was slight. Merely a sliver of a thought, but it was a thought nonetheless. The kind that spoke from the darkness of the mind and reminded her of what she fought not to be.

Jeasin chuckled abruptly. 'Gods, I can hear you thinking from here, girl.'

'I'm no girl,' Mithrid muttered back, knowing she would hear.

'He'll come for you soon. Those in power don't have patience, see? It's what the power teaches them. Loki will—'

As if by magick, the woman's predictions came true in an instant. Runes flashed over the door as it was unlocked and opened. Three Scarred mages waited with shackles and a hood.

'Go fuck yourselves,' said Mithrid.

Jeasin laughed at that.

'Loki wants you,' said one of the mages.

'Tell him I'm busy.'

The Scarred had no patience for her cheek, yet they approached with an amount of caution that made Mithrid smile. Even so, they seized her with unforgiving strength and dragged her back and forth while they got the hood over her head. Mithrid fought their every effort. Of course she did. What kind of prisoner would she be if she did not fight?

A crack of a fist to her jaw put her half to sleep. Mithrid lolled in their grip, smelling nothing but dirty sackcloth and old vegetables. The problem with Loki was questioning everything. It was impossible to tell how deep his plans burrowed, or how many steps he'd thought ahead. Was an old kitchen sack on purpose or a happenstance? Mithrid didn't know, and it annoyed her intensely as they dragged her into another room.

A chair greeted her arse. Manacles and shackles came to wrap her wrists and ankles. Not a candle or lantern showed its light through the gauze of the sackcloth.

'Where's Loki?' Mithrid asked.

A fist answered her, straight to the stomach. Mithrid almost threw up in her hood.

'What is the Outlaw King planning?' The voice was not Loki's. It was reedy, human, and devoid of any of the usual sarcasm.

'I don't know,' Mithrid answered.

Another fist knocked her jaw, clashing her teeth together. 'What is the Outlaw King planning? What is his next move?'

'He and I have had a falling out. He hasn't invited me to council in a long time. I don't know.'

This time a blow to the head, clipping her ear. Mithrid felt something hot drip down her neck.

'What is the Outlaw King planning?'

Mithrid heard the rush of air and the grunt of effort and flinched, but a crack of a door and a shine of light stopped the fist at her cheek.

'No, no, no!' That was unmistakably Loki. 'I said to question her, not beat her, curse you!'

There was an immediate shuffling and recoiling. A golden light shined before somebody was thrown up against the wall. Bones crunched, and a throat was strangled before a heavy thud met the stone.

'Take the hood off.'

'Aye,' said a gruffer voice.

The hood was dragged off to reveal Loki with a horrified look on his face. The gruff man was a burly Scarred, twice the age of the others gathered like vultures around her in the dark room.

Loki flicked a hand, raising shutters and spilling blinding light across the stones. Mithrid winced even though she was glad for it.

'If you want information, I don't know anything, and even if I did—'

'Don't give me that old speech about not telling me even if you did know. I don't want information. I have a much grander job for you, Mithrid Fenn,' Loki said. 'Release her.'

'You put a lot of trust in this collar,' Mithrid said. 'I could still get you with a blade, you know. Or my bare hands.'

'That I do,' Loki said with his trademark smile. 'And I invite you to try.'

Mithrid was muscled down stair after stair after stair until her knees began to wobble and her ears popped. The cobbles of the city were soon under her feet. It was a short walk between the grand Arkathedral gates to the gallows Loki had constructed. What was confusing was there were three nooses waiting for necks.

'You mean to hang me?' Mithrid asked. Despite Loki's promise, she wondered whether one was for her.

'Not you, Mithrid,' Loki said with a chuckle. 'Your friends. Your comrades.'

Mithrid's gut fell as she was led up the zigzag stairs and onto the platform. A crowd had already gathered, and it booed eagerly at the sight of her. She was clothed in nothing but trews and tunic, armour gone, but they knew who she was by the fiery hair that blew in all directions in the wind. Mithrid likely stared upon the same faces who had stood in front of their god while she tried to strangle him. She could almost feel the hatred burning in the multitudes.

Mithrid tried to hold her head proud as Loki had her face the crowd. A few rotten vegetables came her way. She looked into every baying mouth and attempted to sneer. The twinges of guilt within turned to anger, which soon became a rage that matched their hatred toe to toe.

Loki waved his hand across the crowd for silence. They gave it to him gradually, and it was then that Loki brought the others onto his pathetic stage.

Two men and a woman were dragged up steps and onto the boards. The crowd jeered so loud it made the prisoners wince. More vegetables flew through the air. A bottle smashed against a beam.

'For the crimes…!' Loki attempted, but the cries of the crowd drowned him out. Like a humble benefactor, he spread his hands and called for peace before he spoke again. 'For the crimes of spying and treachery, these servants of the Outlaw King and Scalussen will be hanged!'

Another cheer erupted. It was then that Loki turned to Mithrid. 'And you'll be pulling the lever.'

Mithrid spat. 'That's ridiculous. I will not.'

Loki leaned close. 'You either pull the lever, Mithrid, or you'll die before their necks break.'

'Why? So you can fulfil your need for violence and pain? You're sick in the head, Loki. You always have been, from what Farden tells me, and I won't indulge it.'

Loki grabbed Mithrid above the collar, making the crowd hiss and call for her murder. His fingers dug into her throat. His golden eyes bored into hers.

'You have to choose. Your life, or theirs. Just as you decided in the ice fields when you woke Irminsul and chose the fate of thousands upon thousands.'

Mithrid swallowed. 'You can't make me.'

'I think I can,' Loki said as he squeezed tighter, making her gasp. Mithrid remembered a time very recently when he had a similar grip around her throat, but there was no escaping him now.

'It's simple. The spies who came to make sure you were alive. Or you,' Loki uttered again. 'Your choice, Mithrid Fenn.'

Mithrid looked down the line of spies, each of them pleading with their eyes. It didn't matter that Mithrid didn't recognise them. They had risked their necks to spy on the Arka and Loki. And here she was, grasping the lever to kill her own kind.

'You can't make me,' Mithrid said again, even though it was useless. Loki mocked her with his bared teeth. His hand clasped hers, sending a shock and a heat through her body. Mithrid wasn't sure if he pushed or she did, but the gallows' trapdoors opened with a thud, and the three Scalussen spies plummeted until ropes tautened with a snap of bone. Only one survived the fall to wriggle his lungs empty, and Mithrid strained as she watched him choke and gasp. She tried to turn away but found herself frozen.

'Remember this moment,' Loki whispered. 'And consider why you thought their fate was lesser to yours, when you haven't even decided what you'll be.'

To the horrific sounds of gurgling and fighting for breath, Mithrid reeled.

'Back inside with her,' came Loki's order, and the hood was wrapped around her head once more. 'Take her to my chambers.'

The Scarred mages offered no complaint and seized her roughly.

It was the thick leader of the Scarred that bent close to Loki's ear. Too close for the god's comfort.

'Who were those bastards? I don't remember the watch catching them,' asked the mage.

Loki raised his hands to his adoring audience and drank in their praise. 'Who knows, Captain. Merely some miscreants I had scraped off the streets.'

The burly chap laughed, and Loki decided to let him live as they wound back into the Arkathedral behind Mithrid.

Mithrid found herself in a room lit by candles and lanterns. Far too many of them, in her opinion.

The word fate dangled in her mind like a jewel on a string. She refused to let it occupy her; the god had many tricks, and she couldn't fall for any of them. Yet the gurgling of the hanging spies played in her ears and tugged at her insides. She hadn't pulled the lever. At least that's what she told herself over and over.

'Let's talk, shall we?' asked a voice in the corner. Mithrid had thought herself alone and cursed herself for jumping.

'You can talk, Loki, if you wish,' she replied, voice muffled by the sack over her head. 'I still won't tell you anything you want to know.' Mithrid contemplated springing across the room and trying to bite him, but she couldn't do much else with her wrists and ankles still bound.

'Those buffoons treated you poorly before, Mithrid, and you can rest assured I won't be doing the same,' said Loki.

'The softer approach is it?' she snorted. 'Good guard, bad guard? I'll play along. If you want to talk, then answer me this: why am I here?'

'You are here, Mithrid, because you're meant for something other than what Farden has planned for you,' Loki said. 'Something more than the tool he treats you as. You're mollycoddled, doubted at every turn, and I'll wager you don't want that. You've never wanted that.'

Mithrid hated that he had taken the very words out of her mind. 'Your gilded tongue won't work on me.'

Loki approached, wine swirling in a goblet by the sound of it. The sack scraped her face as it was pulled away. The god stared down at her, aglow with a golden light. 'Yet you know I'm right.'

Mithrid tried to spit, but her mouth was too dry. She hadn't eaten or drank in a day. Maybe more. 'You have no idea about me.'

'Don't I? I've known you since you set foot in Scalussen. I was Skertrict, remember? I saw you discover what you could become, saw you taste the first inklings of importance. I mean, really. How Durnus did not notice my name, I'll never know.'

'Am I supposed to be impressed?' Mithrid said with a shrug.

Loki tutted. 'Skertrict. Rearrange the letters.'

'Trickster,' she muttered after a moment, voice flat and unimpressed. 'How very clever of you.'

'Wasn't it?' Loki bit his lip and flashed his eyes before he sat. With a sigh, he crossed his legs and waved his wine in a circle. 'I know you all too well, Mithrid Fenn. A troubled girl with her father and family dead. A thirst for revenge of an orphan against an emperor. A power she doesn't understand. A power that can defy the strongest mage in all the lands, her only ally, or so it seems, now pitted against a god of lies. It sounds like a skald's tale, if you ask me.'

'I don't think anyone did ask,' hissed Mithrid. 'You've no right to sum me up, and you do a poor job of it.'

'Wine?' Loki offered.

Even if was offered by her foulest enemy and could have been thoroughly poisoned, Mithrid needed a drink. 'I'll take some. If only so I can spit it back in your face.'

Loki poured her a golden cup anyway and was kind enough to unshackle her hands. Her ankles he kept locked in iron. Once again, she almost reached for his throat, but managed to hold herself back. Now was not the time.

'What did I really do to you, if you think about it? Aside from setting you free in the ice fields,' he asked.

Mithrid sipped the deliciously cold alcohol. 'You tricked us. Stole magick. Perverted Malvus into a creature that pulled the daemons from the sky. Sent leviathans after those I loved. Threatened to kill me. Tried to kill me, in fact, and forced the death of Durnus, my friend.'

Loki waved his wine about again. 'Well, when you put it like that.'

Mithrid sneered.

'Can't we simply talk, Mithrid? It's better to talk with your enemy instead of clash blades, no?'

'No.'

'I wonder what you know about Utiru.'

The name came like a sucker punch, and Mithrid didn't smother her surprise as swiftly as she would have liked. 'I know you should go stick your head in her cave and see what you find.'

'Her, is it?' said Loki with intrigue. 'A creature, perhaps? I see the fear in those eyes, Mithrid.'

Mithrid chided herself silently. 'The keraken would pull her limb from limb.'

Loki snorted as he rose to fetch more wine. 'We'll see.'

'For all your hatred of us, you act so human,' Mithrid uttered. 'You act like you deserve all of this world like you built it with your bare hands, when all you did was lie and steal. It's despicable. Pathetic. As common as a rogue in an alley.'

Loki splashed wine in his goblet and left the bottle on a table near to Mithrid. 'You're the actor, Mithrid. You are far from normal, and yet you strive to play it every day, hoping they'll accept you when all they do is fear and stare. But while others might see a freak of nature, or a poison, I see the answer to the problem. I see a solution and a salvation.'

Chains rattling, Mithrid shook herself as if it would shrug off his lies. 'What problem?'

'Why, the problem of magick,' said Loki. 'What was it that killed your mother?'

Mithrid flinched at that. 'How do you know about my mother?'

'Like I said: trickster,' Loki said with a grin. 'Answer the question.'

'She was killed by one of Malvus' men.'

'For using magick, is that right?'

'More or less.'

'And what was it that killed your father?'

'Mages.'

'Because you used a spellbook,' Loki reminded her of that guilt. 'And who is it who now holds you back? A mage? How interesting.'

Mithrid held her head high. 'I told you, Loki, your lies and games won't work on me.'

'It's not a lie that magick has interfered and wounded you time and time again.'

'Cut the shit, Loki. What do you want from me?'

Loki raised his goblet. 'Finally, we're on the same page. It's simple, really,' he said, leaning forwards in his chair. 'I want you to kill Farden for me.'

Mithrid was speechless.

Loki stayed deadly serious.

'That will never happen,' Mithrid answered, starting to laugh.

'Now who's lying?' Loki replied. 'What was it that ruined your life again? Ah yes, magick. And who wields the most magick in this sordid little world? Oh, that's right. Farden.'

'You're mad.'

The god scoffed at that. 'So says everyone who doesn't see a different future.'

Mithrid waited until Loki took another sip of his wine before she pounced, grabbing the wine bottle with her hand upended. She smashed the stout end against the table with a crash, then lunged for the god with its sharp ends.

Broken glass was inches away from the god's neck when Loki's magick erupted. A golden light flared that burned her eyes and skin as she was thrown against the wall of the room. A chest of drawers was reduced to splinters and shards beneath her, and she rolled back and forth in its debris.

'My fault, in fairness,' sighed Loki, not the slightest bit perturbed or rattled. He simply looked amused. 'I did tell you to try me, after all. At least we have got that out of the way.'

Scarred mages burst through the chamber door, staring down at Mithrid with knives and hands raised.

'Mithrid needs escorting back to her cell,' Loki ordered.

'Fuck you,' Mithrid wheezed as they hauled her upright.

Loki had the balls to wave to her as she was dragged from the room on her arse. 'Say hello to Jeasin for me,' he said before the door was slammed.

Loki was left to swill his wine. He decided to take the dregs for a walk to what was quickly becoming his favourite place in the rat-riddled town: the rooftop.

Loki smiled at the biting wind as snow stabbed little lances of cold into his warm skin. Perhaps it was the vintage he glugged, or how well his game with Mithrid was playing out, but Loki decided to let down the constant guard he kept up. The guard that kept him from the view of his kin in Haven.

It wasn't long before a shadow shifted in his peripheries.

'You have taken the girl. Why?' whispered a voice.

Loki turned to look at the spectral form of Evernia. She stood with her arms crossed, and she wore the usual disapproving frown the Arka sculptors had captured so accurately on every statue and shrine that now lay shattered and thrown in the Port of Rós.

'Because you underestimated her,' Loki said with a mocking tut.

'I came to ask you once more to put an end to this, Loki. You and Farden will stop at nothing to kill each other. Your battle will split the world in two. That is not a god's calling.'

Loki heard a hint of worry in the goddess' voice. 'You're more afraid of Farden than you are of me,' he surmised. 'Aren't you?'

Evernia stepped closer. 'I wonder if you had been born with us, instead of in Haven, you might have understood. The void turned your mind. There is still time to change your ways.'

'Save your platitudes. Magick and the lie you call sacrifice changed my mind,' said Loki, leaning against the marble. 'You know what I wonder? Why you've come to pay me a visit so quickly? So conveniently timed. You've spent years manoeuvring your favourite mage around. Don't tell me he's spurned you, Evernia, and this is the only way you can feel like you're of use?'

Evernia didn't reply. She merely faded out of view, making the distant lights of the Spire shiver as she disappeared.

Loki turned east with a cackle, contemplating what the horizon held for him. He reached inside his pockets, searched for a moment, then brought out a scroll. He pulled it open with a crackle and angled it to the city lights to stare at its detail. Once again, he took in the daubs of white paint and figures of pale flesh and the charcoal swirls around them. Poison, Azen had called Mithrid, and Loki had heard the word the elf had spat at her. *Lakrimur*. Loki's elvish wasn't as accurate as he would have liked, and he mulled over what it meant.

With a twist of his hand, more of the scroll was revealed, and Loki studied a serpent drawn in bright oranges and ochres. Crimson flame poured whenever it touched the black smudge of earth. Loki tilted his head before rolling the scroll away and clicking his fingers.

Krauslung melted before his eyes and was replaced by a range of different and grander mountains, so tall that snow covered them from base to jagged tip. The Emberteeth.

Snow swirled around Loki's feet as he walked across the barren rock and towards the mightiest of their slopes. A volcano rumbled above him, its peak broken and glowing. A pillar of black smoke poured from its toothed crater, blacker than the night that wrapped it. The mountain stood slightly shorter than it had in the past, and it was wider at the peak where it had been blasted away, but it was no less formidable and imposing. Colours and lights danced in the sky where its smoke met the clouds. Brushstrokes of blues, crimsons, and greens ran across the sky, drawn by some unseen artist. With a wave of his hand, Loki felt the magick in the air, crackling between the dust and wandering cinders. A blotch of fire escaped the volcano to draw a smoking trail in the snow of its sweeping slopes, far too close for comfort, but Loki kept walking.

Rock huts dotted the landscape, newer than any of the ruins behind him. A spire and a city had once stood at his back, but now it was a crater and a smear of rubble beneath a landslide of volcanic rock. Where great glaciers had once covered the earth beyond, only bare rock and blackened tundra remained. The bodies of the last war that had survived the fire but not the smoke had yet to be buried. They stayed frozen, ghosts trapped and fated to wander and howl to the night. There was nobody to build a pyre for them besides the meagre efforts of the nomads who had set up camp on the slopes of Irminsul.

Kharander. Loki remembered their name. He had thought them all dead after Farden and Mithrid had coaxed Irminsul to unleash its fury, but replacements had arrived. Perhaps the eruption had forged more followers of the faith that called the volcano a god.

When they weren't huddled around cooking fires and banging pots with spoons, they built intricate towers of balancing rocks and bowed in prayer to the volcano. The pot-stirrers studied Loki as he strode through their camp, wary but not uninviting. Loki made sure to smile and nod.

A crowd of worshippers spread across the slope as if an invisible barrier stopped them from going further. Loki walked between them while they lifted and bowed their hands, muttering prayers to themselves while Irminsul rumbled away. While Loki watched, another streak of magma came hurtling from its open mouth and sprayed the charcoal slopes with fresh sparks. Pale figures dotted the slopes, forming a faint grey path through the snow, the knuckles of rock like cremated dough, and the spitting, steaming vents. Pairs carried stretchers of frozen bodies far up to the lip of Irminsul where they were surrendered to the fire. Judging by the amount of new bodies dotting the landscape with broken stretchers beside them, it was an unenviable job. A task for true believers.

Loki took a step towards the volcano, eliciting a moan from the Kharander around him. The nearest reached to grasp his coat with filthy hands as they began to chant. Others put their hands to them, until Loki stood with a cape of soot-covered worshippers.

He could have jumped. He could have used his magick and his godly privileges, but something told him he needed to make this pilgrimage himself. Voices rose as Loki took another step, and another, until he marched through the rubble and frozen magma, boots crunching on pumice and snow and wondering whether he was right. Only the mountain's heights would tell him.

CHAPTER 31
A TEST

Though I have spoken of the walking mountains they call bastions before,
they deserve another warning! From their fearsome tusks the length and
breadth of the grandest pines, curved like a bloody sickle. Their long,
serpentine noses are but another arm, designed to reach and grasp and
crush! Beware their stomping feet and terrifying war-cry that bleeds the
ears! And think not to put an arrow in such a beast, dear traveller, for their
hides are thick as Krauslung granite.
FROM 'SURVIVAL IN PARAIA', BY MASTER WIRD

Mithrid awoke with a start to the hammering of the door. An iron
hatch at its base opened and a wooden tray slid into the dark. Two
wooden bowls of slop clanked together, spilling some of their foul
contents on the stone.

Mithrid fetched them with a sigh. Loki chose when to feed
them, chose when to fetch them, and when she would wake. The
monotonous control was growing tiresome, chipping away at her
resolve. The only freedom she was allowed was when to piss.

Jeasin was weaving something out of her frayed threads with a
splinter of wood. They were on their second to last candle, and the
flickering light made the woman's face ghostly. Mithrid put a bowl in
front of Jeasin, and her hands found it immediately.

'What is it today? Brown shite or grey shite?'

'Grey shit.'

'Joy. The food's got worse since you been in 'ere.'

Mithrid sighed as she tried to gulp some of the lukewarm porridge down without gagging. She was glad for the light, otherwise she couldn't pick out the maggot wiggling on the edge of the bowl.

Jeasin put her serving aside. 'He didn't used to be like this, y'know.'

'What do you mean?'

'I mean he was always a twat, but two decades ago, he weren't evil. Just a sarcastic prick.'

'You've known him that long?'

'I met him in Albion. Like I told you, Farden came to kill the duke Kiltyrin for crossin' him. In doin' so, he got me all wrapped up in his dark business, and we 'ad to escape Tayn. Loki was waitin' for us at Farden's hovel on the coast. Him and that gryphon.'

'Ilios.'

Jeasin spoke around a mouthful. 'Loki was always different, though. One night, Loki thought I was sleepin', but I saw him dreamin', movin' all about like he was in a nightmare. Woke up with a start and brooded the rest of the night. I didn't think shadows of gods slept, never mind dreamed, but he did both. And I reckon whatever he dreamed that night changed him. That and starin' at Farden's magick. Now he's flesh and bone, there's a madness in him.'

'And he's got nothing but domination in mind. Got a taste for power and adoration and can't get enough.'

'There's somethin' more. I know minds better than most, and Loki's out to prove somethin'. Better. More. He dreamed of a different him, and now he won't stop until he gets it. Farden simply plays the part of his nemesis.'

'All a game,' said Mithrid, managing to find the bottom of the bowl. One fleck of some nondescript white meat was hiding there. 'He told me he wanted me to kill Farden.'

Jeasin slurped, taking her time to answer. 'And would you?'

'If you have to ask, then you don't know me very well,' Mithrid replied.

'I might not be able to see your face, but I 'ear the hurt in you. I reckon you have dreams just as big as Loki's, that you might be somethin'. And you've been it once or twice, but you've also had a taste and want more. Now you're full of rage. Vengeance you thought you left behind for love and peace, but you're addicted and have no idea who you'd be without it. So you keep pushin' and rushin' into danger, even though you been told time and time again what it would do. Am I doin' well so far?'

Mithrid clanked her bowl on the floor, making Jeasin twitch. *Why did everybody insist on telling her tale for her?* 'Sounds about right,' she muttered.

'I known plenty like it. Farden's the same with death and duty. Me with the finer things. We've all chased a dream to the edge of a cliff.'

Mithrid had heard plenty of problems, but she was only interested in answers. 'Then what do we do?'

'We give up, or we jump and get what's comin' to us,' Jeasin sighed. ' I jumped, and that's why I'm in 'ere.'

The two sat in silence for a time. Jeasin ran her finger around the bowl to get every last trace of the foul porridge. 'Could you do it?' she asked at last.

'What?'

'Kill Farden? And I don't mean in 'ere and 'ere,' said Jeasin, poking her chest and forehead. 'Physically kill him?'

Mithrid had pondered it before, fleetingly and guiltily. Another dark thought hiding in her mind's shadow. 'Truthfully? I have no idea. I am his utter opposite. A poison to his magick. But even without that, he's one of the best fighters in Emaneska, if not the best. Perhaps. Loki seems to think I could.'

'And again, would you?'

Mithrid tutted at that. 'Farden gave me a home. He gave me a new family. We fight for the same thing.'

'Doesn't sound like you believe that as much as you want. Do you think he's dangerous? What could he choose to do with that spear you told me of?'

'According to everybody else, I'm the dangerous one.'

Another fist pounded the cell door. 'On your knees!' an order drifted through its stout wood and steel.

Mithrid did no such thing. She refused to make it easy for them.

It was Azen that appeared in the doorway. 'Lakrimur,' he muttered before he sketched a circle in the air. Sapphire runes sputtered into life. He clawed at the air between them, and blue light crackled around Mithrid's wrists. She fought, making the shining shackles weaken and fade, but the spikes prickled her neck before too long, and she was forced to endure the stinging touch of the elf's magick, making her skin blister and peel.

'I wager you hate that you need Loki's collar for that to work on me,' Mithrid said snidely.

The elf's spell seized her, slamming her wrists together and yanking her onto her knees and then her face.

'You will speak when spoken to, worm,' the elf whispered in her ear as he crouched like a spider, grabbed a fistful of her hair, and drew a line across her throat with his cold finger.

'Get your hands off me!'

With a flick of the same finger, Mithrid was dragged across the floor with the spell leading the way, clammy skin squeaking on the polished stone and marble.

❦

Jeasin listened to her shouts and yells diminish corridor by corridor, stairwell by stairwell. But the door had not yet closed, and she heard the breathing of two others, stifled by masks. The smell of sweat and blood was rife on them, along with the herbed perfume of a tincture. More of the Scarred mages, no doubt. They stood waiting in the corridor, but the footsteps that entered her cell were quieter than leaves falling to loam.

'What do you want, Loki?' she asked with a sigh. 'If you want somebody to whisper sweet nothings and slap your arse, you'll have to pay like all the others. The price is freedom.'

Loki stood over her. Jeasin could feel his light like a nearby fire.

'Delightful as always, Jeasin,' he said.

'I told you, I'm not goin' to help you turn that girl.'

'That's perfectly fine. Then you can stay in here until you rot to bones and dust.'

'You really think she'll kill Farden?'

Loki laughed. 'See? You're nattering away like old friends already,' he said, taking a moment to think. 'And if you had seen what I've seen that girl do, then you would know she could, if she so chose. Whether she will is partly down to you, Jeasin. Help me convince her, and you can go about your merry way. Free as a cloud to go back to that hole of an island you call Albion.'

Jeasin didn't answer. She thought of a thousand ways in which to score a cheap shot and rake her nails across his ego, but she said not a word until the door shut with a bang.

'Shit.'

Loki had chosen the Arkathedral's throne room as his next stage to perform his irritating dance. With no sack on her head this time, she scowled at the sight of him perched on the marble of the Blazing Throne Farden had quenched. His armour glittered in the light of a hundred candles. It was apparently night, and Krauslung shone beyond the stained glass. Only Scarred stood guard. The Arkathedral felt almost empty save for cursed mages and elves.

Azen's magick dumped her at the foot of the stairs, and the glow vanished from her wrists. The pain in her arms and head subsided.

'You look tired, Mithrid. Sleep is good for the soul, they say. Perhaps you're not ready.'

'Ready for what? More lies and boring questions?'

'For a test.'

'What test?'

'I want to see what your power is all about.'

Mithrid grinned. 'Take this collar off, and you can see up close.'

'You'd like that, I'm sure,' Loki chuckled. 'It must be tiring, being so angry all the time, Mithrid. That can't be good for you either.'

Mithrid cast a look at Loki's Scarred, masked and shaved heads gleaming. 'You want me to squeeze the necks of your mages? Fine. It would be a pleasure.'

'Not yet, and definitely not here. I've just had the place cleaned. Do you know how tough it is to get the scorch of a fireball out of marble? No. I thought not.'

Before Mithrid could answer, Loki swaggered down the steps and seized her by the arm. Mithrid swung a punch, but he caught it easily and twisted her wrist. *Gods, perhaps she was tired.*

'And away we go,' Loki whispered.

A pain lanced through Mithrid's skull as a roar of air and magick deafened her. Cold marble was replaced by freezing rock. The candlelit hall had become a black-mouth cavern ringed with driving snow. Blue lights shone within, showing the gaunt faces of smiling elves. Rubble surrounded them in broken towers.

Mithrid shivered in the fierce and sudden cold. Mages' hands dug into her armpits as she was lifted and dragged across the ruined landscape, following in Azen and Loki's wake.

'I offered my good friend Azen here the rooms of the lords and ladies I had evicted from the Arkathedral, but elves don't seem to like warmth and comfort. Besides, there are too many of them,' Loki chatted idly, pointing to the nooks of the cavern walls, where scores of grey figures crept, and white eyes stared.

A wide space had been cleared at the centre of the cavern. Torches of blue fire marked its borders, where either darkness or elves drifted.

Mithrid fought to quell her shivering. It wasn't merely the cold that was to blame. The baleful, hungry stares of the elves kept her skin prickled and bones shuddering. Mithrid bared her teeth at every one, but they only did the same to her, and theirs were far sharper. They were hateful things.

Loki wrenched her head back by her collar, staring at her fiercely before the collar came free with a fizzing of metal. An unseen hinge and clasp broke it from her neck, and he stood with it in his hands.

'Call this a gift,' Loki whispered, turning his back on her for a moment. Mithrid immediately reached with her shadow, but Loki waggled his finger as its tendrils hovered before his face. He pointed above where a hundred elven archers bent their bows, just waiting for an excuse to fire.

'I wouldn't if I were you. You'll be dead before I am. And we all know how much you value your life. At the cost of three of your own spies, at least.'

Mithrid cursed him. 'Test me then, you vile little creature. Bring me your best mages so I can kill them.'

It was amusing how well petty insults worked on the god, especially when his height came into question.

Loki stood at Azen's side and waved a hand, and one of the Scarred mages lumbered into the clearing. He already looked pleased with himself, as if he thought Loki was giving him a chance to show off against a measly, unarmed girl. Loki clearly hadn't told him.

Mithrid felt a wave wash over her and a pain in her head as the Scarred mage summoned his magick. The cold air wavered above his hands and shoulders where his Book burned. The tattooed keys on his bare forearms shone white as he raised his hands and summoned a flame to burn in each.

Mithrid clicked her fingers, squashing the mage's magick so thoroughly that the flames almost blew out in the next breeze. The mage's confident smile eroded, and he pressed against an invisible wall.

Shadow erupted from Mithrid and surged towards him. The Scarred tried his hardest to fight it, but the darkness seized his wrists and started to bend them outwards. The white light of his keys stuttered as he struggled. Mithrid marched closer to him, forcing him down to the bare rock before she kicked him hard in the nose. Bone crunched under her boot, turning the man's eyes up to their whites. He didn't move again.

The burly and gruff Scarred who had interrogated Mithrid stomped his way into the ring, clearly outraged. Mithrid could see the madness in his wide eyes and the wild magick that had seeped into his mind.

He didn't waste time on ceremony. A whip of lightning stretched between his hands before he lashed it at Mithrid. She swerved, giving her time to throw a wall of shadow at his next attempt. The magick was strong, with some of the sparks pushing against her power. Mithrid pushed back harder, withering the spell and knocking the Scarred to his arse. She smothered him with darkness until she found a grip on his throat and began to squeeze.

The mage seethed and raged, but with every struggle, Mithrid got a tighter grip, pressing against his armour and gripping his skull. The effort wracked her tired body, but the old familiar rage rose to keep her steady. She wanted blood.

'Malvus and Modren killed the mages that slaughtered your home and father. You never got your revenge on them. Mages just like this man,' Loki spoke over the clash of metal and magick, as if reading her mind.

The Scarred pleaded for his god to stop her, but Loki stared on without another word. It was only when a crunch echoed through the cave and the mage fell still that Loki began to clap.

'Fascinating. More impressive than I ever expected, don't you think, Azen?'

The elf wore a downturned expression, eyes full of murder as he stared solely at Mithrid.

Mithrid kept her shadow moving, searching for a way to snap Loki and Azen's necks with it. She didn't often wish for magick, but it was then that she wished for a shield spell. 'Is that it?' she asked.

Azen hissed short and sharply. An elf in a pointed hood and runes covering every inch of his pale skin entered the circle of light. Threads of blue magick already circled his hands, mirroring Mithrid's shadow. Mithrid tensed, conscious she was playing along to Loki's game, and yet the satisfaction of breaking her enemies was too much to ignore. She smiled as the sharp shards of light appeared in the elf's hands.

Mithrid threw out her dark magick, stifling the runes

'Enough!' barked Azen. 'This is heresy. She should be snuffed out like the r—'

'Bored already, Azen?' Loki interrupted him sharply. 'Then why don't we give her the true test, hmm? Bring out your Ekidna.'

Mithrid didn't know what that was, but a scrape at the far end of the cavern lifted the hairs on her arms once more. The elves began to hiss in unison, making it worse.

'What is this, Loki?' she yelled.

Foul lights flickered one by one in the shadow, scores of them, each glowing gently with a haunting light. Mithrid had stared into them before, she realised, as the monster showed the rest of itself.

Dripping jaws parted as the giant creature let out a screech. Mithrid stumbled backwards in pure instinct and a terror she did not want to admit. Her shadow streamed from her hands without even a thought, and as the monster's legs pounded the rock to close the gap between them, she held it up to smash into its horrid face.

Ekidna emitted a burbling screech at the touch of Mithrid's dark magick. Its many claws dug chunks from the ground. Great globs of spittle landed all around her. The smell of rot that accompanied the wind of its breath was almost enough to knock her out, but Mithrid kept pushing against it as she had in Troacles.

'How did you beat, Malvus, I wonder? Was it the same old hate and lust for revenge? Was it thirst for blood?' Loki called to her.

It had been to protect those she loved the most. Mithrid knew that, but she let the bastard dig for his answers.

Yet Loki already wore a smirk. 'It was for the rest of Scalussen, wasn't it? Farden? No. Perhaps another. Somebody who has your heart, I'll wager. How I wonder what this beast would do to them!'

It was cheap manipulation, Mithrid knew that, but the mere mention of Hereni filled her with emotion, and her shadow surged like an enormous fist to clobber Ekidna's face. The repellent monster hugged the ground, gnashing its jaws and refusing to fight back.

Mithrid's jaw dropped as she watched it respond to her shadow, leaning this way and that to avoid wherever she made it flow. Ekidna shuddered its spines, but it didn't attack again and stayed crouched like a miniature mountain, half-drowned in the darkness. Mithrid sagged to the rock, breathless and relieved.

Azen was fuming. He stomped across the rock and managed to backhand Mithrid across the face before she could stop him. His blade was already drawn, and he looked ready to skewer her with it. Mithrid felt the split in her lip and the blood trickling down her nose as she held her breath.

'Azen!' Loki bellowed. 'You will leave her alone! I asked for Farden's head, not hers. She is under my protection.'

'I don't need it,' Mithrid said as she wiped sweat from her forehead and flung it at Azen's feet.

The elf cursed something in his guttural tongue before the sword withdrew. His grasping hand didn't, and he hauled Mithrid up by her hair.

'Your days are numbered,' Azen threatened. 'We will not tolerate you for long.'

'That's enough, Azen,' Loki said from behind her.

Mithrid found cold metal around her neck as the collar closed once again. She fought as she had sworn to, trying to spread her shadow to the necks of both elf and god, but another whack from Azen and the sharp touch of threatening needles made her go still, and she held firm as Loki put shackles around her wrists, staring at her all the while.

Mithrid endured a wash of nausea as the spell dropped her back on white marble. The mages picked her up once more and pointed in the direction of the dungeons. Azen stalked moodily behind them, sword still drawn and menacing. Loki stopped the mages at a window to dismiss them. They retreated down the corridor, still staying close. Azen did the same, though he disappeared up the nearest stairwell.

'Elves,' Loki said. 'What they lack in mirth they make up for in their thirst for blood. Almost rivals my own. Even yours. Don't act like I didn't see the smile on your face when the mage's neck snapped.'

Mithrid didn't realise Loki's hands had crept to her shackles until they came loose. She shrugged away.

Loki gazed out across the city. 'Perhaps I should have been clearer with you when we last spoke. I want you to kill Farden, but not with your hands, for that is my gift to myself. No Mithrid, I want you to kill his magick. All magick, if that's what it takes. You want to know your fate. That is your fate.'

'What could you possibly know of my fate?'

'I know more than you,' Loki said with a mocking tilt of his head. 'I know you're not the first of your kind.'

A scroll appeared in the god's hands, and he pressed it into Mithrid's.

'But I get ahead of myself. Before we reach such a glorious end, you're going to help me another way. You have a way with monsters, it seems, and you're going to help me catch a few.'

Mithrid almost threw the scroll at him. 'Once again, go fuck yourself.'

'Oh, you'll help,' Loki said, ever so sure of himself. 'If you want to know the truth about yourself, you'll help. After all, who knows how powerful you are? What an amusing way to find your limit.'

Mithrid did nothing but curse again as Loki summoned the mages. Words struggled to leave her mouth. Loki was like a worm that had crawled in her ear to listen to her thoughts, and she hated him for it. She could feel her strings being pulled, but a growing part of her was discovering she wanted to pull them, too, and see where they led. Mithrid could almost hear Farden's voice berating her, and she shrugged his ghost away.

'You all right, girl? What did he do to you?' said Jeasin in a worried voice. The woman shuffled closer, her figure dark against the meagre candlelight.

Mithrid collapsed to the floor, the exhaustion she had been hiding taking hold as she cradled her splitting head. 'Nothing I can't handle.'

'And how long will that last?'

Mithrid had no answer for that, and it made the nausea within her worse.

'I don't care,' she lied.

'I'm startin' to think the only way out of this mess is to do what he says,' Jeasin muttered, almost to herself, feeling her way back to the bed.

Mithrid spat blood before wiping her face. A dark smear was left on the back of her hand. She said nothing in reply and hunched up against the wall once more. It was the scroll Loki had given her that stole her attention. More tricks, most likely, but her curiosity won over her caution. With weary fingers, she prised the scroll open and found faded pictures drawn within. It looked ancient, full of beasts and horrors she had never seen.

It was on the third twist of the scroll, and the third scene to greet her eyes, that she saw it. Black shadow stretched across a battle-scape, and there, on a hill, stood figures drawn in white with fire in their eyes and on their heads.

It was Durnus' ghost that breathed in her mind then. A faint memory of a conversation, and words he had spoken in the elvish tongue.

Imur, came the whispers. *Imur means elf.*

Azen had called her *lakrimur*.

Mithrid threw the scroll away in a flash of anger and confusion.

CHAPTER 32
TERRITHA

Those that call Sigrimur a fallen hero have no knowledge of his final days, when the spear spoke to him in whispers, and he agreed to sate its thirst for chaos. Though the spear might have god's blood in it, it also had the malcontent of the elves, and nobody listened to me before he threw himself into battle that last time.

FROM THE LETTERS OF SIGRIMUR'S GENERAL TINA, SENT TO A
DISTANT RELATIVE OF LADY IRIEN

The Siren Queen sighed deeply, checking on the pale sun behind the clouds.

'Where is this giant, then, Farden?' she asked.

'Got something more important to do, have you, Queen Nerilan?' Farden tutted, turning his gaze across the desert and palm forests once more. It had been days since they had left Mogacha, and Ossas had still to appear. It was getting to the point of worry.

Rokhelm was studying footprints in the dust, or sniffing at the breeze, or poking at the husks of coconuts and palm fronds that had fallen in the recent storms. The man was incessantly interested in everything his squid eyes saw.

Warbringer was rather amused by the squid-man, as she called him. Farden spared a look for her warhammer and thought again about what she had said. Of the sacrifice needed to raise Dotharadine, if she was even real and not some minotaur myth. Little else had been found of such a great one or goddess in the libraries, but Farden believed her, and that was what made it more painful. Farden shook his head to the unvoiced question and pressed a finger to his eyes to sharpen and lengthen his vision. A last burst of summer had come to New Scalussen and the southern deserts. The rain-soaked ground had turned to mist and a haze on the horizon. The palms creaked and rustled gently in the warm breeze that blew from the north, where the peaks of the Giant's Shin mountains and distant New Nelska poked their heads from the cloud.

'He's making us look bad,' whispered Lerel.

Hereni nodded. 'Maybe he's lost.'

Rokhelm ambled past, making Elessi smile, even if she thought Farden didn't notice. 'We've heard rumours in the depths. Something has been walking across the ocean from east to west.'

'See?' Farden said as he stared at Nerilan.

Behind them, Ilios whistled low as he dug his claws into the dirt and turned south.

'What does the gryphon see?' Rokhelm whispered as he wandered in that direction.

Ilios trilled, and Farden understood immediately. 'He says something's coming.'

'There,' boomed Towerdawn.

A shadow had appeared in the distant mist, far too small to be Ossas, and for a moment their worst fears plagued every mind while they imagined elves or gods appearing out of the haze, but it was nothing but a coelo. An old and greying beast, shaggy around its giant horn, and in full trot without charging.

'Should we move?' Hereni asked.

But the coelo slowed at the sight of them. It didn't seem to be one bit interested in the group of humans, nor even the minotaur, dragon, and gryphon that stood on the sand. It simply gave a gruff snort, sounding out of breath, and came to a halt nearby. Dirt squelched as the coelo shook itself and sat its arse on the ground. It flashed them a tired look before turning east as if waiting for something.

'What is happening?' Lerel asked.

Birds began to gather, too, circling something to the east like gulls to a fishing boat. Some were indeed gulls, but others were vultures, or hawks, even smaller swifts and crows.

'Do you feel that?' Towerdawn asked, and it took Farden several moments to feel what the dragon felt. A thudding in the ground, and far too rhythmic to be an earthquake.

Farden began to smile and made sure to watch Nerilan's face as Ossas finally arrived. The curious soldiers gathered behind them gasped and whispered as the walking mountain of dark stone emerged from the mist, draped in long, withered strands of kelp around the shoulders and ankles. Even though Farden had witnessed the size of Ossas before, he couldn't help but open his mouth and gawp like a frog, eyes roaming from boulder toes to the skull-like head carved of barnacle-covered rock.

Other beasts like the coelo and the birds followed in his wake. Antelope and buffalo trotted alongside the slow sweeps of his cliff-face legs, trying to keep up with his long strides. He cleared a mile in just a few moments.

'By the bloody gods,' whispered Elessi.

Towerdawn propped himself up on his claws. 'By Thron's breath.'

'Told you,' said Lerel proudly.

Even Warbringer had to crane her neck to take all of Ossas in. 'Shit,' she grunted.

Rokhelm was suddenly next to Farden and walking beside him as he approached Ossas. Farden rolled his eyes but didn't complain.

'Mighty Ossas! Glad you could join us.' Farden yelled as loudly as he could.

With the crunching and rasping of stone that sounded like a landslide, Ossas bent a knee to bring his face closer to the ground. 'Fine land, you have chosen. Old land. It sings to Ossas,' he boomed.

Rokhelm bowed. 'And we remember your song, Ossas.'

'I know your eyes,' was all Ossas said, after staring at Rokhelm and then to the city, where Keraken lounged and slept in the harbour. 'Friend.'

'Others have to be gathered before we take the fight to our enemy. The land is yours to roam and rest on. You and all your… friends,' Farden said as a buffalo came to snuffle at him. It seemed particularly intrigued in Warbringer. The coelo had moved to sniff and rub its hindquarters on one of Ossas' toes.

Ossas seemed to grin, with his jaws cracking and crunching. 'Where Ossas goes, the land follows.' The giant did not rise again, but fell to his backside instead, making the earth shake and armour rattle. 'It has been a long journey, but Ossas will not rest again. Far too long, Ossas has spent asleep.'

'Do you remember any others like you? Like Keraken?' Farden asked, straight to business.

'All dead now. Ossas used to hear their songs in Ossas' sleep, but Ossas does not hear their songs now. Though Ossas does hear songs from the north. One too far away to know. Another a small presence. An angry melody of a god that Ossas does not like.'

'Loki,' muttered Farden.

'And one further north still. Old, like Ossas' song. Angry as well.'

'Thank you, Ossas.'

North. That left far too much world for Farden's liking, but as least he knew there was a chance at recruiting yet another Great One.

Fortunately for him, Peryn was working her way through the ranks of soldiers and Jar Khoum who had come to stare at Ossas.

The witch read from a giant tome as she walked. Peryn hadn't yet noticed the living giant sitting on the plain, and when she broke from the group, she dropped the book in the dirt. The finches and sparrows on her shoulder cheeped and flew to join the other birds perched on Ossas' head and shoulders.

'Fuck, you really did find a giant,' Peryn said in a gasp.

Ossas welcomed her with a blink of his burning green eyes and raised a hand for more birds to land on.

'What's brought you, High Crone?'

Peryn frowned at the title and retrieved her book. When she had found the right page, she stabbed it with a sharp nail. 'Another.'

Farden whirled, putting his hands to the book. 'Where? Who? What?'

Peryn produced a map from her cloak. 'Where is all I know. Falkenrath.'

'Falkenrath, you say?' Rokhelm butted in. 'I remember it before I joined Keraken. A northern city, full of barons sitting on gold thrones.'

'I've found it. At least what it's become,' said Peryn. 'Now it's a town called Orklak, and a hundred miles past Vorhaug. The Skölgard Empire changed its name a long time ago. As for who and what, all I can find are fairytales about a shadow that loves to devour travellers. The roads out of Orklak take a wide sweep north and south, avoiding an area of plain.'

'Devourin' travellers?' Elessi muttered. 'Wonderful.'

'You don't have to come, you know,' said Farden.

'And I won't be. I've already found a Great One. I've done my bit for your mad plan.'

'What if it's just a story?' asked Lerel.

Rokhelm grinned, looking between Elessi and Farden, and shook his head. 'Plenty of tall tales have a truth, and that's why they're magickal. Keraken has explored Nyr's Dagger and almost reached the ice fields, not too far from Vorhaug. He remembers the sound of thunder.'

'There we have it. Peryn, I'll be needing you,' said Farden.

'But the libraries—'

'Can wait. The High Crone is needed.'

Peryn frowned again.

'Who else wants to come fetch a Great One?' asked Farden of his generals and leaders.

Warbringer raised her hammer, making Farden narrow his eyes.

'Waking a giant was enough for me,' said Lerel.

Ilios whistled.

'Of course you can come,' replied Farden.

For some reason, Hereni chose that moment to leave, aiming straight at the city. Elessi followed, flashing a look at Farden. Rokhelm, of course, wandered after Elessi.

With the four of them gathered, Farden pointed Gunnir at the sky.

'Don't get any ideas about crushing skulls, Warbringer. I need you alive,' Farden said. The prophecy of Dotharadine weighed on him heavily. Selfish, perhaps, but he wouldn't let the minotaur slip from his grasp. Not now. Not after all they had endured.

But the minotaur laid her giant hand on his. 'Dotharadine will rise, mage,' was all she said as she shut her eyes and waited for the spell to fold her into nothing.

Farden swallowed the lump in his throat and let Gunnir's magick seize them.

Frosted and sparse lands welcomed them. Pines nodded to each other in the howling wind. A cliff fell away before them, and the landscape rippled until it met a walled city squatting in the middle of the flat wasteland like a forgotten hat.

'Vorhaug,' said Farden.

'You been here before?' asked Warbringer.

'Once or twice on Arka business when I was a Written,' Farden said as he put his helmet over his head. The metal whispered as it contracted around his skull and connected with the cuirass. 'Vorhaug is a nest of smugglers, brigands, and thieves, and it's a place we won't be visiting. We are going east to Orklak instead.

That's a place I haven't been, otherwise I would have taken us straight to it. Fortunately, we have our gryphon.'

Ilios was already hunkered down and waiting to carry them. The gryphon whistled as Peryn and Warbringer climbed onto his back. Farden was clutched in Ilios' hooked claws, and they grated against his Scalussen armour.

From their vantage point, the gryphon took flight and used the sheer drop of the cliff to put air under his feathers. Farden listened to the air rushing through his helmet as the miles passed by beneath them. The only features that interrupted the endless bare land were the occasional towering cairn and long trains of wagons stretched across the roads. Some of the trains must have numbered a hundred wagons, and they were surrounded by soldiers who yelled and pointed at the sight of the gryphon. Ilios meandered into the edges of the clouds instead, climbing higher until Farden's ears popped.

It was only when they saw another scratch of existence looming out of the scattered snow that Farden patted Ilios' claw and motioned for them to land.

Ilios put them down in a crater a few minutes' walk from the town of Orklak. It looked like a shrunken Vorhaug, with palisade walls of sharpened pine and a watchtower at each edge of the compass. Smoke leaked in stacks from its chimneys. Ruins of stone surrounded the town, overgrown by dirt and moss but far vaster than the town itself. Farms stretched through the remains, north, south, and west, but not east. A few hillocks and burial mounds were the only breaks in that flat horizon, where storm clouds slow-danced and rumbled.

Peryn and Warbringer stayed silent as Farden examined the walls and defences. 'Peryn and I will go into the town. You can stay here with Ilios, Warbringer,' Farden ordered.

Warbringer slapped her hand against Voidaran. 'Why?'

'There'll be more questions about you than answers about our Great One. But you can watch for our signal if we get into trouble.'

That seemed to appease the minotaur, and Farden and Peryn alone set out towards Orklak's gates.

The silence between the mage and witch was filled with crunching footsteps, and Farden broke it awkwardly and abruptly. 'I'm sorry,' he said.

'For what?' asked Peryn.

'For Wyved. I failed to keep her safe, just like I failed the rest of Scalussen. Like Sipid. Thenerean. Roglurg. Sturmsson.'

'You couldn't predict the elves,' said Peryn, echoing Lerel before her voice dropped. 'Even if you did free them.'

Farden winced. 'Is that what you believe? Is it me you blame for Wyved?'

Peryn shrugged. 'I don't know, I know Loki doesn't have the magick to release them. Maybe it was Malvus. But as much as blame can be thrown around, it was Loki who sent them to New Scalussen, and nobody else.'

'As much as I tell myself the same thing, I can't accept it. I hate that it might be true,' muttered Farden. 'And I can't get rid of the guilt of it.'

Peryn nodded. 'Neither can I.'

'You fought hard, from what I've heard. Though our minds like to tell us otherwise, there wasn't anything you could have done differently to save her.'

'I don't deserve the mantle Wyved left me,' Peryn said while kicking viciously at a stone.

'Why not?'

'It's reserved for the oldest and wisest of witches. I'm neither. Perhaps another witch could have saved her.'

'You're not the oldest, for sure. But who says you're not wise? Strong? There must have been a reason Wyved chose you.'

Peryn lifted her hand, and a finch hopped along it, cheeping at the wind. 'If that's true, then I don't know what it was, and that's the problem.'

'If you believe Wyved was wise, then trust her wisdom. I would imagine she chose you because she knew you are far beyond your years and have more heart than any of your kin,' Farden said with a shrug. 'Why do you think I brought you along if I didn't think you were important? Deserving of the mantle you've taken on?'

'To apologise?'

'You're only half-right,' grunted Farden. 'What are the others saying about the elves?'

'I'm not going to lie, Farden. There's a lot of talk. The blame lies with you as much as it does Loki, but it doesn't change why we fight and who we'll stand behind.'

Farden gritted his teeth. 'I will fix it.'

'And that's why I still follow, and the rest of Scalussen follow you also. We have trust. What I don't understand is why you don't rescue Mithrid.'

'Because I in turn trust her. She's closer to Loki than I could ever get, and I think it's wise to keep her there.'

Before Farden could say any more, a shrill horn bleated at the palisade gate they approached.

'Halt there, strangers!' sounded a voice thick with an old Skölgard accent. A guard stood atop a gatehouse and above a closed gate, with a horn of hide in his hands.

Their cloaks wrapped around their armour and weapons, Peryn and Farden stood still with arms out and empty. Gunnir was already disguised as an old sword at Farden's side.

'Who are you?' yelled the guard.

'Traders from Vorhaug. Come to buy and sell is all.'

'Don't look like very successful traders.'

'Down on our luck. That's why we're here,' said Farden, eliciting a chuckle from the guard.

'In you go, and any weapons you got stay sheathed or clasped, them's the rules.'

'Of course,' Farden assured him as the gates cracked open with a sprinkle of sawdust. Chains hidden behind the walls clanked as the gate of hewn tree trunks lifted into the gatehouse. More guards stood ready, spears lowered, but none approached. Farden and Peryn entered without trouble and found themselves in a shady tangle of buildings that looked fit to burst from the walls at any moment. As if the land around the town was cursed, the architects of Orklak had given up on building outwards and started building up, piling house on top of house in ever more disconcerting endeavours. Scaffolding covered most of the structures and made wandering tunnels from the streets.

Farden and Peryn blended with the crowds that filled the streets, moving from market to market. Whatever Orklak grew was not enough to keep it afloat on coin, and so it had become a centre of trade instead, its scales balanced between where east met west. Cloth and furs seemed the prime trade, and dozens of shops and stalls were littered with all kinds and colours of weave and hide. Farden saw Golikan green and Cathak cowhide amongst Crumbled Empire mail, and even Arka colours, patchwork and faded. The town seemed like a haven for everything lost, and Farden felt right at home.

'Where do we start?' asked Peryn, eyes narrowed. Farden could hear her finches cheeping inside her cloak.

He knew exactly where. Tyrfing had taught him this trick when he was just a boy. 'Merchants always have the most gossip,' he said, eying a grizzled and proud chap leaning out of a window with no interest for the dawdlers at his shopfront. Farden approached, pasting a smile on his face, and made sure to nod appreciatively at the sheepskin wares on offer.

'You here to waste my time or make it worth my while?' grunted the merchant.

'Got a name?' Farden asked the man.

'Only for those buying.'

'Farden, humble merchant. And you?'

'Chidlow.'

'Glad to make your acquaintance.'

'Remains to be seen for you.'

'How long have you been trading?'

'Born and raised in Orklak. Da worked this stall before me. Ain't nobody that got better skins.'

Farden placed a silver coin on the man's windowsill, right next to his arm. 'And why is it nobody goes straight east from Orklak's gates?'

Chidlow took the coin, bit it, flicked it with a chime of metal, and stowed it away in a breast pocket. 'You don't know? See that's how I know you ain't from around here. You wouldn't ask to speak about such nonsense.'

Farden put down another silver. 'Humour me.'

The merchant shoved it away and waved his hands. 'Don't want no death nor trouble on my hands. No more words with you.'

Though he set his jaw, Farden kept his calm, nodded politely, and went on his way.

'We should try over there.' Peryn pointed to a man next to a wooden tree of bird perches. Most of them played host to a hawk or a raven, hooded and belled and feathers shining. He stood by with a smile, twirling a dead mouse around his gloved finger. Piles of parchment sat on a nearby desk, the corner of which was already decorated with a few shades of bird shit.

The man greeted them in a few languages before they heard Commontongue. 'Need a message sent? I've got the fastest wings in Orklak, yessir,' he boasted.

'We need directions. Thought you could provide some,' said Peryn.

Farden nodded solemnly. 'We aren't from around here and need the fastest way east. People keep telling us it's dangerous.'

'Dangerous? Suicide, is what it is,' scoffed the man. His jaw was a lot looser than the previous merchant's. 'Few trains or travellers who go due east ever come back. Most souls are never heard from again. Only the birds can go straight through the storms without harm. Even now they've gotten worse.'

'Worse?'

The man worked his mouth into a grimace. 'Yessir. Ever since the western mountains started speaking. Since the colours started appearing in the night skies.'

Another shadow of Farden's deeds fell like a shroud on his soul. The mage nodded as he felt Peryn's eyes on him.

'Still brings the hunters, though, one fool after the next,' the man was still babbling. He pointed to some fur-clad and bulky individuals busy strapping a ballista to the flat of a wagon.

'What is it they hunt?' asked Farden. 'Does it have a name?'

The man fed the mouse to a nearby hawk and threw down his glove. 'You must be from far afield. Everyone here knows you don't speak its name. Only brings the thunder closer.'

Farden was intrigued. Perhaps that was why Peryn had found nothing but a location in the scrolls. 'What do they call you, sir?'

The chap tugged his fringe. 'Timecks.'

Farden tried the allure of coin again. 'Well, Timecks, would you tell me more for a silver?'

The man beckoned for two coins, and Farden obliged. He then leaned close and conspiratorial, eyes on the guards ambling about the shopfronts. 'I'll tell you what I can. Every time you see lightning on the plain, that's *it*. That's the curse that lives beyond the barrows.'

'It? Is it a beast?' asked Peryn.

'Nobody knows what it is. Plenty of dukes and warlords and hunters have gone to kill the curse, and only a handful of survivors have ever come back. Everyone who's seen it speaks of the same things: lightning and thunder and a swooping death. That's why the traders go around the plains. Takes an extra week, but at least they come out alive at the end of it. So if you're thinking the shortcut will save you a coin or two and it's worth the risk, good luck to you, strangers, and rest in peace.'

Farden placed a final silver in Timecks' hand to thank him for his words and wandered on. Peryn stuck by his elbow.

'A curse and a nightmare. Sure you want to find this one?' asked the witch.

Farden chuckled drily. 'I know we need it.'

'There might be some allies we are better off without, you know.'

'See? Wise.'

While Peryn muttered darkly, Farden was already seeking a gate by which to escape the superstitious town. They found one soon enough and made their way back to the gryphon and the minotaur.

'News?' asked Warbringer.

'There's something to the east,' said Farden. 'We're going to find it.'

'What is it?'

'Something that everybody in that town fears to speak the name of. A so-called curse that kills everything that dares to set foot in its territory,' Peryn elaborated. 'Just in case Farden forgets to tell you the most important bit.'

'Sounds exactly what we need,' grunted Warbringer.

'The High Crone is right. It sounds dangerous. Possibly suicidal. The usual, to be honest. But I have an idea,' said Farden. 'Why was it only birds can go due east without a worry while everything else is killed?'

The others pondered. Peryn took a red-breasted finch from her pocket and watched it look around as it let out little chirrups. 'He doesn't seem afraid,' she admitted.

Ilios trilled.

'You don't count. You're never afraid,' said Farden.

'What in your mind?' Warbringer asked.

'Have your birds follow me and Ilios. I will happily face the curse alone. I don't want to risk a single one of you after…' Farden's words drifted off.

Peryn shrugged, letting the finch sit on her fingers while it cheeped loudly at Farden. 'You think the key is beaks and feathers? Then you need me with you. They like you, but not as much as me.'

'I am in,' said Warbringer with a thump of her chest.

Ilios whistled, sounding almost impatient, as if he was unsurprised and uncaring of the danger that awaited.

'Fine. Then onwards we go,' Farden ordered. Ilios took their weight again, heaved them into the sky, and flapped confidently into the east.

The gryphon kept low and slow, weaving between the towering cairns – marvels of a tribute to the ability to stack stones – and silent barrows. No trees grew in the place, and the remains of those that had tried were burned stumps and fearsome shadows. The drizzle came to soak them, and Farden felt Ilios beginning to tire with the added weight of drowned feathers.

It was then that lightning crackled, drawing the jagged outlines of bubbling storm clouds.

Ilios had them on the ground before the thunder could roll, and Farden landed hard and rolled to his feet as the gryphon skidded through the mud ahead of him.

'Feel danger in the air,' said Warbringer, some of her tufts of hair standing on end. Farden felt the same electricity in the drizzle. He rubbed his fingers together to find sparks crackling between the metal.

'Magick, too.'

'Same thing.'

Peryn spread her arms, letting the dozens of birds she hid away in her cloak and cloth fly. They spun around her, alternating between perching on her arms, shoulders, or bald head and fluttering about making a ruckus. The witch held her hand up for silence as the lightning flashed again, and the thunder told them the storm was coming closer.

'Ilios, see what you can find!' Farden called out over the rising roar of the wind. The gryphon took flight, raising his wings to catch the rushing air. The gale scattered the curtains of drizzle, and Farden and the others saw hideous omens hidden in the mud. Bones. Entire skeletons slumped against boulders and cowering in shallow craters. Some were picked disturbingly clean while others were smashed into unrecognisable shapes and spread over a gut-wrenching distance. Old wagons stood ownerless and bedraggled, with cloth coverings ripped and ragged, wheels broken, and whatever cattle that had dragged them lying in a pile of bones nearby.

'We come to place of death,' rumbled Warbringer, holding her hammer high over her head.

It was at that moment lightning chose to strike Voidaran. A blinding flicker, and the minotaur was on the ground, hide smoking and Voidaran's runes glowing. Farden hammered on the beast's back, making her choke and gasp.

Warbringer's first thought was Voidaran, and she grabbed for it, pressing her hand to its carved skull. 'Bastard,' was all the minotaur managed to say before she got to her hooves and shook herself.

Farden broke the drizzle with shield spells, and the magick fizzed at the touch of the rain. Another bolt of lightning struck moments later, making Peryn's birds hide once more.

'It's fine,' said Farden, as he weathered yet another strike. The thunder filled their ears, but the storm seemed to have used up its fervour, and no more lightning came. Only a chill wind. Farden didn't know if this curse was human, beast, something in between, or something unknown altogether, and that bothered him.

'Ilios!' Farden yelled to the swirling clouds. 'What do you see?'

No answer came from the gryphon, but Farden did spy a shadow rushing through the murk above. Farden stretched his shield spell thinner and wider as he walked, boots crunching on bones. 'Ilios!'

Wind swirled, driving against his shield spells as a great shadow descended, black as night and crackling with lightning. It was not Ilios, and Farden ducked as sickle claws sliced at his spells. They were forced to huddle under the shield as a scream pained their ears. Within a moment, the nightmare was gone again.

Farden bellowed into the clouds. 'We don't want to fight you! We only want to talk!'

'You think it wants to talk?' Peryn asked.

Farden blasted aside gloom with a light spell, filling the storm with daylight. It brought another scream from above them, where a gigantic, winged shape could be seen. It was no dragon. It wasn't quite a bird, and whatever it was, it was swooping for another strike. Farden briefly wondered if he had made a mistake yet again. The mage cursed the storm.

'Ilios!' he yelled, readying his shield spells yet again.

'Farden, put down your magick!' the witch called out.

'What?'

'I have an idea!'

'It better be a good one!' said Farden as put down his shield spells.

'We try the birds!' Peryn yelled as she weaved her hands in the air. Her birds streamed around her in patterns, following the movements of her hand. They forced a cheeping halo above them, and as the fell shadow descended on them, Peryn put a grimace on her face and strained to keep the birds in formation. It was not a moment too soon, and to Farden's relief, the winged thing swooped away. He saw a glimpse of feathers, or lizard scales, and too many grasping claws.

'What in Hel!' he yelled as it looked to come around for yet another pass, skimming low across the mud and surrounded by a tornado of storm cloud.

It was Ilios that broke the monster's charge. With a sharp whistle, he appeared above them, flapping wildly, beak agape and claws splayed.

The nightmare halted at the sight of a winged foe, and Peryn pushed her birds towards the shadow, letting the curious things investigate. The fact their own curiosity led them stilled Farden's hand. Another screech came from the monster, but it didn't come further. Farden felt the thud in the ground as it landed.

'What is it?' Warbringer asked.

Peryn waved them back as she went ahead. Her birds had returned, chittering madly at the witch. 'It's scared.'

'Scared? Scared of what?'

'Of you. And Warbringer,' said Peryn.

Ilios whistled in confirmation, head low and eyes curious.

'You can understand that thing?' Farden asked of them both.

'I'm a High Crone, aren't I?' asked Peryn with a grin as she led them forwards, hands wide and palms up.

The rain and mist faded as the distance between them shrank, and the Great One was slowly revealed.

It was a bird, to put it simply. A humongous, towering, terrifying bird that would have reached halfway up the Dawnknell. Whatever the thing was, it had a head like a stork, perched on a short, sinuous neck and tipped by a long, hooked beak. Its feathered neck gave way to dragon scales on its breast and belly, leading to three legs that gripped the mud with talons as long and as curved as whips. Feathers covered the rest of its back, where two sets of wings protruded and shuffled warily.

'Dotharadine,' Warbringer cursed as she gazed upon the beast with wide eyes.

The monster seemed to feel the mage and minotaur's apprehension and unleashed a scream that left a ringing in Farden's ears. It was correct: he'd definitely made a mistake.

Its head reared back as a finch came to rest on its beak, and it croaked something Farden couldn't understand.

Ilios and Peryn could.

'She won't attack as long as Ilios and my birds are here,' said Peryn.

'She?

'She doesn't like humans. Or magick for that matter.'

The monster croaked some more, and Peryn explained. 'Humans trapped her here long ago as a weapon to break the city of Falkenrath, and she hasn't left since. She has remained her for centuries, defending herself from all those who came to hunt and kill her.'

Farden saw no chains. 'How?'

'An old Skölgard spell. An invisible chain. It pains her when she tries to go too far.'

Farden remembered his lessons of the Manesmark School. 'Then it must have a root somewhere. Something it's shackled to.'

The monster slapped the halves of its beak together, sounding like a battering ram smacking a gate.

Peryn nodded as the finches twittered in translation. 'She says there is a strange rock she cannot harm. One that reeks of magick.'

'Does she have a name?'

The monster lifted its sapphire, violet, and pitch-black wings, pinions spread wide. A dark cloud seemed to emanate from them, waterfalling down its back. Lightning crackled across her feathers.

'Territha.' Peryn smiled as if her true name had a meaning Farden would never understand.

That is almost elvish, whispered the spear in his hand. *Skybreaker.*

Farden liked the sound of that. 'And will she help us?'

'Would you free her if she didn't?' asked Peryn.

'Of course I would,' and Farden meant it. Skölgard magick was cruel, and all beasts deserved freedom just as much as any other soul he fought for.

'Good,' said Peryn, shortly before Territha took flight and knocked them to their knees with the force of her wings.

Ilios struggled to follow as the monster weaved through her clouds, heading north by Farden's reckoning. It took no time at all for Territha to screech and start circling something on the ground. Ilios put them down close by what looked to be another cairn, but this one had smoother sides. Six smaller stones surrounded it in a circle. Magick was thick in the air around it.

'Is that it?'

Farden nodded. 'It must be. I can almost see the runes on its surface.'

'Your turn,' Peryn said with a smile.

Farden approached the stone and it wasn't long before he felt a presence pushing back, as though he waded through deep water. A pain blossomed at the base of his skull. The mage could feel his Book growing warmer with every difficult step. This was older magick, strong and fierce.

Farden led with Gunnir, using the spear to cut through the walls of magick. He could feel their invisible threads snagging and tearing against Gunnir's blade, but it did nothing to stop the pain growing in his head. It pounded in waves, and Farden cursed the wizard who had made this spell.

Gunnir whined as magick flowed, fighting back against the stone. Farden pressed closer, reaching with the blade. Wind rushed and pulled at him as he battled to close the gap. It was only when the blade struck the stone with a metallic chime that the spell broke. With a shower of stone, the cairn exploded into shards and rubble, clanging against Gunnir and his armour. Even the others had to shelter from the blast.

High above them, Territha let out a long screech that faded as she flew into the distance, weaving west with great beats of her four wings.

'Is...' Farden frowned. 'Is she coming back?'

Farden started to walk after her, knowing it was useless but trying anyway. It must have been an hour before he stopped to listen to the air and the rumble of thunder that had moved west with the monster.

'That doesn't sound good,' he said, whistling for Ilios to pick them up, and as soon as the others were aboard his feathery back and Farden clamped in his claws, they raced after the storm.

When they spied Orklak through the driving rain, they saw smoke rising above it. Not from its chimneys, as before, but from its walls and rooftops. The scorch of lightning marked the palisades, and fur-clad bodies lay smoking beyond the gates. A broken wagon and its ballista lay in pieces in the muck. Archers and spearmen on the walls ducked as shadow and storm clouds swooped for them. Farden didn't blame them, but he also knew who was to blame for letting her loose.

'We need to get Territha to stop!' yelled Farden.

'And how do you propose that?' Peryn yelled back.

'Talk to her!' Farden ordered as he tapped Ilios' foot. Farden fell to the ground, striking the mud with his knee and the butt of the spear. The Scalussen armour rang out as he stretched his magick and made a storm of his own down in the mud. Lightning flickered around him, skipping back and forth from puddle to puddle.

It wasn't long before Territha noticed. A crackle of lightning and thunder gave her away as she swept towards Farden. The mage killed his magick and stood ready. For what, he wasn't sure, but he stood his ground no matter what.

A finch landed on his shoulder and fluttered its feathers with a cheep. Before Farden could look to Peryn, circling above on Ilios, a dozen more finches alighted on him, all making a raucous chorus.

Farden was buffeted by hurricane winds as Territha came to a halt barely feet from him, wings flared and beak open. Her giant claws stretched and flexed in front of his face, but Farden still didn't move. With a splash of mud, Farden felt Peryn and Ilios at his side. He reached up to put an arm around the defensive gryphon. Territha screeched again, and Farden was glad he wore his helmet. All he could smell was rotten meat.

'She asks why we protect you,' Peryn shouted over the crackling lightning in Territha's wings.

'Well? Don't leave her waiting,' murmured Farden.

Ilios was the one who answered, in a series of whistles and sharp notes. Territha tilted her head as she listened. It was almost too fast for Farden to understand.

'What gryphon say?' asked Warbringer.

'That I gave them a home, and I fight to keep it that way,' said Farden. 'Ilios, tell her we could give her a home, too. Far from here. There are plains to hunt on. Mountains. And others like her.'

Ilios told the monster, and Territha croaked loudly. Farden wasn't sure it was an agreement, but the monster folded her mighty wings, and the storm about her died away for the first time.

'What about Loki?' asked Peryn.

'I will ask, in time. All that matters is that she and that town stay safe. I don't doubt it and its hunters deserve it, but I won't have more blood on my hands,' Farden said as he held out his hands, and the finches hopped and fluttered back to their witch.

'Wise,' said Peryn with a smile.

With Ilios charged with leading Territha back to New Scalussen, Peryn and Warbringer stood by as the Great One's storm moved southwest and finally left the plains beyond the barrows in peace. Even the rain lifted and gave them a moment of peace.

'Two down,' muttered Farden as he gripped Gunnir tightly and held it aloft.

The spell left sand spinning in their wake. A soldier carrying a stack of spears far too close to where Farden, Peryn, and Warbringer had appeared out of thin air lost his balance and went flying, spears also.

Farden had barely helped him up and gathered two of his spears before Elessi came jogging along the beach.

'Hereni's gone!'

Farden 'What do you mean, gone? Taken or left?'

'Left. She took Irien's flying pig thing and went north several hours ago on her own.'

'To Krauslung?'

Elessi's face said it all. 'Bull went with her.'

'Bull? What spurred this?'

'A hawk arrived from our spies after you left. Mithrid has been seen, injured but alive. Loki made her execute three so-called spies. Since then, there's been not a sign of her. Loki's emptied the Arkathedral. Only soldiers are allowed in, and strange folk have been seen inside.'

Farden cursed, and yet still he didn't move.

'Whatever reason it is you're waitin' for to go get Mithrid, it's not good enough. You need to get her out of Loki's clutches before anything happens to her,' muttered Elessi.

Farden leaned close. 'Mithrid wouldn't want me to,' he said in a small voice.

Elessi scowled. 'What are you up to now?'

But Farden was already walking, breathing out a sigh as he put on his helmet, aiming for the shape of Fleetstar sitting on the dock and watching Keraken pick at a pile of silver fish.

CHAPTER 33
BROKEN PROMISES

Two counts of pickpocketing. One count of breaking windows. One count of grievous injury caused by kicking the victim down the stairs. Three counts of drunkenness.

REPORT FROM THE TOWN OF HALIOS, CONCERNING THE ARREST AND IMPRISONMENT OF ONE LEREL, NO LAST NAME

SEVERAL HOURS EARLIER

'News from Krauslung, General,' said Ko-Tergo, marching up with parchment clutched in his claws. Hereni almost jogged at his side. Elessi had only barely set foot in the Dawnknell's shadow.

'You read it?' she asked of them, before her eyes scanned the scrawled words of spies.

'She's alive,' breathed Hereni. 'But it's not good.'

Lerel took the message from Elessi's hands and tutted.

'We have to get her back,' Hereni urged.

'Not without Farden, Hereni,' ordered Elessi, although she fumed silently in reply. 'He seems to trust she's strong enough to endure until the time is right.'

'Endure is the right word! Think about what she's going through. Beaten, tortured. Loki's playing games with her. Why Farden hasn't gone to get her back is bordering on suspicious.'

'The ships need to be rearranged at the docks, Hereni. Perhaps you should see to that.'

'Ships?' Hereni asked, face a storm.

'Ships.'

Hereni marched away towards the docks, throttling the sword at her side.

'You can't expect her to sit back and do nothing,' said Lerel.

'I don't. I barely want to, but it's Farden's orders.'

'Gods damn it. I hope he knows what he's doing.'

'Unfortunately for us, it never seems like he does,' murmured Elessi.

Whatever Farden's game was, Elessi wished it would end swiftly. She watched a dragon circle overhead.

Hereni did not go to the docks. She went instead to Akitha and her forge, set into the northern walls where they met the harbour defences. The constant plume of smoke was her guide, and she wove through streets and junctions, ignoring every soldier and mage who saluted her.

Hereni thumped her sword down on a cloth-covered table that acted as Akitha's desk. The blacksmith had her boots up on its other side and a book in her hands.

'You got a wasp in your britches,' commented the Siren.

Hereni poked at the sword, and Akitha peered at it without moving. 'A Golikan sword notched my blade. Need it sharp.'

'Tough steel those eastern bastards have got. It'll take me a little while to put a new edge on it, but something tells me you ain't in the waiting mood. You look all fidgety, if you ask me.'

'Can you blame me, when there are certain people in danger that I've been told not to help?'

'Mhm,' said Akitha, drumming her nails on her book. 'I've got something for you.'

The blacksmith got to her feet and went to the far wall, where all manner of sharp edges glittered. Akitha's hands wandered over two swords before she selected a third and brought it to Hereni.

It was barely longer than a knife. A seax, in fact, with a slightly curving, wavering edge like the waves of the ocean. The rest of the blade had ripples like woodgrain in its steel, and a twisted crossguard protected a single-handed hilt. Akitha held up a nearby quill and ran it along the seax with barely a touch. The shaven feather was thrown to the table, and Hereni held it up to the torchlight.

'Fine for cutting an Arka throat.'

'That it is,' Akitha agreed as Hereni changed the buckles of her sheath. Akitha poked at her armour and fastened it here and there. 'Whatever you've got in your mind, you stay safe, Hereni. Don't need any more loss in this city.'

Hereni nodded before swivelling on her heel and leaving Akitha to stare after her. She made short work of the streets, once again keeping her head down and following the walls to where the stables sat. Hereni was only accosted once by a captain asking about arrows and fletchers and all sorts of things she had no interest in. She gave him the barest of answers, enough to keep moving, and left him pondering behind her. Hand on her new blade, Hereni kept her course straight.

The beast that the Lady Irien had brought with her. It was the first idea she'd had, and it was the one she'd stuck with. A grifabore was what Mithrid had called to it, and the big barrel of a beast snuffled at her as Hereni stood at its gate at last. It was halfway through a pumpkin, munching it ever so messily as it mashed it to pulp between thick teeth. Hereni stayed wary of the curved tusks as she circled it to test how bothered it was by her presence.

It wasn't, was the shortest answer. She could have prodded the grifabore, and the thing would have kept on munching. Hereni began to check the saddle that had been left by its side and decided to try putting it on the grifabore's winged back.

'Easy, Saltlick,' Hereni whispered as she hefted the heavy thing up and over the bristly back of the flying hog. As she placed it down, she saw a face staring back at her from across the grifabore's back, sad yet determined.

'General,' Bull said in a soft voice for somebody so large. 'I heard about Mithrid.'

'And?'

'And it looks to me like you're going to go get her.'

'What if I am?'

'Then I want to come along. Mithrid helped me escape once, and I want to save her from Loki.'

'It's too dangerous.'

Bull came into the light of the lantern hanging overhead. Hereni searched his face, noting the faint scales that were beginning to gather on his jawline and cheekbones, where stubble should have been growing instead. There was an axe on his belt and fine Siren-made mail under his cloak.

'I know dangerous,' he grunted.

That Bull did. He was braver than his hunched shoulders and quiet demeanour. He also had a better reason: 'And I also know General Elessi's looking for you, and the longer you argue, the quicker she'll catch you.'

'Fine, but you'll have to find your own way there. This saddle only takes one extra rider, and I need the space for Mithrid.'

Saltlick agreed with a whining grunt.

'Then Kinsprite will join us too.'

'We have to do this quietly, Bull,' Hereni said.

'Dragons can be quiet. Quieter than this hog, I'll bet. Faster too.'

As it turned out, Bull ate his words. The hog was fast as an arrow.

As soon as Hereni poked the grifabore into the street and ordered a path be cleared quick and sharp, Saltlick bounded into a lumbering and lurching gallop as if he had been longing to stretch his wings. And that he did, clipping pots from windowsills and chimneys as he took to the air. After several beats of his strong wings, and a dive that made Hereni cling on tight, he flapped north over the city walls and out into the wastes beyond the forests.

The rocks and dust sped by beneath her in a blur, and Saltlick let out a squeal as his powerful wings drove them faster and towards the mountains. A quick look over her shoulder showed Kinsprite was keeping up, but not as easily as she might have hoped.

Hereni turned northwards and slid the visor of her helmet down to keep the wind at bay. Her heart thudded against her breastplate, but she couldn't calm it, not until she saw Mithrid.

❦

Loki came early, or at least it felt early in the cell. There was salt on the air that wafted through the open door, far fresher than the cloying damp of the cell with the bucket beginning to fester. Another of Loki's subtle tortures. That, and the constant screaming that reverberated through the stone of the fortress from somewhere below, where magick was being carved into backs and driving the unfortunate mad. Fodder for the elves, or so Mithrid imagined.

Mithrid was tired. Mithrid was full of doubt. Mithrid hated that she was glad to see him. Not his face, and not for any reason than answers to her questions, but she loathed that she didn't loathe his presence as much as before. 'What is it now? More tests?'

Loki beckoned a hand, leaving the doorway empty as he strolled along the corridor. 'Another journey.'

Mithrid was left to leave her cell at her own pace, unbothered by guards and unshackled. Scarred mages still lined the hallways, full of scowls. Mithrid followed the god to a hallway lined with carvings of so-called great deeds and important people long dead.

'No guards or mages or elves, Loki?' asked Mithrid. 'What's the matter? You don't fear me any more?'

Loki chuckled amiably. 'Oh dear, I regret to say I've never feared you, Mithrid. Feared your potential? Absolutely. Afraid and all kinds of excited.'

That nettled her and intrigued her in the same moment. 'Where are we going then?'

'Home,' Loki said.

Mithrid blinked. 'What?' she blurted, but Loki had already clicked his fingers, and her question was lost to the rush of magick.

Mithrid collapsed onto wind-worn stone and scrub moss. The light was a different colour, a bluish cold where Scalussen was always amber warm. She recognised it immediately. A deep breath brought her salt and rot.

'No…' Mithrid muttered as she rolled back on her heels and knuckled dizziness from her eyes.

Time had not been kind to the ruined, murdered village of Troughwake, but Mithrid knew the broken cranes gathered around the cliff-edge all too well, and the defiant arms of ladder clinging to the rock.

Loki was standing nearby, arms crossed in disapproval. 'Quite the mess. Why don't you show me around?'

'Why don't you go and fuck yourself? I didn't ask to come back here. How dare you.'

'And yet you can't take your eyes off that ladder, can you?' Loki said, sucking his teeth. 'Don't you worry. I'll have a look about myself.'

Mithrid stood only once he had vanished, not demeaning himself by using a ladder. After some time of teeth grinding and fist clenching, she gave in and put her hands to the rails, as she'd done countless times. Mithrid thought she had climbed those rungs for the last time already. Troughwake was buried. It didn't need an exhumation, and she wanted to curse Loki for forcing her to grab a shovel.

With shaking legs that Mithrid blamed on the travelling spell, she cautiously picked her way through the remains of the village that had been her home. A strange ash covered every flat surface that wasn't sheltered. Most of the bodies had fallen to the sea below with rot or had been picked by gulls, ravens, and rats. Their scant armour and weapons were gone, likely pilfered, and the houses ransacked again by thieves and scavengers. Mithrid saw a pirate's lost boot in one of the doorways, and it hammered another nail into the coffin of that memory. The smell had returned to sea salt and weathered timber, but it hid nothing of the scent of death and burning she remembered. Mithrid ran her hand over a hole in a beam, where magick had once carved through it.

'You found a spellbook, didn't you?' asked Loki, leaning against a corner of a dishevelled house with broken windows. A bedraggled skeleton lay draped over the sill, skull missing. Mithrid couldn't drag her eyes from it.

'That's what drew the Arka mages here, wasn't it?' Loki pried. 'Where did it come from?'

'Are we really going to act like friends instead of foes and chat the day away? Why ask if you already know the answers?'

Loki's glinting eyes became sharp. 'Because I want to hear you say the words, and you'll do what I say.'

'Once again, fuck you, but fine.' Mithrid played his game. 'A bookship.'

'Farden's bookship.'

Mithrid scowled. 'Yet I was the one who found it. I was the one who read its spells, and you can pull at that thread all you want. I've made my peace with it.'

'Oh, I wouldn't dare question fate,' Loki snickered as he wound in through the ruins, avoiding the more rotten planks and rails.

Withered seaweed and sand clogged the lowest levels, where a storm must have washed high and broken most of the ladders and fishing houses.

'Which house is yours?' asked the god.

Mithrid could already see it at the end of the row. No skeletons lay inside its door. There was not a sign of her father's remains. He must have been taken to the pyre or thrown to the sea, or so she hoped.

Loki had followed her gaze and now followed the path, weaving along the cliff face to where her door lay broken. Mithrid spent a few moments refusing to join him before the morbid curiosity drew her. She stared at the floor where she had found him. The memories of her father's grey face and placing the beetle cake on his empty, silent chest rushed over the dams and locked doors she had put in place in her mind. Mithrid felt her throat swell.

'Would you dare to change fate, Mithrid, I wonder? Would you take it back if you could?' asked Loki.

'What game are you playing? If it's sobs and tears you're trying to stoke, Loki, then you can save it. I kept my promise, I avenged them,' Mithrid spat. And that she had. There were no broken promises in her heart, only sorrow for the lost. Mithrid had left Troughwake with vengeance in her heart, and she had given up body and soul to grasp it. If Loki had hoped to break her with his visit to Troughwake, it had done the opposite. It fortified her and rained fire on the guilt of bringing magick to this village in the first place. *How little he knew*, Mithrid thought.

Loki looked offended. 'Not in the slightest. I brought you here for catharsis, for solace, and to remind you why you started fighting,' he said.

Mithrid flinched. All she had wanted to hear was a lie, but somehow Loki was right. She felt a comfort she hadn't known before seeing Troughwake fallen to ruin. Mithrid steeled herself. It had to be part of the game. It had to. She loathed the god had been anything but evil, that he might have granted her – dare she think it – a kindness.

Loki was not done. 'You avenged all of Troughwake and Scalussen, yet since that glorious moment on the Bloodplains when you crushed Malvus, you've wanted more, haven't you? That should have been it, but somehow all you feel is thirsty. Empty. It's a curious feeling, isn't it?' Loki said with a dramatic sigh.

Mithrid didn't answer, not trusting herself to speak.

Loki looked around at the vacant pots and the shrivelled remains of plants. Mithrid remembered her mother singing to them, before she became an empty chair at the table and a desolate side of the bed for her father.

'Where did he die, your father?'

'Right there,' Mithrid pointed at the floorboards.

'Mother slain by mages. Father slain by mages. And an orphan made. Gods, it truly does sound like a skald's tale.'

'Glad it entertains you,' Mithrid spoke through clenched teeth.

Loki had other ideas. 'And yet the skalds will sing of you. These events are the foundations of your legacy, Mithrid. An epic tale of rising and falling where you become the hero.'

Mithrid glowered. 'You'd make me a villain. Something I've been fighting not to be.'

'Only a villain in eyes less discerning and half as wise. If fire and blood is what it takes to cleanse the world so it can know peace, then I say so be it. Farden's made the same choice on behalf of the world half a dozen times already. In Albion and Krauslung before you were born. In the ice fields. Now in Troacles. Hypocrisy of the highest order.'

'Do you really think gossiping about Farden will work on me?' Mithrid sneered. 'As if I'm that simple.'

Loki shrugged as he picked at a gouge in the wall. 'I only speak the truth. At the beginning of the Last War between Farden and Malvus, Farden hounded the Arka for years before Malvus was forced to ban magick in an effort to bring peace.'

'Peace? The Arka pillaged and punished Emaneska in the name of Malvus' law.'

Loki tutted. 'Because Farden recklessly encouraged and glorified the use of magick, swarmed magick markets with dangerous objects, and tried to incite rebellion before the Dromfangar Fealty. Because of Farden's actions, thousands were forced into hiding, and Malvus was forced to hunt thousands down. Many were killed in the process. Other imprisoned. Others put to work. All for listening to Farden and rebelling against a very simple law.'

'It is far from simple. I know dozens who would have been put to death for magick in their veins they did not ask for. Magick is natural, and that should never be governed by law. Malvus would have killed her if Farden hadn't intervened, so don't you try to twist history to—'

'Her, you say? A slip of the tongue, Mithrid. Is *she* the same person you've made a little space in your heart for?' Loki smirked. 'Though it charms my heart to hear of love blossoming in times of struggle and war, magick is far from natural, my dear Mithrid.'

Mithrid took a step and showed him a fist. 'Enough, Loki! Either spit it out or take me back to my cell.'

'Oh, we're not done.' Loki raised his hands and pressed his fingers together. Bereft of choice, Mithrid tensed as a spell enveloped her and turned the world inside out. The sudden cold of her new surroundings stung her lungs as she gasped. Mithrid had fallen again, and this time her hands grasped pale ice. She knew this landscape also, and it, too, had changed since she had left it.

'This,' Loki intoned. 'This is what magick does.'

They stood on a mountain slope caked in snow and ice. Before Mithrid, a wasteland of burned rock stretched outwards until it was reclaimed by snow and glasslike glaciers. Where ash and dark mud didn't cover the stone, bones lay in countless thousands, too jumbled to be recognisable. Dark specks dotted the ice where bodies had escaped the fire but frozen to death. Familiar ruins poked from the dirt and rubble to their right, and Mithrid realised where they were.

Mithrid set her jaw, feeling a throbbing pain in her head. There was magick in the air. 'And why have you brought me back here?'

'Because you need to realise what Farden did here.'

Mithrid swallowed another lump in her throat. She had started Irminsul's fire. Nobody else. Troughwake might have been avenged, but the shadow of the ice fields still hung heavy over her. Mithrid shoved her conscience away. 'It was war,' she whispered.

'It was magick. Raw and unabated. Hel and Haven now strain because of the death that was wrought here and in the Bloodplains, and it has set Evernia's gift loose. Look at the colours filling the sky. Feel it in on your skin. Farden's recklessness has chipped away at the shackles keeping magick under control for decades, and here he finally broke them. Magick now pours into the world, and it won't be long before it tears it apart.'

Guilt resurged within her as Mithrid stared at the mountain above them, now cracked and broken but still able to dominate the horizon. The smoke pouring from Irminsul glittered with threads of green, blue, and scarlet. She winced as pain pounded in her temples.

'It was my doing,' she spat. 'Are those the words you want so desperately to hear?'

Loki waggled a finger. 'Who ordered you to wake the mountain?'

Mithrid chewed the name over and over. 'Farden,' she breathed while Loki beamed. She couldn't stand his grin, so she looked again at the volcano and the glow of the earth's fire illuminating Irminsul's crater. Mithrid shuddered as a flash of her nightmares filled her mind.

'We shouldn't be here. You shouldn't have brought me to this mountain.'

Loki strode ahead with a chuckle as though she spoke nonsense. 'But that's not all it is, is it? You and I both know what lives within that mountain, don't you, Mithrid?'

Mithrid didn't need to answer for the god to clap his hands as if he'd won a round of cards. Her wide eyes and bobbing throat said it all.

'Do you know why it woke for you?' he asked.

Mithrid shook her head even though she answered. 'My dark magick.'

'Because you're the only thing in the world that can threaten it. Just as you did Ekidna. What lives in that mountain fears you. Monsters, Mithrid. Great Ones the world has forgotten just like

Irminsul here. Even Farden has no idea what truly lies in this mountain.'

'You speak nothing but shit. I can't do such things. Not even Farden could fight what I saw.'

Loki whirled on her, looking excited. 'Precisely! Don't you believe you're destined for such greatness? Don't you know what you are? What you're meant for? Magick is what these creatures are made from, and you are their antithesis, Mithrid. If you don't believe me then I will show you. I can prove you're meant for much more.'

'Like killing Farden?' she growled, mind full of the fire of Utiru's mirrors.

'More.'

'If you think you're the only one with the answer, then fucking spit it out!'

'Fine.' Loki's face turned serious. 'One that should not have fallen to Malvus' ban of magick, Mithrid, was your mother. She was a special creature.'

Mithrid approached him, boots crunching on. In her peripheries, she looked for the sharper rocks. 'Don't you talk about her. You know nothing about her.'

'Fire-red hair just like you? Paler than most?'

'Easy guess.'

'Used to sing to your plants?'

Mithrid stayed silent.

'Why did she die?'

'Having a charmed ring on her finger was all the reason an Arka mage needed to kill her. Tell me again how Malvus' simple rule was a good thing,' Mithrid snarled.

Loki nodded. 'I was also born into a world I didn't ask for or like. We've both fought to change what we were given. You with your power. Me with my words and trinkets. Both told we can't and shouldn't—'

'We, god, are nothing alike.' Mithrid wanted to throw up. 'Don't you dare insinuate—'

'Both of an ancient bloodline.' Loki raised an eyebrow.

Mithrid reached for a rock and raised it to crash it on his head. But Loki's lips spread into confidence and mockery as she halted in front of him. She couldn't quite bring it down. The hooks of truth had her, and dead gods told no truth just the same as dead men.

'Talk!'

'You, Mithrid Fenn,' Loki breathed, 'are the same as your mother. You are a lost line of elvish blood. Not dark elves, but light elves who survived the gods' sacrifice and bred with humans.'

Somehow the bastard produced the scroll that Mithrid had left ragged in a corner of her cell. Once again, he showed her ghostly creatures on a hill, surrounded by fire and turning back mighty monsters with their dark power.

Mithrid's eyes were full of stinging fire. 'You think I'm going to believe that?' Mithrid raised the rock to strike, but the chance she had been waiting for and the moment to break Loki's skull had vanished. Loki seized her wrist in an iron grip, and as her other hand came with a punch, he snatched her hand from the air.

'If the magick keeps spewing unabated, soon there won't be anyone not touched by its threads. And when the world senses danger and doom, it seeks to preserve balance by bringing about an opposing force. You are that force, Mithrid. The other side to the coin from Farden. Your mother would have had the same power, had she a chance to use it.'

'You…' *Liar. Cheat. Bastard. Fucker.* The words came in floods, but none made it out of her mouth. Mithrid dropped the rock and stood trembling as Loki let her go. She shook her head over and over. 'It can't be.'

'But it is, and now you know the truth.'

'It's a lie!' she yelled.

Loki stepped closer, but Mithrid shrank away.

'You know as well as I do that if Farden continues the way he is, he will let magick flood the world and shatter it beneath his feet with that spear, just to kill little old me. He already has the keraken, and if I were him, I'd be seeking out more of the Great Ones to raise them. Help me, Mithrid, and we will raise our own with your power, and you will make Farden pay the price for what he's done to us. Magick will no longer hold sway over the world and you will be its hero and saviour,' Loki said, voice growing loud and fierce. 'That, Mithrid Fenn, is why your mother brought you into the world. That is the more I speak of and the more you thirst for. That is the emptiness you feel. That is your great fate. Destiny, if you want to use that word, and where others would stand in your way, I would guide you!'

'You're... you're insane!' Mithrid answered, voice cracking.

'Then so is Farden, and you have to choose.' Loki delved into his pocket once more and brought forth a small and simple copper ring with a square crest and a black gem.

'What is that supposed to be?' demanded Mithrid.

'The ring your mother wore. Lost to all but my pockets.'

Mithrid snatched at it in disbelief. Immediately, she saw the mark of blood upon it, as if her mother's murder had been days ago, not a decade and a half. She thumbed it to dust and stared at the jewel. All it held was the fiery glow of Irminsul's peak, and though it lay low, suppressed by her power, Mithrid felt the magick in it. She slid it onto her finger, and the collar twitched as she tried to push her dark magick away, but the ring stayed dormant. She desperately wanted to know its magick, but she wouldn't dare sully it with Loki's touch.

'What does it do?' she asked, voice tight.

'No idea. But you need rest after such revelations.'

Loki raised his hands to click once more, but Mithrid held up a hand. She looked again to the ruined landscape that she and Farden had wrought, with its dead and its black scorch.

When she dropped her hand, the view melted and splintered before her. This time, she did not fall. Mithrid found the god holding her wrist, and she wrenched it away.

'Don't fucking touch me,' Mithrid snapped, looking around for the corridor to the dungeons. Loki had brought her somewhere else, where an open door waited. It was no glorious chamber of silk and velvet and gilded pillars, but it was better than the dark hole of the cell. It had two beds and a curtain around its shit-trough, but it had the same locks and runes on its door.

'And what of Jeasin? I won't leave her,' mumbled Mithrid. She set her jaw, still reeling from Loki's words. There was a bramble patch of a hundred questions in her head, and it was making her dizzy.

Loki nodded. 'Call her your new chambermaid then, if you so wish.'

'I do.' Mithrid put her hand to the door's frame as she swayed. She staggered backwards until her legs met the bed.

'I'll expect an answer next time I see you,' Loki said with a wink before he slammed the door. She stared at the runed wood and iron with mouth agape and eyes distant, unfocused like her mind. She didn't dare close her eyes in case she saw Irminsul's fire reaching for her, or her mother's face. Mithrid felt like she swam in a sea of night and echoing words, none of which she wanted to listen to. It couldn't be true. It had to be lies. Tricks. And yet the hook of possibility was lodged in her heart.

It must have been an hour – an hour Mithrid spent curled on the bed with eyes wide open in deep thought – before mages delivered a confused Jeasin.

'What's all this?' she asked.

'Our new cell.'

'Mithrid,' Jeasin clasped Mithrid's offered hand. 'Thank the bloody gods. I don't know what you said or did with Loki to get us 'ere, but you're a wonder.'

Mithrid grimaced.

'What did the bastard want?'

'To show me my old home and the ruin in the north. To show me my mistakes. My future. And to thoroughly blame Farden for everything.'

'Light chat, was it?' Jeasin snorted. 'Suppose 'e's not wrong about the Farden part.'

'I hate that he might be right about any of it.'

'From the sounds of it, that god is in your head.'

Mithrid clutched the ring tightly until it pained her fingers. 'You don't understand,' she said. 'It has to be a lie. A foul game. A trick. But what he said... I can't help but hear the truth.' She shuddered as the confession came forth. 'Part of me might even want it to be true.'

Jeasin sniffed at that and searched around the room, getting used to its angles. 'That, my girl,' she said, 'is when you have to be the most wary of a liar.'

Mithrid had promised Loki's tricks wouldn't get to her. Not a tear or a frown or a shout would pass her lips that she hadn't given permission, she had told herself, but today Loki had broken that promise.

Clamping her tired eyes shut, Mithrid held the ring to her chest and tried to silence her raucous mind by repeating her mission over and over.

Stay strong. Keep your hand in the fire.

CHAPTER 34
ZEAL'S FIRE

I am betrayed, my dear reader! I am slain! I pray these notes reach an educated eye and the truth is known of my end. I am undone by minotaurs, no less! What foul curs and savage beasts!
Though they might promise friendship and speak of kindness, they had the cage and spit ready for me on my arrival. What a fool I have been! What sights and miles I have endured, only to end up as the centrepiece of a minotaur's feast!
FROM THE 'LAST LETTERS' OF MASTER WIRD, FOUND DURING THE EFJAR SKIRMISHES

Saltlick truly was an irascible beast. Three turnips, a heap of carrots, some dubious tomatoes, and the grifabore was still whining at being left in the stable. Not to mention the overly large handful of silvers Hereni had paid to the tavern owner to stable the beast and to keep quiet in the meantime. They were beyond Manesmark by an hour and Krauslung by two, on the northeast road to Hâlorn, but still firmly in Arka territory. A cloak and a hood were her disguise and the night her escape.

Hereni left the tavern and its far too curious patrons and marched down the well-worn road. Tucking her flaxen hair into her hood, she kept a hand on her blade, thankful Akitha hadn't made the scabbard as fine as the steel and kept it ordinary and inconspicuous.

Two snow-covered standing stones guarded the road on either side. Runes marked three miles to the edge of Manesmark. The tavern lamps reached far into the night, and they were enough to spy a figure leaning up against one of the stones. It was equally cloaked and hooded, but a faint smile could be seen in the gap between them. A bow was slung over one shoulder and a handful of blue-feathered arrows in a quiver on his thigh, hiding behind the cloak's drape.

'Bull,' Hereni greeted him without breaking a step, and he fell in beside her.

'You think we'll be able to get into the city dressed like this?' he asked.

'Not in the slightest, and that's why we're stopping in Manesmark first.'

Bull understood completely. 'Then what?'

Hereni didn't have a plan. All she had was a direction and a fierce fire burning within her. She was no Written and had no tattoos to glow, but magick raged in her veins. Above them, a dark shape soared silently.

'Kinsprite says she's watching.'

'You already talking to her in your head?'

'I'm not so good at the talking back part.'

Hereni smirked. 'You really have become a Siren, haven't you?'

'Almost,' he said. 'But it's made Mithrid angry and makes me feel a guilt I don't much like.'

'You're following your heart, Bull, and that's all that needs to be said on the matter,' Hereni told him.

Bull whispered that to himself as they walked on.

The miles of squelching in frozen mud and watching the whispering pines along the road fell away all too quickly. Manesmark soon shone brightly before them, but it was nothing compared to the bonfire of torch and lamplight that burned another few miles beyond. Krauslung. Hereni had only seen the city once before, but not at night, and she found her eyes stretching wide. Its lights turned the snow-laden sky orange. Glittering spires poked the clouds. The Krauslung's marble shone white and amber as if it were still day.

Manesmark was busy despite the late hour. Barracks and training yards spread over the hillsides, still in use by smatterings of soldiers. Walls and fortifications blocked off the rest of the town, where smithies and fletches and armourers toiled. Their fires played on the sheer granite walls of the mighty building at the centre of Manesmark. The Spire towered over all. Its dark shape was stark against the city's glow and the low cloud, and its lit windows were a hundred eyes arranged in a jagged, soaring shape.

'Stick to the edges, there,' Hereni said with a wave of her hand, where three guards were loitering on the edge of a stubby watchtower, their backs to the town while they passed a pipe between them. She and Bull left the road for the sparse copses of trees and circled as if they'd come from further in the mountains. An old deer track led them closer.

'Can you take the one on the left?' Hereni asked, nodding to the burliest one through the pines. He looked about Bull's size.

Hereni saw a shine of silver wood as Bull took the bow from his shoulder and found an arrow from the quiver on his thigh. He might have been a simple fellow, but he was not a fool by any means, and it was true: his heart beat stronger than most. 'I can,' he whispered with a smile.

Hereni took the arrow from him and put a cut across the back of her hand before smearing the blood across her fingers and cloak. Bull looked on, deeply intrigued.

'Stay ready,' Hereni said, affecting a severe limp and putting a heavy hand on a hip. She put her scabbard to the small of her back, hidden.

'Evernia's tits,' Hereni cursed loudly as she lumbered closer to the tower. The Arka guards were immediately wary, spears up and one of them holding a torch high above his head.

'Who goes there?'

'Have you a healer close by?' Hereni called to them in a voice that sounded urgent but stayed a whisper. She showed off her bloody hand. 'A healer!'

'What's wrong with you?'

'Bloody sabrecat!' Hereni blurted, not stopping for a moment until the three parted to let her lean against the tower's wall. 'Came out of the woods back there!'

There it was: the moment their gazes shifted back to the woods, and their spears drifted away from her face.

Hereni pounced, a spell already tumbling from her lips. Seizing two of the guards' throats in her hands, she let fire pour from her fingers. Flame melted the metal of their gorgets until fire burst from the visor of their helmets. Unsurprisingly, not a scream came from either of them.

Bull had his eye on the big guard, who had his helmet off and fumbled with the pipe in panic. His head jerked sideways, an arrow poking from his temple.

Crouched low, Bull came running from the forest. 'Drag them inside,' Hereni ordered as she grabbed a pair of dead legs, and Bull followed suit with barely any effort.

Hereni began the grisly task of removing the armour from the cremated guards. Bull had an easier time with his disguise. He was dressed in Arka steel and green cloth and stood waiting with his bow over his shoulder before Hereni was even half finished. With the bodies stuffed into emptied arrow barrels, blood and char wiped away, they pressed on with eyes wary behind their visors.

Lucky for them, Bull's armour held the marks of a captain, and with heads held high, they pretended to patrol the streets of Manesmark as they crossed the town. Soldiers and guards saluted here and there, but none challenged them.

Krauslung beckoned, and with every step she took, Hereni's heart beat a fraction faster. She was having trouble taking her eyes off the Arkathedral, even as its lower levels disappeared behind the rearing Krauslung walls, where jagged crenellations and spear tips stood stark against the amber sky.

It was beginning to snow when they reached the gates. Though they were kept ajar, a multitude of guards and soldiers stood before them. Hereni led the way, raising her spear and muttering, 'Make way,' when she felt bold enough to do so.

'You there!' came a cry. Just as they crossed the threshold of the gates and into the torchlit tunnel that burrowed between the giant stone blocks, too.

'What?' Bull demanded with an officer's impatience, making Hereni smile behind her visor.

A sergeant was standing tall and broad behind them, but he faded quickly as he saw the marks on Bull's stolen armour.

'You got some blood on your cloak there, Captain,' was all he said, drawing a few stares.

Bull stared back for some time, until it almost became uncomfortable. 'Peasant spoke back to me.'

The sergeant's dour face split into a smile. A few chuckles came from the others. 'Aye, Captain,' he snickered before turning back to his post.

So-called Captain Bull and his guard marched into the city as if they were born there, despite having little idea where to go. They were both strangers, but the Arkathedral beckoned like a beacon, and they set to weaving down what they hoped were quieter streets. The problem, however, was that it seemed Krauslung had no quiet streets. Fortunately, the guards' armour made the crowds part and let them pass, and it was only when they came to a pair of lesser gates embedded in the Arkathedral's white marble that they were halted.

'Who are you?' asked a guard in grand armour. He, too, had the marks of a captain.

'Captain… Bull.'

'As in bullshite? Never heard of you.'

Hereni had an answer. 'We're new. From Belephon.'

The captain sneered, showing black teeth. 'More of you weak-spined bastards, is it? God, you still stink of the smoke of a burning city. Thought Loki had sent you all north to some godsforsaken fort in punishment.'

Bull cracked his knuckles. 'Think again.'

'True soldier would have fought to the death.'

Hereni patted the rounded pommel of her seax. 'Want to get some practice? You're making us late. Let us pass.'

The captain flexed his shoulders. 'You going to make me, soldier?'

'Captain,' Bull corrected.

Bull had about a foot on the man, and he finally gave in with a snort and a spit. 'Get out of my sight. I'll watch for you when you're out of armour.'

'Looking forward to it,' muttered Hereni as the gates opened for them. She swore her heartbeat was loud enough for them all to hear, and she tried not to hurry into the warmth of the Arkathedral while the captain stomped and cursed behind them.

'Where is Mithrid?' Bull asked in a whisper as they strode confidently but without direction.

'Up, I'll bet,' said Hereni, spying three sets of stairs leading from the giant atrium. A statue of Loki stood at its centre, and Hereni had to hold herself back from scorching it. Her magick had to be kept low. She had caught the whiff of helbeasts in the streets. Within the Arkathedral, she smelled something else. A familiar scent of death that chilled her. *Elves.*

Striding up step after step, already beginning to sweat, they coiled upwards into the mighty fortress. Hereni raised her spear to every guard they saw, walking quickly enough to evade any questions. At its upper reaches, the fortress became darker and darker. Every other torch was found dead. Guards increased in number. Hereni felt the waft of magick in the air and spied Scarred mages stalking the corridors. At least it disguised her own magick. With her hands spread by her side, she tried to feel a void in the magick's flow, sensing where Mithrid might be. There was nothing, and Hereni felt a nervousness chip away at her resolve.

By what must have been the fiftieth level, every hallway and stairwell was crafted from polished white marble and trimmed with gold. They must have been getting closer, but their course was interrupted by a mage with arms crossed. Their obstacle stood at the foot of a grand staircase that led to vaulted ceilings and tall windows that glowed with Krauslung's flame.

'Where are you going?' the mage demanded at the earliest sight of them.

'Up,' said Bull, moving past him, but a hand knocked against his Arka breastplate.

The mage shook his head. 'No, you aren't. I say who goes up. Only Scarred and Loki's new pets up there.'

'We're needed in the dungeons,' said Hereni. 'Where are they again?'

'Two levels ab—Wait, didn't you hear me, bitch? Why don't I recognise you?' Without a helmet, it was easy to see the suspicion on the mage's gaunt and scowling face. 'Put your visors up, damn it.'

Hereni looked around, seeing no witnesses. A patrol had just gone by, but they would have to be quick. Without a word, she and the Siren struck simultaneously.

Bull seized the arm stretched in front of him and twisted it while Hereni grabbed the mage's head and stuffed a fist in his mouth before much of a shout could escape. She wasn't quite quick enough, and a yelp reverberated around the hall. Lightning sparked in his hand, shocking her, but Bull slammed his clasped hands into the back of the mage's head, and his lack of a helmet was his undoing. The spell died as they caught his limp body and carried him behind the staircase, out of sight.

'Come on. I have a feeling our time's running out!' Hereni whispered as she took the stairs two at a time.

❦

'Well?'

Loki regarded the elf with a bemused smile while he poured himself some more wine. 'Well, what?'

Azen raked a claw along a table, gouging a little wooden spiral. 'You wait and you wait. You talk and you talk. Days have gone by with nothing but waiting and talking. While the mage looks for reinforcements and strengthens his position no doubt.'

'If the Dramath-Ai did their job—'

'You will not speak of the Dramath-Ai!' Azen's fist smashed the table, breaking its leg. 'Their loss still pains us.'

'No doubt. But you forget we are not idle. We're seeking our own strength,' Loki said, sipping loudly to watch Azen wrinkle his lip. 'Mithrid just needs more time, is all.'

'You play too many games with that poison. You trust her too much. A knife will find its way to her hands as soon as her collar comes loose.'

Loki smacked his lips. 'Perhaps you're right. Perhaps you're wrong. That is the beauty of waiting. Time, Azen. That is what you will give me. Our oath had no hourglass turned on it.'

'We have spent centuries waiting, god, and our patience is wearing…' Azen fell abruptly silent, looking sharply to the door as if he heard a knock.

'What is it?'

'Magick.'

The Arkathedral was full of mages and scuttling elves, but the narrowing of Azen's eyes told Loki this was something else, and if he trusted anyone and anything on the subject of magick, it was an elf.

Loki got to his feet, searching with his mind, but it was no Farden. He couldn't taste the mage's scent of magick, and deep in his mind, he didn't know whether to be relieved or disappointed. How enormously he loved torturing Farden, but that bloody spear had come far too close to Loki's neck far too many times. Loki was not quite ready to face him again. But no, this was somebody else.

'At last, they come for her,' Loki chuckled. 'See, my good Azen? Patience is the victor's practice. Wait, and all good things shall come to you.'

Hereni was lost. They had travelled up and down three levels of stairs, dashed down a dozen hallways, and doubled back constantly to avoid patrols. Once, they had even stood in a doorway at attention when they couldn't escape. The deeper they wound into the core of the Arkathedral, the more Hereni felt a trap closing in. Every corridor looked the same. Every door as faceless and uninformative as the next. There weren't even any bloody windows to tell them it was still night.

'These look like prison cells,' Bull said, pulling at a locked door. Something inside it scuttled across straw, chuckling in a spine-tingling pitch.

Hereni looked down the junction of corridors, every one of them delving deeper into the darkness of mountain rock. 'Fuck this. Mithrid!' Hereni began to whisper, softly at first but then louder. 'Mithrid!'

A thin staircase led them through a chokepoint of marble, and they burrowed to where the corridors were dark as pitch without the torches. A man's screams came from somewhere around them, and Hereni didn't want to know why. Bull put an arrow to his bow and held it flat and half-drawn.

'Mithrid!' Hereni yelled.

'Who you bloody shouting for?' called a mage, poking his head around a corner. Another followed him. Fortunately, they were not Scarred, but still very much a problem.

'Prisoner… transfer,' said Hereni, waving them forwards and close enough for her magick. She whispered a spell under her breath, hiding flames behind her back until the right moment.

'Which prisoner?' the mages shouted in unison.

Hereni answered with quick flicks of her hands, unleashing two crackling firebolts. The first mage went down none the wiser, a smoking hole in her armour. The second was quick with his shield spell but was thrown backwards against the wall from the force. Bull's arrow broke against his magick, and so he did as his namesake suggested and charged him like an angry minotaur. Bull threw his whole weight against his chest, and while the stout Manesmark armour didn't crack, human skull against the wall did. The mage slumped to the stone, drawing a streak of blood across the marble.

Shouts chased them down the corridor. Whether the magick had been felt or heard, their presence had been discovered. Their disguises counted close to nothing.

'Shit, shit,' Hereni babbled as she banged on armoured and runed doors. 'Mithrid!'

'They went that way!' Bull yelled to a trio of mages careening around a corner. The urgency of his voice won them over, but only to the end of the corridor.

'Oi!' they yelled, skidding on their heels.

Light bathed them as Hereni and Bull escaped the darkest dungeons, where the smell of sweat and effluence was rank, and found brighter hallways instead. The doors still bore iron and bars. These must have been for the fancier prisoners, and Hereni hammered on their doors just the same.

'Mithrid!'

'All I'm sayin' is that Farden with a keraken and a magick spear sounds like a recipe for the end of the world. What did they call it all those years ago? Ragnarök. Bloody Ragnarök.'

'And Loki says I can stop it,' whispered Mithrid. She still hadn't moved from the bed.

'This elvish business though…' Jeasin reached out to touch Mithrid's face. The girl shrank away for a moment before letting her.

'You got somethin' in you, girl, but never in a thousand years would I 'ave said elvish blood.'

Neither would Mithrid.

Jeasin's face scrunched up, and she let out a shuddering sigh.

'What is it?'

'The best lies always have a bit of truth in 'em,' replied Jeasin. 'Even if you are one of these light elves, it doesn't change who you already are.'

It was Mithrid's turn to sigh. 'What about who I'm going to be?' The choice was looming, closer and closer with every heartbeat. Jeasin's hands fell from her face, and Mithrid clutched at the bed frame as the woman turned and went to the door. Her hands spread across the door.

'What you were always meant to be. That's how fate works, right?' muttered Jeasin, pressing her ear to the wood now.

'You hear something?'

'A ruckus, if I'm right. I hear yellin'.'

Mithrid stood. 'Where?'

'Nearby. Comin' closer. I can hear somebody shoutin' a name.' Jeasin arched away from the door. 'It's yours!'

Mithrid should have cast around for something to break apart. She should have kicked the bed frame and wedged it against her collar again. All she did was stay still.

'Surrender!' came the yell of guards outside her door. A slight pain lanced through Mithrid's head as spells pounded against each other, walls, and floors. A shriek cut the clatter, and the door shook as something was thrown against it. Blood began to seep beneath the hairline crack where door met stone.

'Back up, Jeasin,' Mithrid warned.

The woman did as she was told, clenching her arm tightly.

'Mithrid!' came the cry.

'Hereni,' Mithrid breathed before running to the door. No, it couldn't be. Not now. Not her. 'Hereni!'

Fists pounded on the wood from the other side. 'Mithrid!'

'What are you doing here?' she yelled.

Another crash of magick and roaring of fire came before Hereni replied. 'To get you out. And it's going rather well so far!'

'Where's Farden?'

'Gods know where! It's me and Bull.'

Mithrid pulled at her hair. 'Loki will kill you, Hereni!'

'Not if I can help it.'

The door began to shudder, and Mithrid felt magick spreading.

Farden had taught her all manner of unlocking spells. The problem was that they took time and concentration, and Hereni was running out of both.

'Gah!' she strained as she closed her eyes and pushed her hands harder against the door. The clockwork was clicking, the runes were glowing, but somebody had layered spells on spells, and it was taking far too long.

'Hereni!' Bull yelled from the edge of the corridor. Two soldiers lay dead nearby with arrows in their chests. 'More are coming!'

The door shook as the last latch slid back, and Hereni fell inwards with the door. It was Mithrid who picked her up, and Hereni seized her in the tightest embrace. She held her breath, feeling Mithrid's racing heart against her armour. Yet something felt off. Something grated against her neck.

'What is this?' Hereni pulled at the iron collar around Mithrid's throat. The collar with spikes pointed inwards. She could see scabs on Mithrid's skin where it had already wounded her, and tears sprang to her eyes.

'Something that'll kill me if I use my power.'

Hereni held her face and kissed Mithrid's broken lips. 'I missed you.'

'So did I.'

Hereni stood as somebody shuffled behind Mithrid. 'And who's this?'

'Lady Jeasin,' the woman spat, as if it was a stupid question.

Hereni pointed a finger, frowning in confusion. 'The spy?'

'Much more than that, I'll thank you, but yes.'

'She's coming with you.' said Mithrid.

'Us. She's coming with us,' Hereni answered, momentarily taken aback.

'Hereni!' roared Bull.

Hereni seized Mithrid's hand and led her into the corridor. 'Stay down!' she yelled, spinning a wreath of fire above her and sending it spinning down the corridor behind them. A huddle of soldiers ran for their lives, buying them a moment of time. Another had pinned Bull against the wall with a spear. Hereni rushed him, and before the soldier could turn at the sound of her heavy paces, Hereni had already run him through with her seax. Akitha was right: it was a fine blade.

'This way!' Hereni said as she passed her blade to Bull, trusting in nothing but utter guesswork but at least it sounded confident. All they needed was a window and a long enough drop.

'Bull, is Kinsprite ready?'

'Almost!' he yelled as he wiped blood from his face.

Another mage barred their way, standing at an intersection of two corridors. This foe was Scarred, and Hereni cast a shield spell just in time as the woman's shining lightning skittered along the stone. The impact shook her arms and made her shield sputter. Boots squeaked across the marble as she was driven back. Hereni had almost forgotten how hard Scarred could hit, but it was her turn to show this mage what Scalussen taught.

Hereni reached out with both hands and a mutter of a spell, forming a spear of ice that raced for the Scarred. The shard was aimed wide, too far for the Scarred to meet with her shield, and she began to laugh maniacally. Hereni saw madness in the woman's eyes as she took a breath for a second spell.

Hereni beat her to it, driving her magick before her with a clap of her hands. Walls cracked and spat stone as quake and force spells ripped through the hallway, angled just right to throw the Scarred off her feet and straight into the spear of ice embedded in the wall.

There was no time for pride or congratulations. Thundering shouts and sprinting boots came from all angles.

'Which way, Mithrid?!' bayed Hereni.

Mithrid hesitated for a fraction of a moment.

'Mithrid!'

'That way!' she yelled, pointing to the far left hallway, and Hereni thought she glimpsed a sliver of light in its angle. She wasted no time taking Mithrid's hand once more and dashing onwards.

The marble tunnel aimed for an open hall lined with what looked like statues. Hereni could see more light spilling down the corridor and illuminating the way. A stained-glass window could also be spied, black and amber with the night and city's torches, and Hereni sprinted towards it, readying her spells. A fireball rocketed down the corridor, flashed through the hall, and punched its way into the darkness, leaving the window to shatter in its wake. Painted glass fell like a broken rainbow, and Hereni pelted the marble ever-faster, searching the skies beyond for any sign of dragon. 'Is she ready, Bull?' Hereni yelled.

'She's very close!' boomed the Siren, trying to keep up while hauling Jeasin along so fast her feet barely touched the ground.

'Hereni!' Mithrid hissed, pulling her hand free. Hereni scraped to a halt across the broken glass.

'I can't leave.'

Hereni seized her again. 'What? Have you lost your mind?!'

'You shouldn't have come for me.'

'Mithrid—!'

'I'm not done here!'

'What do you mean you're not done here? But it's Loki!' Hereni shouted.

'That it is!' boomed a voice.

Soldiers and mages flooded from an adjoining hall. Two figures appeared from another doorway opposite, one short and smug, one tall and far from human. The latter was a dark elf, and blue light shone between his claws. Loki stood by his side, wagging a finger back and forth.

Hereni aimed her fire spells, grinding them into blades before she hurled them at the god and the elf.

A ring of blue runes like the Dramath-Ai had wielded slammed into her fire, killing it dead. Another circle of runes chased it, each a blade in their own right. Hereni's shield cracked under their force, but it managed to hold together. Hereni stared through the rippling surface of her spell, counting soldiers. The cold wind howled at her back. Snow flurried past her shoulders.

'Bull?!'

The Siren put a hand on her shoulder. 'She's ready, but how are we—'

The elf snarled as he raised a spear of light and stood ready to throw.

Instead of Hereni, it was Mithrid who stepped forwards. 'Stop! Loki, don't you dare hurt them.'

Loki waved his hands to the elf, who reluctantly let his magick die.

'Your Scalussen friends have come at last to save you, I see! Now where is Farden?' said Loki, hands open and wide.

'He's not here,' said Mithrid.

'How curious. Now, as much as I admire your tenacity, General Hereni, Mithrid is not yours to take. She is under my protection now, and you've made quite the mistake coming here.'

'Let them leave alive, Loki, and I'll stay,' Mithrid blurted, taking another step.

'Mithrid!'

Mithrid threw Hereni a murderous look. 'This is the only way you get out of here alive.'

'I'm not fucking leaving you,' Hereni growled. A dangerous idea came to her mind then, and she didn't question it. She snatched the seax back from Bull and grabbed Mithrid around the neck with one hand. With her other, she held her blade close to Mithrid's cheek.

'What are you doing?' Mithrid complained, grabbing at her arms.

'You'll thank me later.'

'Hereni—!'

'You want her so much, Loki?' Hereni challenged the god. 'Then you stay back, otherwise I'll slit her throat!'

Loki walked closer, not further away. Hereni had never been that close to him, and despite his slight glow, the torches burning in their sconces, and the fire running through her, Hereni shivered. His gaze bound her like shackles.

'Touching, but I see how Mithrid holds on to your cloak, Hereni. Even she doesn't believe you'd do such a thing.' Loki's smile spread. 'Is this the one, Mithrid?'

'Shut your face,' she spat.

'It is, isn't it? The one who holds your heart,' said Loki.

'Back away!' Hereni screamed, inching closer to the window and listening for the beating of dragon's wings. This wasn't how she had planned the night ending.

'Let me go, Hereni,' Mithrid was whispering. 'He won't let you take me, and I won't see you lying dead and bleeding on this marble.'

'You can't be serious.'

'Do we have a deal, Loki?' Mithrid asked the god.

Loki performed a mock bow. 'For you, Mithrid, I'll let them live,' he said, voice slick as oil. 'I couldn't bear to see you broken-hearted.'

Mithrid pulled away, and Hereni was forced to let her go. Without a look, she walked calmly across the marble and broken glass to stand by Loki's side. Only then did she raise her eyes and stare back at Hereni impassively. Hereni shook with enraged confusion.

'You can't be serious,' she echoed.

'Deadly.' Loki sucked his teeth. 'Though I'll be taking Lady Jeasin back. I've grown quite accustomed to having her around, and she's not getting away from me that easily. Hand her over, or everybody dies.'

Hereni took a breath to fill the hall with curses and obscenities, but she clamped her mouth shut and slammed her blade into its sheath.

Jeasin stood tall, and for a moment she didn't speak or move a muscle besides turning her head back and forth, listening. 'If that's the way you want it, Loki. Fine,' she said, reaching for Hereni's hands. 'If you could help me, girl, I'd appreciate it.'

Hereni nodded, walking the woman slowly while she clutched at her arms. Hereni tried not to react as she felt Jeasin's hand slide onto the seax's handle, hidden by the woman's robes.

Loki grew impatient. 'You're not that old and decrepit, you old whore.'

Jeasin paused in front of him. 'There you are,' she muttered, and before Loki could tilt his head in intrigue, Jeasin pounced. The woman's hand and the Scalussen steel it held were a blur, flashing outwards from the sheath and reaching for Loki's face.

Hereni heard it before she saw it: the whisper of steel against skin. And even though Loki's skin sounded more like iron, he reeled back with his hand clamped to his cheek.

'Everybody dies!' came Loki's infuriated bellow.

Hereni hurled out a shield spell to keep the elf and soldiers at bay. She practically threw Jeasin at Bull, and while he helped her onto the sill, he clamped a hand on Hereni's shoulder and began to pull.

Blue light flashed, cutting through Hereni's shield. Pain lanced up her side. Glancing down, she saw blood pouring from her side between jagged Arka steel.

'No!' came a yell that Hereni hoped was Mithrid.

Another light flashed, and though Hereni winced, it was not haunting blue but a sheer white that blinded everybody in the hall.

Farden had arrived.

A blast from Gunnir knocked everyone to the ground. Loki was crouched, a hand on Mithrid's collar.

'Mithrid!' she yelled again, but Mithrid didn't move. Her face was a dark scowl, tortured like Hereni had never seen. By Mithrid's side, the god's hands glowed with light as he held back the spear's fire. Before she and Loki vanished from the shine of battle in a burst of broken glass, Hereni saw it. As did all who stared upon Loki in that moment, she wagered: the streak of dark blood across his cheek.

'Go!' Farden yelled, Gunnir in one hand and the other reaching for Hereni. Bull and Jeasin hurled themselves from the window as a blue dragon skimmed the fortress. Spells hammered the mage's shields from every side, and as Hereni clasped his gauntlet, fire tore from Gunnir's blade. Azen stood before its onslaught, runes burning brightly in his hand to keep from succumbing.

It was then that Farden raised Gunnir and brought its steel down on the marble. Cracks ruptured the hall in all directions, and within moments, sections of floor and ceiling began to crumble. While soldiers were swallowed or crushed by falling sections of stone, wind screeched as Farden whisked Hereni away, a scream of her own tearing from her throat.

'By the bloody gods, Farden,' Hereni gasped, sinking to the snow of a mountainside.

The frigid air made him feel every drop of sweat, every surge of fire that spiralled around the spear and his gauntlets.

'What did you do?' she gasped.

'Taught Loki a lesson, is what. Something I maybe should have done last time, when I should have listened to Mithrid,' Farden said as he gazed through snow and dark to where a faded cloud was rising from the Arkathedral. The faint knelling of bells could be heard when the wind gusted.

Farden turned to notice Hereni's bloody hand clamped to her ribs. He knelt down at her side and remembered an old healing spell. She muttered one for herself, and the magick managed to stop the bleeding if nothing else. 'We need to get you to a healer.'

Hereni was fixated on the ground, shaking her head.

'I'll spare you the "what were you fucking thinking?" speech, shall I?' Farden suggested. 'You're lucky you're alive.'

'She chose to stay. We had a moment to run, and Mithrid chose to stay,' Hereni whispered, taking a moment. 'With *him*.'

'To save your lives, I'll wager,' said Farden in a low voice. 'She plays a dangerous game.'

'She said she wasn't done yet,' said Hereni, and up came her gaze, sharp and accusing. 'This is you, isn't it? This is all a trick. A ploy. That's what you two were talking about in the yards! Evernia's tits, I don't know who schemes more these days, you or Loki!'

'It's all Mithrid, actually,' said Farden quietly, scanning the skies for a sign of the dragon. 'It was her idea to get close to Loki. To wait until his guard came down.'

Hereni wrinkled her nose. 'Then you're a fool for letting her.'

'She said quite the opposite.'

'Loki's in her head, Farden!' shouted Hereni, getting to her feet, 'I saw his hooks in her! She wasn't the same Mithrid. All you've done is give Loki our greatest weapon and provided Mithrid every opportunity to become what she saw in those mirrors.'

Farden's eyes bored into hers. 'And that's precisely what Loki will think. We have to trust her. I already let my daughter fall to dark minds and weave her power for evil, and I won't let Mithrid do the same.'

Hereni said no more. The sound of wings had grown loud, and from the drifting snow came Kinsprite, eyes gleaming. Bull and none other than Lady Jeasin perched on her back.

'Well, I never,' Farden gasped.

Lady Jeasin, whispered Gunnir, equally as surprised.

Jeasin clambered down from the dragon's back as if revulsed by Kinsprite's scales. 'Thought you could just forget about me and let me rot in Krauslung, mage?' she ranted.

'I thought Malvus had killed you,' said Farden.

Jeasin didn't need Bull to find her way across the snow and grass to where Farden stood. 'Unfortunately for you, he didn't,' she said. 'Tell me: where did I get that Loki bastard? Didn't feel like I slashed his throat.'

'Almost,' Farden said with a smile. 'You cut his cheek.'

Farden thought Jeasin might spit, but instead and to his disbelief, she snorted and briefly embraced him.

'I 'eard about Durnus,' she murmured. 'I'm sorry.'

Farden nodded. 'I'm glad you survived,' he replied, before Hereni stood at his side, tense and unblinking. 'And I'm sorry I ever put you in danger.'

Hereni butted in. 'What is Loki doing to her?'

'Trying to make her his, is what, girl,' Jeasin replied. 'He put a collar around her neck to stop her magick. He makes her fight his mages while he feeds her lies and truths in the hope she won't know what's which. About you, Forever King, about magick, even about what she is.'

'What do you mean?' Farden asked.

'Loki thinks she's got elf blood in her. The others like that elf call her lakrimur.'

Gunnir breathed in Farden's ear. *It means light elf. Literally burning elf.*

'That can't be,' Farden and Hereni said in unison, sharing a wide-eyed look.

'Guess what?' Jeasin said, slapping her hands together. 'It ain't my business to figure out. I did my job. Loki asked me to lie to Mithrid for him, and I didn't.'

Worried silence answered her.

'She's fierce, your girl,' Jeasin said, turning to Hereni and not Farden. 'I wouldn't worry as much as you're doin' right now.

Farden watched as Hereni nodded and shook Jeasin's hand silently.

'And what of you, Jeasin?' Farden asked. 'New Scalussen is safe. We could find you a house.'

'Safe?' Jeasin laughed harshly. 'If the last few decades have taught me anything, it's that safe is anywhere you ain't. I've had my fill. I've tried to cut a god's throat, I've survived an empire's fall, and I've survived you, Farden. I'm done. I'm goin' back to Albion and my home. And don't you tell me I have to ride a dragon or use that magick spear of yours to fling me across the sea. You'll get me home some other way. It's the least you bloody owe me.'

'Saltlick,' Hereni muttered.

Jeasin furrowed her brow. 'Pardon?'

'How I got here.'

'Irien's flying boar?' Farden asked.

Hereni led the way up the road, and within a few minutes of silent stomping, they walked between two pillars of stone. A glowing tavern lay beyond, and there seemed to be some commotion going on in its stable. Farden and Hereni began to run.

Beneath the thatch, they found two men arguing, one who looked to be a tavern keeper and the other a merchant swaddled in layers of fur. 'It won't obey!' shouted the merchant.

The barkeep didn't give a hoot. 'Give it some more veggies, damn it! Not my fault you can't handle the beast. Shouldn't have bought it otherwise, but sale's final.'

Hereni lit a flame in her hands, drawing the attention of the two men. 'I'll give you a chance to apologise and step away before I burn something precious off your bodies.'

The barkeep did as suggested, scuttling away swiftly with his hands and arms held high. The merchant was less agreeable.

'What? What's going on? Didn't you hear? Sale's made, interloper! Go find your own... whatever this is. I'm going to stuff it and display it, and you shan't interfere,' the merchant warned as he tugged again at the rope wrapped around Saltlick's neck.

The rage Hereni nurtured found something to target. The flame in her hand grew.

The grifabore had other ideas. With a fierce grunt, Saltlick charged at the fur-clad man and used his tusks to upend him into the mud. Saltlick beat his wings to jump and hit the man square in the face with a hefty trotter. The merchant was knocked senseless. Fortunate too, for Saltlick trampled him a little more for good measure until he was beaten to a pulp.

'What in Hel am I hearin'?' asked Jeasin, catching them up.

'That's Saltlick. A grifabore. And a fine one at that,' said Hereni, managing a smile.

'He'll do nicely,' Jeasin said.

'What?' asked Farden.

'I'll take this Saltlick to Albion, where both of us can be fat and 'appy and far out of the way of your bloody mess, Farden. Maybe I'll even find a way to bein' a duchess. Who knows?'

Hereni shrugged. 'He does need a new owner after Farden got rid of his last one.'

'Of course he did,' Jeasin tutted. She approached Saltlick, clicking her tongue. 'My da used to keep pigs.'

Saltlick came to investigate her. Jeasin found his rumpled snout and tusks and started to scratch his chin. The grifabore collapsed to the ground with a thud as he turned on his side and put his stubby legs in the air. Hereni snorted while Farden bowed to Jeasin.

'It's been quite the tale,' he said.

'That it 'as, and you'd best keep me out of the sequel,' said Jeasin, coaxing the big hog upright again and finding his stirrups and saddle. With some cursing at her stiff bones, she climbed onto Saltlick's saddle and patted the grifabore's bristled haunches.

'Please don't break the world in two,' was all Jeasin said before she urged Saltlick into a run. The speedy hog's wings spread, and the wind got under them, lifting Jeasin in the air and whisking her into the snow.

'You,' Hereni said, finding her next target. The lowly barkeep. 'You tried to sell my grifabore.'

'I thought you'd left him!'

'Lie,' Hereni said, chasing him with quick flashes of fire until the strings of his apron burned. He ran straight to the door of his tavern.

'Home and the healers, Hereni,' said Farden, raising Gunnir. It wasn't an order. It was not a question, but something in between. 'Kinsprite, Fleetstar, Bull, hold on.'

The mage watched Hereni stare south to the city's glow.

'Trust,' was all she whispered.

It was late in the evening when Farden jumped them all back to New Scalussen. Strangely enough, it was Akitha that stood waiting for them.

'What are you doing here?' Farden asked.

'Waiting for them.' Akitha pointed at Bull and Hereni. 'How did the new blade do? You haven't lost it already? Thron's balls!'

'It might be lost, but it made Loki bleed,' said Bull.

Akitha's fierce demeanour faded, and she held her head proud as she helped the injured Hereni stumble towards the Dawnknell. The young mage's chin was on her chest.

Bull and Kinsprite stayed beside Farden. He looked the lad up and down before extending a hand and clasping his tightly. 'You did well, Bull. You always have a home here as well as Sutherheim.'

'Thank you, King,' said Bull, and as Farden turned, he added, 'The queen only wants to keep her people safe, you know.'

'As do I, Bull,' said Farden as he marched away, mind and heart heavy. He couldn't help but wonder if Hereni's doubts rang true.

'Trust,' he repeated to himself.

part three

BLOOD

CHAPTER 35
THE·DEAD WHISPER

*A schism is a cruel fate of the dragon and rider bond. One in several
thousand couplings suffer it, when their minds differ so greatly their bond
becomes jeopardised. And with their souls entwined, only pain and madness
await.*
EXCERPT FROM THE WRITINGS OF SIREN HERETIC AND ONCE SIREN
QUEEN VIVAN SISERO

It was early in the morning when the crow's skull spoke.

Set almost at the centre of the table between Lerel and Farden, between the plates of breakfast the mage hadn't touched, its dead beak twitched.

Lerel flinched. She had been staring at the empty chair across from her, where a fire-haired girl normally sat. She blinked, spreading her hands across the table.

'Where have you been, Irien?' it whispered.

Every eye turned to Farden, from Eyrum's tired bags to Warbringer's narrowed suspicion of the skull.

'Tell him Farden's in hiding after Mithrid's... departure,' Farden said, gingerly pushing the crow skull across the table to Lerel.

'I do her voice once and now I have to play Irien constantly?'

'Anyone else?' Farden looked to Ko-Tergo, who shook his furry head vehemently. Elessi cleared her throat and pretended to be hoarse.

'Swines,' answered Lerel as she picked up the skull, took a deep breath, and touched a thumb to its gem. 'Farden is in hiding… my dear,' she said in her best Golikan accent.

It took a moment for Loki to answer. 'Is he now? And so he should be, after what he did to my Arkathedral.'

Gazes turned on Farden, but he shook his head and put a finger to his lips.

'I heard,' replied Lerel.

'And the others?'

'Preparing for battle.'

There came another pause.

'What of the keraken? What have you found out?'

'It has no weakness. It's not looking good for you, my dear.'

'Find me something I can use, or I'll come down there and flay you myself,' whispered the skull before the gem fell dark. Lerel slapped it down on the table, not caring if it would break.

'It makes my skin crawl,' she said.

'But by the sounds of it, Loki's not in a good mood,' said Farden. 'And that's exactly what we want.'

Warbringer nodded appreciatively. 'A war of mind and might.'

Lerel eyed the whole loaf at the far end of the table, where another chair sat empty. It was normally picked to pieces by finches by now. 'Where's Peryn?'

Farden chuckled. 'With her new pet.'

'It's here?' asked Elessi.

Farden grinned. 'Steel yourself.'

It took the soldiers a moment to notice the king and his council waiting on the gates. Lerel didn't blame them. What lay beyond the walls was far more pressing.

Territha had come to Scalussen.

The bird – if it could be called a bird – was simply humongous. Taller than a ship's mast and double that from pinion to pinion when it spread its four wings. Every soul on the walls flinched when lightning and thunder crackled between its feathers. A few soldiers looked like they might have shat themselves when Territha shrieked, leaving a sore ring in Lerel's ears.

Clouds had come with the huge beast, draped low across the desert and bringing spots of rain. Ossas seemed to welcome it, momentarily rising up from his backside and raising his hands. His beasts weren't so sure, with many hiding in his shadow. Some outright fled with ears back and tails between legs. Once more, Lerel didn't blame them. Fortunately, Territha was more interested in the great Ossas, flapping around his head and cawing at a thankfully quieter volume. Ilios spiralled above them both, wings riding the storm-currents. In the distance, huge and curious eyes poked from the water of the harbour.

Nerilan and Towerdawn were already standing beyond the gates with several of the dragons and their riders, all watching with inquisitive eyes. Nerilan's were so narrowed they were almost closed.

'I hope you can control this monster, King,' she said as the others arrived.

Farden pointed to the tiny figure that stood alone on the plain, utterly dwarfed by Ossas and Territha. It was Peryn, surrounded by a weaving, undulating cloud of birds. 'Our new High Crone can.'

Nerilan sniffed haughtily. 'You had better be right about this farce of a plan.'

'I'd better, otherwise you'll be kissing Loki's boot instead of spitting at mine.'

'How's that dragon egg *we* rescued, by the way?' Lerel asked, getting a stab in. Farden wasn't the only one who was constantly vexed by the Siren queen.

Eyrum interrupted. 'What if Loki comes to New Scalussen and sees what we're doing? These Great Ones are hard to miss.'

'Ossas looks like one of the mountains. Keraken spends most of his time underwater, and his surprise is already ruined. Territha is constantly cloaked by her storms. I say let him flit south and see his doom.'

'And when do we go to battle, Farden?' rumbled Towerdawn, eyes closed and scrunched as if in deep and concerned thought, or even pain.

'Not yet. We have to find one more. I know there's another out there.'

'There is one. Utiru,' said Lerel.

'Anyone but her. There's another. There has to be.'

'What do you mean *another*, Farden? Is three monsters not enough for you?' demanded Nerilan.

Farden shook his head. 'If I don't bring them to our side, then Loki will take them for his,' he replied, as thunder crackled again. Territha circled the walls once more before she flapped towards the Giant's Shin mountains.

Nerilan threw up her hands. 'How wonderful. It wants to live in the mountains.'

Before any more arguing could take place, a Jar Khoum messenger came running across the sand. He babbled breathlessly in his language, and Farden frowned until the boy had to repeat himself. 'He says we have to see something,' said the mage. 'He says something's coming.'

'Loki?' The word was like a crash of crystal, making everybody present tense.

'No,' Farden said, a frown on his face and his feet leading him east along the walls.

Lerel followed close, seeing crowds amongst the palms. The Jar Khoum poured from their underground tunnels and caves. Soldiers flooded the wall tops, some already shouting.

Lerel couldn't believe their words.

'Are they saying what I think they're saying…?' she asked, pausing to feel a shudder in her ground.

'Bastions,' breathed Farden, quickening his pace.

Lerel didn't believe it until they rounded the corner of the walls, and along Scalussen's eastern flank, she saw them and stumbled to a halt in awe.

Each beast was a tower of muscle and cracked grey hide, brandishing four ivory tusks as large as the palms they waded through. Their long serpentine trunks, ridged with muscle, swayed between their slow, ponderous, and determined pace.

The ground shook as Ossas rose to greet them, and in a moment of silent ceremony, the lead bastion extended its thick legs, stretched its thick trunk, and almost bowed to the giant. Ossas bowed back, and with the formalities over, the bastion raised its trunk to the clouds and filled the morning with the sound of a hundred trumpets.

The Jar Khoum queen Kayruka was surrounded by her people. Her normally dour face showed what could have been a smile. Lerel watched closely.

'They have not come to these lands in decades, they say,' rumbled the giant above them.

Lerel searched the sky for lightning before she realised it was Ossas chuckling and not thunder.

Farden cupped his hands around his mouth. 'What do they want, great Ossas?'

Ossas pressed a gigantic fist into an empty palm. 'They want to fight.'

Farden and Lerel locked gazes. 'They what? How?'

'They hear the call of Ossas' song.'

'Then for that I'm grateful,' Farden laughed.

Farden thumped another tome onto the pile.

'One more,' he whispered. 'All we need is one more.'

The libraries felt darker than usual, as if the moths inside the lanterns were half asleep.

'Rokhelm,' Farden said in a hoarse voice. It had been hours since he'd spoken truly aloud. Lerel tore her tired eyes from the scroll and rubbed the ache from them.

Rokhelm had been face-deep in another fat book, and he looked up as if he'd forgotten he was alone. Lerel smirked. She was beginning to like this mad captain.

'It's down to you now,' said the mage. 'We've done all we can here.'

Rokhelm sighed. 'Keraken has been trying to remember, but his memories are old, scarce, and scattered. All he has recalled is a shipwrecked Scalussen Smith. Keraken has a soft spot for mariners marooned, and he spoke with this one awhile in his way. The man said his brother had fallen to a beast of shadow and rage. On islands in colder seas. Perhaps not a Great One, but his only other idea nonetheless.'

Peryn drummed her long nails. 'That must have been a thousand years ago.'

Elessi tutted. 'And colder seas don't quite narrow it down.'

Rokhelm shook his head, quite at odds with his smile. 'I was not with him, but I know the memory. I taste the salt. Somewhere between Albion and the north. A wild and friendless sea.'

Farden roamed the map sprawled nearby and pinned by obsidian pebbles. 'The Lonely Sea?'

Rokhelm grinned. 'Perhaps.'

'Leave it with me,' Farden said, crossing his arms with a clank of his vambraces. 'You all take a few hours to rest. I'll do some more digging.'

Elessi, Peryn, and Warbringer gratefully escaped the library without a word. Only Lerel remained.

'Take a br—'

'I'm staying whether you like it or not because I know that look and that voice, Farden. You're up to something,' Lerel told him sternly.

Farden tried to hide his smile. It didn't work. 'Let's take a walk.'

The mage led her deeper into the Jar Khoum city, where the tunnels opened into huge caverns and honeycomb caves full of cerulean light and the roar of overlapping echoes. Lantern-lined walkways reached between stalactites and stalagmites. Flocks of bats flapped in the lower reaches of the scores of cave chambers, avoiding the spears of light that came from various holes in the cave roof above. Palm-frond houses clustered and weaving alleys bustled with Jar Khoum, from skalds playing flutes to busy crafters, or hooded, dusty figures tending the lanterns rubbing shoulders with warriors and merchants.

Farden stopped on a walkway overlooking a hollowed-out pinnacle of rock growing out of the cave floor. A wooden walkway spiralled around it from base to cone tip and weaved between balconies and windows glowing with blue light.

'Beautiful,' Lerel whispered.

Farden shook his head. 'One mere facet of what we fight to save. One of thousands, and I feel them all slipping from my grasp. There is too much. Scalussen. Krauslung. Warbringer and her prophecy. Nerilan and Towerdawn. Mithrid. Now the elves. Even me,' he said. 'I was so sure I knew the way through this time, but now I'm on that same old knife-edge. Is it the spear, like Nerilan likes to remind me? Is it the same old me, learning nothing?'

Lerel took his hand. 'You are as stubborn as always. You are reckless as always. But you are also as fearless as always. Driven by what's right as always. And I would tell you if I thought you were going mad, as Nerilan thinks, I would tell you.'

'As always.' Farden held her gaze.

'I'll admit, you've come close to worrying me, but by all those measures that spear hasn't changed you. You've changed you. With some guidance, of course,' Lerel said, hiding a smirk. 'It will all come together in the end.'

'I don't disagree with you, but why do I feel that coming together is charging at us headlong? Time's running out for us. For Mithrid most of all.'

Lerel pursed her lips. 'How was she?'

'Bruised, confined, but alive, and I saw the same fierce look in her eyes, but Hereni's doubt has rattled me. She thinks Loki's lies are turning Mithrid against us, and if they are, then we're in trouble.' Farden bowed his head. Lerel watched him closely, wondering if there was more to his words. 'You asked me a while back if I fear her. Well, I'm starting to. That's why we need all the Great Ones we can get. I'll do almost anything to find another.'

'If Rokhelm and the libraries can't help any more, and time's running out, then what? The gods?'

'I said *almost* anything.' Farden shook his head. 'Another idea I've been nurturing.'

'Why don't I like the sound of this already?'

'Because it's pure and utter madness.'

A visible unease crept into Lerel. 'Madder than the Great Ones? I have to hear this.'

'Tyrfing.'

'You remember he's dead, right?'

'Precisely. Durnus used his magick and the Grimsayer to send me to speak to his ghost. With the spear, I—'

'Don't say it,' said Lerel, cutting him off cold. She held up a hand. 'Because it sounds like you want to go to Hel.'

'I want to ask Tyrfing what he knows. The dead whisper, and he might know where to look.'

'Is that even possible?'

'If daemons and gods can go there, then the spear should be able to as well. It's a realm like any other, and my memory and the Grimsayer can get me to Tyrfing.'

Lerel crossed her arms. 'I'm coming with you.'

Farden laughed. 'Absolutely not. It's not safe, Lerel. It's Hel for gods' sa—'

'I haven't known safe in years, don't be ridiculous. It's been far too long since I saw Tyrfing, and I want to make sure you don't go astray, as you are often wont to do,' Lerel said with a narrowed gaze, daring him to defy her.

Farden sighed. 'Travelling to Hel has a cost. You can't forget seeing a place like that.'

'It's final, Farden,' she said in a stern voice. 'Well, what are we waiting for?'

It was only after Lerel and Farden had stomped their way across the hewn stone that a shadow fell across the railing, cast by no light. Threads of fine silk were spun from the air and swirling motes of dust. A goddess watched them leave with dark eyes of shifting mercury, lips pursed tight.

The pedestal screeched as Farden dragged it into the middle of the room. The Grimsayer yawned wide with a whisper.

'Tyrfing,' said Farden to the tome, and the pages once again began to search until they found him. Tyrfing's form became visible, shuddering slightly.

'The first soul to live in Hel and not have died to get there,' Farden spoke with reverence, shaking his head.

'Will this hurt?' asked Lerel, checking her armour and sword for the third time.

Farden tutted. 'There's no going back now, Lerel. You said it was final.'

'Answer the bloody question.'

'It shouldn't.'

'Shouldn't?'

Farden pulled a face. 'We're only visiting instead of travelling there. We don't have to die, if that's what you're asking. Not this time.'

'Do I… do I need a coat?' *Did one need a coat for Hel?*

Farden smiled as he held Gunnir flat over the Grimsayer. A breeze stirred the veils of the windows and made the door rattle.

'Ready?' he asked.

Lerel took his other hand and didn't know whether to shake or nod her head. Perhaps she had acted too rashly. Her worry over Mithrid had spoken for her before she could—

Gunnir's spell drove the breath from her. The magick had hit her hard before but not like this. She fought to gulp air as a blur of rock and fire filled her eyes. All she could do was clench Farden's hand and pray that it would be over soon.

It wasn't, and Lerel started to panic. Her lungs were empty and begging to breathe. Pain radiated from her chest. She clutched at Farden's hand tighter as she began to shake, but with what felt like a cold slap around the face, she was abruptly released. And into an icy puddle, no less, crystal sharp with cold. Her hands crunched on grey pebbles as she forced herself up to take the deepest breath of her life.

It felt like no air she'd ever tasted. Cold as the wind of the ice fields, but strangely thin like soup watered down. Lerel gulped it in nonetheless.

Farden crunched on the gravel and ice nearby, reaching for her. 'Welcome to Hel,' he rasped as they hauled themselves up out of the pool.

Lerel shrank back as she saw what lay beyond, where an endless cavern held a carpet of faint blue mist. A faint light kept it from utter darkness, but without flame or lantern or moth to make it. Lerel rubbed ice-water from her eyes and looked again, now seeing the faces and shapes in the mist. It was no fog, but a crowd as vast as the cavern, never-ending and ever-moving. A constant flow of souls kept coming from tunnels that could have swallowed mountains. The dead shuffled back and forth, and Farden was proved right: Lerel heard their haunting whispers.

'Is that...? Are those...?' Lerel needed to hear the word. She felt nauseated by the sheer number.

'Souls,' Farden replied, grim of face and brow low. 'And far more than I saw last time I ventured here. Maybe that's why it's far colder than it was before.

Lerel agreed and wished she had brought a coat after all. She rubbed her hands together for warmth, and it was then that Lerel realised their breath did not come in clouds as it should have. But before she could speak, a deep voice cut the silence.

'What in Hel are you doing here, Nephew?'

Tyrfing stood over them, casting no shadow in the depths of the world, cloak moving in an unfelt breeze, hands on his hips.

Farden said nothing, instead clasping his uncle with both arms. Tyrfing flinched at first, as if surprised by the feel of something solid after so many years spent shepherding ghosts. It took a moment until he squeezed back, gripping Farden so tightly even the Scalussen metal creaked, and thudded him hard on the back. He seized Lerel next, almost drowning her in the hug, but she held on tightly.

'How are you here? How did Durnus manage to send you both in the flesh?' asked Tyrfing. Farden took in every detail. His uncle's pale skin was thinner, almost glasslike in the way it shone at certain angles. He had aged, but not enough for the years he had spent below the earth. He still carried the same armour he had worn the last time Farden had seen him, albeit dustier and rusted at the edges, eaten at by time.

'Durnus didn't. This spear did,' he admitted.

'This…' Tyrfing squinted at the weapon in Farden's hands, still vibrating from its spell. 'This is new.'

'It's the Spear of Gunnir. Gods-made and a crucible of magick.'

Tyrfing looked suspicious. 'I don't know what that is, but I feel its power. Too much power, if you ask me. Is that why so many souls have come down here to whisper of the great and terrible

Forever King? Of magick in the skies?' his uncle asked, and Farden stood his ground even though he felt a disappointment in his gut. Lerel stayed silent.

'Such is war,' Farden said.

Tyrfing nodded before glancing over Farden's shoulder warily. 'What is it?

'You should not be here, is what it is. You shouldn't have come. Hel is stronger than ever and fiercely protective of her realm. If she barely tolerates the sight of me, she'll kill us all for such an intrusion.' Tyrfing beckoned a hand. 'Come. Follow me. Quickly.'

Tyrfing aimed in the direction of the nearest tunnels, leading them on a winding path where the black and featureless rock ebbed and flowed exactly as Farden remembered, choking them every now and again in a flow of souls. They were constant and innumerable, and Lerel shrank away from their cold touch whenever they came too close. Farden watched a faint and ghostly bear of a man drift past, a crown of spikes still sitting on his brow. Another was a wiry, lanky fellow with a swirling dagger tattooed across his eye. Yet another reached barely to his hip and had the scales and snout of a lizard. Farden didn't want to see Thenerean, or Wyved, or Modren, or any of those he had lost since the stars had first fallen, but still he searched the faces. Even Samara was somewhere beneath the earth, robbed of the void when the Bifröst was broken.

A whisper a fraction louder than the rest passed him by, and Farden turned to listen. It sounded like a bard's song, curious amongst the vacant pleas and mutters, and he had to strain to hear it.

'His world is afloat on ambition and dreams, Long nights of ale spent sharing his schemes. The world is his oyster all wrapped up in shell, But my dear, oysters need catching, and his live in Hel.'

'You look tired, Nephew,' said Tyrfing over the wind of whispers, stealing Farden's attention. 'I see the weight of your crown on you, just like it weighed on me. Lerel, you're radiant as always, even in Hel.'

'Why, thank you,' she said, clearly distracted with not offending the dead.

'And you look…' Farden had seen the difference between the uncle marching swiftly before him and the uncle he had been forced to leave here, but he didn't want to mention it. 'You look surprisingly good for a servant of the underworld, Uncle.'

Tyrfing traced his hand through the passing stream of souls, grazing a dozen of them. Farden and Lerel both shivered as a faint whining could be heard, like voices lost in a gale. It was then that Farden noticed the pale and misty souls wore the vestiges of Arka armour. Others behind them sported Golikan wooden plate and feathered helms, even in death. They walked with vacant eyes as they shuffled, completely unaware of the living flesh passing them by.

'You're as terrible a liar as always,' said Tyrfing with a smile as he came to a halt in a tunnel less travelled. It was a weak smile, unpractised. 'I imagine you didn't come to visit for small talk and a family reunion. Why are you here?'

'We need your help.'

'I imagine so.' Tyrfing's eyes grew stony. 'The dead whisper of strange things, Farden. There are souls I don't recognise that Hel calls elves. What is happening to Emaneska?'

The guilt of the elves still lingered within Farden, but he refused to entertain it. There was no time for regret and blame, only solutions and victory. 'The war with Loki is what's happening,' he said, deeply aware Lerel was watching him. 'He's raised an elven army.'

A screech rang through the cavern, one that made the hairs on Farden's neck and arms stand on end as he remembered the foul creature that was responsible for such a noise.

'We should keep moving,' Tyrfing said, beckoning them onwards while he talked. 'I've heard the bastard's name in the prayers that dead mumble, as if they could still be saved. I know Loki rules Krauslung. I know you fought against him in the north, and I know you killed Malvus in the east, but elves? I have felt so trapped and useless, unable to reach you. It has been my curse, but it has become a blessing now I've seen the death and chaos that's being wrought above without me. Especially now.'

'Then help us.'

Tyrfing squinted again. 'What bizarre plan have you concocted now, Nephew?'

'It's complicated—'

Lerel snorted. 'Farden is raising the Great Ones to fight Loki's elves and a monster they call Ekidna.'

'Great Ones?'

'Monsters of old. Hydras and giants.'

'Bloody Hel, Farden.'

To Tyrfing's muttering, they came to an open cave that Farden remembered very well indeed. A cave whose entire far wall consisted of nothing but pitch dark. The sweeping curves of a broken bridgehead still remained.

Tyrfing's voice was a whisper. 'Without the Bifröst, every soul who should have passed to the other side has been collected here, and it is testing Hel's limits. Even with the half who are sent to Haven, Hel doesn't have to share the power she reaps with the other gods. She is the strongest of them all and could be a powerful ally.'

'Not the gods. Never the gods,' grumbled Farden. Tyrfing looked unsurprised.

Lerel snorted. 'We need another Great One. A creature fierce enough to make Loki shit his godly pants, so to speak. Have you heard any whispers from north of Albion? From the Lonely Sea?'

Tyrfing angled his head. 'So strange you should ask,' he said as he led them forwards, to where the ruined bridge pointed out into the void of the other side, where nothing and everything remained. A lone ghost stood by its edge, and he was not like the others. His form jittered and flickered like a flame in a gale. He looked paler than the rest, and Farden struggled to make out a beak of a nose and a high forehead. He wore nothing but his mist-like skin. His flickering reminded the mage of how Durnus and Tyrfing and once a daemon-cursed Elessi appeared in the Grimsayer.

'What's wrong with him?' asked Lerel.

'He's got one foot in Hel and the other still above. Suspended, Hel calls it, and she loathes him for it. I don't know its cause but it can't be good. Or pretty, for that matter. Necromancy, I'd guess. You'd better ask Durnus.'

Farden didn't know how to tell his uncle the truth. He kept his silence.

Tyrfing paced around the half-ghost. 'He's old Scalussen, by my reckoning, which means he's a thousand years old and should have gone over the bridge to the other side a long time ago. But he's still here. Stuck. When he isn't here staring into the void, he wanders as if looking for somebody. He follows the others around, always a woman of shorter hair, usually silent as a stone,' said Tyrfing. 'But the reason I'm showing you him is the only word he sometimes says is, "Saciath".'

'Saciath,' Farden repeated, dredging up maps in his mind.

'The most western island past Albion and the furthest edge of the Lonely Sea. I only know it because I was sent there long ago by the Arka to solve a trade dispute. There was a part of the island we were forbidden to set foot in. Marshes thick as brambles. The shadows and shades that come here from Saciath – some straight from the marshes themselves – whisper of a darkness between the bogs. It might not be what you want and might be no more than a faerie or a wight, but it's the only answer I've got.'

'I'll take it, Uncle,' Farden said, gaze moving to Lerel. She was staring at the Bifröst with a frown.

'Could it ever be rebuilt? The bridge, I mean. Don't these souls deserve freedom?' she asked.

'That they do, Lerel, but it would take more magick than I've ever contemplated,' Tyrfing sighed. 'Where are you, anyway? Where did you come from?'

'New Scalussen.'

'New Scalussen,' Tyrfing echoed. 'You've come far, Farden. You give my regards to old Durnus and to the others that still draw breath.' Tyrfing's face fell then, and his eyes sought the ground. 'I saw Modren pass me by the other day.'

'Durnus has gone too,' Lerel whispered, making Farden grit his teeth. 'Sacrificed himself in the east to save us all from Loki's games.'

Tyrfing bowed his head, clenching his fists. 'He just had to copy me, didn't he?' came the words, strained and taut. He put a heavy hand on Farden's shoulder. 'I will look for him.'

There was no time given for mourning. None for explaining, either. For it was then that the flow of the dead seemed to waver and slow. A rise in their whispers rushed down the tunnel towards them.

'She's coming,' Tyrfing uttered, wringing his hands. 'Hel. She's felt your presence.'

A pounding tremor could be felt in the rock.

'You have to go, Nephew,' Tyrfing said with urgency as he grasped Farden by the shoulders. 'Use that spear of yours.'

Farden needed no further convincing, but he did take a moment to seize his uncle tightly once more. 'I will see you again.'

'In the flesh, I trust,' Tyrfing said, pressing his forehead to Farden before stepping between them and Hel.

Farden pointed Gunnir to the ceiling, seized Lerel's hand to pull her close, and thought hard of the beach of Sanctuary Bay. The waves. The scent of salt on the ocean's brisk winds. The grit of sand beneath his feet—

'Farden…' whispered Lerel.

'I'm trying!'

'Try harder, Nephew. I can't protect you from her if she catches you!'

'If we could all give me a moment!'

Farden clenched every muscle, letting the magick swirl about them, drawing ghosts like leaves into an open window. Lerel clutched his hand tighter, sucking in a deep, deep breath. He did the same as he felt Gunnir begin to tremble. The spell was catching, knitting itself together, but far too slow, as if Gunnir needed to warm up in Hel's cold breath. The thudding of footsteps grew louder still, marching closer.

'Farden!'

Farden stabbed Gunnir at the ceiling and felt the world turn, but not completely. He pushed harder, letting forth a wordless yell as he thought of waves, sand, and the cold wind of ocean salt. Flame burst around his hands as a shadow loomed at the end of the tunnel, and at last Gunnir's spell went rigid like a grapple latching onto a parapet. Lightning crackled across their bodies as Hel vanished into a blur.

❧

'Voices. Magick. Stench of flesh!' Hel screeched as she stomped down the tunnel. 'Explain yourself, worthless creature!'

Tyrfing stood his ground, arms folded and face blank, painfully aware of the dust swirling around him and the crumbs of rock falling from the ceiling. Hel towered over him, nine feet to his six. Her bones rattled beneath her paper skin and taut sinew as she waved sharp nails in his face, so long they almost curled back on themselves.

'I don't know what you're talking about, Goddess,' Tyrfing asked. 'I exist only to serve.'

'Do not toy with me, oath-bound, or I will finally rid myself of your presence in my realm. Who dared tread in my realm?' Hel hissed.

'You've been threatening for years. Why not do it, and finally release me?'

Hel seemed to consider it. The goddess of death drew closer, her blade of a nose inches from his face. Tar-black eyes swirling in skeletal pits devoured every inch of him. Her nails crossed his throat, slow and cold. Her other hand was poised to strike.

'Better to leave you to suffer the imprisonment of your trespassing,' said Hel, cold breath on his face. She withdrew, face a sneer, and left him to weigh his thoughts and whether he had made the right decision telling Farden where to find a murderous shadow. A dark realisation had wormed its way into his head, darker than the pits of Hel's eyes. There was something different about Farden. Fiercer. Colder.

Tyrfing cracked his knuckles, and the sharp echo faded into the void behind him.

❦

Rock and dirt and centuries of ice whirled around them, crushing and crushing until Farden's skull felt as if it would implode. It was all he could do to keep his mind locked on their destination, ignore the fire in his lungs, and hold onto Lerel as the screeching spear cut a path through reality.

Sand choked him. Farden tried to roll over and found himself stuck. He was buried up to the waist in sand.

'Lerel?'

Farden whirled around to find two hands poking from the beach, waving around frantically.

'I need help here!' roared Farden as he fought to haul or dig her out. The fine sand kept sliding into whatever gap he could dig. 'Lerel!' he yelled again, channelling magick while a horned shape and hooves came sprinting.

Before Farden could whip a wind spell across the beach, Warbringer's muscular hands wrapped around Lerel's arms and hauled her out of the sand so fast she soared above the minotaur's head. She came down in Warbringer's arms with a cough and a splutter.

Farden was next, torn from the beach and left to struggle upright. He wrapped his arms around Lerel as she spat sand.

'That, mage,' she rasped, 'was far too close.'

'You need healers,' rumbled Warbringer.

'No,' she shook her head, pawing at Farden.'Tyrfing,' Lerel whispered. 'What if Hel—?'

Farden was already racing for the Dawnknell.

❦

The Grimsayer was right where he had left it. And yet he had a visitor. The mercury eyes of Evernia were fixed upon him.

'You really should learn to look.'

'Where have you been?'

Farden ignored her, seizing the rough edges of the Grimsayer and barking a name at its pages. 'Tyrfing!'

The Grimsayer's lights got to work, spinning a form that stood upon the blank page. For a moment the form didn't stutter as it always did, and Farden's knees began to buckle.

'There!' yelped Lerel as Tyrfing's glow flickered.

'He's still alive.'

'And why would he be otherwise? Upset a balance, have we?' spoke Evernia in her whisper of a voice from the corner of the room. Her glow was brighter, her face stern, and her appearance utterly unwelcome. 'Where have you been, Farden?'

'You should learn to knock, Goddess,' Farden muttered with a scowl.

'Ah, wonderful,' Lerel muttered at his side. 'Another awkward and tense conversation.'

Two other forms appeared at Evernia's side, coalescing out of thin air. They didn't take such solid forms as Evernia, but Farden could still make out Thron, face like thunder and wings hunched, and Heimdall, impassive and golden eyes ever-moving.

'Release us. This is your last chance,' Evernia spoke.

'That sounds like a threat, Evernia.'

'I have come to offer our help one last time in exchange for the spear's power.' Evernia held up her hand. 'Instead of trading daggers, Farden, I implore you to see sense. You think of us as puppet masters and seek to sever our strings, when all we are guilty of is trying to guide you to save a world we are otherwise powerless to save. Do I regret our methods? Perhaps. You see me as Loki's kin, yet your fears are misplaced. We will see to it that Emaneska flourishes again.'

Farden shook his head firmly, keeping his voice low. 'And there it is. You will see to it. I can't trust you not to interfere, and that is not your right anymore. Emaneska needs no gods, and I won't change my mind, Evernia. My decision has been made. I won't be your Samara.'

'You insolent, ungrateful worm,' growled a glowing Thron.

'Then you leave us no choice, mage,' was all Evernia said before the gods faded into threads of smoke and ash that vanished in moments.

'That can't be good, Farden,' Lerel said, fists clenched. 'Do you ever wonder if you go too far?'

'No, I don't,' said Farden, marching from his chambers.

'You are not invincible, Farden,' Lerel blurted. 'Even with that spear and your armour and your magick. They killed Sigrimur. What do you think they will do with you?'

Farden took a moment to reply. Lerel saw the slight lowering of his head before he clanked into the shadow of the corridor.

'Try,' came his echo.

Lerel let a shudder run through her and spat another grain of sand that crunched between her teeth. She stared at the Grimsayer for a moment.

'Durnus,' she whispered, a thought in her mind. The lazy lights drifted, sketching parts of the old vampyre, but never whole. Exactly like Tyrfing.

Lerel stared at the door, now empty and Farden long gone.

CHAPTER 36
A RETURN TO UTIRU

There are no finer shipsmiths than those who are Arka-born. Centuries spent at sea have gifted them secrets others are not privy to. Both runecraft and architecture they wield, and in ways we other ship-crafters can only dream of understanding.
AN EXCERPT FROM A LETTER SENT TO ALBION SHIPSMITH MIKAL JABROWN

Mithrid stared down at the rift in the marble, reaching at least ten levels to the highest ring of walls. Rubble strewed every courtyard and battlement below.

Farden's work.

'Quite the mess, isn't it?' Loki tutted, weaving his way through the patches of rubble and cracked marble. Servants toiled away to clean it up. The battering of hammers wafted up on the day's winter breezes.

Mithrid's voice was small, her thoughts far away. Thousands of miles south, to be precise. She turned to face Loki and saw a faint scar crossing his jaw and cheek. It had healed before the dawn, but the Scalussen steel had marked Loki for eternity. It should have been her knife, and yet Mithrid had stood by.

'One of Farden's finest abilities,' she said.

Loki clapped his hands at that. 'You're starting to catch on.'

Perhaps too much, and that was Mithrid's worry. She could remember Farden promising to do anything but rip the Arkathedral into pieces, not so long ago. The crowds of people far below, where the rubble had spilled over the Arkathedral's main gate and outer wall, no doubt muttered and cursed his name and the name of Scalussen. If she squinted, she could make out bodies covered in cloth, dozens of them lined up in rows between the detritus.

'I must admit, I admire your change of heart, Mithrid. You stuck by me instead of escaping. I think you are ready, Mithrid,' Loki said as he shifted around her, coming close. 'You're ready to rally a monster to our cause. Farden might not believe your true strength, but I do.'

'Which monster am I supposed to face?' asked Mithrid, trepidatious.

Loki gave her a sideways look. 'An old friend of yours.'

It took a moment for the coin to drop. 'No…' Mithrid said, feeling sweat on her forehead.

'Yes. We're paying Utiru a visit.'

'That's madness.'

'Cold feet?'

'You don't understand Utiru like I do!'

Loki rubbed his palms before beckoning for more servants carrying armour. 'I'm excited to meet her, whatever she is,' he said as the lackeys came forwards with pieces of Arka armour. With silent and swift ceremony, they strapped the gold and green plates onto her limbs and torso. No helmet, of course, what with the cumbersome collar around her neck.

'She is a nightmare in flesh and bone, Loki,' Mithrid warned, 'and she'll probably want revenge in return for escaping her.'

'Perfect. Just south of the Thundershores, am I right?'

Before Mithrid could even squeak out a word, Loki's cold hand grasped hers and whisked her into screaming light.

Gone was the fresh afternoon air. Only a smell of desert's char and hot rock. Mithrid faced a barren landscape under a dome of stars. It was a place she had kept locked away in her mind. Its path only led to Utiru.

Behind her, as she whirled, Mithrid found a familiar wall of rock split by a canyon, like the gutter of an axe-blow. Within, shards and pillars of crystal and quartz punctured the rock and made the path perilous. A cold breath wafted from the mouth of the rift, and it carried a whisper that made her shiver.

Two Scarred mages and two archers waited for them, all similarly clad in Arka armour. All fodder for Utiru and utterly unaware of what waited beneath the mountain.

Mithrid's mission hung in the balance; she could taste it in the dry, sickly air. Worse, her once-clear path was torn in all directions. If she refused the god, she risked raising the stakes for Scalussen and losing Loki's favour. However, this could be her chance to wield her shadow and turn on the god, or perhaps Utiru might eat him and solve everybody's problems. To complicate matters further, there was also a curiosity in her, fuelled by a need to test Loki's lies, and it fought to be heard. And of course, the abject fear of the enormous spider lurking in the cave beyond with her mirrors was ever-present. The very latter won her over as the god stepped into the rift and beckoned for her to join him.

'I won't go, Loki. I can't. Death is the only thing that lives in there,' Mithrid babbled.

'And that is precisely what I want. Are you scared, Mithrid? I've never seen you like this.'

Mithrid hated such an accusation, but it was true. 'It's common fucking sense, is what it is.'

'It's as you said: you escaped before, and you can do it again,' Loki reminded her. 'I only want to set you free, Mithrid. It's a chance to prove yourself, not anyone else. Not even to prove me wrong.'

'Spare me another motivational speech, Loki. Utiru is too powerful. Too wily. Too evil even for you.'

'I'm almost offended.' Loki shook his head, playing disappointed. 'But it changes nothing of the fact that this is what your kind was born for, Mithrid.'

'You're a fool,' she snorted.

'Tut tut, and I thought we were getting along so well.'

The two Scarred stood at each of her shoulders, but before they could take her by the arms, Mithrid shrugged them away and forced herself to follow Loki.

There was no moon to light their way this time. Only the scant glow of the stars, and it didn't have the same effect on the crystals as the scarred sister. The rift was darker than a sewer where the mages' light spells didn't shine. Once again, Mithrid had to duck and clamber over great tree trunks of crystal that lay in their path and made their going slow and irritating.

Finally, the rift narrowed into the mouth of a gloom-filled cave, fanged with crystal. With mages stoking their light and fire spells, they moved into the cracks of the mountain and left the night behind.

'Anything we should be expecting other than Utiru, Mithrid?' asked Loki, ducking under a thrust of sharp quartz.

Mithrid frantically weighed every option again in her head. Perhaps the mirrors might send them all mad before they could even reach Utiru. Leaving her abandoned in Khandri without weapons, water, or a way to get home, of course. Mithrid ground her teeth. Loki was smarter than she liked to admit.

'Spiders the width of your hand. And mirrors,' she replied. 'Don't look into them unless you want to go insane,' she added in a mutter.

A flit of glass caught her eye as they turned a corner in the corridor of rock. *Spiders of glass.* Mithrid's collar rattled as she shivered again, and Loki cast her a look.

'Not yet, Mithrid.'

Up ahead, where the tunnel became straighter and smoother and the rock underfoot was replaced with fine sand, a milky light shone upon glasslike crystal. Reflections of light scattered across the walls, and soon polished mirrors punctuated the rock on either side.

Mithrid watched Loki closely, glancing sidelong in mirrors to glimpse what could be seen of the god, but she saw nothing.

One of the archers chanced a look, unable to ignore his own curiosity, and came to an immediate halt before a mirror cracked and shattered.

'No, no,' he began to babble at whatever he saw in its shards. 'No!'

Loki slapped him, knocking him to the floor before the echoes of his shout could die. It drew blood from his nose, but it had broken the mirror's spell.

Mithrid saw Loki look. A fleeting glance at what the mirror could offer him. Mithrid knew their undeniable magick, but all she saw in the god's face was a stern fire in his eyes and a bunching of his jaw.

'Eyes ahead! I catch anyone looking, I'll skin you alive right here and offer you up as a gift for Utiru,' Loki threatened.

With that dire promise hanging over them, every one of them did as they were told and kept their eyes front. Only Mithrid dared to defy. She had seen what Utiru's mirrors held, and once again, as they moved past quickly, she caught a glimpse of herself staring back, a fountain of fire and rock at her back. Shadow surrounded her, lifting her up above a ruined and smoking city. Mithrid and her reflection locked eyes for a heartbeat.

So nothing had changed. Her path still pointed to chaos.

Mithrid had little time to ponder fate and destiny. Little time to wrestle with the choice, if it had come at all. Perhaps she had missed her moment, and she was already sliding down the scree of doom. A chittering of glass claws on rock was growing louder.

'I'd get your spells ready if I were you,' Mithrid muttered, remembering how those needle claws had felt on her skin as they buried her. She took a long step backwards.

The Scarred needed no encouragement, and she let the mages flow past her. Loki stood his ground at her side with one hand on her collar. His glow filled the tunnel, and in the light, crystalline spiders swarmed in their dozens, then scores, then hundreds, covering the ground, walls, and tunnel roof. Spells of fire and lightning cast them aside in broken shards. Shield spells crackled as the spiders threw themselves like slingstones. With bows useless, the archers set about stamping and using the flats of their shortswords, their yelling growing more and more frantic with every moment. One of them had been bitten by crystal jaws and had started to sag.

Mithrid looked to Loki, whose glow only seemed to be attracting the spiders. A ring of fire ran around them, and the Scarred held off their flood momentarily. Only a handful of half-molten arachnids made it through the flames, fading and glowing on the rock in amorphous puddles.

'I told you,' was all Mithrid said, as the bitten archer slumped to the rock, cracking his helmet on a lump of quartz.

Loki weighed his chances with a quick flitting of his gaze. A curved knife – *her* curved knife – came from his coat pocket and pressed into her spine, between the plates of armour.

'Any tricks…' he warned, 'and our budding friendship comes to an abrupt and bloody end. This is for you, not for me.'

Trying to shake off his lies, Mithrid counted every way she could wriggle out of that situation. Every way she could pin Loki long enough without dying in a cave, a meal for a Great One. All of them risked her skin in a way she couldn't accept, and so, as Loki removed her collar with a clanking of metal, Mithrid turned her shadow on the spiders instead.

The mages' fire died, snuffed by spreading shadow. The spiders recoiled with the scraping of crystal on rock. Mithrid could have crushed the mages right there and then. She could have turned her magick on Loki and fought. Doubt assailed her again. Death hovered over every decision. The frustration pushed her shadow up the walls and onto the roof, driving spider after spider back. Even the mirrors seemed to flutter, and deep in the rock, something shuddered, and the spiders retreated as one. And yet they stayed in sight, lurking in rifts in the rock and waving their crystal claws in protest.

All Loki had for Mithrid was a smile as he poked her onwards with the tip of the blade. 'Bring this one with us,' he ordered the others as he kicked at the fallen archer.

With shadow still swirling around Mithrid's hands, they pressed on beyond the hateful mirrors and to a part of the tunnel where broken crystal and rubble marred the way. Utiru had dug at the rock to catch them during her last escape, but there was still a clear path to her cavern, strewn with sand and pebbles.

The breath of cold air grew into a wind as they approached the impenetrable gloom, no matter how much Loki glowed or how bright the Scarred pushed their light spells. Mithrid held her breath against the stench as she heard one of the archers mumble in horror. Besides the spiders that scuttled through the shadows, all that could be seen were dangling bodies wrapped in fine silver webbing. They hung just on the edge of the gloom, suspended by their heads. One nearby looked the freshest, and Mithrid squinted at it as her heart began to race. She remembered the dreams of Utiru all too well.

There was not a twitch in this one's limbs. She was dead already, but it was her arm that drew Mithrid's attention. It appeared to be wooden, and Mithrid's eyes widened.

'Utiru!' bayed Loki, filling the cavern with his echoes and making Mithrid flinch.

It was then that the bodies trembled on their strings, wavering slightly. A loud scraping came as the gloom shifted. Light spells faltered as a grotesque woman appeared, hovering high above the sand. She had no legs that were visible, but no fewer than six arms protruded from the bony form she called a body, milky pale and glistening. In each of her spindly hands, she held a mask, some of beasts and some more human. Black eyes and a mouth without lips curved upwards, betraying sharp teeth.

Even though Mithrid had gazed upon Utiru before, she still recoiled, forcing the blade deeper into her back.

'Easy, Mithrid,' Loki whispered.

She was not alone. The remaining archer's hands shook on her bow, threatening to loose her arrow at any moment. The Scarred retreated several steps as Utiru drifted closer. Mithrid shook her head. They had no idea what still hid in the shadows.

With a sideways jerk of her head, Utiru shifted one of her masks over her haunting face. The mask was porcelain and bore a smile that was altogether terrifying.

'All know the meaning of the spider's web,' Utiru whispered behind her mask, her voice like paper being crumpled. 'To enter it willingly is no fault of the spider. You trespass in Utiru's shadow. You must pay the price.'

'I bring you gifts, Utiru!' Loki greeted the monster. He motioned for the Scarred to drag the body of the archer closer, and it took the mages a moment to follow his orders.

'Gifts,' Utiru rasped. 'Gifts come with promises. The last one to come promised gifts of power. Alliance. In return for mercy. Utiru cares not for gifts, nor promises, nor mercy.'

The nearest body shuffled on its string, and Mithrid once again looked at its wooden hand.

'That's Lady Irien,' she breathed. Mithrid felt Loki's knife pressing harder at the mention of the name, forcing her a step closer to the monster. Her eyes frantically searched the shadows for the rest of Utiru.

'I see,' Loki said in a curiously strained voice. 'In that case, great and wonderful Utiru, let me be blunt and to the point. I come to ask for your help.'

Utiru chuckled behind her mask, a dry and hacking sound. She switched to another mask, this one of gold. 'Utiru helps none but herself.'

Two gigantic legs stabbed at the sand with a bone-shaking crash. They reached into the dark, tall as pines, skeletal and the colour of shadow. The claws at their ends hooked into the flesh of the unconscious archer and hauled him away into the shadow. The other archer had turned a pale green colour and kept looking at the exit.

It was then Utiru came closer, revealing more of her elongated torso, and where it joined with a bulbous body and the salivating mandibles of an enormous spider.

It was then that the archer decided to flee. She made it a dozen steps before another leg stabbed from the gloom and crushed her against the sand. It didn't kill her straight away but lifted her screaming into the air, still holding a broken bow. She was whisked above their heads into the foul reaches of the cavern, where a crunch silenced her screams.

As much as Mithrid wanted to see Loki quivering or sweating like the remaining Scarred, she was surprised he stood his ground. His golden glow shone brighter as he kept his broadest smile.

'A god,' Utiru breathed, reeling back slightly. Not in fear – far from it – but with intrigue. Another mask covered her face, this one carved of stone, with sharp, raging eyes and horns. 'Long has it been since kin of yours have walked our lands. Utiru smells the blood of an old enemy in you.'

Close, she came again, and the Scarred ignited shield and fire spells. Utiru chuckled, inhaling as if she drank in the smell of magick. More of her horrifying body emerged from the darkness, showing skeletal limbs spread across the cavern in all directions. She was not crouched in front of them, but over them.

'Your dreams will be pleasant to devour. Utiru savours the taste of revenge. Long has she waited for it. And you…' The monster turned to Mithrid. 'Utiru knows you. Such delicious fear. Such rage and desire. Now what will we see of your dreams, child?'

Loki seized Mithrid by the shoulder and swivelled her away. They seemed to slide over the sand as if they were in the grip of one of Eyrum's speed spells, just in time to evade another spider's leg hammering down. Grit sprayed Mithrid's face, and though Loki whipped the blade to her neck, he bellowed over the roaring and screaming of the spider and the Scarred. Lightning lit the cavern in stuttering bursts, showing off all its horror, from the skeletons that hid in great piles to the crystalline spiders swarming from ugly boreholes.

'Now, Mithrid!' ordered Loki.

Mithrid grasped her dark power, wrestling concentration out of the panic. She was a fool for coming back to this lair. A fool for believing Loki could tell the truth.

'Mithrid!' yelled the god when a Scarred was batted across the cavern with a howl. The remaining mage screamed madly as he wrapped a shield around himself that bristled with fire. It barely kept Utiru at bay.

'It's time to prove yourself!' Loki urged Mithrid. 'Forget anyone who has ever told you that you can't. Forget control. Forget caution. Forget anyone who's held you back!'

Mithrid let go. Every grasp of control she wielded against the shadow she let loose. With a convulsion that lifted her off the floor, dark magick erupted from her. Her shadow surged for Utiru, and wherever it touched, the giant spider recoiled with a chitinous clicking.

'A blasphemy!' Utiru screeched.

'Call me what you want, Utiru! You're the one who cowers, not me,' Mithrid shouted. It was no boast. At least she didn't mean it to be. She was testing the truth of the matter: she held a Great One in her clasp. *Her*. Mithrid Fenn of a backwater village, daughter of a woodcutter, orphan child. A skald's tale, indeed. Loki was right.

Utiru challenged briefly and spat and blubbered as she reached once more. Mithrid wielded her shadow in whipping tendrils, swiping away her legs and making her hide sizzle at Mithrid's touch. Sweat poured. Muscles flamed. It took every fibre of her strength, and the weight pressed her boots into the sand, but she managed to hold. Utiru held every mask before her face as she shrank into the rear of her cave. Darkness washed around Mithrid, and not one of the crystalline spawn dared to come close.

'Just as I expected,' Loki said proudly, straightening to dust his hands and grinning even wider than usual. 'Here's the deal, old and fearsome Utiru. The world's forgotten you, but I want you to rise up, glorious as the younger days, and make them remember your name. A great battle awaits you if you fight on my side, and all the meat and minds you wish to feast on. And if you do not, my dear friend Mithrid here will make sure you're forgotten for good—'

Mithrid tutted. 'And remember the mage that dared to stand against you and break your spell? A mage of red and gold armour who freed half a dozen of us from your dreams?'

Judging by the snarl and the circle of masks Utiru arranged, she remembered.

'Then you might get to kill him as well,' Mithrid said.

Loki chuckled. 'A fine touch. She speaks the truth. He's the one I call enemy.'

It was Mithrid's words that seemed to sway her. Utiru tucked in her legs, forming a cage around her bulbous abdomen. Her masks spread apart, revealing her pale face, darkened slightly by a scar of Mithrid's making. 'Utiru has decided.'

'Then north you will go, Utiru, until the mountains spit fire,' said Loki.

Utiru straightened again, and Mithrid flexed her shadow around the hideous creature like two pincers waiting to squeeze. It was enough to keep the monster civil.

'Take this mage as another gift,' said Loki, and the surviving Scarred's head snapped around. 'A tidbit for the journey.'

'Gifts and promises,' she said, as Loki cast the Scarred forwards with his magick. She scooped him up mid-scream, wrapping him in silk to choke his cries and stowing him under her belly. 'North, Utiru will go.'

With tremendous strength, Utiru drove several of her claws into the wall of the cavern and began to burrow. Starlight broke through in faint spears, sending the crystalline spiders running. Not Utiru, whose molten pitch skin glistened in the faint glow. With a scuttling that made Mithrid's skin crawl, the monstrous spider broke from her mountain and disappeared, leaving the girl and the god alone.

Both god and girl turned to lock stares. Mithrid's dark magick still swirled around the cave, and Loki was close enough to flash the knife across her throat if he wanted. The collar lay in his right hand.

'Do you believe me now?' he asked. 'That you are meant for more?'

'I…' The awful truth was that Mithrid did. The shadow swooped closer. 'You almost got me killed.'

Loki was motionless save for his thin lips. 'I had to push you to the edge, is why. And look at what it achieved. A monster such as Utiru, bent to your will.'

Mithrid couldn't deny it. Was it pride? Was it shock? Was it guilt at unleashing such a curse? Inside, she reeled. On her hard exterior, she saw only the god and her chance to unleash her power on him.

Loki was already inside her head. 'There's more. You're only just beginning to walk the path to greatness.'

'And all for what, Loki?' she blurted, hot in her face. 'What is the point? So I can kill Farden and break his spear for you? Save the world? And then what? You rule for eternity?'

'Exactly. All I've ever wanted was to rule in peace,' Loki said, and Mithrid hated how little that sounded like a lie.

'And what of me? What becomes of me?'

'Whatever you please, Mithrid. You and your Hereni.'

Mithrid's shadow pushed closer to Loki, but he held his head high and smirked. Even so, his knife was still close to her side.

'If you want that life, you need me as much as I need you,' Loki whispered, raising up both the collar and the blade. 'I give you something Farden didn't: a choice.'

Mithrid took a moment to look between them and his shining eyes. This was her chance. Everything she had worked for. The reason she had fought and endured, but an iron fist of doubt held her arm and dragged her back. 'If I do this,' she said, 'the rest go free and alive. Eyrum. Lerel. Elessi. Warbringer. The Sirens.'

Loki had yet to blink. 'You have my word. All I want is Farden.'

Thread by thread, Mithrid's shadow died around her, leaving only Loki's glow and the shafts of starlight. Loki held up the collar, but instead of wrapping it around her neck, he let it fall to the sand. Mithrid looked up, surprised.

'I don't know about you, Mithrid, but after some slaying of monsters, I like to drink some wine. Will you join me?' the god offered, holding out his open hand.

Mithrid stared at his gauntlet for a moment. Her thoughts screamed at her, but one pinnacle rock stood firm against their roiling waves.

The promise of destiny.

Evening had fallen on Krauslung in their absence. A fleet of fishing ships had come into Port Rós on the sun's last rays and the dregs of the tide, and the harbour was alive with activity. A halo of gulls and rimelings spun around the spires of trade and counting houses.

The rubble had been cleared from the upper reaches of the Arkathedral. The fortress had fallen silent and still. Only the occasional howl of a Scarred getting runes carved into their back or the screech of vuleguls atop the Nest disturbed its peace. Elves clung to their shadows. Mages and soldiers wise enough to keep their mouths shut patrolled quietly. It was a cautious air. One with its tail between its legs, and Loki hated it. The day had been a victory. It was simply a shame their only witnesses had been eaten. Or half-eaten in the case of the final mage. He had done so well, too.

'More wine?' he asked of Mithrid, sitting a distance away in the same chair she had pounced out of not long ago. Same chair, different surroundings. They occupied a chamber beneath the

Arkathedral, where grand windows looked over the city with nothing but a deadly drop below. It was a chamber a dragon had once crashed into to save a certain mage from a certain pale king named Vice.

Mithrid nodded.

Loki finished his wine with a slurp. A bottle of a Skölgard vintage had already been passed between them. One thing could be said for the worthless worms that infested the world: they knew how to ferment, brew, and otherwise pickle themselves. The drink was slower on a god's mind than a human's, and he enjoyed its attempts immensely.

Loki eyed the worm before him. Mithrid drank like an old veteran, as if she couldn't stand to see the bottom of her glass so drowned. Her flaming hair, still tangled with sweat and dust, lay across her shoulders, and her eyes had barely come up from the floor.

Mithrid snatched the next bottle from him and kept it for herself, and Loki poured his own glass from another bottle. He stared out across the city, watching the occasional light flicker out or spark into life.

'What bothers you, Mithrid?'

The girl met his gaze with a scowl softer than it usually was. Loki could almost hear the churn of her mind. It was to be expected. It was to be encouraged.

'Your plan is flawed, you know,' she said, gulping at her wine.

Loki smirked. 'How so?'

'Let's say I go along and kill magick. Where will your powers go? What of the spear you once craved? Farden's armour? Your coat full of so-called trinkets? How exactly do you expect to rule anything? You'll be one of us. A worm, as you like to say.'

'As the late Irien would say: my dear, I only wanted that spear so Farden wouldn't get his golden hands on it. As for his armour, I'm already immortal, and think I look quite fancy is this blue number, don't you?' Loki flexed his gauntlets. 'My power is gods-given, not magick. Evernia harnessed magick for our uses, and I wield it alongside our own power, born of belief.'

'And souls.'

'Correct.'

Mithrid looked soured by such talk. 'How is it you came to be? Who made you the way you were?'

'Are you asking if gods fuck, Mithrid?'

The girl snorted.

'A shedding of blood, a sprinkle of stardust, and a god is born.'

'Utiru mentioned your blood. Whose blood are you that made her so eager to kill you? Is it the god that once betrayed her?'

Loki decided to tell the truth. He was unpractised, and he kept it simple. 'Evernia's blood.'

Mithrid's eyes widened. 'She's your mother?'

'In a human sense,' Loki said, pretending to be proud for a moment before his face fell. 'Other than using Farden as her tool and weapon, I am her greatest regret.'

'The gods' darkest failure, is what she called you if I remember right.'

Loki raised his glass to the ceiling. 'Too kind.'

'Why did you leave the collar off my neck?' Mithrid asked. 'I can't imagine you trusting anyone.'

'Trust is nothing but a mutual agreement to not stab each other in the back. As I told you in Utiru's lair, I'm the only one who can give you what you want and deserve. And I know you want to see where this all leads. We can walk the path together,' Loki said.

'What if I change my mind?'

Loki saw the slight curl of shadow around her fist, like the sole of an extinguished candle. 'You won't,' he told her. There was no hoping he was right. He was certain, and lo and behold, Mithrid let the threat die and drank her wine. She was too curious for her own good. Too bound to the pathetic ideas of love and fate.

'I told you what I dream of, so what of you, Mithrid Fenn?'

'Fire,' Mithrid said, scrunching up her face as a realisation seemed to hit her. 'At least I used to. I don't have dreams, I have nightmares. The same one over and over, almost every night since the east.'

'That gryphon of Farden's. He sows dreams into minds, you know. And if Farden feared you, what if it was all a game to keep you controlled with fear?'

'He's not that malicious.'

'Is he not? When Farden took his revenge on Duke Kiltyrin, he broke into his chambers, sealed the door, and strapped him to a chair so he couldn't move his head. Then, he took a copy of his Book, which – as you know – drives almost everyone who sees it insane, and carved off his eyelids so he was forced to look. They found him an hour later, a raving lunatic.'

'That was a long time ago,' Mithrid muttered. The edges of her words weren't as sharp as before. Her bottle was almost finished.

'You still defend him, even though you turned your back on him and his kind.' Loki spat his wine on the floor. The vintage was seeping into his head faster than he had expected. 'I didn't ask about nightmares. Tell me what dream you have.'

Mithrid stared into her wine. 'I don't have one. Hereni has one of settling down, and I said yes. My dream has always been either slicing Malvus' throat or yours.'

Loki dangled a thread in front of her. 'You could reign as a queen. You and Hereni both. New Scalussen would be yours.'

Mithrid looked up. 'What's next? Am I ready for Irminsul?'

'Almost.'

Mithrid snatched at her bottle to finish the dregs. Before Loki offered another, a poor excuse for a knock sounded at the door, as if the knuckles had barely graced the wood on their way to the handle.

Azen strode into the room, making Mithrid straighten and the elf's white eyes narrow in fierce suspicion. 'Lakrimur,' he spat. 'You trade wine and wag tongues with this blasphemer.'

'Mithrid here has secured us another weapon for the battle against Farden, in fact,' corrected Loki. 'You should be congratulating her.'

Azen growled deep in his throat.

'What do you want, Azen?'

A single thin finger was raised, pointing to the ceiling and presumably the chambers or roof beyond. 'You have a visitor. It waits in the place they call the Nest.' With that, the elf left the room, muttering elvish words as he gave Mithrid one last glance.

It. Loki tilted his head. The Nest could only mean something with wings or…

'The time of the elves is to be short-lived, you know,' Loki whispered, giving Mithrid a glance. 'Follow, if you can stand.'

Mithrid proved she could, taking another bottle with her for good measure, and together they trod the marble to reach the highest stretches of the Arkathedral. Loki made sure to keep Mithrid in front of him. He still couldn't be too careful, not now that the pieces of his plan were coming together so finely.

A figure waited at the edge of the Nest. The vuleguls around them cawed crankily as Loki and Mithrid arrived. A few flapped into the night. Others gathered around the figure, their featherless and wrinkled heads bowed in respect.

Loki examined the silhouette as he grew closer, and the city lights betrayed the truth when he saw them shining through its shadow.

'Evernia.' Loki saw Mithrid flinch at the name and saw the narrowing of her stare. 'How nice of you to visit.'

'Spare me your cheek, Morningstar. It does not please me to endure your blasphemous presence any longer than I have to, but necessity has brought me here.'

'Kind of you to say.'

'The girl must go.'

'I am no girl,' Mithrid spat. 'And you should know you were wrong about me.'

'Does that give you pleasure, to say that to your goddess? Farden has taught you well, I see. The girl leaves or I will not speak my offer.'

Loki was immediately intrigued. 'Mithrid,' he said, but the girl was not listening. Her shadow had returned, and though difficult to see, he could tell it reached slowly for the god's form.

'How dare you, mortal?' Evernia said with disgust on her face.

'Mithrid,' Loki interjected. 'As much as I wish it were so, Evernia is not your next test. Get your rest instead, for tomorrow we hunt more glory.'

'You were wrong, you know,' Mithrid told the goddess one more time before she stalked her way through the nests and back to the torches burning by the stairs.

Loki turned back to Evernia, whose face was far too haughty.

'What do you intend with her? To breed nefalim?' she asked.

'Spit it out, *mother*,' snarled Loki.

'Farden has become a threat.'

'*Become*? Hah!'

'He opposes us, and so Haven is left with one choice.'

'Say it.'

'To offer you an alliance against Farden. If we help you defeat the mage, then you will use the spear's power to free your kin from the sky.'

Loki could have cackled. He could have brayed with laughter, but he held himself back. 'I must say, Evernia, it's a very surprising offer, to say the least. But precisely how are you able to help me, shadow?' Loki asked as he circled the goddess.

'Haven and Hel are almost full, and combined with a freed gods' power, we have enough to release one of us.'

'You, I imagine.'

'Wrong,' Evernia said with relish. Loki let her have that minuscule victory. 'If she agrees, then it shall be the goddess Hel. With the goddess of death at your side, you will win the day, and once the spear is beyond the mage's grasp, you will summon the rest of us.'

Loki laughed while he shook his head. 'And why would I want to share any of my spoils with you?'

'We will leave you to your devices. It shall be a pact.'

'You know, it's funny. You realise you've just proven Farden's fears about you correct, don't you?' Loki asked. Suffice it to say, he was enjoying this immensely. If Evernia knelt at his feet, it would have been perfection.

'His insolence is beyond measure. If we are forced to choose another evil, then we shall,' said Evernia. 'Give your answer, Loki. Do not make me wait.'

'How many Great Ones has he raised?' Loki asked.

Evernia cast her gaze south to the faint twinkle of islands on the black horizon. 'Three, so far, including the keraken.'

Loki took a moment to think, pacing back and forth far longer than he needed to. When Evernia looked fit to unravel, he stuck out his hand. 'You have an agreement, Evernia.'

With a great look of distaste poorly masked by her stern facade, Evernia reached for his hand, and he pulled her closer as soon as he clasped her cold skin.

'I look forward to celebrating our victory,' Loki said with a sneer before her form disintegrated in his hands. The vuleguls that had gathered around her took wing and soared in spirals to the city below.

Loki stared at the city lights in the space where Evernia had vanished, letting them blur as he listened to the echoes of her voice in his mind.

'How delightfully unexpected,' Loki whispered, as he reached deep into his coat and felt for the crow's skull. He brought it forth to the squawk of a vulegul.

'Are you there?' Loki asked it, waiting as he listened to the moan of a rising wind. 'Farden?'

Beneath the earth, where a ship made of toe and fingernails scraped against a shore of pebbles and vacant-eyed ghosts, a shadow of a goddess fell.

Hel did not have to turn her head to know who dared to enter her realm. 'You seem to be lost, Sister.'

'Far from it.'

Hel arose, bones clicking as she sought the ship's railing. She towered over Evernia, almost lost to the mists of the dead. Hel waved her hand, and the crowds parted so she could stare down at her sister.

'You have grown powerful. I can see it in you,' said Evernia with a voice as flat as a calm ocean.

'Hel, the scales, and its souls are mine. My reward for my penance, and if you have come to take any of them, then we will have a sore disagreement, Sister.'

'Once again, far from it, Hel. I have come to reward you. Haven has made its decision.'

Evernia turned her hand, and the scales she had gifted to Hel on the breaking of the Bifröst appeared in her hands, gleaming with power. 'You are needed above.'

'You release me? Why, after all this time? There is always a catch with you, Evernia. You will speak the truth in my realm,' hissed Hel.

A wind of rustling moved through the endless crowd of souls. Evernia drew closer until the hem of her fraying dress grew dark with the water. Her raven hair flowed as if a gale blew. 'Because Farden will bring Ragnarök with the spear that has driven him mad, and we must stop him as we did Sigrimur. Because you are mightier than the rest of us, and we have but enough power for only one of Haven and Hel to return. And because we have forged a pact with the blasphemer Loki, who will help you to rise, and you will help him with the death and destruction of Farden. It is then we will take back the Spear of Gunnir and return to our rightful place.'

'And what of your blood? Loki?'

Evernia raised her chin. 'Loki will be swept aside by our combined might, and we will wipe the slate of this world clean with fire and water and start fresh. The world will be rebuilt as we first intended. No more Farden and Mithrid. No more Scalussen and Arka. No daemons and elves. Only us.'

Hel crooked her hand, and the scales shimmered above her palm instead. She clutched them tightly as she pondered the end of the world.

'When?'

CHAPTER 37
A THIRD

Runecraft is a wily practice. It does not merely depend on the runes one carves, but on the method, the medium, the chisel, and the intent with which one carves. Mages think themselves the pinnacle of magick. We crafters would disagree.
FROM THE PREFACE OF A BOOK SIMPLY TITLED 'RUNES'

Saciath was a fine place if one's preference was bare, gorse-infested mountainside interspersed with pines standing guard around bogs and marshes. And rain. It was impossible to forget the rain.

Farden's shield spell kept them dry for the most part. Fleetstar enjoyed the wet and walked alongside them with what could be described as a smile on her face. Every now and again she would spread her wings and let rain sizzle on her forked tongue. It made Eyrum smile, as if he remembered his own dragon.

The Siren clunked along by Farden's side, now almost healed thanks to healer magick and witch's herbs. His mighty battleaxe was his walking stick, and he didn't let rubble, mud, or puddle stand in his way. Warbringer stood on his other side, a strange glaze of satisfaction and peace on her face as if she was happy to see marshes once more. Farden caught himself staring at Voidaran before Warbringer caught him. Farden shook his head. The minotaur had insisted on coming along,

Two towns of sharp turrets and towers clung to each side of the sprawling valley, high in the mountain crags as if they wanted to be as far away from the valley floor and its burbling river as possible.

Their torches painted the low cloud that obscured the mountaintops with a marmalade glow.

Farden wanted nothing to do with them. Warbringer's need for blood was not to be tempted, and the speckle of brave farmhouses was all he dared involve them in. Time was short, and the night was deep. They had no use for subtlety.

As they wound along the river's edge, they found a farmhand still toiling in a pumpkin field. It looked like a punishment to Farden. He called out in greeting, but when the lad turned in surprise and took one look at the dragon, the minotaur, and the two fierce, armour-bound warriors, he threw down his pitchfork and fled. Farden didn't blame him.

'We have coin!' called the mage. Such words were more magick than most spells.

The boy halted, torn between the lights of the distant farmhouse and the promise of copper and silver. Perhaps gold.

'Pink-flesh look skittish.'

Farden chuckled. 'Probably because he thinks you're going to eat him, Warbringer.'

'What if he'll say anything for coin?' asked Eyrum.

'Then we will offer to eat him and see what happens,' Farden replied with a shrug.

'I am rather hungry,' muttered Fleetstar. The Mad Dragon even went as far as to lick her lips.

Warbringer rattled her horns. 'I saw him first.'

With a show of a coinpurse and a clink of the contents, the boy approached, slow and wary. He couldn't have been more than twelve winters old. His terrified gaze darted between Fleetstar and Warbringer, and then back to the coins. Always back to the coins.

When he deemed he was close enough, he held out his dirty palm, and Farden flicked him a silver coin. Farden didn't think it was possible, but the boy's eyes went wider.

'I'm Farden. What's your name?'

'Chuxer of Norton. Up there,' said the lad, pointing to the nearest town. 'But mas'er callin' me Chux. Who're ye?' His accent was so thick, Farden barely understood him.

'Travellers and hunters,' grunted Eyrum.

Farden stepped closer, holding another silver. 'We're looking for somebody that lives in the marshes.'

'Plenty o' frog'unters over there on their stilts. Prob'ly abed now.'

'Some*thing*, then,' Eyrum added.

Farden nodded. 'Something that everybody on your island fears. We want to go where it's not wise to tread.'

The boy shook his head, pursing his lips. 'You'd no wanna that, mis'er. No ye don't.'

Farden wanted to smile, despite the boy's fear. 'What is it?'

'The Steel Ghost.'

It was then that a crossbow bolt thudded into the ground at the mage's feet, prompting Farden to slam his wrists together and forge a shield spell in front of him and the lad.

A yell rang out from the farmhouse. A farmer with a tunic on backwards came running, struggling to reload his crossbow. 'Who're you! Get gone, thieves!'

The breath and fight flew out of him when Fleetstar spread her wings, and fire crackled between her fangs.

'By Dalas' foot!' the farmer screeched, raising his crossbow again to fire. The bolt glanced harmlessly off Farden's shield, and the farmer staggered back, tripped on a pumpkin, and fell on his arse. 'What kind are ye? Ain't no dragons or horned devils welcome in these parts! Get gone!'

Farden held his hands wide. 'We mean no harm. All we want is directions.'

'Use a bloody signpost if'n yer wantin' directions, s–sir. Don't be comin' with beasts o' terror to a man's doorsteppin'. In the house, Chux!'

'He's got coin, Mas'er. 'Ready given me one,' lied the lad, holding up one of the silvers. Smart, seeing as the farmer snatched it from him. The mage had to smile, even though his impatience grew.

'Where and what is the Steel Ghost?'

The farmer flapped his jowls. 'Steel… Stuff o' tales and stories, 'tis! What nonsense is this? Am I dreamin'?'

Farden was intrigued. Tales and stories were what he needed.

Chux shook his head vehemently. 'Ye know it's realer than that, Mas'er. Two went missin' last month.'

'Drowned in a bog, they did!'

But Chux was adamant. 'So what 'bout all those wrong-uns the Duke Alxander likes t'throw in there? They're never comin' out! My da said ye can hear the screams at night.'

'Yer da's a drunkard. And scream would ye jus' the same if'n you were drownin' in those bogs! That's all there is, by Dalas!'

Farden cut to the point. 'Excuse me? Which bog?'

'There! The Marshes of Metrada,' said the farmer, blustering as if it was common knowledge.

'Then I thank you for your time, and we'll leave you in peace.'

'Begone, strangers!'

Farden cast a look over his back as they followed the road further on. The master had the lad by the collar and was pointing up the hill to the farmhouse and to the town beyond. Chux broke away into a hesitant run.

'We should make camp and wait for light,' said Eyrum, his one eye roving over the clouds.

'We don't have time.'

'You smell trouble, Farden,' guessed Warbringer, already hefting that cursed warhammer.

'Always,' he muttered. 'Let's get off the road. Fleetstar, would you be so kind as to keep watch?'

'Always ordering me around…' Farden heard the dragon mutter before she flapped into the sky to lose herself in the clouds.

❦

Trouble was right.

Trudging through the rolling grass of the valley's slope instead of the gravel and mud road had been slower going, but a wiser choice. Within an hour, a twinkling procession of torches left the nearest town and wound its way down into the valley. Before long, they could hear the sounds of hooves. But not cows, as expected, but thick and sturdy goats with curled horns and bristling beards braided and beaded.

From behind a lip of a rocky tor, Farden and Eyrum watched them whirl and circle to look for footprints in the rain-churned mud. Warbringer was tending a buried fire beneath an overhang nearby. She had apparently developed a taste for sausages in recent weeks, something the Jar Khoum were famous for. It was bizarre to see a minotaur cooking for once. The only other times Farden had seen it, it had been Arka meat sizzling over bonfires in the Efjar Marshes. What was disturbing was that the smells were far too similar and both hauntingly appetising.

'Who are they?' asked Eyrum.

'I would guess Duke Alxander's riders, and they don't look happy to hear about us,' said Farden, quietly counting between his words. There were fifty at least.

'Wasted two silver on that lad. You should have given him gold. That might have kept him quiet.'

Perhaps Farden should have, but it was too late now. The duke's men were dividing in half and going separate ways, goat horns posted at their mouths to trumpet a warning and hooked spears waggling. One half galloped on down the road and into the night, while the other half stayed put, sending scouts into the wilderness.

Farden looked to the sky, hearing thunder, but no lightning had shown its face. When it rumbled again, he realised it was coming from beside him. It was Eyrum's stomach, and the Siren thudded a fist against his cuirass.

'Get some food, I'll keep watch,' Farden told him, but the Siren stayed put.

'I am fine. Three eyes are better than two.'

Farden could feel the Siren waiting to talk. Waiting for the right moment, perhaps. It couldn't have been waiting for the courage; Eyrum had never been short of that.

'Are we close, Farden? To the end of all this, I mean?'

Farden turned to look at him.

'I remember when you first strode into the hall in Hjaussfen. Defiant. Just waiting for an excuse to swing your fists. You would have fought me if I had not taken you away. I simply wanted to spare a life. Little did I know then that I would be crouched here in the rain, almost forty years later.'

Farden's eyes widened at the count.

'I ask only because I am tired, Farden. Growing old without my dragon's life. We have fought enemy after enemy together, and I will fight for you until the end, but my hope is I will see the end before I go to the other side. My hope is this is the last fight we stand together for.'

Farden winced, thinking of the cold stone of the Bifröst far beneath their feet in another realm.

'It's coming soon, Eyrum, and we'll stand together one last time. I promise you that,' he said, hoping to Hel and Haven and everything in between it was a promise he could keep. Once more, he felt that knife-edge cut into his feet.

Eyrum glared at the rain once more, but his heavy hand clasped onto Farden's shoulder and rocked him back and forth.

'What will you do when it's over, old friend?'

Eyrum thought for a moment. 'Sail,' he said.

'Sail?' Farden asked.

'Sturmsson taught me. I would like to sail and fish. Fly across the waves as I did on my dragon's back.'

'Never took you for a fisherman.'

'And what of you, Forever King?'

Farden sighed gently. 'Try to learn how to accept peace.'

'Putting down the weapons and armour is a start.'

Farden nodded.

'Will you?' asked Eyrum.

'What?

'What you promised Nerilan and Towerdawn and destroy the spear?'

You cannot keep me forever, came a whisper between the raindrops, and Farden cleared his throat. 'They're getting closer.'

It was a distraction, but it was also the truth. The scouts were winding their way up the hill, curious of the tors and possibly the smell of sausage wafting through the night.

Warbringer scuffed at the dirt behind them. 'Do we fight?'

'No,' Farden said all too quickly. 'We walk.'

Though the minotaur grumbled and angled a stare at Farden, she did not complain and went to douse her campfire. She and Eyrum followed Farden as he struck out, aiming higher and keeping behind gorse bushes. Gunnir was stowed safely in disguise as a sword at his side. He kept one hand on its metal and one eye on the goats creeping up the slope. They were faster and more nimble, but they were still poking in the wrong direction for the time being.

Something shifted in the darkness up ahead, between two tors that stood like a flattened gate. A shadow stood between them, and Farden immediately called a halt. Metal whispered as he held Gunnir in a fist, creeping forwards while the others stayed put.

It was a lone wolf. A big bastard with a shaggy coat drenched by the rain, with eyes of amber that shone even in the dark. It held still as the stone that framed it, even when Farden stood and approached.

Not the first time you have traded gazes with a wolf, spoke Gunnir.

Farden nodded.

Another whisper joined the rain. *The lone wolf is not alone any more.*

Growls burbled as six more shadows crept over the edge of the tors, looking down on Farden with curious eyes. Farden stood his ground, putting his hand to his Scalussen breastplate and looking at each of them in turn until, one by one, they broke their stares and turned to disappear into the night.

Warbringer and Eyrum joined him. 'Wolves?'

'The least of our worries.'

'Onwards.'

Their game of cat and mouse lasted for another hour until they were forced back down into the river valley by crags of rock it would have taken a day to climb. There the ground became even muddier than it had been, and the bowed heads of reeds began to crop up in copses. A distant wall of pines cut the road dead further ahead, and as far as Farden could tell, they had lost the duke's men to the rain. If he knew lackeys like he thought he did, then they had grown bored, cold, and wet and gone home a long time ago.

'Steel Ghost. What creature is steel and ghost?' asked Warbringer, devouring a cold sausage.

The name had explained some of what Farden had seen in Hel but not enough. He shrugged. 'Rokhelm said a beast of shadow and rage.'

Warbringer thumped her chest. 'I will take rage.'

'We already have a beast of shadow. Mithrid,' muttered Eyrum. Farden held his tongue. Only Lerel and Hereni were wise to their plot.

A goat-horn blew somewhere amidst the murk of rain. To the north, perhaps, but before they could utter a word, another horn answered with two blasts to the south. They were caught in the middle.

'Shit,' Farden cursed, looking around for cover as he slammed on his helmet. Aside from a few bogs and clumps of tall grass, there was nowhere to hide. Only the pines.

'That way, and quickly!' he ordered, watching Warbringer heft her hammer. Bloodshed and Voidaran did not need to meet that night.

A Steel Ghost didn't sound the bleeding or the dying type, but the duke's men would be fodder for the warhammer, and Farden couldn't allow it.

A little-known truth about goats was that they had better eyes than one might imagine. Especially at night and when a flash of red and gold sprinted along the road in front of them.

The damning bleat of one such keen-eyed bastard came before Farden saw the goat and its rider gallop out of the mist. The man already had a horn to his lips, and he blew three sharp notes on it before lowering his spear and bellowing his orders.

'Stop there!'

They were too far from the pines to sprint for it, and riders were already flooding out of the rain to head them off from both south and north. Horns deafened them as the riders circled like a whirlwind of goat-flesh and jangling silver chainmail. The pennants clinging wetly to their hooked spears were a dull purple. Farden stood his ground, magick flowing through his body in readiness.

A rider with a beard to rival his goat's and shark's teeth lining his helmet trotted out to address them. His hooked blade came dangerously close to Farden's face. Not dangerous for Farden of course, but the man was not to know. A purple tabard across his chest sported some goatish coat of arms that Farden had never seen before.

'In the name of Duke Alxander, for crimes of trespass, put down yer weapons and yer knees in the mud!'

'Not going to happen, but you can let us pass in peace, and we'll do you a favour.' said Farden calmly.

'Favour? Duke wants no favours from yer kind. Magick and empire and dragons ain't welcome in Saciath. Nor is whatever in Dalas' name that beast is,' the rider said as he pointed at Warbringer.

'Dragons, what dragon?' asked Farden, looking around.

The rider spat on the ground. 'Ye can play yer games with the duke, not I, strangers. On yer knees!'

Eyrum spoke up. 'We come to find the monster in your marshes. We came to rid you of it.'

The riders around them chuckled, but their captain stayed serious. 'Ain't no monster, and if there was it wouldn't be yer business. Every blade of grass and drop of rain that falls is the duke's, and nothin' happens without his say-so. Now, I ask you one more time. On your knee—'

Before Farden could raise his sword, another horn blew, and this one had a different tune to it. Galloping shook the mud as another group of riders appeared out of the rain. These did not ride thick goats as the others, but bulging rams with equally curly horns and vicious glares, and were clad in a mail their smiths had tried to make look gold but instead shone like a dull mustard.

'Is it fuck!' yelled the newcomers' captain, who wore a tabard bearing a ram's crest. 'Ye trespass on the land of Duke Reexe!'

Farden looked to Eyrum and Warbringer, who both shrugged.

'Begone! These're our prisoners, and nothin' to do with ye—'

'You begone! Alxander is forever crossin' our borders! These're our prisoners!'

'We should leave you to your dispute—' Farden attempted.

'Ye'll stay right there!' both of the captains roared. Both sets of riders had turned their ranks and spears to face the other. Their argument was reaching fever pitch, and now accusations of sexual proclivities towards their steeds were being made.

'Goat-fuckin' bastards!'

'Sheep-shagging cun—'

A crackle of lightning split the air and lit the night as Farden slammed Gunnir in the mud. It broke the argument and tension in a heartbeat, and every eye turned upon the mage.

'We're nobody's prisoners, and if you want to keep suggesting as much, then you'll find out what magick and dragons and minotaurs can do. Set us free and squabble on your own time!'

'For Alxander!' came the baying yell of the first captain.

'For Reexe!' answered the second, and within moments, the riders were at war. The first volleys of slingshot and crossbow bolts slammed against Farden's armour. One traced a cut across his cheek before he could slam his visor shut, and another dug into Warbringer's arm, but she broke it off without so much as a grunt. Only her warhammer screamed as she began to swing it in a deadly arc.

'Curse you all!' Farden yelled as he drove a wall of force and wind outwards, knocking goats and riders alike aside before Warbringer got to them.

Another clang of metal came as a bolt thudded against his head. Farden whirled the spear and spread fire to keep their circle wide, but the riders were not some peasants thrust atop a goat. They were fierce, as if they had spent their entire lives fighting feuds in valleys.

Four of the goats manoeuvred to surround Farden, and with brave bleats, they charged. A shield surrounded him, but these goats were made of steel. Not all hit at the same time, and he was jostled and thrown between them violently before they pressed inwards to trap him. Spears hammered at his armour, fruitless but enraging. Farden had tried to be quiet. Tried to be civil. He had tried to bargain, but it was no use, and he let his impatience rain down on the fools.

Lightning forked from the clouds to Gunnir's tip, and a shockwave sent riders and goats flying in all directions. Rams, too, and once the riders had picked themselves up and recovered, they were momentarily united against the invaders of their island.

Stones and bolts rained down on Farden's shields. Fire sputtered along Gunnir's blade as he swirled it, cutting down a rider from his mount and letting his cauterised halves fall to the mud, one of which screamed in pain and shock. Alxander's captain came charging, with his goat's horns low and his spear aimed.

A memory flashed before his eyes, and Farden couldn't help but see the fools of Krauslung on that muddy battlefield. They were trespassers on these lands, and despite their stubbornness and cloth ears, they didn't deserve such carnage.

Farden found himself pulling back, maiming where he could have killed, and solely to cut a path to the pines. Eyrum and Warbringer followed at his back, breaking past his shields to sow death with axe and hammer. The minotaur had carved a path of her own through the riders, and didn't slow no matter how many missiles met her flesh or bounced from her armour. Her voice rumbled as she sang her battle song of death and glory.

'Fleetstar!' Farden yelled to the skies as he reached the trees, seeking the dragon's fire and anything but the warhammer. A wall of riders was charging again, spears aimed and crossbows raised.

A shadow punctured the clouds as the dragon swooped, flame streaming from her jaws. Sturdy and fierce these goats and rams might have been, but a dragon was their mortal enemy, and they began to panic as the dragon sowed a river of fire through their horde. Fleetstar even snatched a goat and rider from the ground to prove her point and crushed them both between her jaws.

At that moment, an unholy scream came from the forest. Far too loud, far too long, and far too guttural to be any human, goat, or sheep. Not even a wolf or bear could have made such a noise, and it turned the battle into an eerie stillness. Not a soul moved.

Pines wavered as something shifted behind them. Farden retraced his steps, spear held out straight, as the scream sounded again. The piercing noise sounded more like the shredding of metal than a voice. Through the drumming rain, Farden peered and thought he saw two glowing points of eyes staring back before they blinked out.

Branches and logs cracked as whatever it was surged to snatch a rider from his goat. In the same breath, a boulder came flying out of the woods to crush one of the goats flat.

'Is this the Steel Ghost?' Eyrum shouted as he ran for the cover of a pile of bodies that Warbringer was building. Voidaran screeched louder than Farden had ever heard, and he feared Dotharadine would erupt at any moment.

Farden didn't know, but he knew a tactical retreat when he saw one and ran for the road and the bogs, hurling himself into the nearest pit of murky water.

'Back!' he yelled to the others, spitting mud. Warbringer and Eyrum were wise enough to do the same and sprinted after him. Each of them dove into their own bog as a pine tree came crashing down over the road. Fleetstar soared into the clouds and out of sight.

The air was filled with the bleating and bellowing of riders and mounts. Bodies four-legged and two flew into the air, pirouetting before they came crashing down. The fortunate landed in bogs of their own and stayed still and quiet, or unconscious and silently drowning. The unfortunate fell at painful angles in the mud or flew deeper into the forest.

Farden saw Duke Reexe's captain being dragged through the mud by what looked like a chain. He vanished into the rain and the gloom of the forest, but his yelling didn't stop.

One by one, the riders either scattered or succumbed. The dead were left to bleed and gawk at the clouds, mouths filling with rainwater, but the wounded were snatched by dark and shrouded hands, almost figments of the imagination. A metallic creaking receded.

'Steel Ghost,' Warbringer murmured.

Eyrum squished another gnat against his grey scales. 'You sure about this one, Farden?'

Farden was not, but he had come this far. He heard Lerel's words. *Stubborn. Reckless. Fearless. Driven.*

'We follow it,' he said over the rainfall and the sounds of cries, moans, screams, and other such noises of complaint and horror. The forest thrashed, and distant marshes splashed under the unknown force. It was madness by anybody's standards but his, and for a moment he wondered if he had slipped into the trap of power and pushed too far.

But Warbringer and Eyrum merely shrugged and began to climb from the marshes.

'No complaints?'

'You say we need this one?' asked Warbringer.

'Yes.'

'Then we go get. We trust.'

The minotaur's words and nudge of her knuckles made Farden smile grimly. He grasped that feeling tightly and hoped it would never wither. The knife's edge in his mind grew a little wider.

Farden joined them on the road, soaking wet, stinking of marsh-rot, and covered in a combination of mud and peat. 'At least we have a good disguise,' he said.

Warbringer chuckled at that. 'Old Arka tricks.'

Together, hearts beating a little slower knowing there was a dragon above them, they trod between the dead and the broken – and in some cases the *very* broken, with parts strewn across a disturbingly wide area – to enter the gloom of the pines.

The noises of the wounded could still be heard, muffled by the rain and distance but easy to follow. It turned out that the pines were a thin ring, guarding a sprawl of marshes dotted with stubborn trees that refused to join the rest. In the darkness, lit only by the towns' distant glow and Farden's most cautious of light spells, the bog-water tried its best to gleam. A myriad moss-lined trails ran between the pools, lined with reeds and tufts of grey grass, and they were churned to mud where great ruts had been carved by something large and furious. Moths flapped around him, head-butting his armour while midges swarmed like Peryn's birds. Farden took a breath. At least the trail of the kidnapped wounded was easy to follow.

'No going back now,' he said aloud, and the others grunted in unison. There was something enormously comforting about the two companions looming at his side.

'Feel like home,' Warbringer rumbled.

Treacherous, was the going, and irritatingly slow. The Steel Ghost, if that was what it was, sloshed through the marsh with legs larger than theirs, and to make it worse, weaved a strange path back and forth. They tried to follow the noises and fading screams as much as possible, but the hovering mist played tricks with their ears. One moment they would charge after it only to hear it behind them. All they could do was keep to the trail and continue marching. Armour was fine and well on the battlefield, but its weight was almost a death trap in a marsh. The minotaur was the only one who seemed to be enjoying herself. She had a knack for gauging the weak spots over the firm, and though the others tried to follow her as best they could, they plunged into bogs over and over. Every time, they paused to haul the unfortunate one out and make sure they weren't heard. Farden sweated through it all, as if the passing minutes gnawed at his skull.

To make matters worse, the marshes were not just home to frogs and bothersome flies, but the detritus of the Steel Ghost's carnage. Bodies, some fresh and some ancient, hid beneath the surface of every other bog. Stiff skeletons grasped at them every time they fell. Corpses with flesh peeling leered and reached as they passed. Some lay on knolls, searching for freedom, rotted where they had failed, and they twitched in the corners of their eyes.

Farden was the latest to fall victim to fall into the murk, but Warbringer caught him before he sank. He came up with a skeletal hand wrapped around his greave which he swore held on as he kicked it free.

'We are close. I smell blood,' Warbringer whispered, as quietly as a minotaur could whisper, that was.

'I hope you're right, because I can't take much more of this.' Dawn could have risen, and the infernal duo of mist and rain would have kept it from them. The noise of the Steel Ghost and the wounded had grown quiet. Either death had come for them, or they were lost.

Eyrum spoke nothing of his exhaustion, but Farden could see it in his eyes. And yet he stayed the most determined one, leading them through the marsh with his keen Siren ears.

'Warbringer's right,' he muttered, motioning for them to stay low when the arse of a hill loomed out of the haze. It rose above the marshes in a lazy incline, covered in pine trees like a helmet. Their ears pricked as a lone scream rang out, painfully close.

Farden concentrated. It had been a while since he used his mind to speak to a dragon, and the skill was slippery. *Can you hear me, Fleetstar?*

Barely. You're terrible at this.

Hush. Keep watch and stay listening. We'll probably need you.

Wonderful.

Farden clambered up the hill, using the wandering roots of the pines to keep from getting stuck in the mud. The footprints that had been half-swallowed by the muck were like none he had ever seen before. He recognised the furrows of clawing human hands, however. That was plain enough.

With careful steps and patience they thought all but lost, they crept to the peak of the hill only to find it was the rim of a shallow crater, like a barrow with its grave scooped out. It should have been veiled in darkness and haze like the rest of the marshes, but stones with shining, unfamiliar runes gave off a sickly yellow light that verged on green. Farden could see another ring of pine trees, as if they had been planted purposefully and tended. A huge, barn-sized shelter of logs and moss caulking stood precarious at its centre. Behind it, another structure was barely visible in the mist, and it seemed to shelter a stone coffin, surrounded by more tiny stones lit by runes.

Farden squinted. What looked like stonesmith tools were strewn on stone and log benches within the makeshift and open-ended barn. Bodies were piled at each corner, making those alive babble and yell all the more, plainly heard now.

A dozen survivors were arranged in a circle, chained to stone blocks covered in runes and scars. At their centre was a dais with all manner of chiselled script covering its surface. It was huge. Warbringer, Eyrum, and Farden could have lain head to toe and still not reach its edge. It was scarred with marks of lightning and burned leaves. And blood. Far too much blood. The stones were caked and stained to their core in crimson, donated unwillingly by countless victims, no doubt.

Farden saw Eyrum looking at him from the corner of his eye. 'Once again, Farden. Are you sure about this one?'

Before he could decide, Gunnir whispered a word he understood very well.

Necromancy. A magick made by those who bring back what was lost.

There was more to the murderous power of this Steel Ghost, and Farden wanted to know what it was. Without a word, he shuffled to the edge of the crater to get a closer look.

Hidden by gloom, rain, and the logs of the shelter, a hulking shape moved around between the trees, lugging chains and carving final adjustments into rock. Farden couldn't see its form. He didn't know whether it was a beast or a human or something in between, and all his spells could tell him was that it flowed with magick.

With his extended sight, Farden glimpsed the face of a Saciath rider. It was the Reexe captain. A cut ran from his hairline to his chest, and he looked dazed, but he was the loudest of them all.

'Release us, monster!' he yelled and pleaded. Others took up his cry, and there was a great shriek before they fell silent and whimpering.

A glow that burned blue instead of the wan yellow spilled across the mud and pools of blood. A chain with a spike on the end of it appeared, clutched in a hand made of dun yet intricate steel plates, each scrap moving independently and held together by a faint sapphire shine.

'Steel Ghost indeed,' was all Farden told the others.

Before he could take a stand or voice a shout, the hand drove the spike into the side of the captain's head, turning his eyes up in his skull. The others who were conscious screamed as the same was done to them, and as the monster came to the edge of the circle, Farden glimpsed two legs and heavy feet, all made of clanking and creaking metal.

When each captive was pinned by their chain, the Steel Ghost thumped to the dais and took ahold of a bundle of links, each leading to a stone and a still-twitching corpse.

Lightning crackled over the monster's metal and blasted chunks from the mud and wooden shelter. Farden ducked as a bright fork soared into the trees around them, snipping a branch with a burst of flame. Below, the eyes of the dead opened to glow blue, and heads twitched.

'Thron!' Eyrum cursed as another strike of lightning scorched the mud mere feet from his hands.

It lasted moments. Whatever spell the Steel Ghost was casting collapsed with an explosion of one of the runed stones. The rubble had barely met the ground before a shrieking roar filled the night. Stone, chains, and corpses were cast aside in a rage.

Farden stood.

'What are you doing, mage?' blurted Eyrum.

'Taking a chance,' he said, and at that moment he did feel mad, especially as he put his faith in the words of a spear. Farden trusted it was Durnus' words and not power talking. He strode down the hill, no other plan in mind except to see this monster for himself.

Eyrum and Warbringer bravely followed at his back, axe and hammer ready.

With every step he took down the treacherous slope, hoping he didn't fall on his arse, Farden saw more and more of the huge creature. This Steel Ghost was not as large as Ossas or Keraken, that was already certain, but whatever the glow of runes and the rain hid still stood twenty if not thirty feet tall.

'I come to talk!' said Farden, holding Gunnir and an empty hand out. The monster whirled in the axle of his carnage, hands still dripping, and through the murk, Farden could glimpse those same shining blue eyes staring back at him beneath a giant and disjointed form.

There were no words traded before the monster began to thud across the stone and mud with heavy fists held ready. Farden got a brief look at the beast before it attacked him, and what he saw was a complex suit of cracked and cobbled steel armour without an owner. All that sat within its curves and angles was a faint blue mist, punctuated only by two piercing eyes. With a shriek of metal, bloodied and notched blades slid from its palms, ready to cleave.

Farden held out his empty hand and a shield spell ignited before it. Farden's boots skidded through the mud under the impact, and magick shone as a blade scraped across his spell, but the monster did not try again. It stepped back, eyes blinking and overlapping plates grinding against each other.

'You have magick,' came a voice of churning metal and a haunting whisper.

Farden kept up his shield and held Gunnir flat and firmly. 'That I do, and it'll make short work of you if you try me or my friends.'

The monster leaned forwards, and between the crowned helmet that covered a glowing face of unblemished skin and human teeth, Farden thought he saw a smile.

'Is that a promise?' the Steel Ghost asked.

Farden scowled and got straight to the point. 'We've come here in peace to meet you, and if you are willing, to ask for your help.'

'Help? From me? Nobody has asked such a thing since…' The Steel Ghost trailed off, looking distant before his blade poked at Farden's shield again. With a clanking of hidden clockwork, he stretched taller, and Farden had to spread his shield wider.

'You will fight me,' said the monster.

'Fight you? We don't want to fight you,' Eyrum blurted.

'Give me your best, magick one!' roared the Steel Ghost before his blade came hammering down with the force of a landslide. Farden was bent to his knees under the force, but he thrust upwards with the spear, and a detonation of thunder broke from its tip. The Steel Ghost was sent stumbling back against a pine and cracked its trunk.

'Yes!' he bellowed.

Farden sensed a challenge, and as Eyrum and Warbringer stood beside him, he gave them a simple order. 'We don't kill him, understand?'

'Aye, King,' rumbled Eyrum as he limped ahead with his axe flowing around him. Farden drew his curved Khandri sword and spun it in his hand. The spear in his other crackled with sparks. Warbringer slammed Voidaran down on the mud, making the earth shake with its power.

As the Steel Ghost recovered, it roared from the depths of its glowing soul, and every gnarled and rusted and mismatched plate spread outwards to reveal a storm of blue mist and light, dark mouth open far too wide.

If it was supposed to shock them, it did just that, and Farden was a fraction slower throwing his firebolts than he should have been. They exploded against the Steel Ghost's armour with little effect, stalling him only slightly as curved spikes extended from his shoulders and arms. They were playing to survive, but the Steel Ghost was playing to kill.

Farden ducked as the first of the notched blades swung over his head. He aimed for the gaps between the armour, but when he swung, the plates closed in preternaturally fast and locked his blade between them. With a wrench, Farden was deprived of his sword, and he spun Gunnir instead. Again the plates closed, but this time Gunnir scorched them and made the Steel Ghost recoil.

'Yes!'

Warbringer pounced, soaring across the muck with Voidaran raised. It hammered against the Steel Ghost's foot, bending metal and driving his claws into the mud, trapping him momentarily. Another swing caught him in the hip, battering him backwards so that he almost tumbled, but it was a ploy to bring them closer. The Steel Ghost wrenched his foot from the mud, kicked Warbringer square in the chest to send her soaring, and then spun around, metal shrieking as the plates rearranged.

Farden was quick to duck, but one of the blades clashed against Gunnir, almost ripping it from his hand. Sparks showered him as the spear cut a deep notch in the steel, and before Farden could haul it free, it was the Steel Ghost who did the hauling. Farden flew across the mud to land on his face, and as he scrabbled upright, the monster raised a foot to squish him. And yet Farden saw him pause for a fleeting moment, as if he wanted Farden to get up.

Fine. If the Steel Ghost wanted a good fight, then he would have it. Farden whirled Gunnir over his head and spun lightning that battered against the monster's plates and helmet. Fire blossomed in a ring around them, closing in until Farden was wreathed in flame and the Steel Ghost stamped and roared as it scorched his armour.

Eyrum braved the fire to knock his battleaxe against the monster's blade and knock a chunk of armour free. A fine distraction. Farden saw Warbringer charging from the other side and clenched his fist to quench the fire. The Steel Ghost looked up in surprise for a brief moment before the minotaur collided with him horns-first, sending him sliding across the mud. A blow from Voidaran dented the plates across his back, cracking one entirely, and finally put the monster to the mud.

Farden threw up a hand before the warhammer could descend again.

'We don't want to kill you—' Farden attempted to bargain, but the Steel Ghost was far from interested. His eyes burned.

'More!' he bellowed to the sounds of bent metal popping back into place with sharp clangs. He did not get up, but rather his armour tore itself apart and put itself back together again in a standing position. 'More!'

'Ghost not listen, Farden!' Warbringer roared.

Again the blades came searching, and this time the Steel Ghost really tried, cutting shapes that they were forced to jump and dive through to keep themselves whole. Farden held firm as both blades clashed against Gunnir, sliding down the spear's blade. The mage drove the fire of his magick into his fingers and spread sparks down the ragged steel. Gunnir erupted with a storm of its own, and lightning poured into the monster's soul. For the first time, the Steel Ghost roared in what sounded like pain, and yet he stayed locked against Farden, grinning at the sight of his armour beginning to glow.

'More!' the Ghost roared, and Farden's patience withered.

'You asked for it!' he shouted as he thrust Gunnir upwards, drawing in magick until flame roared across its blade. Farden clenched, bringing a vortex of wind to pull at every piece of the Steel Ghost. With a stamp of his foot, the mud rippled to swallow the monster's legs up to the knees. And with a twist of his fingers, every nearby rock rose up with unseen hands and rocketed for the Ghost. It sounded like a bell being shot by a hundred archers, and their foe rocked back and forth under the impacts, voice rising into a metallic screech. Farden did not let up.

'Farden!' Eyrum yelled.

Gunnir was ready. A shockwave bent the pines almost to breaking as Farden let its magick pour. A jet of white fire collided with the Steel Ghost's breastplates. Fire wrapped around the monster, racing across his steel and iron and drifting soul, and what didn't scorch him set half the pines alight. Flames even burst from Farden's armour.

'You'll kill him!' Eyrum yelled in his ear, daring to put a hand on Farden's shoulder.

'No,' Farden said as he brought the spells to a thunderous halt. 'I won't. And purely because I don't think I can.'

The Ghost's steel glowed red-hot. Black scorch covered the rest of him, the armour dented and broken in a score of places. Blue mist seemed to drift and leak from every gap and tear. And yet, Farden could still feel the inner inferno that had fought against his magick. As daunting as it was to know Gunnir had to struggle to kill him, Farden was glad such an ally existed.

White eyes ignited once again, and the mist snapped back into the armour to make it rattle. Dents once again fixed themselves, and runes glowed just as they did on Farden's back. Whatever spell its ancient makers had written into the metal, it was powerful indeed.

'More,' was all the Steel Ghost whispered.

Farden saw it now: the polar opposite to his own fate. A desperation to perish instead of exist. A struggle against the curse of immortality. 'You want to die, don't you?' he asked, sombre.

'And yet I cannot,' came the growl of a reply, distant and worn from being repeated over the centuries. 'It is my curse.'

Farden stepped closer. Even buried up to his knees in mud, the Steel Ghost still towered over him.

'Fight. You have more to give,' the monster said, waving one of his blades half-heartedly. Farden held Gunnir against it.

'I won't. It's not our way.'

'Virtue,' grunted the Steel Ghost. 'Another curse.'

With little effort at all, he dragged his legs from the earth and began to mutter to himself, turning away to thunder back to his shelter and the bloody mess he had made of it. Fires burned here and there on the sap-rich wood.

With a clench of Farden's fists, he extinguished them all, and the Steel Ghost grunted again. Though Warbringer and Eyrum scowled, Farden decided to follow, watching him clear away the carnage and throw the bodies on the rotting piles. It was as if they had been forgotten in an instant. But not so.

'I am Farden of Scalussen—'

The Steel Ghost slammed a blade into the mud, sending bones flying at Farden. 'What lies are these? Scalussen burned centuries ago. I was there.'

He was a Scalussen Smith after all, just like his marooned brother. 'New Scalussen,' Farden quickly replied. 'A kingdom that desires the same peace as you did.'

The monster loomed closer. 'You,' he rasped, like a saw on an iron ingot, curious at the same time as angered. 'You wear the Nine. Where did you steal it?'

'Some of it I found, others I rescued. The rest I was given,' replied Farden.

'A liar and a thief. You are no better than those who came to pillage the Smiths' forges.'

'I was given it by Korrin, of the Knights of the Nine,' Farden countered, hoping for reason instead of more violence. 'I found him in Hel and set him free.'

The Steel Ghost relented at the mention of Hel but kept his blade close. 'I remember that name.'

'Have you a name? These others,' Farden said, pausing to glance at what was left of the Saciath riders. 'They called you the Steel Ghost, but that doesn't sound like a name to me.'

'Fitting though it is.' The metal beast thought for a moment, distracted again.

'They call this place Metrada,' said Eyrum. 'Is that you?'

The Steel Ghost stared at the pine boughs as they whispered, and slowly his blades retreated into his forearms. 'That was my name, long ago,' he grunted before he gathered his complex chains.

Farden let loose his words. 'A friend of ours remembers a Scalussen Smith marooned on an island the same as this one, and he spoke of a brother consumed by a beast of shadow. I also know of a ghost that stands in Hel, caught between that realm and this one. Cursed. Would you be one and the same?'

'Cursed, you call me, and cursed I am,' Metrada whispered. 'I am otherwise engaged. Otherwise engaged.' The words spilled over and over. Here Farden was, worried to his soul about madness, and yet the haunting eyes he stared into showed him its true face.

'Otherwise engaged in what?' Farden asked, daring to step within the circle of stone.

Metrada kept up his work, toiling brutally and swiftly, as if he had done such a thing several thousand times before. 'Work. Always work,' spoke the monster, beginning to scrape patterns in fresher stone with a metal claw of a finger.

Farden's eyes roamed over the monster's plates again, which he realised now were covered in glyphs, intricate and ancient. A sheer magick Farden wasn't sure he understood. 'What is it you forge?' he asked.

'Death. As I have for a thousand years,' Metrada whispered, and Farden ignored the shiver up his spine at the sound of the word.

'Can we help?' asked Farden. It was a dagger of a question, and it seemed to cut straight to Metrada's core. Farden could see a soul set in its ways, spending centuries shedding blood without hearing a single word that wasn't screamed. Farden hoped he played a friend Metrada had forgotten could exist.

The monster skewered him with his dangerous eyes. He looked Farden and the others up and down while his claws clicked on the stone as if considering how much their flesh weighed 'You would not understand,' he said, words a blacksmith's hammer on an anvil.

'This is necromancy, isn't it?'

'In part.' Metrada had no brow to wrinkle, but Farden saw the memories playing behind his shining eyes. Metrada looked to the coffin. 'My wife Adarta fell to the ice breath. The cold got in her lungs, made her weak and fall into a stupor. I knew of ways to save her, forgotten ways, but the High Smith Aurien and my brother both forbade me to try. Heresy, they called my cures, and so I ignored them and lost myself here in this place. Weeks I spent building this machine and when it was done...'

Metrada carved another rune, and with a rap of his knuckles, they sputtered with light.

'She was already gone.'

Farden bowed his head. 'And how did you come to wear the armour?'

'My design failed. My runes incorrect. The spell broke, and it did not bring her back but took me instead,' Metrada grunted. 'So I stayed lost, and I have tried to reverse my mistake for a thousand years. I have taken countless corpses. I have used animals. I have taken live ones. I have tried few. I have tried many. And all the while, Adarta waits for me on the other side.'

'Is that her?' asked Eyrum, pointing to the coffin.

Metrada nodded. 'Her ashes. And I will join her one day. I must.'

Farden stayed silent about the Bifröst, but what he did do was tell the truth. 'Metrada, we came to ask you to fight. To join us in battle.'

Metrada turned around without moving his legs, plates reconfiguring one by one. 'Battle against whom?'

Warbringer snuffled. 'A god. Elves. Great Ones like you.'

'Great Ones,' echoed Metrada.

'A battle that will either end the world or save it. A battle for Ragnarök,' said Farden.

'A fine place to die if there was one,' murmured Eyrum. 'No better chance of it.'

Metrada looked between them, one by one. 'Why didn't you just say so?'

Farden had to smile. 'Can we trust you, Metrada?'

The monstrous machine stretched tall and then sank with a whine of metal. 'You can trust me to fight. Never fought a god before. And if he does not kill me, then you shall with that spear. Whether it is your way or not. Is it a deal?'

Farden bowed, quietly wondering if he could keep that promise when the time came, or whether it would merely trap Metrada in a Hel with no escape, servant to the gods. Only time held the answer, and he straightened with a firm smile. 'We have a deal,' he said.

Metrada came to loom over him, studying his armour before extending a cautious hand, 'Immortality is a curse, Scalussen got what it deserved cursing the Knights so. Wise to remember that, Farden of New Scalussen.'

Farden clamped his visor down as he held out Gunnir.

❦

It was the early hours when the sand of New Scalussen whispered beneath their feet. A herd of antelope who had been lounging nearby scattered with strange barking sounds.

Metrada checked his plates and mists to see, irritatingly, that he was still all there after Gunnir's spell. He stared at the city before him with a grumble that Farden wasn't sure meant he was impressed or displeased.

'Eyrum and Warbringer will take you to the harbour,' Farden offered Metrada. 'There's room and shelter there.'

'Aye, King,' said Eyrum, saluting with his axe before leading Metrada away. The ground thudded under his metal claws, and patrols came to gawp. Warbringer hung back, eyes sharp and glinting in the dark.

'Problem, Warbringer?' Farden asked, already knowing the answer.

'You cannot stop Dotharadine's prophecy, mage,' she growled. 'You think I not notice. But you have no right. You pink-fleshes have word for it. Inevitable.'

Warbringer said no more, and Farden watched her leave with a sigh. He took a precious moment to be alone with his worries, listening to the winds mixing with the mumble of distant waves.

The whisper came from his pocket.

'Are you there?'

It was no Gunnir, and Farden cursed as he brought Irien's crow skull into the faint light of the city. The gemstone cast a gentle glow, spilling over his hands. Lerel was nowhere in sight, and there was no chance Farden could pull off a worthy impression of Irien.

The mage needn't have worried.

'Farden?' the skull whispered again.

To a gust of wind and a rustle of palms, the mage pursed his lips.

Farden's smile was tight. The ruse was up. 'Loki.'

The rustle of distant laughter made the crow's beak twitch. 'How wonderful to know you still draw breath,' spoke the god.

'How awkward. I can't say the same for you,' replied Farden.

'We appear to be at a stalemate, Farden. Whatever are we to do?'

Farden set his jaw. 'I suggest battle.'

'My thoughts exactly,' Loki said with another detestable chuckle. 'Where and when?'

Farden had been considering such a thing for a week. Not Scalussen. Not Krauslung. Not Easterealm and not Paraia. Chaos had to be forged elsewhere.

'The ice fields, where it all began.'

'A fine suggestion.'

'Three days from now.'

'Then we shall have our war.'

'I look forward to holding your heart in my hands,' Farden replied, lips close to the beak.

Without a further thought, Farden clenched it in his gauntlet and crushed it to shards. Not content, he stamped them into the sand until the skull was unrecognisable.

Three days, he had, before the end of the world.

CHAPTER 38
AN EVE OF BATTLE

There's not a battle that's ever gone completely to plan, but there's also not a battle that was ever won without a plan.
FROM A DIARY WRITTEN IN 806 OF THE NEW COUNT BY ARKA GENERAL GRACE ARES, REMEMBERED AS ONE OF THE FINEST WRITTEN MAGES

'Three days?! You gave Loki three days, and you want us to sail all the way back to the ice fields in that time? Even the dragons can barely fly that far that fast,' yelled Lerel, words like a deluge.

Farden quickened his pace, but Lerel kept up with ease.

'I have a solution.'

'Another idea? You know what? I take back what I said. You *have* gone mad.'

Farden stopped dead, hoping to find a smirk on Lerel's face that would blunt the edge that had just raked him. There was none, and she stood on hands and hips and waited impatiently for an answer.

'A portal,' he said.

Lerel prodded him in the shoulder. 'That doesn't fill me with confidence. Last time you jumped a bookship, it landed right on the beach. A miracle it didn't squish anyone. Now you want to jump our whole army and four Great Ones?'

Farden was torn in a hundred different directions, and he didn't have time to stand still. He held Lerel by the shoulders. 'Not jump, a quickdoor. Durnus did it once with interwoven branches when we brought Tyrfing back to Krauslung.'

'But you're not Durnus. That time and distance magick has never been your power.'

Farden stayed quiet and clenched his spear. 'It is now. I've had enough practice.'

Lerel huffed. 'Nerilan and Towerdawn want to see you. Immediately, is what they said.'

'Don't they know we're preparing for a war?'

Farden broke into the daylight outside the Dawnknell and aimed for the nearest warehouse filled with banging and clanging. Scalussen had risen before the dawn on its king's orders and had not stopped working since. The final preparations for battle had begun.

Formations of tables filled the floors, and at each sat an armourer punishing rivets, scraping with files, or engraving with fine chisels and hammers. Akitha and Metrada had already formed a strange friendship, and the monster apparently had much to say about New Scalussen's runecraft. Akitha had put her own army to work, reinforcing the metal with Metrada's suggestions. The Siren smith wandered to and fro, checking and prying and doling out curses every other step.

Farden nodded to her as he pressed on, back into the daylight and towards the fletchers that sprawled across half the main plaza. Barrels of arrows bristled with gold and red feathers, stolen from the pheasants the Jar Khoum excelled at catching.

Swinging past the eastern walls, they climbed the stairs of fresh stone and put hands to battlements. Witches and snowmads were traipsing carefully between the herds of creatures that had come to worship Ossas. Where the witches and their clouds of birds wandered, bastions knelt their tree trunk legs down in the dirt and allowed the witches to affix the armour and great sheets of mail the blacksmiths had spent days creating. Only the witches and northerners dared come near the biggest of the beasts, and the bastions listened only to them. On their backs, platforms were strapped for archers and mages. Steel caps were added to their tusks, and spikes wrapped around their trunks.

Only Peryn was absent, likely in the mountains with Territha. Ossas wasn't the only Great One to attract a following, and a halo of huge vultures, condors, and eagles circled the smear of storm on the nearest mountaintop. And not too far away, Ossas himself looked on with watchful and beaming eyes.

'How are you expecting to put those on boats?' Lerel said, drumming her fingers.

Farden pointed to the harbour. 'We have plenty of ships and barges, and the dreadnoughts were built big enough for dragons. The bastions aren't much bigger.'

'You've got everything planned out, haven't you?' Lerel might have covered with exasperation, but Farden could tell it was concern that hid beneath.

'Almost. But why does it sound like you're concerned by that?'

'I'm impressed, but it also feels like I'm on the back of a runaway dragon and have to trust it'll land me back on the ground safe and sound,' Lerel sighed, pressing palms to her forehead. 'All right. Where's this portal going to be?'

'You'll see,' Farden answered. 'You'll be proud.'

'Hmph.'

On the flagstones between the walls and the bay, hundreds and thousands milled, running drills, dancing through sword forms, or hammering on each other's armour while chanting. Others queued to collect their sharpened arms and freshly-runed armour.

Sixty thousand. That was the number that burned in Farden's head. Scalussen, Paraian, and Jar Khoum, and all of them were raring to fight. That was all he had to throw at Loki, and though a younger Farden wouldn't have blinked, it hurt to think of a single one of them dying for such a cause. And yet Farden could not have asked them to stand down if he tried. Half the army already flooded the harbour and beaches, eagerly waiting to board the ships of the Bastard Fleet. The blood shed by the Dramath-Ai weighed heavy on them. Farden could almost smell the vengeance in the air.

'She's almost ready, you know,' said Lerel, following Farden's gaze out to the harbour, where a forest of masts crawled with sailors. One stood amongst the rest, even between the dreadnoughts, a dark and heavy blotch in the harbour. The brand new mountain of a ship was mostly free of scaffolding and workers, and Farden led her towards it.

'She's yours to sail,' Farden said as he scuffed sand beneath his feet. 'All you have to do is come up with a name.'

Lerel cleared her throat as if something stuck there. '*Spring's Victory*. After Sturmsson.'

'Couldn't have thought of a better name myself,' Farden said, surging in the dreadnought's direction.

A mighty cheer erupted when the soldiers and sailors in the harbour saw their king and queen, as they fondly thought of Lerel. Farden set his jaw and made sure to smile, even though inside he was a storm of impatience and trepidation. Lerel clasped hands with captains and crew while Farden kept moving, a channel opening up for him in the crowds.

Farden had to crane his neck to take in the whole of the *Spring's Victory*. Iron reached from the water to grip her hull. Between the shields that ran along the bulwarks in their thousands, the snubbed noses of scores of ballistae poked forth. Five huge masts protruded from her broad decks, heavy with black sails, and her fore and aftcastles were fortresses of ironclad wood, reaching hundreds of feet high.

'By the gods,' Farden murmured.

'The pinnacle of ships. There's no finer vessel in the known seas. Certain people can't stop coming to ogle,' said Lerel, brandishing a finger.

Farden saw Elessi and Rokhelm further along the pier, deep in conversation like two thieves plotting a heist.

'What mischief are you up to now, you two?' Farden asked them

Rokhelm chuckled. 'Cannons. Your dreadnought could do with some. Then she would be perfection.'

'What in Hel is a cannon, and why would I want one on my ship?' asked Lerel.

Elessi snorted as Rokhelm scuttled away. 'That usually means he wants us to follow,' she said.

'I'm glad somebody can translate,' Farden replied.

'They do spend so much time together, after all,' Lerel muttered, getting a whack on the arm from Elessi, but it didn't stop her smiling.

❦

'This,' Rokhelm said proudly, 'is a cannon.'

Farden looked again at the thing. Frankly, it looked like an overgrown and unimpressive sausage of black iron, perched in a wooden cradle and poking out of a porthole. There was a hole at one end, and that was it. The ship with no name had six of the things altogether, spread around the middle deck and each about nine feet long. A few runes marked their metal flanks, but they seemed to have no moving parts at all. Next to each one sat a pile of almost spherical rocks and small barrels marked with a crudely-drawn skull. It looked like Rokhelm was hoarding poison.

The ship shifted beneath him again, and Farden found himself looking out of the porthole at the shell of the beast they stood on. He had ridden dragons and gryphons, and yet the idea of riding an enormous keraken didn't sit well with him.

'Are we supposed to know what that means? Farden asked, and Rokhelm answered with his actions. First, he took one of the barrels and upended it. It wasn't poison that seeped out, but a black and grainy powder. Once a measure had been fed to the mouth of the cannon, it swallowed a wad of cloth and then one of the round stones. Farden listened to it rolling down the cannon's throat with a clunk.

'Is this a magick?' Farden asked, though he felt nothing.

'Of sorts,' Rokhelm said as he winked at Elessi. He stood at the rear of the cannon and peeked from the porthole. Without a word spoken, Keraken shifted again until their broadside faced out into the ocean and away from any of the fleet.

'Give me fire, mage,' said Rokhelm.

'Where?'

'Right here.' Rokhelm pointed at a carving at the arse-end of the cannon, shaped like a snarling bear. There was a hole in the middle of its throat. More of the grainy substance was poured into it, and then Rokhelm gestured for Farden to light it.

Farden had many questions, but he did as he was told. With a click, a candle's flame burned at the end of his finger, and he held it to the bear's mouth.

What happened next happened all too suddenly.

First, the black grains sparked into a fierce and spitting fire, and no sooner had they ignited did the cannon emit a deafening bang and lurch backwards in its cradle. Through the billowing smoke, Farden couldn't see anything of the stone, but a splash far in the distance gave him some clue. Incredibly far in the distance.

'What in Hel?' Farden spluttered.

Rokhelm swelled his chest. 'Met a man of the far west many years ago, where sands stretch on longer than seas. He taught me of the ways of powders and what he called *sahr*, and together we built these cannons. Caloms, he called them in his tongue, but I prefer my word.'

'This powder, can you make more of it?'

'I can, if you have the ingredients.'

'Fetch Akitha,' Farden ordered a nearby guard. 'Put as many of these cannons as you can on the *Spring's Victory*.'

Elessi smiled. 'A fine and wonderful name for a ship, but she ain't magick. How is she supposed to go north in three days?'

'That's what I asked him,' muttered Lerel.

Farden clenched his spear, hearing the whisper in his head. 'We're making a portal. A quickdoor in an archway made of rock big enough to sail the *Victory* through.'

Before Rokhelm and Lerel could answer as one, Farden beat them to it. 'The Folly of Elleen. Half a day's sail away by my measure.'

'That's… correct,' said Lerel, squinting.

'Told you.' Farden grinned.

While Rokhelm looked enraptured, Elessi threw up her hands. 'Giants. Terror-birds. Metal ghosts. Now portals. How I can't wait for this all to be over!'

Farden thumped the spear. 'It'll work. Durnus has… used to show me how.'

Rokhelm slapped a beam and laughed. 'If not, then maybe Loki will freeze to death waiting.'

'Farden!' came a cry from below. Farden gratefully ran up the stairs to get some air and be safe in the knowledge he could hurl himself off this strange ship at any time.

It was Bull, standing on the sand with his eyes wide at the tentacles that came to weave around him and poke at his armour. Rokhelm stamped his foot and muttered a warning, and Keraken withdrew.

'Nerilan's looking for you, King!'

'Fine,' Farden sighed, raising his spear to avoid having one of the tentacles wrap around him, as Elessi had become used to.

Bull flinched as sand sprayed his armour and the mage.

'Lead the way,' Farden ordered before Lerel and Elessi could descend from the ship. A blunt blade of worry poked his gut.

Nerilan and Towerdawn waited beyond the walls. A curious place to be, as if they were midway through saying their goodbyes. A dozen other dragons waited with them, filling the drab day with colour and shine.

'Are you leaving? What's going on?' asked Farden.

Towerdawn's head was raised. His scales gleamed in contrast to his dun eyes, glazed over with deep thought and what Farden assumed was frustration.

Nerilan had a foul curl to her lip. She looked to have a wasp in her armour by the way she shrugged her shoulders, eyes darting between the activity in the city and the mage striding across the dust. 'We are here to ask you one last time,' she called to him.

That did not sound promising. Everything had been going so well. Farden watched as his generals caught up. Lerel, Elessi, Ko-Tergo, and Eyrum had arrived. 'Ask me to do what, Nerilan?' he asked.

'You entertain your own thoughts on the gods, but you do not speak for all of Emaneska. We have a right to return our god Thron if we have the power, and I beseech you once again, Farden Forever King, that you do as I ask and release him from the sky.'

Farden had to know. 'And if I don't?'

'We won't join you in this fight,' rumbled Towerdawn, as if he was sad to say it.

Farden crossed his arms with a chime of armour. 'You promised to fight Loki if he reappeared. You gave your word. And now we're at that moment, you want to slink back to your mountain under some pretence of returning a god? Feckless,' he accused, speaking only to Nerilan. He already saw the pain in Towerdawn's eyes. The schism was tearing them apart.

Nerilan's glaive moved from her shoulder to point at Farden. 'How dare you.'

Farden whirled around to those gathered, an unofficial council in the humble scrub beyond the walls. 'Is this what the rest of you believe? Ko-Tergo? Elessi? Eyrum?'

'Not I,' said Elessi, standing with him.

Ko-Tergo's furry brow creased. He, too, took a stand behind Farden. 'I do not.'

Eyrum crossed his arms. 'I made my decision long ago. Farden knows what's best.'

Nerilan bared her teeth. 'None of you see that the spear has infected his mind. He makes decisions with the snap of the finger, whispering to himself when he thinks nobody notices. He raises monsters, and none of you bat an eyelid! It was he that cursed us with elves!'

Heart thudding, Farden listened and waited, but there came not a whisper of agreement from the commanders of Scalussen. With Towerdawn's silence, it was Nerilan alone.

'Looks like you're wrong, Nerilan, and I stand by what I said,' Farden said.

It was normally then that Nerilan backed down or Towerdawn barked a few words at her to make her, but not that day. No such luck.

'I've had enough of your pride, Farden. You're a menace, a curse, and I hear the rumours that you released the eves, and I'm inclined to believe them. We will not be bound to you any longer!' Nerilan yelled. Her sinuous glaive came close and menacing, making Farden bristle.

'You want to fight to decide, Nerilan?' he snapped. 'I'm ready. It's been far too long in coming if you ask me.'

The glaive flinched. It wasn't so much as a swipe but a threat, but Farden seized it in his gauntlet all the same and began to twist. Green light flicked across his armour.

'Stop this!' Elessi cried out.

Farden's eyes bored into Nerilan. 'You've spoken to them, haven't you? The gods. Let me guess, Thron came to you and asked to be set free? Said it was your duty? Perhaps shamed you because of your inaction, as they like to do?'

Nerilan looked guilty. She didn't try to hide it. 'What business is it of yours, Farden?' she demanded, dragging her glaive away. 'Thron is not your god. This world is not yours!'

Farden shook his head. 'They are Emaneska's gods, and you are more of a fool than I already thought if you trust a word those gods say. Not when their power depends on us.'

'Enough!' Towerdawn blurted, a tinge of pain in his voice, but Nerilan didn't stop. She feigned a strike with her glaive only to deliver a punch straight to Farden's face.

He let her, in truth, only so he could hammer her back right on her scaly jaw in kind. It had been a long time coming indeed, and the Siren Queen reeled, spitting on the sand before she raised her blade in a fell strike. Farden raised Gunnir, exploding outwards from its sword shape and thrumming with magick. In his periphery, Farden saw Lerel and Elessi, faces aghast.

'I said ENOUGH!' bellowed the Old Dragon.

Fire filled the air above them, dangerously close, and Towerdawn stumbled as if one of his legs gave way. Nerilan did the same, and Farden lowered Gunnir. The silence of the moment was nauseating. Farden caught the dragons behind them swapping looks with each other and their riders, words unspoken. Farden knew what they feared. The schism.

Towerdawn recovered, standing tall once more while Nerilan pressed a hand to her head. 'You're the fool,' she muttered, stumbling back to her dragon.

'No, Nerilan,' Towerdawn rumbled, so quiet only the mage and the queen heard. He did not speak to the mage but to Nerilan. 'I stand with Farden.'

Nerilan staggered, staring at her dragon with glistening golden eyes. 'We swore.'

'*You* swore, Nerilan!' yelled Towerdawn.

Both of them winced again with unseen pain. Several of the other dragons around them made their decision silently, and Farden stared as they turned their backs and flapped into the sky, heading north.

Towerdawn watched them go with his molten eyes. 'The Sirens will need time, Farden,' he said.

'We sail north tomorrow, Towerdawn, we need you—'

'Time, Farden,' Towerdawn snarled.

Farden knew when not to argue with a dragon, but his heart and his gut ached as the Old Dragon and his malodorous queen turned, carving a path through their remaining fellow dragons. When they took flight, the rest of them followed in a silent and sombre retreat. Only one stayed behind, and that was Kinsprite. Bull stood by her side, hand on her thick neck.

'No dragons,' Farden muttered.

'Kinsprite and I are with you,' said Bull, tentatively, casting glances at his dragon to make sure.

'Nerilan will have us strung up, but it's worth it to kill Loki,' said Kinsprite. 'She didn't fight malice like his as Modren and I did in the wilds.'

Farden's head whirled, but he sharpened himself to a point. 'Then I need scouts. Would you go north to the ice fields?'

'We would,' growled Kinsprite.

Eyrum thumped forwards. 'I will go as well. Fleetstar will take me. Only right I end this on the back of a dragon, as I was meant to.'

'Then it's decided,' said Farden, clasping Eyrum's wrist and meeting his fierce eye. 'You'll be sailing soon enough, old friend.'

Eyrum clapped him hard on the back, and as the lad and the Siren strutted into the city to find Fleetstar, Farden blew a sigh. He was still reeling from Nerilan's grip on his throat. Not the danger of it, but the implications of such a thing. Unforgivable, it was. Less had started the Arka-Siren war.

'Where's Warbringer?' he asked of the others coldly.

'On the beach, near the waves, last I saw,' said Ko-Tergo. 'Why?'

'She is the last piece of this puzzle,' said Farden, already walking towards the beach.

The minotaurs were in a huddle, each of them bowed on one knee. The closest circle had their horns locked together around an object that thrust from the sand. It was that bloody hammer. The rest straightened and bowed in time to their rhythmic chanting. All that remained of the clan – several hundred of them – were gathered there, even the families and the young calfs, as Warbringer often called them.

Farden stood by behind a sharp rock and waited, not wanting to intrude. Warbringer already seemed displeased with him, and the last thing he needed right now was the minotaurs of Efjar leaving him as well as the Sirens.

It lasted an hour before the minotaurs broke their ceremony. Warbringer, previously lost to the inner circle, stood and thumped her chest three times. The whole clan responded in unison, and the sound shook the air, louder than the churn of New Scalussen at Farden's back.

It was then that Warbringer caught the mage's eyes, even from as far away as he was, and she raised her hands, lifting the hulking crowds. One by one, they began to disperse in silence. Some came to touch horns to Warbringer's and put a single, reverent claw to Voidaran. And still Farden waited, nodding and bowing to those who came past.

Only when Warbringer was alone did he approach.

'You come to tell me no again?' she asked.

Farden sighed. 'As much as I want to, I know I can't. I wish for you to know that. Death is not as glorious for me and mine as it is for you and yours. We don't have Bright Fields to go to. Only the cold void of the sky or the endless caves of below. What I'm trying to say is I don't want to lose another friend.'

'Most glorious fight would be dying with friend, side by side,' she replied. 'But I understand.'

Warbringer loomed over him, horns blocking out the afternoon sun. 'But Dotharadine is not the end,' she said as softly as a minotaur could and put a hand on Farden's shoulder. There was no need to wince this time. Warbringer had learned and was as gentle as any human touch.

'Why did dragons leave?' she asked.

'Because Scalussen is alone once again, Warbringer.'

Warbringer snuffled at the air. 'Not alone. We have each other. And to north we go. For last battle, to spill blood of the little god. Many may die but we will not fail. And those who die will be remembered. Sung of. Will be a better end than void or caves. Do not fear for them. Freedom is worth sacrifice.'

Farden wished he could believe her.

Another day inched by, full of hammering and clanging and the snuffling of impatient beasts.

The beach was now painted black by soldiers' formations. The ships of the Bastard Fleet were close to full, but there were still many to board. Even the barges that had been hammered together in days sat low in the cerulean waters. Every inch of deck and mast was covered in the presence of grim and fierce-eyed warriors. The beasts had taken some coaxing, that was for sure, but the witches and snowmads had done their job and whispered their spells of calm.

And then there were the Great Ones.

Ossas stood up to his knees in the bay, a curious Keraken wading around him. Metrada stood upon his own borrowed fishing vessel, a stout hulk that he had already scrawled with runes. Territha was the storm that circled the city and crackled like a whip to the final work of battle.

Farden looked across all the might of Scalussen and took a deep breath. 'Are you sure we can do this?' he whispered to Gunnir.

Portal magick is easier than you think.

'Says you.'

Footsteps scuffed stone behind him, breaking him from his trance. 'Every soul that can and wants to fight is gathered, King,' said Lerel with a smile.

Elessi was with her. 'Everyone else is hidin' in the Jar Khoum caves, in case Loki tries another trap,' she added. 'We're ready if you say we are.'

There was no answer to that question. *How ready could one be, to fight the battle of battles?* Farden murmured, 'We're ready as we'll ever be. No time for doubt now.'

A horn blew from the *Spring's Victory* as he spoke, and Farden clanged his spear in answer, making the metal ring like a bell. The masses of Scalussen began to chant, rivalling Territha's thunder.

'All supplies loaded?' Farden yelled over the noise.

Elessi snorted at that. 'Enough to wage a war never mind a battle.'

'Everyone armed and armoured?'

'To the teeth and dressed to the nines,' Lerel answered.

'Ko-Tergo and Peryn's forces and beasts?'

'Secure.'

'Minotaurs, Jar Khoum, and Paraians?'

'Occupying the dreadnoughts.'

'And the rest of Scalussen? What of the High General and Admiral?' Farden asked with a wry grin.

Lerel rolled her eyes.

'Growin' bored waitin',' said Elessi with a tut and a matching smile. 'And eager to murder a certain god.'

Farden held their eyes for a moment. 'I couldn't have got here without you, you know.'

Lerel pushed him onwards. 'Stop telling us what we already know and get on with it!'

Farden held out his hand as Gunnir crackled. 'Let's go give Loki what he deserves.'

A soaring cheer greeted them as they appeared upon the beach, splashing in the shallows. Farden raised the spear in salute, but it was not a time for speeches. They had thousands of miles yet to travel and ice yet to set foot on before hearts needed to soar, and weapons were raised to the sky.

Farden made for the dreadnought, letting the hands and cheers rain down on him and the others. None dared to touch Gunnir, however, and Farden held it ahead like a plough to break through the crowds.

The *Spring's Victory* awaited, heavy in the water but no less imposing and crawling like an angry ant's nest with individuals. Several of Rokhelm's new cannons poked from its portholes, and Farden caught Lerel grinning. Elessi moved to the nearest empty pier, where Keraken picked her up and placed her atop the ship with no name.

'After you, Admiral,' Farden said to Lerel with a sweep of his hand, who bowed in return and strode up the sweeping gangplank to her mighty ship. A pause atop the deck was all Lerel spared before she took a breath and unleashed it in a fierce shout.

'All hands prepare to sail and make way!' she ordered, and the sailors squeezed between all the passengers went to work with speed and sharp yells. The *Spring's Victory* tilted as she was pushed out into the bay with oars, and wind mages got to work on the canvas.

Farden followed Lerel across the deck and to the wheel, where her stubby second Laroso bowed as he withdrew. Warbringer waited there too, Voidaran strapped across her back and her horns painted black and red. Lerel set the wheel spinning, testing the long rudders of the dreadnought.

'Rokhelm told me something earlier,' said Farden.

'What's that?' asked Lerel, as the wind spells began to blow.

'He says this is the biggest ship ever created.'

'She bloody needs to be,' said Hereni, as she came up the stairs to join them.

'How are the mages, General?'

'Enjoying their new armour and brimming with magick. Can't you feel it?'

'I can. I just wanted to hear you say it,' Farden said with pride. 'It's good to have you at my side again.'

Hereni grumbled but took up her place at his shoulder all the same. 'I won't fight her, Farden. Remember that, if it comes to it.'

'We won't have to,' Farden said, hoping that saying it aloud would make it true.

Lerel turned, hair wild in the wind. 'On your order, Forever King.'

Farden lifted his spear, magick raising his voice above the bay, soaring above the cries of Scalussen. 'To the ice fields!'

❦

'How sure are you?' asked Lerel.

'Pretty sure.'

'Out of ten.'

'Sev–eight.'

Lerel nudged Farden sharply. 'Don't let the others hear you say that.'

Warbringer had already heard. 'Not good odds.'

Farden shrugged. 'If I fail, we simply have to sail, and Loki will have to wait.'

'The barges and beasts won't make it, neither will the smaller ships. You either do what you say, Farden, or we invite Loki south.'

Farden patted Gunnir. 'Trust me. Trust the spear.'

'I'll trust you.'

Lerel waited a moment for Warbringer to stray to the far railing before leaning close to Farden. 'It's Durnus, isn't it? He somehow lives on in the spear, speaking to you.'

Farden threw her a sharp look. 'That's ridiculous.'

Lerel stared flatly. 'Nerilan was right about one thing. I've heard you whispering to the spear as well, when you think you're alone. Is it him you talk to?'

Farden pursed his lips. 'I think so.'

'So that's why you haven't grieved like the rest of us. Why didn't you tell me, Farden?'

'Hard to, with the word madness being thrown around so liberally. He helps. Tells me things.'

'Tells you things like how to make a portal?'

'We'll find out.' Farden said, raising his hand to point. 'There it is.'

The mage was right: the Folly of Elleen was ahead, poking from a headland and half an hour's sail away. They had made good time with the spells and the true winds at their backs, as if Paraia wanted them gone.

The Folly was an arch of stubborn granite that protruded from the coast. It was a skinny thing, long-eroded by wind and waves but clinging on. Lerel had no idea why or how it had earned its name, but the tentacle of rock protruding from a spur of cliff and arcing down towards the waves was a formidable sight.

'You forget. Nerilan said something else,' Farden said. 'You've never asked me about what Irien said of the elves.'

Lerel snorted. 'I've never needed to. True or not, I don't care. I wager most of your subjects have decided the same. They might not trust the spear any more than they did, and they still mourn those we lost to those grey bastards, but they still trust you.'

'If it is my fault, all I can do—'

'Is fix it,' said Lerel. 'And I know you will. Just to try not to create a larger problem doing so, like you have a habit of doing. Try not to break the world in two, for example.'

'You know? That's exactly what Jeasin said,' said Farden, before he clomped down the steps and made for the bow, passing between soldiers hurling their guts up over the sides of the mighty ship, or warriors perfecting the edges of their blades, or those playing dice and spending the voyage losing their coin.

'How comforting,' Lerel muttered to herself.

❦

'You ready, old friend?' Farden whispered as he took a stand in the *Spring's Victory's* broad bow, where two ballistae poked at the iron waters.

Ready.

'Hold them here!' he yelled before the spell took hold, and he jumped to the pinnacle of the Folly.

Old bird nests crunched underfoot, and new bird nests full of bird squawked as he appeared in a blink and the sound of a ballistae firing. They took flight with angry cries, and Farden tried not to breathe too deeply of the stinking, congealed layer of shit around him. It was not as noble as a finely carved and inscribed quickdoor, but it would do.

Think of the destination, not the journey. Durnus' words played over and over in his mind as he twirled Gunnir and placed the post of its blade into the rock between his feet.

Farden searched for the right kind of magick, muttering memories of spells to coax it out. When he found the right thread, he latched onto it and let the spear's magick entwine with it. A slight rumble spread through the arch, and Farden pursed his lips as a nest tumbled down to the waters. He could see schools of dark fish holding in the current.

'Easy, now,' he told himself.

Farden thought of the ice fields and where the sweeping ice met Chaos Sound. He thought of the jagged ice cliffs breaking off into the waves and the razor-billed birds diving deep into the jewel-blue shoals.

Corpses interrupted his thoughts, spread across the ice, burned and charred, and the rumbling in the rock beneath him grew fierce.

Farden flinched. 'Destination,' he said aloud, pressing the magick into the rock once more. The waves below began to stir and slap together. The fish scattered for safety as water began to hiss and steam. The rumbling became a quiet hum that held a haunting note.

It was then that sparks flew from the centre of the arch, trapped between rock and wave. Farden felt the corpses intrude again and heard the wolves howl as they tore at frozen, snow-bound bodies.

Lightning pierced the ocean, and Farden felt a deep cracking run through the Folly.

Farden bared his teeth as he carved the magick with his mind and bent it to his will. He remembered every lesson of the School, every word Durnus had ever said of quickdoor magick, and he let his Book burn as Gunnir's power flowed.

Sparks spat again, and this time they spread in a thin film that began to stretch between the arch. The sea sizzled where it touched, but it held, and Farden clung to the magick as hard as he could to keep it steady.

'Now!' he bellowed.

Lerel heard the shout and swallowed hard as she looked upon the fractured air, broken like a window. Snow seemed to be wafting from the rippling surface of the portal, and if she let her eyes blur, she could make out the pale mountains of icebergs.

'He's bloody done it,' rasped Laroso. 'When will he cease to amaze us?'

Lerel hoped she would never have to see such a day as she raised her voice to her crew. 'All ahead! Push those spells! Let's do this as quickly as we can!'

Bells rang in the masts, and the rest of the fleet swarmed to get close. Lerel let them flow ahead of her, even directing her own mages to add wind to their sails. The first ship was the *Autumn's*

Vanguard, and Lerel held her breath as her bowsprit pierced the curtain of magick with a crackle. Foot by foot, she was swallowed, and Lerel told herself she could glimpse her on the other side of the strange window.

Her relief was short-lived. What was more concerning was that the *Vanguard's* mast had almost touched the arch, and she was riding even lower than the *Victory*. Lerel wished she had some dragons to weigh down the ship even more. At least the cannons were helping.

Three, six, nine, a dozen ships had now gone through, every face aboard them wincing as the portal's surface washed over them. Waves battered them as Ossas came striding past, half-submerged in the water and grinning wide as he delved into the magick. Next came the ship with no name and Keraken, to which Lerel swore she heard Farden cry out with effort. When the twentieth ship had braved the portal, and a loud rumble of stone filled the air, Lerel drove her dreadnought forwards.

'Hurry!' Farden yelled from above, and Lerel bayed at the wind mages.

'We run out of time!' Warbringer yelled.

Lerel did not disagree. 'Give the sails all you've got!'

The *Victory* lurched, gaining speed but slower than Lerel wanted. To her horror, cracks had begun to appear in the portal's veil, and Farden looked to be bowing his head as the strain tried to bend him double.

The portal crackled disconcertingly, making everybody on board hold their breath. Lerel could hear the collective gasp, and she bit her tongue so hard she tasted blood as the *Victory's* bowsprit led the way, magick sizzling over the varnished wood and taut rigging.

'Faster!' Lerel hollered. She could feel the magick washing over the deck from the wind mages' stations. The vast black sails of five masts stretched to their limits in their storm. And it was just as well they did, for as the portal washed over the decks and passed Lerel with a blast of frigid air, she heard a horrendous crack behind her.

The spell had collapsed behind them, snapping shut on the stern of the *Spring's Victory* and breaking the flagpole from the back of the ship. The flag of Scalussen scales had disappeared. Only a smoking broken pole remained, and Lerel felt a weakness in the rudder.

'Njord's balls!' cried Laroso as splinters flew, and the landscape wobbled behind them.

And what a landscape. Lerel almost felt as if she was home amongst the icebergs and fields of floating chunks of ice. Even the knocking of it against the hull was pleasing to her ears, never mind the chill on her cheeks and the catch of the freezing air in her throat. There were few smells beyond salt and fresh air, but Lerel drank it all in.

Farden had done what he promised and jumped them barely a mile or two from the shore. The Bastard Fleet floated in a calm wash between the ice, and not one of the ships was damaged. Even Ossas and Keraken could be seen stirring the icebergs from below. Yet Lerel frowned. It didn't look right to her, as if the ice had shrunk back closer to the rock. The mazes of Chaos Sound no longer existed, but rather a channel straight between the Tausenbar Mountains where a glacier had once stood. Fresh ice, shaped like a flow of a waterfall frozen, had swallowed what remained of the piers and port that had once stood there. Lerel looked for the telltale spouts of steam from whales that used to escort Scalussen ships into the Sound but saw none.

A whip-crack made her flinch, and Farden appeared on the back of the ship, almost knocking Hereni over. He dripped on the deck, and a suspicious trail of seaweed was draped across his shoulder.

'What happened to you?' asked Hereni, wiping droplets off her armour.

'Absolutely nothing,' Farden said, clearing his throat. 'Where are we?'

'Chaos Sound, but it doesn't look like I remember.'

Farden's firm face fell as he stared upon the new fjord that led the way north. 'Irminsul's fire.'

'Your fire,' said Warbringer.

'Gods,' Farden breathed as the cliffs of warped ice passed them by. Boulders and stones of cooled lava studded the swirls of blue and white. Mages used magick to manoeuvre the bigger bergs out of the way, and the dreadnoughts crushed others in their path as they surged on. Night was falling, and the peaks of the fjord had taken on the faint amber of the failing sun. There was a faint layer of cloud above them and a fierce cold chill in the air, one that Ilios spread his wings to feel in his feathers.

A piercing roar rang out as two dragons wheeled around a mountain peak and dove to meet them. It was Eyrum and Bull, and the grizzled Siren looked quite at home on the back of Fleetstar.

'What news?' Farden yelled.

'There's something here. Shrouded with mist and shadow, but it's in the north with its back to the mountains and Scalussen's ruins.'

'Then Loki is early and eager,' uttered Farden. 'We'll make camp as soon as we find the end of this fjord and make him wait the night while Territha arrives. We'll be fresh when we meet him in the morning. Agreed?'

The assenting murmurs and grunts of the others were sharp in the cold air.

As she gripped the wheel and felt the crunch of ice beneath the iron hull, Lerel thought of another time they had gone north, to fight a daughter and to fight for survival. They had thought the world was ending then.

How wrong they had been.

CHAPTER 39
RAGNARÖK

We wage war so that we may live in peace.
PROVERB PENNED BY ARKMAGE DARRA IN YEAR 644

Mithrid held the ring between her thumb and forefinger and framed Krauslung in its circle. It felt as if she aimed a bow, and wherever she stared, she could imagine unleashing it, all unbeknownst to those milling below like specks of ash in the breeze.

First the port, and the largest of the Arka ships and their emerald sails ribbed like dragon wings. They were minuscule compared to the Scalussen dreadnoughts. Then the mountaintop beyond her, where a dark scar pitted its slopes. Her gaze moved to the Spire and the town lights still burning past the dawn, and Manesmark suffered her imagined wrath.

Then the statue of Loki, deep in the city and now a day from being finished. Candles and lanterns were being set around it in preparation for his glorious return, wielding Farden's head. They had even prepared a spike.

Once more, Mithrid placed her mother's ring on her finger and tried to quell her power enough so that it might do whatever it was supposed to do. It gave her nothing but a glint, somehow catching the sun even though it had yet to break over the mountain ridges.

It was hard to miss somebody a grown mind never knew. She knew the tragedy only by what it had robbed her of, but the childhood memories were nothing but a blur of magick and a scream. Even Troughwake was beginning to fade, though her father stood clear in her mind, dark and ominous in the doorway, an axe in his hand, magick burning behind him.

'I won't disappoint you,' she whispered.

'I should hope not.'

'Fuck, Loki!' Mithrid cried as she nearly jumped out of her skin.

Loki was leaning against the doorframe of the balcony, and he held up his hands. 'Old habits.'

A wizened man stood near his arm, eyes almost hooded over by the wrinkles of his forehead.

'There is a saying,' he said, taking the steps one ponderous hop at a time like a bird. 'And though I find it detestably lyrical and one of those sayings that everybody regurgitates at a moment's notice as if they're godly words—'

'But?'

'But it goes like this: today is the first day of the remainder of your life. The question is what will you do with it, Mithrid Fenn? Will you choose glory and do what you know in your heart is right? Are you ready?'

Mithrid clutched the ring on her finger. There was no thinking. There was no hoping. There was only her destiny. She had come this far, and though she never expected to be on this path, she would follow it to the end. The choice had been made, and she knew it in her heart.

'I am.'

Loki stared at her, pouring his gaze into her soul. When he saw nothing but willingness, he clapped his hands and bared his teeth in a wide and wolfish grin. 'You've passed every test I've set you, and now it's time for the final trials: standing against Farden and raising Irminsul.'

'You think I'm ready?' asked Mithrid, in a voice pitched higher than she would have liked.

'That I do, lakrimur,' Loki said, at last motioning to the old man at his side, who seemed to be comprised entirely of wrinkles.

'Sjarvek here has a gift for you. When you're finished, I will be in the throne room.'

'Finished?' Mithrid asked, but Loki's coattails were already whipping into the dark of her chambers.

'Miss Fenn,' said Sjarvek, bowing so low his wrinkled face almost touched the tips of his shoes. 'If you'll follow me.'

Mithrid did exactly that, following in the wake of the servant, who, she might have added, moved surprisingly quickly for a man of his age.

Arranged on the bed was an array of familiar armour, freshly polished and even patched up where it needed it. The obsidian and crimson plates shone in the candlelight, and Sjarvek looked proud as if he had done the polishing himself.

'Have you served Loki long?' Mithrid asked, putting on the padded shirt Akitha called a treyja.

'Since he first arrived, Miss Fenn. I served Malvus and Arkmages Tyrfing and Durnus before that.'

Mithrid was surprised. 'You knew Durnus?'

'That I did.'

'Interesting. And which did you prefer?'

Sjarvek manoeuvred his jowls about before giving her a hushed answer. 'The Arkmages were kinder. Lord Durnus most of all.'

Mithrid nodded as she reached for her vambraces and greaves. The servant helped her with the straps and buckles while he maintained his silence.

Mithrid stretched, feeling the plates slide over each other. It wasn't the most humble of feelings, putting on armour. It suggested an invincibility that leaked into the bones and crawled into the mind, and in Scalussen plate, she felt it raw and fierce. Mithrid clenched her gauntlets and admired the spiked knuckles Akitha had forged.

'Loki killed Durnus, you know. He forced his hand in Easterealm,' Mithrid said as Sjarvek retreated to clasp his hands. She watched the words work their way through the wrinkles.

'It is no business of mine what the lords and ladies I serve do, only that I do what they ask,' he said dutifully.

Mithrid nodded before she looked out of the window at Krauslung one more time. 'Then I want you to do me a favour.'

Loki awaited her, lounging sideways on his throne. A Scarred general of Paraian skin and Azen waited on either side of him, both equally displeased to see her in full armour and free of collar.

'You are a fool to take her,' growled Azen, with no regard for ceremony.

Loki waved his hand at the elf. It was then that Mithrid noticed her axe leaning against the throne and Loki's nails drumming on it. 'I would be a fool not to, dear elf.'

Loki kicked his legs and jumped to his feet to welcome the girl. His weapon. In one hand he grasped the axe, and in his other, he spun the knife he had given her all those months ago. Loki came close to Mithrid, and she stood her ground.

'Trust is a difficult thing to ask of anyone when betrayal is so easy to commit, but I feel you and I have reached an understanding, Mithrid,' he said. 'You've seen my mind, and I've seen yours. You wanted to skin me the first time I dared to compare us, but I feel you have come to see what I see. Am I wrong?'

Mithrid eyed her axe. 'Irritatingly, you are not.'

'Then I return these to you,' said Loki, holding out her weapons.

Mithrid was slow to grasp them and slower still to sheathe the knife at her side. The axe she kept low. She could feel Loki's power hovering inches from his skin, and for all he spoke of trust, he kept his guard up like a fortress wall.

'You can relax, god. I've made my decision,' Mithrid said.

'Then we are ready,' said Loki, stamping his foot with a grin. 'Azen, your elves?'

Azen ran a shard of light across his fingers. His eyes had not left Mithrid. 'Gathered in the north and waiting. Every last one.'

Loki turned to the Paraian general. 'What of the mages and my army?'

The man showed off a gap-toothed smile. 'Two hundred mages and twenty thousand soldiers ready to fight, milord.'

Loki chuckled. 'Then it's high time we joined them.'

'Only if you tell me you remember your promise, Loki,' Mithrid interjected. 'This is about Farden, not the others.'

'I promise to do all I can,' the god said with a grand bow. 'And now, if you will gather.'

Loki smiled at each and every one as he opened his hands wide. Magick blew around the Marble Copse, stirring dust and killing candles.

Mithrid clenched her axe tighter than she ever had.

❦

Ice whirled as the magick broke its grip and left them reeling in the bitter air. It was an air Mithrid remembered all too well, but its cold still caught in her throat and made her cough.

Snow drifted alongside the mist, and Mithrid felt the magick in it prickling her skin as she pushed herself to her knees, dizzy. It had the foul tang of elf-spells to it, and she glanced up to see their dark and insectile shapes juddering through the haze that wrapped them. There was another feeling; one of raw magick emanating from something mighty.

A hissing came as Azen stood tall and raised his pale arms wide. The noise spread through the mists until it filled her ears, and Mithrid wondered how many of the creatures were out there. A scraping of ice reached her ears. A scrape of something large and hideous, lurking in the murk, where two giant shadows loomed.

Mithrid faced the lighter side of the mist and walked in its direction. She could feel the churn of thoughts hiding beneath her skull, but she ignored them all, wondering how it was that she was standing on this side in the war to end all wars.

The elven spells drew back like a curtain to reveal the ice fields, broken and shattered as they were at the edges and around Irminsul and the Spine of the World. A smoothed sheet of ice covered in packed snow stretched beyond. Rocks and boulders dug craters here and there, now almost swallowed by the cold. The swathe reached all the way to the Tausenbar Mountains in the south, and the specks of Scalussen arrayed across the battlefield. Mithrid felt a stir in her gut at the sight of them. They, too, clung to shadow and mist, but Mithrid thought she glimpsed the masts of a ship bigger than she had ever seen. A storm settled between two of the distant Tausenbar peaks, and two glinting dragons guarded it on either side. Mithrid took a sharp breath when she remembered Hereni was somewhere beneath those clouds.

Loki was again at her side, arms crossed and more than an axe's measure apart. 'I'll give Farden one compliment. The bastard is punctual when he was a world to break in half.'

Mithrid turned away from her treachery and looked to the giant volcano instead. She could feel the waves of colourful magick pouring from its peak like wind on her skin. It drifted between her fingers and brought a painful throb to her skull. There was a fiercer power to it that Mithrid hadn't felt before, and she wondered if her mere presence had stoked it.

'You feel it, don't you?' Loki said, holding his fingers up just the same. 'Today is the end and the beginning if you do as I say, Mithrid. You will go down in history as a saviour.'

'You can stow the promises, Loki. I'm here,' Mithrid murmured. 'My mind is set.'

A crackle of lightning came from the distant storm, and thunder rolled across the plains of ice.

Three small figures appeared halfway between the battle lines.

'It's time,' said Loki, as he raised his fingers and clicked.

❦

Boots crunched on the ice and stubborn snow, purposeful, relentless, and uncaring. Those who filled them were keen-eyed and walked with fists clenched around their spotless weapons. The clinking of their metal gave melody to the rhythm with which they punished the ice fields.

They stopped for nothing until the crackle of magick broke the cold silence and until two shadows stood upon the ice before them. A god and a girl.

'Can I stab him in the face now and get it over and done with?' muttered Hereni.

'If only,' Farden whispered.

Farden put Gunnir's haft in the ice with a crunch. He had been here before, staring upon a different girl and a different enemy, also about to wade into a battle for the world's survival. Why history was doomed to repeat, Farden didn't know, but he did know it was high time its fell cycle was broken.

'Farden Four-Hand. Always a pleasure' Loki greeted him with a mocking chuckle. 'I'm sure you know my good friend? Or perhaps you don't, for I present the new, the awakened, the unshackled Mithrid Fenn.'

Farden watched Mithrid closely, praying Hereni was wrong. He searched her defiant eyes, and to his increasing concern, he couldn't glean any meaning from them. They were blank as a cloudless sky, surrounded by dark circles. She was either playing her cards close as she had promised him that cold morning in the training yards, or Loki had won, and she had become all of his worst fears. Farden hated he couldn't tell.

'Are you all right, Mithrid?' Farden asked.

Mithrid didn't answer. She barely looked at them. Even Hereni was ignored.

Loki spoke for her. 'She stands with me now. She's come to realise what an accursed menace and a blight on the world you are,

Farden, and come around to how the rest of Emaneska thinks outside your little sphere.' He paused to smirk. 'If you hoped to use her as a pawn to stab me in the back when it was turned, you have failed once more, my friend.'

'Whatever lies he's fed you, Mithrid, remember they are lies. Remember who you are,' said Hereni, standing at Farden's side with a sword drawn and shaking unashamedly. 'You can still change your mind.'

For a few moments that ached with possibility, Mithrid did not move an inch. She at last decided to speak, and the voice that came from her did not sound like Mithrid in the slightest. Doubt slid into Farden's mind like ice-water.

'I am where I belong,' Mithrid said, in a tone Farden had never heard before, flat as a platter.

Loki beamed. 'All those ideas and grand plans you thought you had about your secret weapon, forget them. Mithrid will be fighting for me today.'

'Then so be it. If Mithrid stands with the enemy, then she is the enemy.' Lerel crossed her arms. 'We'll give you a chance to lay down your weapons and surrender, but I know you won't take it. In fact, I hope you won't.' That drew a glance from Hereni.

'Otherwise you wouldn't be able to call yourselves honourable, would you? Such lofty ideals for yourselves, you Scalussen, acting like the champions nobody wanted or asked for. Pathetic,' Loki gloated as he looked past their shoulders at their hidden lines. 'And disappointing, Farden. I thought you would have brought more of your friends. And no dragons, I see? You call this Ragnarök?'

Farden did nothing but force himself to smile and give Loki his own medicine. 'More than enough to take you on, don't you worry. I've waited a long time to watch you die at my feet, Loki,' he said, 'and I know today will not disappoint.'

'We'll see about that.'

'Mithrid,' said Hereni, voice cracking. 'I know you'll do the right thing.'

'That she will, General Hereni. She will smile as she cuts you all down.' Loki chuckled as he looked to the sun. 'I say it's time we fight, what do you think? All this small talk and threat-making has made me rather hungry, and it's been some time since I last ripped one of your miserable souls from its body.'

Farden slammed his spear on the ice once more, and seizing Lerel and Hereni's hands, they left Loki and Mithrid on the fields.

Farden's mind reeled.

'You really think she's still on our side?' Lerel gasped as the jump spell made her bend double. 'If Mithrid wanted to kill Loki, surely she's had a dozen chances already?'

'I tell you he's turned her,' muttered Hereni.

'You forget how careful and cautious Loki is,' argued Farden, even though he doubted his own words. He watched his other generals gather around them. 'I still believe in her. I have to. And that goes for all of us!'

Hereni forced herself to nod, face ashen like marble and lips white. Farden held her gaze before she nodded firmly and took a breath. 'I believe.'

'Is it time, mage?' rumbled Warbringer.

It was at last.

Farden stood tall and raised Gunnir. He stared at the masses around him, reaching between the ships and bastions, and as he took in the sea of grim faces spread before him, he put a finger to his throat to make his voice soar with a spell.

'Hear me, Scalussen! Hear me Great Ones!' Farden bellowed. 'I could give you a speech of victory and glory, but that is not why we've gathered here today. No! This is for survival and our way of life. This fight is against tyranny and oppression! This fight is for your freedom, to be as you will be, to do what you wish, to live how you see fit and be judged by the laws of right and wrong, not the whims of a god or a murderer!'

A mighty cheer filled the icy air, swelling Farden's heart.

'No matter what waits for us across that ice, we are stronger because of who we are and what we've survived to stand here today. They call this day Ragnarök and say it is the end of gods and the world as we know it. That much is true, for a god will die today, and the world he would have us live in will be crushed beneath our heels, never to take breath again! We begin a new era today, friends and warriors, and it starts with you giving every scrap of strength and steel and magick and accepting no quarter or defeat! Failure is not an option! Defeat is not an outcome! Are you with me, Scalussen? Will you fight the last fight?'

Scalussen answered, and it did so until the ice fields shook, and the thunder above them was drowned out. Voices raised to the storming sky. Feet pounded, threatening to crack the ice. Shields and sharp steel clanged together.

'Fine speech,' grunted Warbringer, raising her warhammer to salute the Forever King.

'You can't start a battle without a good speech, remember?' Farden said, heart throbbing in his ears.

Elessi held her chin proud. 'Tell me again we're finally at the end, Farden.'

'That we are, Elessi. Though I can't quite believe it,' said Farden, taking a breath. 'Take your places. Remember the plan.'

Elessi ran for the ice's edge and Keraken lurking in the cold waters. The beast almost looked excited. Warbringer stomped to her minotaurs, where a cloud of breath hovered over sharpened horns and vicious-looking spears. Ko-Tergo stood with the Paraian warriors, each covered in white and black paint. Hereni joined with her mages, faces like stone. Farden could already feel the pressure of magick growing in them, mingling with the wind that blew strong from the volcano.

The magick was strong, almost too strong, and he felt Gunnir whisper without words as it surged around him. Farden blinked, wondering if he was imagining the rainbow colours that lifted from the volcano's toothy mouth like the First Dragon's Wake.

Lerel still stood by Farden's side, and he took her hand in his. 'I need you to stay with the *Spring's Victory*,' he said in a low voice.

Lerel shook her hand free immediately. 'Cow shite! I'm staying right here.'

'I can't lose you today, and all Loki wants is to make me lose, even if we win. You're too important to me to risk on the field. He can jump where he pleases, and he's too quick with a blade and his trinkets.'

'And this battle is too important to me to miss, Farden!'

'You're not missing it, Lerel. I need somebody to hold the back line and bring the firepower. Somebody I trust!'

'Don't you give me that rubbish.'

'Lerel, that's an order,' Farden said sternly, taking her cheek in his hand, his voice a whisper. 'Somebody has to lead Scalussen if I can't.'

'The fact that you think that's an option only makes me want to stay. After all this time and effort, you doubt if you can truly defeat Loki?'

Farden shook his head. 'I don't doubt, Lerel. I wonder what it will take, is all. Especially with Mithrid at his side.'

Lerel seized his hand. 'You're coming back to me, Farden, and that's final. You hear me over all that noise in your head? You don't get a say in that. Neither does Loki. Nor Mithrid, if it comes to it.'

'I hear you.'

'You promise me!'

Farden smiled as another horn blew across the ice. He kissed her firmly, holding her tight before he broke away, cutting a path through the ranks to the front lines.

'Damn you, Farden,' was all Lerel said as she hurried back to the edge of the ice and the *Spring's Victory*.

❦

Farden came to a halt a short distance beyond the front lines. Streaks of blue sky tried vainly to interrupt the shadow and cloud of both armies. Irminsul's breath brought a fine falling of ash, mingling with specks of drifting snow. At least it was a finer day than the last time he had stood in the north to save the world.

Loki kept to his games. He and Mithrid had disappeared to the slope at his army's back, and once safe, Farden thought he heard the god's fell voice in the wind, but nothing so much as words. There was no chanting. No war-cry. No stamping of feet. Not yet. That took Azen striding from the mist raising his pale sword to the sky. A distant horn blew a haunting blast like a dying scream, and a line of elves emerged from their camouflage, pale and crooked faces leering. They began to creep closer, fog and shadow trailing in their clanking wake, blades hammering against their shields. Farden counted the ranks and files of their enemy. Their spells still hid their true number and the tricks Loki had likely prepared, but Farden guessed two thousand elves marched towards them. Far more than he had expected, and that was barely a third of what he wagered hid in the mist and shadow. And there were Arka, too, what was left of Malvus' empire, still fools for their new god.

It had begun.

Farden could have frowned. He could have cursed. He could have shocked the sky with lightning, but instead, he smiled. For Loki had played his hand early, having Ekidna emerge from the mists as if he hoped to rout Scalussen by fear alone. It would have worked on any other army on any other day, and even though mutters came from the hard-eyed mages and soldiers marching at his back, Scalussen didn't miss a step.

'No rest 'til freedom!' Farden bayed, and Scalussen filled the north with its war-cries once more. Paraian and Jar Khoum drums pounded relentlessly in their ears.

'Show them who we brought!' cried Farden as he pushed the smoke and shadow from the front lines. Spells dropped across half the army, revealing the mighty bastions, coelos, and buffalo that advanced in their midst, and as if they, too, had a war-cry, they bellowed and roared and trumpeted alongside Scalussen.

Beneath Farden's feet, ice shook and rumbled as Territha came forth from her storm, every beat of her wings a thunderclap. A cloud of claws and beaks followed in her stormy wake. The battlefield loomed dark, and lightning spread like tangled branches across the sky.

Behind him, a whine of metal and a tortured soul and the stomping of steel feet. Metrada appeared from the shadow, slower than the rest. The bastard was dragging his boat behind him by its anchor chain, slung over this shoulder.

'What in Hel are you going to do with that?' Farden bayed.

'You'll see!' Metrada boomed before raising it up and saving the soldiers behind him from a barrage of spells and arrows that sprayed the ranks with splinters. With a mighty roar, he hurled it over his head, and the boat sailed over the Scalussen ranks to crash amidst the first ranks of grimacing elves. He must have killed or maimed fifty of them in one fell swoop, and Scalussen roared with cheers and mocking cries.

Sparing a moment to cackle, Farden touched the corner of his eye to stare at Loki and Mithrid on their slope, hoping to see a flicker of panic on the god's face.

Farden was not wrong, and upon the hill beneath the burning volcano, a god furrowed his brow.

'Farden's been busy,' said the girl at his side.

'That he has,' Loki murmured, pursing his lips. 'But no matter. He'll soon stare into the face of death and dreams itself. Prepare Utiru!'

'Fire!' Farden yelled, unleashing a crack of thunder from Gunnir, the second signal. Another thunder answered, this time not of magick, but of shackled ballistae finally freed and of the firepowder in Rokhelm's cannons.

Elven shields met the onslaught, but not as successfully as they had hoped. Flaming bolts and cannon stones ripped through their ranks from two angles, momentarily stalling their charge, and the ice had its first taste of blood, elven black and Arka crimson. The ice turned blue as elven magick sang in reply.

Farden punched the air to spread a spell wide across the front lines. 'Shields!'

Other spells sparked to meet his, just in time to catch the initial elven and Arka volley. Fireballs and shards of light and ice exploded against their shields. Scalussen held firm, but they were not impenetrable. Cries of pain rose from where mages were fewer in number or the overlap of shields failed.

'Hold fast! Farden ordered and pushed his own shield wider as another volley came in.

Hereni's voice rose above the first clashes. 'Front two rows, maintain shields! The bloody rest of you, give them your all!'

Fire filled the murk of smoke and spell. Ice shards glittered. Green tendrils of force cracked like whips. Light spells pulsed. Magick thickened the air as the Scalussen mages gave the elves Hel. A rumble spread from the volcano as if answering Scalussen's challenge.

Farden broke his shield to stride ahead with Gunnir levelled at his hip. Fire burst from its blade with wilful abandon, and Farden had to strain to hold on as it cut through the shining shields of the elves and Arka. Farden didn't stop, letting the ice begin to melt and crack beneath him before he heard Hereni yelling his name.

'Great Ones!' she was bellowing, and Farden lifted his head and halted his magick to watch monsters clash.

Ekidna and Territha had broken ahead of their ranks, surging towards each other like two oceans colliding. The foul elven creature was outmatched, and Territha brought the full force of her lightning against Ekidna, making it screech and writhe in pain, falling into its own army and impaling many an elf.

Breaking ahead with great strides, Metrada waded through the elves as if they were paper. Even their spells barely slowed him. Every piece of armour that was shorn away came snapping back, and his ghostly form reached around his arms of steel to give him more claws to swipe and snatch with. The ice ran red in his path.

Farden had no more time to stare and gawp. The elves were so close he could see the runes etched into their pallid skin. Jaws yawned wide as weapons and spells were raised, and their unholy screeches filled the air.

Farden yelled moments before they clashed. 'Brace, Scalussen! Show these fuckers what this age is made of!'

Like clockwork, the Scalussen lines folded into three prongs, and shields of metal and magick hammered the air as they came to a wrenching halt. The elves' charge slammed up against the barrier, extinguished like a wave against a cliff. Lightning rained as they flailed, trapped between magick and the surge behind them. Arrows flew like hailstones in a winter storm, and the front lines turned to a mire of corpses before the Scalussen walls.

'Lift!' came the order from Hereni and Farden, and the fierce barrier lifted momentarily so that blades, spells, and spears could go to work, hacking and slashing and burning anything they could touch. The music of slaughter filled the air.

'Drop!'

Once again, the shields and vortex spells ignited and drove the elves back foot by foot. Corpses crunched and wheezed beneath Farden's feet as he pressed ahead. First, his magick wrought ruin, and then Gunnir flayed their hides with its burning blade. If there was to be bloodshed, then there was no monster better deserving than this enemy, and Farden let them have every ounce of his frustration, his anger, his revenge, and his hatred. He carved through snarling pale faces and slashed the bellies of Arka mages who thought themselves powerful. The carnage sprayed as screams filled his ears. Limbs and heads tumbled, and steel sparked. Ekidna and Territha battled in a hurricane above him. To Farden it was all a deafening blur, his only focus the next kill. Whether it was the Arka blood in his eyes or a battle-rage, all Farden saw was red spilling and raining.

Farden punched through the first wave, turning his spear back on the elves and cutting them down with a blast of magick that split their armour and their skins and pinned them against long Paraian spears.

The mage stared down his lines of battle and found his forces breaking through or driving back the enemy line in two places, east and west. It was bitter battle, and the Scalussen dead piled together, but not as high as the elves and Arka, and with a savage cry and clang of steel on shields, Scalussen reformed its ranks. This time, they left breaks in the front lines, a tempting proposition for any enemy, or so Farden hoped.

Farden threw a fist into the crackling air as he called a halt. The mist waited for them a stone's arrow across the ice, teeming with hissing and the grinding of blades against shields. Their victory was small and slim, and he knew thousands more waited for them.

Once more, the spear raised to glow blue with lightning. It was the next signal, and the ice shuddered yet again as the beasts began their charge. Cannon fire roared over their heads, viciously close as they approached the limits of their range.

It was then a savage and unholy scream came from within the cliff-face of mist. A shadow reared up a hundred feet or more, made of frightening angles and reaching far and wide.

'Loki has brought another Great One!' Farden cried out. That was unexpected, and Farden wondered if Loki now stared down at the look on his face.

'What is that?!' Hereni called.

Farden already knew. He recognised the scream. His skin shivered as he drank in the scent of death and ancient rot.

Utiru.

Her horrendous visage emerged from the mist, hanging over them and staring down with a sickly smile poking through a gap in a horned mask. Utiru's arms formed a circle around her as the painted eyes leered at them, and her grey, sweaty body convulsed with rage.

Hereni immediately cast the widest shield she could. 'What by Evernia's festering balls is that?' Farden heard her cry.

Warbringer was storming up from behind the lines. 'Utiru!' she bellowed as she led her minotaurs in a charge.

Farden raised Gunnir as the rest of the foul monster exploded from the veil, skeletal arms clawing and spider's legs swarming to crush the lines. The air shattered and popped as shield spell after shield spell broke. Rent armour shrieked louder than the dying voices.

Gunnir responded with a river of chaos and lightning that struck Utiru in what Farden hoped was a softer underbelly. He thought of all the hatred he felt in that cave and pressed deep into Gunnir's magick.

Utiru reeled backwards, arms splayed and her smile a grimace. Although her skin charred and puckered, it did not break. Utiru stampeded at Scalussen, smashing mages to gore left and right of Farden. Another leg reached out to hammer an armoured buffalo in its ribs, sending the poor beast and its witch rider sailing across the ranks.

The mage rolled beneath the creature, striking a heavy blow with Gunnir to one of her legs. Utiru screamed, her horrid body reaching downwards to swipe at Farden with her sickle claws.

'You!' she screeched.

Farden's breathing came short and fast. Her foul scent tried to overwhelm him, but he stayed sharp and murderous and swiped again to draw black blood and dust from her bones.

With a crackle of magick, it was then that Loki chose to appear, in the midst of pounding legs and bubbling screams, and swung a sword for Farden's ribs. Farden whirled to fend him off, reaching out with a handful of lightning, but Loki dodged away.

'My my! Does it appear the mighty Farden's spear isn't so mighty any more?' he crowed.

'You tell me!' Farden snarled as he unleashed the spear's fire at Loki. The coward skipped beyond him, and Farden turned the fire to the belly of Utiru high above him. But a leg caught him a heavy blow, and Farden sailed into the Arka ranks, feeling bodies cushion his fall. He heard Loki laughing before he spied him with his sword balanced nonchalantly on his shoulder.

'Let me show you who else we brought to fight!' Farden barked as he scrabbled upright. 'Now, Hereni!'

Hereni cast a spear of flame high into the sky, the final signal, and no sooner had it left her hands did a rumbling shake the ice fields.

'What tricks are these, Farden?' Loki yelled, laughter dead.

To the west, where the ocean ran under the ice fields, a coiled scarlet fist of muscle and spines rammed its way through the ice as if it was rotten wood. Keraken climbed upon the field, jaws splayed wide and cries of battle faint but streaming from the encrusted ship upon its shell. Cannons bucked in their cradles as the ship opened fire, bringing more screams to the song of battle.

Behind him, Farden heard the crashing of rock and ice as the great Ossas climbed from the ocean and came charging across the glacier, shaking the earth with every stride. Farden could not help but duck as the giant stepped over the front lines with a gust of wind. Ossas did not fuck around and hammered a colossal fist into Utiru's masked face. A cheer ripped from Farden as the monster shrank back, and Ossas kept on swinging. As if his fight inspired them in some unspoken magick, the beasts roared with him to deafen the battlefield.

Loki's face said it all before he vanished into wobbling air. With that, the elves' spell of shadow broke and revealed their numbers. Several thousand more of the foul bastards waited beyond, and with engines of siege and warfare cast from black wood and iron. Machinery clanked as they stretched and bent to fire.

Runes glistened across the whole span of pale flesh. Sharp spears of sapphire light began to rain as the Scalussen lines closed in, and shields locked together. Fire and ice spells followed from the Scarred mages amongst them. The noise was horrendous, and Farden smelled searing flesh in his cold-burned nose. Yet the lines did not falter, and wherever bodies fell, more flooded to replace them.

A final volley of cannon stones and ballistae bolts arced over their heads to carve furrows from the elven and Arka ranks. The ship with no name, born by its fearsome wave of red tentacles, strafed them from the western flank, cutting deeper with her larger cannons and finer aim. Cannon stones tied by chains ripped through spears and necks and ploughed straight to the heart of the elvish numbers.

Their cries were music to Farden's ears. A melody of carnage that he wanted to push to a crescendo. And so he did, bending his spear into a wedge and driving a vortex spell behind it that flattened an Arka contingent. Flame poured from his fingers to engulf them, and before the ranks behind could wade through the burning corpses, Farden was amongst them, spinning Gunnir into screeching and snarling elven faces. Wherever his blade didn't touch, lightning pounced, punching burning holes in breastplates or opening up glaring wounds.

'Charge!' Farden yelled breaking into a run with steel pounding the ice. Metrada outstripped him, surging towards Ekidna and any elf or mage that stood in his way. Magick rocked him back and forth as his blades cut a path. He began to lob anything he could find at the elvish monster. Stones, chunks of ice, and even corpses flew from his steel fingers to batter against the spines of Ekidna while it lashed out at swooping Territha. The monster was on the back foot, crawling further and further away, and Territha scorched it once more with a terrifying bolt of lightning and a clap of her wings.

An ululating cry flew past Farden, along with a looming shadow and mountain of mail-clad flesh as thick as oak. Peryn stood atop a bastion's head, her bow bending and straightening over and over as her arrows found their marks in elven necks. Arka soldiers tumbled through the air as the bastion swung its trunk and sharp tusks in vicious arcs. Witches at her back threw vial after vial of powders that exploded and plumed in bright greens and oranges amongst the enemy.

Warbringer and her minotaurs followed in the bastion's wake with Voidaran a screaming blur around her body. Nothing could stand before it, not elven magick, not Arka steel, and not the sheer mass of colliding ranks. Warbringer scythed through the fields that stood before her and roared with her kin. Before the fray dragged them from sight, Farden saw one minotaur rip the head clean off an Arka soldier before flinging it at his comrade. Ko-Tergo was there in full and terrifying swollen form, his lycans at his back, sowing fear and panic as their claws slashed and hooked halberds devastated. The elves might have towered over a human, but the yetin and lycans could stare them down eye to eye.

Above them, Fleetstar and Kinsprite weaved between the elven ballistae and catapults and carpeted them with fire. Kinsprite even went as far as to rip one of the catapults from the ground and hurl it into the packed masses pressing against Scalussen's lines. Arrows flew from Bull's bow while Eyrum lopped off any head his axe could reach.

Another bastion thundered past Farden as the shields of elves and Scalussen met, and the fighting grew even fiercer and bloodier. An Arka mage was impaled on one of its sharp tusks, and before he could die, another was slammed next to him, and another, until the bastion's head hung heavy with its skewered spoils.

'Why isn't Mithrid getting involved?' Hereni barked in Farden's ears as she worked close, a shield tightly wrapped around her and flame in both fists.

'Be glad she isn't! Either it's a good sign, or she's Loki's last trick. Either way, we'll be ready!' Farden told her and himself. It was all turning out too much like the last battle for his liking, when Samara had stood distant and in the company of evil before wielding her terrible power.

Farden pressed ahead with the bastion, trying to break a hole in the elven defence. Magick and blades and arrows hammered against him, but Farden was unstoppable with godblood cladding his skin and burning in his hands. Scarred mages ploughed fire against him, but if there was one school of magick they shouldn't have wielded, it was fire, and Farden stole their spells and made them explode in their hands. Flesh sizzled. Armour melted. Farden wielded his hands in intricate patterns as he filled helmets with forge-hot flame and wilted weapons to liquid. Gunnir cleaved them while the burning writhed and danced.

It was then that he met Azen on the field of battle.

The elven king stood with a bank of a dozen elven mages, shields bright and runes spinning. Farden wasted no time on smart words and threats and cast Gunnir's fire across the sneering faces, breaking their spells and bringing their number down to eight.

Azen blasted the ice with spears of light, casting snow into Farden's eyes while he charged. Farden met him with a clash of sparks and sheared the tip from his sword.

'You don't belong in this world any more, elf!' threatened Farden as their faces drew close, magick burning in between them.

'You never did, worm,' Azen spat.

Azen kicked out, the claws of his feet raking the Scalussen armour. Farden staggered, but a quick force spell held him firm against the ice, and with a twist of his hands, spikes of rock thrust their way from the tundra. Azen moved swiftly, bones clicking as he dodged the granite blades. All but one, which carved a line across his cheek that bled black.

Azen's fury boiled to the surface as he summoned two fierce runes that shone white. His elven mages did the same until Farden was almost blinded by their fire.

Farden raised his shield and Gunnir as their magick fell upon him. He wondered momentarily if Ossas had turned and rained a barrage of blows upon him. Farden was thrown left and right, back and forth while bell-clangs of magick and metal filled his skull.

'Enough!' he cried as he dug Gunnir's blade into the ice.

The magick was trickier with ice and freezing water far beneath them, but Farden didn't care. He dragged the magick from the air and every mage around him and built it into a wind that drove the elves skidding across the ice. With shaking hands, Farden pulled on the earth and its deep fires and brought his shivering gauntlets together in a clap, pointed solely at Azen.

The elf threw rune after rune, but nothing he did could prevent the pillar of fire from erupting beneath him, spraying steam, blocks of ice, and flame in all directions. Even the Great Ones paused their battles to glance at the fire that momentarily pierced the hurricane of battle.

Farden moved quickly, pounding across the ice to where Azen had stood. Runes broke against Gunnir as he whirled the blade to slice throats and bellies. Elves writhed and sputtered as they became corpses. But Azen was nowhere to be seen, and Farden cast around with shields strong for the bastard.

There he was: marching for the rear of his lines and Loki like a true coward. Farden surged after him with Gunnir taking on a fierce glow. Jar Khoum drums thundered afresh as Scalussen pressed its luck across the ice. The elves, for the first time since Troacles, took a step back.

'With me, Scalussen!' Farden yelled. 'Death to Loki!'

Scalussen took up the cry, crashing on the elves in a wave. The bastions and larger beasts had already broken them into three crowded contingents. Ranks and lines and order had died alongside the thousands that already lay vacant-eyed and bleeding on the ice. It was now nothing but a sea of open battle, and Loki and Mithrid let it crash on their shores without moving a muscle.

A shivering scream split the air from the west, where Ekidna had found itself the target of not two but three of Farden's Great Ones. Metrada stood in a waterfall of blood as Ekidna reared and dragged its spiny body from one of the Steel Ghost's blades. Territha filled its face with lightning while her legion of feathered allies clawed at her hundred eyes and extinguished them one by one.

It was Keraken who delivered the final blow. After a volley of cannon fire that jolted Ekidna, Keraken wrapped his tentacles around the monster, caring not for its gnashing jaws or wriggling, clawing legs. Foot by foot, Keraken dragged Ekidna to the hole he had crawled from and began to drown the hideous beast in the ocean beneath the ice. Enormous fountains of seawater exploded, but Keraken was relentless. When his tentacles finally re-emerged, they slithered back onto the ice without Ekidna.

Farden raised another cry from Scalussen. A premature cry of victory, but Farden did not care. The battle was beginning to shift, and he could feel it in the press of elves against the Scalussen shields. They stayed firm, refusing to retreat any further and fighting more bitterly than before, as if they could sense their doom. For a horrifying moment, Farden watched his section falter beneath a whirlwind of slashing blades. No one soldier or mage could stand against an elf, and when pressed together in a pack, they fought with their backs to corners like vicious animals, and it had stalled the Scalussen advance. Further down the lines, Hereni stood like a dam against a section of Arka soldiers and Scarred. She had a hundred mages at her back, and their fire spells became a second sun on the battlefield as they poured bolt after bolt upon the Arka, but they, too, held fast rather than advancing. Utiru had also swivelled around so Ossas looked to have switched sides, and her trampling legs wrought carnage on the eastern flank.

Utiru was the target Farden levelled Gunnir at, and he let that foul beast have everything the spear had to give while Ossas battled her fist and claw, green eyes aflame. Territha's lightning descended once more, flickering over Utiru's limbs.

Utiru unleashed a scream, but for all the fire that scorched her bone-pale skin black, she kept fighting, forcing Ossas back with three simultaneous blows to the head, scraping rock from his face and making him roar and reel.

An unspoken order flooded through the beasts and the army: one to press forwards no matter the cost, and Farden momentarily lost his forces in a rush to claim the slopes. Farden fought his way amongst them, but it was no use. Scalussen hurled itself against the remaining elves, and he almost lost Hereni in the flood of bodies. The battle reached a fevered peak.

Utiru, spoke the spear, clear as day.

Farden realised then it was Utiru's magick washing over them, driving them to fear and frenzy. He sought out the beast to end her once and for all, and to bury all his hateful fears and memories with her.

'Warbringer!' Farden bellowed, and the minotaur came running.

Mithrid watched it all from above, trying desperately to keep track of Hereni and Farden amidst the struggles. She couldn't have helped them even if she wanted to.

'When is it my turn?' Mithrid asked of the god, finding her hands sweating in her gauntlets. She resisted the urge to wipe her forehead.

'Very soon, by the looks of it,' Loki said, without an ounce of joy in his voice.

Farden and Warbringer aimed for the same leg, pouncing while Utiru grappled with Ossas and put her weight on it. The old giant refused to be beaten no matter how much she carved from him, as if he had some ancient and unknown grudge against her. If that was true, then Farden was glad for it.

First, a howling Voidaran struck, breaking bone and filling the north with the monster's scream before Gunnir sliced. Black blood and yellow ichor sprayed as the dry flesh and sinew burst apart, and the weight of Utiru came crashing down.

'It will take all of us!' shouted Farden, ducking the press of her enormous writhing body.

Territha swooped, landing claws into Utiru's back and prising away flesh. Cannon stones from Keraken smashed the masks from her hands and broke her claws. Metrada waded in to see to another leg and bring her belly to the ice.

It was Ossas who finished Utiru. Great and wonderful Ossas who raised his fists and brought them hammering down like a falling island to break whatever spine she had.

Farden tried to thrust Gunnir into her throat as she thrashed around. 'Sweet dreams,' was what he had planned to say, and he was even prematurely proud of it as the glaive blade reached for her skinny neck. But Utiru lashed out again, swinging one of her front legs at the mage as he approached. Farden was ripped from his feet to fly above the masses.

'Farden!' he heard Hereni scream as he spun head over heel.

Scalussen armour was fine for keeping one alive, but its weight did nothing for a soft landing, and all the air was driven from Farden's lungs as he collided with the frozen slopes behind enemy lines. He retched as he pressed himself up, and blood dribbled from the fine gaps in the Scalussen visor. He reached with the spear but in a moment of horror, found it missing.

Farden dragged his visor up in a panic. He reached with his hands and felt its presence to his right, where it was embedded in one of Irminsul's unwanted rocks. Farden's gaze flicked to Mithrid and Loki, closer now. Close enough Farden could almost see the god's eyes widen.

A rune of light smashed into the mage, grating a scar across his pauldron and sending him skidding. Farden tried to hammer a shield spell into the ice, but another rune clattered into his chest and threw him onto his arse. A circle of blue fire sprouted around him, and over its flicking tongues, Farden saw Azen standing in his way.

A whip-crack drew his attention. The god was gone, and no sooner had Farden's eyes flicked back to the spear did he see Loki looming over it, reaching cautiously.

Farden bounded to his feet, rushing to put himself directly between Loki and Azen. Only then did Farden reach for the spear, bending all his will around his grip of empty air.

With a burst of stone, the spear broke free, only grazing Loki's fingers as he tried to close a fist. Gunnir whipped back to Farden point-first, but he didn't seize it. He stepped aside at the last moment and let the spear rocket past to collide with Azen.

The spear skewered the elf through his side, just above his hip, and ran him completely through. Gunnir collided with the ice beyond, soaked in black blood. Any other enemy would have sagged to his knees, but Azen fought on ruthlessly, runes sputtering in his hands. They came crashing against Farden's shield once more as he sprinted to attack. Magick surged across Farden's back and hands. Original magick bereft of the spear's power, but more than strong enough to deal with an elf.

A quake spell shook Azen's feet from beneath him, raising him up only to bring him crashing back down where Farden's firebolt was waiting to plough into his chest. Farden leapt with him as he reeled backwards, seizing his skinny throat while Azen's mouth froze in a snarl.

Farden brought the creature down on the blunt end of Gunnir's haft with a spray of blood. When he looked up, Azen's mouth was wide open, and the haft poked a good foot from between his sharp jaws. The odd light in his milky eyes faded as dark blood poured from the corners of his lips.

'Good riddance,' said Farden, straightening to look at Mithrid, who still stood alone on the hillside.

A snap of magick brought a sword to clang against his helmet. It would have cleaved any other metal than Scalussen steel, and it forced Farden onto his hands and knees. Another blow came searching for a gap in the armour, driving against his ribs to bruise the bone beneath the metal.

Farden drew the spear from the elf king's mouth and whirled it in a wide circle, making Loki duck out of reach.

'It is time, Farden! Time to see what your protege has learned of the real truth!' Loki crowed as Mithrid marched down the mountainside towards them.

'You told me once I'd fallen for the oldest trick, but today it's your turn, Loki,' said Farden.

'Have another Great One in your pocket, do you?'

'Better,' said Farden, looking to Mithrid.

Loki laughed at that, wiggling his sword. 'Oh, how you cling to hope! I hate to dash your plans of betrayal again, Farden, but whatever loyalty you expect from Mithrid has already long gone, hasn't it, Miss Fenn?'

Mithrid said nothing, only lifting her visor so she could stare at Farden as shadow began to leak from the hand wrapped tightly around her axe. Her lips were thin and taut. Farden felt his gut tighten. This war for the world still rested on the girl's sharp shoulders and the trust that he had finally given her, and here she was: the very spitting image of what he had glimpsed in her mirrors. He could not tear his eyes away, even while the air shook with the battle behind him and the lightning Territha sowed.

'Mithrid, we had a plan!' Farden yelled.

'Plans change. People change,' was all Mithrid gave him.

Drums pounded behind them as Scalussen broke through the centre of the elven ranks and began to pour towards Farden.

Warbringer, Ko-Tergo, and Hereni led them, while Ossas cleared a path by barging the wounded Utiru towards a waiting Keraken, tentacles curling around her skeletal appendages as cannons hammered her hide. Utiru screeched like the very world was being shredded, but she did not go easily like Ekidna. Keraken's tentacles battled her flailing limbs, and Farden gritted his teeth as he strained to catch a glimpse of Elessi.

'Mithrid!' came Hereni's cry. All it conjured was a flicker in Mithrid's eye, nothing more, and Farden felt the void yawn wide beneath him. Failure began to chuckle in the darkest corners of his mind. His truest and greatest fear.

As if the mage's panic washed across the battlefield, the other Great Ones swarmed to him. Ossas kicked elves like fallen leaves with his giant feet and pointed at Loki as if he too owed him a debt. Metrada sprinted at full pelt, breaking ice beneath his steel feet and almost unrecognisable beneath all the gore that showered him. Territha soared above them, both dragons on the tips of her wings, closing in fast.

'Hold!' Farden roared, raising his visor to let the words fly, but his orders were useless and unheard amongst the cacophony of the charge.

To his horror, Mithrid raised her hands and summoned shadow to pour across the ice and rock. Tendrils of it reached high and low to meet the Great Ones, stronger than Farden had ever seen her wield.

The moment the shadow touched Territha, the winged terror screeched harshly and wheeled away with lightning shivering across her feathers. Fleetstar and Kinsprite shrank away from its touch with discordant roars. Even Ossas skidded across the ice as the shadow wrapped him and stuttered the light in his eyes. Every one of the beasts mired in battle behind him cried out in chorus as he stumbled.

Only Metrada seemed remotely delighted. 'Yes!' he bellowed out as he fell to his knees, and Mithrid's shadow encircled him. The soul within the Steel Ghost's armour shivered and writhed as the metal began to buckle and crack.

Mithrid was grinning at her work. Farden couldn't believe it. He was stunned at her power, and worse, Loki could see it in his face.

'You see, Farden?' he laughed with a harsh crack of his gauntlets. His glow grew brighter in mockery. 'Gods, do I love it when I get to see that horrified expression of yours! A rare one, to be fair, but so delicious when it appears.'

'Mithrid!' Hereni stood in the midst of the chaos, shield spells in both hands and face raging with emotion.

Mithrid ignored her as she spread her dark magick further, and Farden took a step back as the waves of her power reached to his feet.

'I told you I was always meant for more!' Mithrid shouted, in a voice colder than the ice beneath them. 'None of you – not even the gods – believed in me! Only Utiru's visions and Loki saw the truth. All the while you pretended you cared! You pretended you loved me! And yet all the time you smothered me and corralled me into something weak and obedient. No more! Today I show the world what it made me, and you will rue the day you held me back.'

'Not like this, Mithrid! Loki's poisoned your mind!' Hereni cried out as the shadow reached for her. She ducked as two elven spells slammed against her shields, breaking the magick like glass. 'I know the woman you are inside, and she would never cause such pain and suffering to those she cares about! Remember who you are, Mithrid! Remember the truth, not the lies Loki's fed you!'

Mithrid sneered at that, and Farden's heart crumbled. 'I've seen the true face of evil in this world, and it stands in front of me, not next to me. It's not Loki that will end the world, it's you, Farden, and the magick you unleashed here, It's the spear in your hand. My fate is to stop you,' Mithrid answered, making Loki beam. 'I wonder if that's truly why you've held me back all this time.'

'And she's barely getting started!' Loki brayed. 'I think it's time to show them who you really are, Mithrid!'

It was then that cries and shrieks came from the crags of ice above them. White eyes appeared in their hundreds. Elves began to spill down the slope with shrill yelps and weapons springing. Their arrows rained on the brave Scalussen, and only half their shields were quick enough. More dying screams filled the air at Farden's back before he spread his shields wider. Mithrid's shadow made them dissolve at their edges, and Farden fought back as hard as he could, and together their magick roared.

Loki joined his new disciple and blasted Farden with magick more powerful than he had ever felt the god wield. The wave of golden light knocked the mage back, boots grinding on the ice. His shield held, but every Scalussen who had broken through to the mountainside fell flat. Farden looked at his warriors, from Hereni sheltering behind a rock, to Warbringer spinning Voidaran in a blur and breaking the elven volleys to splinters. Or Peryn, now dismounted and fighting around the hulk of her fallen bastion with her witches and vicious swarms of birds. Or Eyrum, slicing elven heads from shoulders as Fleetstar raced over the battlefield in a stomach-lurching spin. Or the broken Utiru and Keraken locked together in vicious battle, crashing across the ice and threatening to crush the western flanks. Farden's heart clenched tightly as he saw the fresh elves pincer around them and slam into Scalussen lines, somersaulting over his warriors and mages. Ossas and Metrada did their best to break their charge, but they were spread too thin. The vicious creatures even began to climb Ossas' rocks, hacking away at his stone piece by piece with steel and magick. The great giant roared.

Farden fought to his feet, teeth gritted and eyes burning. With a slam of his visor, he held Gunnir in front of him. If he was to fight Mithrid, then so be it. 'I will need you, Durnus!' he yelled to the spear.

For a moment the spear didn't answer, and Farden hammered it on the ice to make its magick ring.

You keep calling me Durnus, it whispered.

Farden's eyes shot to Gunnir. 'What did you say?'

You keep calling me Durnus. But I have never been Durnus. Not wholly. He is within, but he is not I. I am Gunnir. The Skyrender. The God-Corpser, and together we will drown the world in blood.

Farden felt a chill spread from the spear into his veins. Gods, did he hate being wrong. Worse, he hated the new Mithrid could be right.

Though his gut was in his throat, Farden was given no time to answer as the ice trembled beneath him once again, almost driving him to a knee. Keraken alone tried to break through Mithrid's dark spell, but the monster recoiled from her touch exactly like the others, and no amount of his colossal rage could drive him through. Cannons fired, but their stones fell dead against the shadow.

'What are we going to do, Farden?' Hereni yelled, reaching his side and clamping a gauntlet onto his wrist. Their shield spells joined together as shadow lashed them.

'What I must!' he replied.

'We can't fight her!'

Their choices were nil. Mithrid now had her arms and axe held wide as shadow streamed from her, reaching high into the air to rival Territha's storm and wither her lightning. Waves of it washed up the slopes and into the plain, crushing elven and Scalussen magick alike and reducing the fight to steel, teeth, and knuckles. Behind Mithrid, as her shadow reached Irminsul, the volcano belched smoke and vomited fire.

As a boulder cracked from Irminsul's jagged crater and came tumbling down the slopes, thoughts of the last time the mountain had spoken flooded Farden's mind like its fire had filled the ice fields. Farden fought over trembling footholds to reach Mithrid, Hereni at his side. He had been too late to save Samara, and he refused to let history repeat itself.

'What are you thinking, Mithrid? This is not you!' roared Farden over the sound of rocks and ice grinding.

'You're right!' Mithrid cried out. 'It's not me! It's who I'm supposed to be and have been all along!'

Loki stood beaming by Mithrid's side, weathering the shadow swirling around her in a tornado. He bellowed unheard words in Mithrid's ear as her dark magick reached deeper into the volcano. A roar tumbled across the battlefield, and the fighting came to a crunching halt as all eyes turned to Irminsul. Even Utiru and Keraken fell still.

Farden was incredulous. 'What are you doing?!'

'Seizing her future, Farden!' Loki bellowed above the deafening tumult. 'All these years and all that searching far afield, when a Great One sat on your doorstep the entire time, Farden!' Loki mocked. The god's eyes were fixed on the sky, where Territha and dragons fled.

It was up to Farden and the strange spear in his grasp, the one he no longer put his trust in. Its magick roiled, crashing against his instead of flowing with it.

'You can't hurt her!' Hereni blurted beside him. 'Even if she's turned, you can't, Farden!'

Farden wondered if he could, if it came to it. The dark fate Farden had always feared for Mithrid now stood shrouded in shadow with the world bowing before her. He was powerless. Useless. A fool for letting her throw herself into the mouth of the beast. A fool for trusting her. All he could do was fight to take step after step. Elf after elf fell before the spear's thirsty blade as Farden struggled closer, and all the while, Irminsul's rumbling became a roar as fire spewed into the sky.

'Mithrid! Stop this!' Farden cried out again, hoping she could hear him. Hereni yelled by his side, but even her voice was lost to the cracking of the mountain.

Irminsul broke the sky with a thunderclap. Aghast, they lifted their heads to the sky, where the great mountain seemed to be breaking in two. Lava and fire spewed from its shuddering slopes. And there was Mithrid's shadow, pressing deeper into its fire and urging it on. Crimson lightning crackled amongst the growing tower of ash reaching upwards. Rock tumbled down to shatter against the lesser mountains as a storm of fire broke from its surface. Farden dragged his strongest shield into the sky as an enormous serpentine river of fire and boiling ash surged down the slopes, weaving back and forth in ways that shivered Farden beneath his armour.

The fire was alive. A Great One, Loki had threatened, and a Great One it was. Farden felt the blood drain from his face.

Longer than Ossas and Keraken combined, the monster within Irminsul was a dragon without wings and made of coils of shining, burning magma. The fiery gust that came roaring across the battlefield was deathly-hot and thick with sulphur, and terror spread between both Scalussen and elf alike. Its jaws could have swallowed the *Spring's Victory* whole. An inferno burned amidst tusks and fangs of black and molten rock as it snapped at Mithrid's shadow. Her dark power was wrapped around it like a harness, and the colossal monster writhed, breaking the mountain beneath it with its thrashing before it set its sights on Scalussen. Once again, only Metrada stood before it, his death-wish brand of bravery holding him firm and blades ready.

'Mithrid!' Farden bellowed once more in futility, frustration, and – though he didn't want to admit it – fear as the gigantic jaws of Irminsul widened.

Farden did the unthinkable. Even as Hereni screamed behind him, he threw a spell at Mithrid. A searing firebolt to burst at her feet, but nonetheless a spell. For a moment, it looked as if the fierce spell would reach her, but Mithrid's shadow effortlessly dissolved it to threads of withering fire, and in reply, she sent a whip of shadow to lash at him. The fire that burned along Gunnir spat as it vied against it. Farden loathed the struggle he felt in his shaking limbs as they fought each other's blistering strength. Vortex and quake and lightning spells streamed from him as he battled her dark and terrible power. Even Hereni joined in, driving force spells against the towering cliff face of shadow.

It was then – between the flames and quivering bolts of lightning – that Farden thought he saw Mithrid flash him a look. The same look Mithrid had always given him, but most all the misty morning in the training yards, when she had snorted at Farden's trick of bowing before Malvus in these very same ice fields. Before she had spoken her plan to kill Loki and taken Emaneska and Scalussen's fate into her hands. All of Farden's fear melted in that one instant.

With a twitch of Mithrid's hands, Irminsul swerved, scorching the Scalussen ranks with its proximity but leaving them unharmed. With waves of melt-water flooding behind the monster's coils, Irminsul charged into the elven lines instead. Farden watched open-mouthed as he saw pale bodies scorched to ash beneath Irminsul's breath and gargantuan weight. Great rafts of ice broke from the fields and reared upright, leaving elves to slide down into the inferno of Irminsul's maw with shrieks. Shadow shrank back across the battlefield, allowing Ossas, Metrada, and Territha to recover and shrug off the touch of her dark magick. Keraken used the moment to pin Utiru, bring the ship with no name and her dread cannons to bear, and fire a volley straight into the horrid spider's face. The stones reduced her to pulp, and with a creaking of bones, Utiru at last fell dead to the cheers of Scalussen soldiers.

As the smoke and mists receded at their rear, the rest of Scalussen's forces proudly charged across the ice, led by Lerel. Though she had defied him, Farden's heart couldn't help but soar again, and not least because at her back, a fleet of Siren dragons beat their wings against cold air and belched clouds of fire as they began to dive. A shimmering golden dragon bedecked in armour from snout to tail led them.

And even more delicious, Loki's beaming grin died a brutal death as he watched his elven horde decimated in several blinks of the eye. The smart ones amongst them began to fall back or flee in several pathetic cases, and with a roar of Great Ones and warriors, Scalussen pressed its advantage. For a rare instant, the god was speechless and frozen to the spot, long enough for Mithrid to swing her axe.

'Mithrid!' came Loki's deliciously panicked roar.

❦

Mithrid bent every iota of hatred, every dagger of punishment and torture, and every second spent thinking of Hereni into that swing. The god had tried to crush her with every word he'd spoken, and he had almost won. Mithrid cursed him for waiting for Irminsul to let down his infernal guard. For the blood on the fields and brave Scalussen fallen. She cursed him for Malvus and Durnus. And she cursed him for the inexcusable and incurable rot in his heart, if it could be called such a thing. Cursed him to Hel.

The blade bit deep into Loki's shoulder, missing his neck by an inch but crashing through his gorget and carving into his collarbone. The look in his golden eyes as his glowing blood dribbled forth was of pure abhorrence and shock.

'Tricked you,' Mithrid said, so close she could breathe on Loki's face and watch him search her gaze, cold and dark. There was disbelief in there amongst the pain and hatred, and Mithrid could have laughed in his face for an age. Instead, she snatched the knife from her belt – Loki's knife – and thrust it into his side, and as he tried to peel himself away, she pressed her shadow around him to shackle him in place.

The air shook with Loki's cry, pure magick leaking forth that threw Mithrid back under its force. She landed hard on the ice, armour creaking and gasping for breath, and for a moment her power flickered. Irminsul's thrashing coils broke free of her harness, and it was all she could do to hold on. Mithrid could see Hereni and Farden slogging up the slope to reach her, and behind them, Scalussen began to draw itself together into ranks, all faced towards the greatest of Great Ones: Irminsul, a storm barely tethered by Mithrid and Mithrid only. For all his lies, she hoped Loki was right about her power, and she dug deep with a cry.

❦

Farden bounded across the rock with his eyes wide and a victorious cheer in his throat. Gunnir was raised over his head to strike as his boots pounded the ice. This was the moment he had dreamed and pined and planned for, and he refused to slip now.

Loki was wrapped in shadow, hands pulling at Mithrid's axe still lodged in his shoulder. A curved knife lay on the ground. The blows might not have killed the bastard, but they had already ruined him.

Every Arka left on the field had seen his fall, and they began to flee for their lives, anywhere the east would take them. The blood Jeasin drew had cracked his foundations, and now his might came tumbling down. Loki was not a god to them any longer, merely meat for the slaughter, and Farden was set on doing the slaughtering.

Tied around Irminsul and now Loki, Mithrid's shadow broke Farden's magick but not his ferocious leap across the ice. Gunnir was thrust ahead, point aimed for Loki's chest, but as Mithrid fought against the serpent of fire, her shadow released him for a blink, and the god skittered to a heap a dozen feet away.

'Mithrid!' Farden yelled.

'I'm bloody trying!' Mithrid pushed her magick after the god again, snaring him by the leg. She threw a rock with a spare hand, catching Loki across the head but causing nothing more than distraction, more was the pity.

Farden marched, visor up and Gunnir whirling. Even then, as he knelt there bleeding shining blood upon the ice and rock, Loki had a hateful smile for him. 'You don't know when you're beaten, do you?' he told the bastard as he took aim with Gunnir.

'Funny! I was going to say something similar of you!' Loki slammed his fist on the frozen ground beneath him and made rubble rattle. The swirling smoke and shadow wafted around a shape, and a dreaded one to see in that moment.

Evernia stood between Farden and Loki, her form twitching any time Mithrid's magick grazed the goddess.

'Now is not the time!' Farden cried as he tried to step past her, but Evernia held up her hand.

'We are sorry, Farden, that it has come to this,' she said, voice sonorous.

Even though the blood still gushed from his shoulder, Loki was laughing and hissing, and he dragged himself with one arm. That foul twist in Farden's gut returned.

'Now, at the end, you prove yourself the traitorous scum you always have been, caring only for yourselves. Perhaps that is what Ragnarök has always meant. The death of the belief in gods,' Farden spat. 'I only wish the whole world could hear your treachery.'

'But they will.' Evernia gave Farden a grin that showed far too much of Loki's origins. 'You are but a blink of a distant lighthouse passing in the night, Farden. A falling star forgotten moments later. You and Mithrid both. We were here before your kind was an inkling, and we will be here long after you perish. That is our promise! Who do you think you are to fight it?'

Mithrid spared a tendril of shadow to dash Evernia's image to pieces. Her shadow was still raging, but there was a shudder in its onslaught. Mithrid looked weak, half-broken, and punished by what her power demanded, and once again Farden saw Samara standing there instead.

'You know,' Hereni called out behind him. 'I'm starting to agree with you about these fickle gods, Farden!'

Evernia reappeared beside Loki, with the faint shadows of Thron and Heimdall. The goddess' face glowed incandescent with rage. 'You have mocked and defied us for the last time! You will be but another tale for your skalds to sing while we return this world to what it was, free of heretics like you!'

'And what a glorious world it'll be,' said Loki.

Farden reached for Hereni and Mithrid, but something fierce broke the stone and ice at their feet. They managed to share a concerned look before the ground split, and a spike of iron came forth to stab at the sky and drive them apart. Black smoke fumed, battling Mithrid's shadow until Farden couldn't tell what was dark magick and what was the earth belching. Farden hurled himself across the growing rift for the others as the spike kept coming, reaching a dozen feet at least and refusing to stop. And yet it was no spike, but the blade of a sword.

Faint wisps of ghosts spilled from the edges of the rift, making steam of their breath. Their wailing escorted the crash of crumbling rock as a mighty head and shoulders thrust above the earth. Steam hissed wherever the ice touched the haunting form emerging from the depths beneath the mountains. Gushing smoke wrapped its skeletal form.

'What in Hel is this now?!' Hereni cried out as she clung to Mithrid's hand. Shadow streamed from the other as she fought to keep ahold of Irminsul and Loki.

'That?' Farden said as the truth struck him like a minotaur's warhammer. 'That's the fucking goddess of death.'

They tried to stand tall as Hel ruptured the stone with one last thrust to tower over them, skeletal arms reaching and feet taking her first steps on the battlefield. In one hand, Hel carried a sword of black iron. In her other, she held a set of scales Farden had seen almost every day since his birth. They were Evernia's scales, and the unadulterated magick that poured from them thrummed across the landscape.

Hel had no ultimatum or challenge. The goddess of death spat no bloated threats nor gloated over her own strength. She sought murder, pure and simple, and she swung her sword at Farden with wild abandon.

Pushing Mithrid and Hereni out of the way, Farden tried to meet the twenty-foot sword with Gunnir. The spear held firm and unleashed a shower of cinders, but it also threw Farden across the slope to crash into and pulverise a boulder.

Metrada was quickly amongst them, burning with the bright glow of his soul. Hel seemed to welcome him with a grin as if she recognised him. Sparks flew as their blades clashed over and over. Hel duelled against the Steel Ghost, taking not a single step back as Metrada threw everything he had against her. His blades were blurs of steel. Hel's sword burst with black smoke with every swing. The shriek of magick clashing split everybody's ears.

With Gunnir spitting lightning, Farden looked for a gap to drive the spear into, but Metrada and Hel didn't give him so much as an inch as they whirled together.

Hel towered higher, growing above the Great One to break his guards with huge swings of her sword. Metrada didn't dare capitulate in favour of death; this was a fight he seemingly wanted to win, as if Hel was the one responsible for cursing him so, and Farden was glad for it. Momentarily, at least.

Metrada sailed over his head the very next moment, and steel crashed against ice to shake the mage's bones. The Steel Ghost lay worryingly still, and with a cry, Farden levelled Gunnir at the goddess and let her have all the bloodthirsty spear strained to unleash. The force of the spell drove him back through the grit and slush beneath, but he held firm.

Hel met the blast of magick with her sword until it glowed orange with Gunnir's fire. A cackle came from Hel as she held her guard. 'Weak as your uncle,' she uttered before a blast of lightning scorched her.

Territha screeched as she swooped, wings spread and claws outstretched to draw black lines across Hel's face. Yet the goddess was not quelled in the slightest, and Evernia's scales crackled in her hand as she held them up.

'No!' Farden yelled before a wave of magick momentarily drowned every clang of steel, stamp of foot, and scream in a heavy silence. Farden felt Gunnir explode with fire as it washed over him. He struggled to stay upright, digging the spear deep.

Territha felt the brunt of the shocking spell, cast away in a flurry of wings and shedding giant feathers. With a shrill wail, she crashed against the black rock of the Emberteeth in a huge storm of ice and rock. Eagles and vultures tumbled with her, dead weight to add to the scree sliding down the mountain slopes.

An inferno filled the sky as the dragons descended, fire streaming from jaws and dragon-riders standing tall in saddles with bows bent and spears ready. Farden saw Nerilan upon Towerdawn, leading the charge with her glaive held straight.

A volley of spells from the surviving mages struck Hel at the same time as the dragonfire. For a moment, the goddess was utterly consumed by flame and lightning, but instead of breaking her foul hide, the spells seeped into her skin, swallowed whole until Evernia's scales once again rang with power.

Farden roared for them to back away until his voice cracked, but it was already too late. Hel's sword swung with vicious speed, smashing one dragon to the ice before sweeping another rider from his saddle and ploughing him into the earth, but not before the brave bastard lodged a battleaxe in the face of the goddess of death. A familiar battleaxe, indeed.

'No!' Farden unleashed another stream of fire from Gunnir as he realised he recognised the riderless dragon and the fallen warrior. It was Eyrum, and he was struggling to get up.

Farden broke into a sprint, finding Ko-Tergo beside him, the monstrous heap of white fur stained red with blood. As he ran, the yetin raised a discarded spear over his head and put every one of his giant muscles into throwing it. The spear struck Hel in the collarbone, momentarily drawing her sword back from Eyrum's throat while Farden dashed to the Siren's side.

'Eyrum! Don't you dare die on me!' he yelled.

'Been escaping death for so many years, she's finally come for me herself,' Eyrum said, coughing blood. Farden clamped a hand to his neck where it flowed freely, slashed by a shard of black rock.

'I won't let you!' Farden said, moments before he heard the whining of steel against air. He ducked, letting Hel's sword graze the steel on his back with a shower of sparks. As the goddess fought against the swing's momentum, Farden raised a mighty fireball in his hand, wild with the magick that flowed from the spear. He could feel Gunnir's thirst for more, and if it helped stop Hel in her tracks, he had no choice but to feed it no matter the danger.

The spell hit Hel so hard she reeled for several steps before the magick folded into her. She grinned her dark teeth once more as Ko-Tergo hurled himself in a mad leap for her sword.

With arms whirling and claws shredding her leather skin, for a moment, the yetin drove death back across the ice. A moment just long enough to drag a broken and unconscious Eyrum down the slope and away from the carnage.

'It's been an honour, mage,' he told Farden before he was out of earshot.

'Don't you dare say those words! Get him out of here! Get him to a healer!' Farden yelled to his soldiers. He could see Lerel fighting towards him through the remainder of the elves, and he waved her back frantically.

A screech from Hel turned him back around. Ko-Tergo had dragged the battleaxe from her face and clung to Hel's arm while cleaving at her bones. In a fit of rage, Hel swiped him aside and sent the yetin barrelling into a boulder at a speed that made Farden feel sick. Hereni rushed to Ko-Tergo's side, but Farden could already tell from the angle of his neck he would not rise again.

'Die!' Farden roared madly at death as he cut at her with Gunnir's blade. Their blades clashed over and over, and Farden was forced to heave himself back and forth, duck, dodge, and roll to keep out of the way of the black blade. Every scrap of magick he poured onto her only fed her power, just as it seemed to make Irminsul struggle harder. It was the fight of his life, and he barely escaped it.

Sparks showered again as Hel switched her sword at the last moment of a swing, catching him across Farden's arm as he ducked. A foot swung like a landslide and crashed into his breastplate, and once more, Farden felt himself sailing through the air.

Between the ringing in his ears, Farden heard Hereni baying at soldiers and mages. 'Back! She's too powerful!'

In his blurred vision, he saw a humongous shadow over him, Ossas moving in for the kill. But Hel raised Evernia's scales again, and Farden felt the hammerstrike of their magick crash through the battlefield. Waves of Scalussen fell to their backsides. Stone crumbled from Ossas' fist as he stumbled backwards and scattered soldiers.

Keraken was equally powerless. The tentacles reached and cannons roared, but Hel stood fast, holding a wall of sheer magick before her. When Keraken overpowered it and sought to strangle the goddess, the black sword spun and sheared the tips from his tentacles. The roar of the great monster, twinned faintly with Rokhelm's, brought Farden upright.

Amongst it all, he saw Evernia, her whisper loud in his ear even despite the muddled sounds chaotic in his ears.

'Every soul you have sent to Hel comes back to haunt you now, Farden Forever King! You have forged Hel just as the same as you forged Loki.'

Farden stared at his gauntlet where Hel's sword had clipped him, and he saw the smallest finger of metal missing. Fortunately he had already lost the finger that would have been beneath it. His eyes followed the mark, a deep scratch that ran up his vambraces and to his shoulder.

It mattered little. Only Hel mattered, and her despicable kin shackled by shadow behind her, still grinning and basking in the glow of chaos. Farden fought to his knees once more and filled his lungs with the perfume of death and fire. But before he could charge back into the fray, Farden felt a heavy hand on his shoulder, holding him back. He looked up to see Warbringer proud and dark against the tumultuous sky.

'Not this time. It is my turn,' she growled as she stepped past him, Voidaran whining in her grip as she spun it. Her minotaurs emerged from the ranks with her and began to chant, their voices deep and resonant and shaking the ice.

'Warbringer!' Farden yelled, but the grim smile on the minotaur's face was indelible. 'It can't be time!'

'Dotharadine has waited all along. She was ready in Troacles,' Warbringer said, her eyes and sharp grin beaming at Farden as he struggled to get up and reach her. But he was powerless to stop her, and Warbringer hefted her warhammer once more and brought it down into the ice.

Even Hel and Evernia flinched at the bell toll that spread through the bedlam. Farden felt the ground quivering beneath him as a white flame began to sputter across Voidaran's sleek faces. The minotaurs' chanting grew as the fire spread to Warbringer. If it caused her pain, she did not show it, eyes closed and body shaking worse than the ice.

Farden fought towards her, but the minotaurs held him back as their voices joined in one solitary note, the same with which Voidaran vibrated. The note became piercing, causing Farden and the others to wince and shy away as the air split. Even Hel recoiled as she pounded forwards, sword raised. Only the minotaurs stood tall and raised their claws and weapons, chanting a name Farden could barely make out above the roar.

Dotharadine! Dotharadine! Dotharadine!

'Warbringer!' Farden bellowed as Voidaran grew blinding, whiter than snow and brighter than the defeated sun. Scalussen and the elves disappeared in a breaking wave of light as the battlefield reeled. Even the Great Ones shielded their eyes.

Hel swung her sword for the light before Farden could summon a shield. Another bell toll came, even louder than the first.

Farden blinked, expecting to see the worst, whatever bloody form it took. But as the light died away, his jaw dropped.

Fifty feet of muscle and ancient iron armour stood before them, towering over the crimson mess of the front lines. A ragged kilt flowed and flapped on magick and fire's breezes in the dying ringing of steel. Horns as tall as flagpoles and curved like sickles poked at the clouds and caught Territha's lightning. Farden glimpsed black eyes, grinning fangs, and a snout breathing clouds of steam into Hel's face. The goddess of death's sword had come to a stop against the towering haft of a warhammer like a dreadnought's mast. A square mountain of iron sat atop it, glinting with the glow of battle-fire.

'By Evernia's balls!' cried Hereni at Farden's side, drawing a look from the shadow of the goddess herself standing on the ice. Was it Warbringer still in that mighty shell? Had it consumed her? Farden was too busy craning his neck to ponder.

Dotharadine raised a fell voice, slamming the new Voidaran into the ice and rock to bring light once more. To Farden's astonishment and delight, more minotaurs appeared with every flash of shining aura. Some wore crowns of iron feathers. Others fish tooth and scale armour. All lifted axes and scythes and hammers to their goddess with deafening roars.

As the minotaur clans set to carving the remaining elves to pieces, Dotharadine knocked Hel backwards with Voidaran, slamming its steel into her gaunt cheeks. A bellow without words came from her as she kicked the sword up to rake against Dotharadine's chest and armour. But the minotaur goddess only laughed like a mountain moving and swung Voidaran again. For the first time since Farden had been introduced to the warhammer, it did not scream. It merely dragged the very wind behind it as every soul on the ice fields, even Farden, ducked involuntarily.

Voidaran met Evernia's scales with a thunderclap. Shards of white light pierced the sky as the scales shattered before the speed and sheer weight of the warhammer. Voidaran did not stop there but continued until it collided with Hel's skull. The snap of bone and magick was like a punch to Farden's chest, and all of Scalussen winced under the force of the blow. Hel's sword clattered at Evernia's feet as she followed the path of the hammer and collapsed to a skeletal heap, a shining light bleeding from her broken face.

With a mighty cheer, Farden followed as Scalussen surged one last time, like a wave crashing on a shore of thinning pale skin. Black blood stained the ice as the last of the reborn elves were put to death.

Farden sought only Loki. The bastard was moving now, even though Mithrid's shadow surrounded him. He didn't need magick for what he had in his heart. He didn't flee, but instead crept towards Mithrid with a sword in his fist, using the struggle against Irminsul as his distraction.

Farden hurled Gunnir as fast as his exhausted body could allow, and it came just in time. As Loki pounced for her, seizing Mithrid's wrist and crumbling her concentration, the spear sliced across his temple with a crackle of sparks. It sent him sprawling, long enough for Mithrid to recover her spell, though not before Irminsul managed to surge closer to gnash at Scalussen.

'I can't keep this up, Farden!' Mithrid yelled, drenched in sweat.

'You'll have to! Even if it makes this fucker right!' Farden snapped as snatched Gunnir back to his hand. Loki was smiling despite the fact he clearly seethed. His golden light stuttered as Mithrid fought against him. Farden levelled Gunnir at him and poured every inch of hatred into the fire that burst from the spear's edge.

Loki roared in kind, loosing his magick against it. Farden pressed and pressed, but neither one of them won, and they found themselves at an infuriating stalemate. With Mithrid's shadow in the mix, Gunnir couldn't fell the god, but without it, Loki would slip away to fight another day.

'Loki *is* right,' shouted Mithrid.

'What?' Hereni called out, eyes full of Irminsul's fire.

'About magick! About balance! About what I am! Magick has been leaking into the world since before I was born, but after the battle on the ice fields and the discovery of Gunnir, it's become a flood that threatens to end us all. It's our doom, not a weapon of victory, Farden,' Mithrid yelled. 'I am a light elf, and I was born to crush magick. That is my purpose, and the longer that spear exists and magick is allowed to pour unchecked, the closer we come to losing everything. Magick has to be stopped.'

'She's learned well, Farden,' called Loki, holding fast and still shining. Mithrid pressed him against the rock with a snarl.

Farden bared his teeth, fighting to ignore the echo of Gunnir's voice. 'I don't need magick to end this!' he promised as he stabbed the spear into the ice and threw down his helmet. 'You keep Irminsul at bay. I'll deal with Loki.'

'He's mine to kill as well!' Mithrid snarled, but Farden shook his head.

'Those were some strong words you spoke not too long ago. About believing in you. Were they true?' he asked.

'Not any more,' Mithrid said after a beat, eyes wide.

'Then you're a damn good actor,' Farden said with a smile. 'I believe you. Let your shadow loose, Mithrid Fenn, as you say you were born for. Just don't you dare die on me.'

Farden held her fierce gaze for a moment. It was heavy with a deluge of emotion and struggle but, most of all, the strength he had always seen in her, since the very first day they had met, when her eyes had burned even in the darkness.

Mithrid nodded. 'Everything's ready. Just as we planned,' she muttered, stare searching his face.

'Then let's finish this,' Farden said before Mithrid threw her head back and let the shadow flood the day.

Farden felt Gunnir shrieking in protest. He could feel his own fire dying in his veins. He could taste it in the bitter air and in the pounding it put in his head. Even the Scalussen armour creaked and whined and complained. Shadow and dust whipped around him in a hurricane as Farden marched for the god, sweeping the Khandri sword from his belt while Loki brandished a sword and circled. Shadow wreathed their arms and every step they took back and forth until Farden thirsted for the god's blood.

'I've waited for this moment ever since I met you!' Farden spat as he thrust and swept the hooked blade to the side. Loki was fast even without his magick, uncaring of the gaping wound in his shoulder and hole in his side. His skin was still stone. His bones iron. His eyes two flaming jewels of defiant golden light. And yet Farden still grinned and beckoned him closer.

'I've waited since the moment I first heard Evernia whisper your name amongst the stars,' Loki retorted. 'When you were nothing but a whelp playing with magick. They put their hooks in you so long ago. Did you know?'

It was Loki's turn to strike, whipping his blade down, feinting, and then dropping the sword to his other hand to strike low. Farden saw it coming and raised a knee to block. With a clang, he clamped the blade between his gauntlets and ripped apart, breaking the blade from the hilt before head-butting Loki in the face. It hurt like Hel, but Farden regretted nothing. He felt that old bloodlust in him rearing its ugly head once more. If only it hadn't taken so long to find its truest target.

'No, but it's a shame for you that I've had so long to practise,' Farden mocked as he aimed a kick at Loki's side. The god's fist came striking down, but Farden was already swinging his sword. The Scalussen steel, Akitha-wrought, carved a line from Loki's chest almost to his waist. The god clicked his tongue as he circled again, armoured fists now weaving in circles.

'Farden!' Mithrid yelled through the tornado around them.

The mage snarled. His heartbeat pounded in his eyes. The shadow was becoming nauseating.

Loki struck swiftly, landing two blows that Farden blocked and a third that snuck around his guard and put sparks in his eyes. It was a lucky shot, or so Farden told himself as he felt blood trickling from his forehead. Farden cackled as he threw his sword aside and waded in with punches of his own.

The first went straight for Loki's side, driving deep until he heard the god's armour and flesh crunch. The second battered Loki around the face as Farden had on the beach so many years before, and once again he drew the god's blood. Loki swung wildly to keep him at bay, quite unbecoming for a deity, and Farden gritted his teeth as he swung harder and faster. Loki's armour buckled under the raining blows of red and gold steel. Shining blood speckled the ice. The god managed to batter him back several times, but Farden, deep in the grip of fury, barely registered the impacts. Within moments, he had the god's throat in his grasp at long last, and with vicious strikes, he swiftly reduced Loki's face to a puzzle of cuts and bruises. Only then did Farden cast him to the ice, where he spat blood, defeated yet not dejected. That fire in his golden eyes refused to see his failure, but Farden had a plan for that.

'Now, Mithrid!' Farden bellowed, reaching for Loki with one hand and Gunnir with the other as the shadow swept away like the eye of a storm. Shackles of dark power pinned Loki, and metal pounded against Farden's palm as Gunnir flew to him, already aching to be let loose. Farden raised it over the hateful god and let the light of its blade burn with a blinding ferociousness, until even he couldn't bear to look and the ground shook violently around them. All Farden could do was hold tight as he thought of Krauslung.

Loki spat blood and bile at him as the spell burned, eyes squinting yet teeth bared. His forked tongue lashed in a desperate attempt to save himself.

'Even now you can't finish the job, you weak-willed worm!' Loki challenged, voice dripping with contempt. 'Is it because you need me, Farden Four-Hand? You can't be the hero without a villain, is that right? Perhaps you and I are destined to war for ever more! I will sow ruin while you hatch your little schemes, each of us pushing and pulling while the world burns around us.'

Farden brought the blade closer, fighting not to cut the god's throat.

Loki turned bitter, legs and arms thrashing as Farden squeezed tighter. 'Do it, Farden! Do it! Claim your victory! Turn me to ash if you wish! But you know I won't ever truly die away. I'll be there in your mind. A memory to wake you in the darkest hours. A splinter you can't worm free. I've started a fire you can't ever put out. Those pathetic fools of Krauslung would eat out of my hand if I let their mewling, putrescent mouths near me. Kill me, and the shit-stained dolts will see me as nothing but a martyr, and my death will give birth to a thousand statues in my name. I will be worshipped for centuries. I will be sung of and written about. I will be remembered as the kind and powerful god who stood against your tyranny. You see, Farden? I have feasted on their souls, and they still adore me even now! The roots of my lies have grown deep. Unreachable. Unbeatable. I will be cast in gold and you, Farden, you will be forced to hear my name on the lips of priest's prayers and in the tuneless wailing of skalds for as long as you choose to run from death. And then, when the cold embrace finally reaches you, I will be there in Hel for you, waiting to laugh with all those who were sorrowfully late in realising how pathetic and futile your life has been.'

Down the spear plunged, but not into his throat. Loki didn't deserve a quick death but rather a slower one with a blade to the gut. Gunnir sliced through the Arka armour as if it were molten glass and pierced deep to the god's spine. Loki fought not to grimace as they stared, eyes deadlocked.

'Only fitting,' Loki said as he dribbled blood, shining fainter than before. It almost looked human. 'To die in the ice fields where I was born.'

Only then did Farden smile and release him to slump to the flagstones. Only then did he let his own subtle shadow and shield spells fade. Only then did Loki realise the icy breath had vanished from the air, replaced by salt and bilge. Only then did the god understand the ice beneath him was finely tooled stone instead.

'But we're not in the ice fields, Loki,' Farden whispered. 'We're in the place you've dared to call home.'

Farden drank in every flicker across Loki's face as the god stared around at the sounds of shuffling feet. Crowds had begun to appear from the fading shadow and sea-mist. The crowds of Krauslung, and they had heard every word.

'You…' Loki gasped.

'Didn't you notice we'd jumped?' Farden smirked. 'I guess not. I wonder how the trickster feels about being tricked?' The mage stepped back as the people came closer, closing in around Loki, silent to a soul and yet fuming in the eyes and clenched fists. Steel flashed in some hands. Clubs of wood in others.

'You think I would let you die and leave your legacy intact? Do you think I would let Krauslung keep living the lie you sold them?' Farden asked. 'No, Loki. When my enemies fall, every part of them falls. That's what you failed to learn in Albion, so long ago.'

Loki felt a great many things, it seemed, in those final moments. But fear was the most satisfying of all, flashing across his blazing eyes as the people loomed over him, pressing thick so Farden could barely see.

The god didn't deign to cry out on the first blow. Nor on the second or third, but by the time he reached a dozen, he began to shout and plead and scream. It was then that the blades and clubs rained down. Loki's dark blood ran beneath the crowd's feet and along the seams of the stone, seeping into the very city that had turned on him.

In the end, they made hideously short work of Loki. When there was nothing left of the god large enough worth trying to recognise, they turned to Farden. It was then that a wizened and wrinkled fellow Farden vaguely recognised shuffled from the crowd, bearing a shredded and bloodstained leather coat. Farden couldn't feel a wisp of magick in the thing.

'Miss Mithrid told us it was you who would be delivered for justice here tonight. And yet you bring us the truth. Why?' asked the old man.

'What's your name, friend?' asked Farden.

'Sjarvek… King.'

'You want to know why, Sjarvek?' Farden stood tall in front of them. 'Because now you have your truth, all you people of Krauslung. You have the truest freedom you've ever known, and that is all I've ever fought for.'

'And what now?' the greying man asked.

Farden looked around at the faces, some hopeful, others bloodstained. 'Appoint those who know nothing but care for this city, as I have. As Arkmages Durnus and Tyrfing once did.'

'Somebody like you?' came a brave shout.

The mage shook his head. 'Not me. Not a lord or lady or merchant. Not a warlord. One of you. Grow. Prosper. Flourish. Be what Krauslung has always been.'

'And what is that?' enquired the old man.

'A home.'

Farden stepped back as he raised Gunnir above the stone. He didn't blame them for shrinking back. He looked only at the bloody mess left of Loki on Krauslung's stone.

'But I'd start with throwing what's left of Loki in the sea, and tearing down that temple. Just a suggestion,' Farden said before Gunnir whipped him back to fire and shadow.

Fire and shadow was all Mithrid knew. Her body shook so violently she wasn't sure if it would ever stop. Blood didn't pump through her limbs any more, only pain.

All of Scalussen save for Hereni and Lerel stood behind her. Shields thrummed at her back to keep the searing heat of Irminsul at bay. The volcano behind the monster was beginning to crack deeper than it already had, spreading for the ice. The Great Ones that remained could barely stand against the fire.

Mithrid chanced a look over her shoulder to where the smear of battle lay dark and heavy on the ice. On the fringes, where she had steered Irminsul, charred bodies lay floating in the meltwater that poured from beneath the monster's inferno. Her mouth had run dry a long time ago, but now it positively cracked as she thought of the Scalussen that lay there burned and disfigured. She was no better than Farden and the sacrifice he had wrought on that same tundra not a year ago. Mithrid felt the guilt wash through her, and it was in that simple, fleeting moment that she knew that Loki had truly failed. That Utiru's visions were false. The crueller Mithrid would not have felt such a racking in her heart.

Shadow flowed anew as Mithrid set her jaw, dragging Irminsul back mere yards.

'The magick is too strong!' she yelled to the others standing at her side. 'The harder I push, the harder it pushes back! We're running out of time.'

Lerel shielded her face. 'We have to wait for Farden!'

'Where in Hel is he?' demanded Hereni, wilting under the force of her own spells as they fought to keep a landslide of rocks and glowing cinders at bay. 'We bloody need him.'

'I hate to say it, but he's the last thing we need right now!' Mithrid spoke the truth, drawing a stare from Lerel. The admiral's sword angled towards her.

'Is that Loki talking or you?'

'It's me, Lerel. Magick is breaking the world. Every moment that Gunnir exists, the more danger we face. It'll all be for nothing if I don't kill magick for good! Irminsul. The volcano. The spear. Everything has to go!'

Hereni was aghast. 'My magick, Mithrid? What makes me who I am?'

'Only through tragedy, Hereni!' Mithrid urged. 'Loki might have spouted lies, but the occasional truth snuck through. Magick has been the source of every struggle Emaneska has faced! Can't you feel it in the ground? The air? Ragnarök is magick. Evernia created a curse. It just took several thousand years to bite. But I was born to break it, just like my mother before me. That's what I'm meant for.'

Hereni searched Mithrid's eyes, where shadow leaked to trail amid scarlet locks of hair.

'This is madness, girl! Heresy!' screeched the shape of Evernia amongst Mithrid's shadow, only existing where it didn't reach. Mithrid found herself wishing she could have hurt her.

'Fucking Hel. If she thinks it heresy, then I trust in you,' Lerel snarled over Irminsul's roar of frustration. 'But if you kill Farden—'

'I wouldn't dare. The world still needs that old bastard, whether the world likes it or not,' Mithrid growled as her foot slipped back through the bloody slush. 'But he better be quick—'

A whip-crack of magick brought a bloodied Farden back into the fray, and all he needed to see was Irminsul before he unleashed the spear's fire. It cut dark scars through its magma, but it only made the monster thrash more, trying to shake Mithrid's shackles and shields. Fire fell upon spells as Irminsul whipped its tail back and forth.

'Farden!' Mithrid shouted, but her voice meant nothing over the roar. The mage left her with no choice.

With a twist of her hand, Mithrid spread her shadow to Farden, wrapping around the spear and his wrists quicker than a blink and drawing the fiercest of looks Mithrid thought she had ever seen.

Mithrid turned a cheek as she felt Irminsul inch closer and the heat grow fiercer. Hereni and Lerel were forced back out of her reach.

'What are you doing, Mithrid?!' bellowed Lerel.

'It's the only way!'

Farden fought back, spinning a shield of fire against her magick and forcing her power back. He seemed to be mouthing something, but Mithrid snarled and pressed harder. Irminsul crept ever closer.

'Mithrid!'

She had no choice. She couldn't battle both monsters of magick at once.

'I have a plan!' Farden shouted over the roar, and even though his voice was faint, it made Hereni snarl as her arms shook beneath her shield. Sweat poured from her brow.

'If I ever hear those words again it'll be too soon!'

'Magick has to die, Farden!' bellowed Mithrid. 'It's ripping the ice in half! That spear has to be destroyed!'

'I know!'

'But—' Mithrid flinched. Perhaps she had misheard. 'What?'

'Durnus is in that spear!' Lerel blurted, drawing Mithrid's wide stare. She withdrew her shadow from Farden to hold Irminsul instead.

'*What*?' she yelled.

'No, Lerel,' called Farden once he had fought closer. His shield shocked the air as he raised a fist, armour glowing with Irminsul's fire once again. 'He's not. Durnus died that day. I don't know what I've been talking to, but it wants death and destruction. Mithrid's right: magick does need to die, but not before I keep some promises.'

'What are you doing, Farden?' asked Lerel, seizing him by his collar.

'What I should have done a long time ago, but right now I need you to run. You too, Hereni.'

She laughed in his face. 'I'm not leaving Mithrid's side.'

Farden's grin unsettled her. 'Believe me, you'll want to when you find out where I'm taking us.'

'Farden!' asked Lerel, eyes narrow.

The mage held her hand as he prised it from his armour. 'You can't get rid of me that easily, remember?' He thrust out a hand to Mithrid. 'I trusted you. It's time for you to trust me. Truly.'

Mithrid hated that she saw her father there, helping her up from a hundred falls and ladder rungs. Even though she bared her teeth, their armour clanged together as they clasped each other's wrists. 'Go, Hereni,' she said.

Hereni shook her head, grasping for her. 'You don't get to make that decision.'

'Go! Otherwise we'll all die.'

Hereni let her lips graze Mithrid's before she cursed and pulled Lerel back.

'Just like old times,' Mithrid said, looking to Farden. 'What do we do?'

'Hold still,' answered Farden. 'We're going to put this Great One back where it belongs. Kill your shadow, Mithrid.'

Mithrid did as she was asked and trusted in the mage.

Gunnir shrieked as the magick poured from its blade, breaking chunks from the mountain above them to tumble onto Irminsul's back. Farden could barely keep a grip on the shaking steel. He knew the spear had heard him, but it couldn't know what was in his mind. That was pure madness. A rat's nest through and through, and he wished it luck finding its way.

It is time to break the world, bellowed the spear in his head, just as Farden wanted.

Farden pointed the river of shining fire and lightning at Irminsul's jaws, holding the monster at bay long enough for Gunnir to rip every scrap of generous magick from the air and hold it tight. The steel glowed between his fingers. Farden poured his all along with it. Every rune and scratch in his book. Every scar, until the very air shook, and his feet left the ground, and even Irminsul hesitated a fraction before it opened its volcanic jaws as wide as a chasm.

'You'd best be coming back to me, Farden!'

Farden barely heard Lerel's shout above the din of pure magick, but it still curled the corner of his mouth as he brought Gunnir down in a striking blow. Not at Irminsul, already swollen and fattened on magick, but at the ice, and the great chasms that lay miles beneath it.

The ground broke before the spell, cutting a rift straight down that swallowed Farden, Mithrid, and Irminsul faster than any gravity could have. Darkness and rock and grit rushed by them in a kaleidoscope, all while Irminsul gnashed at the air and writhed to feast upon them in free-fall. It was all Farden could do to keep ahold of Mithrid's hand as the abyss drowned them in roaring darkness.

Ice water bathed them, filling his lungs, but even though Farden retched and coughed, he dragged himself to his feet. He found Mithrid still gripping his arm, helping to lift him up.

'You're getting too old for this,' she muttered, looking around at the sight of Hel and its sea of muttering inhabitants, and for a moment her breath caught in her throat, and she went even paler than usual. Her legs buckled at the knees.

'You might be right!' Farden yelled as he fled for the nearest tunnel as the fading spell brought Irminsul crashing into the rock pools with a burst of fire and molten rock. Fiery jaws missed them by an inch before they weaved behind a pillar of rock and down a narrower tunnel. Irminsul's breath reached for them, hotter than any dragon's, and it scorched their heels and seared their necks as they hurtled across

'Do I want to know where we are? Because it looks a lot like Hel to me!' Mithrid bellowed.

'Then you'd be right!' answered Farden.

'And these are…?' Mithrid cried, trying her best to weave around the ghosts in their path. 'Are these dead people?'

'You still trust me?'

'Wavering!'

Irminsul's heat burned through the rocks behind them, and with every enormous thrust of its coils, the monster was catching up, crushing the shades of crowded ghosts in its path.

Farden barrelled around a corner while a quick shield held spattering fire and magma at bay. 'This way!' he yelled. Mithrid did her best to let her magick trail, but Irminsul was free now, and it wanted their blood for their blasphemy.

Farden's lungs were full of vinegar. Every inch of his body wanted to slump into the cold ground and be done, but not until there was peace for all, and that meant the shades they raced through like the thinnest, coldest fog. With every turn and weave and every vaguely-familiar tunnel, Farden pined to see the nothingness of the void beckoning to him, but it took several breathless minutes of pelting the stone for their lives until he saw it, yawning wide at the end of a tunnel and cave. And at its edge, the ruined Bifröst. The world's greatest wound.

'Hold it back as long as you can, Mithrid!' Farden yelled.

'What are you doing?'

'Something I hope works!'

'You *hope*?!' Mithrid bellowed as she slammed her shadow into Irminsul's gaping jaws as it filled the tunnel with fire. The heat alone drove her backwards, but not before Farden skidded to the foundations of the bridge Loki had broken with his first betrayal. His greatest. Farden prayed there was some magick left in it after all. This was the mightiest gamble he had ever taken, but his faithful blind belief propelled him forwards, as it always had.

You cannot destroy me, hissed Gunnir. It almost seemed to twist in his grip as Farden put his feet onto the dead, glasslike stone of the bridge.

'That's how I know you're not Durnus,' Farden hissed right back. 'If you were, you'd know I've never accepted being told I cannot do something!'

You cannot!

But the power of a weapon had always resided in its wielder, and so it did then. Farden raised Gunnir, almost scraping the void with its blade. 'Goodbye, old friend,' he whispered before he brought the spear crashing down on the roots of the Bifröst.

For a wrenching moment, nothing happened.

'Any time, Farden!' Mithrid yelled, skidding back foot by foot and already nearing the bridge.

Gunnir quivered. A snap of metal came from within it. Something hammered against his palm as a wind began to blow, and not one of Irminsul's inferno, but one deathly cold, as if they had brought the ice fields with them. The spear changed shape, bursting with spikes, then blades, all of which crashed against Farden's armour. His grip dragged him to his knees as it became a sword. Metal shrieked as it bent and bowed under an unseen force. Beneath its blade, spiderweb cracks of light began to spread through the Bifröst.

Farden didn't dare let go, especially as the wind now became a hurricane blowing through Hel. His boots squeaked on the stone as the bridge bucked and sent a shiver through his spine. He could feel all the magick in Gunnir fighting and clinging to survive, but its own power cursed it. The pressure of the dead was greater, and the Bifröst had lingered in hunger for far too many decades.

Grain by grain of steel, Gunnir began to melt into the stone. Lightning sputtered as the bridge grew in jarring leaps, its stone jutting outwards into the empty void where it belonged. A ripple spread through the darkness, showing distant faces of lost, forgotten stars.

'It's working!' Farden yelled with equal parts joy and terror as the hurricane grew even stronger, spinning him around so he had to hold onto the shrinking Gunnir to keep from being swept away. The dead began to flow as the Bifröst reached halfway like a dam released. Farden heard their whispers rush past him.

'Farden!' Mithrid yelled as she was plucked from the stone and sent tumbling across the foot of the bridge. With Mithrid's shadow dead, Irminsul howled. But not for them; for the countless ghosts that flooded past its fire. The monster writhed against their touch as if it drowned in their flood.

Farden caught Mithrid's hand before she could tumble into the void. He roared with the effort of holding them there, but the mage refused to let go, even when Irminsul came hurtling towards them, flames swirling in the unholy wind.

All they could do was duck as the Great One soared over their heads, scorching their armour in one last feeble attempt to ruin them. Irminsul's thunder faded as its flames unravelled to dust to join the flood of dead drifting like sand across a black canvas.

'Get us out of here, Farden!' Mithrid cried.

He was doing just that, with every shred of magick he had left and that he could sieve from the Bifröst and the dwindling remnant of the spear. But it was then that it shivered into nothing but a splinter, and Farden's grip broke.

Mithrid's scream was cut short as Farden jolted to a stop. Something strong gripped his wrist, and his eyes shot up to see Tyrfing holding onto him, standing firm against the streaming dead as if he barely felt the rush.

'You're a lucky bastard, Farden,' was all Tyrfing said as a fierce and foreign magick shot through Farden's arm. 'But it's not time for you yet. Neither for you, Mithrid Fenn.'

Before either of them could speak a word, a shining jolt of lightning blinded them, and the Bifröst seemed to swallow them whole into its riot of dashing rainbow colours.

❦

'She's here!'

The sounds of voices were a muddle. Mithrid barely felt alive. It took the touch of strong hands to remind her. And how she regretted it. A searing pain burned at the centre of her mind.

Magick.

She opened her eyes, and as she had the night after Troughwake, stared once more into the sapphire eyes of a huge dragon. Mithrid sensed the char of her breath and smoke leaking from her snout, now armoured in fine steel.

Bull had a hand under her arms and lifted her to her knees. Barely a heartbeat passed before Lerel burst into view.

'Where is Farden?'

Mithrid blinked at her wrist, still aching from holding on so tightly. 'He was right next to me,' she croaked. 'He rebuilt a bridge in… in Hel. He gave up the spear…'

The memories were as frail as the ghosts Mithrid still felt against her skin, cold and empty, yet refusing to be nothing. As did she, and she stumbled to her feet. Hereni seized her close and held her up as the ground shifted beneath them. Numb tears found her eyes as she saw the dead strewn across the ice and rock around her. Yet not all had died; the rank and file and beasts of Scalussen were flooding back to the ships while a widening rift spread through the ice as if chasing them. A fountain of fire now spewed from the volcano along with ribbons of green, blue, and scarlet light that flooded the sky and made Mithrid's eyes ache. Geysers of steam burst from its slopes, creeping closer.

Only the dragons and the Great Ones remained to see the world end. All but a recovered Territha, who shrieked at the cataclysm as she headed for quieter mountains. Ossas and Metrada stood close while Keraken swam in the rift, swatting tumbling rocks away from retreating soldiers and picking up fleeing elves to throw at the volcano. Elessi bellowed orders from the prow of the ship with no name. Only Dotharadine remained close and towering over the corpse of Hel, which was starting to fade to dust and cinders the same as the monster of Irminsul. Her clans gathered around her in their thousands, refusing to move.

'Ragnarök,' Mithrid breathed with a shudder. She caught sight of a bloodied Ko-Tergo, dragged on a snowmad sled, hauled by

Paraian soldiers. Her knuckles popped as she clenched her fist. 'I have to stop it.'

'Where is Farden!' Lerel yelled over the roar of fire and magick, not even a question.

'He's alive, I can feel it. It's not his time,' answered Mithrid, wincing and swaying. She could feel every stinging thread of magick washing over her, and there was something to it that felt like Farden and the raw magick inked on his back. 'But it might be ours if I don't stop the mountain, or every one of us will die. Farden can't save us now. Only I can!'

'And what if it kills you like it did Farden's daughter?' demanded Hereni. 'What if it kills the mages or the Great Ones?'

Mithrid said nothing, only seizing Hereni in a fierce embrace and pushing her lips to hers before shoving her away towards Lerel. 'Balance, Hereni. And if it doesn't work, then sing a song about me!'

'Mithrid!'

But Mithrid was already marching for a spur of flat rock that jutted out over the ugly remains of battle. Shadow wreathed her fists as she forced herself to look at the sheer magick streaming from the broken peak of Irminsul's mountain. Taking a deep breath and planting her feet, Mithrid spread her hands and splayed her fingers wide. Her bones jolted as the shadow exploded from her body, as if hungry and ravenous to eat into the magick.

The volcano lurched, cracking wide to spew rocks and lava, but Mithrid kept pushing even though her footing shook violently. It felt as though the whole world tripped. Flaming stones reached high into the air to scatter the dragons. Streams of molten rock dribbled down the slopes around her, forcing Hereni and Lerel to retreat.

Mithrid narrowed her eyes with effort and pain as her shadow collided with the fountain of pure magick raging from the earth itself. It was an aquifer unstoppered, and Mithrid somehow had to contain it. With the spear alive, it would have felled her, and it almost did as she drove her shadow far past Irminsul. Her dark power reached into the sky and assailed the slopes in tidal waves.

Freak, they had called her. *Lakrimur*, the elves and god had branded her. But Mithrid knew who she was now. Cinders and ash swirled around her while the world burned at her feet, just as Utiru's visions had shown her. Her fate had come true after all. The end of the world was her doing, but Mithrid was also its cure.

Mithrid's teeth chattered. She felt blood streaming from her nose and trickling from her ears to warm her clammy neck. Sweat blinded her. Her knees felt as though they would buckle at any moment. But in the whirling storm of her power, Mithrid saw a figure trudging from the murk, hands low and empty, hair wild in the gale of magick duelling its antithesis. Its poison.

It was Farden, and Lerel's cry was nothing but a faint whine against the hurricane of shadow.

Farden stood amidst it, not a blade in his hands or a protest on his lips. He raised his chin to hide the fear and torment in his face and stretched his arms wide and welcomed the darkness with a nod, as if he knew what had to happen. Biting back a cry, Mithrid forced her shadow to wash over him. She saw his mouth open in unheard pain as fire began to flash across his skin.

It was as if his Book fought for its life. Farden clenched every muscle as Mithrid's shadow racked him in waves. His jaws clenched so tightly he felt his teeth would crack. He could barely breathe even though he roared in agony, and already he felt the weakness in his legs. He could not move, and yet in his peripheries, he saw the crimson shine of lava reaching towards him.

But Farden was not alone in that deluge. Another glow dared to brave the shadow alongside him, and this one was of sapphire and turquoise. Farden wrenched his head sideways to see the looming hulk of Metrada, his spirit a cape in a storm and dust streaming from his armour.

'You kept your promise,' Metrada boomed before he passed Farden and stood between him and the lava. Even as the Steel Ghost took a knee, with pieces now flying from his armour and his ghost a fading shimmer, he seemed to smile in his odd way. 'We will see each other again in the void one day.'

Despite the pain, Farden had to smile at the truth Metrada had spoken. *Save them.* Durnus' last true words and the promise Farden had clung to, fretted over, and fought for ever since.

Feeling an enormous weight fall from his soul, Farden bowed his head as he joined Metrada in a guttural cry. Dust and cinders now rushed from his armour, and the flames darting across the metal crumbled to nothing as Farden let go, and let Mithrid win.

An explosion of power knocked him to his knees, slamming his head against the rock, and the last Farden saw of the end of the world was a sky full of shadow and the volcano's fire bleached white as all colour faded to memory. Smoking rocks and molten lava filled the sky, and faint shouts of panic drowned in his ears as Farden shut his eyes and let the roar of Ragnarök envelop him. Fitting, perhaps, that the last he heard was the cry of a gryphon.

CHAPTER 40
NO REST UNTIL FREEDOM

I am being sent a Written mage from Krauslung. Tyrfing's nephew, gods rest him. Whether he will cause trouble or solve problems, I do not know, but we will see.
FROM THE DIARY OF DURNUS GLASSREN

Finches.

Their curious yet demanding cheeps were what woke Mithrid, and once her crusted eyes cracked open, she saw two beaked faces peering down at her from a porthole, puffing up their red chests. A dark day spitting with snow and ash waited beyond.

Mithrid took a breath to find everything that could possibly ached did so. The last glimpse she remembered were dragon's wings and claws closing around her, and the spitting cinders of dimming lava as a mountain fell quiet and light died in the sky. The force of the spell had racked her almost to pieces. She had felt her bones splinter, and the glimpses of splints and poultices across her body were proof of that. She wore no armour, only a soft tunic and trews.

Even so, the chaos had been but moments ago to her mind, and Mithrid flinched and tried to stir her aching body. Broken and bruised things protested as she fell out of the healer's cot. The pain soared, but not as much as her panic. Her axe was propped up against a drawer, and she seized it, but when Mithrid slammed her spare hand on the nearest cot for balance, she came face to face with an ashen Farden. The mage's eyes were closed, his split lips parted slightly, hair across his face He looked dead, and Mithrid raced to put a hand to his chest and feel for a heartbeat or a flicker of magick. There was nothing.

'Don't you touch him,' came stony words from the doorway. Lerel's shadow loomed there, red-eyed and fists clenched.

Mithrid pushed herself to her knees. 'Is he…? He can't be…'

Lerel moved to clasp Farden's limp hand. 'We found him lying next to a dead Metrada, half-buried in dust and colder than the ice.'

Mithrid's eyes began to water.

Lerel sniffed. 'He's alive. But barely. He might wake tonight. Maybe tomorrow. Maybe in a year. We kept his armour on to see if it could heal him, but you did what you said you were going to do, Mithrid. You killed the magick, but you almost killed Farden along with it.'

'He wanted this,' Mithrid whispered, remembering the look on the mage's face as he stood wreathed in shadow and the nod he had given her.

'But I did not. I didn't get a say,' Lerel spoke through her teeth.

'What of Loki? Did Farden kill him?'

Lerel looked to the door. 'We don't know yet.'

'And is the mountain—'

'Quiet, thank the… something other than the gods.'

Mithrid thumped her axe on the wood and used it as a crutch. 'I have to see. I have to know.'

'Mithrid,' Lerel said, but she ignored her. Leaning heavy on her axe, she tottered along a passageway to the nearest stair. The frigid air was a shock to her clammy skin, and though the world was fuzzed and dark at its edges, Mithrid forced herself onwards and upwards until she staggered across the deck. Here and there she caught the eyes of solemn soldiers and mages slumped across the deck in varying degrees of bandage. Dozens bowed to her, but not all, and those that didn't whispered her name and scowled. Mithrid hobbled faster, aiming for the prow.

She fell on the steps, and a sailor helped her up to the gunwale, where she could look across the blackened, bloodied, melted mess of the ice fields. Where the ice turned to rock and dirty glacier, where the slopes turned to jagged range and mighty peak, Irminsul's mountain still remained. Its glory was no more, now a pitiful remnant of its former height. Smoke still drifted from its silent summit, now splayed wide like a ragged tree stump, but no riot of colours nor magick spewed into the sky. At the volcano's roots, a channel of water cut from Irminsul to the Tausenbar, as if a shelf of the world had tried to peel away before they stopped it.

She stopped it.

And yet Mithrid did not dare smile. The wounded aboard weren't the only ones to have paid the price. A sea of tents spread across the edges of the ice, where braziers burned fiercely and ships swayed calmly. And far out on the ice, pyres in their dozens waited for the torch. Hundreds worked to pile corpses and keepsakes.

Boots came clattering across the deck. Hereni stomped to Mithrid's side as if she were fuming. She took Mithrid by the arm, but she did not pull her away back to her cot. Instead, she pressed her forehead to Mithrid's and put a shaking hand to her cheek.

'You should not be out here. You should not even be upright,' she whispered.

'I had to know it wasn't a dream.'

'Unfortunately not.'

Mithrid clasped Hereni's hands. 'Who did we lose?'

Hereni's voice rasped with emotion. 'Thousands. Five dragons. Metrada. Ko-Tergo is with his snowmads, down on the ice. Eyrum…' There her voice broke. 'Eyrum's on his own pyre, made the Siren way. His wounds were too great. Hel was too strong.'

'To think the gods betrayed us makes me want to start up a whole other war,' Mithrid murmured, drawing Hereni's narrowed eyes.

'Even those who survived have paid a price. Your shadow took our magick, Mithrid. My magick,' she said.

Mithrid pursed her cracked lips. 'Has it all gone?'

Hereni glowered at the Spine of the World. 'Not quite, but it's weaker.'

Mithrid swallowed but she stayed firm, not giving up Hereni's eyes. 'I had no other choice. It was all for balance. Otherwise—'

'Ragnarök,' said Hereni with a shallow nod.

'Better the world continues without its magick than ends because of it. Farden knew the same.'

'So does Lerel, even though she blames you at this moment in time.'

Mithrid took a deep breath of the bitter air. 'That's a burden I can carry.'

Hereni was looking at her sidelong. 'I doubted you, you know. I told Farden that Loki had changed you. For that, I'm sorry.'

'He almost did, and for letting him and making you fight for me, I'm also sorry. The plan couldn't be known by anyone. It had to look believable.'

'Almost too believable.'

'I'll take that as a compliment.' Mithrid tried a smile.

Hereni scowled. 'Could have sworn I saw my death in the jaws of Irminsul. I should never have doubted the power in you. Seems you were right: you were born for this. Gods, you even went to Hel.'

'That is something I'd rather forget,' Mithrid answered in a whisper. 'What I want to know is where you found all these monsters.'

Hereni snorted. 'Stories for another time.'

Mithrid nodded, her gaze working from the moving mountain of stone to the humongous eagle-beast crackling with lightning on a distant peak. And to Dotharadine, for whom Warbringer had sacrificed herself. Even now, the minotaur goddess stood like a guard upon the ice, keeping vigil with her claws on her towering warhammer and her eyes facing north.

'I swear I saw him down there, you know,' Mithrid murmured.

'Who?'

'My father. In the rush of the dead, I thought I saw a familiar face staring back at me with a smile for the faintest flicker of a moment. At least he's with my mother now. And speaking of...'

Mithrid took the simple ring from her finger – one of copper and holding black gem – and gave it to Hereni.

'What's this?' she asked, raising an eyebrow.

'Loki gave it to me.'

The eyebrow crept higher as she moved the ring closer to Mithrid.

'No, it was my mother's, once. It's the magick ring that got her killed, and I've been waiting to know what it does.'

Hereni took a moment to watch the ash fall around the circle of copper in her palm before she let Mithrid slide it onto a finger.

For a moment that ached Mithrid's heart, nothing happened, but it started so faint she almost missed it: a single note of a singing voice, pure and clear. It ebbed before flowing louder, weaving a melody to float across the deck and the icy waters, and everywhere its echoes touched, conversations died, and heads turned to listen.

'Who is that?' breathed Hereni, as if it were a spell she feared to break.

'My mother,' said Mithrid, as a tear rolled down her cheek. She wasn't the only one.

❦

Nine days passed before Farden awoke, and he did so with much spluttering, cursing, and fighting until he realised who and where he was. Pain wracked his broken body from his half-healed wounds, and it took both Lerel and Elessi to calm him.

'Did we do it? Did we win?' was Farden's only question, hoarse as a stiff brush against a stone floor. He clasped at Lerel. She gave him no words but a nod instead.

Farden raised a weak hand and immediately winced. The pain was quickly explained by the sling around his shoulder and arm. He lifted the other hand instead and stared at the skeleton key tattooed into his forearm. He clenched a fist to feel something, anything, but all he was gifted was nothing. 'And what did it cost?'

Placing a kiss on his clammy forehead, Lerel made for the door.

'Come on deck when you can, and see for yourself,' Elessi whispered as the latch clicked shut.

Farden was left alone to try his shaky legs. He put bare feet to cold plank and clicked his neck from side to side before his gaze rested on a familiar glint of red and gold arranged on a trunk in the corner. Farden's instinct was to rush to it, to feel its chill pour through him. A painful flinch was all he mustered before he caught himself. The mage simply stared instead. The helmet was missing, and gouges and scratches crisscrossed the scarlet and gold. Magick's char had turned some of the gold to a mud-brown.

Farden bowed his head.

When he finally stumbled onto the main deck of the *Spring's Victory*, Farden wore almost none of his armour. Almost none, that was, except for his old vambraces, now beaten and scarred after the battle. It could have been the overcast skies and the linger of campfire smoke, but the lustre of the metal seemed to have faded. Lerel and Elessi quickly came to help him, standing at each shoulder to gently hold him up. Ilios was behind them, whistling low and worried, and Farden pressed his forehead to the gryphon's beak.

'He saved you, you know,' breathed Lerel.

'He always has,' Farden murmured.

Silence reigned on the deck. A reverent quiet gripped the thick crowds who left a narrow trail to the *Victory's* railing. Farden searched every face for familiarity, and his heart had begun to ache when he saw Hereni and Mithrid. Though they were still wrapped in bandages and looked as if they had been dragged through a hedge backwards, the relief almost felled him, and Mithrid came to take his hand. Farden seized it so tightly her smile turned to a wince.

'You did it,' was all Farden could say. 'You saved us.'

'So did you,' Mithrid said in a whisper, eyes wide. 'Loki's dead, isn't he? Tell me he's dead. Not a single hawk has come from Krauslung.'

Farden nodded and stretched tall. 'That he is.'

Mithrid bared her teeth in a fierce grin. 'How did he die? Just as we planned?' she asked.

'Battered, beaten, stripped of his coat, and ripped apart at the hands of Krauslung. There's nothing left of him,' Farden said, and it had never felt so good to utter such words. He and Mithrid held each other's stares for a moment.

'A light elf,' Farden murmured at last, shaking his head. 'Who could have predicted that?'

Spread across the glacier and the decks of the Bastard Fleet, every soul that could stand or raise their fists for the mage did so. Tens of thousands of voices joined in unison, far more than Farden's dark worries had expected.

Paraian warriors led the chanting until the air shook with stamping feet and victorious voices. Kayruka and Peryn stood at their fore, blades stabbing at the sky. The Sirens and their dragons raised their heads to roar, and Farden caught sight of Towerdawn's gold wings spreading wide. Beyond them waited the Great Ones and the minotaur clans, clustered around the dark and ominous pillar of Dotharadine.

Bethel! Bethel! Bethel! cried Scalussen.

Farden felt a stinging in his tired eyes as he knuckled a would-be tear away. Normally Farden would have waved for them to stop and be silent, but this time he let them, not least because his shoulder had been dislocated and his fist partially broken.

'I think they want a speech, Farden,' said Elessi, a smile lingering.

'It'll have to be a brief one.' Farden stood at the railing, taking a breath and a moment.

'Loki is dead! The daemons and elves lie defeated! Death herself is dead!' he managed to say, his throat still full of rocks and his lips split in half a dozen places. 'We have won, Scalussen! We have our freedom at last!'

He and Mithrid made quite the battered pair as he clasped her hand and lifted it to the sky, and the cheers and chanting soared even higher until the Great Ones joined in. Ossas and his beasts filled the air with their bellows and trumpeting cries. Voiceless Keraken thumped his tentacles against the water in his own celebration. Territha lit up the clouds with her lightning. Dragons spat flame. Even the distant Nerilan – if Farden's eyes didn't deceive him – clenched her fist in victory.

'And now what?' asked Elessi when the roar diminished.

'Now we go home, my wise friend. I imagine New Scalussen missed us,' said Farden, taking Lerel's hand. 'What's the point in surviving if we don't get to live in peace?'

Farden sensed their silence and locked eyes with Mithrid, whose smile was slow to spread.

'I bet we go a week before you find a warlord or monster that needs killing,' she said.

Farden shook his head, but he couldn't hide his grin. It was a brief thing. His gaze kept sneaking to the missing gaps in the army. He counted each of his generals and felt the loss like a dagger. He clenched his fists as he remembered the angle of Ko-Tergo's neck, Eyrum's blood on his hands, and Metrada's defiant grin until the end.

'Where's Ko-Tergo? Eyrum?' Farden demanded. 'Metrada?'

Lerel was the first to answer after an uncomfortable pause. Soldiers around them had bowed their heads. 'All down there, Farden,' she said, as her glistening stare moved to a dark patch of ice where pyres stood unburned and waiting.

'No.' Farden's hand flew to his side where he expected a spear to be sheathed in disguise. All he found was an empty belt and leather trews.

'Guess I can't do that any more,' Farden whispered. 'You'll have to help me.'

❦

As soon as Farden slid from Ilios' feathers and his feet touched the ice, he stumbled towards the pyres to see the cloth-wrapped and ice-kept fallen. There were thousands of them waiting for the fire. Staggering through their rows, it wasn't long until Farden saw the battle-axe lying beside one wrapped shape, and he fell to his knees beside its pyre. A hulking shape lay still next to Eyrum, where Ko-Tergo's form rested.

'We waited for you to light the pyres.' Lerel's voice was small beside him. 'Ko-Tergo died on the battlefield. Metrada sacrificed himself to protect you.'

Tears ran freely down Elessi's cold-pinched cheeks. 'Eyrum died of his injuries the morning after the battle. His last words were for you, Farden. He warned that if you dared mourn for him instead of honour your victory, he would come back to haunt you.'

Farden let loose a sob. 'Fine words.'

'At least their souls can rest on the other side now that you fixed the Bifröst,' offered Mithrid, face also scrunched up in sorrow. 'All of the fallen can.'

It was scant comfort, but it was comfort all the same, and Farden raised his head. 'I've had enough of ghosts,' he managed to say, trying to smile.

A tremor in the ice offered a distraction. The minotaur goddess was approaching, as terrifying in victory as she had been in battle. Voidaran swung by her side, handle spearing the sky over Dotharadine's armoured shoulder. Farden found his mouth go drier merely looking at her.

Before Farden could say anything, Dotharadine raised Voidaran to the heavens and began to shrink, her warhammer along with her. Her minotaurs flocked to stand around her feet and chant in their harsh tongues. Wherever the other clans hailed from, they all spoke the same words as Dotharadine's horns shrank behind those of the others and vanished. Farden found a worry spurring him across the ice, and he winced as he slipped and hobbled, trying to outpace the others.

'Warbringer!' Farden yelled, not knowing what to pray for.

When the minotaurs stood aside to open a channel into their circle, he saw Voidaran sitting alone, steel in the mud, handle pointing to the clouds. Farden sagged to his knees once more.

'Not you too…'

'Do not cry, mage!' boomed a deep voice as a huge minotaur stepped into view and marched down the channel. At first, Farden didn't believe his eyes, but it was Warbringer for certain, with all her scars and trinkets around her horns. There was an ethereal power that eked from her, and it made every minotaur bow as she passed by. Farden struggled to his feet with Lerel's help.

'You think I would sacrifice myself? Life too good. World too wide,' Warbringer called out.

'Does this mean you are a goddess now?' Farden asked as he fought not to hug the beast. Instead, he clasped her huge hand with his, but she thrust it aside and wrapped him in a crushing embrace.

'Everybody underestimate minotaurs, but who struck down Hel? Who brought all clans together? Who saved day?' Warbringer gloated, voice rumbling through his bones.

Farden found himself grinning with gratitude as he peeled himself free. More tears were knuckled away. 'You did,' he replied.

'You kill little god?' she asked.

'Eviscerated.'

It was Warbringer's turn to grin, and she showed off fearsome sharp teeth. 'I like this word.'

Farden didn't want to ask the question, but he already knew the answer and needed to hear it aloud. 'What happens to you now?'

'We go to Efjar. Where we all belong. Thanks to you pink-fleshes and me.'

Farden nodded. 'I'll miss you keeping me heading in the right direction.'

'And what for you?' Warbringer asked as she nudged him with a knuckle.

'Home.'

Farden heard the rumble of feet behind him. A crowd of Scalussen, Jar Khoum, and Siren were gathering around the pyres. Great Ossas came to kneel over Farden. Territha descended to the ice with a shriek, and Peryn approached in a whirlwind of finches and sparrows. Rokhelm stood close to Elessi while Keraken poked his head above the ice and waved a tentacle.

'How can I ever thank you all?' Farden asked of them.

'Don't call on us again, for one,' said Rokhelm with a chuckle. Elessi whacked him on the arm, and Ossas boomed with laughter.

'Ossas likes your Paraia. Ossas will see what its deserts hold,' he said, and by his giant foot, the Jar Khoum Kayruka nodded emphatically.

Peryn stepped up as the winged nightmare behind her squawked. 'Territha has had her fill of gods and ice. She will go east once more, and it's been decided the witches will go with her. There's plenty of forests and places for us to build our own home.'

Farden bowed in the witches' manner, with a swirl of the hand, and Peryn smiled, standing tall for the first time since Wyved had been taken. The mage looked between Ragnarök's survivors, lost for words. 'The world will always owe you a great debt. We could not have won this battle without you.'

'And we couldn't have won without you, Farden,' said Peryn. 'We wouldn't be here without you.'

The whole army stamped its feet on the ice in agreement, once, twice, thrice. Ossas held out a cliff-face of a fist, and Farden put his own against the rock.

'And so it ends,' boomed the giant before he turned away.s

As all of the Great Ones except Keraken chose their paths, Ossas to the sea and Territha to the east, Farden turned to the others, led most of all by Towerdawn and Nerilan. The Old Dragon lowered his great head and showed off the new scars the battle had gifted him. Nerilan was missing an ear.

'Thank you for helping to save our arses when we needed it most,' said Farden. 'What changed your mind?'

Nerilan sighed. 'Towerdawn trusted you would keep your promise about the spear. It pleases me to see he was right,' she said. 'And, when I thought about it, I decided I preferred you and Mithrid over elves and gods. The lesser of two evils, we shall say.'

'More than anything, it was the example of a young rider and dragon, who stayed true to the ideals of allegiance,' said Towerdawn, looking to where Fleetstar, Kinsprite, and Bull lurked. Bull had a sheepish smile on his face.

'So I don't have to say we told you so about the gods?' asked Farden, making Nerilan cross her arms.

'Ouch,' said Mithrid with a glint in her eye. 'That must hurt.'

'I will certainly not miss your cheek in Sutherheim, girl,' replied Nerilan sharply.

Farden felt pride swirling in him. It was a new feeling. 'Ignore her, Nerilan. It's the light elf in her talking.'

'Light elf?' Nerilan blurted. 'What have I missed?'

Hereni chuckled. 'Oh, you have no idea, Queen,' she said as she turned away, back to the warmth of the braziers and the ships. The others and Nerilan followed her, while Farden remained alone with Towerdawn.

'And what of you, Old Dragon?' asked the mage. 'What of the schism?'

Towerdawn exhaled smoke. 'The Sirens and the court of riders agreed to follow us until we cannot rule. And, as it has always been, the next dragon and their rider will take our mantle, and Nerilan and I will fade into song and memory and tearbooks.'

'Sounds almost peaceful,' Farden murmured.

'My tearbook swells with memories, Farden. I have lived a long life, and I have seen too much of the world in chaos. Now that you and Mithrid have bought us peace, it is a gift to choose how its final chapter is written, however short it may be. That is all we can ask for, is it not?'

Farden had to agree, and he put his hand against the dragon's warm scales and closed his eyes. 'That it is.'

New Scalussen gleamed in the full winter moon when the Bastard Fleet returned home a week later. When the dragons soared east towards Sutherheim, roaring and spouting fire in tribute and farewell to the ships and warriors of Scalussen, Elessi found Farden at the bow of the *Spring's Victory*. He did not stare north, as she expected and as the rest did, but west.

'Heavy mind?' she asked.

Farden hummed. 'Not any more. I'm wondering what's across that ocean out there, as I often have.'

'Rokhelm could tell you.'

'Is it rude I don't want him to?' Farden answered.

Since the burning of the pyres and the voyage home, Elessi had noticed something curious about the mage. He was the same Farden, but he moved slower than usual, as though he had nothing to rush towards. He spoke quieter. He even stood taller, as if for once, the weight of the world's fate didn't weigh on him.

'We're leavin' you know,' she whispered.

'You and Rokhelm?' asked Farden, surprising Elessi by matching her smile. 'I knew you would. We don't need to say anything of the past except that Modren would want you to be happy.'

'I know,' Elessi replied, sighing deeply. 'And that's why I told you first. Scalussen will do just fine without its High General. I never had a lust for war like you did. I fought because I had to, but for the first time in years I don't feel that shiver in my skin whenever a daemon or an evil creeps closer, and I would rather enjoy it than play ruler for a change.'

Farden chuckled. 'The strange thing is, so would I.'

'You're leaving too?' asked Elessi, taken aback.

'The Bifröst is repaired. The gods' power has been stolen. The daemons, elves, and Arka have been reduced to bones. Magick has been cured. The spear is gone. Krauslung is finally free at last. Emaneska, Paraia, and Easterealm will know a freedom they've never known before. The Sirens don't want to skin me alive. Mithrid saved the world instead of destroying it, and most importantly of all, Loki is dead. We won,' Farden replied with a shrug. 'So why not? Peryn is taking the witches to their new lands. The snowmads and lycans stayed behind in the north. Warbringer has united her kin and will soon return to reclaim her home. The Great Ones are at peace, and seeing as Scalussen has Hereni and Mithrid now, I'd say Lerel and I are entitled to some of the same peace and quiet.'

Elessi's eyes gleamed. 'I would say so too, though to hear it all comin' from your mouth I feel like I've gone mad. Maybe Mithrid worked too much of her elf magick on you.'

Farden narrowed his gaze at the city lights.

'Still nothing?' Elessi asked.

'Not even a glimmer of my magick. I know Hereni and many of the mages can still cast basic spells, but me? Nothing. Korrin's armour? Simple steel. My Book remains in ink and form, but that's all. I'm barely a mage any more,' Farden admitted, and Elessi searched his grey-green eyes to see if there was a hint of regret, but the mage was a blank book.

'Do you miss it?'

Farden nodded solemnly. 'Hard not to when you've used it your whole life, but for what it caused, what it dealt, what it brought the world, I'd rather have to worry about lighting a candle with something other than my bare hands.'

'Farden. Finally human after all,' said Elessi. 'Where's this peace and quiet of yours going to be then? Don't say Albion.'

'West,' said a voice. It was Lerel, standing with arms crossed and a smile on her face, leaning against nearby rigging. 'Voyaging past the Cape of Glass and being guided by new stars is what any captain dreams of doing. Maybe we'll prove there's not an edge to the world beyond that horizon.

Lerel wasn't wrong about the stars. There was something different about the skies after the battle, as if the dead had spilled into the void to light their own candles, and the night sky was full once again.

'Sounds like a fine adventure to me,' murmured Farden.

When the ships docked and welcoming arms wrapped around the thousands who had survived the north and Ragnarök, when beasts galloped into the streets and from the gates into the wide open and familiar scrub, Scalussen finally knew peace.

Hawks had preceded the Bastard Fleet like heralds. A feast was already laid out across the harbour and beach in endless tables and crates, and Farden had to smile at that. Victories and feasts could never be separated.

A moment of silence fell as Farden, Mithrid, and their generals set foot on harbour stone and finally returned home.

Farden raised a fist. 'To the lost!'

'The lost!' thundered the crowd.

'To freedom at last!' Mithrid bellowed at his side.

'To freedom!' echoed the multitudes, and Farden swore his hair stirred in the gale of their voices.

As Scalussen was swarmed by its returning warriors, pyres and braziers were lit to remember those who had burned in the north, and after a silence, the business of celebrating victory was seen to swiftly and riotously. Scalussen had celebrated before, but soldiers had always been kept on walls, bows and magick taut and ready. With Loki dead, Ragnarök quelled, and the scales of Evernia broken, there was an abandonment of worry like Farden had never felt. He found he could even stare at the oldest stars without scowling for once.

From the corner of the plaza, he watched his generals and captains weaving and dancing to the pounding of drums that had only recently hammered a last charge across the ice. Mithrid and Hereni whirled together, hands clasped and outstretched as they spun, laughing freely. Elessi and Rokhelm danced much slower, a quiet conversation between them with hands on hips and smiles on their faces. Farden raised his cup to her as she caught his gaze.

Warbringer – or Dotharadine, Farden hadn't yet decided – stood amongst her minotaurs and Bloodmongers of other clans and stamped their hooves while others locked their horns. Peryn and her witches weaved patterns with their birds. Those that weren't stealing crumbs from the table and seeds from the loaves, that was.

Ossas and Keraken occupied half the beach, playing some sort of game with knuckles and slapping tentacles. The sound of a keraken chuckling was quite disturbing, but there was a childish glint in the monster's yellow eye that Farden enjoyed.

An enormous beak nudged him, and Farden didn't have to turn around to stretch a hand and scratch the feathers of Ilios' cheek. 'What will you do, old friend?'

Ilios whistled sharply, and Farden smirked. 'Of course you are. Then I'm glad. I don't know what I'd do with you.'

Ilios clacked his beak before he trilled.

'I have no idea if they have gold in the west,' Farden replied. 'Who knows what awaits us? Perhaps you can dream our future again, now magick simmers instead of boils.'

Ilios stayed suspiciously quiet. Farden put his hand under his jaw to stare into his eagle's eyes.

'You weren't the one giving Mithrid dreams of fire and Irminsul all this time, were you?' he asked.

Ilios shook his head, but his eyes gleamed devilishly.

'Bloody Hel, gryphon,' Farden said in an exhale. 'I would be livid if your meddling hadn't helped. But you're explaining that one if she ever asks.'

Another trill.

Farden nodded. 'She's ready. Mithrid never needed me to learn who she was. Nor you, for that matter. You don't become a god for a moment without wanting nothing to do with it after. Take it from somebody who's tried.'

Ilios whistled a short tune. Farden snorted and ruffled his feathers.

'Yes, that's really how I feel.'

Lerel emerged from the crowds with a bottle of wine in her hands and a smile on her face. A finger crooked towards Farden, beckoning towards the harbour wall. Farden was powerless to resist, and he followed with a slight limp. Ilios wasn't to be left out and insisted on tagging along.

As they journeyed, the others noticed them and left the festivities behind to follow in their wake. Elessi and Rokhelm nodded subtly. Fleetstar put her haunch of goat aside and weaved between the crowds. Hereni and Mithrid drifted through the dancers after them. In a silent file of footsteps, they wandered to where the lights of New Scalussen faded against the edges of the shadow, where waves crashed on the rocks and owls hooted in complaint of the distant ruckus.

Mithrid stood with her arm around Hereni. 'Why do I feel this isn't going to be a pleasant conversation?'

'It's time, Farden,' said Lerel, lips blue with Jar Khoum wine and charcoal around her eyes. Farden almost lost himself for a moment.

'We're leaving,' he said.

Hereni looked confused. 'Who?'

'Farden and I,' spoke Lerel.

'And me,' said Fleetstar, making Farden smile. Ilios trilled.

'And Ilios, clearly.'

Mithrid stared between them, red hair waving in the sea breezes. 'To go where?'

'West,' said Lerel. 'Across the endless ocean to see if it really has an end.'

Hereni shook her head. 'You? On a ship for that long, Farden?'

The mage snorted. 'If that's the least of my fears right now, then I'll take it.'

'And what of Scalussen? What of the Forever King?' asked Mithrid.

Farden held up his bare hands and his nine fingers. 'Not so forever any more. He can stay a lyric of skalds' ballads. A memory. And in my absence, I leave Scalussen to you two. I can't think of anybody better to lead the city and these people. And trust me, I've tried,' Farden said with a smirk. Mithrid matched it.

'Well, I can't say I'm surprised,' said Hereni, swilling her wine. 'At the nomination for leader, that is. There's clearly nobody better suited to the job.'

When the laughter had died, Elessi clasped her hands. 'It's probably a good time to bring up the fact we're also leavin',' she admitted.

Lerel looked to Rokhelm, who grinned awkwardly. 'Where are you going?'

'Anywhere Keraken and Rokhelm want to go,' Elessi replied as she took Rokhelm's hand and clasped it to her. 'It's time to be somebody other than General Elessi.'

Rokhelm bobbed his head. 'There is much to see beneath the waves.'

'I'm happy for you both,' said Lerel, voice tight as she choked something back.

A silence dragged between them as gazes were shared. It was Hereni who spoke first. 'When will we lose you?'

'Soon,' said Lerel, and Elessi nodded in agreement.

'It's time to put Emaneska behind us. Before you're proven right, Mithrid, and I find another war for us to fight,' said Farden.

'Then I pity the west, if you find it,' said Mithrid, with a glimmer of a tear in her eye.

The night was filled with laughter and song and the crashing of waves as they embraced tightly.

❦

The next morning, the witches, Sirens, and minotaur clans departed New Scalussen. It was a bittersweet parting, but Elessi made sure every single soul got the sendoff they were due, and all those who remained formed ranks beyond the gates to cheer and clap them on their journeys to homes new and old.

Peryn wasn't the only one who wept as she bid farewell to the others. Bull tried to pretend he didn't as he said goodbye to Mithrid and Akitha. Even Nerilan was suspiciously quiet. Warbringer and Farden embraced until the clans almost faded into the dust and mist.

'I name you Promise Keeper, Farden, and you are always welcome in Efjar,' Warbringer had told him, with bowed horns and glistening eyes.

'Go easy on us pink-fleshes. We're not all bad,' Farden had replied, to the minotaur's grin.

'That is the truth.'

Farden hadn't known how to thank her, and Warbringer hadn't known how to say goodbye. In the end, Ossas ushered the minotaur away before bowing his forehead to the soil. As he departed, he broke into a low and sonorous song that the beasts who followed in his wake bleated and lowed to.

The evening hours brought rain, and Scalussen rested in the truest sense of the word, with not a hand lifted in work or training. A silence gripped the city as gutters flooded and fires and braziers were stoked. There was mourning and healing to be done, and the future was resigned to wait until tomorrow.

It was almost midnight when Mithrid heard a knocking at her door. Hereni merely groaned into a pillow, still feeling the effects of the barrel of wine she'd drunk. With a mutter of her own and a hand pressed to her throbbing head, Mithrid got up instead and shuffled to the door.

A creak of hinges showed her a dark corridor shrouded in shadow and not a soul in sight. Only a small object covered in a silk cloth greeted her. Mithrid whipped it aside to find a small wooden carving sitting on the stone. It was the length of her hand and whittled into a mirror image of her.

'Farden?' she whispered to the shadows.

It was a moment before a voice answered. Mithrid caught sight of a hood and cloak and a glimmer of red and gold.

'I never had a chance to save my daughter Samara. I failed in that regard. I never even had a chance to know her. I know you aren't my daughter, Mithrid, but if you were, I would be honoured to call you so.'

Mithrid blinked to keep a tear at bay. 'I think you'll find I saved you,' she said, her throat tightening.

'Never change, Mithrid,' said Farden as the shadows swallowed him.

'Farden!'

Mithrid chased him. Hereni appeared at the doorframe, eyes bleary, but she understood what was happening. She almost overtook her as they urgently searched the Dawnknell, but the mage had disappeared.

'The beach,' Hereni whispered, and they surged towards the waters.

They found nothing in the sand but another silk-clad carving. Hereni found it first and brought it into the light of the Winter

Fortress. A scrap of parchment was wrapped around it. 'There's a note.'

'To the new Arkmages,' Mithrid read aloud, thin trails of shadow leaking from her fingers and swirling around the parchment and its words.

Hereni studied herself carved in wood before her eyes strayed to the rainy haze of the harbour. The stern of a ship was on the verge of disappearing, and if Mithrid wasn't mistaken, tentacles carved ripples as they submerged. She swore she saw two shadows waving at the ship's railing, and Mithrid squinted at the runes carved above its rudder.

Undaunted.

'Looks like it's up to us now, Mithrid,' Hereni murmured. 'You up to it, lakrimur?'

'More than you know. I've had enough of gods and magick to last a lifetime,' said Mithrid as she reached for Hereni's hand and felt the ring around her finger. She sighed, feeling a peculiar calm run through her. 'You always wanted to build a home. I say we build the greatest.'

Hereni kissed her then, in the rain and firelight, before they watched the ship catch the wind and race into the night.

It was dawn when Lerel found Farden on deck, staring west as she had most of the night. The vambraces on his bare arms shone even in the faint, cloud-mired light.

'Regrets?' Lerel asked.

'None,' said Farden as she slid her arms around him. 'I keep expecting a hawk to bring bad news, but there's nothing left for me to fight. It's taken me sixty years, but I'm finally right where I should be, doing what I wish and with no leash of meaning around my neck.'

'And all it took was killing a god for you to realise,' whispered Lerel. 'And you still look younger than forty, damn you.'

'Not for long,' said the mage, as he watched Ilios and Fleetstar pirouetting around the clouds. A storm hovered on the horizon and beckoned towards them. 'Shouldn't you batten down the hatches or something?'

'You better leave the sailing to me. I'm still High Admiral, after all. I outrank you now,' said Lerel as she placed a kiss on his cheek and headed for the aftcastle.

Farden angled his face to the cold air that blew across the featureless ocean. After so many years chasing a road to glory, redemption, or revenge, it was a strange comfort seeing no road of any kind. Ilios and Fleetstar sang above as the storm winds hit them, and the *Undaunted* bucked against the waves.

Farden searched the sky for storm giants, as he had on the journey to Nelska all those decades ago, but all he saw was the swirling carvings of wind and ocean. Snow began to fall, sticking to his cheek. He felt a shiver run through him, and old habits followed. Farden raised his hand to cast a spell, but he caught himself and smiled. Yet curiosity won, and Farden stared down at his fingers as he clicked them once, twice, but no magick was glimpsed.

A third time, Farden tried, and it was then that the smile spread wider across his cold cheeks as he watched the faintest spark and flicker of flame burst from his fingers, and felt the weak bite of magick in his veins.

Burying his hands in his cloak pockets, grinning wide, Farden lifted his head to feel the chill of the snow on his skin. It had taken him far too many days to come to know the strange feeling that had taken over his soul. Yet as the waves rocked him back and forth, and the wintry air hugged him close, Farden knew what it was that resided within him.

It was peace.

THE END

DEATH AWAITS ALL WHO ENTER THE MARSHES OF THE MINOTAUR CLANS

Get a free short story from the world of
Emaneska and find all of Ben's books at:
WWW.LINKTR.EE/BENGALLEY

Other Books by Ben Galley

THE EMANESKA SERIES

The Written
Pale Kings
Dead Stars - Part One
Dead Stars - Part Two
The Written Graphic Novel

TALES OF EMANESKA

The Iron Keys
No Fairytale
The Weaver & The Wyrm
A Feast For Wolves
Blood For The Forest

THE CHASING GRAVES TRILOGY

Chasing Graves
Grim Solace
Breaking Chaos

THE SCARLET STAR TRILOGY

Bloodrush
Bloodmoon
Bloodfeud

THE BLOODWOOD SAGA

Demon's Reign
Demon's Rage
Demon's Ruin

STANDALONES

The Heart of Stone
Shards